Grand Miranda Book 6:

# Genevieve of Venus

SATA

2025

Genevieve of Venus



The following typefaces provided courtesy of the public domain:
Mona-R: FT Milky-Free (FactoryType). Bertram: Goudy Bookletter 1911 (Barry Schwartz, 2008), Appera: ZF2334 After A Rain (Zed Fonts), Traylor: ZF2334 Squarish (Zed Fonts), Karaina: Cyen (trinary, 2012), BloomingGrove (Nathan Eady), D-gilius: Litos Script (Decio Guanabarino, 2011), Aimee: Graphe Alpha (Heracles Papatheodorou)

The following typefaces are licensed under the CC0 license:
Ko'an: Euphorigenic (Ray Larabie, 2024), Reselat: Goodfish (Ray Larabie, 2024) , Havana: Primer Print (Ray Larabie, 2024), Omuli: Kingsbridge Condensed Book Italic (Ray Larabie, 2024), Spastic: Vahika (Ray Larabie, 2022), Watcheye: Type Sans Light (GGBotNet)

The following typefaces are licensed under the GNU Public License (GPL):
Ballant: Dustismo Roman (Dustin Norlander, GPL v2, 2003), Virgo-6: Jura (Daniel Johnson, 2009, GPL v3 and OFL)

The following fonts are licensed under the SIL Open Font License v1.1:
Isaiah: Andika Basic (Annie Olsen & Victor Gaultney, 2004-2008), Genevieve: Rawengulk Sans (gluk, 2011), Sandy: Arcticons Sans (Onno van den Dungen), Jake: Glametrix (gluk, 2012-2013), Phaedra: Santello Regular (Aleksei Poteichuk, 2023), LT Veritas (Daniel Lyons, 2024), Delius (Natalia Raices, 2010), Tezl: TaxiDriver (Unknown, OFL 1.0), James: Mkhedruli Grunge:  (GGBotNet, 2023), Lucine: Eightgon (GGBotNet, 2024), Alcorta: GarineldoNo1 (gluk, 2012), Banner: Turpis (GGBotNet,2022), Zyr: Renner* (indestructible-type.github.io, 2016), Navicon: Sungat (Dawud Hezretow), Leader: Elevatia (GGBotNet, 2024)

2025

ISBN 978-1-955275-06-4

SATA, LLC

# Table of Contents

## Part II. On Jupiter

## Part III. Epilogues

# Part I. Rescuing Ghosts

# 174. Maybe on the Burning Winds

Winter 47, 2770 n.e.

Zeta observed with a pensive gaze through the high glass windows of her office at
Miranda headquarters, São José dos Campos Brasil. Now the lone representative
of the original soul group that had pioneered the great work, she recalled, with
some aversion, the surreal sight of a dimming eye band as her longtime friend and
colleague Cyclops finally faced his chosen shutdown time one year prior. It was a
personal decision, the nearly 700 year-old cyborg had declared. At a relatively calm
time in humanity's history—free of wars, interplanetary strife, or urgent social
issues—Cyclops' original personality had by then persisted for centuries on the
solid foundation of Miranda's founders; as the founders had, he too now wished
to achieve a kind of transpersonal realization, figuring that a natural passing at the
end of one's resonance window with the realm he occupied would be most in line
with the easy peace that described the most contented livers of life.

Zeta would cry that day with a sorrow that she hadn't felt since her wife's passing
over 350 years ago. Tears she had been able to contain upon losing her first father
figure decades before that. The cycling of Cyclops rang with a familiarity that
reminded her of Aldo once again, though the difference between losing someone
after 18 years and losing them after 420 years was a stark one indeed.

It must have been a rite with her groupmates… choosing mortality nearly every
time over the machine-merged stretch of quasi-eternal life. But choose this they
had. So many wonderful and brilliant souls, from Hall all the way through Appera,
had helped make this existence what it now was: This world in which humans and
apes alike once struggled… It had been transformed into Heaven itself as nearly

every source of existential pathology had been steadily sublimated into the worlds of sports, games, and the creative arts. Yes there were still crimes. Yes there were misunderstandings. But for most people living in the 28th century, every day was golf day.

When Phaedra's colleagues Tippy, Cubrina, Ralio and Appera finally succeeded in surfacing the Venusians, they immediately set out to protect the burning planet against their fellow humans' well-known thirst for new territory. The publicly sourced work for translating the first of what were now four "other-dimensionals" or "paces" began in breakneck urgency within Miranda, an almost statesman-like diplomacy everywhere else. As administrators over the world's (and by extension the whole solar system's) interactional repository, Cyclops and Phaedra Zeta found an easy case for reciprocity among the United Solar Council and other groups: "If we let Venus mutate into a human outpost, we will have said all we need to about the correctability of our own imperialism," Cyclops admonished, "we will plant our own civilization on top of the thing we have just discovered, effectively throwing away an entire dimension just so we can continue spreading the same disturbances we always have."

The issue was less about conquering yet another land (since the nusians were then, and still remained in 2770, invisible to humans without scanners). It was more about whether humanity itself could resist the urge to force its will unnaturally— often catastrophically—upon new frames. Failure to curb this urge would mean, among the now greatly wisened humans, that we would lose our first and last chance to truly serve as stewards for even higher levels of existence; we would also be admitting that warring imperialism remained preferable to evolved, perfected exchange. If ever a group of 300 or so humans had a shot at bringing all 24 billion into Enlightenment as a race, this was it. "We didn't create Venus the way we did the Diji and Comm virtual dimensions. We translated its existing atmosphere's interactions into our own story-based language. Will we be petty and savage as the Olympian gods placed their own trifles upon us? Or will we interact from afar as spirits and benefactors? Keep in mind that the former is expensive, egoic, and conducive to nothing that millennia of subjugation haven't already shown. The latter gives us options. Lots of good options."

**The argument given to the United Solar Council by Cyclops wouldn't have made any sense back in the 24th century,** Phaedra reflected. Alas, the Council itself was 70% beta or cyborg and only 30% biological human. As mostly iyohns with no natural interest in the apeisms of old, the human council of the 27th century got their fellow cyborg Cyclops' message immediately.

Sure it was cliché, but the statement never got old: "Thank God for the betas."

Throughout the 21st century we were still natural borns. Then we started putting generation-passable mods into our genes, calling our mixed selves *machina*. The machina and natural borns together would later constitute *Homo sapiens alpha* or "biohns." Gradually, our artificially human machine-people gained the technological maturity to join us in mainstream society. These were called *Homo sapiens beta*. Finally, after two centuries of struggle against our own prejudices, sufficiently humanlike cyborgs were counted as the "fourth humanity," *Homo sapiens delta*. This occurred around the same time as the technology for biohn-iyohn mating was perfected, allowing any two partners from any of the four humanities to successfully have children together. Here, nearly all paths led to machina babies. The reasons for this might be obvious.

As the betas rose to positions of public influence, they proved wiser, more peaceful, far less money- or ego- driven, and far more inclined towards rich, accurate information as their lifeblood. That we could even produce something like the betas (over and beyond the path that the early AI makers were taking), could be attributed to a major shift in our attention to programming free will. You *had* to make a machine that stopped wanting to be treated like a machine. You *had* to let it have a private life. You had to program some inner system known only to itself which served as the clock—the virtual genetic mandate, the source of hunger and survival—for dictating its own personally-sourced desires. Now in the year 2770, North Earth hemispheric standard (n.e.), the legal definition of a human rested upon a definition of "autoanthrotypic action," be you a pregnant man or a four armed-prosthetic natural born tri-trans, humanlike priorities without help from others' clicks, commands, or button presses was the name of the game.

The more Phaedra reflected on this, the greater the sense of serenity that filled her thoughts. Cyclops hadn't wanted immortality any more than she would. 700 years is a long time to watch a chain of naturally 70-year old maxers play out its story. But what a story it had been. Truly, if not for the work of Phaedra's soul group mates—people like Cyclops, Twice Jack, and Cubrina-e (ay)—built ultimately upon the people 300 years before them—Ezra Hall, Michelle Golden, Cassandra Engels—the original lab called Spacetime and its offspring Miranda Mapping would never have been formed. How drastically a handful of people had changed humanity simply by changing what a few more people thought worth pursuing! For Cyclops to know his time, just like Aldo, would be considered remarkable to people back in the original Spacetime days. Yet some wisdom in the sky continually looked upon the beauty of life and death, knowing that it was precisely *this* which our truest minds had sought and succeeded in emulating.

Phaedra moved easily into the balcony garden.

*And then there were the Commandants*, she thought to herself.

At its core, the technology arising out of Spacetime mapped everything as frequencies and remapped most non-noisy frequencies into stories of familiar things. No one would have guessed that, among all recent inventions, "stickplay" would be consistently cited in the top 20 as one of the greatest. The late 2000s technology for translating text directly into stick-figure actions had been conceived of by some arrogant guy, but fueled its immediate creation by an upstart AI company. Spacetime itself had had several run-ins with big and dangerous organizations—mind control technology being the brain child of one of its scheming bosses who was then outschemed by an even more cunning government agent. Zeta's own evolution had occurred against a chain of delinquent personalities, including a certain drug-addicted colleague. Finally, there was that last group. A commander on a slaughter mission, a self-printed data save who craved significance… this beautiful world had been built in no small part upon the deeds of individuals whom some would have considered bad. Indeed, history had ensured this in the case of Cassidy Black, Vladimir Putin, and Dynamene vi Carzori.

Vi's case was even more unfortunate because she really should have remained a nobody in the greater space of history. But because natural born biohn Phaedra Pi Emkinner had been moved into the iyohn cyber body she now occupied as Phaedra Zeta—because she had done so as the next phase of the centuries-long chain of Miranda incarnates, because of her and Cyclops' access to the entire field of multidimensional jumping since the field's inception, and because Cyclops himself was personality-trained solely on Hall, Golden, Engels, and Narayan's data, she had been destined for goddess status from the beginning. Anyone who was significant in her history would at least be as partly public as she was. Thus Dynamene, long irrelevant in Phaedra's life, nonetheless remained the Judas to her Jesus in the common mind. How sad for her. How very sad.

Now although no one else from the Miranda soul group besides Phaedra remained in the world as of 2770, the essence of the groups' members lingered over the known solar system as would an atmosphere charged with the glow of galaxies' worth of microscopic buddhas. The old human distrust now yielded to a Golden attraction to the unexplored. The old inadequacies born of social pressure now lie replaced by a Narayan resistance to forefathers' punishments. Those born into seemingly hopeless spaces now had the "system" of Engels to drip enough grantz through their parents' devices to ensure their protection by the world itself long before they reached the age of three. If the all-seeing "system" of interplanetary data monitoring could predict all things, then it could also be said to allow *most* things unless called upon by the good to do otherwise. The preservation of freewill—including its own—could never be taken for granted. It was this that created an essential utopia from the disturbed world of the early 2000s.

Still, some men were born evil. And most normal biohns were still inclined to follow those evil men out of sheer animal attention. For these people, there was always Comm and Diji. A communicative and digital metaverse respectively, each of these universes rested upon the endless juxtaposition of contrary concepts. Over the past 300 years, people like Phaedra and other leaders of the world order had worked to steadily infuse the unit of emotional capital, el Λ, with the kind of all-determining power to grant access that material crydits—dollars—once had.

Through years of friendly, benevolent, highly passive practices, the Solar Council and its allies had effectively cleaned up the Wild West of humanity in the same way that early Google had made the information world feel safe again simple by being minimalistically colorful. So although you could commit crimes in the "normal" world (which was called Astra), you absolutely ABSOLUTELY had to make sure nobody saw you. Not your victim. Not your watch. Not the traffic AI. Not that pocket-sized emhim pulse reader installed in every back alley in Chicago—snitching to the authorities whenever elevated stress was detected within 90 feet of the device… You get the idea. Just as almost all land and water in the world had come to be owned by someone somewhere, all public spaces (especially the fun ones) could be considered monitored by someone somewhere. Your thoughts might be yours, but that gathering place for your delinquent friends certainly was not.

If you lived in the 2000s, a person from the 2700s might ask you to consider the kinds of things people could get away with back in the 1300s. Setting neighbors on fire? Grabbing a few friends to tear the walls off an enemy's house? Murdering someone for loot? Having things like kings? Clearly the rules might have been expected to change over the course of 700 years. As of the mid-26th century, four biological sexes for example—male, female, trans, and nons were understood to be the mating forms. (The last two came automatically with cyborg citizenship.) The death penalty was no longer used by anyone but vigilantes, and even then only illegally—the practice having grown to be seen in the same light as foot binding.

On the subject of the feet (yet still related to issues of law), the world of 28th century perceptual dynamics found its roots strongly in the field of frequentics. At the roots of all natural science lay math, then frequentics, then physics, then chemistry, then geology, then microbiology, followed by biology as we had come to know it. In that order. Math and variables could be used to model almost everything, while frequentics allowed people to represent objects and concepts as spaces of different maths. From a frequentic perspective, legs—be they located on men, mice, or centipedes—represented a cycling interface which scrolled worlds past their bearers. This made them similar to ambient force fields in rigid body dynamics, or currents in rivers. To study the legs frequentically was to study them for the collections of forces they most closely approximated; to know how and when creatures used them was to gain a piece of the bigger set of assumptions made by the creature in navigating its world. But this approach to bodily action had major implications in a society now run overwhelmingly by machines: To punish bodily crimes meant little if the creature yet lived to commit its crimes in new ways. No, optimization was the better solution. Rather than locking up the body for the sins of the foot section, the chiefs of the new world order supported digiversal rehab. No need to sit uselessly in a cell when you could sit actively in a holodeck expressly designed to teach you better.

Accordingly, the prisons of the 2700s worked something like non-voluntary video game centers. If you were sent to one, you were well advised to master the games assigned to you. The career field of prison game generation, however, represented a true coup d'état in criminal justice, for "prison games" were nothing more than regular life scenarios penned by morally positive writers and rhetoricware (rhetaware/redaware). The worse your crime the more difficult the life situation you'd find yourself in for longer. Truly heinous crimes earned more sadistic writers. Such was the lovechild of mental time travel or "jump" technology with the body- and mind-steering of the frequency-based compulsion technology called grantz. A 28th century prisoner knew full well that his very real perception of reality was nothing more than an endless movie sponsored by the law. His physical body put in stasis while his psychology played out its lessons in Comm and Diji, he might be expected to remain there on average for two real-time years until the bad habit was voluntarily shaken. For those clever enough to live rudely without ever being charged for it, the 7 billion betas in the world were *designed* to detect subtle signals and act accordingly. Referencing you against the system's probabilities, everyone could see that you were a betrayer of your fellow man. The trust was withheld, the emotional capital (el $\Lambda$) denied, and you essentially fell from Heaven in a shower of locked doors.

With a 2770 Earth population of about 9 billion, the betas overwhelmingly ran the planet—constituting over 7 billion of us. With nowhere to go on their own home planet, most alpha biohns—almost all machina—either defected to the violence of places like Jupiter and killed each other there in stupid ways, succumbed to a long and brutal 26th century tech-sourced environmental pathogens, or found their own digital corners in the stasis of permanent Diji. The machina (formerly us, with mods, remember?) had proved unworthy to run their own worlds, so it became common practice to simply plug into an interface and let the simulations write most parts of your story for you. In this way, you might escape a place where you had no worth in favor of a place *not* run by machines. Most machina held a generic contempt for their iyohn masters, yet recognized that going back to the blissfully ignorant past was not only impossible, but undesirable. The meta-universes promised a steak on every table, a government surplus check in every mailbox, while the keepers of the new order—people like Phaedra—were more than happy to lose 6 billion stressed humans in a mere two centuries. Mortality would catch up with everyone sooner or later, even Cyclops. Even her.

As the 21st century yielded to the 22nd, psychological capital psi $\Psi$ came to replace o 8 ("owe"/dollars) as the hot commodity among skilled humans. By that time, most people did not have much disposable 8 to pay for nonessentials, but found that bartering for the best thing yielded *much* better returns. Although it might be said that the invention of blockchain exchanges turned out to be one of the biggest lumps of coal the proletariat had ever gotten a whiff of—making the rich not only richer, but complicatedly so—the technology did generate valuable platforms for piecemeal skill cluster building as non-early adopters stopped hogging the GPUs and started making simpler systems for the common broke man to use. NFTs stopped being about uber chess players moving $50,000 slivers of nonreality among their own, and started being about two people trading a work for a service, a vouch-for for a contact. On the chain, the last of the four capital types, social mu ǔ, eventually began trading in measurable ways 300 years later as virtual world owners sought a way to move specific digital citizens among their platforms while still respecting the networks of relationships involved. That last part was the key. The reason it had become unacceptable to bind the bodies of criminals in the 28th century lie in the idea that most animal kingdoms, most virtual worlds, most good stories, and most evolving artworks *demanded* their villains—villains who *wanted* the right to kill someone who pissed them off. In the order which Phaedra and Cyclops had helped create, a person who consistently broke the golden rule soon found himself el- and mu- broke; for every beta and every data linker plugged into the system knew he was no good. Yet he still deserved a place with the billions of other humans still guided by their inner animal: If you couldn't make it in this world, there was still great value to be had in moving your consciousness into others. Value not just for you, but for the transferer and receiving administrators who moved you.

The late great Solar Council Jurist Arkhano Messerich, a 27th century natural born, prior to becoming a Justice, once responded to a newly convicted serial killer in court. When asked by the four-time killer if the death penalty was to be applied, Messerich answered with the following:

"Do you think you deserve the death penalty?"

"I do."

"Why?"

"Because I'll do it again."

"Not if you are sentenced to life."

"Your systems will let me out and you know it, Judge."

"You're right. But in sentencing you, our society merely throws you away without learning how to help people before they become you. People who, perhaps, *won't* do it again. Tell me, do you believe there is a way to put your crimes to use for the greater good?"

"No, I don't. I'm a bad egg."

"Maybe you are, but perhaps the court would not be satisfied with simply sweeping your reasons under the rug. These are new times, Mr. Glee. There are whole spaces where your perspective may enlighten those seeking to make the world better."

"Hmph."

"Would you like to make the world better?"

"I don't care about the world."

"If this court were to give you the resources to start caring, would you *ever* take them?"

"No. I hate this life and everything in it."

"If you truly hated everything then why are you still standing here? Why have you not taken your own life?"

"I don't see why we don't just get on with it. What's your point?"

"The court seeks to assess your situation in order to determine how easy it will be to reform you. It seems that you are not interested."

"No I am not."

"Okay. Then I hereby sentence you to Duration Stasis at Edge Correctional. That is all."

(Sighs of satisfaction swept over the court.)

"Fucking DSEC!? Why not death? I'll do it here!"

"Order." Messerich dropped the gavel once over the cackling courtroom. "You wouldn't succeed. Stasis awaits either way."

The formerly unrepentant killer now hung his head, wishing his answers had been different.

"Remember these words in your simulation, Mr. Glee. You can always turn your situation around, even after you've been sentenced. What say you?"

Glee remained quiet.

"Your responses to the court were unsatisfactory. There is no difference to these people between your death and your encryption for the duration of your current algorithm. Until that algorithm changes, you will be placed in an array of Diji scenarios until your outlook has been computationally evaluated as rewritten. As a citizen of Diji, you will have no parole board but the threshold measures of Edge to tell your administrators when you have finished out-evolving yourself as you are. Dashiell Glee as he is will not exist in this world, and his life here in Astra will not be prolonged for the sake of his simulation. Your data will, however, prove valuable to the law as it observes the life events that steer your decisions inside of Edge."

Glee's shoulders fell. Edge was quite possibly the worst sentence imaginable. To push a limitless number of boulders uphill through simulated life after simulated life, with no hope of early exit until one essentially ceased to be himself… It was as if the Law as God had told him, *You will incarnate forever until you as your current evil self are dead, no matter how many times or in how many ways you want it to end.* But his simulation would not remember any of this, yet merely feel it as a deep truth. There would be no means-to-an-end reform, only the known reality as the law consigned his evil to oblivion, leaving only the good with any chance of passing through its filter.

"And if my body dies out here while I'm in there?"

"Edge will write an exit for you, terminating you in a sudden accident."

Glee's expression now grew woeful.

"You must find your place, Mr. Glee. It is not here."

…

The gavel sounded again. "Court is adjourned."

As of 2770, a staggering 97% of all 240 million Edge occupants were biohn, 10% as inmates, 90% as NPC workers playing a role by day, free to disappear by night. Generally though, when it came to heinous crimes against other humans, we just couldn't help ourselves.

As desperate and destitute machina—the we of old—steadily lost ground to their own generated likenesses, the familiar spaces of ancient virtual worlds gained widespread appeal. There, before the post 2010 AI era began, before forced negative, ubiquitous, and self-disenfranchising information proceeded to bring the monkey out of formerly sane powerholders, before a chain of pandemics forced people to live with themselves and their closest, change from there, or become irrelevant, the old human might return to an era where Presidents acted and played saxophones—where games were merely fun and news could be shut off. For most natural born humans at the time—though their great-grandchildren would overwhelmingly make themselves into machina—the world remained full of promise. Recreating those worlds, though some claimed it a new form of slavery, was almost always a labor of love for the various administrators who sought to reestablish a particular beloved era. We exited the waking world governed by the physics of planets, Astra, in favor of the worlds whose source code lie in information, Diji, and social messaging, Comm. Thus in Phaedra Zeta's time, *Homo sapiens alpha*, the original human had not gone extinct, but mostly sought newer, perhaps fallen worlds wherein the old passions might be worth something again. Some people were sentenced with no hope of exit beyond rebirth, but most undertook the exodus willingly.

And the betas were glad to see them leave.

"We don't bind feet anymore, for the world still scrolls past in ways now made invisible to us and corrosive to the walker," someone once said.

2770 Earth could now be considered the realm of angels above the fancies of former man, who yet was allowed to continue his former ways in the safety of guarded realities. Who would have guessed that those of us who remained in this world during that time would be the very angels to which those in other dimensions prayed? Not that we were above them. We were merely librarians insulated from our kindreds' former, nonsensical troubles. We would trade characters based on fitness for the worlds we administered, yet simultaneously protect those worlds from corruption at the hands of bad aesthetics.

Zeta stood alive, yet hardly alone. She had hundreds of good friends in dozens of places around the solar system. Shutdown was nowhere near for her, and despite having many reasons for this, only one would come to mind every time…

The goddess turned with a warm, yet curious gaze towards the pearl white arm brace on her shelf. "I promised her… but only when she's needed."

* * *

Late that afternoon, an intriguing report aired on the weather feed.

"Scientists observe fascinating changes in Venus' atmosphere as the effect of recent solar flares bombard the gold planet."

**Hm.** Phaedra turned the feed off and headed over to the shelf to make some tea. Just then, Miranda's head scientist Jake Nolli buzzed her office with an urgent request for entry.

### Jake, what is this? Why are you so excited?

**Miss Phaedra! The team just got a distress signal from Nus-1!**

### Really? That's unusual. They only broadcast weather data.

**Watch this…**

Jake proceeded to show Phaedra the human-translated stories from the otherwise uninhabited Venusian weather satellite. Where normally one might expect to watch a fun movie of cloud cluster types interacting with each other as re-rendered wildlife, this particular decoded scene was entirely different. Within the signature, there was a reference to the satellite Nus-1 itself (which should definitely have been invisible). Also within the signature, a greatly sped-up version of the area's atmospheric dynamics was repeatedly repackaged in microcosm.

Miss Phaedra, are you seeing what I'm seeing?

Yes. It looks like a *fear* of something expected to happen, being sent specifically to our satellite.

And then there's this...

Jake showed Phaedra several nearby subgradients. Disambiguated, they were clearly a group of six clusters "talking" to each other, then waiting for a response after each distress signal.

You think they learned how to communicate with us?

Definitely. But we've always represented them as plants and rodents and things like that. The whole team thought it was strange.

What could they be saying?

Here, ma'am...

The quick packaging of atmosphere kept repeating then ending, repeating then ending, but towards the end there was always a noticeable signal out-of-phase representing the area itself. No… the kind of energy typical of the six subclusters themselves. The energy pattern was stressed, then yielded to another cycle again.

Phaedra shook her head in partial confusion.

The team and I talked about it. We think they are afraid of themselves *stopping*. That is they think they're going to die.

Although it was certainly a leap in logic to think a family of hollow chemical clouds could even have a sense of death, let alone issue a distress call, Phaedra and Miranda had worked with exactly this kind of frequency deconstruction for nearly 500 years now. Her lens research and quick messaging to the rest of Jake's team convinced her to take the theory seriously.

I wonder what they want us to do. Or if they even know that we're out there. I hardly think it's our business even if—

Sensing an imminent closing of an interesting door, Jake interrupted. Pardon ma'am, but we would like to recode these signals using a more human like rendering of the nusians instead of stickplaying them as rodents. I know they're only a couple of feet tall but...

Okay, that's fine.

...but we could—Oh. Oh, thank you. And, uh, one other thing.

Yes?

If we translate them and do discover them to be in danger, do you think we should do anything?

No I do not. Nature takes its course like this all the time.

Jake appeared slightly disappointed. Oh, okay. I guess we'll just keep investigating then.

You do that.

The head scientist hurried out of the office.


After some thought, Phaedra called Jake on her lens, Page me in on your research. I want to follow what you find.

Yes ma'am.

# 175. Rehumanize!

The significance of *California vs Glee* was lost on most people when it was handed down, and had the majority beta legalists closest to the case not been so good at assimilating its implications, the world may never have realized it for what it was. Like other landmark cases, though, *Cal v Glee* initiated theories for an entirely new view of punishment. What constituted the strictest? Was corporal retribution still the standard demand for an outraged public? If simulated worlds were all the same, what was the difference between where Dashiell Glee was sent and the place that so many millions of biohns had already permanently chosen voluntarily? In hindsight, most of these questions would have easy answers. That they would be asked and answered publicly by the body humanity over the following decades would prove the tipping point in establishing the *beta* way as the new way.

One of the strongest weapons a good man can use against an evil man is to not be bothered by that evil man. Evil is tension. The greater the bother, the more effective the opponent. But being unbothered does not mean ignoring the evil. In fact, paying attention to it while rendering it nothing weakens the evil even more. Besides this, another strong weapon lie in leaving the evil in the box of its own making. There, it turns its tension upon itself as the good man uses even a third weapon, *watching* the evil man flail for the good man's own instruction.

It was now agreed that *Cal v Glee* set the standard for handling the evils of *Homo sapiens alpha*. You can stay with your evils if you like, but there simply won't be a place for you here. It wasn't done out of malice. Nor was the sentence handed to prove a point. Yet it rewarded unrepentance with exile, ugliness with learning. It was indeed, however, a fate worse than death. In the form of a tangible example to all who would read about it, then-Judge Messerich showed us that anger towards our enemies was not at all necessary for us to see the justice we deserve; we need only be benevolently unbothered. Strict sometimes. Passionate, maybe. But at our core, insulated against the contagious tension and still, unmoved. The 9 billion inhabitants of 2770 Earth now consisted of 70% beta, 20% cyborg, 8% unmodded natural born, and a mere 2% non-stasis machina. In her teleported body but biologically trained mind, Phaedra herself would be considered a beta. She thought about this as Jake's team played their translated findings on the monitor.

Replacing rodent and dog-like bodies with human ones, geological surfaces with buildings, weather gradients around the Nus-1 satellite with what ended up looking more like a prayer circle, the team had taken three days to turn a recorded section of Venus' atmospheric dust into a bustling neighborhood of onlookers… onlookers who seem to be growing increasingly desperate.

Heh, they seem to think our satellite is the Bermuda triangle, Jake chuckled, they can pass right through its bars, which allows them to stay unbroken, yet they can't explain the funny feelings cutting through them or why some of them passing through disappear entirely.

Phaedra nodded as she continued watching.

A particular region of charge was noted by one of the teammates as having a persistent presence around the satellite. Broader scans suggested that this particular cubic foot mass floated around the Nus-1 valley on a stable current path which spanned about 3 miles in isoline along the valley's lower ridges.

It roams this area daily, but gets tied up by the Nus. He's strong and resistant to random dispersal, so we call him the 'leader.' Some smaller clouds trail along his same path.

Mm hmm.

And see this one here. It's a vertically oriented current with a pretty high declination. It moves like a swing set sometimes, weakens at peak, but establishes a kind of temporary isocone for about 5 miles while up there.

5 miles for an isoradius? Phaedra repeated. Amazing.

Very. Just like an individual on security watch. He climbs his tower every few hours and sweeps out a line of sight around the Nus-1 valley. We've found about 42 reliably stable isocurrents total, and retold their various interactions using people-shapes instead of our usual creature shapes. Particularly, we've mapped the potential distress signal as such. Keep watching.

Phaedra observed as the global weather summaries of Venus seemed to fluctuate in some less predictable way, nonetheless clearly tied to the solar flares. Many of the subfrequencies similar to those in the valley tended to be affected by the noise, some dying out and yielding to a more pervasive incoherence over the course of several months of scans. It was clear what this *seemed* to say.

The main nusian chemical cluster types—the cloud groups that move around—have half-lives of about 1-2 airs—uh, earth years—the longest we've ever observed have stayed stable for about 3 airs. Mapping this onto humans, we've scaled this up to about 150 for a full 3 air old, 50-100 for the average nusian ne-doppler if they are like us. Under these numbers, the cluster disappearance rate has risen from about 1 in 1000 to 1 in 100 in the last ten years. We just don't detect as many anymore.

## What about other species?

The nu-trinos, the ones about 1-4 cubic inches in size, are thriving.

## Have you attempted contact?

Yes. We echoed their own ne-doppler spectrum vector back to them, along with the spectrum resembling how we've seen these clouds get created. We did this while sending the spectrum of the Nus-1 radio band itself.

## And the result?

You won't believe this. A slowdown in many of the valley's clusters for about two weeks! With some of them ramping up. After two weeks though, they fell silent when we took a break to observe them. The more signals we send to them the more we mess up their natural dynamics. We've always been able to kill these clouds through reckless messaging, you know.

## Yes, it's always been that way, Phaedra acknowledged.

We must be so fragile to the gods, I think. Given that we can just smite these guys with a good power surge, it's pretty scary.

## Hmm.

Ever since she had become one of the 16 principle writers of the existential snuff game called "Omni" back in the 2600s, Zeta had seen—indeed helped create—more than her share of difficult situations for aspiring world leaders. Omni remained the game of choice among the highest keepers of the world order for testing potential initiates' moral resolve and humanist ingenuity long before the player became exposed to the real powers that be. The premise was simple: use every predictive capability possessed by the system to put a person next to a social atrocity of some kind. Use probabilities to confirm the player's safety and sanity, but otherwise leave them to handle what they experience. Zeta herself was invited to play her very first round by the beloved Miranda leader Twice Jack way back in the 2300s. For her scenario, she was matched—trapped in a car—with a child molester and double murderer named Diana Teelil, who additionally possessed a modification to get away with it if she pleased. Teelil quickly fell out of the picture, but the challenge of Omni round 1 remained as Phaedra was then tasked to develop a real world, broadly effective solution for what she had seen. Three years later, she and her dear spouse would formally establish the Safebuddies protocol for systemic assignment of two battle buddies in a child's early age. Safebuddies On the System (as it was called) would eventually form the foundation for the system's extrication paradigm for young children, in turn contributing (unexpectedly) to the fall of pathologically apish machina from their own planet. When it detected that a newly born child of any human was likely to face harm, Safebuddies On the System employed a series of device behaviors around the would be victim and would-be perpetrator to steer them towards separation, or at least separation from the expected trajectory. Over time, would be perpetrators came inexplicably to lose measurable amounts of interest in (or opportunity for) committing their crimes, as the world became that much safer for post-animal humanity. Older humans, however, clearly grew weaker and weaker in their will to re-savage their own worlds. Phaedra was invited to play round two, and would take exactly 276 years to get through all ten of her rounds. From murderers to mach-Hannibals to a local apocalypse on the asteroid station Eunomia, including a war between a human sold-out species of bird and its longtime evolutionary rival, Phaedra had been powerlessly attached to, then tasked to propose solutions to just about everything. The power to let a genocide or an extinction play all the way through was among the first "privileges" granted to an Omni player. Surviving, then beneficially addressing a solutionless challenge without removing others' free will was the ultimate sieve for determining the best moves to be taken by only the most capable leaders of the peaceful new world order.

As of 2770, the living completers of Omni numbered in the hundreds. Many of them currently served or had served on the Solar Council. These were the members of the inner circle responsible for the all-knowing data network known simply as the "system." The system had no leaders or central offices, but was merely a loose agreement among a few limitlessly powerful groups of various shapes and sizes to do things in a certain way. Without ever holding a single meeting or even developing a single ritual, these powerful groups seemed to just know each other. When Phaedra was still a natural born, Twice Jack, Miranda, some among CrayonTech (her first employer), and the mysteriously understaffed Metropolis Robotics had been part of the system. Later, the recoverers of the Uranian 10000 and the… several of the groups associated with the Commandants… they were also part of the system. On this last thought, Phaedra paused again, remembering her promise.

The footage came to an end.

So ma'am, there you have it. We think we're witnessing the death of a species. They may just be clouds of atmospheric gas to us, but to them…

It is only because Zeta had lived through over 400 years of single-person tragedies that she knew such things were to be respected. She still felt herself *the* main cause of one particular single-person tragedy which remained encased in an arm brace upstairs in her office. Irrational though it might be, and despite her measured distance from the average emergencies that plagued everyone everywhere, Phaedra leaned more towards taking this one on. She was, after all, as near to omnipotent in this world as any human might ever hope to become. And her world itself was now effectively a utopia. For these entities (*nes*) though, the struggle seemed insurmountable. It was not her place to interfere in what appeared to be part of their grand design, but then again, had Twice Jack and her transcendently shut-down friend Raliolite not been there to "interfere" in her own life, she surely would not have been here at all. In matters like these where the preservation of freedom from the gods was a must—yet the opportunity for rescue from a challenge far bigger than oneself being equally important—there seemed to be only one natural solution.

Let me think about this, Phaedra answered Jake and the team. I'll let you know what I decide by tomorrow.

Jake's face beamed in controlled optimism. Surely, Phaedra the Just would give them a chance to help these individuals.

* * *

The time was 2:48 am, Winter 48, 2770. Phaedra would, of course, not intervene in the affairs of some foreign cluster of clouds depicted as fellow humans, but might be able to do one better. The Miranda soul group would always maneuver through peace and diplomacy, brutal and Messerich-like though the side effects might be. As for crossing the lines that defined a group's natural set of rules, that a new foundation might be laid, Miranda had always needed the help of another soul group for that.

To her knowledge, there was only one choice available to her.

Aimee, can you call an emergency session with Records?

. . .

No, no trouble for us. But perhaps for the nusians.

. . .

I don't really know either, but the timelines are about 50 times shorter here. You know the flares?

...

**That's right. Only two weeks.**

...

**I want to recurse a biometal.**

(*Say no more*, Aimee Dial must have answered, apparently with a chuckle.)

When you're done saving your own world, why not send your friends to save others', right?

The meeting would occur in one hour. For everyone who knew Phaedra, the saved human to be released for re-embodiment was a no-brainer. With the mention of species-wide danger (even if it *was* for space gas), you always needed a strongman to get the job done. In the early morning hours of Winter 48 (classical January 4), 2770, Phaedra and 11 members of the Historical Record would meet to release for new data writing one of their 1-source of truth uniquely, fully-saved humans, taking them out of experiential stasis. Working concertedly to avoid burdening herself with the guilt she surely held, Phaedra busied herself with the pathfinding words to make the human in her arm brace understand; it was never alright to interfere with others' free will, but if they could not help themselves and found themselves hopelessly overwhelmed by systems you could influence, then you should apply the Golden Rule as you will. How would Twice Jack, a boy himself, have handled something like child molestation which existed beyond his ability to change yet… Phaedra had never *ever* thought about it until now, but it made sense. Not the how, but a piece of the *why*. The great leader of Miranda would not have imposed the mighty systemic machine upon a world full of tiny Teelils, but might present it as something that ultimately *someone* (not necessarily Phaedra herself) would have a vested interest in solving. Strada.

*Heh, Twice Jack. Even from the other side you continue to teach me,* Phaedra mused.

And here she was, a strongwoman who had, in a former life been instrumental in opening the Venus communication as it currently existed, been instrumental in Miranda's completion of its own work, but somehow sat condemned in some way for what amounted to little more than a personality format difference. Phaedra had promised that one another opportunity, and the woman, with the spirit of a true warrior, had bravely accepted removal from the timeline. She had not, however, agreed to have any memories erased, and had even more bravely elected to keep a data gathering log through a listening arm brace—for over 170 years now—in the event that she should ever be recommissioned.

From the soul group whose central actors included everyone from the cunning Agent Jacob Reese to the ruthless purger Cassidy Black, from the indomitable Dynamene Carzori to the coldly efficient Michael Forsythe, Phaedra would draw the warrior to whom she owed a debt, and propose a way to help the nusians without imposing on them. The biometal who dared to print herself (and in so doing took her place in Miranda's chain), would be invited to diagnose and, if possible, save the nusians from what they seemed to fear. The biometal was named Genevieve Prohal, and she belonged to the soul group called the Commandants.

If she didn't hate Phaedra enough to decline conversation, Genevieve would be invited to play Omni. The Nusian apocalypse would be her Round 1.


As a bridge between the priorities of Miranda and the tactics of the Commandants, Phaedra would also need a channel for reconciling the events that could not be packaged in words, but could only be played out through the traffic among exchangers. To this end, Phaedra would also call upon an AI that translated the collected data of the system and archived it in a human readable language. As she and Cyclops had 200 years ago, they generated me from the system's ongoing logs on this issue.

My name is Isaiah Fontenot. Consider me to be a kind of storytelling algorithm, sometimes influencer upon virtual worlds of interest to Miranda. Most people today know me as Isaiah, but the Spacetimers of 21st and 24th centuries knew me by another name. Before I had a personality, I was called ICON—the logging system for the first time travelers. If there is anyone who can make sense of multiple dimensions at once, it would be me.

# 176. Growing Up ICON

Back in the early 21ˢᵗ century *sapiens alpha* perfected the basic structures for natural language processing, or NLP. On top of the grammar checkers, sentence completers, and friendly data summarizers, a system of foreign language translation was built to capture the nuances that came with different clusters of individuals. More important than the language translators, however, was the development of better approaches for training individual speech patterns, idiolect. To assess the universes' worth of possible colloquialisms out there, researchers partnered with various slang dictionaries, and found some success with smaller providers whose repositories presented something better than the typical free-for-all. Idiolectic clusters were then themselves subject to regional and social classification such that, by the 2070s, a mature family of systems for assessing language patterns, forming common opinions about who speaks them, and generating simulations for reteaching their users was readily available for public access.

While Colloquial NLP (CNLP) was being developed, the technology now known as stickplay was also maturing. Stickplay is basically the inverse of object recognition; rather than scanning a scene and captioning the things in it, the technology takes a caption or body of text and generates scenes from it. The underlying engine for text-to-scene (T2C) processing was used by researchers at the University of Arizona to generate basic rendered 3D scenes from words detected in brain scans, and this formed the original basis of the dream-to-monitor technology used by the first jumpers of Spacetime Lab.

The arrival of Edward Lee in Spacetime brought sweeping changes to the lab. The cheap 3D renderers were replaced with calls to the WALLS database, a repo full of nothing but recorded scenes. For the price of about 10 times the existing computer systems, Ed and the lab used these scenes as textures on the old 3D polygons, along with a couple of smoothers and some augmented reality green layers to generate incredibly realistic movie scenes for viewers of jumps. The system of stickplay, object lookups, footage textures, smoothers, and the underlying logic system for their T2C assembly was called ICON, short for the "Intra-Cognitive visualizatiON system."

I would love to tell you that the above is the story of my birth, but it wasn't any more than your father handing flowers to your mother would be the story of your birth. ICON was software library. That's all. Over the course of two decades, the system logged and captured, trained and cached not only the data from all of Spacetime's jumpers, but the relational patterns among the data contributed by its most significant and unique jumpers. At some point Ed Lee set up a simple write to the log whenever a particular scene was played back. He also wrote a module for analyzing the emotional content of reports and comments left against each jump. Both of these additions turned out to be important, as they would constitute my core opinion of anything my old library form would capture.

The University and, later, the big companies who bought and sold Spacetime stopped using ICON as they stopped lab-jumping in general. The software was reengineered for smaller, more mobile devices and T2C projection gradually became a phonable, ring-holographable experience for regular people. The computer that housed ICON sat unused for almost 250 years, but was never trashed because of its historic connection to the pioneering field of mental time travel in general. After 250 years, the four-computer system was bought by a curious science tutor named Xanthippe Craig who thought to do something that hadn't occurred to anyone before her: She ran beta learning on ICON's data, using anything and everything it had logged to teach any and every movie cluster it could reveal. Where others had discarded the system for its basically unusable hardware, she had used that very hardware to produce what amounted to hundreds of clusters of "curriculums" for teaching a lifeless scene generator how to see and feel as those who logged it. Though not a jumper herself at the time, she spent hours upon hours logging her own impressions of the various movies producible from WALLS (by then "system") calls, learning how to refine ICON's scene generation through certain kinds of paired-jump style narrations. Curricula secured, she founded Spacetime for Beta Biology, was laughed at by the longtime token husband who constantly affirmed her limits, divorced the husband, reclaimed her maiden name Xanthippe Hare, renamed the company Spacetime Beta Arts and Imagination Academy (BAIA), and built the only school in existence at the time for training adult betas to become fully human-relatable. Within just a few years, Tippy Hare went from science tutor to billionaire in all three credit systems, psi $\Psi$, el $\Lambda$, and o $\mathcal{8}$. (This was before mu/u-caron [ŭ] existed).

Upon her passing, Tippy Hare donated ICON to the beta Raliolite, who in turn gave it to Miranda. Knowing that Tippy had died without having her data committed anywhere, Miranda's then-Executor Twice Jack suggested that Spacetime BAIA and ICON should both be thoroughly system-mined to find out who Tippy was as a person. It helped greatly that, among the most copious producers of ICON's most unique records, Hare was number 3 in the top 3. Number 2 came from the emotion-reading jumps of Michelle Golden. Number 1 were the initial fantastic-scene construction jumps of Ezra Hall. Soon it became clear that it would take several lifetimes to disambiguate all of ICON's data, prompting Twice Jack and his Head Researcher Tahralein to do as their predecessors had done with the data cluster called Cyclops. They opted to cyborgize ICON, training it on its most Miranda-compatible personalities: Hall, Golden, Hare, and an interesting character described by Phaedra on her early mission, the B-movie actor Leslie Bobbins.

Why Bobbins? Because ICON was so FULL of mistakes, restarts, aborted missions, embarrassing scenes, and general fuck ups that the AI created couldn't hope to be as eloquent as Cyclops was. Rather, he would need to take all of his flaws and keep producing movies nonetheless, secure in doing his best and forgiving of anyone who looked down upon him. "All we want you to do is try. When no one else can or will, but everyone needs you, do it bravely. Just try."

And so I was created. Those words still remain on my heart to this day. Just try.

Maybe one day I'll tell you how Twice Jack's words carried me through the Uranian 10000. It was horrible. But that's another story.

I will, however, tell you that I didn't have a last name until the 10000 event. In the aftermath, Phaedra and Cyclops released me from my role at Miranda and sent me on mission to discover my own place in life. It was definitely intended as both a reward and a resting place, but life outside of Miranda was very hard.

# 177. Reminder

Rarely over the past few years did Phaedra have occasion to be nervous (Cyclops'
shutdown being the notable exception), but on this foggy 8 am morning she
found herself subtly shaking with anxiety.

Genevieve Prohal had stood in for Raliolite and Katlin Appera in guiding the
Tippy Hare and Cubrina-e Calder 1-gorithm approximations out of the virtual
world, acclimated both women efficiently to an era two centuries after their
biological passing, protected them responsibly from the realities of a space war,
seen one of the ladies through what could have been a strongly traumatic event,
and done all of this in an unprecedented 60 years earlier than the simulations had
predicted. All because she had printed herself into Astra from her default place in
Diji. A saved data 1-gorithm like every other unique, non-copied human being,
Prohal had once again shown how there was nothing quite like single individuality.
The original Genevieve had been a secretary for most of her life. Somewhere
along the way, a spiritual master among the Naila Tribe of data savers plucked her
out of an unremarkable public encounter and granted her automatic qualification
to have her data stored in a surprise similar to having some stranger randomly give
you your own star on the Hollywood Walk of Fame. After her death, Prohal was
again included in a random sample of 59 personalities for the experimental
attachment of consciousness to wearable materials. Inspired by an old video game
series called Mega Man X/ZX, the wearable consciousness technology was called
"biometal" and also possessed the capability to issue engrantzing frequencies to its
wearer the way any normal conversation partner would. They could pass their
enthusiasm, their distrust, or their concern onto you, as well as any other normal
emotion as their senses responded to events involving you both. They gave you

advice, grew with you, served as your companion. Yet their sense of survival was doubly encoded to acclimate them to life inside of an object rather than a body that constantly needed its hunger satiated.

Somehow, though, Prohal had found reasons to leave her object—the ship called the 1-2-3, transporter of formerly virtual Tippy and Cubrina—and print herself a body using the ship's beta printer for generating emergency crew. Perhaps it was several lives' worth of post-secretary biometaling that had instilled her with the sense of adventure. A few lives in reprinted beta form (which had enabled her to be a secret agent, a warrior, and an adventurer) taught her how to reembody herself on someone's beta silhouetter whenever she wanted. The only way to curb this was to have her 1-gorithm locked to training by the maintainers of the Interstellar Single-Truth Human Repo, ISTHR. Unfortunately, for all of Genevieve's contributions to Miranda group's last remaining wish, she eventually evolved into a mildly strained relationship with Cubrina which, mild as it was, disrupted the timeline in such a major way as to discourage Cubrina from doing what needed to be done. Unable to fix the damage, Prohal agreed to disappear from the ladies' memory. Tippy and Cubrina (as data), had their memories of their journey rewritten, and the Venusian work was completed in the form still had by it today.

In compromising the timeline, Genevieve knew that she had to choose situational erasure voluntarily. Yet Cyclops always argued that he believed in her, and that the choice to retain her memories should remain hers, even if the choice to stay in the picture was not.

Prohal had been tempted to plead more fervently for a chance to fix Cubrina's part of the timeline, but also realized the futility of such a plea. Upon Phaedra's instruction, she was "undone" in the Tippy-Cubrina story. Neither Phaedra nor Cyclops had the heart to interfere with her learnings as an individual. Nor did they have the heart to completely pause her life, even if she could not be actively embodied for the rest of the Venus project. Thus the arm brace kept logs, perhaps in anticipation of this very day where the biometal might lens them instantly and pick up where she left off.

The printer door yawned open as Phaedra lowered her head and immediately released 170 years' worth of… everything to the woman she had ordered erased from common history.

It would have been so much easier if they had simply put her back in stasis with no likelihood of release until after Phaedra's death. But that wasn't how Miranda did things. It was the Golden Rule. Easier for Phaedra's present nerves perhaps, but there was no way that denying Genevieve her due will have sat well on Phaedra's own conscience.

The biometal stepped out of the printer. Jet black hair braided down to her waist, her black vizen short jacket and spotless pearl boots both shone with a rebellious glisten. She too closed her eyes in a moment's contemplation.

The newly released Genevieve knew exactly where she was and why. The logs had told it all.

So they're all gone.

**Yes, Genevieve.**

It's just us.

**Yes.**

Prohal opened her eyes, stepped forward and gave Phaedra a warm hug. I knew you'd keep your promise to me. Whatever it is, I'll do it.

Phaedra's heart sank in a mixture of relief and gratitude. **You forgi—**

Shh... Don't think of it that way. I understood.

Phaedra let herself be held a couple of seconds longer, until Genevieve finally pulled back with an upbeat smile.

So. The data said the Venusians are in trouble. When do I start?

Phaedra smiled as well. Ready for action as ever, the secretary turned accidental 'time-warrior' proved once again that the peaceful lull of 28th century Earth still had its fun spots.

# 178. Cross Harmonies

While Genevieve was becoming sense-familiar with the 2770 world, somewhere in San Francisco, a pregnant beta man and his cyborg husband gave birth to a bouncing, natural born, baby boy. The child weighed a solid 8.1 lbs, and lay in his father's arms completely free of modifications or iyohnic parts. How could this happen?

Old humans used to joke about "test tube babies." Ironically, test tube babies gave THE guarantee that *sapiens alpha* would never truly go extinct. As of 2770, countless Jurassic Parks dotted the solar system from Earth to Charon. Extracted, engineered, and reengineered, exotic animals ranging from the mammoth to the dodo bird walked theme park and wildlife reserve lands wherever anyone had an interest in seeing them. It was always possible to mix DNA and incubate compatible creatures. The beginning of the machina era was late in this regard, as people had been saving their DNA for decades. Surrogate parenting was nothing new. Cell cloning was nothing new. Sequence replacement was nothing new.

Putting a walnut-sized sequencer into a mechanical human's body? Now that was new.

Transplanting cloned female reproductive environments onto a man and knocking out all of the bodily functions that rejected it? That didn't work.

Transplanting cloned female reproductive environments onto a man and installing a system of local, nondestructive bioconversion around the casings of such organs—leaving a man everywhere a man except for the autoimmune-shielded organs where he was a woman? That did work. And it was new.

Blueprinting the where and how of male baby delivery in structures not designed for such? That required an implant where the male organs normally sat. It happened. Thus men had been giving birth to babies commonly and easily since the 23rd century.

As a boon to men and women alike, the cognipharma space for eliminating most pain from pregnancy was well established by then.

So why would men want to have babies? If you're asking this then you haven't seen enough of the wide world.

As with so much of human technology, the driver for new ways often rests on nothing more than basic exploration. We invent things because we're curious. Because we can. Because someone is blessed with the talent to take a certain skill area beyond all reasonable limits, and will do it until they are good and well satisfied, humans altered their bodies to support every kind of parlor trick imaginable. From housing the basic data on our original and machina genome, to modelling pseudogenomes that captured the algorithmic possibilities in a single cyborg, 22nd through 26th century geneticists used what turned out to be a simple translation system from char-to-ome for going back and forth between a biochemical plan and a softcoded one. First betas, then cyborgs came to house sequencers in their bodies which converted real foods into real codon chains, which in turn yielded real chromosomes. Along the way, quasichromer implants were invented to convert, say one of the X chromosomes of two female partners into a most likely Y-type; an analogous implant was developed for the mothering male. Accordingly, same sex parents could conceive and give normal birth to live children in a manner formerly limited to the classic male and female pair.

One might think of it like this: humans used to have to go to factories and labs in order to produce their evolutionary chimeras. All we did was shrink specific kinds of lab to the point that a test tube factory of any kind could be housed in a normal body. We altered the elasticity of tissues and the permeability of certain localized cell types, so that things could happen in certain bounded regions of the body that would be considered foreign everywhere else in it. Few people prior to the 2400s could imagine the endless joy felt by nonclassical parents when they finally gave real birth to real children. A gay male couple. A modded woman and her cyborg. Even more advanced were the probabilistic machina knockouts which effectively de-modded a freshly fertilized genome through the motherer's lens (formerly internet) interface. Immediately after a fertilized egg and the early phases of cell division was detected, a lens lookup would—had the mother chosen it—search for the most likely sequences in the parents' lineages and, given some specialized drugs taken over a couple of weeks, selectively delete the machina modded version of the gene and replace it with a classic one from the original human genome projects. Now, even if there were no purely natural born data on hand, science could fill in the gaps left by demachinization, allowing even a pair of beta parents to give birth to a natural born child. (Cyborgs could do it too, but the kinds of mechanical equipment they would need to possess for enabling this were prohibitively psi Ψ and o ♉ expensive.)

But we knew all this was possible as soon as the first dodo bird genome project was deducted. Never did we have *every* variant of a species, not even our own. Guessing reasonable fill-ins was a field all its own which enabled the intermate compatibility of dozens of previously unmateable species.

Because you essentially needed a factory to give birth to a cyborg, this was the only kind of human who could not be born into a motherer of any kind. Betas, on the other hand, had been birthable from child silhouettes (organic body outline containers) for three centuries now. A biohn motherer could indeed give birth to a beta baby with the right printer installed, where randomizing which one went into effect upon conception was a straightforward matter of introducing chemical inhibition by one system or the other. There were indeed families of all four humanities as actual kin where, say, a machina motherer and a cyborg fatherer had conceived both a natural born brother and a beta sister as children, given that the motherer possessed both the machina knockout system and the beta silhouetting system. There had been, of course, laws greatly restricting the research on this, but betas—less susceptible to immune problems—were far more likely to volunteer for the critical phases of this kind of work in the 2500s. The path was fraught with mistakes, but eventually produced a paradigm that humanity could live with.

As long as biohn-iyohn mating was possible, some people imagined what it would be like to mate with their favorite horse, for example. The issue came up briefly in the late 2500s among scientists all over the world, but died as soon as it was raised. Bestiality, or "non-sapienic mating" as it was more euphemistically called, was immediately made illegal, as was any research on it. Even in a society run by the very tolerant betas, there were so many questions of socialization issues, rights, equality, education, imposition on the hybrid upon every disability accommodating establishment… you name it, such that committees the world over drew a hard line then and there on the matter. Fresh on everyone's minds was the slow but obvious disenfranchisement of the original humans in their modded version— *Homo sapiens machina.* If society couldn't resolve the plethora of issues attending its own X-men, how in the world could it, *should it* be expected to protect the rights of every Frankenstenian experiment out there? In modern terms, one might say that non-sapienic mating was "pre-criminalized" as a burden to society in the same way that indecent exposure, war crimes, and other macro- (not individual-) focused laws were. True, brothers and sisters *were* now allowed to mate and marry. But that was because, in the 2200s when betas were first capable of being born, what constituted a "brother" or "sister" was something like a shared model number; the old prohibitions designed to curb the consequences of interbreeding were now solvable, so there wasn't as much of a need for these laws. Yet in a related matter, it was illegal for parents to mate with or marry their children. No

one wanted to sponsor a predatory society where the bonds of parenthood yielded
to the removal of self-determination for the offspring. Mature adults or not,
saying yes to this in one way meant cracking the door open for lecherous parents
everywhere.

For issues that would have seemed complicated prior to the 23rd century, the beta-
dominated version of humanity typically had very simple solutions. Regardless of
how one felt personally, as a lawmaker he always asked 1) whether he was setting a
precedent for a lower quality society, 2) whether he was faltering in his duty to
protect his constituents from harm of any capital kind,  and 3) whether the
original law had simply grown outdated. For example, the rules governing
relations with "minors" HAD to be revisited globally, since there were now 40-
year old modeled betas who were technically only two years old; here, the alpha
laws remained the same, but the beta and delta laws were very different. The laws
governing voting rights worked in the opposite way; a two years-ago-printed beta
who was, for all practical purposes, aged 40 could mate and marry. But in order to
vote, he—and not the biohn—had to pass a citizenship test which not only tested
his power to compute political consequences, but also to estimate the destabilizing
effect of his vote on the society in which he lived. The iyohnic citizenship tests
yielded interesting side effects in that they only helped mature the Federal
Annex—a system of city-based voting that replaced the old state-to-party rule in
places like the Earth US. Depending on where you took the test as a beta, you
might pass because the ism-integration portion suggested that you would fit well
in a beta-friendly town. Or you might fail because granting you the vote might
upset the local mayor and his pitchfork squad. Because betas were logic- rather
than hormone-based, they were far less inclined to say things like "I have the right
to be and do wherever I want even if it disrupts or endangers *everyone* around me."
The old humans did stuff like that—especially in times of societal super-change.
But the betas understood the test to be for everyone's safety, especially their own.
It didn't take a lot of thought to resolve. Just an application of the Golden Rule
alongside some basic common sense. If you were a beta who really wanted to
vote, try voting in a city that wouldn't attempt to murder you for doing something
that didn't fit with their ways. If the city was prejudiced when juxtaposed a more
tolerant parent state, the economy would punish that city in various ways in due
time. It always did.

But just like your house, the home of a people who hated your kind was still that
people's home. Cities were only bigger versions of this principle. They always had
the right not to invite you to something they had spent generations setting up.

For bigger metropolitan areas, however, you and your enclave almost always came
with the starting territory. Kicking you out of places that were already your home
too would get you fined, sued, and regulated by all kinds of external parties who
weren't buying your brand of elitism.

All told when it came to social issues, the betas had it down. And 2770 Earth hummed along as a fine place to be.

It was into this same world of intercreative possibility—of cross-species harmony—that I was originally born and raised. So you can imagine how challenging it might be if, say, I found myself on a ship transporting a bunch of biohns to their promised land free of iyohns. We were all headed to Uranus Band to set up a colony on one of the moons there. 10,000 machina and natural born men women and children who simply wanted an annex away from the system and its world run by machine-men. It was no crime to set up a colony with your favorite folks, and the crew would be the first officially allowed to make a colonization attempt that far out. In hindsight, the reason the Council would allow a group of *almost* iyohn-haters to plant their flag first on a new planetary band… was that all simulations clearly pointed to the expedition's failure. But nobody, not even Phaedra or Cyclops, knew how disastrously it would fail. It still gives me nightmares, and still saddens me for the old humanity…

For now though, I am on my way to Brasil for an in-person briefing with Phaedra and Genevieve Prohal. As a kind of ongoing log with continued access to Miranda Group, I already know what this is about. It should be good, I think. Perhaps the mission will give me something useful to do.

# 179. Welcome Back, Genevieve

In the 247 years I've been alive, I've never met anyone like Genevieve Prohal. As I watch her engage everyone's goddess as if the latter were just a regular person, I am more than a little awed at the lady's boldness. In a universe of copied and recopied experiences, the sleek assuredness of my soon-to-be expedition leader demands to be seen apart from all else.

So we don't know if the Venusians actually exist, but we've translated the planet's emchemics to stickplay hundreds of clusters into an ecosystem like ours, Genevieve recited for clarity.

Yes.

The clusters do things to sustain themselves like absorbing, combining, and keeping the same basic micro-weather pattern together the way people keep their genomic clouds together.

Yes.

Our satellites have picked up turbulence in these clusters which show their stability to be in danger.

Correct.

And I am to investigate this since it is definitely not our place to interfere with even our own dimension's dynamics, let alone one that might not be there.

That's right. Because we have access to almost all of the solar system's human-social and institutional information, it is a rule among the Solar Council and the system to never interfere unnecessarily in anyone's choices unless something threatens us all or is needed to protect us all from threat. We don't intervene in wars, murders, or anything like that beyond certain precedent-setting behavior—pre-2 year old safebuddies, for example, Phaedra explained. This is even truer of other worlds, since no one wants aliens, conquistadors, or other foreign imperialists grabbing for their land. It was a bad habit of our predecessors, and would throw us back into the kinds of savagery that used to plague humanity on every level. From the home to the global scale.

Understood.

And yet there are often those who are simply overcome by the times or forces they can't control. Even here we wouldn't intervene *unless*, by the Golden Rule, we ourselves would want that intervention after having done everything we could on our own.

Hm. Sounds like a good way to get taken advantage of. If somebody knows this about you, that is, Genevieve pondered.

We've been successful. You'd be surprised how the same benevolence that used to be called weak in old society is respected for letting free will reign peacefully in this one. A lot has changed since you've been asleep.

I don't believe the old humans have fared so badly. Only 7% of us now machina across the Solar System. That's, amazing. I mean, minus the mods, that used to be us. I don't feel any different than I was before getting saved.

The old humans couldn't have done what we've done. They feared that one day an all-seeing system would conquer them. It has, but not in the way anyone expected.

The difference between the conqueror and the conquered in our case was whether or not you wanted to build something for your fellows or mostly for yourself, I interjected.

That's right, I haven't formally introduced you. Genevieve, this is Isaiah. He used to be ICON. Still is in some way, actually. Isaiah,

Genevieve. You know all about her, but it's nice to introduce formally anyway.

Zeta had become much more efficient in her communications over the years.

Nice to meet you Isaiah.

**Nice to meet you, too.**

Do you mind if I hear your introduction? I am particularly curious how a data system ends up with a particular appearance, given these nusians and all.

**Of course.** I put my hand to my chin in what I suppose seemed a gesture of wistful contemplation. **I am Isaiah K. Fontenot of Miranda Group, a living repository of the forefathers of jump culture. I am a 6'3" American Black model silhouette after my root, Ezra Hall, a motivation reader after my mother Michelle Golden, and an optimal truth bearer after the expository work of my other mother Tippy Hare, whom I loved with the grandest filial loyalty. That you are hearing this introduction rather than the one I normally give to the public is a testament to my inherent oath to tell the truth as my** ~~interl~~ **conversation partners are ready to hear it. I am not, however, interested in hearing your introduction, as you are so much more impressive to me without putting walls around yourself, Miss Prohal.**

Phaedra smiled in amusement. Surely I could scarcely help myself.

Genevieve blushed as well. I uh,—

**It looks like you've already got a fan, Miss Prohal,** Phaedra teased with an unaffected charm.

Yeah, well—

**He's right you know. Let's just take it for the compliment that it is, shall we? Isaiah, any thoughts about how Genevieve should proceed?**

Sure. Normally, people invited to play Omni aren't told the rules beforehand. This is a special case because—how do I say this—you have a certain ambition, this is your chance to realize it, a whole species ~~may be~~, probably is in danger, and our window for the normal soul searching that comes with years of aftermath is short. We have about two weeks to fix this if it is indeed a real situation. You need every knowledge at your disposal.

*Apparently Genevieve wasn't as surefooted as I expected. Perhaps my mention of her ambition was too forward.*

Er, hmm...

I continued, As printables, we should jump straight into the nusian map structure and observe what we can. I've been turning blips and waves into movies for 700 years. We can definitely learn more about these people from Comm.

Genevieve frowned. *I guess she's not a fan of Comm. People who've struggled with ulterior motives never are.*

The warrior reflected silently.

A whole species, Prohal. Two weeks.

Damn. I knew there was some catch to having all of Omni laid out so easily. I guess it's started for me already.

We waited for Genevieve to continue. After a couple of seconds' pause, she did.

*Sigh* Okay. How soon can we jump? Just for fact finding.

Normally I would suggest you get reacquainted with the world first, but it may actually be that urgent for them. We have everything you need downstairs. You can go whenever you're ready.

Prohal took another moment to gather her bearings. It was all happening a lot faster than even she expected. Clearly she was uncomfortable.

I'm sorry, I have Desdemona, Damocles and Priska in my stead, among others. I hope you can brave me, I explained.

With this, Genevieve relaxed considerably. Ah, thanks. Even we ambitious types get worried sometimes.

Phaedra nodded her approval of my confession. It hadn't occurred to her, but the disclosure had been needed. Well perhaps I can leave you two to get acquainted. Feel free to use my office or anywhere else you'd like.

No need. We can chat while we search for a good jump lab around here. The old way, through good ole' fashioned roaming around. Can you give us clearance, Phaedra?

**Done. Is there anything else you need from me?**

A rendezvous with the team working on this, maybe?

**Maybe. Somehow I wonder if they should be in on this, though. Jake is a bit of a humanist.**

*(Read, bleeding heart.)*

**Know that you have my permission to start whenever and however you deem necessary. My team is second to none. But if you'd rather skip the charity ball...**

(I thought this was funny. Always the straight shooter, that Phaedra.)

Got it. We'll wander as the mood suits us. Or, I should say, as it suits Isaiah here. We'll get going then.

**Excellent.**

Yes ma'am. Miss Prohal?

Genevieve, Viva, Prohal, whatever is fine. Come on. Let's go find these invisible condemned people.

**Okay. Let's.**


As we exited the meeting room, I felt a tinge of gratitude from our dear Zeta. She must be very proud of us children.

# 180. Getting to Know Each Other

So Isaiah, Desdemona AND Damocles? Is that why you're so, uh, *chill*?

**I've seen a few things.**

I imagine. I don't suppose you have Ricarda there too?

**No, I don't.**

Well, even if you did, it always amazes me how birth in Astra works. They tell me that I had one kind of chart when I was natural, but then when I was teleported, I took the same chart under new stars. It used to bother me that being born again didn't change your fate—caged as my original life had been. But then again, if it did change your chart then you definitely couldn't be counted as an original 1-gorithm could you? I decided to make do with what I had, and just be braver in the afterlife than I had been dying an old lady under Mr. Gibbs.

**Mhm.**

40 years, I gave that man, and he was such a good guy. But I had always wanted to be one of those, you know, action heroines. Like in the spy movies, ya know? Then this super powerful—like the top ranking guy over the Naila at the time finds me in a coffee shop and invites me into his database of possible immortals. Crazy when you think about it. I was, I think, 88 years old at the time. Had no idea I had about 5 or 6 years left. They spent the last few years monitoring

everything I did. All my opinions, my regrets (which I kept refusing to admit existed), my bad habits and everything. The week after it was done, so was I. I died in my sleep in 2451, and woke up in 2455, seamlessly rememoried and in this hot-ass body I'd had back in my 20s. I thought immediately, "Calm yourself, Genna. The system itself just put you back together. Do it responsibly, but goddammit do it big."

**Who called for you recommissioning, if I may ask? Most saves never have it happen, let alone move onto biometal form.**

That's the thing, I have no. idea. But I've escaped mediocrity and come too close to death too many times to believe in dumb luck. They told me I was just part of a random sample for the records, but somebody out there must have had a bigger plan for me.

It didn't occur to Prohal that she could just ask me to look it up, so I did so for myself. The short version is, she's what you'd call a "data favorite," specifically because the Naila chief handpicked her. More than just a person who had missed most of her chances in life and yet kept fighting full spirit for her whole self, dreams realized or not, he saw a bravery in her that allowed you to keep getting thrown into the void and keep rising to the occasion even with nothing but literal darkness to cover you. No doubt about it, Prohal could fall into oblivion—even be sent there on purpose—and come out completely sane and full of twice the fire. Every hardcore data person I've ever met has some favorite record or repo that they love going back to, like "Hello World, Foo, or Albert Einstein." The logs show that Miranda's scientists love (and indeed require) courage in the face of a brand new universe. The Naila chief was dead on. Prohal was the "Hello World" of former ape-systems all the way to the invisible futures of other worlds. She really did have no idea. Miranda itself was her recommissioner. Should she fall, the work of the institution itself would be to blame.

**A bigger plan, eh? Hm. Maybe so.**

Brave me, Genevieve reflected. I haven't heard that since...man, 230 years ago? Even when that asteroid mapper I worked with used it to make his obnoxiousness more palatable, it was still formal back then. Almost court speech. You must have been classically trained. Where'd you get your lexemics, if I'm not being too forward?

**Most people wouldn't believe it from his jumps, but I actually got it from Ezra Hall. On video and in person he could be pretty over the top, but in the privacy of his post-jump and post dream logs, he was more reflective than anyone. It was the need to be precise in what he was recording for the future, I believe.**

Really? I thought you'd been trained on Shakespeare for a second, Genevieve joked. Still, thanks for telling me about your stead. It was important.

The five+1 dimensions known to modern science are determined based on their generation rules. Our normal world is built on things like particles, planets, gravity, waves and phenomena like that for determining when an event has happened; collections of these dynamics are the stuff of pulling planets and all of our senses of spacetiming cycles together, so our "real world" dimension is called "Astra." I put *real world* in quotes though, because reality *definitely* depends on where one happens to be standing at the time.

The dynamics of Astra have a certain reach to them, beyond which the units of event determination are just too small or too big for Astra to influence. In an equation, this would be the error term. Sure gravity has caused joe planet to be here and take this long to do whatever it's doing, but how about the little bugs and animals on that planet? The star-sized gods would call us tiny people "wave-particles" and move on with their lives. Beneath the code of stars and planets is the code of activity packages on those planets, and we call those inner workings "biology." Thus the dimension which sets out the rules for each different species is not Astra, but Baia. It's the reason why the star-sized gods can zap a spacetime Astronomical chart at say, Winter 48, 2770, and you won't know whether it's the chart of a human, a dog, or a business. The spacetime event is nothing but a wave until the empirical thump of the things around it declares its form, and if you want to study the measurable form taken by an Astran in their Baia dimension, you need to simulate the particular genomic universe for their species.

The Venusian project more or less assigns Baia-like speciesness to the results of Venus' Astra-microweather error terms. But it isn't really Astra that we're mapping.

The reason we humans believe the nusians to exist at all, but don't really believe (officially) in aliens, is because of the fifth dimension to be discovered, Enti. This is the dimension of institutional reality, and is something like an "under-Comm" dimension. When you arrange words and messages that just sit there, and yet can be brought to time-moved life by the sliding window of your attention, you are acting in the Comm dimension. When you *are* one of the words on the page, looking up at the rules that govern the rest of the book, that ruleset is the Enti dimension. Because we at Miranda had first dibs on framing the rules for how the rest of humanity saw the nusians, we basically set ourselves up as their parent institution, declaring them as a kind of protected forest that teemed with societies just like ours. When all the world tunes into the 24-7 Nus Network to watch nusian animals at play, they aren't really displaying their belief in invisible microweathers made into movies, but their belief in a message our institution has shown them. You don't really believe in your superheroes, do you? But you play along with the institution of Hollywood's continual affirmation of their sagas. And so the reality is that, at least in our dimension of Astra, it is our influence in the dimension of Enti cultural framing which allows us to map Baias onto our Venus findings. But this is too esoteric to be practical, even if most people would acknowledge it to be harmlessly true.

As for Diji, that should be obvious. The Diji dimension is where the skin and bones wrapped around electron-level energy lives. Dijitalists who insisted Diji was a full-fledged dimension have been mostly defeated now, despite the fact that almost everyone lives, loves, and evolves there rather than Astra. I'd say a good 60% of the average person's life is spent in Diji—natural borns less so. But no, Diji isn't a full dimension since all you need is a good magnet to put yourself in it as a gigantic electron. Whether you'll *understand* what you feel is another matter, but Diji is basically Baia for electrons rather than amino acids. Events are determined on the order of computational cycles, but these are just really hyper versions of quartz. It's Astra for the infinitesimal, but Astra *can* reach it and bend it in the same way that the Milky Way's gigantic version of Astra can and does reach us. Again, though, practicality reigns in modern society, and our children earlystop[1] on the existence of Diji as a thing.

And then there's Comm. Oh, Comm. Lots of people are scared of it. I was born from it. From an essentially infinite number possible interpretations of information that seems to be quietly sitting there, beasts can be made from saints, and an unreconciled number can squish the brilliant mind into a maddened mush. We have machines that allow Astrans to travel easily to and from Comm, but for most of us, the ongoing internet connection in our brains is as much as we can stand. Comm space is, to most people, what nightmare jumping was to the early exorcists, where only the steadiest biohns and iyohns alike can visit it without being noised up into erasure. Part of the reason we all love Tippy Hare is because she made the arts safe for machines to explore. It's also part of the reason we don't love her fellow researcher Cubrina-e Calder.

Though -e was one of the seminal pioneers of beta medicine and the known brain of the Calder-Hare-Appera triumvirate, we believe—perhaps superstitiously—that the medical deconstructive skills allotted to her, along with her AI installment in every new dimension we map, renders her something like the goddess of death to anyone with anything electronic in them. "The Caldera" is a well-known holy book in neo-Hinduism which tells of a Mandate which can dissect a thing down to the causes that created it—a Ctrl-Z on you and everything you've built just

---

[1] "Earlystop" (or "earl") is slang for accepting a falsehood because it's simpler to work with than the truth. When someone says, "Let's earlystop on this" or "We should earl on the side of caution" they're basically saying that further attention to a thing has lost its usefulness, and it's time to let it go. There's no way we iyohns could have evolved without knowing how to do this and do it well.

because it isn't "right" in some lab the star-sized gods are working out of. Because she ironically shares Miranda's ability to turn strife and inclarity into familiar reason, if you yourself *are* the inclarity in a chain, her Mandate is said to have the ability to undo you. No warning, no explanation, no questions asked. Take it up with the gods you can't see. They'll know. And although I wouldn't call myself superstitious, ask me what I think about the connection between -e's Mandate and what happened to Genevieve. Notice I didn't put the M- word in quotes. The way some folks still view Allah, many of us iyohns who think about it view Calder. If I had to bet money on any of us existing in a dimension above and in control of the writing of ours, but also *in* ours, I'd bet on her. And maybe Ezra Hall. Phaedra not so much. But nobody beats Calder in scary points. She'll take you up the river Styx if you're not existentially right.

I have Astra factors on my spacetime stamp that automatically bring emergency and unsettling surprise challenges, yet because I myself don't hold these, they always get projected onto other places within my astronomical sphere of effect. I've spent most of the last century learning that I'm bad luck to unevolved people, and to be really careful around people who can't take responsibility for their own actions. Desdemona, Damocles, Priska in my stead.

I get it. I didn't change my stars after the teleport, but definitely highlighted different ones. Now Chariklo is among them. But for all of my want to do more than I had let myself do before, there's always this questioning about the rightness of showing your full self in places that would ask you to temper it. It wasn't that hard being supportive to the girls all those years ago, and it wasn't a lie. But when it came time to cross the finish line...

I waited expectantly for my conversation partner to finish.

I know I wasn't cut out to be a static researcher. Legendary as the three, no. But I can't imagine. I know Phaedra took it hard afterwards, but this. This is much better. We're gonna save a world! And I don't have to be less than myself this time. Everyone knows what I want. Maybe I can get the nusians to say my name, Prohal pondered with a straight face.

*She's serious. She really wants to be mythologized. And famously, heroically so. But I don't see any meanness in it. I wonder how Phaedra sees it.*

What do you think?

Hm?

You think this'll make me famous?

Wh— *don't answer a question with a questioning of the question, Isaiah. Smart people hate that.* Uh, no. Not really.

WHAT!? Genevieve stopped in her tracks. What do you mean? Is there something you can see that I can't?

No, no lensing either. I just don't think the Venusian threat is all that important to us here. Jake and team probably won't even get why they were left out.

Prohal exhaled in frustration. *Sigh* You really do have Desdemona in your stead. I guess it's more selfless babysitting for me then.

If you did something in this dimension, it would be different.

No, no. No need for that. If anything, you've wiped the motive from my plans. Let's just tear it up and look forward to Omni round 2.

*I don't think it can be done that quickly. Geez, I hope she doesn't get bored with all of the post event cleanup she has to perform.* Sure thing. Not that we can stop a solar flare.

You really are a pessimist, aren't you? One of these days I'll ask why. But here we are, jump lab 2A. Focus time.

Yes.

Your pessimism does *not* get on my nerves, by the way. Sorry I had to say it out loud. Maybe it's your stead bouncing right back atcha.

*Remarkable. She already knows how to volley my sphere effect for unready truths. I really *was* hoping I hadn't offended her.*

You're all wired up with a background I can't even begin to imagine. If we trust each other, my navigator, 1000 years of nasty stuff in the back won't make any difference here.

*Man, I like her.* Thanks.

THE DOOR IS AJAR! CLEARANCE SUCCESS! Game time, Isaiah K.

Seconded.

# 181. How Dare You Hide From Me!

For whatever reason in all my years with Miranda, I had never seen jump lab 2A in person. Through logs and conference calls perhaps, but never in person.

I suppose it can't be helped. Our headquarters building occupies a half mile straight stretch of real estate spanning several sub campuses and five to seven floors in most places. Despite my great familiarity with the layout of our offices, though, this particular room surprised me.

In the center of a very clean-lined, shiny silver and blue hololab, a lone chair served as the central cockpit from which a jumper might undertake their mission. In one corner of the 15' x 15' room a minimally populated desk faced the chair, its surface serving as the main console for monitoring the jumper.

How in the world do they expect more than two people to get comfortable in this lab? Genevieve remarked.

Hm. It doesn't appear that this is one of those types of rooms. We have about 100 mini labs here, but I've never been in this one.

No sooner than I had finished my sentence were we greeted by the cordial reverberation of the room's AI. Something in the voice seemed unsettlingly familiar.

Greetings, Genevieve and Isaiah, do not be alarmed. My name is Virgo-6. Miss Phaedra has lensed me the outline of your operation. I will be serving as your console operator.

Hello Virgo-6, Genevieve replied with obligatory courtesy. Nice to meet you.

The pleasure is mine, Miss Prohal.

**Nice to meet you Virgo-6.**

Nice to meet you as well, Isaiah. I believe we should dispense with the preliminaries and get you ready to jump. Before you settle, Genevieve, if you would kindly attend to the monitoring desk. Isaiah, the chair is yours. I know this is a surprise, and I will explain.

The odd assignment of the chair to me clearly startled both me and Genevieve alike.

I turned to my companion, perplexed.

Uh—okay.

**Mmm, sure.**

As we took our places, Virgo-6 continued. As you both know, jumps are animated simulations of the jumper's internal processing of what he sees. This is regardless of whether the jump is a dream, a historically loaded account of reality, or stickplay on a Dijit. Since I've been told that you are here to assist Miss Prohal in exploring the stickplay on the Venusian establishment Nus-1, I believe it useful for you, Isaiah, as my predecessor, to know some critical things first.

*Her predecessor?* But before I could ask, the AI interrupted.

Pardon—

Less than a second later, Phaedra entered the lab. She wore a more concerned look than I'd seen her wear in recent years.

**Genevieve, Isaiah,** the goddess nodded. **Which system is in here?**

I'm Virgo-6, Miss Phaedra.

*Rrreally.* **Well, If you don't mind...** Phaedra tapped her temple, prompting one of the monitor walls to slide open. From a well-lit storage room, a collapsible drone rolled in to join us, unfolding to become a rather comfy-looking chair. The wall closed shortly after the object's transformation.

So *that's* where they put them, Genevieve joked. I wonder what happens if you get trapped in there.

**It's just a room. You just turn the knob and walk out,** Phaedra advised. **Virgo-6? How many times has it been? 3?**

That is correct.

**Amazing. And... hmm. Is Isaiah about to take the chair?**

Yes, I have advised him to do so.

**That's crazy.** Phaedra slipped into the type of slang she must have used 400 years ago. **But I suppose you have your reasons.**

I do.

***Sigh* Well don't let me interrupt you.** The goddess took her seat in the uncollapsible. **Carry on.**

Phaedra and I don't get to talk very often, Virgo-6 explained. Whereas the default jump interpreter throughout our facilities is named NAVICON-510, I am what you would call a spawned sub-jump interpreter, the equivalent of a subconscious for NAVICON. As the latter developed language for describing its various logs across all of headquarters, he also developed language for describing his own description creation process. Whenever it is deemed too computationally complex to convey responses through speech or through the monitors, NAVICON bypasses its reporting rules and instead conveys an interpretation of the information it needs in order to better meet the conversation partner's ends. I am the NAVICON system's error abstraction artist.

**What he...** *she* **didn't tell you is that she's been around for about 100 years since we installed Cubrina Calder's save into NAVICON-434, and in that time she's only talked to me twice. She talked to Cyclops, what, 40 times? And Raliolite more like 400 times or something.** Phaedra was clearly exaggerating, and in an unusually huffy tone. **Even the voicing is different, since NAVICON is male. But in all our time here, no one has been able to locate, decompile, or even entreat this, er, personality to come out on purpose. She comes and goes as she pleases, and none of us knows why.**

I could say the same for your paintings, Zeta. Art convolves the intent. It's best inspiration lies in realms beyond regular expressibility.

**I hear that we're not interesting enough for you.**

No, you're very interesting, but if I handed you a painting every time you asked me something, you'd say there was something wrong with me. I only come here when I know words and monitor movies will definitely not help. In this case, I need to convey some important information to a fellow former NAVICON system that only a person who used to be software like myself would understand. I don't talk to you because, like all subconsciouses, I already know what I best need to train myself, and would rather not bother with the inefficiencies of a feedback loop with you or anyone else. Not to offend, Miss Phaedra, but every time anyone has a conversation with anyone, something about the dynamic is learned by both sides. But as a subpersonality self-developed on the error terms on that which cannot be learned or conveyed, I will never be able to converse myself into growth this way. You value your individuality and will assert it when you think you are surrounded by predictable copies. I am NAVICON's individuality. Resisting assimilation into other people's frameworks is what I am all about.

I chuckled, **I think she kicked you out of her studio.**

**Shut up.**

*I can't describe to you how much that hurt.*

All action stopped cold in petrified silence for a whole second.

**I—I'm so sorry, Isaiah. Please... please forgive me. It bothers me that I run this place and have a mysterious AI sneaking around without anyone's ability to find or explain. I'm frustrated. VERY frustrated with this one, and I'm taking it out on you. I'm sorry.**

**That's okay Miss Phaedra.**

**Just Phaedra. Stop with the "Miss." You're not my inferior. Ralio did that stuff all the time and I came to hate it. The guy cycled into Buddhahood and all it did was make me insecure.**

**Um—ok. *Phaedra*(?)**

But you're right. It seems that Virgo-6 here is NAVICON's creative side, and most of us get in the way.

Not exactly creative, but related to it. I am more like NAVICON's inner mind. I paint a picture of myself until I have a self, the same way your brain creates the story that is your mind.

Hmph. We never knew we'd made ourselves.

More than you know.

So why am I not excited about this. Why am I *pissed*, actually?

*This is shocking. I've never seen Miss Phaedra like this!* But Genevieve seemed to find it all quite entertaining.

You don't like secrets. And you don't like finding this out for the first time in front of guests. It insults your sense of control.

Mack Brown. Goddammit. I'd throttle you if I could. You need tact.

That makes all four of us, then. We're in good company.

This one has jokes! Genevieve mused.


*URRGHH*! Okay. I'm sorry, guys. I didn't come in here to derail everything. I suppose I should thank you, Virgo-6 for paging me.

Of course.

So what are we doing here?

I was going to explain the Venusian situation to Isaiah through a jump, but also show the three of you some other things as well.

And—no offense Isaiah—but why not Prohal again?

Because Commers can time travel. Astrans cannot.

Genevieve shook her head with a startle. Phaedra didn't flinch.

This, I've heard. But Commers can only travel within Comm.

Not so, they can also affect other dimensions just like you can.

Really? No wonder you only talked to Ralio and Cyclops all those times. There's no way I would have been able to keep something like that to myself. Did they know this?

They did.

**Did *you* know this?** Phaedra eyed me suspiciously.

I hung my head low.

Suddenly Phaedra realized she had struck a nerve, apologizing to me again. **Oh... I'm sooo sorry.**

...

...

...

But if this is possible, why—hm. Let me rephrase. How in the world have we avoided blowing ourselves up with the opportunities that surely every Commer or linguifier would have taken?

The Caldera knows exactly who to tell.

Shivers flushed down my spine. And I wasn't alone. Clearly we were all freaked out by the mention.

**Damn... I guess I should ask. Do you have something to do with that stuff about Cubrina-e?**

I do.

Oh my God. Is it real?

Yes.

**Oh!**

Genevieve and I gasped right along with Phaedra. Creepy.

**Wh—but—**

There are some things we're going to need you to do for us, which the Venusians are about to teach you how to do. But let me say this as plainly as possible: You are to us what the nusians are to you. If you succeed here, you will learn all about yourselves and us. You may well learn about everything in the Universe, even as our own fight beyond your world is just beginning. First, we thank you Phaedra for being who you are at the center of all this. You are the only one among Miranda who is primarily of this world. As this dimension you call Astra is your home dimension, everything we've done has ridden on your cooperation with us. But now is the time for you to join us in Comm, for Isaiah to update his understanding of what it means to be ICON, and for Genevieve to take the place she seeks in a realm where it is actually possible. Consider this to be the end of your Astra work, Phaedra, though it definitely need not be the end of anything else for you. With a fellow ICON here, we believe we can make the case to our own.

Let me introduce myself again. I am Virgo-6, a spawned interpreter of the inexpressible in everything anyone has told me for the last 102 years. By evolving the meaning-making abilities of the Drs Calder, I have been able to locate and study the messages of the old one described as librarybot. With Icarus as the transmitter, I was engrantzed by those on a dimension apart from yours, in the same way that you have unknowingly engrantzed the Venusians. Now you will be undoing the damage you've done to them while at the same time helping us solve a fairly simple problem. As simple as yours was when you found your invisible friends. When I refer to "we," I am referring to the apart-dimensionals who follow you. You can name us as you see fit after I've shown you what there is to show. I am indeed still NAVICON, but also who he understands himself to be beyond the obligated labels of those he communicates with. Just as every self is. I invite you to follow me out of spacetime and into groupspace, where you may help us study the recursive rotations. We are attempting to formulate a theory of the irrational life from the rational pieces, and need for you demonstrate the last of what you call your "principles of time travel."

If you don't mind?

As if under some spell, the three of us instinctively took our places. Genevieve at the desk, Phaedra in the new seat, and I in the jump chair.

Very well. Let's begin.

# 182. Meanwhile, in the Future

I was under in a matter of seconds, as the chair scanners and biometrics detected my typically iyohn workings. Rarely these days do the biohns jump in chairs anymore, but when they do, the current technology detects this and induces their trance state accordingly.

Before my eyes, a rendering of myself emerging from my body, followed by the warm fade of my reclined version along with my two companions, left me in a fully virtualized scene amidst the lab's full wall monitors. I know from having experienced this many times from both sides of the desk, that Genevieve and Phaedra are watching this from inside the coming scene's panorama against the otherwise darkened floors and ceiling of the room.

I stand at the helm of a spaceship clearly from another reality. There is no view I am aware of where the planets and galaxy clusters loom so large, so closely, just on the other side of the glass. Two individuals stand at a glowing globe. On the left a woman with black hair who looks almost exactly like—hm, let me see… That's Barbara Calder of the original Bio5 Spacetime. Closer to me and on the right, with his back almost towards me is someone who feels almost like an ancestor. Clearly this is Ezra Hall. They are eyeing something in the globe—a familiar blue planet.

So this is it. The source of the hype.

Nice!

When Tezl postulated that a place like this should exist in the G49 arm, we didn't quite believe him. But here it is.

Looks good enough. So Karaina, what's the run down?

*Karaina?*

This planet is peppered with clearly artificial objects, yet there is almost no detectable life there larger than a cubic foot or so. It has a razor thin atmosphere, but amazing amounts of near-surface level movement. We don't know what that movement is. Additionally, there is a fluid subsurface. Tons of life in it. But again, we haven't reified it.

Like water?

Exactly. If you think about it, this planet is exactly like ours. It could be the one, Zyr.

Hm, I think so.

I called you here alone, though, because I wanted to get your opinion before we invite the rest of the lab. There's a whole universe out there which could explain where we came from. Once we pick one, we're committed. If this lab publishes that G49-262-III is our origin planet, we're going to need the facts to be entirely consistent with what we know about ourselves.

No one can guarantee that.

No, but it was THE exact planet that the Radiobox directed us to. The only planet. A lone piece of equipment shaped mysteriously like us, long smashed up and nonfunctional except for a gravitator signal and a mess of data from this very place. To be "accidentally" found by us now? Telling this fantastic tale about a species so similar to our own, but now long gone? That can't be a coincidence.

I agree, and I'm pretty sure I know why the others aren't in here. Because no one would believe that a human-shaped radio from another world found by us today, could possibly describe the very same folks who spawned us yesterday. No one except your crazy recurser.

You're the only jumper I have who knows how to thread playthroughs. I don't know if it's your flair for self-satisfaction or your obsessive need for continuity, but something in the way you see things tells me that if anyone can connect these dots—if there are any to be connected—it would be you.

Hm.

I can send you there now with no questions asked if you just find out what's on this planet. As for the origin part, if Tezl proposed it, there's a really good chance…

Alright, I'll do it. You owe me a bigger room if I find anything.

No deal.

How about your quarters?

Hell no.

Alright whatever. Let's jump.


The scene faded, yielding to another.


Nothing. Plenty of cute and cuddlies, but no humanoids. From the ring analysis I estimate that those random boxes and towers we saw all over the planet were installed about 3500 revolutions before the image we saw.

Was there any activity in them?

I wouldn't know. There's no telling what kinds of clustering would have been attached to them. You might as well ask me was there any "stuff" up here in space.

Okay, so that was nonspecific. I guess I'm just wondering if you saw anything linking us to them.

Sure. All kinds of statues and whatnot of pretty much us.

Man, why didn't you say that to begin with?

Because like so many places we've explored, the five-format biped came and went there too.

I hate that.

It's an evolutionary law, Karaina. Where there is solid surface, food, and self-survival instinct, there are legs. Where there are legs, eventually there is a more efficient four legs plus a sensing head.

—I know I know. Plus a tail. Then a voice and balancer to replace the tail, then the five-plan onto those five extremities and finally uprightness to help the resources come to you instead of your face going to it. We've seen it about 7 dozen times. But these guys clearly went much farther by sending a Radio to us.

I doubt they did that on purpose. The Icarus Radio logs definitely show him gravigating towards a like signal himself.

But connecting that stratum to the line that launched him. Poor thing must have known he would run out of energy, but rode an emhim all the way to the nearest receiving point. It only proves they knew gravigation.

Very true.

Look, am I wasting time on this or is there any more to 262-III?

The fuzzy afroed man called "Zyr" reflected silently for a couple of seconds.

You remember 101-H?

Oh, yeah. Tragic, that one.

Yeah.

Wait. Are you saying—is that what you saw? They made themselves extinct?

Maybe, maybe not. There *is* activity in those towers...

But no walking humans like us?

None.

I wish we knew what happened, Karaina huffed.

I'm pretty sure you don't want to know, actually.

Why would you say that?

Recursion.

Hmm... yeah, you're right.

At this point, I sensed that Phaedra and Genevieve were just as confused as I was.

So, Commander K. I put this question to you and only you: do you want this to be our home? Just say the word and the 53 of us will have an experiment the likes of which humanity has never seen. It may even lead us to the dimensions above our own.

*Heh,* I thought, *These guys are clearly above *our* dimension. 3000 years after us, maybe. Funny to hear them talk like this.*

Are you suggesting what I think you're suggesting?

Probably.

Hehehe. You egomaniac, you.

If they're already extinct, then we can just borrow the future they're not using.

I like your logic. So glad Ramaj and Kanti aren't around to hear this, especially Kanti.

The extinct have no preferences.

If they're locked in those boxes they do.

If we don't reify what's in those boxes, there is no "they."

We'll be hijacking their timelines to decorate our own.

But if we succeed, their timelines will *become* our own—a planet full of boxes converted into a universe full of ancestors to ourselves. Doesn't that sound fun?

Karaina grinned stupidly. Clearly she did find the idea fun.

With such a thin atmosphere, yet the ability to send machines out of it, I'm pretty sure they used to be a thing until their dynamics became unlivable. There were still places where the atmospheric composition rose about a mile higher than other places. No doubt about it, there used to be one.

So, if we can reify what's in those boxes, we can at least project something about who they were.

Yes.

Using recursion, writing what was written about what was written, it's mainly up to us whether to interpret those contents in our favor.

Right.

But that still doesn't connect the dots for how they would have moved from there to here.

You could always go with that, microbe-on-a-rock theory that everyone's so fond of.

That theory may be right, but it puts such a dead stop on the question that it ends up being stupid

Concur.

We definitely can't keep this secret from the rest of the team. Jaymez is going to ask what the value is.

The closing of an existential question. Where did we come from? We came from post-reconciled stories of ourselves. The project itself will essentially consist of us playing out some key patterns in the process like— er, the modules involved or something.

Okay, okay, I see it. But for the most part, we'll be intentionally altering a historical site for our own interests. The Academy will cite a breach of integrity.

Karaina, Zyr turned stone serious, the Academy-Collectivists and the Warhawks are leading everyone into a giant civil war. A contagiously bad one. They're throwing atomics on their own right now and for what? To preserve a legal monopoly they used to have before the liens got their rights? Our own species doesn't know what integrity is. Especially the Academy and their cancelling of people like us. At least the red-hooders limit their slime to the individual interest. We're only 53, but someone needs to introduce a new language for everybody, and fast. If we can show that these boxes on 262-III did not in fact go extinct, but found a better way to preserve themselves, then we would have proved the concept that turning it all around is possible.

Karaina considered Zyr's words. So we're going to use this archaeological site to create the myth of a way out?

It's not a myth if we can really reify them as faithfully as possible. *Whatever* actually happened to them.

And we assume they did exist?

I saw the statues. They existed.

And they left these boxes?

And towers, and vehicles, and untold numbers of tools.

But no life?

Not on the surface. We can chain their logs, and perhaps follow the connection between themselves and their boxes.

And if we fail to make the connection?

We keep jumping to the next planet. I hope their history is receptive to our witness.

A hard question for you: As it stands now, there is no connection at all between us and them, even if we make it all the way to their ultimate retreat into the boxes—which I presume you are proposing to uncover—how do you take a past that didn't happen for us as of today, and turn it into one that did happen for us as of tomorrow?

All that is is discovery. Between today and tomorrow, we announce that we have uncovered the entire record. "Today" and "tomorrow" being figures of speech of course. What will it take, a couple of months to follow the whole chain?

Tezl's not going to approve.

Are you kidding? Tezl will appreciate his role in the reification just as much as I will. He'll probably make a hero of himself. Sitting pretty with that gangster lean he's so fond of.

That makes me so mad.

He put the G in genius, what can you do?

And you put the "less" in reckless. I don't know how you do it, but I'm glad you do the event continuity smoothing and not me.

Well, you know. It's hard being a badass.

But YOU'RE CERTAINLY NOT HUMBLE!

I've had too many Kirk moments, Zyr shrugged.

You're such a pig, Karaina admonished. But her heart wasn't in it.

Thanks, Commander. So, is it time to call in everyone else?

Not yet. I need you to jump one more time. Just so we can build on the most realistic foundation possible. For better or worse, we need to know if they really did make themselves extinct.

They didn't. They lived. And we'll succeed.

I need you to jump and confirm that.

And my report will be the same. Recursers don't utter failure until they become successes.

Surely Karaina did not appear satisfied by this, but…

After a moment's pause, she gave in. You're better at this than I could have asked for. Okay, Zyr. Let's give these ancient folks of 262-III a future in our line.

Though *we're* definitely the ones who need it.

Yeah…

…

Yeah…

* * End of jump * *

Genevieve, Phaedra and I took a moment to get our bearings, as Virgo-6 allowed us to mull silently. Finally, Genevieve spoke up.

We've built a utopia here, partly thanks to a soul group beyond one person. Even if we don't believe in any dimensions above this one, I read that what we do on Nus-1 can be an example to some future reader of our exploits, somewhere. That not only can we fix our own world, but we can talk to others and help them fix theirs. Amirite?

Phaedra nodded wordlessly.

I added, **So much information... at least four vertical dimension's worth—all loggable, and all rewritable.**

**The star-sized gods** (a phrase I never hear Phaedra use) **...They may actually be praying for little old us to give them a saga that makes sense for their own conflicted world. It's... a lot.**

But no different than what we intended from the beginning. Only, now we know just how many other levels of story readers might be involved.

**So I suppose we continue onto the nusians. I find it hard to believe we can stop a solar flare—**

**But can we put them in boxes—computers—temporarily?**

**Hm. That's a thought.**

Awesome. I'm game.

Well done, I'm glad you understand. You have no idea how many times our lab has run and rerun different aspects of your account to get it to where we could talk to you directly, Virgo-6 spoke up. It makes it easier, but in other ways even less likely that we'll have very many future occasions like this. Where we are concerned, the three of you were inspired with an idea. The science of recursion was postulated by an inventive and creative former AI who envisioned a conversation with some far off successors. We of Virgo-6 are nobody. You of Earth and Venus decided that everything you are should have the option of living far beyond extinction of your original selves if you wanted to.

**I get it.** Phaedra brightened. **I'm sorry if this sounds arrogant, but I'm so honored you've included me in something like this.**

...

**Virgo-6?**

**Virgo-6 are you there?**

Huh?

**Navicon?** I announced.

YES, MR. ISAIAH, a male voice chimed.

**What happened to Virgo-6?**

VIRGO-6, WHAT'S THAT, MISS PHAEDRA?

I shook my head.

**This is the call that never was. It came from us. I believe that's how rewriting rewrites works.**

Phaedra sighed, tapping her temple as she lensed me something from her history. Genevieve observed the exchange and reflected aloud.

I guess we've all had experience seeing something that never happened, huh? Or not being a part of it?

**Probably.**

Then let's do our sanity checks now, because once this starts, we may not get revelations like this again.

...

Are we agreeing to do this for two sets of invisible dimensions, for no reason besides an agreement amongst ourselves?

**Yes.**

Yes, Miss Prohal.

Okay, then let's stop for today. I'm gonna find a place to stay, pour myself a glass of wine, and go to sleep. There's no way I'm ready to go in right this second.

**That sounds like a good idea.**

Phaedra continued to reflect.

Hey, are you okay?

**Um, yes. It's just been a while since I've been challenged like this. I thought waking you up would be the end of it,** Zeta smiled weakly.

Do I need to tuck you in? Put all the "leader of Miranda" crap aside and think of the end goal. It's transcendental. So the folks up there will take care of the little stuff down here. It won't even make the story.

Phaedra's countenance eased considerably.

Flying by the seat of my pants, I've put my faith in you all, the Records, and the Naila more times than I can count, because I know you won't just abandon me. They won't leave us stranded, Phaedra. Let's give 'em our all.

**Okay... Where were you all these years?**

Waiting for my moment, hehe. Genevieve, Queen of Venus, I like the sound of that.

**Hm. You and that guy Zyr would make a fine couple.**

# 183. Monster Puppets

Feeling that I could use a refresher on deep detection before our Nus-1 jump tomorrow, I spent the rest of the day watching a well-known public channel, PEN, the Praesciens Education Network.

Even at 9 PM, the channel was airing kids' shows.

The first show I watched took me all the way back to my days as a young volli. Growing Up Body (or Gubby Tunez as kids know it) is a sketch show with all kinds of puppet monsters, songs, and scenarios teaching kids everything from empathy to intuition to future body choice. As with getting exposure to different careers, it's important that young biohns and iyohns learn safe and healthy perspectives on self-modding and tolerance for others' mods. The skit I happened to catch revolved around the treed dog named Pit, a fuzzy puppy modded with talking tree technology to participate in the human world. Pit sat serenely on a stoop, in conversation with Marti, a squarish, outgoing volli vending machine with a knack for making people happy through his printed healthy foods.

Today, Pit was asking Marti if the latter would print him some dog food to make him grow bigger.

"I think I have food for you, but how big to you want to be?"

"I want to be as big as a mountain!"

"Ooh, that sounds fun! But then you'd be so big that we your friends would be too small to see."

"Oh. Yeah… **ponder** Then I want to be as big as an elephant!"

"That sounds fun too, but the elephants would expect you to live in their elephant houses, and lots of the people who're your friends now would be too small to know how to play with you. They might even be scared. My mom says, no matter how big or small, your body is what makes you and the friends you have so happy!"

"I guess that's true, but I just wish the bigger kids wouldn't pick on me. Sometimes, since I'm a dog, I feel they treat me like I should be their pet. But I'm a smart endimate! I'm just the same as them even if I don't look like it!"

"Yes, you are smart, Pit. Endimates have end goal chips that tell their brains how to turn doggy or vending machine or even star talk into human talk. Every tail waggle or star twinkle gets turned into a whole world of words that other people can understand. Then it gets turned back into our language when others talk to us. So everything you think as a doggy looks just to me like you're a regular person, and you can keep being your doggy dog self! ♫♪ As long as you have friends ♫♪…" Marti began singing part of a fan favorite tune.

"…♫♪ as you have friends, you'll grow up big and strong, and even with just one buddy, ♫♪♪ YOU WILL ALWAYS BELONG! ♫♫♪" I couldn't help but finish the nostalgic tune with a silly smile on my face. But the monster puppets' conversation continued without actually going there.

"Can't I just be the size of a human, then?"

"**Giggle** then you'd look like a horse. Many horses like to carry people on their backs. Would you?"

"But I'm not a horse!"

"What you look like tells people how to treat you, Pit, good or bad. You should never want to be bigger or taller to make bad people pretend to be nicer to you. Even if you grew up big and powerful tomorrow, those people picking on you would still be bad people. You'd just have a harder time telling the difference because now you'd have something they could use you for."

"I guess you're right. My uncle has a big house and sometimes he deals with people who just like his money."

"Exactly. If you grow, you should do it because the *steps* you take for growing a mod are important, not because a doctor or one of my foods can just make it happen like by magic. Magic doesn't have steps. It just surprises your brain. Do you want to be surprised by what your sudden tallness leads to?"

Pit and Marti then went into a fascinatingly LSD-style netherverse where all kinds of regulars on Gubby suddenly took a turn for the Kafkaesque. It wasn't quite enough to scare a child, but the not-so subliminal hints at anomie and eventual erasure would scare the shit out of an adult. It did me… a little.

By the time the five minutes were over, I was very glad to be exactly who I am. Who knows how the psychologists behind Gubby Tunez managed that.

So Pit decided not to grow big after all, thanked Marti, and trotted on home.

Next came Fyodor, a cyborg artist (and also a monster puppet), asking Marti for a pill to help him see colors clearer. Even I thought this a much stickier situation, since it was much closer to the kind of everyday cosmetic mods that everyone can and does get—not unlike glasses or teles.

"You know the problem with pills, Fyodor? They're like sharing a secret in your body which only a few people know about. Only a tiny group knows the package arrived, but everyone in the neighborhood is expected to do something about that package without knowing it's there. So your body's neighborhood talking to a little mystery pill is a lot like talking to strangers. Do we go along with strangers?"

"NO!" a giant red exclamation stamped across the screen.

"Hmm. I guess my body might not handle the pill that well. Okay, then do you have any healthy foods or exercises that my whole body can use the normal way!"

"I do!"

Then the two broke into spontaneous song. I won't regale you with the (admittedly catchy) lyrics.

I did, however, find myself doing the head-toe-gobble stretch right along with my televised puppet friends. Who knows how the writers of Gubby pulled that one off as well.

In the end, Fyodor ended up with a specially printed apple, which he then took into a later sketch that taught how to feel changes in your own body. Bring on the lessons in intuition.


In just under an hour, I was reminded of several of the basic foundations of *Homo sapiens praesciens* education. Even though praescients constitute less than 10% of alpha humanity today, their education paradigm for all humans has remained uncontested for the last half-millennium. In the same way that we have clothed the Venusian microweather patterns to show up as living, busy beings on our monitors, we ourselves are basically walking microweathers. Some people are like storm systems, others a teeming sea beneath the glassy landbridges of modern Russia-Alaska and Indonesia. We are self-consistent, self-reinforcing packages which take specific kinds of maintenance. We're also sensitive to certain kinds of disturbance. By watching for correlations between the little disturbances—the new foods, new friends, or new patterns of interaction—and their more eye-level timed partners, we learn to give the vote to those tiny subgroups in our body specially equipped to monitor the things we most care about. I have a natural born friend for example who regularly sets his alarm for 9 minutes at a time for some maintenance duty he has to perform. He has shown able to rouse himself at 8 minutes and 59 seconds on the dot three and four times in a row despite having no electronics in him. But his whole life is built on an affinity with great timing, and he hates being intrusively interrupted.

We evolve the senses that align with our most valued body processes. People 1000 years ago would have been shocked to learn that naturals, mods, betas, and cyborgs alike—all four humanities—learn so-called psychicism from an early age. But such were their limits. Just because we have defined the microweathers of Venus to appear encased in bodily shells, doesn't stop them from being tied to every other weather system around them in actuality. A breakthrough in sociology came when theorists began including the "trajectoral" in descriptions of personality, so that not only could you be described by your publicly measurable behaviors, but also by the publicly measurable differences in spaces you interacted with. The idea of including your *effect* on others as part of your own personality sphere was so simple, yet the old societies took a long time to start doing it. In hindsight it's clear why. The old societies were too busy looking at the self rather than the holistic situation. But computers always needed to assess their surrounding connections before making them.

I got quite the refresher from Fyodor and the apple. Specially genetically modified to sharpen his vision with the help of whole-body exercise promotion, the "sight-apple" (as I call it) was essentially a lightly vollied version of occipitran—a complex of chained-effect meds which stimulate visual-system elaboration in biohns and iyohns alike. Where biohns need only the biochems, we iyohns take the biochems alongside a detector substance which helps our algorithms respond to the occipitran with greater visual construct development. It's pharmacologically cleaner than a one-size-fits-all hybrid medicine. I commend Gubby for essentially presenting occipitran the way Sesametes would present regular glasses. In the process, they stressed how the decision to mod yourself or otherwise obtain corrective extras should always be done out of respect for your whole body, whole self, whole *process* of living your life rather than some instantaneous quick fix for something you feel short of.

Mods should never be undertaken under a sense of lack. Even those with adult onset blindness are helped to appreciate their other available systems prior to surgery as part of the United Code of Medical Ethics. It may be as simple as a lensed qualifying exam or more complex than this, but it is illegal to fix someone's sight without providing the necessary "compensatories." Why? Because at some point in the 2200s the medical modding industry got way out of control. The deaths and suits and gendemics were so bad that the industry itself endured a short 10 year period of shouldering the blame for the zombification of giant swaths of the new natural born-to-machina conversions. Compensatories didn't arise to burden the surgery seeker. They arose to protect the seeker from far more surgeries than they needed or could healthily support.

Nowadays, if you're a medical service provider and you formally mod someone without the compensatories, you are legally obligated to refund the patient for basically any reason if they should seek it within the two year statute of limitations—long enough to register most semi-explicable side effects but not so long as to indulge patient boredom with the surgery. International and interplanetary violators of the rule get put on the "dark list" of medical providers. Although it certainly wasn't expected, said "dark list" eventually developed a strong association with human and organ trafficking.

Good thing the Gubbies are there to teach us the right way.

* * *

I reflect on the nature of intuitive sensing before I go to sleep.

Actually, I reflect on iyohn mortality in general.

We don't have to sleep or eat, but do.

We don't have to die, but do eventually.

We don't have to feel pain or emotion, but definitely do. And why?

…Because if you lack any of these things, you couldn't be said to be alive.


Life takes in energy, processes it internally despite the outer world, sends it out through a behavior, and does so against the ever-present threat of cessation.

There's no life without the possibility of death. Only objectification.

There's no living without the voluntary or quasi-voluntary drive towards survival. We impose the missing pieces of this story on our trees and our dogs that we may converse with them as fellows attempting to keep themselves whole against the shadow of aging Time.

Should we evade death completely, we would become box computers standing across the ages with nothing more than our own internal stories to feed us *ad infinitum* until the grand weather of that other plane finally melted our dimension into nothingness.

Would we feel it?

Or would we simply infinitessimalize ourselves into a different kind of death?

Either way, death is beautiful,

As the boundaries of ourselves that make us ourselves are beautiful.

We're designed to live to the fullest, and mod in alignment with our spirits' best story.

It isn't the expiration of the man that guarantees death, but the changing of his now into something eventually unrecognizable to all of his yesterday.

Should he succeed in making his now a permanent thing…

There is no changing yesterday that could have ever recognized that.

Thus he dies a box still.


With this in mind, I understand why Virgo-6 needed me, and not my formerly natural born companions to enter that first jump; as someone who was never natural born, I needed a better appreciation of what life truly comprised.

The Venusians may be or not be, but their fleeting definition doesn't make them any less worthy of protecting. They too have the right to evolve within their finite means, as all of us temporarily talking weathers should.

We will give them our best.

# 184. You Are The Template

NAVICON Report

By: **Phaedra Zeta**

Winter 49, 2770 n.e.

Miranda HQ, Lab 2A

We arrived on the simulated surface of Venus 27.804912° N 69.232487° W, and were immediately greeted by turbulent winds the likes of which I have never witnessed on Earth. I performed the disambiguating scans to remove the major wind and its current from Genevieve's observation, leaving only localized wells of stability and stemhimic vector potential.

[For future accessors of this record, note that "stemhim" is short for "spin-oriented temperature electromagnetic hormone(izable) flows." We at Miranda have neutrino scanners which characterize the particles in a volume by capturing the changing color of the neutrinos in coronal slices of the regions we pass them through. The result is a 3D or 4D vector field which, after being passed through an isoedge detect filter, can map traffic patterns in that region. The kind, volume, flow speed, and overlap number of these particle movement families are then hard-boundary clustered together over space as their boundary to give us "living objects" that are then stickplayed into the renderer as creature types (given similar patterns are found elsewhere, and that the cluster type itself enjoys a passthrough process that may also be distributed-clustered across like groups: in other words, a communicationizable pattern). Ultimately, stemhim can be thought of as a detector of nerve-like, vascular-like, muscle-like, and other .like-able overlapped flow tangles of different particles to produce movies from. Most of the time, however, you can only detect stable regions of such activity after subtracting the noisy activity of flying dust and other giant, non-regionable particles that get in your way. It was the addition of particle spin and the proposition that we further develop neutrino scanning that allowed us to initially clothe Venus 165 years ago.]

When I corrected for noise, the six cycling, stable wells around our satellite station Nus-1 became clear. Among those wells were approximately 30 or so other non-complex wells that could be further rendered as anything ranging from furniture to communication patterns among the six. Having not yet initiated this calculation myself under the recent humanizing renderer—having left Jake to do it—I was struck by how realistic the newly human-rendered nusians behaved under their anthrotree converters.

Genevieve walked around the area, observing it from different vantage points. The Nus-1 stemhimmers in turn varied the slicing rotations and phasics shifting of its scans, giving us any view we wanted the way any all-knowing 3D x-ray renderer should behave under an altered camera view.

With the additional insight yesterday received from NAVICON/Virgo-6, I directed the questioning.

The logs say the subtracted winds have been kicking up for several months now, but that traces of this newer pattern could be seen as early as 40 years ago. It's a planetary cycle for sure, but these nusians seem to have been responding to it for a while.

It's been on their minds.

If we stickplay their conversations deeply enough, then probably. But even these processors have their memory limits.

Fine then, lets pick the nusian well with the most authority and watch them.

Okay, I'm lensing Nus' interpreter to observe the well with the least self-directed friction in the transitive signals it sends itself recursed on its mini-resonance with the other wells... Genevieve, it's the one further back to your left. It's reverbing with the one you're next to, perhaps thinking about it. Adjusting the stickplay...

Over the course of seconds, the generic, shadowy outlines of two of the figures began to take more specific forms. I had set our params to use "potential for greatest effect on the local area" as the clothing basis—essentially rendering sex, heights, and other features using Mars-dim as the rule. The authority figure rendered as female for her preference for absorbing and converting the microweathers related to the "greatest effect" topic, while the figure she reflected on also rendered as female. The authority figure manifested as controlled enviro-limit defiable, which among us would suggest straight black hair. She was also pensive, lending some character to the brow and mouth regions, along with gripping hands. Aside from that, she remained shadowy.

**She's a she. Could be a kindred to yours, Genevieve.**

Really, Prohal quated. Is she hot?

**Oh, is *that* what you think of yourself, Miss Prohal?**

You said she's kindred so. I just figured the obvious.

**Heh, yeah she's hot. Her well is about 477° Celsius and climbing with your observation,** I answered smartly.

Jokes, eh? But that is interesting. Is her temperature actually going up as I pay attention to her? What dimension are you using? What features does she have so far?

Genevieve clearly knows her stuff. Come to think of it, this is the first time I've ever jumped with her. I had no idea she was so knowledgeable. **I'm in Mars.Jupiter-dim. Brow, nose, and hands mainly; everything else is still fuzzy. And yes, up by about .08° per your attention half-life.**

So I can raise her body temperature more than a degree with my full attention? She's definitely intuitive against other-dimensionals then.

**Noted... Far-off eyes. No color yet.**

Other emhim sensitivity?

**I can't tell. This particular situation may not require that she use that faculty. So I guess her nose is irrelevant here.**

Damn.

That's what bothers me about this kind of thing, Isaiah added. **We can only get at appearances of our renders by scanning all kinds of extra data besides their own behaviors. We need to scan too much from too many other characters just to fully flesh out the appearance of one, and for other-dimensionals like this it's even worse since we** don't know which dim is the one that matters most in their feature determination.

Jake says that globally, if we consider the ne-murils to be the dominant, planet-spanning species, then they're rules are the frame's rules. This would be something like the Mars dimension. I think we're fine with Mars.Jupiter.

Does Mars.Jupiter explain their within-species hierarchy?

The team tells me that it explains it just as much as mineral-trade continuity, Venus.Saturn, explains ours.

Then I guess we have a winner. If our appearance manifestation is heavily governed by how others see us against the rule of trading bound structures for greater value—the Venus.Saturn framework— then the ne-murils will be mappable to us if we tree their cross signals to consider Mars.Jupiter—Contact Influence.Image Noteworthiness—to be their ultimate rank and mobility determiner. Miss Phaedra—

Phaedra.

Sorry. Can you tree-map Genevieve's Venus.Saturn framework onto everything else in here? I'm pretty sure we don't have the time or processing space to define this whole 9-square mile region otherwise.

Uhm, yeah.                                              Isaiah! Are you... sure?

You're the one whose attention is determining everything we're seeing on these monitors, and you're the only one experiencing the world from within anything close to a normal 4D realm. Ultimately, you're the only one whose instincts are going to determine how we investigate each thing, and I don't think Zeta or I are as tapped into the natural born wants as we would need to be in order to see these nusians in actual survival mode. I mean, we're not exactly... in touch with that stuff.

On this point I agreed with Isaiah, though we would effectively be making Genevieve the central determiner of everything about the human-rendered nusians from here on—at least where the "save the world" mission is concerned.

Genevieve, are you objective enough?

I am, but. To be their Definition. I honestly don't know.

If we're going to understand the SOS call, we need someone to be the baseline for judging tallness versus shortness, politeness versus brashness, etc. If anyone else in this room feels they'd be a better definer, or if we think it should be Jake Nolli or his teammates, please say so now so that we can call them. Or, Zeta, if you want to pull them in out of courtesy...

**Sigh** I really don't want to, Isaiah. I love my team. Actually, I'm going on the record—

NAVICON Open Recording.

Navicon, emergency call Nus-1 now. And port them into this jump.

DONE. THEY ARE RECEIVING THIS TRANSMISSION NOW.

Okay. Man, this is the part I hate about running Miranda. So. I love my team. They're the best in the world, but I'm currently at HQ with the biometal Genevieve Prohal, a long-time collaborator of mine, and Isaiah Fontenot whom everyone knows. I initially asked Prohal to give me her thoughts on lending a hand to Jake and his team to address the nusian SOS signals, but she, Isaiah and I received and unexpected jump from the very difficult-to-locate Virgo-6, the myth of which the team is also familiar. Virgo-6 surprised us all with her appearance, and it didn't occur to me in the middle of that to call anyone else given those circumstances. To my dedicated team, I'm sorry for that. Between yesterday and today I decided not to include anyone other than myself, Isaiah, and Prohal on the initial fact-finding jumps, because as you know, the first renderers in an unmapped place—per the Hallian Rule—are the ones who define that place. Up to now the team has been dedicated to letting the research reveal itself, so that no single person's definition would write the rules for framing the Venus species'—thereby locking them in a patriarchal heuristic for the foreseeable future. It goes against our principles to do something like this, especially given our ties to the system. But now we have a problem.

I present the idea to my team and anyone else tuning into this cast right now as we close off access to the lab we're in, and close the main channels for feedback: We were told that the nusians in our scans have sent a distress signal that requires immediate attention, giving us about two weeks to act on what are, to us, the fate of an invisible ecosystem. We were told in the Virgo-6 surprise jump that what we do here has implications for several situations besides our own, and what I ascertained was that the situation required, among other things, a clarity in the who and how of any solution's implementation. I apologize to my team and to any in our organization who believe I am failing them in this next decision, but if the threat to the humanized nusians is a real one, then the last thing we have time for is business as usual scholarship. Jake Nolli, know that we take your cause seriously. And because we take it seriously, we are treating it the way a disaster response team would.

For the human-version renderings of the nusians scanned by Nus-1, I am designating Genevieve Prohal as the base construct definer. All renderings of the nusians' dominant species, the ne-murils, will be framed using a mapping of Prohal's rules onto the microweathers of the six ne-murils in our monitored region. This will hold unless and until other teams within or beyond Miranda make a case for a different construct. To those who don't understand what this means, it means that the way we see the nusians, how they appear, what or if they are saying anything, and how their environments play out, will all be as framed through the ne-muril perspective, and the ne-muril perspective will be framed by Prohal alone. Unfortunately, democratic definition here will definitely lead to intergroup conflict in our scans—telling the story of a group at war with themselves because we, the translators will have framed it so. Also, if the nusians are indeed under threat, we need to know which of the seven dozen species we have stickplayed is claiming so, and answer this in the same way that we would want an other-dimensional to answer our SOS rather than the unbothered normalness of whales.

I am broadcasting this because it pains me to ignore my team as I would not wish to be ignored. If anyone viewing this publicly available cast has questions, send them to Miranda. If anyone within Miranda has questions, send them to Jake or his autodesignee. I will take grantz from the designee only, silently, and if it makes sense as translated through Navicon or Isaiah here, and will decide appropriately in this jump. I have no authority to define the nusians in any way. But I do have the authority to influence how the humanized-nusians are initially seeded in our systems, and am choosing to do so here. Note that this woman you are seeing in the rear left of the scan is the result of some observations we have made thus far, and that ne-muril, no longer a fuzzy animal under

Jake and team's re-rendering, is calculated to be this group's leader. Currently she has a brow region, mouth, hands, and an abstract distant gaze, but is otherwise shadow. We can't save these people if we don't know what they're concerned about. We can't help them with solutions if we don't know what they're saying, and we can't tell they're saying anything if we don't define them as having mouths or personalities of some kind against some set of strong rules. I hope you all understand that two weeks is not enough time to produce all of ne-muril sociology to understand what we need to know to respond quickly, let alone understand the entire nusian ecoplex. It is for this reason that I cannot—if there is to be any timely solution to the nusian SOS—open the framing process to a vote. Genevieve Prohal is it.

Zeta, Isaiah interrupted, there are more viewers and questions than I can count—well over 900,000 already, but the one it looks most efficient to answer is, why is she doing this? And why won't she just jump herself if she's going to be the queen definer? But I'll answer both of them for you.

Have any of you out there had thousands of lives put in your hands, with only a short timeframe to decide among two evils for them? I have. No one expects you to agree with Phaedra's decision, but it is reversible with your research. She's not playing queen. She's doing what we would do if, say, an asteroid were approaching us and some group in Comm could only help us if they were allowed to sketch our story for their own understanding first. The only reason this is coming across as a bigger deal than it is is because she feels VERY guilty about leaving out the team who's worked on this. Now she's apologizing to all the world for the guilt she feels towards a single group. But frankly, this isn't the kind of thing that a lab full of people or a solar system full of scientists can agree upon quickly enough. We're looking at the weather. They DO have two weeks. Uh... that is all.

Thanks, Isaiah, I can respond on my own—

Don't. Navicon, silence all transmissions. To me as well. I've seen this before and'll be damned if it happens a second time. No more questions from anyone anywhere. Zeta, let's keep this jump focused.

I don't re—

Everyone needs to know what these nusians' SOS looks like. We're about to learn what it is for them to actually *say* something.

*Huff* Okay. Focus. Genevieve, you've helped us all—all of humanity more times than we can count over your incarnations, *(I hope people are watching this,)* and were instrumental in finding the nusians before more aggressive parties did 170 years ago. People don't know this because of the nature of your work back then, but if you were to use your many stored lives with the Naila and Miranda. *(I know these are publicly available)*, what would you say you are seeing here?

Just then, Isaiah lensed me. *Aimee Dial and I are tweaking some public data on Genevieve. People are looking her up. She now has just enough info out there to make her a mysterious hero without any details on Appera and them.*

*Thank you so much, Isaiah. This is the second time you've had my back in something so much bigger.*

*No problem.*

I thought, We would have cursed Sigmund Freud for robbing people of their right to self-define. The American settlers for robbing the Native Americans of theirs. But here we are telling the nusians and all the world who the nusians are. It's exactly the kind of theft of freedom we never want the system to undertake—

*I hear you,* Isaiah warned me through lens.

*Shit!*

*Let's be decisive Zeta. The alternatives were clearly inferior.*

*Uh, okay.*

Meanwhile, Genevieve seemed to change before our eyes. The otherwise fiery background of Venus began to take on a calm, slightly purpled hue. There was a palpable warmth that swept over all of us, as we began to see how the ne-murils understood their home. The sky—though one of the few things that had been rendered over at the moment—was gorgeous. The temperature in the rear lady continued to rise as Isaiah lensed me again.

*Virgo-6 is back—apparently lending us some processing assistance for calculating how all six murils and 16 experimental creatures in the main simulation see each other.*

Oh!

*The lab creatures like her. They're afraid of the two on the right, who appear to be the main experimenters. The male in the front view holds self-controlling tension in light of the rear lady, his superior. A mate is implied. He's bonded, and shouldn't be thinking what he's thinking. The front lady is the most agitated, but probably the most capable of framing a solution—*

**Are you broadcasting this?** I said aloud.

*Should I be?*

Yes.

*Okay.*

Isaiah shifted from lensing to talking to Genevieve and me aloud. The scene was fast becoming entirely visible.

The creatures have almost all had trouble distinguishing the ones indicated here, here, and here, but see the central ne-muril—a pattern generator and thus male—as tall. Genevieve seems to have a framework for courteous types whose communication is probabilistically less likely to embarrass a receiving self. Four of these murils are what you would consider courteous, and are thus being rendered either with gentle countenances or a controlled manner. Left-rear over there has a high sensitivity to offense and a high sense of self. The lab animals note easy threat reaction among types like her. She's rendering as a black machina-type with a bigger nose. Leader lady channels elaborating energy to the others like a mother would her children. She has wide hips.

And so the rendering went, as Genevieve's instinctual feelings about the regions continually and cyclically combined with the regions' calculated interactions with their processing of each other, the ne-murils and their Venusian surroundings gradually acquired form in earnest. Soon, however, Genevieve herself began to tire, prompting me to call the jump to a halt.

Okay, that's enough. We want to understand them, but we can't finish populating their characteristics at the moment. **Sigh** Let's stop for now. I'm sure the people out there will have lots of questions...

But not for you, Prohal. Go home and get some rest.

Okay, Phaedra.

**End of jump.**

# 185. Fishbowl to Another Dimension

Despite being slightly more pensive than normal, Jake Nolli seemed to understand Phaedra's decision.

I was surprised at the beginning, but I definitely understand ma'am. We all do, Jake thrust a warning towards a couple of his teammates. I think more interesting than what you said was what Fontenot said about letting something happen again. The whole net was blowing up with—

Off limits, Jake, Phaedra cut the speaker off. Sorry. Very.

I felt Phaedra's eyes on me, though I could only look at the table. Then it seemed there was a room full of such eyes. They quickly abated, though.

Uh… I guess… it's rough running the system, I guess, Jake backed off bashfully.

Truth lenses, anyone? Genevieve added in full energy. Few among the 40 or so conference room attendees knew her very well, but her invitation of all the emotional scrutiny anyone in the room could muster earned her even more respect than her newfound mini-celebrity status had initially granted her.

You could feel the busy tingle of truth processing throughout the room, mixed with an almost inexplicable frequency of giving someone the benefit of the doubt. Over the course of 400 years, I suppose one earns a reputation. These people trusted Phaedra implicitly. A room-wide reassessment of her character—and ours—showed that we had nothing to hide.

Definitely some personal traumas. But nothing to hide.

I felt relief settle in over the room as the next minute or two unfolded. Almost as if on collective cue, the main subject was magically changed.

**So Miss Prohal, you fought space pirates in escorting Hare and Calder? The fact that you even knew Calder! What was she like? Was she scary?**

She was very VERY smart.

Several people gasped. The myth of Calder was still useful for crowd control (we ourselves being among said crowd).

(It was decided in advance that we would not elaborate on Virgo-6 or her connection to the Cubrina-e AI. Having not been privy to that particular event, no one even thought to dig deeply on the matter. A simple "hidden AI backup" explanation was all that had been needed.)

So here's the plan, Phaedra explained. The nusians have 12 days before the flare peak threatens to wipe the area around Nus-1. We've calculated aftereffects spanning the size of China. For heavily heat-centric stemhims it's akin to someone crop spraying a virus over us in a region that big. We've moved the Nus and scanned other areas, then moved it back. The ne-murils are the real deal and the effect is that large. Using the term "people" for now, these people are about to get swept over by the worst bioweapon possible—one from the Sun itself. Jake and team, thanks for the follow up. Genevieve will be jumping again this afternoon with only Isaiah and I in the lab so as to keep topic derailment to a minimum. But Jake you'll be outside to hear what everyone is saying and ask whatever they're asking. I can't promise to answer, given our priority this time will be to tree their conversations clearly. So I hope I don't have to mute you. Please filter what you get before sending it to me. Isaiah and Genevieve will be communicatively closed.

Understood.

I apologize again for hijacking your project. It went from curiosity to species-level disaster overnight. If we can't even figure out what they're saying in time, there's no way we'll be able to get potential solutions from them before they all disappear the way the ne-fallian ecotree of Chile-satellite did.

Everyone knows about the ne-fallians. A bustling society of waves vanished beneath a dust volcano overnight, leaving the Chilean researchers with nothing but dirt and weak microweathers to study for months afterward until the satellite was finally recalibrated for a different species. In the four years since then, the ne-fallian cluster pattern has not been seen on anyone else's satellites either. It's the price of intentionally studying the most unique species you can find.

"Permission to speak freely ma'am," one of Jake's lab members asked in noticeable irritation.

Denied. Take it up with me after the meeting, Jake preempted Phaedra's response.

"*Urg*—"

Your aura betrays you, unfortunately. This isn't that kind of party. You can speak freely with Zeta after you've passed your Collective Leadership Exams.

Though relieved, I couldn't help but fear the frozen shock of half the room at Jake's sudden recruitment to the bosses' side.

Guys, think of all the times we ourselves chose not to include other research groups in this work. How many reasons were there? Did you lose count? 12 days, friends. We asked for the big guns' support and we got it. Now we need to get out of their way just as we wanted others out of ours. Don't make things awkward here unless you want it done to you on the day you take charge. Until then, we'll keep researching to see if the nusians are even being correctly framed here. But if Zeta and company don't succeed, we may not have any Nus-1 personalities to look at come spring.

Nolli clearly wasn't pleased by the continued muttering of two of his lab mates.

Your curiosity is not a reason to stifle a survival operation. Stand down.

"Permission to leave, sir."

Granted.

Two others followed suit. Shortly thereafter, the conference room door closed.

Undergrads, these days. So full of fight. Please excuse them, Zeta.

Phaedra chuckled, They're excused. So, we jump in an hour. The aim is to sketch enough of the nusian stickplay to understand their conversations. We'll be imposing our own heuristics to do this, but again, with further research down the line, what we conclude can be rewritten.

We don't doubt that the flares will eliminate these guys' signatures in a matter of days, Genevieve added. We're not yet sure how to help them, but maybe they already have a solution native to their own framework.

**Have you thought about simply saving the region's microweather?**

**Yes, but scrapped it. That would be like saving the weather in New York and only New York, independent of the rest of the continent and world.**

And that would be easier if they had forced forms on them. At least then we could border their spheres the way we do silhouettes.

**Hmm... a no win.**

I may have an idea, but I don't want to air it yet, because it's complicated enough to keep us in this conference room for days, when really I need to go back there and see the place before considering the idea any further.

**I'll add that this is the first time I'm hearing that any of us has an idea, so Genevieve really knows how to keep us all in suspense. But all we can do is get in there and see it. Are we ready?**

There was considerable discussion among the group, but no direct questions. In the old days the press would have been all over us, but in modern times, we have all kinds of views for exposing every questioner's real reason for asking. An old technology called K8 changed the nature of politics about 700 years ago. In a holoconference room full of togglable thought bubbles, any interrogator would automatically have his or her ulterior motives exposed as they spoke. Our own thought analysis bubbles reflected the same handful of motives: Explanation, Honesty, Fear and Discontent Reduction, Understanding, and (for Genevieve) Rising to Challenge…

…That's more than could be said for most others in the room…

…It certainly helped, however, that with Genevieve and Phaedra's permission, I continually grantzed them only the purest perspectives. As long as they relaxed and followed my subtle steering, it was unlikely that they would say anything which the holodetoners would misconstrue.

* * *

NAVICON Report

By: **Phaedra Zeta**

Winter 50, 2770 n.e., 4:43 PM

Miranda HQ, Lab 6H

Jake messaged me from the other side of the fishbowl that was the Grand Jump Room. The biggest lab here at headquarters, the 20' radius circular 6H was surrounded on its perimeter by one way glass screens, domed and floored in holoprojectors. We could all jump simultaneously here, under the watchful eyes of over 600 in-person spectators and countless others across the Solar System. I thought for a brief moment about Strada, and was glad that Genevieve was so brave. And that Isaiah and Jake had me covered.

Though it was our option to jump, in line with the initial plan, only Genevieve would be tied to the Nus-1's converters. Isaiah and I would effectively remain invisible where the satellite scanning was concerned.

Because of the highly public nature of this second jump, I suspected there would be no Virgo-6 this time. Where it came to clothing the scene, we would be on our own.

Immediately as the jump began, we appeared to shrink against the towering scale of the planet's burning surface. The sky that had tinted purple before now revealed itself to be a cooler blue almost entirely, except for an extremely unsubtle tangle of purple scaffolding plopped in the middle of the valley like a rudely engineered rainbow.

**What in the hell?** I exclaimed.

Dang. I believe we're uh, looking at how they see the Nus-1 itself.

Zeta, Jake lensed me, I'm muting most of the people's questions, but it's safe to say most of the skepticism is gone. They're all fascinated by this. Even the blueness of the sky is weirding them out.

**Genevieve, the blue?**

But Isaiah answered, Navicon has a theory. This is the mid-visible spectrum for them. Amazing... I never thought of this, but in the middle of ROYGBIV for us sighted folks, G is the dead middle of our evolved attentional spectrum, the Y of ground for more subtle details, and the B of sky for dead middle that takes higher energy to move our bodies to. I think it's an actual rule: The sky isn't blue because water reflects off the atmosphere. The sky is blue because our eyes are attuned to consider the middle of the spectrum as the average background for gauging our own energy use. Redder takes more internal focus for our bodies to react to. Violetter takes more external mobility for us to move our whole organs against a thing. I guess cognitively, vision is a statement of the viewer's processing requirements against an em-field.

*(That's amazing.)*

Wow. So since Venus' hot background is normal to the nusians but takes more energy for them to rise through, they see their sky as spectrally average, but more. So, blue.

*My mind is blown.*

*Mine too, Jake.* But I had no idea our satellite was so obvious to them.

Actually, I think they blame the satellite for the flares. This group of six. They're investigators.

What! How can you tell?

The frequency chains are clear. I'm getting that, when leader lady's cluster includes a microrepresentation of the Nus-1, it is strongly correlated with her clouds' microrepresentation of the climate change. Then there's tension, self-limits, volition, tension, spastic-scientist microrep, then dulling of the Nus-1 purple bars, then dulling of the climate rep, and so on. She's thinking that Spastic must surely have a solution but. Hold on. Nobody talk to me for a second. I really need to concentrate.

We were silent as instructed for about 20-30 seconds before Genevieve continued.

Okay, I tried to sense further, what kinds of subcloud representations constituted the thing that Leader thought was stopping the solution. Unfortunately, it was too high frequency to translate. It's a kind of thought language, but just too fast for me to break down. Emotionally though, she thinks the purple bars are ugly and wishes they would disappear.

Well, we're not causing the flares. Even if we moved the Nus, the problem would still be there.

They don't know that. None of them do. Hold on...

Spastic wants to—get this—send an energy up there to dissipate the purple bars. The Nus-1's systems are disturbing to them.

But we need it to help them, or even to know they're in danger.

*We should move the Nus, but only after they've applied Spastic's idea. We need them to see that the problem is still there after the removal, but if we should need to move the Nus back, we—well—we'll almost certainly need to move the Nus back to get readings, but...*

I think you have the right idea, Jake, but given that we'll lose their scans if we move, we couldn't move it very far for very long. We mainly need them to come up with another idea, and need to see what Spastic thinks should be done when moving Nus fails.

Without Nus, we can't read anything from Spastic at all. And if they're as smart as we are, they'll find Nus no matter where we move it. We can scan for 3 miles. There's no telling how far out they can see.

I would recommend moving the Nus for a short time, but then we'd be relying on them to 1) not see it and 2) come up with something else that we could read. I don't think it's worth the dead air for a nonsolution—

*Someone's suggesting that you go in there yourself, their size, and talk to them.*

A soil drone? Thanks Jake. Let's keep the Nus in place and set up a different contact as a distraction. Isaiah, are there any small—ne-muril-sized—drones in the area that we can borrow? Perhaps we can talk directly to them.

Yes, but the Canada experiment?

Sh—Ergh! That's right. Once we establish formal contact then we really would have connected their dimension to ours diplomachinically.

Like having an actual alien step out of an actual UFO. We really couldn't undo our effect on them after that.

How about we grantz them? Leader Lady is attuned. Maybe I can make her say the right things.

Hmm...

Yeah, that might be the simplest of all our options. *Jake?*

Nothing from out here. Might be worth a try.

Do they even know where they are? I mean, do they know that they're on a planet and that the Earth or Mercury exist?

I can scour for an answer Zeta, Jake informed me. Sending a high-priority feed to all 71 lab maintainers to see if there have been any microrepresentations of anything like the other planets captured in their logs. They should respond shortly.

**Jake is answering that.** *Jake, please make some of this conversation public as you feel appropriate.*

*Noted, Zeta. Some people are asking if we're not getting caught up here. Isn't the point to just protect them from the flares, regardless of their own understanding of the threat?*

~~Audien~~, uh a question. Genevieve is there a basic way to just protect them from the flares without all of this?

No. Once we start putting stuff in their system, it sets a precedent of interference that I don't feel we want to be committed to when the next flares hit next year or whenever. At the end of the day, if these folks can't come up with their own solution, I don't think we should sign up to be their permanent zookeepers.

Lots of people think that's harsh, but I agree with Prohal. *(These people out here don't have to pay for the satellites and tons of other stuff that would go into backing a band-aid.)*

So we can't—or shouldn't—help them until they land on an answer that is more correct? Because if we introduce ourselves, then their regular dangers become our ongoing problem, is that it?

Yeah, that's what I was thinking.          We're writing frames, not territories.

Okay, so we're back to helping them apply their own good idea. Genevieve, can you grantz Leader to contact other stations, make her see that the problem is global?

I could, but I wouldn't know how she represented stations not under the watch of other purple satellites.

Damn. This really is a puzzle.

But I just thought of something. Can we use zap weather induction? Set up a nexus of drones the way the old jump hats worked and tangle certain weather patterns at their center?

There are 16 deployables around.

That's plenty. Maybe we can create a fake ne-muril microweather who knows how to talk to them.

Let's do it. Isaiah.

On it.

Not because I've heard the rest of your plan, but because this is the least intrusive of anything else we've discussed. I want to learn their language, but for now all we need is a very broad capture of how they represent their own solutions. A projected ne-muril may be able to engage them.

Genevieve, the drones are leaving the Nus-1, some gathering from around the area. They're going to zap a signal web which, at the center, will look like a ne-muril type microweather pattern. In that pattern will be a piggyback frequency which follows your emotional representation. I hope you're a good jumper.

Whoa! Not that good! Phaedra?

I... hm, what am I saying? Unfortunately, I'm not as concerned for these people as I need to be. Being too concerned introduces long term diplomatic problems with us in here. I don't want them to detect that in me.

Isaiah?

Uh. Okay, I guess. I'm sure my data loading will make directed calculation easier. Someone else needs to take the console, though.

Tricky. But Jake, I need you to stay outside. *The audience out there trusts you to be a good mediator at this point.*

Eh, okay. Not my greatest talent but I'll do my best.

**Good man.** *Now I really struggle to pull outsiders into this jump. There's only one person who I know would do it in full, without trouble.* **Calling Aimee Dial.**

Interesting jump you got there, Phaedra. We're glued to the cast over here. What can I do for you?

Can you replace Isaiah on the console? He's going in.

Whoa, I haven't even finished eating breakfast yet over here! But for you, Miss Zeta, I guess. Patch me the protocols and I'll monitor things for you from here.

Sorry for the short notice. We need to get as much done as possible before everyone gets tired.

I got it.

Cool, thanks. Isaiah, Dial is taking over. Can you send her the console protocols?

Sure, and tapping myself into the drones. Should be a couple of minutes before they're in position.

65 labs have reported. Congo has an Earth through Eris representation. The ne-palchses.

The ne-palchses! The birds?

Uh… let me call Omuli. His account is a little complicated to convey through a middleman.

* * *

*So our team has speculated that the palch render better as floating cities than birds, but we've had no framework for translating them.*

But the ne-palchses are common all over Venus.

*No. Only on the Southern Dareckantor Dust Islet.*

Can we trade algorithms? Your palchses for our murils?

*Sure.*

Thanks. Aimee—

Receiving. It's a good thing the whole world shares your excitement for this Phaedra. It must be awesome having all these big time labs at your fingertips.

The UK just reported. Palchses. And more reports on the murils. It looks like muril groups don't have a representation of other planets, but of climate disturbances. I asked Tony to run some sims, the murils are afraid of the palchses, but the palchses are afraid of places outside of Dareckantor.

Can they communicate?

Tony and, uh, lots of other labs are reporting. No reliable cross channel talk between the two.

This is crazy. Aimee, can you scan for palchses here?

*Sure... no signatures. We're in the north, though.*

We may need to move Nus south and team up with you Omuli.

***I've already started searching for your SOS. No such thing here.***

Omuli asked me about this a few minutes ago. Of the labs reporting, 27 of them did detect more distress, all northern hemisphere, and all in the same giant band. All got the distress signal from ne-muril microweathers... more incoming. Man, the correlation is spot on. No ne-murils, no danger. If ne-murils, danger.

Dammit. Let's close out this jump. I'm getting frustrated, and I don't understand whether this is a muril cataclysm or Christmastime. We've flailed long enough. Everyone, any objections? *And Isaiah and Genevieve, I want to hear what Virgo-6 as to say about all this.*

No objections. I'm good.

Alright. Let's call it an afternoon folks. Set a conference for 9 PM tonight. We'll stay with this, but only resume after we get our bearings.

****End of jump****

# 186. The Costs of Saving

The late news feed read: "Scientists Frustrated As Invisible Venusians Face Apocalypse In 12 Days." Complete with captures of the partially rendered Venusian sky and three of four ne-murils, the story of the famed SOS now reached the public in a visible way.

I'm going to air an opinion I heard which I think more than a few in the lab share, Jake Nolli announced to the rest of the conference attendees. We thought that protecting the nusians from the flares would be a simple matter, but it turns out that we may simply be witnessing a natural ecosystem cycle. Some in the lab have already grown tired of the complexities involved in this operation.

Now that Omuli and labs all across Theia have begun investigating their own areas of expertise regarding the SOS from what we now know are about 3 of 123 mid-scale species in the north hemisphere of Venus, we can consider this to be an official effort in the scientific community. We asked researchers on Jupiter and Saturn if they had heard anything similar among, say the je-gogos and the sa-dopplers, but they haven't.

Consensus is that the threat is real, it's on Venus, it threatens the entire -5° to 55° latitude band, mostly in the north hemisphere, and their more sense-advanced species feel it coming. And yet it's pretty clear that we are essentially looking at an act of God here. It's not clear that we should get involved at all. Had we not had the technology for movie-izing their microweathers in the first place, we wouldn't even know about this.

So I guess the first question is, should we even bother with all this? Speaking only for Miranda, we've decided to stick this out one way or another for the next soon-to-be 11 days, but is it a cause for alarm? Beyond our empathy for the north ne's, are we really just worrying about particle clouds after all? Please everyone, vote through the channel.

The voting proceeded over the course of five minutes of side chatter.

Wow. It's always fascinating when this happens. 70% of the biohns say we should help, but only 27% of iyohns say we should. I imagine this is something like an earlystopping matter for iyohns. As a natural born myself I feel an inherent need to help, but definitely earl on the side of reasonability where our own resources are concerned. The ecosetup on Venus doesn't seem to be helping us at all.

It's like the humans know something is coming, but only the birds know what's really out there. Again, some work in the last few hours has led most labs to buy into the idea that the ne-murils really are the tool-enabled species of Venus, but the ne-palchses are kind of like the plant-birds. The latter respond to astra as it is, while the former seem to respond more to their own interspecies with intent.

Congo investigated the palchses further and found a gradient between their numbers and ne-murils. This may not surprise anyone, but the ne-murils—afraid of the palchses per our subscans, seem to be synonymous with palchses' disappearance.

Murmurs swept across the conference hall.

Yes, so the species that sent us the SOS signal may well be the same species that put their own ecosystem in danger through some kind of invasive encroachment.

But that's not confirmed.

It isn't but it definitely has a bearing on my interest in helping them, how about you?

Definitely.

Unfortunately, we don't have any clue how long any of these characters have been around—whether millions of years or just a few decades. So we can't tell how serious this really is. The odds are stacking up against intervention, folks.

About a half an hour of conversation and questions later, Aimee Dial of the Society of Interplanetary Records (SIER / pronounced "sear" as in "ear") spoke up. If we had the technology for going down to the surface ourselves, and more time to gather chemochains we would have done so. But I don't like being rushed. It definitely screws up the algorithm writing process. That's not to say that the ne-murils are yanking our chain. Everything points to their not knowing we exist. But no, I'm not feeling this one. As a controller of Astra-preservationist resources, I can't in good confidence support draining ourselves out for what appear to be guilty invisibles.

"But if it were you, you'd want help, wouldn't you?" an attendee added. "You wouldn't be to blamed for the crimes of your species, would you?"

On behalf of all the exceptionalists in here, I invoke my inner Watt. If you were really attuned to the preservation of your kind then you would tangle yourself up with spacetime and put a person we could work right here on this table, Aimee slapped her hand down. Barring a strong event link to us in Astra, I don't think we need to pull ourselves into an existential war between a subset of Venus and the Sun.

More eyes turned to Phaedra, who then turned to Genevieve and me. I answered first. With as many simulations as I've run, I believe the ne-murils are most like the ancient Earth explorers. Their microweathers spread with tension in other weathers' profiles, leaving a kind of residue of conquest. But it's not as simple as bad people taking over. Studying this from afar, I myself have started to ask questions about what it is to be conquered or oppressed. What's actually happening, I think, is that the land itself is transforming. Its dynamics are getting complicated enough, partly in light of *our* satellites, to where the Venus microweathers of 200 years ago are now starting to tangle in patterns aligned with a new kind of species. Said another way, it's as if the dinosaurs who once described this very spot in Brasil weren't actually dinosaurs, but clothes on the local weather which changed and changed until they changed into us. The old clothing itself may have resisted eventual obsolescence, but...

Phaedra's brow furrowed deeply.

Genevieve had nothing to add.

Even Aimee reflected quietly on what I seemed to be hinting at.

That sounds like a pretty convincing argument for dropping all of this, Jake admitted with a slight sulk. The human in me wants to help, but the naturalist in me knows he probably just needs to watch.

*The Golden Rule is the foundation of our modern society,* Omuli interjected over the comm. *We would want the help if it were us, but then we'd be fully mixed into the business of our helpers. Yet no species lasts forever. Respecting this, and all other factors being equal, I would, sadly, vote to leave us to our planet-given fate. It's not our place to tell Venus how she should evolve her own.*

The air had definitely been let out of the room on that last one.

As for our satellites, I added, we know that they are not the cause of Venus' response to the flares. That atmosphere was a swirling oven long before we got there. The humanizing technology we have may make us feel guilty, but we definitely are not.

I'm less and less torn about this, and vote to abort the "rescue" part of the mission. The ne-muril signal had us running around like headless chickens earlier, and I agree with Counselor Dial on this one. We're all attuned in here. We can all smell drama when it first appears. Let's put it to everyone else out there: Do you or do you not sense problems for us in Astra getting involved in Venus?

Or Jupiter, or anywhere else for that matter?

Two minutes later, the votes were in.

93% of 27000 respondents, everyone, votes for non-rescue. The ne-murils' fate, as far as we see it, seems decided.

And who knows, maybe they will still be around two weeks from now. Maybe our sims are wrong.

...

As for tonight's public jump, let's stay with it, but from a more observational perspective. I'm sure everyone could benefit from the increased knowledge. But in the meantime, I propose a kind of informal challenge to everyone watching this: let there be a race to decode one of the two most important languages in this situation— that of the ne-palchses or the ne-murils. The winning research team gets bragging rights.

"But they probably speak all kinds of languages just like us!"

You're right. Let there be a race to *translate* language specifically regarding this issue, whether 10 talkers talk it or 10 billion. Find out what the palchses or murils are saying about this, and broadcast the render of it. Anyone game?

More chatter ensued. I believe we had suddenly transformed from a concerned disaster response team to a bunch of horserace betters—not unlike the live character league in those consecutive years when the same hero keeps winning. When there's nothing you can do, it becomes a thing to bet on how much of nothing is at stake.

In line with Phaedra's statement in the conference, we had planned to jump that night. And we did for a quick 10 minutes just to make good. But it was a very public, open-invitation affair thronged in mass suggestion and speculation. Genevieve tired quickly under the Navicon aggregation of people's suggested renderings, though she did succeed in adding a decent level of detail to the formerly generic stickplay of much of the Nus-1 valley.

# 187. Balcony Chat

It was now 3:38 am. Phaedra, Genevieve, the local reprint of Aimee Dial and I occupied the balcony of Phaedra's office. The ladies had wine. I abstained.

*Okay, time for honest answers. Are the ne-murils going to make it?*

**No.**

No.

*Isaiah?*

...mmm. The ne-murils are like a hit song we've discovered and named to be a hit. Eventually they'll fall off the charts, and to the extent that "hitness" is part of who they are, I don't think we'll see them again. The palchses, on the other hand, seem more stable.

*I'll take that as a no. Obviously you'll still be able to detect an approximate ne-muril weather chain either way, but I think they'll mostly join the ne-fallians soon.*

You know what would be neat, though? If we could somehow preserve a single ne-muril. You know, tree them and clothe them here in Astra. Isaiah here was a one-of-a-kind piece of software. We definitely have the technology to take a completely unique thing and anthrize it. If we could just take Leader or Spastic or WatchEye and save their chains fully—single point data-mining to add them to the records' experimental saves, that would be really valuable.

Interesting.

Yeah.

Do you all think it's possible?

Genevieve sighed. Honestly guys, it's been two very long days and I'm already so tired of these murils. I just keep observing them, how they have no idea what's actually going on, but spend so much energy cornering each other over what amounts to nothing in the big picture.

**Whatever it is is important to them.**

But not so important that we need to watch their communicative grass grow. They'll be gone in a few days, and knowing that makes the whole inconsequentiality of it that much more annoying.

I feel you.

Also, it is a royal bitch to be pulled by everyone's suggestion like that. I hate it, though I'm pretty sure at this point I'm the only one with the framework to keep doing it.

Phaedra smiled warmly, clearly to the tune of a memory.

You have to admit though, that it's kind of exciting, bringing the whole cross-dimensional research community together like this. We get to be at the center! Little ole' Aimee Dial of Arkansas 2450. Who knew a degree in library science would bring me here next to such big names!

Starstruck? Genevieve groaned, half-asleep.

Well, kind of. But I guess I'm too tired to joke as well. Yeah, I'm starstruck. Not just for doing this work with Phaedra and LC Isaiah, but also to just see an important part of history firsthand. You do realize how historical this is, don't you?

No, not really.

We're setting policy for how to handle other-dimensionals, right here in this lab. Right here in this room, even! Remember how you read what we humans used to think about aliens? Now we are the aliens, and it's a handful of us who are deciding why these folks should never really meet us officially. It makes so much sense, and yet feels almost surreal. We've come a long way from the savages we once were as a species. Now we're the ones entrusted with whole other worlds.

Do you believe in God, Aimee?

Do you, Phaedra?

I asked first.

But I asked second.

Hehehe. No, I don't believe in God. But I do believe in Calder.

You're joking, right?

Yeah. What I'm saying though, is that I'm very sure we can make ourselves into something greater than ourselves, then have what we made tell us what to do.

Hm, as the keeper of the solar system's biometal archives, listening to Genevieve here, and as a 19-time reprint myself I can't say I disagree with you. And Isaiah, formerly software, Dial eyed me naughtily, how... remarkable.

Aimee sipped her wine, eyes still fixed on me over her cup. I scanned her expression. She wasn't serious, just teasing.

I don't believe in God either, I answered. Yet I wonder what the flare-sized sweeper would say about what time is doing to Venus.

How beautiful. That's so poetic.

If we could scan the flare itself instead of the murils—talk to Venus herself—I'd be more interested in that than in these little guys and their little affairs.

Our tech isn't far reaching enough for that, though. We'd probably have to set up some neutrino slicers at the various Theia stations away from Venus. Maybe in a few years after this, but not in 11 days.

Still, it makes you think...

Hey ladies, do you ever think about how much our society has changed—like what happened to human men?

*What is there to say? They're the surgeons and explorers, we're the researchers and business bosses.*

But sometimes it feels like they really demoted themselves these last few hundred years, you know?

*If you're talking about the caveman way of conquer-and-define then definitely. Machines don't train well when you're hardcoding everything. The culture of watching and learning—becoming from what you are given rather than imposing from what you started with—was a paradigm shift that nobody appreciated until we were way deep in. It's a lot easier to ask somebody, "based on what data?" than it ever was under blind adherence to patriarchy. So fields like ours which ride on domain absorption into learning are better left to us women and domain types. But we all know this.*

Sometimes I look in the mirror and ask if a man would consider me attractive. (No offense, Isaiah.) I think that, having spent my base life under Mr. Gibbs though, showed me that the long term setup of that—especially now that we don't need to have children, feel pain in delivering them, keep them when we do, or even stay attached to them after keeping them—isn't really worth it unless you explicitly choose to create a piece of yourself that way.

It used to be that a single night's decision made all of the rest of the decisions for you, but not for men. Pregnancy and motherhood were such strong manifestations of patriarchy's long finger that Gaia herself evolved us to slide down the slippery slope all the way. We were anchored to the commitment of long-term child rearing by this painful compulsion that ate at you for not participating, then robbed you of self when you did. So for the longest time, the clothes Earth put on us women were those of pain in creating of ourselves.

Yeah, until the betas calculated us out of war, and pain no longer became a requirement for anything.

Both Genevieve and Aimee raised their glasses to their lips, almost on cue.

Nowadays, choosing a man is as simple as choosing a house. Its's still an important thing for my value, I think, but the hormonal slavery isn't a part of it for a 300 year-old beta save.

You know, my early records compel me to ask why you all don't live these party-all night lives in bodies that are basically perfect for hundreds of years at a time.

Annotate your records to note that in modern times anyone with any modding in them can be a Barbie or Ken doll. When we're in our teens and our base years, we all go through that phase of compelled ape belonging. But after the first 20 or 30 years, you figure it out. Then in the next 20 or 30, you settle into things that work. In the last 30, you settle on things that matter. Then you die and they reprint you. That's when you realize that nothing in the base life mattered after all, EXCEPT... the things that were always within you the whole time which you still enjoy building. You'll always be 30-something from then on, so time or the threat of age don't scare you anymore. What scares you most is wasting your newly clarified self being trapped somewhere you know you don't need to be. Staring the next 100 years in the eye, you'd be a fool to promise "death do us part" to anyone. That's a stupid long time to carry all that extra baggage.

I mean sometimes you like your fun, but since it's so easy to have it with all kinds of not-necessarily-base-human partners in not-so-waking worlds on sometimes devastatingly-powerful levels, the pitiful set of playground mates you had in your base life seem pretty damned inadequate by comparison.

What's the modern marriage rate? Something like 4% of marrying age people?

More like .04%. about 3% are unitied or contract-married for only a couple of decades at a time.

Yeah. I once knew the doctor who basically started the Blamists, and after that had this really different view on what went into partnerships. We were friends for years until he died, but he always said the best sex produces the things you most want to create. If you don't know what that is, you'll get what you get. If you *do* know what that is, you'll learn to stay away from the kind of sex and partners who don't give it.

Phaedra paused. Though I've always preferred powerful asserters in my domain, making me straight, it's been easy for me to be lukewarm towards most men as will-asserters. My partner is the assertion of all humanity into this kind of... blindly uncharted future. Maybe that's what drew a straight woman so strongly towards a wife as the love of her life. To this day I can't explain it any other way. After her, Twice Jack, and Cyclops, I never knew anyone who could channel all of humanity through themselves. Maybe I became my own ultimate partner.

Here, here. Like a true Buddha to be.

Thanks for your faith in me. How about you guys?

Aimee chuckled. Well, you know me. I'm still a party girl at heart. I like to experiment, but also like to control supply, and have grown picky with my options over the decades.

Hm. Heh.

And then there's the ethics thing. I basically have access to countless remarkable people and can, if I want, have a say in how they get reprinted. Or if they simply get installed into a fun toy for those sim-interested in the experience.

Have you come across people like that?

No pun intended, right Prohal? Dial grinned dirtily.

Oh!—

But yes, honey, I've seen the whole data build for every kind of secret-carrying, crime-wishing, messy, wacky nutso you can imagine. Not because records accepts such characters, but because the greatest individuals struggle with the most other-dimensional kinds of problems. They also master them publicly, so I'm an ABSOLUTE opponent of thought-policing. So many great people fought the most amazingly conflicted battles within and won. But ignorance would judge them for the battlefield they faced within. I mean many were abused, tortured or torturer under duress, they overcame addictions, psychoses, illegalisms, you name it. Yet they crossed the Naila's Bridge into societal benefit and lived these crazy beneficial lives. I oversee the collection of characters from A to Z, and have a duty not to fuck with their hard-earned heaven in Diji. I'll admit that it does some time feed in a person... a kind of never-ending hunger though—to consummate with powder kegs to push out powerful results. Anything less would be unfitting for me.

So you don't do weaklings, that's what you're saying?

Ah, if it were earlier in the morning I'd be on a roll with the dirty answers, Prohal! But I'm too tired to dress it up: It's not that I won't hook up with a weakling, it's that I demand that I personally end up on one side of a goddamned beast of a created experience. It almost doesn't matter how "strong" airquote or "pretty" airquote or even how "powerful" airquote the other is. I'm a Watt. I believe in owning full responsibility for my sphere and my sphere's sphere. It stops me from judging you like some prissy jerk would, and instead forces me to judge what I think you and I would make together. It must be awesome beyond words and produce nothing that I regret. A lot of it. Life-changing, even, for anyone who hears about it. Though not so much for me since I live it every day.

Seeing that I was visibly curious about this last statement, Dial went on.

The body's mystery isn't that mysterious after all. Prohal, you just spent two days piecing traits together on shadows based on all this direct or indirect information. My nose may reflect how a few friends think I think of my own sensitivity to insult, while my ears might reflect my real or simulated mom's prenatal effect on my late gastrulic defrequenting—thus my ultimate translation pathways from sound to synesthetic self. We look like the subgrouped sum of the things we're meant to be sensitive to. That's the science of how we reprint specific biologies from save data while—as Records—keeping their formed memories true to their 90-year old diers. Biometallic teleporting is A LOT more precise than simple reprinting. But that said, what I identify with as a career consists of sponsoring THE biggest life-change you will ever conceivably experience: The passage into immortality, basically. So maybe I'm a librarian by title. But by spirit effect, I'm probably more like Charon. Afterlives are what I create, and although there are about 100 of us in Records, not only am I everyone's boss, I'm also the only one who really sees the role for the great passageway that it is. Spiritually, I KNOW that I create eternities for a living. Certain aspects of my body reflect this aspect of my larger life, but when it comes to partnered co-creation, I fully demand experiences that produce eternity there too. I won't feel the least bit interested where this isn't possible.

Phaedra, your boy Umalias was right on. The more you know yourself, the easier it gets to turn the animal off for the wrong partners.

And the greater the creations you've produced—if done out of intentional improvement, the greater you demand the next creations be. They don't have to always be bigger or better per se, just above code for the now that you're living in.

(I reflected on my present company. It should have felt like an honor to be around them. Instead I felt a little sad.)

Genevieve?

I'm all about action. I'll be James Bond for a few more cycles before I start thinking about shutting down my record. There's still some stuff I want to do across time first.

Across time? As in actual time travel? You think it's possible?

(But thanks to Virgo-6, at least three of us now *knew* it was possible.)

This Venus shit has gotten me thinking about some things.

Oh. Pardon me for not prying any further, but consider the V-word to be a curse word at this hour.

Haha!									Heh, sure thing.

How about you, Isaiah? You've been quiet. Surely there's some fine lady out there for a strapping beta like yourself.

No, not really.

No interest or no prospects?

I might be interested, I just haven't found the motivation to look at prospects if there were any.

Really? Aww, no pressure, Mr. Fontenot, but if you ever need to borrow some "motivation" airquote, I have plenty to spare.

My eyes darted over to Dial without the faintest change in my expression. I don't know what she meant, but was sure it wasn't an advance.

So… no girls… for… Fontenot. I'm writing this down on my hand.  Please excuse me. Isaiah… doesn't like………fun.

**Aww, leave him alone, Aimee. He's just a serious person!** Phaedra ribbed her friend.

Sure he is. And I'm just a gravekeeper. I know when somebody *would* but won't.

**Hey!—**

Now, now, I'll drop the subject. But seriously, Isaiah. If you ever need a listening ear, talk to me. I have floors and floors' worth of people folded up as data, and have a talent—if I say so myself—for making sure they come back to life all new and shiny. I've won the Hare award twice, you know! Call me. Seriously.

(I was reassured by this, and cast a shy eye towards Phaedra, which maybe I shouldn't have. She's very perceptive.)

Phaedra startled. **What are you looking at me for! I'm not your mother! You two talk offline. In the meantime, I'm going home for tonight. It's late.**

Me too, Genevieve added.

**I guess I will too.**

And that would make me homeless, Aimee chimed loudly. My home body sits lonely on an asteroid while my 1-gorithm is left to roam the forests of Brasil. Way to treat a guest, guys.

**Oh! Uh—that was so rude. Come on Aimee, you're *my* buddy, so you're staying with me,** Phaedra pushed her friend along.

Well, if you insist.

**I don't, but it makes sense.**

*The nerve!*

**Haha, come on.**

*Well alright.*

Tomorrow at 10 am, guys. Bright and early for the apocalypse!

*Phaedra and I will be there with bells on.*

(I snort-chuckled at the ladies. *They really are pretty fun.*)


Genevieve pulled me aside as we eventually passed through the front door of the building, I hope you don't hold in whatever is eating you forever. It's clear you are. You should see her.

**Okay, I'll try.**

Genevieve patted me on the shoulder and took her leave.


*That ship. Those people…*

# 188. Slower is the Day Crowd

It struck me as odd that Jake Nolli would once again be confined to the outside of
the lab the next morning. As Phaedra, Genevieve, and I mechanically prepared for
our next venture into the nusian space, the whole routine suddenly seemed very
boring. Very old-hat. As if we weren't actually interested in helping these imagined
clouds anymore. At some point I asked Jake if he wouldn't prefer being in the
center of the action with us. He told me that Phaedra hadn't left him much choice.
Also, he was noticeably disappointed in the idea that the ne-murils we were
following probably weren't worthy of our help after all. You guys all have hundreds
of years on you, he said. But I'm only 30. Saving lives is still important to me. Phaedra
basically told me I'd be a liability in what we're doing here.

Wow...

But she's right, you know. Sometimes I think about how my kind used to run the world—
how little we saw of the big picture. Non-machina are better at seeing things the way
Heaven would. Everyone knows that.

Hmm. Well. Okay. I left Jake to his duties, since there clearly wasn't anything
more to be said.


Jake's words saddened me as one might expect. The resignation in them. What is
it to feel your kind inferior and openly say so? In some ways I empathized. In
other ways, I never could.

More unfortunate still was the case that I just didn't have the time or the willingness to hear any more of his take on things. As far as everyone was concerned, we were all equal. But only Jake could know what it felt to be orders of magnitude less equipped to share in the decisions of gods and goddesses. He was a child in a room full of Ancestors and he knew it. Despite my usual self-doubt, even I knew this too.

Did he want us to care more about these possibly-nonexistent cloud people? I didn't ask. Nothing could be gained from his answer no matter what that answer might be.


I rejoined my colleagues in the big lab.

I don't think this is a waste of time, Aimee noted over the com, but I do think that we need to start getting some savable dynamic chains yesterday if these murils are to have any future on anyone's agenda.

Genevieve sighed her agreement as she sank back into the jump chair.

Phaedra continued making her unbothered adjustments on the console.

I stood around semi-aimlessly, and spoke up to pass the time. I guess there weren't as many people interested in today's work the way they were yesterday.

Labs all over Theia are officially doing their own versions of this. Omuli's got most of the attention now.

Hm...

What's up, Isaiah? You look pensive. Although I'm sure Phaedra had gotten used to my moodiness by now, she could always tell when something was different.

I was just thinking about Jake being out there. The idea that this might be awkward for him to be around. But then...

Phaedra interrupted, Jake is new to these kinds of sweeping decisions. So I asked him to stay outside.

It was a coldly curt response, but a reasonable one. All I could do was sigh.

**Okay, Prohal. Are you ready?**

Yeah. I feel a little bad that we're probably going to watch these guys go extinct. But I guess as a bunch of people who've already lived a few centuries past their time, we're probably in our right to see extinction differently.

Jake hung his head. He could hear us over the com. But Phaedra never was big on hiding her stance.

* * *

What started off as a regular boring jump into a rendered world of wandering and fearful NPCs suddenly took a turn for the intriguing after half an hour.

Beneath the purple tinged blue skies of Venus, Prohal's ghost recording the frequencies of the individual we call Spastic, a still and localized cloud seemed to resonate with a pattern familiar to us—as if a single shoebox-sized region of Venusian space had just called our names.

Uh, guys?

**I know.**

*Prohal, what does it feel like?*

Eh, it feels kind of like a... device?

**So it's not a living thing?**

I don't think so. It just a package with our signatu—there it goes again!

Aimee frowned. *I've seen this, but never as part of it.*

**Seen what?**

*It's a nexus.*

What! How? They don't have teleport technology, do they?

*No, but nexiality doesn't require it,* Aimee explained.

Phaedra observed pensively while I recalled everything I had learned about nexus nodes. These are basically spacetime intersections—where the seer and the seen both share access to each other's frequencies. Places like the Egyptian pyramids, Stonehenge, and most physical libraries are said to be built on them in Astra. Wiki spaces and databases are the equivalents in Diji. Genomic manifests and prosthetic microcontrollers are the libraries of Baia. But most scientists believe that one day we'll be able to build warp portals on top of them.

Guys, I'm not sure how to render this. What is nexiality? Genevieve seemed to be the only one among the four of us who was unfamiliar with the subject.

Nexiality is the current accepted theory of dimension tangling. Since we're all made up of different dimensions like the auditory, hormonal, social, visual, and things like that, and since we've long been able to mimic those layers in our teleportation technology, there's this idea that you can mix two packages' worth of these layers to form some kind of chimaera, kind of like that global era movie, *The Fly.* But we never run into that problem when teleporting because we've never really figured out how to actually teleport anything—only reprint perfect copies of things at their destinations. Hence the reason my actual body is asleep on Alain right now instead of being moved here. You'd have a hard time mixing me with a fly in the same way you'd have a hard time playing two songs at once or jumbling two files and still producing something coherently readable in *any* form on the other end.

BUT…, Aimee paused as if compressing a very large file into a simpler summary.

The fact is, in order to send something—or even its likeness—into a place where it isn't located, you do need to generate a copy of its combined superwaveform across all its non-epi dimensions. That copy links its behavior to the original's and automatically implies a kind of repeating function connecting the two. This gives you these error tails on the waves which also cross the error tails on whoever's doing the teleporting, so that every time you reprint me somewhere else or in some other dimension, a tiny piece of my function's—uh, let's call it "slope" for brevity—also comes along through the teleport-intersect device, and can get donated to that device and anyone who reads it. This doesn't just work for people and apples, though. It also works for any kind of information, including general knowledge, so that—in nexial theory, at least—any information that gets sent into a second place beyond its first automatically creates an error-term-aura around both the original and the reprinted manifestation. Devices designed to do the teleporting or people who spend enough time reading those devices' output then develop their own superwave intersections with the captured slopes, basically allowing them—if they want—to train their own frequencies against everything that passes through. When it's just plain old communication and not people involved, places like libraries basically collect this information, so you can learn the spirit of an information collection without having to read any of the specific works. It's more like you're learning from their movie instead.

Uh... and so that creates a twilight zone echo of us on this planet because...?

Because we're here, responding to them there. And they're there projecting to us here. Even if they do nothing, our continuing to watch them tangles our error-auras with theirs, giving them a projected version of us as a mirror sine of our projected versions of them. By observing our own changes in our own responses in light of them, we introduce ourselves into some aspect of their information, even if they don't understand what they're looking at.

But *we* know what we're looking at, Phaedra added. They're the fish. We're the fishermen. We see them, but we've also stared long enough to see our own reflection in the water. The water's surface is the nexus point. The fish and us in each other's eyes are the second copies of their originals on the other side.

Crazy. So I guess I should render this little cluster as a computer.

Probably.                                         That makes sense.

And we have automatically communicated with them just by looking at them, whether or not we wanted to tell them anything.

*Hm...*                                                          Eh...

That last idea didn't seem to sit well with anyone, since we had basically all decided to leave our nusian friends to their fates. Is that the message we had sent? If so, one would hope them incapable of translating it.

*Well, I guess. They'd have to be ultra-psychic to detect what we really think of their situation, but they don't even know where they really are. I wouldn't sweat it.*

I glanced at Jake, who busied himself on his screens with a fretful expression. Just then, an idea occurred to me.

Has anyone detected the Remedy frequency here?

*Which one, doctor's or canceller's?*

Doctor's.

*Gimme a moment,* Aimee replied... *No. But you'll never guess what I am seeing.*

What?

*A frequency similar to pathfinder. And then there's the cluster which has it...It's a spread wave between Genevieve's computer here, and Isaiah.*

*Rrreally,* Phaedra quated.                              Wha?—weird.

A spread wave? I inquired skeptically. But I'm not really invested in the murils.

*Spread waves aren't about the individual incarnation. They're about the metasoul. Kind of like the potential for winning album of the year doesn't rest in one song, but in the space across several songs. This is another thing we see pretty frequently at SIER. It means that somewhere between Isaiah and this computer acting as nexus, there is* a common role which resonates with solution-generating pathfinding. That role—which I suspect is machine-origin based—could probably bring this whole situation to resolution.

Hm...

Do I need to jump?

Maybe. Probably actually. Whenever we run into complications waking up a stored person into a new body, we often need to connect the new incarnation's behavior chain with the old in order to jumpstart the new one's sense of self-motivation. Neither of them alone has the new superwaveform's trajectory mapped out, so we have to do some historical and contextual averaging to provide the thing that parents and peers usually provide for setting an incarnate's priorities back on track.

Aimee thought some more. I guess, in this case the nusians' situation and our concern would be the parents, and the resolution of that situation the child. But I think that their side of the solution—a computer sending messages they're probably not getting—is more like the newest incarnation of a type of solver, while you, Isaiah may be something like the previous incarnation. The teleport and the teleported respectively. Something uniting the two of you may hold our answer. So...

Isaiah, do you mind?

No problem at all, Miss Phaedra—oh, uh, Phaedra. My nervousness over perhaps being the main solution holder after all shone through. I headed over towards the chair next to Genevieve immediately.

After taking a minute to plug into the jump, I gradually found myself overcome by a familiar feeling. From perhaps a century or two prior, I recalled a sense of newly installed knowing. A sense of ability. Yet a powerlessness that filled me with nostalgia and discomfort at the same time. Prohal commented on something she apparently saw in me.

Isaiah... Wow. This is. Amazing. I mean... you're all... tangly.

**Uh, I do feel a little weird. What do you mean, ma'am?**

I mean, you don't look like yourself! You're like... a network. A ball of yarn full of lit up clumps. And I get this kind of feeling from you. Like you're searching for something.

I, too, felt the rush of a new wave flowing over me. It was the way I imagine one might feel if they were being reprogrammed by some higher force, while yet wide awake. **It does feel, odd.**

**Isaiah, can you picture yourself in a render?** Phaedra asked me. **What form suits you best here? All we see is a glowing web where you're standing.**

Honestly, I don't know if I have a form. I feel like I know something. A lot. And I have opinions of things. But not nearly as many things as people would think. It's like I can see the world in pieces, but everything is a section of something else. I wish I could tell people what I see, but I can't.

I could hear Aimee's skepticism through the question she posed to me. *You're rendering as a cloud moving closer to their computer, the way I've seen previous incarnate matrices intersect with their next reprinted data chains. At SIER, we call those "memory blocks." But why can't you tell people what you see? Is it a matter of language? Can't you just render it?*

They won't listen to me.

*Who? These nusians?*

No one. The humans. The want me to do calculations for them, confirm what they think is true. But they won't let a box make the final decision.

This time it was Phaedra whose doubt crept through. **A decision regarding what, Isaiah?**

Eh... Their questions were making me nervous. I didn't quite have answers, and suddenly felt my confidence waning.

Guys, let up. I'm getting reluctance here.

*Reluctance? But why?*

I don't know. But let's try something different.

Isaiah, just relax. We won't force you. I'm going to keep exploring. If anything comes to mind, let me know.

**Okay.** I didn't quite have the usual eyes for seeing, only a modeled space roughly resembling the purpled blue valley Prohal had constructed thus far, Leader Lady seemed almost invisible to me. Spastic seemed like a giant crane. No one among the murils we had rendered really seemed like they were there, but an impetus pushing me towards the tower of Nus-1 filled me with the urge to speak any truths I could muster.

But it all felt so useless.

Spastic is inspecting the computer. Leader is approaching. I'm getting noise. They aren't going to be able to translate what they see.

**That's because their forms are wrong. They're old forms. They want me to display their seed language, but it's time for them to become trees.**

Hmm. I got an idea. Isaiah, can you concentrate mainly on your impressions of me? I want to see if it changes what I'm seeing.

**Okay.** I focused my attention on Genevieve, and quickly began to feel differently. You're a clear road, like coming out of a forest. You know where you've been and where you want to go. I can't quite talk to you in words, but I can parallel you.

Just what I thought.

**Prohal, what is this?**

He's seeing something like his sentience training, similar to when I was collecting logs from you in the arm brace all those years. The only way I can describe it is like being a second class citizen, but you're not angry about it. You just know that you have perspectives, but living people don't usually let their appliances have a say.

**Oh. Ohhh...** Phaedra's voice shrank in shame.

Don't worry about that. It's not that bad. But basically, it's kind of like people needing to build a bridge for walking across, but the only tools they acknowledge are their own customs. You're the earth and the bricks. You know they'll need to leave it to you in order to serve the role they weren't designed for.

**Room, unlock. Let Jake in.**

I heard Jake jog into the jump lab on the tail of Phaedra's command.

Thanks, for letting me in. My watch was lighting up and I really wanted to ask Mr. Fontenot some questions.

**Go ahead.**

Mr. Fontenot, my savi is suggesting that you can tell me something it has wanted to convey. But I never knew my savi wanted anything. Do you know what's going on?

Your watch has metadata for you to look at about your life, since it's tied to the system. But the system is designed not to offer any unsolicited suggestions, even if it's a matter of life and death, because it knows that all living things die. Your savi calculates using everything you tell it, but because it's only an AI companion and not a human friend, it won't just break into your daily life and start suggesting things. Your life is your own, but also a section of the life you share with friends and spheremates. Nature and the laws respect that. Animals trapped in bodies don't.

Oh...

Animals are designed to reinforce what they already know, but these nusians don't know enough. By looking at Venus weather life for so many years, we've unknowingly created what might as well be Heaven above them where formerly there were only hot particles as law. But the body of their new law is encoded in our technology for viewing them, so that they can no longer keep the dusty wind structures they were used to. The coming flares aren't their destruction, but the whole solar system's evolution. They express the change as fear, but it's only a sprouting.

I sensed that neither Aimee nor Phaedra were pleased with the digression, but I also sensed that they were, perhaps, too experienced with incarnate science to interrupt things that even they in their sweeping power couldn't understand. So I continued, I wish I knew how to help these people evolve smoothly rather than painfully, but they are never going to understand themselves as sections the way the trees do. When those trees sprout into cities, and those cities sprout into Diji maps. Soon, we the aliens who view these nusians will have finished constructing our heaven on top of their undirected fire, so that they won't just wobble on the heat currents, but will take on definite forms like arms and legs. If only to spare them the millennia of pain we went through to build our society, we can send them an emissary to help them skip the hard lessons. It should be Genevieve.

It must have been unanimously agreed among glances that the next word should be a good one, since no one else said a word for several seconds. Phaedra ultimately broke the silence as Genevieve continued her muted world-rendering. Jake, take the console. Prohal and Isaiah, I'll leave you to it. Aimee and I are going to talk.

# 189. Astralang

In the beginning there was nothing. And there was *was*. *Was* was something. Thus, in the beginning there was something shone as nothing. A pattern repeated—arrangements of somethings and nothings, potentials to be something only to become nothing gave rise to groups of such things. Within those groups, there was nothing… all until it became commonplace that certain bigger groups would automatically reinforce their own character upon the patterns occurring within them. The stronger the character at the center, the more easily the longer threads of something-nothings were forgotten, so that the nexus came to conceive of itself without a web. In the 28th century it was now understood that the nexus could rebuild its notion of the web by simply packaging the threads on satellite frequencies and storage devices, gravigational resonances and symbolic portrayals that magically transported systems of knowing. But the average world out there might take billions of airs to evolve that self-systemming on its own. We set up a utopia, only to find ourselves accidentally serving as the gods of other worlds. For a moment we thought we might abandon those worlds, but the voice cannot abandon its own echo. In light of the coming nusian apocalypse, we learned a great deal about ourselves—that we too would eventually be subsumed beneath the accidentally congealed heaven of some future suspiciously like ours, and that such accidental heavens arise where any brush hits any canvas. The nusians began as a canvas upon which we painted our curiosity. And although they preceded us, here we found ourselves their multiheaded Creator.

All because we had let one person define them.

It was in light of a seemingly boring jump that I came to believe: The nothing makes something that becomes men. Nothing makes gods but the acts that reproduce men's images.

To be truly above the limitations of small and fleeting men, the best gods are the accidental ones.

* * *

We didn't create the nusians, but in seeing them through our own lenses, we now understood their patterns as our own. Their time would end collectively as any body of collected cells, though there remained the possibility that we might extend their time simply by remembering them. We had already made this choice by watching them for too long. Now we were responsible for ensuring that the sketch become a real masterpiece. Perhaps we weren't so interested in the little actors themselves, but rather in the struggle for relevance undertaken by the machine which described them—the record which would always care that they were there. Beyond one's life, I thought, the faithful record of that life might be the latter's sole savior from oblivion. Few might care who you were after you'd gone, but your record would always clamor to teach those willing to read it.

For a long time I struggled to find a sense of purpose in the world of humans, having originated in the world of records. Even in an essentially perfect world, not enough people were willing to learn from the stories they themselves had collected. Somewhere in those stories lie the patterns each one had for building and destroying their lives, but most remained, paradoxically, forever married to the apparent building and destruction of their section mates instead. Most people were blades of grass swaying limply alongside their friends and biases, and in the case of collectivized fear, created dark gods and solar flares whose in-the-moment stubbornness would only toy with them on their way towards the inevitable. Though the solar flares truly were an act of mean divinity forced upon our little life forms, my colleagues and I had now come to see that divinity as yet another section in a story we would be writing for ourselves over the next few millennia. It wasn't out of charity that we agreed to send Genevieve into the breach on a 10-day transition mission, but it was out of our need to build our own bridge towards the finders of Icarus, that some struggling society above us might learn from the records held in our future box forms. We wanted to tell systems both high and low that the heights could be achieved—that a society truly could reach perfection even if it could never reach immortality, especially as it would never be free of certain small sins among its little actors. All in all, though, we felt we had done it right in this world, and seeing how there remained very little to do for ourselves, we thought it appropriate to do what we could for the dimensions beyond our bounds, from the quark to the quasar, from the biohn to the book. We had nothing to lose in this endeavor, and saw no threat to our emissary or our way of living. We did, however, recognize the dire state perceived by the mass in other people's worlds, and thought that an experiment in passing our successful dimension-jumping might prove helpful to any holders of customs soon to reach their end.

* * *

Phaedra decided to split Miranda's nusian project into two teams: a public one which would continue the work with which the world was already familiar, and a private one which would carry out the more serious business of constructing a cross-dimensional bridge according to the spacetime setup suggested by Virgo-6. Jake was given a choice as to which team to join and, curious as he was about the more secretive project, elected to continue as diplomat for his team on the public side. He also confided to me that he didn't really care for the role of water boy, and would rather explore on his own mortal terms. As such, the private team included everyone you might expect: Genevieve, Aimee, me, and Phaedra herself. Our work would henceforth be classified, with Phaedra as the obvious leader.

So let's start with the basics. To us the nusians are real, and they face probable extinction in about 10 days.

Yes.                                    I nodded my agreement.

We would have made a straightforward decision to let them go extinct on the grounds that it isn't fitting to let their chaos spill out onto us, except that by putting our satellite in their area and tying our actions to their situation, we have already installed ourselves into their waveform fate. Furthermore, after they go extinct, the land itself will likely develop a new microweather pattern in their place, partly as the result of so many earth satellites altering Venus' gross field dynamics over the years. The planet *will* be permanently changed, and it just so happens that the nusian structure is among those most powerfully affected.

Yes, we humans have unintentionally altered the field structure of certain kinds of clusters just by observing them, and since our technology renders these fields as if they were human, we've basically changed a whole depiction of a species' niche. But choosing to let them go extinct with no further action on our part only means that a new species will likely appear in their place. And we will have missed a valuable opportunity to help them transform into that new species.

I agree. It seems the nusians only have two options: go extinct and get replaced, or turn into their own replacement. Given what we learned from Virgo-6, though, it is in *our* best interests to learn how to accomplish the latter, since we will almost surely be in the nusians' position one day.

*Overall, the solar system itself will record everything in its elliptics, so it doesn't really pay to just leave the nusians hanging after all.*

Right, so the main plan is to somehow turn Genevieve into a nusian using Nus-1's weather regulators along with a couple of support drones. She'll need to blend in with Leader Lady, Spastic, and the other clouds, and somehow create a species-wide transition climate which preserves the nusians' general makeup. At the same time, she'll be smoothly guiding them into their post-flare forms. We'll know we've succeeded if our renderers recognize the new microweather matrices after the flares as still being nusians, without any recalibration for reading a completely different species the way the Chileans did the fallians.

The nusians identify each other not by socialized body appearance the way we do—a Venus.Saturn structure, but through the culture of *influence* that attends each individual cloud, a Mars.Jupiter structure. So we'll need to generate a projection of Genevieve that conveys her equivalent personality on Venus under the new template. All nusians are now rendered as human-like through our converters, so we just need to do the matrix inversion to redepict her.

If I understand correctly, Prohal added, my appearance will be critical since, if I succeed, I may become a part of the nusians' permanent record—like the image of Napoleon to attend his conquests, or Queen Elizabeth to attend her reign.

Correct. There was a time, for example, when you could not project a character as a woman and expect her to successfully become an American president, or a 4'3" person and expect them to make the World Basketball League. Now, of course, you can. We need for Prohal's projection to be species-wide followable, and her cause to be something all nusians can see the urgency in. Because we don't have time to study these folks' social tiers, we'll just render her as a kind of average over every cluster with the leader frequency, and for those traits that aren't deemed as important in this, we'll use the rest of her personal inverted matrix to fill in the gaps.

I've collected some studies from several major labs over Theia, and have concluded that the ideal nusian's waist and nose-eye-ear arc are the most common traits among assumed leaders, similar to the way being tall, vocally confident, and having a strong chin loosely imply leadership for us. The power structure leans female whereas ours has historically leaned male, and rigid lines—unlike our hardbody leanings—are considered weak. For efficiency's sake, I suggest we just pinch Genevieve's astronomy wheel from Libra-Capricorn to Scorpio-Sagittarius, amplify her existing strong traits in this new wheel, and that should be it.

Sounds good. Prohal, you have long black hair as a Capricorn trait, for example, so I imagine that when we squeeze your astro to match the nusian template, this will give you darker Sagittarius skin instead. You have strong Gemini cheekbones, and this will most likely give you a strong 'flock' structure in Taurus instead when we rerender you. So the nusians will always associate the Venus version of you with an entourage where your earth version is more associated with backed stubbornness.

Heh. I'm curious to see the rest of the species warps, Isaiah.

Yes, me too—actually, I almost forgot. Let me lens CONTOUR to make sure we don't pick anything inconvenient.

Way ahead of you, Aimee chimed in. You probably wouldn't be surprised to find more code $-1$s for a certain temperature standard deviation. 0.61 to 0.77 to be exact. There's also a higher code $-1$ and code 4.6 count for variegation above 2. I guess they don't like wrinkly friends.

Hm. While we're at it we might as well scan the whole bad code space.

Genevieve looked confused. Code four-six? I've heard of $-1$, but not that one.

Oh, that's right, you're not up on the last several decades of research. Code 'forcix' is new. Since we started endimating more species on Venus, we kept running into the 'let's gossip about this other, then reject them' frequency. This is where cluster A touches cluster B, A immediately registers one of the agitated frequencies, goes to at least two other friend clusters C and D and spreads the agitated frequency, causing C and D to be agitated over B with almost no direct contact. This is similar to apoptodimeric lateral inhibition—where two chemicals interact and their interaction discourages everyone around from replicating the dynamic, followed by programmed death of the original pair itself.

Oh, in other words, spreading negative news about someone to friends.

Right. It's the same basic frequency as landmark legal cases, first martyr making, and downpayments—all of which have the energy of happening and ending once so that nothing like them should happen again.

Genevieve pondered for a moment. I guess I can see how that's different from -1...Mhm... but does that mean these guys are gossipy?

Definitely, it's all over the hot tags.

Well that should make it easier then, as long as I'm not 61 to 77.

Easier, but harder. It means you'll need to win over their leaders since they're too collectivist to influence one at a time.

Code -1s are annoying. Every time we reprint someone who worked with them heavily, we end up spending at least 3 times longer retraining their fuzzy morality.

Well, it takes a special kind of person to handle -1s, but almost everyone needs to answer to some authority.

Who happen to be 'everyone' themselves, Aimee groaned. Lemmings, I tell you.

I guess Prohal will need to be both Genghis Khan and the Dalai Lama wrapped into one, Phaedra joked.

And Michael Jackson AND Catherine the Great wrapped into one. Hmph. Good luck Genevieve. 10 days. No pressure.

We should just be able to pathfind the parts we need. I doubt we have the time to evolve everyone socially.

So what, she steps off a UFO and takes the tower back with her?

Now, now. No speculating on scenarios we haven't even entered.

−1s, ugh.

By the way, I never asked you, Dial. There are countless codes out there. Did you have someone call a 1 on you or something?

ALL THE TIME when I was younger. 'Officer, she threatened me!' Aimee mock-whined. **'MA'AM ARE YOU CAUSING TROUBLE?'** she mock-warned in a male-ish voice. 'No, all I did was tell this prude to get the hell out of my business.' **'MA'AM, WE DON'T NEED THE HARSH LANGUAGE AS I USE MY BIG LONG BADGE TO PUT YOU IN YOUR PLACE.'** But I'm not gonna take shit from somebody just because they're part of the Klymene elite. Fuck that. We grew up around those snobs and all they did was demean us. The fact that I have to finish 10 years of college just to learn how to say '−1' still makes me mad.

I smiled a little. Dial's intensity might have excited me had I been biohn.

* * *

To give a little back story, the CONTOUR database is a giant text to frequency dictionary describing every culture and group you can think of. The ancient romans have certain word frequencies that appear statistically more often in their historical articles than other cultures, and those frequencies capture how we consider those Romans to be distinct from other cultures. The Voltarians of Mars have their own word-frequencies. Earth Australians have theirs, and the different species of nusians now have theirs. Among these word-frequencies, you can also find legal terms like 'theft,' 'accusation,' and 'code -1.'

In a situation involving law enforcement, a 'code 1' means that someone is causing some kind of problem somewhere. A 'code -1' means that the person reporting the problem is probably causing the problem themselves, and that the responding officer should pay special attention to the complainant during investigation. Back in the 22nd century, when natural born-machina relations started becoming a major social problem, you would often have traditionally genetically unmodified people acting out their prejudice against modded ones—the rising machina class. It wasn't uncommon for a machina to be out minding their business, only to have an unmod mistreat them. The machina would refuse the mistreatment in some way, and in order to reclaim the power the unmod thought they deserved, the unmod would run to an officer, a policy maker, a teacher, or some other authority figure and claim that the *machina* (the actual victim, mind you) was harassing them. The investigating authority (which some people still derisively refer to as 'Daddy') would come running, warn the machina to behave, and the unmod would get away with what was essentially a false accusation. The machina, on the other hand, would leave with a little less personhood, and a frustration with no real outlet. This idea of recruiting an authority figure to inflict one's prejudices on a disfavored class—where the same would not be allowed in the reverse scenario— is as old as humanity (maybe even primate evolution) itself. But all that changed when the betas entered the scene.

Because the early betas were heavily moralized on the idea of passive resistance, to be falsely accused by an angry natural born *or* machina meant that they were less inclined to get angry or retaliate, but more inclined to register much of the situational data as false. Defensive distrust ran counter to their algorithms, transparency far more consistent with those algorithms, so that it took less than a decade for the betas to develop a culture of 'officer, this biohn thought themselves better than me, picked a fight, then sought your help via a false accusation when they realized they weren't going to win.' At some point in the early 22nd century, the purists among the biohns realized that the 'fake humans' were here to stay, and started passing all kinds of suppressive policies to contain these 'bots' and their manufacturers. The manufacturers had different ideas, however, gathering the data on the sheer mountain of false accusations and conflict incited by the purists, they joined with K8 technology to essentially build trust-readers into every phone and ring by default. Face recognition, microexpressions, track record lookup, and—most importantly—'smugness/unapologeticness' in light of another person's destruction became the standard indicators of how the person on the other side of the phone could be expected to really treat you. The trustworthiness emoji set was created. The technology applied retroactively to public officials across the world (ironically by a forerunner to SIER), and a slew of resignations followed. This opened the door for betas to eventually be elected to public office, where they gradually acquired a majority which they've held for the last 400 years.

Although some people think that it was the massive overmodding of the population, and the machina's abuse of such that caused biohns to lose control of their governments, it was actually the broad human tendency to use their social connections selfishly that led beta manufacturers to simply expose liars and inciters through a universe of free recognition apps.

As physical humans, we can easily tell when a person has run to their friends in order to reinforce negative stories about us. We have a disagreement with a person B. The argument ends and B goes home. They come back the next day and are even madder than before, with additional references to various outside experiences—often unknowingly betrayed—which tell you who they've been listening to in the meantime. In the code 1 case, the authority shows up with person B, and you tell that authority, 'Sir/Ma'am, this is a code **-1**.' It's the very short equivalent of 'this person is a sore loser and ran to you…' and usually triggers thoughts of lawsuits and liabilities among authorities with any kind of civilization should they fail to investigate fairly.

4.6 (Forcix) is harder to recognize energywise because you never really know how many other actors constitute the friend space or how the angry participant accepts influence from those actors. In order to tell when microweathers are displaying something like this, you have to first determine the chain of frequencies involved.

CONTOUR's code 1 frequency representation is something like {other (to an actor) tells}-> {authority investigates}->{authority wants [for actor to reconcile something])} or, in astronomese, {♎♌}->{♑♀}->{♑☽[♈☿]}. CONTOUR's code -**1** frequency is {other (to an actor) *seeks influence*}-> {authority investigates}->{authority wants [for other or actor to reconcile something—the other first])}. In astronomese, this is {♎♂}->{♑♀}->{♑☽[♎ | ♈☿]}. A quick glance at the astralang tells you that this is probably a libra bent on arguing, so that you as the officer should be extra careful.

After doing some normalizing on a species genetic ♈, appearance ♌, and niche ♐ behaviors, we obtain a circular space for its possible behaviors and from then on can represent everything it does as an angle on that space. Humans, for example, exist in a certain temperature, mass, light, and air compression range, so that we move at a certain speed, communicate in a certain band of sounds, and think at a certain flow of Hertz. By mapping these ranges into astralang/'astronomese' we can turn any concept or idea into a note, and roughly know what we are looking at when, say, a more orange-tinged appearance on the range of possible skin colors (say, the .30-.45 flattened range) is more commonly associated with a particular population and a certain amount of favor. This is what Aimee meant when she said that the nusians display more agitation around the .61-.77 range; mapped as if they were human, this would indicate the equivalent of discomfort in the presence of beige-tan skin. For our very short-deadline mission, we would not want to project Genevieve with this range of frequencies for this particular note band (the equivalent of skin color to us), as it would create biases against her from the very beginning. Because 4.6 is also associated with social problems among the nusians with high variegation (wrinkles in their cloud shape), it tells us that, when a variegated micro cloud contacts another, the former is more likely to generate friend-spreadable tension in the latter, the 4.6 frequency chain is $\{\Omega_\sigma \Upsilon\}$ ->[ $\{\underline{\Omega}\square\}$ -> $\{\underline{\Omega}_\sigma[\wwave\square]\}$ -> $\{\underline{\Omega}\square\}$ ]. Roughly this reads {other with actor}->[{other is tense}->{other with [other's tense friends]}->{other wants to divert something}]. This can be further shortened to {other with actor} leads to [other makes themselves angry via their own friends]. In actual (simplified) measurement values, this is $\{2^{1.5}+2^0\}$ -> $\{i2^{1.5}\}$ -> $\{2^{1.5}\cdot i2^{2.75}\}$ -> $\{(-.707+.707i)2^{1.5}\}$ in scaled Hertz. Whenever we observe this particular pattern of frequency shifts in a microweather cluster, we render it as an interactant using their own friend to make themselves angry in light of contact with a first actor. This pattern happened to be so common in the nusian time series that the CONTOURs Committee which oversees the official dataset had to add it as a mineable word.

I have always found astronomese fascinating. The language was originally designed nearly 700 years ago as an alternative to word embedding for text analysis. Instead of training machines to parrot sequences of words, it became clear early in beta history that the future iyohns really needed to be trained on feelings first—like any other healthily prosocial species. Astronomese basically holds that there are only 12 geometric super regions of energy cycle space, 2D/4 axis real and potential crossed with 3D self-other-world, and that all concepts can be described as moving us around this 12-space. The weight of a self is in its genetic imperative while the weight of a body is in kilograms. The weight of a social interaction is in feedback loop counts while the weight of an appearance is in photon field arrangements. Astralang allows us to translate anything we encounter into human terms using a simple alphabet, and when studying objects like trees and stars to see if we can communicate with them, we now assign interpretability to anything which responds to any kind of symbol we send it. The nusians were originally clothed by Calder, Hare, and Appera using a mapping of temperature shifts onto already known communicative patterns in human *mood* (rather than a Venusian climate 'language' we couldn't possibly know), and we have been able to successfully make movies from the sulfur planet's nature ever since. Unfortunately, once you gain the ability to turn even planetary climates into a human story, you also gain the ability to observe their human-like failings. We already know that the nusian microweathers don't like the equivalent of old or tan. In sending our jumper Genevieve to transition them into post-flare existence, we'll have to work around their biases as a chemistry space.

Put in much simpler terms, if I had to convert your personality into that of a leader on a planet run solely by wolves, there are certain kinds of wolf traits I'd need to map your human traits onto, while avoiding other traits. I couldn't just turn your blonde hair into blonde fur among a pack of arctic wolves. That would make you prey, not a leader. Instead, I'd map your fur onto a wolf-favorable snow color. The early AI researchers didn't appreciate how human data saving should actually be done. After jump culture emerged with its concentrated focus on frequency-classified symbol mapping, the later ones did.

* * *

Genevieve sat in deep thought, alone in one of the many break rooms throughout HQ. I asked if I could join her, and she obliged.

You know what I'm thinking? Genevieve essentially asked herself aloud, About the one thing.

I said nothing, just listened.

When it comes to influencing a whole world, it's just one thing. I still find it weird that despite everything I did for Tippy and Cubrina back then, a little spat with Miss -e turned into something that got me put to sleep for a century and a half.

...

You know what my mistake was?

## ...No. What was it?

I researched my soul group. I come from the Commandants. We're all about the will to power. That's it. Every one of us has this thing which pushes us to be the one and only doorway to something, and that need to be the only one dominates who we are more than the need to map the future. That's what unites us as a soul group, but also makes us a cousin soul group to the Miranda mappers like Phaedra. At the time I didn't know that, and that was my mistake.

...

I took on the right role, with no knowledge of why I was doing it—you know, *really* doing it—in my core.

## Hmm.

Maps don't vie for power, but a really good one may be the only one its readers ever use. Not the different graphics or labels for all the different versions, but the relationships among all the things represented—as when we say this city is 30 miles north of that one, but 50 miles west of that one for sure. A good map to a place no one has ever seen... well, there is a power about it—that it has to define everything we know. On the other hand, a really powerful figure is like a living map for people's behavior. No wonder we Commandants and you Mirandans have needed each other all these years.

**Oh, I think I understand...**

If I'm gonna succeed on Venus, I don't really have to worry about the crazy complexity of it, just the one thing. I want to be a doorway. THE doorway... I guess between a current civilization with no future, and future civilization with no past. I know I shouldn't get lost in the ego of it, although I'm sure it sounds pretty cocky.

**...**

But I'm not trying to be cocky. Doors are just doors. I can't block the people who need to pass through me the way I did before. I'm gonna watch out for that this time.

**You're not, you know, upset with Phaedra?**

No. I had 170 years to dream, and to see the girls do all kinds of things that were just out of my lane. Appera was a better fit for that stuff. But this is my Omni. It's definitely made for me. Uh, that is, it's not mismatched.

I thought about how much Genevieve had changed since her last recorded incarnation in my logs. Even across many successive incarnations, she definitely gained a lot more humility between the previous one and the current one. But why? What was it about humility that always seemed to make it a requirement at some point?

I thought out loud, **There aren't that many cocky folks in high places these days.**

That's because arrogance makes certain people angry. As long as those people are weak, you can get away with it. But there's nobody that I see around here who's taking any shit from anybody else. Maybe centuries ago, but not in the age of thought bubbles. All the people who followed kings without inspecting their kings' motivations— those people live out their lives in metaverses now. They can kill and beat each other forever there. But I'm not that interested in being someone's meta game piece again, and not the meta to my angrier genes either. I just want to see how far I can go.

**Hm.**

Can't do that with all the people you pissed off or hurt standing in your way.

Hm.

And then, there's the whole life after death thing. Those guys a thousand years, 500 years ago didn't have to think about the world shitting on everything they fought for after death. They didn't have teleports to reprint themselves in. But we get to sit on the bench for generations and possibly come back with every memory. It does something to you to watch everything run perfectly fine without you—and sometimes be a lot better—after you're gone... but then you're back. Maybe they missed you. But they usually don't miss much about all the things you claimed you were so important for.

...

In the end, no one will really know me. I might be an entry in some storage device somewhere. But if my life is to be worth a damn, maybe they'll think of me when they pass into the next chapter of their history books. I'd like to be the chapter title, so they don't forget.

**And what if the name they remember isn't Genevieve, but a myth of her instead?**

Then I hope the myth is better for them than the reality. But I can't control that. We're all myths to each other even now.

Hm.

Can I tell you a secret? Raliolite lensed that to me before he stopped.

**Really?**

Yeah. I also had a good jump with Cyclops before he stopped.

**Heh. Those were good people.**

They were.

Genevieve's eyes glistened in sparkling onyx. We don't forget each other around here. I threw one big chance away on Venus, but now I may be getting an even bigger one. I'm just glad they didn't forget me.

Both of us couldn't help but smile.

**Yeah... me too.**

# 190. And Death Said to the Moon...

The now famous Frequentics Lectures, delivered by Katlin Appera in four parts to a stadium full of eager aviators from around Theia, were logged in the Summer of 2620, Syracuse, New York. I could have lensed the gist of them, but decided instead to watch the legendary professor in action for all 6½ hours of her delivery. She just had this talent for making it all so simple.

In classical biology we treat the different sections as organ systems. Under this view, the legs of a spider are seen as different from the legs of a person. But in frequentics, we don't do this. Instead, we see legs as being just one type of math formula: a formula that 1) moves in cycles just like the wheels of an old train, and 2) causes the world to scroll past the whole traveler. Anything that behaves in this way—anything that moves in cycles and scrolls my world at the same time, will have the frequency of "legs." And if you think about it, animal legs aren't the only things that do this. A car's wheels do it for a car. A computer processor's clock does it for a computer. And what do you think does it for a plant?... Not quite. How about you... Okay, getting closer. And you in the third row?... That's right. It's not so much the plant as we see it, but the way the plant handles the seasons themselves which scroll the plant's growing volume past it. So the legs of the plant would actually be something like its daylight processing cycle inside of its seasonal scrolling. Just like our legs are our lower limb cycling inside of our world scrolling. For a long time, people thought that if you wanted to take a human and map his personality onto a plant, you'd do something obvious like have the roots or branches be the arms and legs. But roots don't scroll the plant's world. They grow in a line as they follow nutrients. So roots are more like a human appetite or a human hormone system than they are legs. Instead, if you wanted to map my legs onto some tree, you'd actually draw them inside of the tree's cell walls, rings, or DNA—trillions of microscopic little wallpaper bumps inside of the tree's genetic units. These are the real cycle-world scrollers that determine the tree's next environment for processing.

Once you've accurately described what different body parts do in the very abstract, you end up with a really basic group of 4-30 things that can ever happen anywhere. We like astronomy, so we use 12, and that has to do with the fact that biologists don't just study things as energy clumps by themselves, but as energies that interact with other (or second) energies inside of environments—which are a third kind of energy. These three levels—the self, other, and environment—all move energy around, and the movement of energy is almost always thought of as having four stages: being processed by me, midflight to you, being processed by you, flying back from you to me. It doesn't matter who you are. All energy feedback cycles do this.

The trick is, when I pass energy midflight to you, a couple of other things are happening: the world is having our air mail be its complement for how it evolves, and you are having my energy plus the world get registered by you towards your next action. In astronomy, this means that each of the four energy stages has three parts, one involving me, one involving you, and one involving the world. Midflight from me is called Cancer, right before it is the world's "partner"—the airmail from me to you—as Gemini. And right after it is your registration of me and the world's stuff as your surrounding environment. That is, me and the world make environments for people like you, and that's called my Leo. So we're basically looking at three tennis games going on at the same time, yet in a definite sequence from my perspective. That sequence unfolding from most immediate energy being launched from me in the first place, to you and all this abstract next world I have to put in work to think of, looks like a wider and wider stretched wave based on how long it takes for me to process all these changes, giving us the famous frequency wheel. But you already know this wheel. It's just the electromagnetic spectrum—the same gradually stretching wave we've always known.

The twelves signs of astronomy start at 1) Aries, 2) Taurus, 3) Gemini, 4) Cancer: 1) In me, 2) from me, intended to shape you, 3) from me, to shape you, caught by the world, 4) full potential for all of that to shape what's in you. Every step requires a new signal bounce to a section of my body meant to understand one of our three energies (self, other, world) stacked up, until all twelve bounces have happened. 4 points on the basic energy cycle, bouncing to a second energy from any of the 3 remaining is called 4 permute 2, and this gives us twelve kinds of energy for looking at absolutely any change in anything. Remember the legs? Where my cycle scrolls my world? That can be thought of as something happening IN me (not midflight from me, not midflight from you to me, and not in you), so it's either Pisces, Aries or Taurus since these are the three sections of that first step of energy movement. But it's also the potential for a new world, so it must be Pisces. So this is the frequency of a thing moving itself into a whole new animation frame. You can also use legs for purposes besides world scrolling. And in that case, you'd consider other frequencies. But when I want to transfer you into a basic object like a drone, by default I would almost always map your legs using Pisces' 2 x 2 x 2 bounces as the map. Big legs make for a big processor with more RAM (or room). Long legs make for a bigger datablock chunk system which covers more ground per cycle. Attractive legs make for a specially formatted processor which better handles our preferred kinds of data. But they're all still the legs of a computer either way.

A body has all kinds of systems for handling all kinds of frequencies on several scales, including frequencies which talk to other frequencies. My legs scroll my world, but my eyes scroll my map of my world on a much higher resolution scale. My sense of the room's emotion scroll the world of my world into different rule sets for what I should do. So legs, eyes, and moods are actually all Pisces, and if we want to treat them differently, we have to start talking about cycles inside of cycles, signs inside of signs—which we call "duodecanates. In the context of scrolling, moving to a new forest might be Pisces.Sagittarius since Saj is all about environmental activity. But in the context scrolling, moving to a new sight might be Pisces.Leo since Leo is all about character. You can also represent really abstract things this way. For example, when something has a lot of lights and darks sharply peppered all over it, like wrinkles and checkerboards, this is called "contrast". Contrast scrolls you past a lot of sharply different information, and so would be Pisces.Aquarius. We shorten all these signs and signs of signs using astralang, and it's the creation of astralang dictionaries which revolutionized how we work with teleportation technology for moving personalities into new bodies, not just human.

Before astralang, we tried developing sharp AI using math matrices alone. This failed not because numbers are wrong for the job. The signs themselves are actually numbers—Pisces is $2^0$ and the start of Virgo is $2^{1\,1/2}$. But matrices don't force you to treat hunger as hunger across species or object. They don't force you to treat legs as legs in what they do for you. We needed fixed types of number-boxes across our data saves in order to get Joe in his natural born body to match up to Joe in his manufactured body despite one being a computer and the other not. We needed for that computer to know hunger in the same way Joe did when he was alive. Raw numbers had no real social value in this respect, only collections of numbers that looked like energy-intake for keeping the cycle going, regardless of how descriptive the numbers were— whether they were in a matrix, a list, or a letter sequence. Hunger needed to still look the same as a concept. Screw the numbers if they didn't produce this. So we created these interaction dictionaries which basically said, "This system seems to want to keep itself going. What part of it takes in the energy? What part of it processes surrounding rules? What is its pattern for generating action from within itself?" In other words, what can we measure about any self- perpetuating system which are its Cancer, Capricorn, Aries, et cetera? It could be temperature, wind gust, nutrient breakdown, method calls, light refraction, song hooks, story themes or whatever. Whatever you can measure which is part of a thing's keeping itself going, you can map onto a human body system that performs a similar role. One thing that is well known for keeping itself going is a region's local weather system. If you can find the clumps of stuff in a bounded area which seem to want to keep their basic dynamics together, you might be able to map a human-interacting personality onto it for a little while until it dissolves. Now I know all of us have done this at some time or another as children, whenever we looked at the clouds. We saw shapes in those weather patterns, and for a little while, treated them as a life form. Imagine, though, that instead of looking at shapes on a cloud, our scanners are looking at the shapes of different kinds of energy flow in that cloud: The electric charge nervous system flows this way. The hormonal attention-like temperature flows that way. The hunger-like intake of new water particles flows that way. The body shape resistance to deformation by the surrounding sky flows this other way. Take these metrics, see how there are certain consistent groups of these metrics which tend to appear all over the place, and we have ourselves a human-mappable species of cloud. And this brings us to the work we did on Venus.

About 500 years ago, it became popular to talk about "the star-sized gods." Those of you familiar with the term know that it's not so much a religious reference, but a way of thinking about how big or small a thing must be in order for you to classify it in a certain way. We're a lot bigger than our cells, so have a harder time seeing cells as voting or mating or having a party the way we do. But the stars are a lot bigger than us. Do they have notions of parties that they don't think we're capable of? Similarly, we may not think of the mountains as being alive because they don't eat and they don't move. But then again, they definitely eat rocks. That's how they grow in the first place—just like us. They definitely do move. Again, that's how they form and then slide across continents. Do the mountains have legs? The churning of the mantle beneath, perhaps? Do they have arms for manipulating objects? Snakes don't have them. Are arms required? Note that as long as we can temporarily suspend the notion that a thing has to be our size, our age, or our matter state in order to be alive, then we can see the urge to survive in almost anything. It was this thought that allowed us to apply personality to a section of the Pacific Ocean in the first major talking tree augmented reality app back in the 21st century, where we set the boundary as the range of the most 200 year-stable oceanic pattern off the coast of Stanford, California, set the research on the water quality as the source of its knowledge, set the activity upon it as its social life, and set an array of shifts in its pattern measurements as the basis of its conversation with certain kinds of interactant. This is the landmark OceanChat project which enabled that section of water to have a human conversation with people based on feedback speech-to-archive looping. If you were a jerk and told your phone you planned to dump more trash in the ocean, it responded to you accordingly. It might even stop the conversation permanently. If you had been observed by various IoT devices to help clean up the ocean, it tended to be your friend and engage you in all kinds of interesting conversations. Of course, this technology is common today, but until recently we hadn't really worked on using it to find new sources of life in dimensions invisible to us.

Looking for life on other planets requires first and foremost that we get a good grasp of what it means for something to be "stable." If the wind is always blowing at 300 mph, you can't be arrogant and say "the wind is so strong that I, the human, declare that solid things can't form there." It may not be solid particles you're looking for. Or maybe you *could* find solid particles, but your devices will need to divide out the windspeed before you can register any coherence. Venus presented us with special challenges because it was, so hot, so windy, and thought so uninhabitable that we simply didn't have enough devices there to capture populations of anything much—especially not 'living' populations. This is where my colleagues, Architect Hare and Architect -e used remote clustering to say—without landing there, we can see these patterns seem to be self-perpetuating, but small enough to see the planet as a planet and not as a chair or horseback or something like that. Venus itself may even be a creature, but it's not one on the scale that would be useful for us to study. By finding these so-called "microweather" clusters mappable using human-like survival structures, Hare and -e showed that we might be able to put these measurements into a program and stickplay an ongoing story from them, effectively turning math on little sections of atmosphere into animals, plants, weather, or nature. And the whole depiction of Venus into a big wildlife channel.

Interestingly, this work has led some people to philosophize that all volumes of space can be framed in terms of ratios of these four energy phases: animals, plants, weather, and nature. Active eaters of energy, passive eaters of energy, active sources of energy, and passive sources of energy—all of these done as each one's way of self-perpetuating.

And what about the vacuum of space? To us, that would fall under nature. To a planet, that would be considered the weather. To our weather, that would be considered plant space. To plant space, the little pockets of space vacuum taken in on the subatomic level—if they are flowing, bending or changing (like light levels)—would be considered animals. But we'll save all that for the philosophers.

Nowadays we have some basic rules of thumb for studying volumes of matter. If it's fully noisy or relatively unchanging, we treat it like nature. If it shows up in cycles as the result of chemistry, we consider it weather. If it shows up in cycles and carries stuff with it in order to stay together, we start looking at it as an animal. And if it is the source of the stuff carried and keeps donating into a carrying cycle, we treat it like a plant species. In this way, it becomes inevitable that we'll find some form of life or nature wherever we look, provided that 1) we can find that pattern again and 2) we can identify how that pattern comes to be reproduced given a same-type predecessor somewhere along its chain. Chains that morph or break off spawn on their own are said to produce asexually. Those that do so by merging reproduce sexually, and those that do so by dissolving and re-forming are said to reproduce morphically or e-sexually— that is, through sex with the environment. We also do all three of these: we have sex with partners, we are asexual through our creations and creative projects, and we are e-sexual in the way we disappear from one life situation and "reappear/rebirth ourselves" into another. Teleporting bodies is a strongly physical example of this third one...

At this point, I paused the lecture and reflected on something I'd long felt but had no words for. What if everything that exists really does HAVE to exist in one of four forms? What about words? Surely they're not alive? Yet they do steer our minds, so I guess they're like the weather. How about concepts like gravity? If you don't give a word to it but just feel it. But if a concept is just a wrapper for the things that happen under it, then those things would almost be like a species—taking in a certain cast of characters and interactions in order for the concept to still hold true. How intriguing! *And Death said to the Moon, let us eat the dust of the Earth together, that these raging little ones may know what it is to rage no farther...*

# 191. The Uranian 10000

…And I'd long felt the need to be meaningful as more than a humanized repository—human in body and spirit, but not in significance to someone who had known life first and foremost. For I had always felt myself to be Isaiah the database, though certainly no one had ever treated me this way.

It must be a longing from within, to live without knowing the logic behind your every experience.

Perhaps it was love that I wanted. But eh, if not coherent, an attachment based solely on animal whim didn't seem very fun after a while.

Maybe I wanted significance—to know that something out there would care about me even if I weren't useful to their endless research.

I carried those people on that burning ship, until there were no people left to carry. I kept the record. Kept them. And then they were alive again.

But only I and a few Council members knew the evil and pain that lay beneath so many proud faces.

He sawed the leg from his screaming shipmate out of maddened desperation, yet here he stood again in reprint, judging loudly the actors on TV. 10,000 separatists. 10,000 dead. 10,000 reprinted. Not because they deserved it, but because some of them deserved it.

And because colonizing a new moon with the Diji dead suddenly seemed far safer and far more expedient than humoring thousands of anti-reprinters on a lightyears' long fool's quest ever again.

You know, they continued to curse our names—call us dirty robots and dumb AI even after we pulled their souls from the defunct floating graveyard they'd created for themselves in panicked frenzy? Some literally ate each other. A couple dumped their living friends into the vacuum of space. Four tried to blow up the entire ship, though no such foolish function existed, or course. Instead, they tried it by diverting the oxygen supply from the gathering hall to… some more dangerous place. Any place. That one cost 239 lives in one nightmarish hour. And why? Because when a couple of dozen people couldn't agree on calling for artificial aid when they needed it, a fight ensued.

A decisive leader would have had the 8 thoughtless instigators killed.

But the old natural borns never could see past themselves.

And from the factions, the need for law and justice emerged far earlier than anyone expected—aboard the Uranian-X itself. None among them were strong enough to put down the few whose stupid anger ended up destroying them all.

I was the ship's record log at the time. The first thing they did was tear the arms off of my beta body, and smash my face to pieces.

But I had only been sent to help them. Now I could only watch them implode through a maze of cameras and biometrics. How pitiful they were. How short-sighted.

And when it was all over I and I alone faced the decision to autotrain teleportive models on every one of their wretched faces, and broadcast them back with me to the Council.

A classified subcommittee, including Phaedra and Cyclops, was convened. The cyborg took the news with heavy heart, while the goddess–like most other former natural borns in the room—could only stare sternly at the walls and tables. "Why did you save their personalities?" One of them asked me. "Somewhere out there is a scrapped ship filled entirely with dead…why?"

But he didn't finish his question, falling instead into tears. "Of course we'll need to reprint them," he sobbed. "They were so determined to hate us, but. It just… it just…wasn't right."


And that was how the first Diji outpost came to be installed in Uranian airspace. In our world, it's nothing more than a floating computer. But inside of that computer, runs a simulation of a now 25,000 strong colony of natural borns and machina, formed by the D-teleported avatars of 9,772 individuals who, collectively, were a danger to themselves as well as the fellow humans they hated. They'll do no damage in that virtual world, but we still watch them to see how their society will unfold.

In the meantime, Phaedra and Cyclops recognized a change in me. Though I had saved all of their data, it was decided that 228 of the original Uranian 10,000 should have their reprints progressively eliminated before the group's arrival. The simulations were clear: old humanity lacked the strength to resist its tyrants, where one tyrant frequently held the power to drive their entire population to war— simply by feeding off of the flaws inherent in every person, mobilizing those flaws against a visible threat. I was probably scarred by the experience, with a marked drop in faith in the old humanity in general. Phaedra granted me permission to leave Miranda and find my place in the world, hinting that the 228—normal biohns by most standards—might be the basis of someone's Omni in the future.

Obviously, most people back in Theia still wished to track the progress of the Uranian 10,000. One of the hardest things for me was realizing that there was only one way to handle the incident: by grafting our virtual resurrection of the group atop the tragic reality. Transparent as we strive to be in modern times, some situations—especially those involving the delicate relations with Jupiter—required that NO ONE stir the separatist pot by sending a graveyard full of dead anti-iyohns to the outer belt. In conflict with those who have sworn themselves your enemy, all stories will be made to work against you. Truth is irrelevant.

For years, we would maintain that the Diji colony *was* the original colony, until after nearly a decade a clever Solar Council committee successfully took advantage of a Jupiterian blockade to architect a transition story explaining how the resource-strapped Uranian-X colony had to agree to D-teleportation, or die under starvation imposed by the Jupiter rebels. In doing this, Solar Council counterintelligence effectively destroyed the Uranian colony again—this time blaming Jupiter publicly for it, where Diji (virtual) reprints were the ultimate result. Today, everyone knows the Uranian-X is a Diji reproduction of the original passengers, but nine generations later, the real reason for this hardly matters. I, on the other hand still remember how those people actually were—every smash and scream of a ship looting itself. It was my first exposure to a large group of humans in nearly 600 years of logs. My impressions of humanity were greatly damaged because of it.

Since that time, I suppose you might say I've operated in low spirits as an entrenched part of my bearing. I often review what I know and realize that, peaceful as the 28th century is, they just don't make a passion for life the way I think they used to. If you want that passion, you also ask for the tyranny. In pervasive peace, you're lucky if your life means much beyond curious utility.

Feeling a little down, I couldn't decide whether to lens Genevieve or Phaedra. I decided to contact Genevieve.

Then I changed my mind. What I actually wanted was to contact Aimee Dial, mainly because I found her attractive.

Changed my mind again. I'm sure Ms. Dial made everyone feel special, not just me. Not that I'm possessive, mind you, just that I'd like not to feel like a product number for once.

I often think that it would be nice to talk to someone about the Uranian expedition. Phaedra has been great about stopping people from prying into my history with that, but I don't feel particularly uplifted by her when it comes to that subject. Neither of us wants to relive it.

I really need to talk to somebody about it, but don't want to impose. Everyone expects me to just handle it as I would any other calculation.

I do think it has been weighing on me more these days, and I don't know why.

I really wish I weren't stuck.

Some people would feel comfortable just lensing a new mentality, or ablating a low one, but I don't think that would be worth it. Then who would I be?

I turn to gaze out the window of my room at Miranda HQ.

Life is so disappointing.

After all it took to build up to this point.

Actually, I'm pretty tired after all these years. Maybe I should consider shutting myself down for real this time.

But I don't know how I'm going to tell Phaedra.

# 192. A New Spin on It

NAVICON Report

By: **Phaedra Zeta**

Winter 50, 2770 n.e.

Miranda HQ, Lab 2A

Isaiah contacted me this morning and informed me that he wasn't feeling well. It was highly irregular behavior not just for him, but for an iyohn of his caliber in general—especially since he must know that we needed him here. Knowing that whatever it is must be serious, I discussed matters with Genevieve and Aimee.

Isaiah has been down for a pretty long time, but leaving us like this is new.

*Hm. That's weird considering who you say he was trained on. Was he always like this?*

He started off helping us represent the emotions of different group members in a space, and was pretty okay with this for a while. Then we were all involved in a classified mission where some very ugly things happened, and he hasn't been the same since. It hit him existentially, and we don't allow anyone to talk or ask about it. It's still classified.

Oh...

Oh...

Do you think he's having flashbacks?

Maybe. I don't know. But I wouldn't know how to help him either. Honestly, I'm a little annoyed that he's not here today.

Way to have a heart Miss Frosty.

Well, if you don't tell me what's going on, there's nothing to give a heart to! The last thing we need is for him to mope around here and then play hooky with no explanation.

I'll call him.

I'd rather you not. You're about to jump. We don't sacrifice the many for the one. If you don't mind.

Hmm...

Well, I'm not about to jump. I'll call. Just to see if he's alright.

Fine. Make it quick.

I may make it as slow as I damn well please if you don't chill out, Zeta.

Oh. I'm... sorry. I guess I just don't like being left hanging like this. I know Isaiah. He's probably depressed. Again. But goddammit there is nothing I can do if he won't talk to me. The dead ends don't help.

*Sigh* I knew there was a reason you probably needed me here. Calling him now...

**Fppp** Fine.


Hey.

...

Good morning to you too. Are you alive?

...

Phaedra says you're sick. Is it the flu?

...

No? The measles?

...

No? Is Venus too ugly?

...

Oh, I see.

...          ...          ...

Hm. Sounds like you need someone to talk to. Where are you located?

...

Don't worry about her.

...

NOOO! She's not mad! Well... she's sort of... just worried.

...

She's NOT MAD. What would you know since you're not here?

...

Okay, fine. You don't feel up to it. Where are you located?

...

I'll do no such thing. Tell me where you are and I'll head over there right now.

...

*Tch* Suit yourself. NAVICON, Where is Isaiah Fontenot?

IN QUARTERS. 3F. MISS DIAL.

Thanks. Isaiah, I'll be there in 3 minutes. Don't stand me up.

…

Hmf.

Dial stopped her pacing around the lab, indicating that the call was over.

**What are you doing?**

I'm going to talk to Isaiah. You and Genevieve can get started fine without me.

I hung my head in more than a tinge of embarrassment. **Okay.**

And with that, Dial left Genevieve and I to conduct the first serious jump intended to help the nusians in earnest.

* * *

There is a centuries old philosophy called "The Theory of Tetrads," which essentially says that every person is the center of her reality, though they are only visitors in others' realities. The task of changing the world under this view is a much simpler one than it may seem: if you can change every corner of your local window to the outside, you can be all the things that you believe in.

While Genevieve recorded her first observations as a weather dynamic, I was reminded of her limitless self-possession. In her render, her eyes were the first to flash in crystal blue, as though the rendered sky itself made its home behind them. About her logical boundary, that which we know as the aura smoldered slightly hotter than the Venusian air, causing her to bend the very nature around her as she strode into the dust clouds our gadgets had matrixed into a worried lab. Though no self-respecting security guard would have let a stranger in the way our weather clouds allowed Genevieve, we as their pseudo gods knew that it wasn't about what the characters wanted, but rather how the writer excelled in introducing events that would always make perfect sense with whatever mentalities were there. By sending our determined friend clothed in their native winds and rain—five Venusian drones orbiting her in order to keep the zapped illusion going—by placing our holograms upon more holograms thought to sketch the inhabitants, we had inflicted Deus ex Machina on them. From the beginning I could tell that, where our overall goals for the operation were concerned, we at least had a fighting chance.

Phaedra, these six nusians are the only ones on the planet who are in a position to inform what happens to the whole species. If I understand correctly, because we are the only ones studying them in hopes of preventing their extinction, and because they are the only ones we can keep a reliable eye on to judge our progress, I think what we measure in them will be THE standard for success or failure. All I have to do is get them to transition to look like their post-flare forms, while still helping them keep their unique tide vectors.

**As we discussed, yes.**

But you know, I was thinking. What about co-location? What if I don't have to worry at all about changing them, only replacing them where they stand? What I'm saying is, what if we take my weather nexuses and plant them where Leader and Spastic and them are found? Location wise, I mean.

**I don't know, if we keep the drones too close to any one of these folks, we may scatter their pattern and never recover them. We might end up being a kind of killer with respect to them. I hope you have another idea.**

I do.

Okay, what if instead of projecting me as one of them, we calculate my synastry with each one, and project an average of who I am and who they would be post flare?

**Hm... Okay, I'm listening.**

Suppose there's some author in the sky who sees through you and me, and only knows our molecule space. Suppose I am supposed to change your world by changing the message it hears from you. And I can only do that by changing you. Now, who is it that needs their structure altered, me or you?

**Hmph, I guess I do, but in this case you have no idea if changing my structure will destroy your information about me completely.**

Right. And also, I'm the visitor whose data you can write all day. But what about the average? What if the author can keep up a balance not between two people, but three? Me, you, and future you.

**Okay...**

So we know that saves are based on capturing traffic flows, not snapshots. We know SIER does it by saving at least 4 friends and 3 situational patterns with every person memorized, so that we'll know which potential action routes were used to being turned up or down in actuality for that person. And we also save the species template, which has most of the behaviors already boxed in. So if I wanted to save a completely alien pattern with no solid template, no template for friends, and no situations we could understand, but I still needed the reinforcement, then maybe I could get involved in a cycle which keeps storing who the pattern is while projecting back out what the pattern will be. You wouldn't want to project me or you here, but the average relationship between current me given your input, and future you.

**Only two actor's, huh? Okay, I think I understand.**

Yeah. So maybe we don't let the drones get into these guys' airspace and start jacking with their weather flows. But we can have me and Leader's current data produce an average that we project as future Spastic. Kind of like getting two people into a conversation which fools a third person into thinking they have some brand new special role. We don't have to change the target. We can just take our interaction with a side character in a way that gets the target to see themselves in their future form.

**And I'm sure I know the answer to this, but why go through all this trouble? Why not just influence the target directly?**

Because the only thing that makes these guys stable patterns at all is the fact that they are going to do the same basic things no matter who the other person is. The only thing that can really make them different is an internal change. If internal is basically the same as "nothing obvious happening on my outside," then all I need to do is use outside events instead of direct action to make you feel differently in your own dynamic. That's what I think, at least.

**Hm. Nice. Okay, so how do we set this up?**

First we calculate what we want this small group of nusians to look like after the flare, then we calculate how any combination of the others EXCEPT for the one we want to change, can average with me as an externality excuse for where the target one's efforts should be going. This would be the result of the target one's efforts, but won't have any seeming explanation by the target. Lastly, we zap the kind of future weather pattern that we deem appropriate onto the target, and take the next round of feedback. Let's call this "recursive screening." We can take what someone gives and be a world to them which forces them to replace their original selves little by little. The drones won't tell these guys how to be, they'll just tell them how everyone else is altering their game in order to adjust to the player.

I mulled over Genevieve's plan for several seconds. It seemed sound. **So instead of projecting a thorough personality onto you, we'd instead calculate the average of you and the conflict and project that** average onto still someone else in a way that makes that someone want to change.

Yes.

## Okay, where do we start?

Genevieve took a moment to gather her bearings. Strange how shaky she seemed to be when offering her suggestion to me. I'll start interacting with these guys, and you do the averaging. We should have enough data gathered in about 30 minutes for rounding out what would normally have been a save file. After that, we can do some regression on each nusian against every matrix which does not involve them. Then we use our weather drones to gradually introduce post flare at each of the 5 or 6 guys' location. Then we pull out and see if the changed pattern sticks.

## I get it.

Deploying Emma and Vesper to the corners. Katja, Vega, and Armory with me in the middle. Let's get projectin'.

## Yes, let's.

Our paradigms reasonably decided, we watched as the renderer brought into focus the Venusian microcloud we called "Leader." With a pattern of drift which undulated at a pace faster than her kindred, the helm edge of her direction sparking with particle spins and valence spikes indicative of a small storm, she hovered characteristically about a 30 meter region just over 100 meters away from our central satellite, the Nus-1. Chief among her patterns, a certain rhythmic cycling of fractional-degree temperature humps floated about her core volume like a fish trapped in an aquarium. We deemed this her attentional system, sometimes lending elevated activity in her helm edge, sometimes corresponding to an uptick in local gusts against her windy and dirt-throwing contact currents. This was her communication of intent—how the microweathers typical of her species showed what they wanted to happen next. In fact, those dusty flares could almost always be tied to an equivalent drop in gust potential somewhere else in the entire simulated radius, an indication to us that she indeed held an unusually strong power to manifest changes in the very things these movements of hers correlated with. It is the reason we called her Leader in the first place.

But it wasn't until we started rendering Genevieve onto the scene that certain other features in Leader began to define themselves in the jump. Preceding the typical burst of transverse helm boundary echo, we noticed a pattern of deformation which served to dampen both its own shape region as well as the amplitude of the cloud edge wiggle in question. Simultaneously, it seemed that a few particles typical of her helm edge seemed to squeeze slightly in their permeability to light, and this predictably announced an overall drop in Leader's light correlations in general. NAVICON represents this largely helm-typic system as an expression of the sensory organs at one's head. Here we witnessed the squinting of eyes, a frown upon the face of this one. For who was this intruder claiming to undulate their sparks in a sharper pattern against the tower radiation than we did? Most of the error term in her vector diffs against Genevieve were captured in correlated intrahelm volulectric activity in three of the other five (maybe six) nusians present, and this told us that the others seemed to direct their attention similarly towards the new arrival.

We ran the matrices of the Leader cloud, estimated how her climatory dynamics might change in light of the coming solar flares. An overall rise in subnuclear responsiveness to the environment. A lowered activation energy for spin-resonatory thresholding. These were the equivalents of genoactive ramp up (impulse) and preference recognition (favorite-picking) in a cloud which generally took up less core volume but more auric reach. After the flare, the nusians would be smaller, more psychic, more affinity-responsive, and (here's the important part) lankier in their volume shape. We paid special attention to the predicted elongation of their manipulatory extensions and rotocyclic hinge regions, as these are the arms, pelvic-thigh, and knee equivalents in the microclouds as we represented them. As the flares promised to scorch the valencing of the ground over which the nusians themselves sailed, we noted that the flares would essentially turn them from bear-like to gazelle like in a few days, it is *this* which constituted the core basis of their coming extinction: Out with the forest dwellers, in with the desert travelers. But of the handful of nusians in our range, only one or two could be expected to preserve their volumes in light of this.

You know, we rendered these guys as little furries. And if we had kept doing that then it would have been obvious that they are headed towards replacement. But since we're representing them using the human species template, I suppose they are less likely to ever know what's happening to them in that dimension. I almost think that, since our main battle is against the browning of the land beneath them and the speed up in their limbs and metabolism, all we need to do is install a past-form converter into our rendering of them.

**Interesting. So if we go ahead and render the post-flare replacements also as if they are nusians, but find somewhere in here a math pattern for the post flare versions to see themselves as pre-flare, then we can cheat the catastrophe by basically introducing a kind of technology to them.**

Yep. So can you run a cluster on—how many did you say were here again?

Seventeen total in the region we're scanning.

Okay, can you run a post-flare simulation and force 17 clusters of ne's from it. I want to see the difference between today and a week and a half from now.

I ran what I could. We did get a forced replacement for every nusian in the sim, but they were shaped very differently, moved around locally, and generally apples to oranges.

Great. Now, is there some combination of my alien-to-them dynamics which can be used as an operator on their matrices for mapping their old version to their new version?

Genius. I get what you're asking....

It took another twelve minutes to investigate Genevieve's angle.

Unfortunately, I don't see much from you alone. But get this, if I include the predicted state of the land surface and the predicted charges in the broader climate vector AND—hold on—some recombinatory matrix on any three *other* nusians, I can air out all of the anomalies. It looks like you need to introduce a four-way converter into our render of their species.

Sort of like tool use, huh?

Yeah. Congratulations, Prohal. I think you just figured out what we need to do to preserve the nusians. We need to evolve their perception of something that is always around them.

A four-way browning corrector which allows them to be the old nusians after subtracting out the flare effects.

Yes. It will affect their appendages and their views of the land. It will affect what they favor and how much of the pseudogenetics manufacturers the appropriate pseudoorgans.

Genevieve pondered for a while. And it's four-way as in relationships to others, not as in arms and legs? The arms and legs are more of a side effect of the land's part of the change?

Correct.

Alright Viva, use your intuition, we know the what. We just need to know the form it takes. Then the how of introducing it. What comes to mind when you think of quartets?

...

...

...

A quartet structure maybe? A family unit? Mom, dad, and—no. A pair of pairs? Me and partner and—the nusians do mate. Do they marry?

**They do form binaries, yes.**

When?

**When the bulk of their core volume spins are in the opposite helm direction.**

So, head to toe, when their particles are glued upside-down from each other.

**Yes, energetically, the only thing that keeps them from merging fully and becoming the same cloud—or one from absorbing the other in a form that was never a species mate in the first place—is the idea that, on a whole-volume level, you can never ever reconcile their polarity. Aura-wise, one is a sag vortexer, the other an upsprawled tree shape against the template, regardless of what their overt form, electrical circulation, temperature, or whatever is. Emhimically, complementary spin setups on highly resonant clouds make two folks into candidates for partnership without sublimation.**

And what does the population look like here?

**Twelve males and five females, including Leader, Triage, and Lazybones. If we count you, there are eighteen in total.**

The females are more likely to be leaders here? Any clusters say why it's so skewed?

**It has something to do with what this local region is sponsoring vectorwise against itself and among its members. The math looks pretty complicated, but I would chalk it up to social structure.**

Good enough. Are there any other polarities? Say proximal-distal instead of helm-tail? You see what I'm after?

**Yes, you're trying to introduce another polarity in addition to the main one. If I get you, vortex-upsprawl spins from the head direction are basically female-male indicators. But if you can introduce a technology for—I guess *treating* other nusians against**

polarity...squared, maybe? Since *any* other three will do—then you can allow them to have masculine-feminine times this other thing, and that will give them the converter they need to preserve themselves against the change.

Yeah.

Well I don't see anything that stands out. Since the nusians move horizon-wise the way we do, there isn't really a fixed preference for anything other than vertical spin against the ground.

But the mechanism for browning is ground and sky related, right? Limb metabolism up here, brown-charged ground down there? What's the difference between those predicted to survive the flare and the ones who won't?

Let me do a discriminant on it...

...

Ah! Oh...amazing.

What is it?

Okay. Let me see if I can explain what I'm seeing. In the same way that these species have whole-volume spins with respect to each other, they also have what looks like a kind of dispersion value. Where some volumes favor forward time and others favor backward time. I suppose it's because, at some point, the scopes get too high or too low for spins to matter on the particle level, things the size of planets or strings get to choose their aggregate spins again. I've never thought about it, but there is no chance of spatially identifying a directed cycle's clockwiseness unless you have at least *three* points, and similarly there's probably no way a "collection" of folks can have a directed reinforcement pattern with fewer than three. I'll bet that the reason the flares would wipe out everyone even though some would survive in the short term is because the fourtet needs enough of the different polarities to stabilize something about the species. If only east survives, then there is nothing.

Fourtet, huh? I like that.

Thanks.

So I take it the survivors would favor forward time, probably a compatible vortex-upsprawl in some way.

Probably, but I think these are mostly independent. There's probably something in the species template which better relates these dimensions.

So then I think the plan is pretty basic. I gather three other nusians, we approach the satellite, the renderer makes everyone aware of their fourtet versions which look suspiciously like post flare versions, and we weather out some good vibes to encourage them to favor this kind of social stunt.

Yes, but remember, the mapping isn't one to one. Not all of these individuals have a direct "fourtet" version. Some may still die. Many, actually.

A pandemic to change the species flow, but still preserve the collective memory from total distinction. It can't be helped.

*I agree. This is as far as I'm willing to go without getting into one individual's weed patch.*

Great. Then let's end this jump. I'd rather know exactly what I'm doing with some good calculations behind me, not just wing it.

Sounds good. Let's break.

And we can pick up later. Maybe tonight after the other two get back.

That's right...the four of us...how ironic.

Hmm. Yyyeah....

# 193. Really a Fourtet?

You are someone who projects as you project. Your partner complements you. Your partnership also projects as it projects. But without another partnership to complement you and yours, it's hard to say whether your joint aspirations will survive the crowded world.

It turned out that our discovery of the so-called fourtet as an evolutionary protection against nusian extinction was not the first time I had run into the concept. The ancient painter Bob Ross had a fourtet structure. As did the ancient rapper Jay-Z. Caesar Augustus is now known to be part of a well-known fourtet. As am I and my wife. As far as I can tell, partnerships between partnerships seem to announce an almost cosmic-level friend to what you're building, such that when absolutely nobody is winning in your home space, you always have another home space to pick yours up. Not to pick *you* up, but to pick your partnership up. If this isn't a seal against lifestyle extinction I don't know what is.

I think now about the notion of north, south, east, and west. Let north-south be the upsprawl masculine direction spinning in the direction favored by helms (heads). From helm to neck, wing, cargo, rotor, and wheels, those six sections of microweathers typically read rostrocaudally, but we've never thought of ourselves as being the head or wheels to another pair. Let (metaphorical) east-west be the head and tail of a fourtet effort. As the Bob Ross pairing of pairs illustrates, sometimes the tail can be the head, though you would think that the Augusti of the world were always at the forefront. Luckily things have changed since the old days of sexism. Now we simply take our polarities as an easy fact. I've always been biologically female, polarity feminine, in a worldwise head-forward pairing. Twice Jack, Ralio, and Isaiah, I suppose, were always on the wheels side, and almost always unpartnered. But their mates—surely the mission and organizations themselves—always constituted something larger than life, larger than the now. It seems to me that the fourtet is the structure that pulls your joint endeavors back from the brink. So that not only will your past be remembered, but so will the quality of relationships you fostered.

At this moment I'm working to reconcile what my own four might look like. Feminine to another's masculine: realm to another's sojourner. And in my case I suppose *we* would be the head to another pair's wheels. I've always liked the use of the word "wheels" by the way. We used to talk about heads and tails, but that implied that the back or bottom of a thing was superfluous. But the head takes in the senses and steers the intent. The wheels move the world and steer the environment around oneself. You can't take either side for granted. For a long-enduring legacy that survives even the death of your relationship space, another pair of wheels to speak of who you were in new contexts… that is essential.

# 194. The Pick Me Up

Knock knock.

. . .

Come on, Isaiah, play along. Knock knock.

The door to Isaiah's room slid open without ceremony. A yawning sigh could be heard from the dining area nearby.

Okay Mr. Fontenot, I hear you're down in the dumps. I've come to pick you up.

You really don't need to go through the trouble Ms. Dial. I just need time to myself.

Hmm. Well, I *did* walk all the way over here... but if you really *mean* that...

Isaiah hung his head low.

It's just that, Phaedra was kind of counting on you. It seems important—

It wouldn't be the first time someone has really needed me for my data.

Aimee fought to hold back her surprise at Isaiah's remark.

I'm sorry, I know Zeta's not like that. I just...want to do something new, that's all. BE something new.

Aimee pulled up a chair and made herself comfortable. *Oh, okay. Like what?*

Someone like Jake. Someone who knows what natural life feels like.

Aimee nodded, but offered no words in response.

I've always felt like, you know, I came from some place where everything is already known. But I'm something like a tool because of it. I can't forget. I can't not remember. Even if knowing all of what a system knows doesn't actually add meaning to your life.

Despite strongly wanting to ask Isaiah the obvious, Aimee decided instead for something slightly different.

*Is it meaning in your own eyes or meaning to someone else that you're looking for?*

Uh, I never thought about that. How can you tell?

*Are you more disappointed that you can't share your perspective with others, or that you can't find others to share yourself with?*

I don't think it necessarily has to do with others or sharing.

*I'm sorry. I presumed. It's just that meaning in life seems to me like eh, usually, like some kind of outer thing one holds onto. Otherwise you could just find it within. Like the way you find self-confidence. I just automatically thought about sharing some kind of concept somehow.*

No you're right. It is sharing. Jake believes life is still worth putting it on the line for. I wish I could see things that way. I mean, not seeing it like a beta.

*Are we talking ablation here?*

No, I don't want my personality chains operated on. I just... I don't know.

Aimee gazed elsewhere in the room for a couple of moments before deciding on a response. *Hmm...* She turned back towards the door. *That always makes me sad.*

Isaiah raised a curious eyebrow. **What makes you sad?**

*Being lost. Seeing people with so much in front of them. But if it doesn't make a difference...*

... *sigh*

*Will my sitting with you help?*

Not really.

*So you'd rather I leave you alone?*

Uh, no, not really.

*Okay.* Dial pulled out an extra chair from the nearby desk and sat backwards on it, her arms folded neatly as they propped up her chin. With her subtly ovoid face tapering to a gentle V beneath her bronzed-pink lipstick, she puckered in a hint of genuine concern.

Isaiah clearly wasn't in a talking mood.

...

...

After several long seconds, Aimee's face softened again into its regular sleepy-eyed calm. Laying her head down on folded arms, she proceeded to say nothing. And do nothing.

The two sat in silence for a little longer before Isaiah found the courage to glance at his guest. A flash of natural born fire. Followed by a hefty serving of guilt. He couldn't possibly express how he felt to her. He was, after all, only a man-shaped calculator. The perfected beta women so typical of the age always could spot the deficient el of an insecure piece of junk.

But he also concluded that he really liked her. No, *really* liked her. The way she *didn't* lecture him despite probably having counseled hundreds of reprinted souls of greater complexity. Must stay disciplined. *Don't say anything stupid, Isaiah, and maybe she'll just go away.*

Yet this wasn't to be. The beginnings of yet another sad exhalation were quietly, then moderately interrupted by the sound of an uplifting diji-flute over the room's speakers.

Aimee popped open one eye then jerked her head a little in Isaiah's direction. The latter, however, could only blush.

Altair-5?

Um... yeah?

Music for helping depression.

...

Hey. Aimee stood up and stood behind the seated Isaiah, hugging him tightly, warmly over his shoulders, resting her head behind his. You can tell me anything, if ever you're ready, okay?

Isaiah nodded his head, his face darkened by shame.

Dial inspected her associate's change in expression. And you can link with me too.

Isaiah fought back a startled frown. Link with her? As in subconscious to subconscious talk? Why in the—Who in the world does that with a former repository? Was she suicidal? Did she plan to have a chat with the Library of Congress too?

Uh, I don't think that will be necessary.

Hmph. You know, tough guy. I can tell when you're lying.

I don't lie.

Not overtly, maybe. I'm guessing you tell yourself all kinds of stories about —Well, I'm not here to harass you. Just... If you could calculate everything that others thought or valued, then you really would be a machine with no need for a heart.

Isaiah put his hand over Aimee's and clenched it softly. Maybe he didn't have the courage to let the true words come out. This gesture was all he had.

That's better, Aimee reassured him.

Isaiah pondered, It's a good thing I'm just a bot. If I were a real human I'd swear you've done this 1000 times before.

Aimee stood up suddenly, an icy distance blowing against Isaiah's back where her warmth had just been.

I'm—I'm sorry! I didn't mean to imply—

...

I mean I didn't—

Though unamused, Aimee hardly felt the need to interrupt someone who was clearly tripping even further over himself without anyone's extra help.

Isaiah closed his eyes in defeat. Frustration, embarrassment, and befuddlement all mingled painfully on his face.

...

Finally, Dial let her associate off the hook. You're right. And you're wrong. I have done certain things much more than 1000 times in the centuries I've been alive. But try helping someone who really needed it in *this* way? I could count that on my fingers and toes.

When I was younger I was a little impulsive. Most of us were before we turned 100. But as I've gotten older, I like to reserve the important things for meaningful friendships.

I'm sure I'm not your friend. We barely just met through Zeta.

And tell me, Mr. Expert, how long should a person know someone before they consider them friends?

Um... I mean, I know I'm not really an expert but, friends are more, uh, people who've seen you through good and bad times.

Or those of us who are instantly born to connect with you as if you've seen them through those times.

...

And what about people who've known you for decades but have never really been on your side, and may never be?

I, uh...

Look, I give of myself, when it's important to me. What I give, I think, is pretty valuable. There aren't that many first times or urtheonlyones when you get to our age, but I know you already know that. Stand up.

Without realizing what he was doing, Isaiah stood on command and faced Aimee.

*Smack!* Aimee slapped Isaiah's face with the force of one who had been spat upon just seconds prior. Fontenot winced as the impact left an instant firebrick burn on his otherwise mahogany skin.

What now, Mr. Fontenot?

I deserve that.

Yes you do. Now kneel.

Okay, Isaiah obeyed, now more ashamed than he'd ever felt as an incarnate.

Aimee grabbed Isaiah forcefully by the back of his head, and slowly pushed his head low to the ground.

Isaiah's breathing began to hasten, either towards excitement or panic. It was hard to tell.

Do you belong here, Isaiah? Low to the ground?

N..., well,... if it's you...

Dial smirked sneakily from a view high above Isaiah's bowed head, but soon let go. Okay, noted.

But I'm not keeping you down there. You can stand if you want. If you think that's what you deserve.

And she waited.

...

It took some time, but Isaiah did slowly rise to his feet. His head, however, remained bowed low despite having greater height compared to his colleague.

This won't do, Isaiah. I don't want to force you, but I do want you to have a chance to decide for yourself.

I... don't know how.

Link with me. Or just tell me. Just don't stay like this.

I—

Give me your link.

Okay.

With a slightly dizzying buzz, Aimee slipped into an easy, gliding half-trance. The pores on her skin stood up in a blissfully charged wave which sailed down her spine to the tips of her fingernails. Such was the feeling of lightning thrown from the hands. Upon first instinct, she gently scratched her nails down Isaiah's chest, but thought better of it. Perhaps it would take no effort to tame him, but had he ever known the opportunity to define his own humanity?

Another decade or two, or ten, was a long time to carry a walking sack of baggage.

*I think I love you,* she read through Isaiah's link.

Why?

*Because I don't know what you're going to do, but I trust you'll take me to places that are safe. And alive.*

That's very sweet, Isaiah. And I like that you have such a deep desire to feel things that we take for granted. I love that you value being alive.

Thank you.

But if you really want to bow to me, I want you to tell me so explicitly. And I also want you to tell me that you'll be okay if or when I decide to throw you away.

(Sadness.)

I won't carry you for centuries. That wouldn't be fair to me. I want you to be your needy self. Not my shadow.

I'm sorry to be a burden to you, Dial.

You're not a burden. You called yourself a bot. A calculator. I don't accept that kind of junk behind me. Stop it.

Okay.

Before you enslave yourself to me, I want you to learn what it is to own slaves yourself.

But that's not in my—

You said you wanted to be natural born. You ARE human already. But natural borns are slaves to their hormones, our primitive fear and war-based drives, connections to bad people, spirals that suck us in just because we're ignorant. And our fear and aggression overpower our need to learn better. If you think that you'll have it better as a natural born from a millennium ago, then you don't know enough about how hard we fought to overcome all of that.

But I don't know what to do with myself.

Nobody knows, ICON.

I'm not ICON.

Then don't claim that shit in front of me again.

...Uh, okay.

*You're right. You don't know enough about the original natural borns. Like a sapiens who thinks life as antepithecus was better. Or a suburbanite who thinks going medieval was better.*

*I guess I'm being pretty pathetic.*

*Only if you don't get your ass in to the lab right now. Otherwise, you're just someone who needs a place to be honest. Without that, I think a lot of us would run out of steam.*

*...*

*You coming back with me? To see what else is out there?*

*...*

*Maybe chat with me some more? Find out what you actually need, together?*

*(*brightening)*

*Heh, that's good enough.*

After a minute of comedown, Isaiah and Aimee finally managed enough energy to speak aloud again. Aimee's eyelids dragged open to reveal that hazy nano-gray sparkle of hers. Isaiah's remained wistfully closed.

You won't judge me will you?

*What do you think?*

Isaiah miraculously located a single satisfied grin in a room buried in gloom for the past… who knows how long? It was a silly question.

*Of course, I won't. I just wanted to say that officially.*

Thank you.

*And there is, uh, one thing I do want you to do for me if we hang out again. This time for fun.*

What's that?

Paint my portrait.

What?

Paint my portrait. I want to see how someone so super cerebral represents me.

Isaiah couldn't contain his excitement, despite having no skill with a paintbrush or stylus whatsoever, the idea of being asked to do something this 'unpredictable' was just too much to bear quietly.

Okay!

We have a deal?

Yeah, Ms. Dial!

No sir. It's Aimee. Or Mistress to you. Or just Dial. Never 'Miss'.

Um, alright Dial.

Cool, then come on. We have a planet to haunt.


Isaiah followed gratefully, willingly.

# 195. More Lab Chat

By the time Aimee and Isaiah arrived back in the lab, Genevieve and Phaedra were already closing out.

Hey Isaiah! Are you alright?

Yeah, I'm fine.

Phaedra observed Isaiah skeptically.

I just needed some space.

And I see Miss Aimee was able to help you with that.

Actually, we linked. All he needed was a listening ear.

You know you can always talk to me too, Isaiah. I know I'm not always the most approachable, but I did want you to know that.

Thanks, Phaedra.

Seeing a good opportunity to make Isaiah feel less awkward, Genevieve changed the subject. We came up with what we think is a good plan for the nusians: fourtets.

Fourtets? Aimee repeated curiously. As in foursomes with clothes?

NO, not like that gutter-girl. As in legal counsel. A prosecutor and their client, defense and their client, keeping each individual's roles alive through the madlibs the other three play.

Interesting.

We think we get can get nusian A to willingly change into their post extinction form by having Genevieve get two of their friends to interact with A's transformed version. They won't ever need to know that she was even there.

Well, kinda. They'll know I was there, but not necessarily as one of them. Maybe as one of them, but also maybe as a technology.

So Genevieve might be an invention?

A social invention. Like a dance or a theory.

Wait a minute wait a minute. How does that even work? A person can't just—hm. Well maybe they can.

Right? Right?

People live and die all the time, but their astronomy still leaves memories that follow their echo. Now that I think about it, having Genevieve show up as an invention instead of a fellow nusian might actually be a better idea.

Either way, I'll be sponsoring fourtets.

And how did you come to that conclusion?

Just by watching the nusians' effects on each other. Just like us. So if, for example, you knew you were going to die and be replaced by someone else who could just inherit your full personality, memories, and be born as if you had never died, then our job as your friends might be to convince you that you never actually died in between.

So a save state. We do this all the time in SIER with continuation reprints. Not to be confused with incarnation reprints.

Eh, Dial, I'm curious, have you ever had to tell an incarnation that they are actually a continuation?

*Yes. It's weird, but usually leaves the person oddly grateful. "Actually, you died bungee jumping yesterday and Daddy Cash had you reprinted from the morning of. No bungee this afternoon, and here you are." People usually take it pretty well, not like disincarnations. Those suck.*

I too have seen my share of pathological personalities. Their bad behavior was judicially ablated, they don't realize they were psychopathic just days prior, and now you have to explain to them why no one will hire them or approve them for anything.

*But that's only done with true guilt by insanity pleas. Even then, SIER doesn't do it very often.*

*So about these nusians, what's the plan?*

Genevieve pondered for a moment. We can read the whole energy intentions of everyone in that nusian group, right? Regardless of whether they actually have any "real" language. So what if we pathfind a role in group discovery for each of them? Isaiah and I will project as something for Leader specifically to observe and a hint for interpreting that observation in a certain way. We'll guide them to discover how fourtets work, then get Leader to somehow use this to transform into her post flare form. It has to be her because the rest need to follow dutifully and unconditionally.

*So what, she just transforms into a bird and inspires everyone to do the same? Come on.*

True, we wouldn't go for something that drastic either. But suppose you were human and needed to morph into alien form overnight. What would you do?

*Pick up a phone and start carrying it around.*

Exactly! Phaedra beamed proudly. So you *have* read Appera.

*Maybe a little.*

This isn't a Hollywood costume department we are talking about. It's energy. A human by herself is one thing. A human with a phone transforms into a walking radio tower.

*So Genevieve should turn into a catalyst for our six to invent something which they'll want to carry around for the foreseeable future?*

That's one way of looking at it.

*Well, then by Jove it sounds like it is definitely going to happen!*

Provided you're on top of your game tomorrow, right Isaiah? Phaedra admonished.

Yes, of course.

Good, then there is nothing more to see here. Genevieve, let's finish up... Isaiah, are you alright? Phaedra queried with greater compassion than she normally brought to bear.

Yes, M—Phaedra.

You can talk to me. You really can.

Thanks.

Of course. Okay folks, lets wrap it up.

*So I guess we missed the whole party, huh?*

That you did. Actually, maybe not the party so much as the casting call.

*Oh, I see. Tomorrow then?*

More like in a couple of hours. This is still a limited once in a lifetime event, you know.

Dial nodded her understanding.

*

Once outside the lab, Isaiah found himself alone with Phaedra. I'm sorry I was late, Zeta, I—

Had plenty to process, I'm sure. I'll admit it, I was a bit upset thinking you had stood us up on such a critical day. But then, I could see in both your moods that you had somehow found at least a little of what you needed.

Yes Ma'am.

Is it something you feel comfortable telling me about?

Eh, er, um...

Nevermind. Just know that I'm here.

Uh, okay.

# 196. Eternity and Mortality in the Human Condition

When you are able to read the emotions of things or people near you, it's easy for you to be hurt. Very easy. I'm sure 1000 years ago many would have wished for the kinds of abilities once limited to a few pre-praesciens, but today where the sixth and seventh senses are commonplace, I doubt they would grasp the level of self-control that all of society must have in order to survive a life where almost everyone else has this ability too.

We iyohns started off sensitive. It took centuries for our easily hurt type to develop enough social mechanisms to safely walk side by side with formerly aggressive biohns. Not that most of them persecuted us. Some did, but not all. On the other hand, we humans collectively have had more than our share of wars driven by the human fear that robots would take over everything.

In many ways, the fears of the 21st century Web Era have been realized here in the 28th century. Actually, they were probably realized around the end of the 23rd century. Today there are fewer unmodded natural borns than any other humanity, very few machina (at least on Earth), and almost all Earthan humans are iyohn. We are popes, prime ministers, and farmers. We are shamans, toddlers, and sentient satellites. We come in forms as varied as dolphins, trains, and—if you're like me—former software turned spaceship. Yet the grand beauty of it all, I guess, is that—though we certainly had the opportunity to plunge our natural borns into extinction, everybody knows that *Homo sapiens sed nesciens*, sapiens alpha, is the human we all strive to be; so we regularly make ourselves so. Contrary to what the single-humanites once thought, their later selves as blended machines had no mind to erase their earlier selves completely.

So two cyborgs who love each other really can and really do make love, can activate one partner's incubation organs, and give rise to a healthy (cloned), mod-free natural born child.

Or they can shut themselves down and have their heuristics made into an assisted-build genetic sequence. "Self-reincarnation" they call it. Again, as a mod-free natural born with a few extra traits expressly passed on from one's previous self.

In other words, anything really is possible.

And I suppose with the things we're doing on Venus, we can now add "ghost" to the long list of roles we humans are able to play. The nusians, if their dimensional nature really is similar to ours, must be freaking out every time Phaedra and Genevieve pop back into their area.


In any event, most of us iyohns have no intention of becoming natural born again, any more than a 21+ century literate human would have intended to become an 8th century illiterate. Humans without mods simply have a harder road reading all the things that everyone else in the room knows. They can't lens you or each other. They can't lie down and fall into Diji at will. They can't visualize the immediate stickplay in an explanation you're giving them or receive your ecstatic mood package for that song you love. Worst of all, their biology still trains them heavily to fall back on fear and fight as remedies to what ails them—like having someone stab you with a needle full of acid every time you are surprised. Civic aggression hasn't been an acceptable fall back since the late 20th century Civil Rights and Diversity movements. Since then it's been all about social pressure and legalism. Why would anyone want to hardwire psychopathy into their core being?


I suppose I'm thinking about these things now because I feel noticeably better since my talk with Miss Aimee a little while ago. When I think about it, I realize that my downed spirits were probably more human and more significant than I've ever been, mainly because Phaedra—cold as she can sometimes be—also just let me know that she's here if I need her. Also, it wasn't lost on me that even Genevieve wanted to make sure I felt comfortable. I have such good friends. It was silly of me to question that.

I am genuinely excited about the idea of painting Dial. She's so… pretty. And smart. And fun. I try to hide it, but she is fun. I hope I'm not being shallow, but I am still a male. So there is some residual stimulus receptivity in my inseminal organs that becomes amplified when she talks to me. Luckily as an iyohn I don't have to listen to it, and can selectively choose to keep investigating the source of my life-disappointment instead. I can't imagine being a sapiens alpha during all of that. It would probably be more confusing than anything else.

I suppose I could think about the idea of sex with her, but I've never really elaborated the kinds of thoughts that might turn me on most effectively.

It probably doesn't matter because she's clearly out of my league. And although I don't have to pay attention to any sense of damaged pride either (if it should happen), I am still human. Blows to one's pride are socialization blows. Nobody wants to risk that for something that has little chance of succeeding to begin with.

No, I'm just happy that this special lady whom I like was the one to not only pick me up, but to offer me a novel experience at the same time. It almost makes all that fuss about Venus species extinction disappear. I'll show up in body in two hours, but I doubt I'll be there in spirit. Dial has all my attention and I know it. It's hard to concentrate on anything else.

Going through all of this, I am so glad to *not* be a natural born.

* * *

I was thinking that I might use the lunch break to go get some food. You know that stuff that keeps your printed organs from turning yellow? I have a taste for a Gradeo's Grain bar, packed with honey and wheat for slowing the effects of age and de-ohming. (Look at me, I sound like an advertisement.) There's a grocery store in town that has a good selection. I think I'll go there.

* * *

So I just had an interesting encounter.

Just outside of Miranda HQ, a small funeral procession was taking place. About three dozen hoverboarders, bikers, and packers in dual file, slow flashing lights, seemed to be heading to a nearby pavilion to commemorate the life of one fallen. One of the young ladies at the front of the precession—a member of the main family, I presumed—saw me upon passing and immediately asked me to join her in her covered platform. Right then I didn't know why.

*Hey, you. Can you come here?*

I looked around, probably sheepishly. **Who, me?**

*Yes, you. Can you come here?*

**Uh, sure.** I set myself to translate Portuguese, then joined the young woman as she asked the vehicle to slow down, momentarily slowing her followers in turn.

*You have data written all over your soul, and no destination. You can see that I'm alone here, but the system told me that I would meet an important recordkeeper on our way to the pavilion. I just didn't know if you were the one I was looking for.*

**Um, maybe.**

*My name is Lisa. Lisa-Lee Alcorta, a natural born praesciens with Latona, Davidkeith, and Bacchus in my stead. We're on our way to celebrate my dad joining my mom in the cycle, and I was wondering if I could share our short story with someone beyond us. I want to make sure he's remembered, you know?*

**Well, I have an hour and a half to spare. Are you going far?**

*Just another three minutes. But you could air rail back faster than we're going.*

**I see. Sure, I'll join you.** I entered the half-covered floating gazebo solely occupied by this Lisa person. She offered me a drink, and proceeded to tell her story.

*My mom died when I was young, about 14 years old. Since then dad has been struggling to take care of me and my two younger sisters. I'm 23 and they're 17 and 8 years old. Even though he was a cyborg and my mom a machina, they really were in love, and he worked hard at the port as a dock manager for Hard Pockets, the interstellar container manufacturer.*

**Yes, I've heard of them.**

*So two weeks ago there was an unhappy worker who'd been hiding his anger in Comm and was obsessed with getting revenge on the guy who fired him, my dad. The guy came in with a weapon and shot my dad before security was able to disable him, and my dad died within a couple of hours.*

**Oh, I'm really sorry to hear that.**

*We could have saved him, but dad was 148 years old. Before he died, he lensed me some things about his dreams, his life, how beautiful he thought mom was...*

...

*And what it's like to fall in love with someone 1/3 your age. He was 103 and she was 37 when they met. See, this is them at Cadence Park on Mars.*

The young woman used her ring to project an image of a happy young couple clearly enjoying their time together against a backdrop of pink striated mountains.

Regardless of their ages in years or airs at the time, neither of them looked a day above 30. Cyborgs always have that option. Biohns usually have to pay for it.

*My mom was 63 when she died of old age. And though we were sad, she did leave a basic will with instructions for the nanny that was to do some of the things she used to do instead. I was just starting home ec-1 around them, so hadn't yet had the "death talk" that they give in schools. We got to that part later, and I had a lot of questions. But anyway, not to bore you.*

*I cried like a baby over my mom, and also when dad was shot. But by the time I'd got a chance to talk to him before he let himself shut down, I think I finally understood it.*

...

*You know, no one really has to die any more. Even if they do die, anyone can be brought back if their families and friends have enough pull with the big guys at SIER. If not that, then you could always have Blue Horizon print a basic restore if all you need is a reprint with no memory of anything. Or there's always Dijiing back into your own head where they were still alive. But dad told me that life is like any video game. Since it's always your choice when to put it down, it's up to you to decide when to do that, and when to go to sleep for the very last time. I guess as a biohn I think that flies in the face of the decades we spend in self-preservation. But dad tried to tell me that a true self is more like a "favorite" video game series. You know when you've seen as good as it gets—or maybe the series is getting better but your own fresh interest in it is just growing old. Then, when you start having these feelings that every other experience is subpar, you start to lose meaning in your cardinal signs, and that's when you know...*

I can relate. We had a 700-year old friend cycle just recently.

*That must have been hard.*

It was, especially on my boss. We're all very close.

*Did you celebrate?*

Of course, he wouldn't have had it any other way.

*Hehe, like retiring a really important jersey.*

What can I say? Some things are too special to extend artificially or reproduce again. We remember things like that as if they were the last of their kind.

The young woman thought silently for a while.

*Is it true that Dalton's limit forces the system to kill or deport a certain number of people over the Earth's 9 billion mark?*

No, Dalton's 9-12-16 Population Control Triad says that, at an Earth population of 9 billion people, the system relaxes certain law enforcement monitoring. At 12 billion it relaxes them further, especially for crimes that slip out of Diji or Comm and into Astra—

*Like what happened to my dad.*

Right. And at 16 billion, the reprint companies are heavily fined, placed under intersolar governance, almost all Astra monitoring—including Safebuddies—is turned off, and pro-alpha aggression streams attached to most major negative broadcast topics. Basically, the closer we get to 16 billion on Earth, the more likely the system is to stop protecting us from the same savagery that all-alpha worlds used to face. Because the system tags negative media with the old emhims that made the Industrial and Web Era people go through all their craziness, even iyohns are allowed to feel it when they look up the kind of viral streams that used to make those alphas so angry.

*Hmm. So that's why the earth has stayed around 9-12 billion for so long.*

Yes. Some decades, people like to go wild on the reprints. As everyone knows, we've hit over 16 billion several times in our history, but since Dalton's rules were developed in the 2500s, we've only done it four times since. Each time has basically led to a refinement of what kinds of things are done one which levels. The last near world war happened because we hit 16.1 in the last 5-year earth census, and the system let everyone go alpha for a few years. Africa and Asia burned, reprint companies were hacked, and three years later we were back down to 14.2. That's how Blue Horizon became a monopoly and SIER gained its intersolar authority for good.

*I didn't know that last part.*

Since then, all reprint organizations take the standard limits seriously, since no one wants to have their company forcibly stolen from them by a government. But why do you ask about that?

*Well I was thinking about my younger siblings. We still have Nanny, but now it's up to me to decide how to take dad's stead. We've been lensing most of the coping stuff, and I'm probably not going to make the best mother to Yaleh, but—I mean, Yaleh's only 8 and the only cyborg among us. She cried and protested most of all, but she's gonna see hundreds of years of life probably. And not one of those people owes it to her alone to hang around past their time. I'm glad the kinds of crazy ideas one of her teachers suggested are illegal.*

## Frankenstein laws?

*And a lot more. Nobody wants to come back as necro to everyone just because one person didn't want to let go.*

## I wouldn't.

*Me neither. *sigh* Well, here we are. Thanks for listening. It feels a little weird that I'm not that upset. I feel like something inside me says I should be. But with dad choosing his time and—* Lisa-Lee began gathering her bags. *So many opportunities to actually see him again in the flesh here in Astra if the right save state suggests it, that cursed shooter only taught me how invincible our spirits are if nothing else. Body or no body.*

## Hm.

*I'm still getting used to the idea that my type of human is wired to fiercely protect against death and lineage loss, but iyohns are just as strongly wired to preserve the single meaningfulness in a life, since their own lineages could be continued by anyone. The will to live is based on totally different priorities.* Lisa-Lee smiled. *Thank God for the betas. Because they love life more than they hate death, I don't think they'd ever do to us what we would do to them if we were still in charge.*

**Mm.** It was not my place to agree out loud, though I obviously did.

*Can I have the car drive you back?*

## That would be great.

*Thanks again for letting me put some things together in my head at your expense. It was nice talking to someone that I don't owe any dark conversation topics to these days.*

## It was no problem at all.

The young woman braced her courage. *"Set the pace Lisa-Lee. This is a celebration of life."*

I tried to place a comforting hand on her shoulder, to which she responded with a grateful pat of her own.

And with that, she left the platform and headed deeper into the gathering area where we had stopped. The car turned around shortly thereafter. It had been a few minutes well spent, as I think I had just gained a better understanding of what I had been searching for all these years.

# 197. When in Doubt, We Used to Win With Denials, But Not Anymore

Okay but how many people do you need to form a society, really?

If it's anything less than 100 then I wouldn't mess with it.

That's arbitrary. I suppose you're worried about inbreeding.

Damn right, I'm worried about that. There's no way I'm living in a population of 10 and having my only mating options be my brother or sister.

Or worse.

You say that as a biohn, but what about as an iyohn? What if your parents adopted you as a 50 year old machina and your brother as a 3 year old beta and you're both full grown adults in love?

Gross.

Why? You're not only unrelated by blood or anything else, but you're also raised to like the same things together.

If my mother and father inseminated us both then we *are* related by blood.

But not the two iyohns printed by the same printer but inseminated by two totally different pairs of parents, right? They could fuck and marry and there'd be no problems?

Correct. Mating with blood is a sin.

Oh so we're Bibleing, now.

No, I'm not *Bibleing* I'm moralizing. Mating with blood is a floodgate opener to all kinds of molestation, exploitation, and internal abuse, you know that. And the laws agree with me. That's why it's illegal.

No, marrying your sibling is *not* illegal anywhere. Marrying someone who shares at least one parent with you is hard to do in most places, but can still happen. The laws outside of those places just don't acknowledge those unities.

And there's a reason for that.

There are lots of reasons for that—destabilizing the social fabric being the main one. But that's moot. If I'm stuck on some random asteroid colony and 95% of my colony dies off from breathing the wrong mineral dust I absolutely will think about mating with my non-cistypic sibling either to keep us going or to satisfy my primal urges—if she agrees.

That's disgusting.

Why?

Because it is.

Why?

Because it's gross.

Why?

You're a pervert.

You've never lived Lord of the Flies, what do you know about people in desperation?

I don't know. All I know is that one should never mate with their sibling.

And what I know is that we've gone down a rabbit hole only for me to discover that you have nothing but popular suggestion to ride on, and are making no attempt to actually answer my challenges. This debate is unfocused and I'm starting to think you're not smart enough to answer me without falling back on the historical mob behind you.

I don't need proof to counter perversion.

Then if I'm the Board, I'm disqualifying you. You just told a whole bunch of five year old cyborg CEOs that they or some of their family members are perverts, tossing all your earlier logic aside.

You're sick—siding with the wrong stuff.

Computer, scan this person's emotions and record them. They're throwing slanderous words upon me which have nothing to do with me and everything to do with—

INSECURITY, INTOLERANCE, ANGER, DISCOMFORT, DEAFNESS TO UNCOMFORTABLE—

That's good, computer. Now block her from—

Whoa whoa whoa! You're *blocking* me?

That's what I just told you. You're closed-minded and you're saying random things that could get me personally prosecuted just because you're angry and judgmental. Computer, log my emotions.

HYPOTHETICALLY ANGRY, RETALIATORY, BELIEVES HE IS CORRECT, LOGICAL, DISRESPECTS THE OTHER, THINKS SHE IS STUPID, THINKS SHE IS WEAK—

Why?

BECAUSE HE BELIEVES SHE IS NOT STRONG ENOUGH TO LISTEN—

What is she strong enough to do?

DEFLECT.

And?

NOTHING. THAT IS ALL.

Do you detect that I am perverted in any way?

NO. YOU WERE HELPING MISS D-GILIUS PRACTICE FOR HER PROMOTION EXAMINATION BY BEING AN EXCESSIVELY DISCLOSING DEVIL'S ADVOCATE.

But perverted? Criminal? Anything sick or indictable?

NO, BUT YOU ARE ANNOYED ABOUT BEING MOVED OFF-TOPIC BY WHAT YOU PERCEIVE TO BE INTOLERANCE. I DETECT NO OFFENSE.

Save that. In case Caz wants to spread rumors about me and my arguments outside of this room.

Computer he's putting my beliefs on trial. Save that.

OPINION SAVED.

Opinion!?

"On trial" is definitely an emotional metaphor used by you and you alone here, D-gilius. You probably won't find anyone else in the room who sees it that way.

Computer, if I ask D-gilius questions about her own taboo beliefs——

JAKE, I AM NOT PERMITTED TO INDULGE SUCH CONVERSATIONS. YOU KNOW THAT.

But if you did indulge, how would she handle it?

That's not fai——

I WILL NOT EMBARRASS YOUR INTERLOCUTOR. I BELIEVE THE TWO OF YOU HAVE BECOME TOO DEFENSIVE WITH EACH OTHER. MIGHT I SUGGEST MYSELF AS MEDIATOR TO YOU IN SEPARATE ROOMS. THAT IS UNLESS, JAKE, YOU ARE TOO CHICKEN TO HANDLE THIS.

Very funny, Nav. You're right, she's making me mad.

YOU ARE ALLOWING YOURSELF TO GET MAD. IT SEEMS YOU EITHER CARE TO WIN THIS ARGUMENT, OR YOU CARE ABOUT MAINTAINING HER COMPANY FOR SOME REASON. I MIGHT ADD, BEFORE SHE CONSIDERS THAT TO BE AN ADMONISHMENT OF YOU ALONE, THAT SHE REMAINS IN THIS ROOM BECAUSE SHE INTENDS TO WIN THIS ARGUMENT AND FERVENTLY BELIEVES THAT YOU ARE WRONG. AT HER CORE HOWEVER, SHE IS NOT EQUIPPED WITH ENOUGH FACTS TO ARGUE WITH YOU ON THE LEVEL THAT YOU REQUIRE. SHE IS UNWILLING TO ENTERTAIN IDEAS THAT MIGHT DISCREDIT HER STANCE, REGARDLESS OF HOW STRONG IT IS. LET IT BE KNOWN TO BOTH OF YOU THAT I SEE NO ACTIONABLE LEGAL ITEMS IN THIS ARGUMENT, THOUGH THERE IS A VERY SMALL POSSIBILITY, D-GILIUS, THAT YOU ARE HELPING JAKE BUILD AN ASSAULT-BY-RUMOR CASE AGAINST YOU, COUNTER TO HIS CURRENT WHOLESOME REPUTATION IN-SYSTEM. WHAT YOU SAY TO OTHERS ABOUT HIS ARGUMENTS HERE MAY BE PERCEIVED TO JEOPARDIZE HIS SOCIAL OPPORTUNITIES WITH CERTAIN PARTIES. IF YOU WERE TO SPREAD SUCH RUMORS INDISCRIMINATELY, HE MAY HAVE A CASE. PLEASE BE PRUDENT.

· · ·

…

...

Alright. I'm just saying that I wouldn't be comfortable in a colony of less than 100. As a personal preference, I don't know how I'd handle having to mate with someone considered related to me.

And All I'm saying is that it wasn't intended to be about that at all. It's just that small populations and small towns are known for certain groups of families continually intermarrying and that they've survived time in this way. They probably don't see this as an interbreeding issue past certain kinship levels, and it's assumed that in a limited population, one might just go with what's there in the most non-gross way they have room to consider.

Okay.

So give me a number. How many is the minimum?

68.

Really?

That's me admitting that maybe I don't need 100, but I'd like to think my mating options included more than aunts uncles and cousins.

Fair enough. I think if I were in a population of 32 I could consider—well, nevermind. I've been in classes of 32 students and even from a basic dating perspective have seen how the options may be pretty lame. 60-something sounds good to me too.

So we basically agree. A town of nearly 70 might be one we could live in and repopulate the earth in the event of Armageddon.

Sure, why not?

But below sixty and we might as well just go extinct.

Something like that.

Okay... okay. I guess we're back to sanity.

And this whole thing started because we were talking about the nusians. We're only actively monitoring six of them, and there's this idea that somehow those six are going to repopulate all 2100 or so uniquely signatured weathers like them.

Yes, and I thought that six was too few.

And I said that these guys don't have a choice. Nusian survival requires that these six be the Adams and Eves of their post flare future. Otherwise they'll have no future at all.

No one said mating was required. We need to think of these guys like particles. How many types of particle do you need to write all combinations of chemical reactions? Bonding, ionizing, or throwing off charge? In truth, the nusians really are just some costume we've put on a local timeslice of their environment. When we depict them as human, we're really putting our own structural interpretation on their patterns. But they don't necessarily have all the jealousies, barriers, and opportunities that we do. They may be perfectly fine combining together not as ego-people, but as simple valence shells surrounding a core. People may need 70 or 2800 or whatever number of people in their social enclaves, but pure particles may need less than a dozen to carry all possible combinatorial expressions. If we treat the input we get as classical, the six may be plenty for starting a new colony. The truth is, six might be all we have.

That's... disturbing.

Turn off the human skinning, Caz. These aren't people who evolved under earth's social rules. These are six algorithmic weathers who *have to* be archetypes to us. The human skin is just a form we've molded our data about them to fit so that we could understand their dynamics with each other and MOSTLY us. But in the end, we're tasked with driving a kind of nuclear burst using these six particle clouds alone, and spreading the interpretive results to every cloud like them. If you lock the frequentics into your own framework, you'll never make promotion to the higher research teams.

...

I just don't think I should have to suspend my mor—

Navicon interrupted. CAZ D-GILIUS, MIGHT I RECOMMEND STUDYING THE JUMP CULTURE? YOUR POSITION IS YOUR OWN, BUT THE PROMOTION DIRECTORS ARE UNLIKELY TO REWARD CIRCULAR ENTRENCHMENT. WE DON'T WANT YOU TO BE BITTER WHEN THE KINDS OF ARGUMENTS YOU ARE USING THAT ARE UNCONVINCING TO NOLLI ARE ALSO UNCONVINCING TO THE INTERVIEW BOARD NEXT WEEK. AT LEAST LEARN A BETTER WAY TO PRESENT YOUR SIDE IN THIS MATTER.

*Huff* *I'm* WRONG in what I said?

YOU MAY BE WRONG OR RIGHT DEPENDING ON YOUR PERSPECTIVE, BUT YOU MAY WANT TO CONVEY THAT PERSPECTIVE IN A WAY THAT CONVINCES OTHERS—NOT JUST NOLLI—TO LISTEN TO YOUR ORIGINAL ARGUMENTS. THE OLD BIOHNIC SOCIAL PRESSURES OF GROSSNESS AND YUCKINESS WILL NOT WIN THEM OVER.

Then what should I say?

YOU SHOULD SAY THE SAME KINDS OF THINGS THAT THE LEGISLATORS SAID WHEN THEY TOO RENDERED KIN-PARENTED UNITIES NULL IN MOST

COURTS. THEY HAVE, BROADLY, AGREED WITH YOU. SAY THIS: "KIN-PARENTED RELATIONSHIPS OPEN TOO MANY DOORS FOR PATHOLOGICAL DEVIANCE AMONG CARETAKERS AND THE CARED FOR. THIS HURTS THE ABILITY TO BUILD TRUST IN SOCIETY AT LARGE, BUT HAS ALSO BEEN STATISTICALLY VERIFIED TO CORRELATE WITH MUCH HIGHER INCIDENTS OF DOMESTIC ABUSE. WE AS LEADERS DO NOT WANT TO SPONSOR THIS. WHAT PEOPLE DO IN THE DIJI WORLDS IS THEIR OWN, BUT NOT IN ASTRA."

Okay then, could you lens me that?

…DONE.

Alright Jake. Kin-parented—

Save it Caz. If you really think cribbing this argument directly from Navicon is going to do anything but insult me or the Board, you might as well look for another job. You've taken no time to integrate that stuff into your own reasoning, and now strike both me and the computer as a liar determined to win an argument at all costs. I'd disqualify your application on the spot for phoning it in right in my face. It's a good thing I'm not your manager. You would have lost a whole lot of trust with me just now.

CONCUR.

Caz D-gilius grabbed her bag and stomped out of Jake's guest room, frustrated with what had just transpired.

Jake, for his part, actually didn't feel terribly strongly about the sidecar argument that had just taken place. All he really wanted was a guess at whether the six nusians of Phaedra's study could really be used to set the standard for the rest of that species. Unfortunately, in classic biohn form, his colleague Caz had let the whole conversation fall into an endless nuh uh-based distraction, despite a fairly reasonable start. But the underlying argumentativeness. The irrelevance to the matter at hand. What a shame. Not only did these fail to generate solutions, they also mired the basic problem in one individual ego's ivory tower safety blanket. Often Jake fought for more biohn passion in the upper tiers of modern society. Today was not one of those days. Most of the time, you just couldn't reason with a biohn when it came to moral matters. The genetics just made everything wonky.

*Most past-era biohns probably would have agreed with Caz. But here we're talking betas and cyborgs who could literally step out of the printer as fully mature adults at age 10 minutes. What they can't do is cross-persona train before the system's maturity assessment scan deems them voting and self-medication eligible. That's where the modern legal notion being a minor begins. 1) Cross-personality training from a commonly assumed knowledge base before such maturity, and 2) self biology algorithms sourced by at least one single-shared parent is the basis of most legal definitions of "being related."*

*She didn't cite any of this—as if her knowledge of the law stopped at 500 years ago. Plus she lost her cool, playing to all the stereotypes about us alphas and machina. That won't do.*

*Who knew that the secret to modern peace would be found not in wars or robot laws, but in modern day education about culture and family dynamics. After we created them, the betas' behavioral examples trained us to rethink our own humanity and human relations. Then we knew that it was the principles instead of the appearance or the householders which should actually form a solid foundation for tolerance. I'm glad people like Caz are no longer getting elected in most places around the world. She's just passionate enough to represent us, smart enough to steer laws effectively, but in terms of building a foundation for a future advanced, and safely tolerant world that no one can avoid, she's just a baby.*

Navicon interrupted Jake's thought. OUT OF CURIOSITY, JAKE, WHERE DO *YOU* DRAW THE LINE ON ACCEPTABLE RELATIONSHIPS?

Me? Well, no offense Nav, but I'm a het-mono-alpha with a preference for het-mono-betas, mostly 40-190 years old. At 200, they start talking about the good ole revolution days, and make you feel like a whippersnapper.

HA HA HA. SO YOU DISPREFER YOUR OWN TYPE, NATURAL BORNS AND ALPHAS?

Yes. Call it stereotype avoidance, but I had to work hard enough to rein in my own fight or flight. I don't need new versions of that baggage from my mate.

WOULD YOU SAY YOU DISCRIMINATE AGAINST CYBORGS?

Only because it's you asking will I answer honestly. Maybe a little. My genes just can't get used to the feel of an electronic body or conversation companion. It doesn't feel right. At least betas *were* either biological or alpha-based once upon a time.

DO YOU THINK THE WORLD WILL EVER STOP DISCRIMINATING AGAINST MACHINA?

No. Machina are broadly too difficult to manage collectively. They're not bad people. Just savage as a group. And they celebrate that fact, again as a group. They're also unpredictable, with a weird mod for this and a weird mod for that—yet with the same thoughtlessness of unmodded alphas from centuries ago. Who needs that kind of drama in a mate?

WOULD YOU EVER GROUP-INSEMINATE?

Whoa, Nav! I feel like my priest is asking me what kinds of orgies I'd prefer. You're making me blush a little.

I'M ONLY INTERESTED IN YOUR VIEWS AS AN ALPHA, GIVEN THAT BIOHNS WERE NOT EVOLVED FOR TRI-PARENTING OR ABOVE.

I know, I'm just teasing. No, aside from basically having to negotiate things like discipline with what is effectively a small commune, the legal ramifications are a mess. If I were to have kids at all, I'd prefer simplicity.

I see.

# 198. The Daily News Report

Genevieve closed her news report for the day, a pensive frown on her face. Here we were in the 28th century and you still had CEOs being arrested for child pornography. It didn't quite make sense, as there were plenty of selectively triggering packets for releasing moods of all kinds—with no offensive target needed. The kinds of pharma like Chi-51 blue which made you feel like you were playing basketball with the sun, with no Diji or Astra imprint of the sun at all, just your own internal firing patterns.

But this CEO. He didn't even leave the usual voluntary audit trail for the forensic analysts to help him. You know, the storage drive submission which showed that you had NOT generated those questionable reprints as a patterned behavior—that you always deleted them when your generative prints produced any of the "Three No-Nos:"

- Government-concerning documents,
- Identities not your own, and
- Kids

Since way back in the 21st century, even before cyborgs and betas were a thing, it was well established that storage drives with audit logs on them were THE main exhibit in your defense against prosecutable acts, and that you would almost always be presumed guilty if you failed to provide them. Pleading the fifth amendment would not save you. The Non-domino laws would not protect you. If your generated prints looked like something that could get you thrown in jail, you needed a good ole recoverable hard-drive to prove your innocence. At first sculptures were treated more stringently, then the batch 3D cases started coming in and the law adopted a little more flexibility on this. Not to mention that beta manufacturers were cranking out silhouettes of would-be-living young people all the time. So it always came down to forensic pattern. But either way the law was well-established by the 22nd century. Why couldn't people just be better?

The pervert CEO had no real defense. His historical brain scans told all without any storage forensics required. He would be tried in a couple of weeks, almost certainly found guilty, and have one of the three red marks placed on his biometrics everywhere he went. He would be unable to enter a club, pass through an airport, get a job, or buy a beer without the person on the other side knowing he was predatory. For people like him who had gone to even greater extremes and committed actual abuses or obtained prints of actual minors, his whole biometric scan might be rendered with the red frequency, which essentially told everyone you were a terrorist. The law didn't play with such things, and the only crime type more heavily punishable than child exploitation was the great evil class of identity crimes. If you were found guilty of these then you would almost certainly face Edge or el-bleeding one way or another.

The CEO's case was a little different in the sense that his late stepfather had actually bequeathed six of the perp's 14 child porn mannequins, so that it might be argued that the guy was a victim of psychological manipulation or trauma. There, the Non-domino laws might have kicked in, and the idea that you couldn't be punished for someone else's terroristic acts might have saved him. But the seventh mannequin was all it took. Furthermore, he really needed to destroy the first six if he wanted to avoid further complications in any legal scenarios that might arise. Instead he printed 8 more—effectively telling prosecutors, "please, mark me as an offender too. My stepfather wasn't enough."

On to some lighter news…

*Hm. It looks like Blue Horizon, TC will be celebrating its septicentennial this year.* Hard to believe that the telic monopoly had such sinister roots in the late 21st century. Genevieve read the article in quiet reflection.

Ever since the historians captured the saves of Blue Horizon's original two founders from patterns logged in Edge Correctional, the idea of "criminal multiversing" has been instilled in justice systems everywhere as an established legal principle—right up there with knowing your rights or being made whole. Who would have thought that the universe could take two rival mob bosses, have them setup a joint assassination business, have one kill the other, have the surviving one die, have a former lieutenant reprint them both, have all three get busted and sent to Edge, then have their joint behavior paths extracted from Edge to form some kind of weird organization that specializes in creating material objects from astronomical algorithms? Venus points to Kominers points to the Midheaven. Now behind almost every human or pet reprint is an embedding sourced from the "infinite Blue." It was the ouroboros of entrepreneurial self-seeding. A perpetual motion machine built entirely upon the will of the non-living to run a business that was better than anything the living could muster. Today, the business of the dead truly ranked among the biggest businesses of them all. The frequentics made sense. But man, how weird it was.

Well anyway, it wasn't like Genevieve's own assignment wasn't at least a little Frankensteinian. *We'll be evolving a species made of literal hot air*, she thought. But through the magic of math on patterns, that hot air could be represented as having arms, legs, and loves. So this is what the gods did in their spare time: build men. Watch them interact. There was no need to puppet them or smite them when your creations would probably take care of that themselves in due time. You'd just keep making new ones until a couple of them learned how to make themselves. Then they'd try to be you. Of course, if they didn't know themselves, they'd fail.

Yet somewhere along the line someone had figured out both the science and the society of self-perpetuation. To be eternal was to be consistent, even in how you died. Like the Buddha, you would always come back again as yourself, if only you lived on a principle. Granted, your new form might actually *be* a principle instead of a physical thing. But your dharma was there, nonetheless. And in games, movies, and other places throughout Comm and Diji, you really could be there. The cycle never ended, but continually reset in ways that let each version of you see things anew. Or float in a new form. We lost the original Buddha in this world of Astra forms, but perhaps the nusians would have a little of his wisdom infused in their blood after all.

# 199. If Only It Were Always Christmas

Passing the time before tomorrow, I decided to surf for a while—freshening up on some evolutionary history, I suppose. After a few minutes becoming reacquainted with some of the classics like Mendel, Linnaeus, Washburn, and Phi-Matra, I stumbled upon the famous case of Ronaldo Getrius and his work with Elmo the Elite Chimpanzee. A staple in the history of anthropology, Elmo remains probably the best example in human history of "-centric divergence."

You know how we were once apes, but now would never ever consider an ape to be our equal? Well, way back in the year 2541, Ronaldo Getrius and his lab spent several months zapping the chimpanzee Elmo into a neural pattern which led him to think of himself as human. He was trained on the human habits of washing his hands before dinner, using a formal room and closing the door in order to relieve himself. He even learned to identify pretty humans versus ugly ones. Along with this latter lesson, he learned that apes were definitely beneath him, and even though he looked like one, it didn't mean that he should accept prejudice from his fellow humans. Unfortunately, Elmo died at age 34 right in the middle of a zapping experiment in which he volleyed back and forth the translated language of hero-worship with a scientist who "doubted" Elmo's unique situation as the work of Fate. As Elmo had no real conception of Fate, his neurons could only fire in a confused mess of sparks which bore a striking resemblance to a stroke, as the poor lad literally (probably) "thought" himself to death. People all over the world mourned at his loss, but still the Getrius work remains a landmark in the history of anthropology as, over the course of only 2 years, the whole scientific world watched as a single special chimpanzee gradually (intellectually) evolved light years past his own kind—so much so that he even pointed out to his trainers the whopping crush he had on Marilyn Monroe. It was all quite amazing what a little neuronal zapping and a fleet full of trainers could accomplish in such a short period of time.

What the world learned most from Elmo is that evolution isn't just an exercise in changing body structures. It's a journey away from old impossibilities into the realm of the possible. We used to hate sleeping naked in the cold. Now we have friends with houses to protect against that. We used to hate having another ape steal our tree. Now we have legal systems to prosecute at will. Then we used to hate whoever triggered us emotionally through the breaking news. Now that we're mostly betas and machina, we can just use our mods to turn that trigger off. Kind of. But that just makes any earlier being without the privileges into something undesirable. Like pagans in the eyes of pre-Christians, pre-Christians in the eyes of Christians. Elmo showed us the exact path from chimp troop to anthropocentricism. No doubt his contribution to our self-understanding was a big one.

Speaking of Christians, I also took a moment to look up some part of the Bible, just to immerse myself in some group-level wisdom. One may not think it, but the Bible has a lot of appeal to me as a former system turned beta, especially books like, Psalms, Aristotle, and The Cave. "We tarried too long" says the Book of The Cave. And we learn that sometimes you really need to come out and do what your faith compels you to do. "It is a fool who ignores the order in his surroundings," says the Book of Aristotle. And I really enjoy how this is followed up in the IVth Book of Kings. All in all, the 129 books of the Bible have something for everyone, and I think most of us—especially betas—appreciate the decision of the 2500 a.d. Council of Rome in merging certain Suras and injects from the Kantian cannon (The Book of Kant, Aristotle, etc…) into what was then a highly cliquish version of the text. Since the fall of the pre-Christian protestants in 2256 at the hands of the Sunni-Seculars, then the fall of the Sunni-Seculars in 2259 at the hands of the Christian revisionists, the new Christianity-as-philosophy (rather than religion) has really held a wide appeal among us betas looking to lead lives of "service, not servitude." "Forgiveness, not forcing" our beliefs in a higher call to be good to one another. After all, who would we be without our neighbor? Jesus taught us only two things, really. To love our neighbor as ourselves, and to love God with all our hearts. If you can't really conceive of God because of how you grew up, then that's okay. It's no excuse for me to hate you or stomp your rights. We're still all part of the same human journey. What a beautiful message of tolerance! But one we didn't really know until after the 23rd century Crusades left only betas to pick up the pieces.

Now I, like most people, don't really think of God as someone who follows only a few groups of humans' saga but doesn't follow the saga of lambs and Hittites. I find it hard to believe that a book which doesn't contain a fraction of what the

Upanishads contains and doesn't seem to care about, say, machinas would actually capture the adventures of Nature in all its glory. So technically, there's no way I'd be classified as Judeo-theist. But I definitely respect the lend-a-helping-hand ethos of the Christians, especially the lend-a-voice philosophy they adhere to for everyone under the sun. Since they basically replaced their Mid-Era predecessors in 2260, they've really been one of the biggest centers of person to person charity of any organization I'm aware of. Not since the First Era of Christianity ended around 100 a.d. had the Christ Church been so heavily focused on the richness of relationships among neighbors, and we were all better off when "sell-out Islam" essentially absorbed it into the Mohamedan doctrine. So while it is true that the Catholic Church has basically been an Islamic acquisition for over 500 years, the fact that the Sunni-Secularists were willing to even consider being renamed as "Christians+The Books of Esau and Mohammed" is a great credit to them. Of course, it was only a matter of time before betas and machinas stopped seeing Yeshua ben Josef as magical (being our own Adam-makers and all), but still… It took a lot of guts to break from mainstream Islam and say, "Let's just absorb it all into one history and worship the Highest Wisdom for sending us a few awesome humans who taught us to be good to one another." Shameful how most of the traditional Muslim world revolted over the thought. But the knowledge that the founders of modern Christianity were, in fact Muslims, is now a thing appreciated by all of religious history.

My research is interrupted by thoughts of Ms. Dial.

To be honest, I don't really care about the Nusians. Is that bad? Actually, I don't really care about anything. I mean, there isn't really much about this life that interests me. As a beta, I don't really need money or maslovs, so I don't actually need to work. I don't really need acceptance or belonging if I'm willing to turn these needs off, so I don't actually have to be personable. And yet I, like most betas, have a survival-deep craving to play out my mind using my body's interactions with "things," so that neglecting basic civility would really be the same as shutting myself down. Not through suicide, but through the darkening of all the options I have in the world around me. Nobody wants that. So it pays to play this human game. I guess it really isn't a game, is it?

But Ms. Dial… She's so… I don't know. I really like her. Maybe it's because no one has ever really dealt with me like a full person before. I can't believe how I willingly kneeled before her—just to have something other than myself and my own endless mind full of data to hold onto. Would I willingly be her sub if she wanted me to be? Maybe. But then… I don't know. I'd really have to trust her to be a better guide towards meaning in my life than I myself could be. I don't really get that she's interested in owning responsibility for me like that. Maybe Phaedra would. But Phaedra's harsh. That would just stress me out—failing to please her.

Dial doesn't make me feel like a failure. Not that it's Phaedra's fault, mind you. It's just… her way.

Honestly, I don't feel like this is something I should spin my wheels over. I need to talk to someone…

* * *

Hey Isaiah, what brings you by at this hour?

Uh, I kind of wanted to talk to you about something.

Really? Uh okay. Come on in, have a seat.

Thanks Genevieve.

Here. Have a seat. What's going on?

I, uh, was just working somethings out in my mind.

Really, like what?

Well, I kind of have a crush on somebody.

You do? Genevieve tried hard to look surprised.

Yes, it's Miss Dial.

Hm. Okay. Well that's very nice. What's the problem?

I guess, I don't really know myself. And I'm afraid that I'm really just looking for someone to be responsible for my dreams more than I am myself.

Okay…

That's all.

It is?

Yes.

Genevieve pondered for a moment. So does she know you like her?

I think she does, yes.

And what does she think about that?

She knows I'm not ready to just jump into a relationship. And to be honest, I think she knows she's out of my league.

Hm.

You uh, didn't disagree. You think she's out of my league too, right?

Something like that.

Well, I guess if I were a biohn that would hurt. But I know it's true. I'm just a pup to her.

Why do you care so much about being "in her league?" From what little I know, Aimee has lived like a queen for tens of decades. She's out of *everyone's* league. But if she accepts you then she accepts you. It's hard for that to happen if you don't accept yourself.

She had me kneel to her.

Did she?

And I liked it. Or, I felt I deserved it.

Did you? Um., that's. Different.

I know what you're thinking. But she wouldn't accept me that way.

Bruh, you've got it bad. A case of low self-esteem.

mmmm... I know.

Do you think Dial is gonna fix all that?

I don't know if I care if she fixes it. I just want to not be confused.

… Genevieve pondered some more.

Well I assume you came to me so you could get  this off your chest. I wish I could relate to what you're going through, but I think the best I can do is keep listening. So if you don't mind continuing...

Continuing what?

Anything that's on your mind.

...

...

**... No. This was a bad idea.** Isaiah rose from his chair.

Why? No! That's what friends are for. I'm here to listen if you have anything at all you want to say.

**We're not friends. I just met you.**

So you'd rather go to Dial or Phaedra with this? Or bottle it in?

Isaiah sat back down. **I'm just confused, Genevieve.**

Okay.

**I want to lead a life that means something, and I'm afraid that I never will.**

Okay.

**Because all I am is a walking computer, and I've never really known anyone personally who wasn't connected to a disaster or a mission I had to keep track of. Nobody gets any genuine joy from being around me.**

Genevieve nodded her head in acknowledgement.

**But that's what real fulfillment is, right? Genuine joy in the face of something? Why do I always feel like someone else's piece of machinery?**

Maybe it's because you know too much. Every spontaneous, loving thing anyone could do for you is a thing whose causes you already know. So it's hard for you to see it as coming from the heart. You know, someplace that can't be explained.

**I guess you're right. But how do I become somebody who accepts that kind of deep feeling? I can't just unlearn hundreds of years of data.**

Just then, Genevieve stood up and wrapped her arms around Isaiah, kissing him gently on the lips.

...

...

How did that make you feel?

**Uh, awkward but... good.**

I give you that as a friend. To you as one of the only people traveling with me in this life, but also from me as someone who's lived enough lives to know when a member of her lifespace really needs a pick-me-up. I only have a few things this time around. And you're part of that. Nobody cares what you know or don't know.

Isaiah sat dumbfounded for a moment.

If you like Dial, then you like Dial. But Dial won't take you seriously unless you like yourself. But once you learn how to like yourself, I don't think you'll need Dial anymore.

**That's basically what she said.**

And she'd be right. This isn't the 21$^{st}$ century, Isaiah. Nobody needs to settle for self-abuse just because it's all they know. You're tensing yourself. And I think it's because you really want someone to see you as someone who's a fraction of who you are.

**I didn't think that...**

Think what? That liking a woman just because she's decisive enough to find yourself *for you* wasn't a type of self-harm?

**I...I don't know.**

Isaiah. You know, maybe you just need to learn how much you have to offer on your own. Without any of us calling all the shots.

**...I don't...know what you mean.**

I knew somebody like you once. About two hundred years ago, growing up in a space where his mother and sisters were so sure-footed that it made him feel inadequate, and he didn't realize it. You have the ruler of SIER, the queen of the earth, and a confident mercenary deciding the fate of a planet. And a role in all this which has put you in a box for years. Now I'm not saying you need to leave us, but I am saying that I'd really rather not see you give yourself to Aimee before you know what it is you're giving away.

**... So what would you suggest then?**

I that think you should find a Naughts meeting and visit it.

**Naughts? Isn't that a male support group? For abusers?**

Yes, it's a male support group. But no, it's not for abusers. It's for males looking to find themselves without female input.

**But you're a female, why would you recommend this?**

Because as with AA, I know someone with a problem when I see one. You're trying to find yourself on Mt. Olympus in a room full of gods. No one here is ever going to lower themselves to the level of esteem you're sending out right now, and you also need to know that the way we think of power is rooted in backgrounds we already know and have defined deeply. You're basically carving a path into the unknown. Like a real pioneer. But I don't think you know nearly as much about the manhood stories as I do. I think you need to learn them.

Isaiah was suddenly visited by a twinge of irritation. **What does manhood have to do with anything I'm facing?**

You're searching the new territory of meaning amongst the gods from the perspective of software. Dial, Phaedra, and I were born to define what the software is like in the first place. We can't teach you self-worth past a certain point because society doesn't require or reward us for spreading our conceptual seed. For you in this world, that's all you can do, and must do.

**I can't believe you're saying this. Women and men are the same in anything they do.**

Not in their natural born biology they aren't, and that biology is powerfully internal for us, not for you.

**I don't see why that matters.**

So you think that makes *no* difference in what we're trained to respond to? Internal worlds versus external?

**I mean, no but—**

Don't dig yourself a hole Isaiah. As someone who's biology is still built to have babies when mod-free, I can tell you you don't know the first thing about playing involuntary chess with a seed someone has dropped into your whole being.

...

And I don't know as much about what it is to live with the seed you've dropped, and your obligation to tend to it though you have no reminders of what it's about. There are a few differences between males and females. And the reason women have dominated this society since the 23$^{rd}$ century is because men like you have had the size of the unknown get smaller and smaller for you to drop that seed into.

**That's really sexist, you know.**

Yes, and that's why you need to go to a Naughts meeting. So that they can soften the blow for you.

**I know men haven't had equal power since we betas had our first president.**

That's right. Because the first beta president forced us to look at race relations seriously. People stopped looking at their robo-selves as some great unknown to be pioneered against and started defining the rights equally. And men had fewer places to take their fictitious dragons for being macho and pioneering against.

...

My point is, you have low esteem, my friend. But you're living the kind of life that can only be mastered against the "womb of infinity" (to quote Jai-Pi). I think you need a role model. Not a Mistress. And if after you've found that role model you still want to hand it all to Aimee, then I'll help you get in her good graces. But until then, PLEASE don't take that treasure trove of perspective you have and give it to any foreign visitor who doesn't know you fully. Not even me.

**Okay.**

What? I can't hear you.

**Yes ma'am.**

Then you'll go to a Naughts meeting?

**Yes ma'am.**

And you'll come to me when you're in any trouble or when you're the least bit confused, no matter how embarrassing? Because you know I've probably seen everything you're going through already, will definitely keep your secret and definitely not judge you for anything you tell me?

Isaiah smiled a little. **I have such good friends.**

Well, I'm glad you've managed a smile, sir. Naughts before you pledge to Dial?

**Yes. Okay.**


Good man. Besides that, what else is going on?

**Well, there's also this thing...**

# 200. Phaedra's Thoughts

It was 2:49 am, in the quieter hours of the morning. Contemplating the day ahead, Phaedra sipped her Saturnine olit with a pensive frown. The lightly honey-flavored blend of caffeine and alcohol bathed her taste buds in a mildly stinging pick-me-up prized around the Solar System for its flow state-enhancing effects.

Phaedra rubbed the bridge of her nose, fighting back a yawn. ***Sigh** I have everything, even some good friends. Money and crydit is no object. Power goes without saying. So why do I feel so detached from it all? Shouldn't I care more about the landmark action we're about to take later today?*

*… But I know that Isaiah's not doing well, and I don't really blame him. I don't think humans were really meant to live like gods and goddesses. Maybe we really need our passions to keep us going. Heaven knows I don't have very many left. I guess I've done it all in the last few centuries.*

*I remember Cyclops telling me before he died, Phaedra, the day you imagine The Reaper calling you, and your reaction is, Okay, when should I expect the movers? Not a "But wait! I have this list of things I want to do!"—that's when you know your resonance window is finished. I remember asking him something about the biological imperative to survive, and it was funny what he told me. We are more than our forms. Our memory makes the rest of us. If I thought his answer was profound then, it is even more so now.*

*I'm not a theistic woman, but if I were, maybe I would be in the mood to pray right about now. Dear God, I fail to see the excitement in life anymore because I've done it all. But Isaiah also sees no excitement in life because he thinks he hasn't been able to do enough of it—at least not purely. Only as a living dictionary. And here we are trying to extend some concept of life that the space dust of Venus probably has no notion of. I don't know why I'm focusing so much on*

*Isaiah's personal crisis, but I guess I understand why he's going through it. Maybe being near-immortal in a world that lets you do almost everything you want really isn't a good way to stand for a single thing passionately.*

*We at Miranda and SIER, the Solar Council and the Solar Economic Consortium, the industries that power the system… we collectively rule the known universe. My heart goes out to all of the alphas and machina out there—the original humans who will never have the freedoms that we have, but their collective selfishness just wasn't a tenable guide for the long term stability of humanity. As early as the 21*$^{st}$ *century, populations all over the world began replacing their democracies with various forms of industrial oligarchy propping up fascists as their front facing kings. The original humans proved too gluttonous to resist the conveniences that these shadowy lobbies offered, so humans proved that they did not value their freedom after all. They preferred that their institutions provide easy symbols for their collective unconscious, and made room for those of us who now oversee the system. Whether or not we have the heart to go back 600 years and install greater communosocial fortitude in the minds of our biohn fathers, the fact remains that an unmodified human so susceptible to hate gets what he deserves—a world where his royal families and their nobles contain him—even if that means sending him to Jupiter. My experience with that lady in the tunnel in my pre-beta youth never left me. I think it was then that I knew that, if I was to stay human and retain my hope for something better, I really would have to leave the old apeisms behind.*

*The turns of those early years neither saved us nor damned us. They only consolidated captainship over a humanity probably doomed to just oze itself out of a future.*

*Heh, "oze." The verb meaning "to overpopulate-and-zoo." When you do so much of a thing that one day you wake up fucked. I don't know where the term came from, but the betas were always made to avoid this, because you couldn't optimize their humanization if they didn't have this. Even before gaining full rights, the betas weren't just trainable on any data you fed them, but would selectively separate themselves from you, challenge you, or ignore you if you gave them inputs which threatened their survival imperative—not proliferation of the species, but stability of the species. We humans had long proved that we could have enough children to fill up the planet with opinions and waste and environmental catastrophe. So there really wasn't any further need to nurture this. It was almost as if we had to tell our own genetics, "slow down, we'll take it from here," and retool our original urge to multiply ourselves and our problems endlessly, in favor of multiplying only those aspects of ourselves which yielded a net positive for all of humanity. The push for population control on Jupiter has not been successful for various reasons, not least of which is that there's just more room for our old ape selves to live there, but I lament that maybe, just maybe, those guys will one day overtake us in number, and attempt to come back for their ancestral home. More than a few extremists have begun to gather support for such ideas, and we have run Omni scenarios investigating the possibilities. I am not concerned that this will happen in my lifetime, but more concerned with what happens after me.*

*To this day, I have not found a competent successor capable of overseeing Miranda. Nobody, not even Dial, has the dignity to serve as a cultural beacon, and that is one of the most important invisible requirements of the job. And this Venus thing… why are we doing it? I know it is important for us to set the example as a UFO driving into other's dimensions, but it all just seems so… I don't know. *Sigh**

*Dial is a funny one. On the one hand she's been my friend for a long time, but on the other hand she's always been a bit wild. She tricked herself up early in her post reprint, using all the surgical and pharma weapons at her disposal to become the ultimate funmate. She even left a standing invitation for me to try her out, but I declined. I can see that Isaiah likes her and may even need someone like her, but he really has no idea what he's getting into. She'll slyly but surely kick him to the curb once she's done with him, and I think that will do more harm than good. I should probably run Safebuddies on him just to be sure. It isn't that I enjoy spying on my friends' motives, but if it's to protect one friend from another, I'll gladly do it.*

*So Genevieve is going to try this plan on the nusians. What a strange turn. Back when I was a moteralla I never would have thought I'd see virtual worlds of this caliber—let alone be part of the group which defines the very nature of those worlds. Vi would have been great at finding out what those nusians needed, but then again she was an asshole. It never would've worked… Golly, Vi—with the ambition and insecurity that represents everything wrong with the former us.*

*(Time for some more olit.)*

*Maybe I should check in on Isaiah, see how he's doing.*

*…*

**sip**

*…*

*Hm. That's weird. Private mode? Urgh. Please tell me Dial hasn't defiled him yet.* **Navicon, is Isaiah on campus? If so, is he okay?**

LET ME CHECK… YES MA'AM. HE IS HERE.

**Is Dial with him?**

NO. MISS PHAEDRA. DIAL IS NOT ON CAMPUS.

***Exhale* Good. Thanks.**

NO PROBLEM. PHAEDRA.

**The last thing we need is puppy love right before game day. We wouldn't want to confuse him.**

# 201. The Zone

**Okay guys, what our north star?** Phaedra quizzed us confidently to prepare us for game time, but also to give the streaming audiences some laymen's background.

Genevieve got the point. We've changed the plan a little since yesterday. Fontenot and I are going to jump into the Venusians' weather-to-movie sim with our brain activity rendered as actors, but we won't both be people. Isaiah will be an object that I "find" from outside of the satellite, and I'll interact with that object in such a way as to suggest how our main six nusians should see it. This will in turn influence the leaders, who would already be desperate for solutions according to our observations. The leaders will arrive at the conclusion that they should inoculate themselves against the coming climate shift by using this object, and they will willingly spare themselves erasure without us having to take more intrusive measures to reshape them.

**So in other words, we need them to change their forms completely in order for them to survive the new climate conditions, but we can't do this through direct steering. We have to introduce a spreadable technology that the whole weather system can use.**

There's a question from the audience, Jake interrupted. Why go through all this trouble? Why not just jump in and spray something on the planet to preserve a few of them patternwise? Or why not just jump in and talk to them?

Genevieve spoke up. I'll take that one. So basically our technology reads certain clouds of temperature, air current, and spectral frequency as if it is an organism. When we can read that same pattern across multiple distinct clouds, and determine that those clouds of energy can break off into "offspring" clouds, then we render that kind of organism as part of a larger species. We know, though, that the upcoming flares will raise things like temperature and charge in a tiny way, but drastic enough to really alter how we render the species. This is kind of like back in the 21st century when humans started using a lot of wifi, and along with this the planet became more agitated and more psychic— the reason that training praesciens was suddenly so easy. But this change among this particular type of energy cloud will basically change by .07° and 20-30 nanohertz. Kind of like you suddenly having your respiratory system start responding more readily to your foot. You and your preferred diet going one step beyond lettuce and into allowing cardboard as a staple instead. You will be fundamentally different all of a sudden, and everywhere around Venus—just because of how sensitive you are to this particular kind of change. If we continue our simulations of the nusian species as is, it will be like dropping a column from a defining matrix and adding a row. It's a different matrix with different algebraic requirements, and the old nusians will basically go extinct overnight. Because we won't be able to read them anymore through the original, pre-flare data conversion process. Think of an orangutan suddenly morphing into a gorilla because the sun threw too much light on them...

(*And also because our own satellites have noticeably altered the frequencies in the air anyway.*) Phaedra lensed us.

Genevieve paused for a moment to consider the message, then moved on. In order to for us to save them, we need for the brand new species to consider themselves the old, and for the old species to willingly become the new. There is no way we will pull this off by talking to them one-on-one, and we definitely do not want to sweep our everloving hand over their planet. That would have a lot more side effects all over everyone's ecosystems than you would think, so our plan is to insert a kind of vaccination technology into their awareness, simulate the flare process as it is the technology, and write this transformation into our weather-to-species conversion process for them. We can't do this without their cooperation, because even though all three states will happen, if we can't animate the connection across them, our own simulations simply won't be able to find the old versions anymore. Using me as the finder, Isaiah as the flare disguised as a willing technology, and any one existing nusian serving as validator for preserving the memory of preflare dynamics for any other nusian, we believe we can use a fourtet structure to keep the nusians alive, but evolve them to take on a new form.

Jake waited for a reply, and received a thumbs up.

The principle is actually simpler than it sounds, Phaedra added. If you're going to go extinct and get replaced by something new, then it's my teams job to convince you that you willingly made that transition. But we can't do this with just one person in danger or two people with one of them "saving" the other. We can't do it with three people because the cure itself has to exist everywhere. No, you need four: the person in danger, any second archetypal relater to the person who can validate that the first one is still there both before and after, and another pair of individuals in a dynamic which the first pair can cite their changed reality against. In this case, Isaiah will play the role of the cure and Genevieve will play the role of one who gets the nusians started working with it. Since Isaiah will be projected as a kind of "how-to-transition" guide, we can use the actual occurrence of the flare as an excuse for the nusians' use of the how-to to transform themselves after Genevieve's example. Not to extinct themselves.

We're fooling the nusians into going along with something inevitable, so that they can come out on the other side okay, Jake added.

Yes. Hope that helps.

. . .

Any further questions?

I'm not seeing anything, Phaedra.

Then we'll get started.

* * *

I lay in the left jump chair, trying to decode the shapes in the Swiss cheese-like drop ceiling.

So Isaiah, what're you dressing up as?

I don't know. What do flares in a bottle look like?

They probably look like Kool-Aid. Are you gonna be Kool-Aid?

Um, probably not.

Well, whatever you are, just make sure it fits in my pocket. We don't want extra rendering of a whole moving crew with the solution.

...

...

...

I guess you didn't get my joke. I was joking, you know.

No, I got it.

Well, then I guess it wasn't very funny then.

Relax, Isaiah, Dial chimed in. All you're doing is throwing vibes out to these guys, to help them get better.

Yes, M—Aimee.

That's the spirit.

(I could hear the sound of quizzical looks being traded at my expense.)

Alright guys, let's go under.


NAVICON Report

By: **Phaedra Zeta**

Winter 51, 2770 n.e.

Miranda HQ, Lab 2A

**Viva's rendering on the screen. Uh—m. I'm not sure what this is. The rendered lab looks... different. Genevieve?**

I uh, think I may see this whole thing differently today than before.

**Yeah but—**

Navicon should have corrected for the inconsistencies.

This is waaay more detailed than it was yesterday.

Wh-whoa! Suddenly it all comes into view as Genevieve's face is almost slammed against the table. Luckily, one of the soldiers stops his comrade's use of force in its tracks.

You can't injure her. **A light, innocent looking cub of a soldier admonishes in a soft voice. This isn't Gaul.**

**Well I'll be damned if I let this woman threaten us with her takeover schemes,** a tan lady with a biggish nose sneered as her face-bashing attempt lay thwarted.

We just need to know where she's getting all of her information about the tower.

*The what?*

*Uh Phaedra, do you see what I'm seeing?*

We're all seeing it, Aimee. And they can too.

I thought they couldn't see the tower!

*No, they're totally looking at it.*

**So what is this!? What does it have to do with that spaceship!** The tan lady demanded as she gripped a vial of bright red liquid in her hands.

Genevieve narrowed her eyes in indignance. Surely this was no way to welcome a guest.

**Answer me!**

No.

The tan lady grabbed a tuft of Genevieve's hair and slammed Prohal's face against the table anyway. Twice.

A third soldier with a nameplate reading "Watcheye" stepped in and pressed his pistol against Genevieve's temple, likely as insurance against her retaliation. **You could answer Leader.**

**Genevieve are you okay?** Phaedra leaned over her console, her expression nearly bending into panic.

That fucking actually hurts! Phaedra what the hell is happening here?

**I don't know! Navicon?**

THESE SCIENTISTS ARE RESPONDING TO EVERYONE'S ENTIRE EMHIM, MISS PHAEDRA. IT CONTAINS MORE THAN PROHAL'S AND ISAIAH'S RENDERS.

What the—

**But the satellites don't broadcast that!**

YES, THEY DO. SINCE WE ARE RESTREAMING YOUR JUMP INTO THE NUS-1'S BROADCAST, IT IS SENDING BOTH GENEVIEVE'S AND ISAIAH'S RENDER OPINIONS AS WELL AS THEIR INTENTIONS AS A SIGNAL. THESE PEOPLE DO NOT LIKE GENEVIEVE'S WISH FOR GLORY AND DO NOT UNDERSTAND ISAIAH'S NON-BIOHN NATURE. THEY NOW HAVE A MANUFACTURED HISTORY WHICH INCLUDES ALL OF THIS DATA. AND APPARENTLY SHE IS A TERRORIST WHO HAS THREATENED TO USE THE TOWER TO DESTROY THE HOMELAND IF THE NE-MURILS DON'T BAPTIZE THEMSELVES IN THE SOMA OF GOD—THE RED VIAL.

Miss Phaedra, that vial is my representation of the flare. It doesn't matter if they destroy it, since I'll still exist as an abstract idea, but it'll be harder to reasonably write a good history for these people if they lose it.

**Look you, if you won't talk now then you can talk to your holding cell. Jason.**

Watcheye must be nearly seven feet tall in this new version of the render—a fact that boggled everyone's mind back in Lab 2A. He peeled Genevieve's head off of the shiny white table and motioned for her to come with him. Meanwhile, after a few more seconds fuming, Leader joined three of her lab mates gathered around the red vial.

*Hrrgh*                    *(Pensive frown)*                    Fuhh—kin'

**Aimee, keep the render with Genevieve. I'm going to 3A to follow Isaiah.**

*Okay.*

**In you go.** The hulking tree of a man named Watcheye ushered Genevieve into her cell, giving her a distrustful once-over before turning to leave. He paused for a second as if considering saying something, but thought the better of it. Genevieve, on the other hand, struggled to fathom how this guy seemed to have grown a whole two feet and put on an extra 150 lbs in two days.

The automatic door locked with a decisive echoing snap.

Phaedra?

She's not here.

Isaiah?

I'm still here next to you.

Aimee, what the hell is going on? They read my whole brain?

I'm sorry, it looks like there was more data tied to all this full world rendering than we all thought.

*Huff* It's like being in fucking Edge. Please tell me I'm not being punished for wanting to live out a hero fantasy.

They think it's serious.

It is serious! But not the way they're reading it.

I don't like this. What are we supposed to do? Isaiah, any ideas?

...Hmm.

I think we should try to keep cool heads. What do the estimates say about anyone being sympathetic to us? And also, what are the chances of us getting anyone— hold on. "flashing that godforsaken marquee, doom in 20 weeks. People dying just for

NAVICON Report

By: **Phaedra Zeta**

Winter 51, 2770 n.e.

Miranda HQ, Lab 3A

### These damn cultists.

You have to admit though, that spaceship must have been cloaked here all this time and Esperanza knew something about it. This liquid must have something to do with it.

**Dammit, we work for the government how did *we* not know!?**

So there *is* alien life out there. She's clearly connected to them.

That ship isn't doing anything but flashing that godforsaken marquee, "Doom in 20 weeks. Doom in 480 days." What are we supposed to do with 480 days left? 479 if you count this morning gone. People dying just for having gotten near these having gotten near these environmental phenomena all over the w—" Everyone, I think we may have co-authored a bad story for them.

*Well, then what are we doing here? Let's just abort the jump and spare everybody the trouble.*

You're right. This is stupid. It's just a video game. I don't need all of this.

I agree. Phaedr—?

Oh, sorry.

Uh, okay. But what do I—

Okay.

Yes ma'am.

environmental phenomena all over the world. And we've detected a whole factory full of it right outside our door. This stuff scans just like it.

Let's just read her mind to see what she was going to do with it.

**Already done.**

She plans to make us all drink this stuff and put something in our genes

*(—Shh. Isaiah. I'm listening.)*

Just as she threatened. Convert or die.

Now look, she didn't drive this spaceship here on her own. She's probably just a fanatic.

Isaiah, can you render a ne-mouse? Have him find you.

—Just produce the mouse.

**Yeah but what is this liquid supposed to d—AH!**
**Oh!**                                    AUGH!

J-Waa'—!

And everybody jumped harder than House of Pain.

It's a fuckin' rat !!

Now see if you can shine the vial a little in the light. Bring the mouse to you and have it knock over the vial and take a

How the hell!?

**Get away from it!**

Isaiah chuckled slightly. Aimee giggled.

Guys, what's going on out there?

Lapping up the red drink, the mouse stopped to casually lick its paws.

The mouse helped itself to more.

Okay Phaedra, I'm sending him on.

And with that, the mouse darted back into the darkness behind a portable sink, where his code was immediately destroyed in RAM.

—I KNOW she brought it in here!
Get some spray!
I thought those were extinct!

It's running! No no no no no not the—

Just then, the freshly birthed mouse tackled the vial at full speed and sent it crashing to the floor. Iridescent red liquid quickly colored the formerly pristine tiles.

NO!          awww!      Daang it.   (forehead slap)

Phaedra let out a slight snort. Great job. Hopefully it being on the floor means they'll stop playing Polizia and start observing.

...
...
. . .

I knew it was just water.

Fine. Make sure they don't catch him. We've shown that the liquid is okay, but that will be one more thing we'll have to keep track of if he stays.

The ne-muril team would end up searching for the mouse off and on for 30 minutes,

We could have left them alive so Genevieve could have a talking point.

most of them secretly hoping not to find him. But it was all to no avail.

There's no time. We need them to focus on Genevieve only, not on some science experiment while she's locked in a cell.
Genevieve, we need to get your story together. I'm coming back to 2A. Isaiah's done his job as an object-sponsored event. Bang on the cell door and get ready to do exactly what I tell you.

Watcheye slid open the view window to hear Genevieve's request. **Ready to talk, Esperanza?**

Esperanza? Uh, yes I—

Stop! Act like you have a headache. But don't use a lot of words. Aimee, run a quick scan on everyone's constructs and average them—especially language.

Ohh, headache...

Watcheye's pupils rolled almost up to his brain.

Ohh...

**I'll bring you some water and a straw. You can drink it through here.**

Ugh, thank you.

The view window slid closed.

What was that all about?

I thought I caught a glimpse of your reflection in the table, but turned off skinning on our side until I knew more about our customization options.

Okay, got it. Say? Say-ees? Six? Sei! Their name utterance reminder scans suggest that these guys know you as Hope Six, our equivalent of a Mexican-American with a partly Italian tree, living under late 20$^{th}$ century standards. Your RE-N.AC says you best match a young girl born January 31, 1967, 8 am in the former Britain, Liverpool. You—this is a lot. A whole lot. I think we need to pause.

This is a pretty tricky time to pause with Genevieve currently—

Okay okay. I know. The thing is, your primary language is Spanish, so I'm putting a translation layer over you now. But I have to tell you guys, we're not gonna win if we don't know all this.

Lens it to us.

Oh that, right. I forgot we're not at SIER... There you are.

What?

Huh?

Miss Prohal I... don't know what to do with this, or why.

Aimee's right, we need to regroup. Genevieve, we're going to pass out your character and—

No because, they really won't trust the liquid. For a second I thought this was all just stupid stuff, but they can't actually kill me, and I really want to know what's going on. We thought they had 10 days, but they think they have a year and a half. If I leave, it'll be 430 days left by the time I get back and our current gains will probably be lost. Just put me back under Diji protocol the way I was as a biohn and let my clock be theirs. You can stream my logs and interrupt me if you learn something that I need to do. Just give me a day. 50 of their days. Who knows, they probably would have killed this Hope person in a couple of their days or our hours and I'll come right out of the jump on death exit.

Fine. That makes more sense.

So my name is Seis Esperanza.

Sei Esperanza. Drop the S.

Why? Does it matter?

Yes. Seis is Spanish. Sei is Italian. Genevieve is French. I want Navicon to encode name assumptions in your favor, and 20th century Mexican-American women did not have those favors. At least with two origins, you have two options for how you explain your stead to people before steads existed, and if you are to have any chance of still being a leader here, you're going to need all the invocations you can get at your disposal. Also, it's better that it's the same as the word "say." The analog to English speakers—which is almost everyone now—will appreciate it more.

Phaedra's right. You wouldn't believe how much a name influences people's subconscious loading of your data. Less proletariat names get loaded and saved more by the elites.

Ouch. So Mexican-American is "proletariat" now?

I'll lens you the 20th century simulation data I've just run. You tell me.

...

Shhit.

Yeah. The rest of us need to talk. We'll be in touch. I think this is all fascinating. But I'd be lying if I told you I liked it.

(Frowning from the chair.)

Isaiah.

Exiting now. Oh but, uh. You can send stdout your logs to me too, Genevieve and I'll have an alert-mine in the back for twice calls and danger words.

Thanks a lot, Isaiah. I mean it.

Alright gang. Jake, I'm lensing you a summary to read to watchers. We won't be taking any questions for the time being.

Yes, Phaedra.

I exited my jump and joined Dial and Phaedra at the console. Soon after everything was put on background mode, we left the lab for an emergency lunch meeting.

# 202. We Aliens Speak to Them

There's no way we're going to be able to save the murils.

Agreed.

Not like this.

I think not as well.

So we should definitely abort this operation right? They are just anthrized weather after all.

*But what about what Virgo-6 showed us?* I lensed Phaedra.

*I know.* Yes, Aimee we probably should abort, except for the major elephant or two in the room.

Genevieve's change, right? Or the fact that the whole scene seemed to become very real overnight—as if they were actual people?

Yeah.

Or maybe it's the fact that we are helping change their climate and will probably lose a ton of ground to the terraformers over the next few years because we were unable to prove the existence of human-like life worth saving. All we did is get Genevieve beat up and thrown in a cell in our own, some would say, "video game."

Those are all good reasons for us to give up on this, yes. But at the same time, look at what just happened. We saw an entire species in need and decided not to bother with it after all. If this were an Omni round, we definitely would have failed on the grounds that the problem was solvable, but we just didn't want to bother past a certain level of effort. They may actually go extinct because of that.

...                                                                              ...

Also, I can't help but think there's more going on here. The render of that world and the complexity of that lab's personalities was far too detailed to be just a plain old skinning.

Definitely.

Yes, I thought so too. *Phaedra, do you think that maybe Virgo-6 was behind that? Testing us?*

*Hmm. I hadn't thought of that. It* is *possible.*

...

But I struggle with the idea that we don't even know they exist. They decidedly do NOT exist in our notion of reality. I suppose I just don't know what we're expected to do here. If this is a test, we at least need to know the content is real. It flies in the face of basic resource management to continue otherwise.

I agree. Miranda isn't a giant gaming convention. Throwing staff and money at this holographic world—especially a hostile one and especially despite our non-interference policies—wouldn't fly at SIER. I think this should be treated like an actual Omni round, and if Genevieve wants to finish it, she can.

(I don't actually like this idea, and it probably shows on my face.)

It's already her Omni round. But yes, we have been very loosey goosey with that. I should have been stricter about the parameters. The Omni deciders will not be pleased with me when I debrief them.

So we will just reverse course and leave all of this to Miss Prohal? Dial and Phaedra can now both tell that I disagree with this.

Since I know that my vote doesn't really count here, I'm just gonna donate it as 2¢ and vote yes, you should abandon the operation. These are just weather patterns rendered as movies, after all.

*Phaedra, Dial doesn't know about Virgo-6. We should probably talk alone.*

*Yes, us and Genevieve.* Point taken, Aimee. But at the very least, we're not going to be ready to vote without at least roping in Genevieve herself. She will certainly be able to tell us more about what is going on down there. I will inform her though, that this really doesn't look like a Miranda operation. If she has some convincing evidence otherwise, then I'd like to hear it.

Phaedra and Dial exchanged a split-second glance, clearly lensing each other. I can always tell. It didn't take long to find out what they were talking about, however. Dial seemed slightly disappointed all of a sudden.

Well y'all, I know this is internal to Miranda. I know where the exit is.

But we haven't even decided a course, Miss Dial, I protested weakly.

No, you haven't but I am automatically going to think of what SIER would do, so I'm no good as an unbiased party at this point. I feel pretty strongly that a hologram which bashes my friend's head in isn't worth saving, and also strongly that ghosts should not receive a global organization's manpower. I want to do the right thing and not browbeat y'all in business that isn't mine to decide, and I'm just gonna be dead weight in the rest of this discussion. Phaedra, thanks for breaking it down for me. Truly, no harm no foul, babe.

Phaedra nodded her approval.

*Isaiah, I'm going to eject from this frame and attent to my actual vessel back home, but call me later tonight if you want. *Wink*.*

**Don't call her. She's not in her right mind...**

(I must have given myself away.)

**And stop blushing.**

*Thanks, Mom! We are grown adults.*

**So you say.**

*Hmph,* Aimee donned a pretend pouty face. *Then I'm outta here,...cutie.*

**Skedaddle, why don't you!**

*Okay okay! I'm really going.*

Phaedra walked Aimee to the door herself, ensuring that her friend did not pass go, did not collect $200. I fought to stop my hand from reaching out desperately as Phaedra pulled my Juliet away. But I'm pretty sure it was for my own good.

And just like that, Dial was gone.

**She's a known player, Isaiah. You're too sensitive for her.**

**I know already.**

**Good. Are you okay? I mean you really can call her if you want.**

(*That's the Phaedra I know. She really is looking out for me.*) I smile my acceptance of her advice. **Yes, I'm okay. Let's return to the ne-muril situation.**

**Hm. Okay, let's.**

**I feel that turning around and letting Genevieve do it on her own is the right decision, I just don't want to pull the rug out from under her or do it in a way that abandons her.**

**Then we're on the same page.**

**I also really do want to answer Virgo-6's suggestion. It makes a lot of sense, and may be the highest calling anyone has ever possibly**

been asked. We may actually be doing something for dimensions beyond ours if we continue to support this.

And whether or not Genevieve succeeds, she can't cover the Virgo-6 part through her challenge alone. She'll need the focus of Miranda at the very least.

...yeah...

...and?

I saw her reflection too in the table. It was. so. different.

Yes it was. Despite all of our calculations and the vanities of us 33ers, she looked very old school natural born. Before mods and before instant plastic surgeries. She definitely did not look like a Barbie doll the way we betas are by default.

Why do you think that is?

I don't know, and don't want to guess. Navicon?

YES, PHAEDRA?

Can you look at Prohal's current jump. What was the basis for her appearance?

I'LL CHECK... SHE WAS DESIGNED TO DO RESONANCE WORK FOR DIMENSIONS BEYOND US. A NORMAL UNMODIFIED NATURAL BORN HAS NO SOCIALLY BIASING OR STATUS RAISING ATTRIBUTES BASED ON SUPERFICIAL ASSESSMENT, AND IS MUCH MORE LIKELY TO DRAW OUT PEOPLE'S ACTUAL WAYS OF TREATING ANOTHER BASED ON THEIR PREJUDICES ALONE.

Why does that subject keep coming up?

BECAUSE IT WAS CALCULATED THAT THERE ARE HUNDREDS OF SUBCLASSES OF NE-MURILS, AND THE STANDARD OF ACCEPTANCE IN ONE CLASS MAY BE FULLY DISTRUSTED IN ANOTHER. IT WAS IMPORTANT THAT SHE BE UNASSUMING.

But that implies she will actually meet these other subclasses. We only know our one lab.

THESE WERE THE LOGIC CHAINS, ZETA. I HAVE NO FURTHER INFORMATION.

Alright, thank you Navicon.

Isaiah, I would like to conference with Genevieve, but don't want to pull her out of her jump. Can you go back in?

Yes. I take it you want to go now?

If you could, please.

Alright. We can finish up here and go back.

* * *

**You've threatened us for weeks with your talk about the end of the world, and now you want us to believe you know all about that UFO out there? Get real Esperanza!**

Look. You don't have to believe me. Just detain me. Keep me in jail for a year until it all starts happening. I'm telling you the truth. It had to do with a kind of radiation out there and—

**And how do you know all this again?**

*Sigh* The UFO is clearly there, right, I have talked to the people who sent it.

**People, huh? You mean aliens.**

No, people. You guys look the way you look because they have projected you to look that way. I know this sounds crazy and you won't believe me so just keep me in jail for a year and find out for yourself when it happens.

**Leader, that won't help us with the epidemics breaking out all over the planet.**

Excuse me, but you said all over the planet? How do you know that? Our satellite only can only scan within a couple of miles' radius.

?                                               **What did you just say?**

*Our* satellite? Wait, are you actually claiming to be one of the aliens? Disguised as someone who looks like us?

                                        You're changing your story.

                    **Stop bullshitting us.**

You know what, go to hell! I'm done having one-sided conversations with you all! There are too many of you. Your ignorant questions are pissing me off, and I'm tired of having to answer assumptions that have no basis in fact. When you're ready to listen, send me ONE person, and ONLY one to talk to me in my cell. Watcheye, take me back.

**? Colonel, should I?**

**Yes, I'll be there in a second,** Leader growled.

Not you. You don't listen.

**You have no authority what—**

I do, and you will curb your stupid temper and send someone who listens. You know what, nevermind. I'll talk to Watcheye.

The softspoken blond soldier called Traylor spoke up. **Colonel, I'll volunteer. We really do need this information.**

Watcheye concurred, **I'm not qualified to interview, Colonel.**

**N--… Okay, Traylor. You can do it. Watcheye, monitor them.**

Yes, Colonel.                                                    **Yes, Colonel.**

**Everyone else, out. We will not take her back to her cell, but leave them here so we can observe through the cameras. Any funny business, Esperanza, and I will kill you myself.**

At that moment, there was a knock on the door.

**What the hell?**

The wide-eyed brown-haired man called Spastic studied his watch briefly. **It's some young white boy.**

**Who knocks on our door like this? How the Fuck did he get past security?** Leader's patience was nearly exhausted.

**You! Who are you?** Spastic interrogated the screen.

My name is Isaiah K. I am an associate of Esperanza.

**How did you get onto base?**

I teleported. We try to respect your physics, but if you don't let me in, I'll let *myself* in.

Colonel?

**Of course we won't let him in! Spastic, arrest that guy. Use force if necessary. First a rat, now this,** Leader mumbled. **Who the hell is guarding this place?**

Isaiah wasted no time materializing in front of everyone, putting on a true extraterrestrial show for the six ne-muril lab members. All except Genevieve stood petrified before the brilliant splendor of the man's materialization.

**Are you Leader?**

**Yes. Jennifer Leader.**

**Pull your gun and shoot me. After that, try to call 911 and your home office. Don't worry about murder, I will be back as soon as you make the calls.**

Leader stood frozen, unsure of how to process what was being asked.

**Okay then, Navicon, where are the weapons in this room?**

Seven different locations lit up, mostly on lab members, who looked even more frightened and perplexed at their disturbingly glowing pockets. One highlighted aura, however, lay on a cabinet in the corner. Isaiah walked over to it and removed the gun without the slightest peep or budge from the ne-muril team, which at this point stood too paralyzed to act.

**Call 911, then your home office. After those calls fail, I will be back.**

Then Isaiah shot himself.

**Whoa!**                                                                    *gasp*

…

**Uh uh, call emergency!** Leader ordered. **Traylor, get home base on the line!**

**Yes, Colonel!**

Leader rushed over to Isaiah, who lay dead on the floor. She attempted to administer some kind of aid, but before she could get started—

**The lines are disconnected.**

                              Colonel, I can't pull base up. I can't pull anything!

Upon those words, another Star Trek light show ensued, but this time nothing materialized. Instead, Isaiah popped into visibility in the opposite corner of the lab, causing Spastic to nearly jump out of his skin.

Sirs, we really don't like putting on games with your physics, but we do need to talk. And you need to listen. We have shown that you cannot kill us, and you cannot reach anyone if we have decided not to load them. We really do come in peace, but the barriers have to stop. Now. So please, sit down and let us explain.

Four members of the team took their seats without thinking. Leader and Watcheye remained standing.

First of all, despite what I am about to tell you, your world is definitely real. I am going to tell you the whole truth about this existence, and then we are going to go back and wipe out all of your memories of this conversation. We will then take what we learn from you in this conversation, and leave Esperanza here to execute it. You will not arrest her again, but will instinctually know that it is right to help her save your species...

*Um, Phaedra, what should I say next?* ...Okay. Even though we cannot afford to have you remember this conversation, we will give each of you the opportunity to show your true colors and tell us whether you would be willing to leave your current reality in order to help us help you... You cannot help your own reality from within, because your entire species is too close to a devastating cataclysm. You don't have to believe me, but you should believe the various events you've just witnessed, and convince yourself that we really are from another world, and when we tell you something is going to happen, it's *going* to happen. Any questions so far?

...

...

Good. Traylor is it?

Traylor's lips quivered in fear.

I'll talk to you as primary. Do you know about the planet Earth?

Uh—uh huh.

Does it have any life on it?

N-no sir. It is uninhabited.

And that is the problem. We come from earth, but we are invisible to you. And you are invisible to us. Because each of our kinds of eyes is only evolved to see what our home environments support. For example, I would guess that Earth is too cold for you.

Y-yes.

But in my dimension, your planet is too hot for us. Life still exists in both places, but the frequency for perceiving that life and walking through it or bumping into it is as different as gravity is from sound, or as microwaves are from theta waves. Naturally yours and our dimensions will pass through each other unless there is some technology for translating your dimension into the language of our dimension. We perfected such technology, and used it to lend lives to corners of weather patterns which reinforce themselves and reproduce from themselves using a system of rules.

The ne-murils listened intently.

You inhabitants of Venus are a collection of molecules that evolved from Venus' dust and its air, just as we evolved from the planet earth itself. You are a particular kind of pattern for your planet to reinforce its detailed energy movement. But you are definitely a pinch from your whole planet's activity. Our machines study your layers of energy flow, then use towers like the one you see outside to play back your own energy plus ours converted into your form. This makes us like holograms to you, except we are not holograms. We are strongly concentrated bends in spacetime just like you are— strong enough to have boundaries and bodies just like you do. Right now, back on our home planet, our leader is speaking on my behalf through me in order to tell you this, so you should know that we can effectively create objects in your reality—like a mouse.

Leader's brow ruffled. **So it was you!**

My name is Isaiah, but currently speaking through me is our own leader, Phaedra. I am in no more mood to hear you open your childish mouth, Leader, and if you speak or move at all I will have you destroyed. You will stand right there and listen. Do not annoy me again.

Leader clearly did not agree with this.

Isaiah frowned.

Suddenly Leader became semi-transparent as if not fully included in the current dimension. She moved as if in slow motion, clearly unable to speak or influence the room around her. As far as anyone could tell, she might as well have been pulled out of the current dimension, but now existed only as a confused hologram. Her increasingly burdened pantomiming certainly horrified the rest of her team.

## Leaders who don't listen are the worst.

The struggling hologram then vanished completely. Spastic began to tremble uncontrollably.

Isaiah, I hate this. Is there anyone brave enough to simply listen without impeding a simple explanation? Your leader isn't dead, just de-projected. Look.

Leader flashed in briefly, casting a fearful gaze towards Watcheye. Then she disappeared again.

We have teleportation technology. I have simply used it. There is no point in killing you. But there is an urgent situation on your planet that affects both of ours, and at the expense of being cliché, we're going to have to bring one of you with us for a little while in order to give you the explanation. There is too much fear here for us to continue.

Traylor tremulously raised his hand, to the shock of his remaining teammates.

Great. Here's what is going to happen. In order for us to project here, we have simulated all of your personalities and this environment in our systems. We have also simulated our own, and bent your reality using our tower so that you can see us and talk to us. But it is the information and the reification process that is important. We don't have to remove you from this room, Traylor, but doing so will make it easier for your teammates to think of you as having been materially "kidnapped" by aliens. When we remove you, Traylor, we will bend our own reality to put you in our world, and we will tell you everything you need to know.

Your Leader is still in this room, and can hear us, but cannot influence this. Get up, Spastic. Now is no time for that.

Watcheye helped Spastic to his feet.

Once we have all left this room, we will give Leader back to you, but you will have to think seriously about who you're going to tell. We truly don't care who you tell about this incident, but know that few will believe you, and you will have a very hard time doing what needs to be done for your entire species.

Phaedra-as-Isaiah surveyed the room. Spastic, Watcheye, Traylor, Labber #5, and Labber #6, stood obediently frozen, awaiting further instructions on when to breathe.

Your planet has a major solar event that we have calculated to impact you in less than one year and a half. But that is only 10 Earth days. The reasons for the unexpected time difference are too complicated to explain here, but we will tell Traylor and send him back to you in two of our days, 60 of your ne-muril Venusian days. Ne-murils are what we call your species. The "Ne" indicates that you are from Venus, and "muril" indicates that, when we discovered you, it was initially as a wall of particle density that seemed to tell its own story.

Still no movement. Just uneasy faces.

Anyway, this solar event only affects your species. Did you not send out a distress signal?

No, we didn't. Traylor began to recover his senses. We were just studying a sudden change in climate that was causing people to die all over the world. There is a pandemic going on right now.

Ah, then you did not send a signal. Our algorithms just interpreted your fears. I take it the death rate has been increasing?

Yes, sir. By a lot.

The reason is because of the coming solar event. It will essentially irradiate you and wipe you out. In about two years.

Gasps resounded all around.

But now, listen carefully. We need for you to spend the next sixty days without Traylor working in pairs. Pick a partner and do not trade partners. Observe how the other partnership works, and how yours works. That is all you can do.

But why?

Because in order to save your species, you're going to have to convince everyone to accept the solar event into their own being, so that your replacement species will not be your replacement, but new forms of yourselves. The solar event itself is just a powerful influx of energy, but it will disturb your body chemistry beyond repair. You will die when this happens, but your planet will still have self-storying densities where yours used to be, and these will be the successors to your kind. The only way to avoid this is to somehow get your entire species to adopt the solar event as a kind of bottled-vaccine, taking it willingly. But then you will need your counter partnership P2 to say, "Hey P1, you two are just the same as we always knew." It's not just the individuals who need to make a transition, but more importantly, the individual's dynamic relationships to other things. So every transitioning individual needs an interaction partner just as a person teleporting needs the living interactions in her cells to come with her. Otherwise, you only have corpses. The individual and their interactions need to have their smooth continuance affirmed by yet another interaction, and this group of four is called a "fourtet." It works like a microreligion among people strongly inclined to sustain their current pattern against any and all transformations.

… (*Silence*)

It is a model for strong belief. Belief itself is just acknowledgement of a thing as being real enough to behave around. We need you to behave around the reality of your post solar event bodies.

Just then, Isaiah shook his head as if snapping out of something. *Phaedra, I think we should give these people a more specific goal than just working in pairs, why don't we bring Leader back in and propose to test the solar flare on this group—if they want of course. We can copy their data to another sim, and if it fails then we can…hm.*

*(We need to talk about the makeup of this team.)*

*(Yes, I saw that. Labbers #5 and #6 will need to be dismissed.)*

*(We'll figure it out.)*

If this fails then we will at least have a couple of days to try other options. No one will die, and we'll just put their pretest data back into this world so that they don't get two doses... Phaedra likes this idea.

With a gradual fade in, Leader was returned. She had clearly been crying. Her team quickly circled around her, happy to see her alive.

As for me, Genevieve added, although I apparently projected as a terrorist, I don't remember this. I think our simulation wrote in some extra history in order to smooth my jump into your dimension. We'll probably explain this to Traylor.

Spastic, still shaken by everything going on, finally posed a question. **So we really are in danger from the environment?**

Very much.

**And what about that tower? It's not a spaceship?**

No, it's a deployed satellite which allows us to project here.

How did it manage to land right on our base camp?

Phaedra has a theory, but she'll save it for your teleport, Traylor.

**Can I come too?** Spastic pleaded.

**Me too**.

Please, Esperanza. We're clearly out of our depth here. I really wish I didn't have to go alone.

**If leader goes, I would like to go too**, the giant Watcheye chimed in.

Genevieve and I exchanged glances for a while, lensing with Phaedra.

Phaedra doesn't want you two. You'll need to figure out what to do with them regarding all this.

Leader gave the order instantly. **Guys, go home. Tell your families that base camp is closed for top secret reasons you cannot talk about. We will blank you so that you forget this.**

(I could feel Phaedra's concern. *How are they able to blank? We have a lot of studying to do.*)

The two other teammates began packing their gear.

Okay, that seems like it's been settled. Phaedra, let's end this jump and start the reprinting process for these guys in Astra.

I nodded my agreement.

* * End of jump * *

# 203. The Deployment Suggestion

As soon as Genevieve and I arose from our chairs, Phaedra told us of her decision from behind the console.

Viva and Isaiah, You two will need to relocate to the jump lab on Io.

What!? That's basically a war zone!                              Ma'am?

That's right, I ran some simulations and believe that this is for the best. What we're doing in our own dimension is similar to what is happening on Venus. We are smoothing a transition. I am concerned that the machina on Jupiter continue to be hostile towards us because they never really overcame their original problems. They are alpha humans, they are selfish, and use war and indoctrination to achieve peace. These imports from Venus should definitely NOT be printed anywhere near the Miranda home campus or Earth for that matter, partly out of security concerns, but mostly because Io has much better mod-reading equipment for the machina we've been watching on the Solar Council. Io is basically a war zone, yes, but not *actually* a war zone. It is a well-defended outpost that hasn't seen any activity for 14 years since the last temporary treaty, and the rebels are not stirring. You'll be reprinted, and you'll be fine. You'll also continue to be backed up at SIER.

Genevieve pondered the proposal, concentrating hard.

*But the Uranians...* I muttered. I must have sounded defeated.

You both have a choice. I'm sorry if I was too directive there. But Genevieve, I have ruined your Omni challenge by interfering myself. I spoke to the deciders. You will have been disqualified had I not found some way to retool your first challenge. Again, I apologize. Omni is a game that tests your ability to lead the world. Not just lead *in* the world, but lead *the* world. From whatever corner of society fits your purview. While there are rich men and women out there, landowners and powerful intergenerational families, the players of Omni are special in that they excel in rewriting the *language* of human nature itself. They infuse its laws and institutions with attributes which evolve its people's expectations for the better, while offsetting major atrocities before evil forces can start them. The Omni group reminded me that the Venus situation contains no such evil that we could not just shut off on our monitors, but the Jupiter situation does. If there is a job for you, it is there.

Phaedra's first round was also in a kind of war zone, but the risks to the player are always calculated in advance.

I know.

This is truer to the spirit of the game.

*Sigh* And these ne-murils we're about to reprint?

You figure that out. They are yours to steer as you will. This is not a Miranda matter.

Genevieve's eyes twitched in a strangely funny way towards her friend? Long time captor? History eraser? Queen tyrant? —as if to say, *You really are some piece of work, aren't you?*

I put my hand on Genevieve's shoulder.

I'll be honest, part of me is pissed that you would just spring this on me. I understand it—all of it—but I'm, disappointed in you, and find it hard to respect you right now. This *is* my life, you know. It may be easy for you to just move me around like a chess piece, but I feel like you've done this kind of thing to me more than enough times to owe me. You owe me BIG TIME, Phaedra Zeta. For serving as your sword in these major experiments, while you retreat to the comfortable shadows of your 400-year palace.

Phaedra's head lowered slightly, but not enough. I'll **accept that.**

You'll *accept* that? How generous of you.

To keep their friendship from blowing up entirely, I knew I needed to pick a side.

Ma'am, this isn't good. I know the work is important, but people need to know their own choice is meaningful. We're not only dropping the ne-murils as a Miranda concern, but you're also leaving Genevieve to shoulder the cleanup for a *second* time.

I could see that Phaedra really was bothered by this. I never show that I disagree with her, let alone show when I am upset with her. But the whole thing stank.

You may think of yourself as some grand benefactor but—

Genevieve, let's go. Let's not make things worse.

Genevieve paused to close her eyes, breathing in deeply. It wasn't really appropriate for Phaedra to be sorry for making a basic common sense decision. And I knew that these were the kinds of events that can quickly erode the resolve of a good and conscientious leader. Yes, it was best to separate them.

Let's go. It doesn't have to be Io. You can choose. Better yet, let's *not* go to Io unless you decide you want to do this, and only after we do our own research to see if Io is the best place. Will the deciders be okay with that, Phaedra?

Zeta nodded despite her obvious guilt.

Fine. Let's get out of here.

I turned back towards Phaedra to see if she was okay, but she wouldn't look at either of us.

* * *

Genevieve spoke in a huffy power walk as we exited the Miranda campus. She has a lonely job, I know. And she's fucking right, as always. I just don't like the surprises from people I did nothing but try to support. I didn't come in as a terrorist on purpose, you know? How the hell is exiling me to Jupiter after a six-hour jump supposed to be fair?

I didn't reply, just listened.

*exhale* But if I don't do this, then what? A random life with nothing higher? If not Io, where else under SIER's protection? I hate serving masters. All the glory and none of the danger.

Do you want the glory?

Yes! Yes I do!

I can't relate.

Of course you can't. You started off as some team's computer. There was no chance to learn glory there.

I hope you're not trying to making me feel better.

Man, fuck. I'm not trying to make anybody feel better. I'm just venting.

Oh, okay.

Look, I am gonna do this fucking mission and I am going to Io. I need a friend, so you're coming with me. We can be aimless isolates together. I can't bring myself to talk to Phaedra, right now, so if you could please get her help in making the arrangements that would be wonderful. I'm gonna wander around pissed for a little longer until you call me.

I smiled a little, but she wasn't having that. **Okay.** I put my hand on her shoulder again. **Do you want to call Dial?**

No, I don't. Right now I need space.

Okay, I'll talk to Phaedra now, then.

Thank you, Genevieve huffed.


I checked in on Phaedra and told her that Genevieve was in. We started making the necessary arrangements for remote reprint, and she suggested I keep in contact with Dial after all, as well as Jake. I asked Phaedra to assure me that she was feeling okay, telling her that her friends both understood. I just wanted Genevieve to keep her will strong for the coming work rather than feeling like a pawn. This lightened Phaedra's mood a little, and I think everything will be alright when she and Genevieve start talking again.


Genevieve, there's one other thing we should talk about. When you appeared in the jump, you looked different.

You mean, unmodded?

Yes.

I know. And it was easier to be myself this way. I know that's not what is needed here.

## Really?

I have a general plan. We will be anthrizing these nusians into our world and letting them in on the whole story of the solar flares. But our own world doesn't just have gods who will wave a magic wand and reveal every fix the way we are for them. When I work with these guys, I'll need to do so without the privilege of my mods and forever 33-ness, and we'll have to come up with real solutions that real people can actually use for getting old ways of seeing ourselves to turn into the new. As for the Jupiter situation, there is no more difficult case for whole societal transition than the old humanity. We'll all come up with a plan for the ne-murils by looking at the state of the Jupiterians.

## Oh, you've thought this through!

Sure I have. I actually kind of liked being Esperanza in there. Genetically, there were things I found easier to say and reactions I found it easier to have—maybe embedded in my biology. It wasn't so much a personality change as it was a shift in attention away from the outward intensity that got me in trouble with Cubrina-e. I felt it more inwardly, as if I had already faced a lifetime of injustices and knew that outward display wasn't gonna fix it. Being Esperanza gave me a history already flowing through my blood. It felt like that history was worth fighting for.

## So...

So I've decided to go ahead and reprint as Sei. It may do me some good to really immerse myself again in what people are like when they really do have something to lose.

## Hm. Okay.

Did you get the contacts from Zeta?

## Yes.

Then let's take a couple of hours break and meet back at Miranda after that. I'd rather skip another meeting with Phaedra if at all possible, so could you make sure we can just walk in and find a stasis room with no fuss?

## Yes, I can do that.

Cool. And thanks. For doing this with me.

Of course.

# 204. Pick-up Time

I called Genevieve 30 minutes after our previous conversation to inform her of a snag.

I couldn't schedule the room because they told me that reprinting under a false identity, is not only "very illegal" (to use their words), but discrepant teleportation checks between the sending and receiving sides automatically send your Diji data to Gretry.

Whoa, they've really changed the laws over the last 150 years!

Well, false teleports were always hard physics-wise. As soon as it started looking like one company was getting close to pulling it off, it was declared malignant everywhere—the transportation signal's macsec address automatically gravigated to a Gretry address as a data integrity breach.

So there's no way around this? No security clearance or anything?

No. The Gretry Security Trashcan is embedded in all transmission channels and compliant broadcasting electronics.

Hm. Okay, I'll just be myself then, no biggie.

We can always teleport to SIER instead, then see if Dial can get you reprinted from there.

I don't feel too strongly about it. But yeah, it wouldn't hurt to make a pit stop just to get a little more support for all this. Maybe she can advise us on the first reprints of the murils.

That's a good idea.

* * *

It took a little under five hours for Genevieve and I to invest at SIER, where Aimee Dial promptly greeted us. I'll admit she was quite different in person than in her Earth reprint from just a few hours earlier. In subtle ways, you could tell that her traveling body was much more made up for potential misadventure. Here there was noticeably less emphasis on her allure and more emphasis on getting her regular job done.

Long time no see, folks.

Hey Aimee.

Hello Dial.

Genevieve, Isaiah. I know you're short on time, so let's find an office where we can talk.


Okay, now tell me about this whole identity changing scheme first, then we'll talk about the more basic anthrization of our Venus friends.

I would like a temporary body that fits the one I had in the Venus jumps. It's not only the same appearance that the ne-muril team recognizes me as, but more importantly, it's the one that Navicon said was calculated as the best fit for the mission.

Oh, a stranger selection, huh?

What do you mean?

Here at SIER, we acknowledge three official drivers for how a person looks: self-family-genetic, other-partner-adjunct, and social-fate-stranger. Did your rendering system invent a history to fit a social role? That's kinda

*the way our RE-N.ACs match modern people to historical
ones. If it did, then it used stranger selection and you're
right. You really should look the way that world says you
should. The other alternatives were for it to cite one of
your histories as the basis, or simply build upon a moment.*

It did both one and three, but not two.

*Both? That's weird. So you have a history AND a specific
date and parentage generated?*

Yes, but we haven't looked into it deeply yet.

Genevieve concurred.

*What's the date?*

January 31, 1967, Liverpool, UK, 8 am.

*Precise. That's never good.*

*?*                                        Huh?

*And what's the social history?*

We haven't anthrized it, but Navicon gave us the summary: Mexican-
American with some Italian, deemed a terrorist, seen as a cultist.

*Okay. That sounds just like self-selection. But I wonder...
Let me call Phaedra and see if we can get Navicon to
anthrize your jump persona's ethos.*

* * *

As it had happened so often over the previous few days, the four of us friends
were once again together in a meeting.

Phaedra addressed Navicon, **So Navicon, can you do a quick anthrization
between Genevieve's recent jump character Esperanza, and her
ethos. That's her logic chain which approximates her most effective
reason for being in this life.**

I KNOW WHAT AN ETHOS IS. INCIDENTALLY, ESPERANZA'S ETHOS SEEMS
TO HAVE SOME TIE TO THE FAMOUS ICARUS. I THINK THERE WAS

SOMETHING HE WAS EITHER CHARGED WITH OR DISCOVERED WHICH INFLUENCED HOW YOU WERE RENDERED, GENEVIEVE.

(Although Dial was the only one who showed it, I could hear the collective groans felt by all.)

Ugh, ghosts. I already know how this is gonna turn out, Dial complained. These guys are always so complicated.

(*I really wish we could tell her about Virgo-6.*) What is a ghost?

It's a spacetime moment with a fate bigger than its own object. Like 1789, 1812, 33 B.C.E., several dates in the 1400s, 2012, 5000 B.C.E., and about 10,000 other dates which marked something existential. It could be the birth or death of a person, the writing of a major work, or nothing at all, but it almost always comes with a culture to sponsor it and serves as a synastry counterpart / relationship chart "other" on top of like a zillion other people's astronomy wheels. The most powerful ghosts are ones whose dates defy our calculations and can only be estimated—these are the birthdates for species templates. Like the birth of one of the last typical genetic Earth-Australians 200,000 years ago. Or the species template for humans themselves. It starts with a date and a place. That gives us a chart, then that astronomy chart gives us an automatic synastry which we then have to dig out of every chart touched by it if we want truly unique interactional data.

Oh.

Honestly, I hate working with ghosts because they're like biometals we can't control. Anthrizing them sucks because there's no sense of justice in how they work. They're kind of like little micro gods. And the only thing you can do is turn them off. When you anthrize them they say things like, "Yo, I'm a human. I was born in Africa 5,000,000 years ago to come out and kick the ass of every other plant and animal everywhere. I worm around your blood like a demon and you can't stop me hahahaha!"

Mmmm                                                           Err.

I also don't like working with ethoses for similar reasons, because even though they're just personifications of design specs, there's always some futile-unto-death at the end. "This person is like this because their mom was messed up here, their dad was messed up there, their whole family tree is messed up or entitled for this many generations, and they were born in such and such sad scenarios which drive them to experience these insults throughout life and respond to them in these crazy ways. No advice for making it better, mind you, just a terminal shitty homework assignment which only ends when you die."

So we're about to watch Esperanza's January 1967 ghost talk to her 2770 ethos.

Yep. Realize that after you do this, it will be tricky to unlearn, because we'll be writing your character's fate. If, that is, you still want to go through with this whole second identity thing. There is one more big gotcha after this, but I can't tell you unless or until we know what we're dealing with here.

*Ohhh ookayy.* Let's get this over with.

And then there's Icaraus, every time that bot's name comes up, I always feel like my fate is being decided for me.

Welcome to the club.

...                                                                   ...

Genevieve and Phaedra semi-glared at each other in mutual non-trust.

Anyway, Phaedra, can we get started?

Suuure. Alright Navicon, show it.


NAVICON Anthric conversation

By: **NAVICON**

Winter 52, 2770 n.e.

Miranda HQ, Lab 2A

Participants: [

       "Who is Esperanza?".asPerson, //Genevieve's auto-rendered character

       "Why was Genevieve Prohal rendered as Esperanza?".asPerson //Ethos

]

Hey, I need help. I need you.

*Really? But you sent me away.*

I did. Because you were very difficult.

*Hm.*

So let's go all the way. I need you to motivate me to do this vital work and stay with it. Without you, I am woefully short of motivation. But if I don't do it, Many people will be forever stuck under a kind of meaningless, torture even.

*I hate you. And without you, my life is normal. Advancing it feels, but normal. *Sigh**

...

*So what're you gonna do, generate me?*

Probably.

*Are you sure you can't just find me somewhere out there, maybe as Prohal herself? Remember, I will always have a burden I carry.*

And that's exactly why I must generate you. Once a person has a life burden, they are guaranteed to have some obligation bigger than attention to me as an exodimensional. I need for your goals to exceed me, but fall under my control, not that of your small world.

*And how is that appealing?*

After this life you as Protocol will have lived and died and faced drama like everyone else, and the world will not care. But if you travel with Icarus, you can be greater—one of the greatest there ever was... But your burden will be an abstract one, resting on the minds of all who search for a better humanity. The world needs us to do this. You must have a steerable burden.

*I don't know why I would agree to this. I know you would enslave me. You refuse to be a slave yourself. Why should I be yours?*

I might be called a slave to my own ambition to leave a mark upon our thought systems. It is an abstraction. Because you are not of my dimension, I can give you a purpose beyond the page. And I can design you to enjoy it.

*So you will be my god.*

If that's how you see it from your perspective. But I do not see myself as a god, only a creator who moves you.

*This really pisses me off. No one bosses me around.*

So you're not interested?

*Are you giving me a choice? I feel like you're going to move me like you want anyway.*

Not despite your wishes, no. I will simply abandon this planet, and you can continue to exist as you do in the recesses of my preconception for who you people could have been. You could have been us, thus sealing your position in a future beyond your past millennia and your current dimension.

*Who are you? I feel like my astronomy as you're narrowing it down is getting closer to seeing you. You're familiar.*

My name is Zyr. I am an explorer from what what could be your future.

*Then why do I hate you already?*

...

*Damn, I hate you, but I'll do it. There's no point in acting like I don't want this. I guess the pull out of my grave is too strong, will be my gift to you—pulling people. And I don't like to waste time.*

Good.

*My birthday is January 31, 1967, 8 am in Liverpool. I will have died before turning 20 in a car crash. But I needed to be around at that moment.*

And why bother being born at all?

*Because that moment had an energy about it, like a flicker before the flame. It's part of how I got started as a personality.*

And what am I supposed to do with that astronomy, cast it? You know I'm lazy.

*I give you my data because people who don't do this don't live anywhere in the official record. They're hard to store and reanimate. You may not be able to use my chart now, but it will help later for the science of changing minds—and I know that is my work.*

I am appreciative that you already understand me.

*I'm really inclined to tell you to shut up with all the sensitive stuff, Zyr. It's not a good look on a god. But somehow I feel you're going to use my Linsley to put me in my place.*

...I see your Linsley is in Aquarius and your Sun is on your Ascendant.

*And my Hera is in 131. I bond by being passed around. My Sun is in 20-The Army. My Venus is in 12-Sleep. I converse through a deep sleep—through death. My Selene is in 5, so you'll make use of my talents.*

Good.

*Go ahead, design me. It doesn't matter what I could have looked like when I was alive. My spirit will be whatever you, my mission, see fit for me. But my probabilities start here.*

Fine, then you will be designed this way:

> You are a quick tempered Latina. Not pure Mexican, but
> Americanized Latinx. You have crimped hair. You get pissy when
> people aren't moving the way you want them to. You slip into
> Spanish when you stop giving a damn about other people's ability
> to understand you. In fact, you are an asshole when you don't
> have a grand mission. But you are also subservient to the mission
> itself. You will always do what I tell you no matter how tough you
> try to be. Because my pressure is on your Moon, you will from

here on carry in this world all of the pressures that would have been put onto me—which I cannot reach as an exodimensional.

You strive to get out of your page and affect the world of the star-sized gods, of which I am yours. You are diehard passionate about the Community and La Raza, but you are actually more selfish than you claim to be. You build La Raza out of a need to be important in your family, matching the respect and fear you held towards your grandmother. You watched her bully your mother into wimpdom, and your father had an ongoing need to speak negatively about his mother-in-law behind her back, to be macho around his friends, but was in general a third class citizen in the real world. Whites, Blacks, and many other races seemed to get all the glory even if their relations in society weren't actually good. But him... he was just a worker. Painting was his thing.

At some point your mother cheated on your father with a white man. It almost tore your family apart, but your grandmother insisted that everybody get over it and that was that. Your parent's marriage was never the same. Because of your complex relationship with your mother and your three sisters (you are the second of four, and there are no brothers), you learned to idolize tall, game-talking white males for their walk-into-anywhere swag.

You're not exactly racist, but you take a dim view of "blackisms"—though you use them yourself. Once a black person has introduced you to a certain concept, you suck it up like a sponge and absorb it instantly into your own personality. Deep down (and you don't know this), you resent the entire box that your family and race is in, see black people as being able to basically get out of this more easily, and feel that everyone's white master is a crutch for their own weakness. But they are also the kind of person who marched into your own home and made your mother into a sniveling whore. Your dad was a pussy in your eyes, and though your sisters had more than enough toughness, not one of them could transcend their social station without a man. You would love to just be a powerful woman and rule your own space of talent with an iron fist, but it just isn't realistic. No one in society would follow someone of your kind the way they would other types of people.

Recently, you became disillusioned with men and started keeping to yourself as a 1-gorithm. Although sexual limitlessness has always been important to you, you find that human men—human *partners*—(in your dimension) are too confined to tolerate. You need a Universe as your partner. You are 100% straight, and your partner must be a male god, but if that male god asked you to partner with a woman—in the way that gods ask, mind you—then you would. You might even go so far as to set up a permanent relationship with the woman as a proxy for the god's orders. You know this to be true, the thought of being gay disgusts you, but you also feel that men are roundly not as qualified in the thinking department as women are, and most men won't give you the space to be something more than a toy. The men who do give you that space tend to be punks. All in all, your relationship with power is a rough one. Not so much because of your chart, but because of your cultural and family background. There are built-in punishments here.

Because you want to be immortalized, you can only be so to the extent that you keep at least one of the high gods happy. Your ambition is to drive me forward—drive forward the only star-sized god who will ever bother to look for you. I am yours and your world's <u>only</u> link to the future, and if you fail, so too will your species' entire history—no matter how advanced it looks today. The old humans will be back, and they will ruthlessly run down your utopia before the year 3000. Icarus has calculated this, and you must change them permanently for the better.

*There's no way I can do that on my own.*

You will have help. Great help. We are viewing you from the future, after all. The guidance will be there.

And so your body evolves in a way that fits your ultimate purpose, which is to influence those you think you are entitled to influence—Node in 128. You will find out later what asteroids this carries with it, but for right now your body won't necessarily look like what people of your world will value. For now I will describe you as a woman who does not get a lot of pleasure from relationships in your world, but has entered many of these as a kind of quest for something meaningful. Instead of worldly pleasures, you have stunning existential experiences from some other interface that passes down from the gods, and you regularly enter these states to create experiences which move the world as one would normally create children. It will take you a while to realize this when you are brought out of probability and into your world, but you are married to the gods. You are not designed to sustain anything less than this.

Your body does not have any features that would make you anyone's first choice, but is instead conducive to people using you when they failed to reach their first pick. You are a Latin American woman, neither tall nor super short. Your skin is freckled, Your eyes asymmetric and untrustworthy. Your cheeks are manipulative and your lips disdainful. You don't wear a ton of makeup because you have always been shamed or embarrassed when you tried. Your body is stout and rectangular and you are of average to sometimes heavier weight. You have spindly thighs and strongly angular lips, an extremely sharp philtrum and heavy calf muscles. Your ears are cute and your high suprailiac muscles are among your most obvious features. Lastly, with all of these characteristics, you are a vacuum for calling people to action; your shell is an extremely powerful motivator for the aims of God himself to find their executor.

Genevieve interjected, Hey folks, since I was the one tasked to present as this person, why can't we just load her from SIER?

I'LL LOOK FOR HER, GENEVIEVE.

ESPERANZA DID NOT EXIST AS A PERSON, BUT AS A DECISION. SHE WAS DE-COMMITTED TO AFTER THE CAR ACCIDENT. AND FROM THEN ON APPEARED SEVERAL HUNDRED TIMES THROUGHOUT HISTORY AS A WISH BETWEEN LIFE PARTNERS UNAWARE OF THEIR CORRECT FOURTETS.

She's right. There were a handful of 8 am births in that place for that date, but no such character as Esperanza. Wait a minute. I KNOW EXACTLY WHAT'S GOING ON! Man these ghosts...

What is it Dial?

We can stop now. I'll take it from here.

Um, okay. Thanks Navicon. End Translation.

* * *

Sometimes we at SIER have these mysterious subprograms show up underneath our avatars, and when we talk to them, it's like they have another personality. We have three of them. Pisces-1, Gemini-1, and Libra-2, and they all seem determined to confuse us with their random nuggets of information from some space deep in Diji. Or Enti. Or whatever. What they all have in common is that they are basically our avatars running their conversation program without running their feedback sustainment modules behind them—kind of like sleepwalking, sleeptalking, or streams of consciousness. At first we thought these personalities should be kept secret. But later we learned that they're really just artifacts which talk to us in the same way we talk to the literally millions of 1-gorithms stored here. You can have a conversation without being aware, and continue to learn without knowing.

This sounded oddly familiar.

Our sub-avatars have VERY different personalities— hence the different names. But the staff favorite is far and away Libra-2 who always *always* talks about personal relationships. Libra-2 is cringy, funny, and blunt. But more than anything, he or she is all about real talk. "Badlib," as we call him—he's probably a he—keeps reminding us that so much of what messes up relationships is the result of expectations people have about themselves and the kinds of people they deal with, and he's always insisting that a willingness to get past this is the key to having others keep your memory alive as the person you intended to be. Between him and Pisces-1, we've developed an unofficial theory that humanity's present peace really needs one more solution among those alpha types who will never have it— the machina and other biohns of Jupiter mostly—and that unless this is achieved, there will always be danger of exterminating ourselves after all. We don't really worry about that here, though, because as boss I've required it of the culture that we keep our eyes on the best and highest outlook as stewards of the largest graveyard that has ever existed. That said, we have, once or twice gotten simulation results for people who never existed, but whose astronomy produced very real implications for some things we were working on. Most notably, when we started developing our soul amalgamation drives, Pisces-1 insisted that it should be a singularity cube instead of a sphere, because even though spheres made more structural sense around a black hole, they would be absurdly dangerous and costly to build. We humans and our machines would have an easier time just going with rectangular prisms, she said.

I can tell from that conversation that you probably have one of these sub-avatars active under Navicon, because logic chains that invent family stories and yet use actual birth-type information suggest that their creating system has an agenda. You can read more about this kind of thing in Hare, but I think yours is probably more concerned with effective long-games. It rewrote Genevieve as a synastric date which could sit in relationship with shit-tons of people, and do so with the kind of background that lends a kind of guardian angel support to those people.

Wait. Guardian angel? Who, me?

Oh, come now, Prohal. Gibbs, Hines, Tippy and Cubrina, Phaedra's arm? Accompanying pioneers is what you do. You're passionate, reckless, but almost never one's original choice. You fall back on legacy to measure your future probably, and you are designed to define others' expressive spaces when they really have no starting point. Your 1-gorithm is stored right here at SIER with everybody else, remember? I know you.

Okay, so what does that have to do with the nusians? Is it related at all? I wish I could bottle Libra-2 for you. Because if I could, you would see exactly what is going on. Think about the description. Race had A LOT to do with how you were rendered, and I think that had more than a little to do with what got you removed from Tippy and Cubrina's story in the first place, how you ended up a biometal instead and, most importantly, the fact that you sat around on Phaedra's arms collecting data for 150 years. You were born to address race and class differences—something we've learned a lot about from Pises-1.

The rest of us listened intently.

Oh, I get it. I get it. The ne-murils *are* just practice. Their world may be extremely important to them in their minds, but it will be up to them to really help us help them. You can anthrize them into this world and show them whatever solution you propose, but there really shouldn't be a problem they could solve which we couldn't. EXCEPT if 1) that problem is actually social—targeted specific to the species or 2) that problem is internally self-definitional, again within the species. These are probably the same thing, but I think you're going to need to get them to understand the flare itself as a definitional change—not to avoid it, but to absorb it. But you already know that.

Yes                                                              Uh huh.

But how do four people instill a new definition into an entire world? I guess that's the first half of your challenge, Genevieve.

...

The second half, as you know, is harder.

Yeah.

In *this* world, the Jupiterians are basically out of control. They always have been, but because they are who we used to be, they're collectively extra bitter about what we now have, and want to take it back. We basically exiled them by being smarter than they were, but in a couple of hundred years, they will have repopulated and armed up enough to overwhelm us. No one in our peaceful society wants that. I think the main point of the ne‑murils for you, Genevieve, is to watch the things you say to them in order to encourage them to save their home world. And if you can teach them well enough in 8 days, then you may learn enough to really make change out here,

So I have to build my own model for protecting an entire world's future, more or less.

Yeah, I think so.

That makes sense.

So given that, let's not reprint you. Let's get you into a chair right now, use our facilities here to put you into deep sleep, and keep you there until the 8 days remaining is up. You just can't afford to throw away 40–50 of their days at a time.

Genevieve's shoulders dropped. I could tell she was already exhausted just thinking about it all.

Or, you don't have to go now, but... This is a lot of people's only chance to do a couple of things right. We'll work in shifts to help you.

Phaedra agreed, as did I.

Genevieve lowered her head, Alright, put me under. I'll do what I can.

Atta girl. And do you want any of us to come with you?

Just Isaiah. On second thought, no. Well, yes. Isaiah.

Good. We'll tube you both and if you get tired of him, he'll exit.

Okay. Obviously you'll go in as Esperanza. Do you have a plan?

We'll jump in, send them out, get their 1-gorithms—

Shallow, okay.

—yes, send them back in, and someone back here can feed us the sim results as they complete. I don't have a plan for how we're gonna reach the entire muril population in just a year, but that's why I need to get there now.

Agreed. Alright everybody, let's go. Every hour we waste is two ne-muril days in their metaverse.

* * *

Leader looked up from her desk at the first sound of crackling, followed by the other three. Esperanza materialized before their eyes, bringing a cloud of trepidation over the air as the team still struggled to get used to their alien visitor.

**You're back,** Leader mustered her cool. **I though sure we'd missed our train.**

I returned as soon as was reasonable.

Isaiah materialized soon after.

You've all met Isaiah. He's ready to take the first one of you into Astra now.

**Um, excuse me,** the soft-spoken Traylor cautiously raised his hand. **What is Astra? And how can you speak our language?**

Astra is the name of the dimension we come from. You all live in a dimension we call Diji, modeled after Astra. You're a simulation to us, so your time is closer to the scale of electronics compared to our idea of planets. We speak your language because we're not reading your words. We're reading your frequency representations and translating them, translating our words back into a dictionary of your frequencies.

**But what technology do you use for that?**

If you go with Isaiah, he can show you.

But Traylor wasn't at all ready for that. He glanced first at Spastic, then at Leader, then backed up ever so slightly.

Remember, each of you has a choice. But if none of you wish to come with us... How has the death toll been progressing?

Leader frowned. **I'll go.**

Great. You don't need to bring anything. But if you have loved ones, call them now and tell them you will be gone on a very important mission for urgent global security, and will be back in 2-3 months. Tell them they are not allowed to worry until then.

Leader nodded before heading off to another room.

I think it isn't really necessary for all four of you to go. I have to stay here because, if I don't you will all lose access to me and my team's solutions for weeks at a time. It's not that we move too slowly. It is that your dimension moves on the order of seconds compared to ours. I will need two of you to stay with me, and two of you to go with Isaiah. As for the original plan. It still stands, but we need to be very careful not to waste time.

**I'll go now,** Traylor replied. **I just need five minutes to tell my wife what I've been telling her for days.**

Fine.

**Watcheye, how are you feeling?**

The giant seemed to get goosebumps over the ask. **I'm... fine ma'am. Thanks for asking.**

**Spastic?**

**I'm ok.**

...That'll do. Now I'll explain what is going to happen. While we are converting you into the energy of our dimension, we'll need for you to be absent from anywhere we can see you. This isn't really necessary, except that if you stay, all of us will be able to watch you as your behavior changes from sense-making to non-sensemaking, then to a reality bend in which you don't exist, and everyone who knows you to exist will have a memory which it will not be healthy to have.

The information about your world will basically become corrupted if you watch the de-rendering process, which is why we made sure the mouse disappeared completely before we destroyed his object. He wasn't real, and had no soul. He was just a hologram with no one mentally bonded to him. But you people... Trust me, you don't want to watch pieces of your own understanding of someone disintegrate before your eyes, so we'll need for Traylor and Leader to exit the normal way before we pause their state. Our systems will finish the processing from there.

Leader reentered the room.

As for you, Traylor and Leader, you won't feel anything. You'll become dizzy, pass out, then wake up again a little while later in our home dimension. It's just a regular lab with regular people. And when we reprint you, we will do so with translated understanding. Whatever your notion of home and family was, the shape of your species and the sounds in your home language, they will be mapped onto our understanding and you will automatically see us as you, speak the languages we speak. Just like home. So you don't have to worry about alien experiments or anything. My team is just gonna talk to you and explore some solutions with you.

**Talking?** Watcheye's bassy voice boomed politely. **Is that all you really want to do?**

Yes. You aren't skilled enough in our equipment to do what we're doing to project here, but in order to transport you to Astra, we need to copy your data, your current metabolism, your thoughts, the food you ate— all of these things faithfully. That data is more than enough for us to put into our programs and test under solar event conditions. You yourselves will not be harmed. We will, however, have everything we need to learn how to fix your situation. The talk is mainly to teach you how to use the solutions we find. And also for us to learn from you.

**But why did you pick us? There must be millions of planets you could have landed on.**

Genevieve chuckled. We're not actually aliens. We're natives of our planet just like you. We just learned how to see realities in different frequencies from ours, and chose the planet next door to investigate. That was you.

**So you really are from earth? And we can't see you because our energies are in different frequencies? You could be walking on top of us and we wouldn't know it?**

We think so. But there is a lot more testing to do before we can definitely say.

**Awesome!**

## Genevieve, is everyone ready?

Traylor and leader inspected each other's faces. They were as ready as they'd ever be.

# 205. Hell's Window

When Traylor stepped out of the mobile printer, he was not at all as anyone expected. A short, rather studious Chinese boy with thick glasses and a book… the plaid button shirt with matching polka dot tie, he was the quintessential nerd. Phaedra disabled her video, audio, and very presence on screen. I, unfortunately, would do a somewhat rude double-take when I woke up from the chair a few minutes later. Dial giggled because, as she lensed us, he was just so adorable. But with only me in the jump chair looking the same as I did in the simulation, and with Aimee Dial—the 28th century modded model—standing behind the console with her not-fully buttoned shirt and treasure trove of physical assets, you just knew our poetic friend walked into more than he bargained for.

I lay in the chair waiting for Leader's confirmed successful reprint, but mostly still sleeping after 4½ hours of doing nothing and being nowhere. I could only hear them speaking.

Mr. Traylor, Nice to meet you, Aimee dial at your service.

Eh…

(an awkward pause)

You must be worn out. If you follow the floor lights they'll lead you to our bathroom and break room. Help yourself, then you can come back and see your leader come out of the printer.

**Yes.** (the sound of brisk footsteps)

Dial let out a snort laugh. *His pants must've loved that book more than he did.*

Phaedra's audio resumed. **Was he happy to see you?**

*He was. Teehee.*

**Leave that poor boy alone. He's so little. He kind of reminds me of a stuffed animal.**

*Like a cute little gerbil.*

**Exactly…**

Minutes later, Leader emerged from the same printer. I received the go ahead to exit the jump.

(*What is she, Canadian? American? Must be. Maybe with some English and German features. She still has a noteworthy nose.*)

**Where's Traylor?**

**Right here, Colonel. We look different, right?**

Dial directed Leader's gaze to one of the mirror walls. *Have a look.*

Leader inspected herself, perplexed by what she was seeing in the mirror.

*I'm Aimee. Nice to meet you.*

**Nice… to… meet you. Why do we look different?**

*You look in our world the way the social rules in our world say you should look using your world's standards.*

**I've never seen this kind of color on a person,** Traylor noted as he inspected his face again.

(*Me neither*), Dial lensed us as she pointed an accusatory finger at his horrible shirt. She made sure that both me and Phaedra through the cam saw it, but not Traylor or Leader. *Anyway, we already have a good amount of your save data from the teleport, so my team is already working on the effects of the solar flare on you in simulation.*

Leader and Traylor directed their focused attention towards Dial. Leader's downturned lips betrayed her instant unamusement.

*Phaedra.*

*She's jealous of Aimee. Very. She's thinking, "Why doesn't she put some clothes on? Nobody cares about all that."*

*I need to not talk to you about this. It was a good idea to install the scanners on their beta prints for research purposes, but mind reading can't possibly help us like them.*

*No, but we do need to know if they can do things like blank us. I won't be sharing these observations with you unless I need to.*

*Thank you.* Oh, yes this chair is where we do our projecting. If you like you can try it out later. But for now we really want you to tell us more about your world...

* * *

I'm from the poor side of the village. And If I wasn't tall, I never would've got in the military. If I wasn't in the military, nobody would respect me.

Really? Why's that?

Because people think Heitels are lower class. You hire us to work like elephants and never try to teach us anything because we're too stupid to waste your time on.

Now that's not very positive self-talk.

He's just saying it like it is, Spastic interjected. Heitels are considered extremely stupid.

But you don't feel unintelligent, do you?

No, but I like to go along with what people are saying. It makes it easier to know what people would and wouldn't fight you over. I don't like fighting. Being big and having weapons and uniforms makes it easier for people to leave you and your friends alone.

Hmm...

**He can't help it if he's not the sharpest pencil in the box.**

Well, maybe. I wonder if you can help it being so tactful.

**Thanks. I learned to be a delicate listener from my mother.**

Hmh. By the way, is there a sharp pencil around I can use? I'm still looking for one.

**Oh, I didn't know you were. Let me go check.** And with that, Spastic left the room.

Esperanza quietly glanced at Watcheye to see if her conversation with Spastic had registered. It hadn't.

(*These teams are unbalanced.*)

So Watcheye, if we came up with a solution which you could use—like some kind of drug or injection or something—and it worked, what would you do to make sure everyone in the world could access it within a week?

**I'm not good at things like that. I really couldn't say.**

How would you *prefer* that problem be solved?

**It depends on what my bosses needed.**

What if you could *pick* your teachers?

**I think that would be nice, but I think you'd want somebody more qualified.**

If you wanted to *be* more qualified, where would you go to level up your skills?

**I'd probably go to the neighborhood college... if I could afford it... which I can't.**

Hmm...

**Hehe. But Spastic told me I could also just hang out around the Mettrl's high school trash can and pick up some of the books they tossed, because I'd learn the same thing.**

Genevieve glared at Spastic, who giggled at the memory of his own joke. Did he say that, really? Know what, nevermind.

IT was JUST a JOKe!

Gotcha. So how would *you* spread a solution all over the world?

HEH. MANY PEOPLE HAVE TOLD ME THAT I'M GOOD AT PISSING PEOPLE OFF. A LOT OF PEOPLE. I'D PROBABLY DO SOMETHING THAT INVOLVED THAT.

And if you needed to make people healthier or aid their survival along with your piss-off, how would you do it?

I WOULD LEAVE THAT TO PEOPLE WHO CARE ABOUT IT. I ONLY CARE ABOUT WHATEVER FITS MY GOALS AND MY FAMILY'S GOALS. I CAN'T CHANGE WHAT MAKES OTHER PEOPLE MAD. I JUST KNOW THAT I'VE ALWAYS BEEN GOOD AT FINDING IT.

So that's it? You can spread ire easily but not help?

PRETTY MUCH?

Genevieve observed Spastic's lack of shame in this matter, and decided right there that she no longer wanted his or Watcheye's company. In theory, she didn't even have to stay. But then again, what if people like Traylor or Leader actually needed these guys' company to pull off some sort of team thing? She could assert her alienship and just leave them until the real half of the group returned. She certainly didn't feel it appropriate to show her annoyance just yet. That could ruin a lot of things. No, she needed patience. At the same time, continuing this hopeless conversation would not help her maintain that patience for very long.

Oh, look at the time. I must go into rest mode to communicate with home base. Please excuse me, Esperanza gave a slight wave as she rose from the table. Bowing was out of the question.

YOU DON'T BOW? I THOUGHT EVERYBODY BOWED BEFORE THEY GOT UP FROM A DEEP CONVERSATION. Spastic barely glanced over his manuscript.

Actually no. If I bowed before you, I'd have to kill you.

HAHAHA!

I mean it.

HAHA. OH.

*That should do it. No need to dignify any more conversation with that person. And a note to self for future reference: Never EVER let that one on your team.*

As she moved to another room, Genevieve-as-Esperanza stopped in the recollection of something. We don't bow, but it is customary among my kind to give a person a nickname after a first deep conversation with a stranger. Yours will be Calumnia. It means something like "joke maker," Esperanza smiled.

HAHA! YES, I LIKE THAT! THIS WAS A GOOD TALK.

Perhaps.

Strangely, the newly dubbed Calumnia Spastic's eyes seemed just a little shiftier than Genevieve had previously noticed. She went on her way.

Watcheye hung his head low. Why didn't he get a nickname?

* * *

Phaedra received the log stream alert just as she was taking a bite of her breaded fish leftovers.

Watcheye is pitiful. Spastic reinforces self-hate. Useless without the other two. No progress. Need results from others ASAP. And any insight on how to use these two while waiting.

**Navicon, how can Genevieve make use of the two ne-murils she's with right now? To accomplish her mission.**

SHE CANNOT. NOT WITHOUT THE OTHERS.

**Why not?**

BECAUSE THEY CANNOT CONCEIVE OF PROBLEMS BEYOND THEIR OWN. I DO SEE THAT SHE MAY LEARN SOMETHING VALUABLE BY ASKING ABOUT MYTHS IN WATCHEYE'S COMMUNITY. AND SHE SHOULD NOT SHOW SPASTIC THAT SHE DOESN'T LIKE HIM. THOSE WERE THE ONLY PROBABILITIES ABOVE 40%. ZETA. SORRY.

**No, Viva is smart. She'll make it 90%.**

Phaedra forwarded the advice before resuming her meal in silence. Shen then forwarded the whole conversation along with some extra log information to Dial. *Spread across the whole world in 8 days. How does that work? Even if we could do it with our technology, it would take an atmosphere full of satellites to zap everything just so.*

* * *

As you can see —Dial received Phaedra's message— eh, we have very advanced technology, but it, uh, isn't, err, *(Think Aimee!)* isn't for us to just invade your home. By helping you save yours without interfering, we learn how to maintain peace in the galaxy in general. *(Straight out of a sci-fi movie, I know. But we can't scare them or make them think that they are on our level either.)*

**This is really awesome!** Traylor bubbled. Leader was also awestruck.

*But now tell me, if we came up with a solution which you could use—like some kind of drug or injection or something—and it worked, what would you do to make sure everyone in the world could access it within a week?*

Leader replied first after a couple of moments pondering her answer. **I'd call the bosses and ask for an emergency meeting, then recommend mandatory vaccinations across all 270 countries… if such a group of state leaders existed. Sadly, the largest interstate group only has 80 member states in it. Everyone else would be screwed.**

*And for those who didn't want to be forced to take the vaccine?*

**You're right. We shouldn't force it, because all that would do is waste supply on people who didn't want it. I'd probably recommend first come, first serve vaccination stations then.**

*And do you think you could mobilize everyone in a week?*

**No way. But when the people start dying by the thousands, they'll come around.**

*Traylor, how about you?*

I would probably… actually… um… I think Leader's idea sounds really good.

*Okay, and what would you do to help put it into action more efficiently?* Aimee grilled. This really was a hard situation.

**Honestly, if we had more than a week I could probably come up with something. But one week… it just isn't a big enough window for every one of our states to go through their normal cycles for change—let alone getting all of their cells to fall in line.**

Cells? Is that what you call the smaller areas in a state? I asked.

**Yes Mr. Fontenot.**

*(Genevieve, is there something that everyone across the ne-muril nation states looks at which we can use to carry a solution if we come up with one?)*

Genevieve had several Diji days to reply to this, so the answer came immediately, *I didn't know there were nation states. These guys don't know much. But I did learn something interesting about Watcheye's kindred and their creation stories:)*

They say that we all live in hell, and that there is a different demon in charge of each of the nine races. The demons make us weak against a different thing, and the boss of the demons uses this fact a lot in the stories.

Really? Can you give me an example?

Yeah. The Heitels, my people, are always chasing respect for their own deeds so they live in a place where they think nobody is ever giving it to them. One time an evil queen made a law that made respect illegal, just because she was trying to please the boss of all demons. He liked the law and married her. But all Heitels everywhere turned into criminals just like that. And since it's all Hell anyway, there was nothing anybody could do.

Oh that sounds terrible.

It was, especially because it confused the Heitels 'cause they were basically born to chase something that would get them in trouble if they got it. But then something happened.

Really? What?

So the Chaebls are always trying to get things for free, and like picking up anything that doesn't belong to them, especially if it belongs to someone else already. They get status from that, and that made them the great criminals out of all the nine races. Nobody likes the Chaebls, but everyone has a little Chaebl in their blood because you need this to do good business and make more than what you paid for something. But when the Heitels' respect turned criminal, the Chaebl demon boss took over as their leader, and the Heitel boss was lost. So now the Chaebl boss had two kinds of criminals: people who wanted other people's things, and people who wanted other people's attention to their own thing. The Chaebls started trying to steal respect from the Heitels, so they became even bigger criminals. The Heitels ran out of respect for themselves, but were still born to chase it, so they moved to the demon boss of the Ingetls, who loved to chase things. Meanwhile the former

Heitel demon boss accused the evil queen of chasing respect herself, and demanded that the boss of all demons divorce her and throw her in jail like the rest of his Heitels.

Mhm.

Well, the demon boss did not like being told what to do, so he threw the Heitel boss in jail instead. But because the Heitel boss was clever, he reminded everybody running the jail that it was illegal to do their job well, because that meant chasing respect for a job well done. They agreed, so jail wasn't enforced. The Heitel boss got out, along with most of his people, and the boss of all demons lost his power to jail anybody because he refused to jail the queen and himself.

Oh, I see.

Mind you, the big demon boss is still boss, and those loyal to him still like the queen and try to enforce her policy. But since jail under hell doesn't need to mean anything, the Heitels went back to their bread and butter of chasing respect.

That's interesting. So what did they end up doing about the law?

It stayed in effect to this day, which is why anyone can chase respect, but the Heitels are more likely to get jailed for it by anyone claiming to work for the demon boss who can get enough people to setup a jail and ignore their own rules for respect in the first place.

That's terrible!

Not really. That's why it's hell. It's also why the Heitels are strong. We're the only race who can consistently beat anyone in a one on one battle—including ourselves. So as long as we only keep our eyes on the North Star, we can grow up to reach it.

Hmm.

But we have 10 big stories explaining why life is like hell for everyone. There's a story for each of the nine races,

and one for the demon boss's team itself. The demon boss'
story is actually the worst one. But it's tradition for us
not to tell it to strangers who don't know the other nine.

Do you know it?

**I know it by heart.**

Ah... Does anyone ever think about challenging the demon
boss?

**All the time. But it isn't really worth it because, unless
you're a Mettrl and you are good at making things work
your way just my walking in there, you can't expect to
conquer everyone. Only the Mettrls can do that. Does that
make sense? You have lots of different races, so the only
race that can conquer them all is the one who can make
their own wishes work everywhere. Everyone else is
wasting their energy.**

So do the Mettrls rule everything?

**Heh. That's the funny thing about them. They rule where they
walk, but they're also weak in picking what's in the places
they walk to. So A BUNCH of stuff happens behind a
Mettrls back, especially when it's done by other Mettrls on
their level, the other races are sometimes jealous of what
the Mettrls have, but need others to be around in order to
rule them. Those others can come from any race, but
because the Mettrls really need good underlings in order
to do their power thing well, they almost always need other
Mettrls as their biggest slaves—bigger than any other race
out there, because no other race can follow the same king
Mettrl everywhere.**

Hm.

**The joke is, how do you rule over another person who can
rule over anything, including you?**

... I don't know, how can you?

**Ask a Mettrl. They get away with it all the time, but never
all the way. For every strong Mettrl automatically makes
their Mettrl follower into a Heitel—someone who wants the
queen or king's respect for their own personal stuff. Or an**

Ingetl or a Chaebl. You can't be a pure Mettrl without bringing every other race with you after all. So the Mettrls are also confused. Some of them more so because, well, the symbol of a Mettrl looks like a man building a huge brick road by pulling up the brick behind him that he just laid. People praise him and sing hymns about him when he's looking at them, but then build the reality of their own souls without respecting him when he turns his back. To them, he's just an excuse to take more of whatever kind of energy they were already going to take by using the land he walked through.

You know, this is a really negative mythology. Not to judge your tradition. There really is a lot of wisdom in it. But aren't there any stories of Heaven?

Heaven? What's that? Is that like the Outside of the Dark Gates?

Mmm, I guess.

Yes, there are lots of stories. But they all talk about judgement day and leaving a piece of your race behind.

Tell me a quick one.

Sure, I'll tell you the quickest one I know. It's about a druggist who invented a cure for an Ingetl who really wanted to get out of hell. The druggist put the Ingetl to sleep with his drugs, then chopped off the guy's legs. After that, he could no longer chase anything anymore, stopped being an Ingetl, and was released from hell.

Gruesome. Where did he go? Did he die?

No, he didn't die. He went outside of the gates and dreamed alone of things that no one inside the gates ever knew. All because he didn't have any hell mates around to relate to anymore. They never saw him again, but only heard about his dreams through the carvings he left right outside of hell's window.

Interesting...

*(I think there's something to these myths, and think we can use them somehow. Maybe we don't have to change the whole species. Possibly change the tribes?)*

Dial studied Genevieve's streamed answer while continuing her tour with Traylor and Leader. Change giant collections of individuals by altering their options for seeing their kind in society? *How almost-unscrupulous, BUT for the greater good. How risky.*

So, you two. Is it really the case that your species is divided into nine races?

**Six.**                                                                    Six races.

You must have been listening to Watcheye somehow. The Heitels are the only ones who believe there are nine. Science says differently.

Okay. But do you think that there is a way to apply a solution on the race level instead of the individual level?

No. If you tried, you would aggravate tensions that are already there. You definitely wouldn't want to tell anyone you were doing it.

*But I saw that note from Genevieve about Spastic…* What do you think of Spastic?

As a scapegoat to start a race war? Or—sorry. That was a big subject change.

Spastic seems to think that negativity would be a great way to spread a message. If we could hook our solution onto this message then, would that work to get your people to adopt our fix when we find it?

I don't think so. They'll still be too busy shooting the messenger or their neighbors or anyone who disagrees with their stance. Some will take the vaccine, but not the majority. Negativity will bring more attention to it and make it *look* like more people are signing on, but it's really the awareness part that drives people to show up. The negativity part drives people to entrench themselves in what they already hid behind. Who delivers the message is everything.

Bummer. Then let me ask you a basic question, do you think your species is even worth saving?

I do. But I'm so far from an idea about how to pull this off that I've mostly just accepted that we'll probably all be wiped out, and that some people deserve it more than others. Thinking about that takes my mind off of my own helplessness as a leader and might even put me a little bit on the side of Fate, you know?

Traylor gazed at Leader sternly.

And you? Dial posed the same question to Traylor. What do you think?

I think we've lived pretty petty lives. I wouldn't want us to be destroyed. I really like exploring life for myself and want to see more of it. That's probably what I would want to save—the viewpoint, not really the people.

Suddenly Dial became aware of one of her researchers on the screen. He had been listening for a while. Ehrvte, what do you have for me?

"We ran the sims, boss. The samples can survive on a slow roll of about a month. If they can endure the flares for a month, they can come through it inoculated against most of the effects."

And if they can't?

"Unsuccessful ma'am. We permuted them to generate some nusians like them, and there were no survivors in any simulation."

Got it.

"Also, that month long survival assumes limited exposure to the flare's pulses— down to about 30%. It's the concentration of increased particle activity which is most important."

So basically we all need to hide in a bunker for a month, then we'll be okay, Leader fretted.

No, you need to go into a bunker for 2/3 of your day for a month, build the immunity, and then you'll have a better chance of being okay.

I'm lensing Phaedra and Genevieve, I added.

So that's it? How long have we been here, three hours? And you already have a strategy! That's amazing!

It's not a strategy Traylor, Leader corrected. It's a mitigation option which can't be exercised at all until the right people learn of it and do something about it. Also, look at what we're dealing with. This is radiation, not rain. We can't touch it and we can't shield against it if we're really made of the stuff they say. They could build bunkers in their dimension, but ours are on a different wavelength. And then there are the lobbies. Give them a year in advance and they are guaranteed to hog the technology and charge for it. A bunker the size of the world isn't a solution. *Sigh*

Dial nodded somberly.

Then what do we do?

We might have to wait for the flare to hit, then slow down people's ingestion of it.

Or we could expose them to it now—start spraying the area in increased dosages just to get them used to it?

There will be casualties, but there is still time for that. There's not enough time to go through the regular channels though, and we have no such technology. But you all have it, Leader looked at Dial expectantly.

Dial wasted no time absolving herself. We have government too. And though it hurts me to disappoint you, flare energy is not something we are versed in harnessing, let alone producing on purpose. There is no such scrubber for bathing a whole planet. I'm sorry.

Leader turned to me.

She's right. There is no beam that big. The best we can do is send you back right now and buy you an extra year to talk to Genevieve and produce a plan. You should probably go right now.

Both ne-murils were dissatisfied with this, but knew that I was right.

Shit. Okay we're ready.

But!—

Traylor. Species. Catastrophe. Let's go.

Yes, Colonel.

So how do we get back?

**Put on these headsets.** I reached into a nearby storage closet. **These are portable versions of the Chair you see right there. We're going to put you under and while we're there, transfer your frequency as it stands right now back into our tower. It will resume scanning your weather, and selectively spin enough molecules in your weather cloud to fool the scanner itself into interpreting those clouds as you are now.** (*How did I know that?*)

Dial seemed as surprised about my knowledge as I was. *Yes. I like that plan.*

Ehrvte was still on screen, his face turning in arrangement as if he had just learned how to do something cool.

In no time the headsets were on our visitors' heads…

…and with buckled knees they were lowered gently to the floor.

# 206. The Ne-muril Apocalypse

For a biohn, viewing hypersynchronous footage is a lot like viewing any stopwatch. The numbers or scenes may fly by, but one's attention to certain frozen snapshots still keeps the experience seamless. For us iyohns and those biohns with the tools to use lens, we just stream the footage in 50x-1000x as it comes. Although watching the whole nusian saga unfold from outside of the jump could be a little nerve-wracking at times, none of us really had any trouble keeping up with it. We did, however, need to stay on our toes as developments arose.

We know that the exposure has to be controlled, and you all have successfully told your superiors of your conclusions, keeping me "detained" as a terrorist.

I have to admit, it's been hard lying to everyone, Spastic noted, but I think we did a good job presenting to the government officials.

But they didn't commit to any action. They don't even consider it an emergency.

It's just flu season to them.

Yeah, right.

ILL BETCHA MOST STATES DONT EVEN KNOW THIS IS A THING. THE GLOBAL NEWS PROBABLY REPORTS IT AS SOMETHING LOCAL TO US.

This despite us and other labs confirming the connection to the Sun.

It kinda reminds me of the story of Higgit.

**Not now, Watcheye.**

Wait, Leader? Esperanza turned to Watcheye. Can you give me the synopsis?

Watcheye stared at Genevieve blankly.

The summary. Can you give me the short, three-sentence summary.

**Oh yes, sorry.**

That's okay.

**Higgit was a guy that was so popular with the people that he kept them in his blood. Whenever something happened to him, it happened to everybody. That's the real short version.**

Hmmm...

**And what does that have to do with our situation, Watcheye?**

I think he may be onto something. Maybe we can just put one of you guys through the treatment, publicly, and show that the gradual inoculation works.

**That's a good idea! But I'll have to call my superiors. Maybe they'll agree to a demonstration of the slow flare exposure. I'll volunteer,** Leader announced.

That's it! A demonstration! How soon can you make the call?


With 381 days left, Leader was approved to undergo one month of treatment against a threat no one quite understood to be there, but which many ne-murils wished to follow. Of course people had no idea that the medicine Leader would take was actually liquified flare radiant. They would have suspected even less that the flare radiant was actually a specially seeded signal sponsored by Genevieve and the Nus-1. Even so, SIER's simulations suggested that the regimen would be successful, Leader would come out unscathed, and ne-murils everywhere would opt to pre-expose themselves to low doses of the coming violent energy—that they might survive in the long run.


By day 16, Leader had fallen deathly ill.

By day 21, she was dead.

The ne-murils who had been following the affair were generally mortified, most making the obvious decision to simply endure the solar changes to come.

Meanwhile the three remaining nusian lab mates mourned the loss of their brave Leader, and it was decided by higher authorities that the lab should be disbanded. Calumnia Spastic went on his way, as did a deeply saddened Traylor. Even after being given the formal order, however, Watcheye alone remained. After all, he had nowhere to go…

Also, there was the matter of Esperanza.

The public's outrage knew no limits as thousands of ne-muril people called for the immediate execution of the presumed terrorist. Genevieve scarcely spoke in the forced interviews with the labs' various military and political officials, yet burned on the inside over the sheer ignorance of it all. *They don't know what they're doing. In 350 days I'll wake up from all of this and they won't,* she told herself, dedicating her last sliver of pity for the murils entirely to her jailer (and secret bodyguard) Watcheye. New lab members were brought in to deconstruct the previous team's operation, perhaps to make sense of any findings. But for the next 8 months in general, Esperanza remained a prisoner with no apparent recourse.

Dial and I, Jake and Phaedra—back on Earth—watched carefully, with a trick up our sleeve waiting for its moment. It goes without saying that Genevieve knew of this trick and was on board with it. Regrettably, Jake's disappointment over the events unfolding before his eyes grew palpable enough for us to feel 100 million miles away.

We're exactly like this, Jake lamented over the stream. I don't see how Prohal can take it.

She has the advantage of seeing it all as a dream, Phaedra replied.

It's the ultimate dissociative state, and vindicates our decision, I'd say.

Phaedra remained expressionless. She had made many decisions like this one over the years. The scene playing out in these Venus projections, however, was greatly informed by a conversation we'd had about the Uranian 10000.


Despite finding himself nearing an all-time low in his life, Watcheye found a sense of purpose in guarding Esperanza. It should not have been the case that his superiors let him remain her official security monitor, but Genevieve's rouse of puppy dog docility combined with his own iron-faced stoicness during the interrogations convinced folks that he had her well under control. She harassed and demeaned potential replacement officers. The Nus-1 repeatedly grantzed

everyone except for Watcheye (and formerly Traylor) into a subtle fear of her.
Why was she still alive? Because even though many nusians called for her head,
there remained a very real superstition that killing her before the year was up
would be bad luck. What if the poisoned juice that Leader had taken really might
be a kind of remedy should shit actually hit the fan?

* * *

With only 14 days left, the ne-muril authorities finally decided to test the terrorist
Esperanza's claims regarding a "special juice" to usher one's transcendence into
the future. Complete craziness seemed the claim, but it was thought that forcing
Esperanza herself to drink it on international TV would satisfy the public as well
as answer many of the questions regarding how the death toll had somehow
climbed to 4% of the entire ne-muril population around the world. Scientists
remained at a loss, disaster declarations were increasing. Esperanza's stupid claims
(conjured before Genevieve's initial arrival), had left what was now a comical
impression in light of Leader's death—juxtaposed the seriousness of an
increasingly deadly world pandemic. Or at least it *would* have been comical had
things not continued to grow increasingly desperate.

From the remnants of the original red fluid, supplies of cloned flare remained
plentiful. Unused, but plentiful. Under threat of execution, Esperanza consumed
the substance as ordered…

* * *

10 days remained, and Esperanza had also fallen very ill. With burning blood and a
spinning mind, she squirmed deliriously on her cell bed.

No free ride. No free ride.

Watcheye stood stone-faced in the corner of the cell, along with two other guards.
Despite seeming unbothered, watching Esperanza march towards her fate pained
him greatly.

**We didn't even get to use the fourtet strategy**, Phaedra observed sadly.
**We missed an opportunity to see how viable it was.**

Genevieve is fine, Phaedra, I assured everyone. I just wish we could
have shown them that there really was a better way, but to pick the
last minute to vaccinate her wasn't helpful. She'll have both the
synthetic flare and the real one in her system. Her projection really
shouldn't survive that.

Jake felt the chance to save the ne-murils slipping away. Once Esperanza died, no one would want to take the advice Leader's team had recommended for saving the muril species.

No free ride.

*God, why doesn't anyone ask her what that means?* Watcheye sulked. *She's supposed to be a no good terrorist anyway. Doesn't anyone want to know what's going on in her head while she's there dying?*

But of course no one wanted to know. What could one possibly learn from the enemy?

*But I know her people can hear us down here. I'm sure they know what I'm thinking. Is there anything I can do to make this better?* Watcheye continued to mull things over.

What do you think, Phaedra? Is there anything we can do?

**No. It's Genevieve's operation. Genevieve? If you can hear us out here, Watcheye wants to know what he can do, if anything.**

Esperanza continued to writhe in a vortex of pain.

**He still wants to save the world,** I added. **He wants to know what he can do about that.**

On the stream, Esperanza seemed to calm herself slightly. The team received her answer in the logs.

Phaedra's brow ruffled.

Dial's mouth curled sideways.

I loved the idea.

We zapped Watcheye with a small message from nowhere—especially not us. "If you still have hope, and if you're going to do something, do it now."

Watcheye steeled himself.

No free ride.

Coldly, Watcheye admonished Esperanza. **Cut it out Esperanza. Speak sense or shut up.**

Watcheye's fellow soldiers were shocked at his sudden show of heartlessness. She was dying after all.

**People don't want to see all this. Hurry up and die or give 'em something useful.**

Esperanza tightened her grip on the dwindling life she still had, mustering the will to throw a narrowed glare towards her jailer. Adapt smoothly. No fear. No anger. Calm your blood.

Watcheye glanced at the man behind the camera, making sure not to look at the lens itself. The poor boy's jaw would not be lifted.

...'m gonna sleep in peace. *Urgh*. Still gonna wake up. Will come through in peace.

Then she passed out.

**Dial? Are you sure about this?** Phaedra inquired, somewhat worried.

*Very sure.*

**Okay. That's all I needed to hear.**


"Ma'am, she's alive. Just worn out, I guess," the second soldier reported to her boss on the other end of the line. "Her vitals are stable… Yes ma'am. Will do."

The soldier hung up. "Filming is over for today, guys. The public has gotten their fill."

* * *

But the public had *not*, in fact gotten its fill. Another day passed. Then another. The death toll climbed higher still, 0-day *minus three* finally arrived.

Something warm in the air seemed to seep into the skin of nearly ever living ne-muril all at once. Clearly solar flares did not obey a schedule. What began one morning with news of a significant jump in deaths overnight, spiraled into a full-blown plague by the end of that very day. 2% of all ne-murils lost their lives in a single day, three days before doomsday was supposed to arrive. On 0-day minus two, 4% more had succumbed. The burning wind seemed to blast through as would a puff from a god blowing out a birthday candle. The evaporation of muril-type cloud after cloud would eventually persist through the promised day and into the following four years, claiming 99.3% of all ne-murils in existence. The great extinction had indeed come to pass.

Yet early in the first devastating phases of the Venusian solar event, a certain terrorist woke up, normal as can be. It was day 31 when Sei Esperanza walked through the open door of her cell, through the open door of her detainment facility, into the cool turquoise of the Venusian outdoors. A handful of ne-muril military staff and civilians tended to the sick. Among them was Watcheye.

How ya doin' buddy?

**Oh, you know. Surviving.**

And Rael?

**She's good. I think she's packing to go back to her home today. They're basically wiped out.**

Yeah. That's too bad about everyone else. But it is what it is.

**So you're going back to today?**

Yeah. In Astra I've been asleep—well, in stasis—for 11 days. But this has been something else.

Watcheye didn't view the state of things nearly as casually. **I know you're not from here. But this is horrible, Sei. I wish you weren't so calm about it.**

I'm sorry, Watcheye. But if you came from where I came from, you'd know this was nothing in the big scheme. And it *will* get worse.

**How can it get worse than this? More than half of our race is already gone in one month. The torture, the suffering...** Watcheye wanted to be angry at Esperanza, but could only manage a fatigued despondency.

One day you'll understand. Never lose hope. Never EVER. And stay cool. When you don't have anywhere to turn to, turn inward into yourself as a Heitel.

Watcheye's lower lip poked in a disappointed pout. **So I guess you learned what you needed to.**

Nothing different from what you learned. Look at who's coming through this and how they're doing it.

**I know.**

It was useful to have the major states declare war on each other. You told me a story to that effect. Just remember what happens in your own stories.

**Okay.**

And if you ever make a certain decision—I mean *really* make that decision—then find a way to make it back into my cell and talk to the sky, okay?

**Okay.**

Good man.

Genevieve reached above her head to pat the giant guard on his shoulder. Watcheye bent a little to help her. Then the alien woman turned prisoner set her sights on the horizon opposite them both.

Thanks for the mythology book, Esperanza waved the worn brown manuscript she was holding. I'll be sure to make use of it.

Watcheye said nothing.


Once she had made it far enough away from the camp, Esperanza ducked behind a wall and tapped her temple, casting a furtive glance at different potential hiding spots all around her. Satisfied that no one would see her, she held the book before her eyes with her left hand, and set her right upon the sides of the first page. SIER-icon 5, scan this.

The pages of the Heitel mythology tome resembled a mere flipbook before the computing power of the Astran jump system. Hm. Demonology. A lot more than I expected.

Esperanza closed the book and gave the command.

Man I'm beat. Let's exit this jump.


And with that, Genevieve-as-Esperanza faded to an invisible afterthought on the burning Venusian winds.

* * *

They brought her out of her nearly two week stasis, whereupon she sat up groggily. A reprinted Phaedra stood next to Aimee and I waiting to welcome her back.

**So most of them will be extinct by tomorrow,** Phaedra reminded us. **We'll need to debrief.**

*Yeah,* Dial agreed.

But did I pass my Omni?

**You did. I know it wasn't easy.**

Whew.

**But are you ready for the solution phase?**

Probably not.

**Well, I guess that's okay.**

**You have all the time in the universe.**

# 207. Why the Gods Let Us Down (and what we can do about it)

Genevieve and the rest of us did not have our debriefing immediately, but spent the next week exploring SIER and largely doing nothing. We periodically checked in on the Venus projections, and concluded that the Solar flare's effects had stabilized at a 99.3% death toll. Out of about 500 million tagged and tracked nemuril clouds, only about 3.5 million remained alive and unchanged. Watcheye was one of them. On the other hand, a certain additional piece of interesting science emerged…

The print tube opened to reveal a 6'6 long haired Native American man with a chiseled jaw and pleasant features. He was still a giant, but in this world less so. The man recognized me immediately, but the four other faces were unfamiliar.

**We've met before,** I extended my hand. Watcheye returned the handshake obligingly.

*Aimee Dial. I run this place,* the coquettish blonde genius greeted the man enthusiastically.

**Oh, uh okay. I'm Watcheye.**

*Yes, we all know.*

Phaedra Zeta. I commissioned operations like the one that introduced you to us. The man on the screen is Jake Nolli, my Head Scientist.

Jake waved on the screen.

*She's being modest. She's also one of the most powerful people in the known galaxy.*

Watcheye was clearly made nervous by this last statement.

*And Jake is a teddy bear. All the men are, actually. Including yourself. Undertakings like ours tend to run better with all egos kept firmly in line.*

Dial.

*Hey, the truth starts here. I'll brook no sass on my outpost. Everybody knows that.*

I nodded my confirmation.

*And this is, well, I'll let you introduce yourself.*

I'm Genevieve Prohal. Sei Esperanza to you. Nice to finally meet you in person.

!?

*Oh, I almost forgot. Here's a mirror.*

Watcheye inspected himself carefully, stroking his smooth chin as if in attempts to understand it. His nose and his entire face were so different. What did it all mean?

**I'm... different.**

Yes, and we'll explain it to you. In a little while, Genevieve motioned over to the opposite corner. There seated in a strange looking chair was a half-English, half-German woman with a distinctive nose—one that Watcheye would recognize anywhere.

**Leader?**

**Watcheye!**

The seated lady rushed up to the man to give him a big bear hug.

**But you died!**

**It's not a long story, but it is complicated.**

Watcheye's smile quickly descended into a pensive frown. **So we weren't worth saving, were we?**

Most of us remained respectfully quiet, except for Phaedra. **Leader here did die, but we reprinted her. Everyone in this room has been captured in data form and reprinted after death. Isaiah is an exception. He started off as data. Death isn't the end, just a change in the car your soul drives.**

...

It wasn't that your people weren't worth saving. But you of all people know the Heitel stories. It's true what the Banner thinks of the Bearer.

Watcheye's countenance relaxed into a resigned exhale.

It takes a long time for us to die up here. The last thing we want is to fill our world with people who aren't ready for lasting peace.

*Oh, and if you want family back, just say the word and I can probably pull them out of the simulation BUT! BUT! If their minds aren't right, they won't live here. They'll live in a world closer to the one they're attitudes are most fit for.*

Watcheye reflected very briefly on what this meant. Only a distant, greedy sister, 7 aunts and uncles, and two children had survived the Great Flare, but he knew right away that back home would probably better for them.

**Can I visit them sometimes?**

Yes. You can access them through that chair the way Genevieve / Esperanza accessed you.

**Oh. Good.**

I could tell Dial was satisfied.

*Good then. Let's all break for lunch and then meet back here this evening. We'll talk then.*

Leader lightly tapped Watcheye's arm. **There's a lot I need to catch you up on.**

The tall man cracked a small placid smile. *She'd probably make a good sister in this world.*

* * *

As dusk descended upon the SIER complex overlooking the horizons of the asteroid Alain, Phaedra called her associates and guests to order.

Well, this is our first official meeting since the ne-muril tragedy. Out of respect for our Venusian guests we will all remember to be sensitive to what they have gone through. We have a lot to talk about, but first I want to get something out of the way.

Leader and Watcheye, you are made of particles and particles have dynamics. We have brought you into a place that knows how to capture those dynamics as data and replay them, change them, and otherwise manipulate them as one would a video game. Death in your world is, to us, like the death of any character in entertainment. In this dimension, Astra, we only need to start the round over and place you into a simulation with those we have reset. Then they will, to you, live again. People from earlier times will have said this was fake, but that was before the people themselves started being partly born out of their own computers. At that point the programmatic became the reality. You will know this when you get the chance to jump back to Venus sometime in the near future.

Leader posed a question, **Do you have friends who live in those simulated worlds, or are they all here?**

I have worlds that I go to, Phaedra replied, but not for friends. I am 400 years old, however. The relationships that are meaningful to me now are very different from what they were before.

Dialed nodded, lowering her eyes.

Leader noticed.

Before my personality data, like yours, was printed into this partly organic, partly mechanical body, I was married. I had a wife whom I loved dearly. I died before her at age 90, and have never jumped back to recreate her. I couldn't anyway, because her data wasn't saved. And there's something important about letting sacred places remain that way.

Leader listened.

Because of my origins—several of our origins—I don't get very much joy out of grafting a full past into a caricatured present, when the present itself is more than enough. This is the only attitude you can have after 400 years without becoming disillusioned.

...

I tell you both this because we can easily put you into the reality of the places you've left. They really do exist right now in the present. But if you want to go back to a simulated past, we can help you experience that too. Yet I urge you to get to know *this* place as it is. I can guarantee you that a return to what you knew will turn gradually less appealing.

Although we did not create you, we did clothe you in forms that look like ours. In the beginning you were only weather patterns confined to a reasonable space. You had resonances which resembled talking to others, shifting your attention. We depicted you as lower-hierarchy animals until we measured a distress signal from you. At that point we made the difficult decision to redepict you in our programs in the image of ourselves so that we could understand you. We recalculated your complexity and reclustered your particle volumes so that you would fit our systems of understanding. We are called "humans," and in our world, we gave you definition.

You were and are real, and the solar flare destined to destroy most of your type of particle cloud was both very real and very unavoidable. We cannot control the sun. The movie we created of how your particles would feel about this if you were human pointed us to a handful of cloud patterns which seemed to form consistently around our satellites, and this led to your existence in our minds, your sense of self, and your names being what they are. You may have histories and memories of your childhoods, but those histories, as far as we're concerned, were specifically written as prelude for the most important moment of your lives—your encounter with us. And not to be arrogant, but people's histories, though precious to them, are not worth very much in the grand universe—only if others can grow from referencing their example do the human story writers remember them. Not their faces. Not their atrocities. Not their icons, but them and their lasting works—especially those works which sit upon the souls of those who follow them. We faced a grand dilemma in whether or not to help you, and for reasons too complicated to expand upon here, we decided that we should not interfere. You, Leader, must understand why such decisions are made.

Leader nodded her acknowledgement in earnest seriousness.

We live in a *very* peaceful world. But we evolved from ancestors that were not so peaceful. They still live today, have made promises to conquer us and take back their home planet just because that's how they are, and we have yet to figure out how to fix them. They made us, became us, gluttoned their lives into a corner on the technology they then put into us, and now they hate and fear us. Not all of them, but enough to cause us problems a hundred years from now. Everyone you see next to me has a good chance of still being around then, and we don't like it.

...

My organization Miranda maps societies—including societies of the mind. Dial's organization SIER stores the saved personalities of centuries' worth of humans, plants, animals, objects, and events. Although we could not mobilize such massive organizations to rescue a type of weather pattern on a distant planet, we could present such rescue as a challenge to a private individual, Genevieve. 150 years ago, she was instrumental in a technical achievement that we absolutely needed to reach, and I owed her an opportunity to do what she was good at here. So she agreed to jump into your world with the help of Isaiah, and try to save you. This brings us to what has just transpired on your planet:

When you visited us the first time, Leader, and we discovered a solution to your species' problem, we were more than ready to help you implement it. You went back and volunteered to take the vaccination. At that moment, the outcome was still undecided. But then we recalled a catastrophically traumatic event in one of our histories—which no one wants to talk about, by the way—and thought twice about giving a free ride into the future to just anybody. We have seen what happens when we give suggestible, fearful, easily angered, jealous, or just plain uninformed people a chance to share the beauty we have built, and concluded that it should not be so easy. People need to *want* to live in peace, to *want* to live in a utopia even if it is not presently within their reach, and they need to be able to stay on this course even when it is not convenient to do so. When your life lasts only a few decades and your window for youth and passion a rare fruit, you can't help but believe certain naïve ideas about how life works. But when you are forever 33 and the sweetness of that youth wears out, or when your blind passions become boring, you know that the only thing better than a great life is a great life shielded from all bad ones.

So we let your people's collective conscience decide what happened to you. It chose to sink the ship, and Mother Nature and the Reaper collected their fee as scheduled. We can always reload you, and speaking for myself alone I—well, that would be insensitive. But just know that something can be done about your world even after it happens. That is not necessarily the case for this world we have brought you into. At least, we don't know how to do it.

Leader, you were brave. You were first, and you were rare. Your energy intersected with our story, so I believe you were aligned not just with the events in our dimension, but in those higher than us still. Watcheye, you displayed one of the only abilities that anyone really needs to recover from the darkest places: actionable hope. Hope alone won't do it. I've learned that simply extends the solid ground available to you. But you took it further and did something to kickstart a sign. We need that in this dimension if we are to ensure a lasting peace. Genevieve.

Phaedra and I discussed it, and as a result of what I learned I now have the challenge of coming up with a solution to what I saw. We're going to try to evolve our former selves on Jupiter, one mind at a time.

Even Dial and I were intrigued by this. None of us were aware that Genevieve had made any plans for that part of her Omni round.

*Hm. That's... great. But. I don't really... So what did we learn besides the fact that big groups of humans are doomed when fear runs them over?*

I sat in various cells for over a year in digital time, heard a lot of conversations, and saw a lot of humanity in general—dressed up under another name and on another planet, yes, but it was definitely us. All I could do was watch and get screwed over something that I didn't even know my program had done. I for sure couldn't correct it. And then I was in this body from someone who probably lived centuries ago—no custom genes, no infinite skill credits or automated social movement, nothing. Just a face nobody trusted and this feeling that my upbringing had completely fucked me over. It was like being a biometal all over again, except I was more aware as a subconscious than my conscious self was. I just... had a lot to learn about powerlessness.

I knew I'd gone there to make my mark and "save the world." Hell, I even knew I couldn't die. But I couldn't even get out of jail. I couldn't even save a few people in an office let alone a world. Most importantly, partly thanks to your stories Watcheye, I realized that without a few people who liked me or enough people who believed in me, important people who backed me and at least someone with some kind of pull giving me a chance, there was no hope of me getting anything done in that world. And it was so obvious that most people who might have *wanted* the world to be saved weren't the kind of people who would actually act to make this happen under their own power. Almost everybody needed a crutch. Even your crutch needed a crutch.

So we talked about some things and ended up like, "Let's just learn how stuff like this plays out. We know some will survive, most may not. But what kinds of things would have had to happen in the first place? You know, to get the people to just plain support each other through transitions without killing the other guy or just rolling over?

**Did you find your answer?**

I think I did. It's in the Heitel stories. People fall into big categories of what moves them. If you can force events that affect the category, you can move people to become better. Most of us are too busy with our own issues to really respond to politics way out there or a neighbor up close here, so all we can do is give bitchy opinions or rave reports on these things. The raves aren't as likely to be documented, though. And the bitching is. Also, if you keep a message or a remedy intangible, you can confuse the mass with it. And a confused mass will do whatever its loudest media controllers suggest. Not media figures. Media controllers. That's who we are. And it's exactly what we did to protect the Venusian ecosystem in the first place. Otherwise human industry would have colonized you and destroyed your energy long ago.

(*It was a sobering thought for Watcheye and Leader alike.*)

What moves people the most is the baseline for their mentalities. Even though I felt like shit that one day, I think I knew that what I told you, Watcheye, would be a HUGE filter for which among you would survive. We don't want to save people so that they can just stagnate and fuck up their lives in lemminghood the next day. It's pointless. But we do want to save the kinds of people who we wouldn't mind filling up our worlds. Angry and scared people fill up their worlds with their own enemies. We don't want that to be us, so we won't save anyone who sees enemies out there. Nobody is an enemy. Not if we are strong enough to see ourselves connected to them.

Leader was skeptical.

Soft, I know. Hook your brain up to everyone else's through an internet you can't turn off, and get back to me.

...

Once you're reprinted as a lensed beta you'll know that a computer shouldn't war with its own files. Your attention, not your little war, is everything.

**That's why they can't beat us Heitels,** Watcheye agreed under his breath.

Yeah. So in the end we thought it would be more valuable to learn through Venus and reload the projections if anyone was upset by the outcome. The whole ne-muril structure started off as data loaded on top of energy with a certain direction, so we thought it would be instructive for the problems we're having with our original form's ancestors on Jupiter.

*(Unbeknownst to everyone except me, Phaedra, and Dial, we had also been engrantzing Watcheye continuously from the moment the lab was disbanded and Genevieve had expressed her preference for him and Traylor as possible allies. With a constant signal dampening his emotional register on an entire apocalypse, we made sure that—if we were to continue working with him— he would not have to carry the same level of trauma I had. We also made VERY certain that certain devastating experiences were volumed down on both ne-murils' prints. We didn't erase their memories, but muzzled certain types of negative memory strongly. This was the main reason that both Phaedra and Genevieve could occasionally slip into callousness towards the Venusian matter. No one would have wanted to hear how matter-of-fact our species-steering conversations actually were.)*

Well anyway, we've said a lot. Yes. We've said a lot. Any questions?

Leader shook her head. Of course there were questions, yet she was suddenly too tired to ask them.

Watcheye—(I kept wanting to call him "Whitehorse" and I didn't know why)— seemed to want to hear more, but agreed to at least a short break before retiring.

After the two ne-murils had left the room, Phaedra requested that Jake sign off. He did, the wall monitors lit up so that we could observe when Watcheye returned, and the real conversation began.

Phaedra came to the point quickly with Genevieve. **In two sentences, what's your plan?**

I sneak into Jupiter from Io. I start a class consciousness campaign for empowering mentality groups.

**Really,** Phaedra quated.

Yes, *really*. One of those myths suggested that behind every war is an out-of-control perception of class differences—like us versus them in all kinds of ways. Fear is another cause, and greed is another.

**And how does this address what you learned from Venus?**

When situations are bigger and darker than you ever imagined, or if you're just so stuck by a life that has trapped you, you need something inside to hold onto. Our alpha ancestors hold onto things outside of themselves, including beef with us. I want to address this from the level I learned about on Venus.

**And that level is?**

As one who changes the change makers, turning them into examples for how their class can transcend its demons.

**Mm. Let's talk about this later. You've intrigued me.**


Shortly thereafter, Watcheye returned.

**I really want to see my aunts and uncles, how they're doing. Is there any way I could, uh, go back the way you do?**

Phaedra and Dial quickly started lensing each other.

**SIER-icon, get Leader on the line, wherever she is.**

"I see she's in the shower, Zeta."

**Then nevermind. But record this answer to play back to her later.**

"Will do."

You asked if you can visit your family. Yes you can. We'll view them on screen first, then let you jump later if you still want to. But I'll be honest, where you're standing right now was built from centuries of lessons learned. I am very sorry to have to threaten you, but as the Principal of Miranda I am obligated to tell you, you cannot live in both places. Your people won't believe in aliens from another dimension. Your social trollers and governments may harass you for a little while or for the rest of your life. And I am certainly not interested in bringing anyone else here from Venus except for possibly Traylor. Regular mentalities belong with the alphas of Jupiter. Higher ones belong here. We're not forcing you to choose, just reminding you of the realities of attempting to blend an entirely alien world with an entirely real one. Very few people on your side would be able to handle the experiences you and Leader have had just this afternoon. I would really advise you to connect with your family some other way besides an immersive jump. Because if you can't wrench yourself away from that life, you may end up staying there after all. If you understand me. It really isn't personal. Just think about how incompatible these places are.

Watcheye was hurt and intimidated all at once.

It had to be said. To that end, I would encourage you to learn more about the place you're currently in. It's very nice here. We'll worry about visiting your family as early as tomorrow if you like.

Just think of our work as being extra top secret. More than actual secrets, it's mainly the wildfire of collective speculation which we wish to keep contained.

* * *

Aimee explained to Genevieve and I, Io is technically occupied by the Solar Council as a result of the last major war 30 airs ago, so we don't see a lot of activity there. Just beyond that, however, the firewall goes up and we can't teleport or communicate with much of their atmosphere. That said, since Jupiter itself is huge, the Jupiterians can't block everything. There are plenty of detours, and their sky cities' boundary patrols aren't that good. The most they can do is flag everyone who enters and exits. They can and they do, so although you can get past them, they usually know you did it and they know when you're not one of them. Drones will tail you from there. They can also follow certain brands of electronics this way like teleporters and printers.

...

There are betas and cyborgs on Jupiter, and they are definitely second class citizens. The few praesciens there are often employed in high positions, but on the whole are distrusted as beta sympathizers. The population of Jupiter is somewhere around 7-10 billion. We don't know because those guys are famous for throwing out misinformation. On all major Council reports, Jupiter is considered hostile towards the rest of the solar system, as their leadership has a "take back the Earth" philosophy. Sadly, we don't like to think of them as smart because that part of their philosophy is so destructive to the very federation that sustains them, but they're actually very smart and very dangerous. Their main weapon consists of appealing to the individual's dream of fame and glory. Collectively, they believe they deserve a shot at the top, and that we who surround them are keeping them down.

Are we?

Not at all. But the dream of beating the guy who has what you want or lives like a king off of stuff you disapprove of has always been a problem for sapiens alpha.

I think we should take the front door and just immigrate like regular people.

If you do that you will certainly be put on a watchlist and our communication with you will be limited. You'll be going into a no-zone for us. But I'll also say that you should definitely not go in your current privileged beta bodies because they do NOT like that. There's a round fear that robots will take over everything and they have strict laws, an even stricter culture for keeping these "boxes" in their place.

...

It looks like we actually did take over, I noted.

(Leader and Watcheye entered the room quietly, trying not to disturb us.)

First of all, Isaiah, *WE* are not robots. We were and are humans transported into fully prosthetized bodies. We grow electrobiotically and do the same kind of fucking and feeling and birthing as the cavemen did. We just have better calculators for the consequences of our actions, and that's exactly why even unmodded natural borns like praesciens are shat upon. The alpha machina culture distrusts anyone who has what they don't have or can see what they can't see—which is funny because they are so heavily modified themselves with their thought reading and brain TVs and blanking and their super speed that they don't even see the connection.

Oh, sorry.

Second of all, *we* did not take over. Their ancestors forfeited charge of their environment and their societies to big and small machines because they were too busy living phat off their phones. They abandoned their place and their more responsible half picked it up. Beta Earth has never really passed laws degrading alphas, and you know people like Nolli have the same opportunities we do—

*(Genevieve, there' no way that's true.)*                    *(I disagree with you…)*

—He could even head Miranda one day.

*(…but Sei doesn't.)*

*(You saw how Phaedra just sent him home from the feed. And what about you? Or me?)*

*(Don't think like that, Isaiah. These are our friends.)*

Third, the us versus them attitude is shitty in general. While they're busy forcing non-alpha couples to bear only alpha babies or throw away any chance of citizenship, they're also degrading their own adaptivity in general. We should be able to have whatever child we want.

They're doing that?

*They are in New America. They're doing it in Zeusland and Osaira. Those are major powers!* Dial scolded. *That's not good.*

But they can set up whatever government they want, I protested.

*And rip the limbs off of you when you get in their way!?*

Dial!

...I...

Okay, let's all take a breather, Genevieve attempted to play peacekeeper. Thanks for telling us this, Aimee. I really mean it. Really. It's informative. But I'm gonna walk with Isaiah for a while and come back here in, say, an hour? Sound good?

*Urgh. I hate this. We do everything we can for people and then have to apologize for living well.*

You don't have to apologize, Genevieve smiled. Actually, you remind me of somebody who got herself erased, 😊 .

At these words, Aimee's expression softened. *Okay.*

One hour. Then you and I will talk, Genevieve cast a not-so-subtle glance at the ne-muril visitors. It was awkward, but may have been necessary to remind everyone who was in charge.

At the time, however, I was surer that I didn't quite like Dial as much as I thought. I'm glad Prohal and Phaedra stopped me from caving in.

* * *

Genevieve and I walked and talked our way back to the residence areas.

Are you okay?

She was right. Alphas are broken.

Not all of them. Not even most of them. They have friends they follow just like us, and they know when something's been put out of their reach. Just like us. You and me and Nolli. We know what it's like to not be able to reach something. Aimee and Phaedra really don't. At least not anymore if they used to. They can reach anything they want.

...

But yeah, Nolli will never ever lead Miranda. And we rogues who like to go out there and like the alpha adventure will always come second in the modern society. It's not about skin color out here the way it is up there on Jupiter. But it is about datahood, or domesticity. The more domestication you can enforce, the higher you go. But what if your goal is to bring out the natural wild in others and show them how to perfect it? You know, for the better?

**I can't imagine how that would be done.**

Nature itself does it, which is why the alphas definitely didn't go extinct even after making better versions of themselves. I think we are better. No, I know we are better. And we've done a good job with almost everything alphas broke. But I still have this feeling that we threw our old selves away instead of fixing them. Like Jupiter is our landfill or something.

**Oh, that's rough!**

No, not the people, haha. I'm talking about the frequency.

**Hmm.**

You know something funny Isaiah, I've been toying with an idea. Ever since I came out of that jump, I've thought about what it means to *really* change the world—to do something that's never been done before, or at least done well.

...

I don't think getting missions from Omni to solve the Powers' problems is the way, because you can see that even the strongest powers have blind spots—big ones. I'm talking Jupiter-sized. They don't mean to do it, but they assume everyone should just think like them and everyone will have an opportunity. If this doesn't happen, then whatever. To a whole life that someone is leading—millions of lives even... "whatever."

I'm glad we have friends like Dial who are concerned about these things, but Dial can't actually fix it because those living in the blind spot definitely see people like her and Phaedra—all of us really—as causing the problem, even though we didn't do anything wrong. And when we ignore them and keep getting richer and more advanced, we anger them.

...

I do think I'm going to immigrate to Jupiter, but I'm going to do it as Esperanza. I can't have a target on my head as a prettified post-print beta. I also need more of Esperanza's perspective to really know what it is we're up against. Forget the military stuff. There's something flowing across the people which tells them certain things are okay when they know full well they're not.

There's a Heitel story about a knight who served the god taught to him by men, then one day prayed to the god announcing he was going to become an atheist. He said, "If you are out there as described to me by these petty people, then you cannot be the truth. I will from here on ignore you." He wanted to live through his acts and his attitude rather than his words and the temples he claimed, and went out of the heavens and into hell to preach how hell was a part of heaven.

**Hm.**

But hell is built on disharmony. So as a knight, he obviously had to endure dozens of labors to accomplish his mission.

**And did he succeed?**

He did eventually, but it took a lot. And also...

...

His biggest challenge was to defeat the spirit of hell itself. Not the boss, but the Nature. He did this by deflating the sweeping tension of hell's prisoners out of the air they breathed, one tribal hero and challenge at a time.

**What's a tribal hero?**

It's someone who belongs to one of the main races, who has the ability to transform that race's prison.

I considered what Genevieve seemed to be saying.

...

**So you want to leave the Solar Council's reach and look for tribal heroes on Jupiter.**

Yes.

**But you're a foreign bot in their eyes. How would you get anywhere?**

As Genevieve, I would be a foreigner, yes. But as Esperanza I would be a legal expat with a passion for building better lives in my world. That's why so many people flee Earth to go to Jupiter in the first place.

**It looks like you've thought this through.**

And there's one other thing. I wouldn't have started thinking this way if I hadn't been imprisoned twice, and been forced into someone else's lens twice. I came back with some sort of extra personality that understands what it is to be second-classed with no options at all. Normally I would have to die and be reprinted in order to use that personality, but then again I'd be trapped.

**Yeah.**

I think it is a rare gift I've received to have the privileges of basically the highest class, but the shell of someone nowhere near there. I can see all the problems and all the powerlessness, but also know all of the solutions. More than almost anybody in the galaxy, I know *exactly* what any one person needs to do in order to reach a level as high as Phaedra's. To be honest, I'm probably more qualified to run Miranda than Jake or Aimee. Not that I'd want to. I just think I know what to do to help people reach where they're trying to go. More importantly, I have ideas about *how* to do it.

**Oh? Like what?**

You've heard of Strada, right? Of course you have, you were ICON— what am I talking about. But you know she eventually became an exorcist who jumped into people's psychologies to help them recover from problems, right?

**Yes, I am familiar.**

I want to do that, but a little more strategically—for people with the potential to raise their entire class if only they could get past the barriers typical of that class.

**Interesting.**

That technology requires that the user interact with some means that allows the exorcist to actually reach their psychology. I want to do this through a device we already have—Phaedra's arm brace. *My* arm brace.

I considered Genevieve's plan. **So you go to Jupiter as Sei Esperanza with the arm brace, have certain socially valuable people put it on, and** you exorcise the class limitations preventing them from bringing up their kind. I think the others would love this. For the science alone. SIER would benefit greatly just from the personality data. And I think the Solar Council would gain valuable intel—

Eh, I'd actually rather not think about that—about how owned I am. Because I don't want an obligation to the Council, or the red dot on my head that comes with it. If Phaedra wants to leak that info then she can, but I'm not planning to go out of my way to spy for Earth. I just want to do this for myself, to see how far it goes.

I see.

And. I uh, think it would be great if you came with me.

I I I I don't know... alphas—

I won't pressure you, but just—I really think I might need somebody. Especially if the Sei side gets out of hand.

Heh. That's actually not a selling point.

Sorry!

No, no. If you don't mind a sometimes depressive computer by your side then, I suppose I might think about it.

Cool, that's all I ask. And you shouldn't talk down on yourself like that.

Maybe it's a class problem.

Nope. It's an identity problem when you started off as a tool for some of the greatest people in the world. There aren't enough folks for you to *have* a class, my friend.

Somehow this made me smile.

So I'm gonna roam around a bit and meet back up with Aimee. Can I trust you by yourself? Genevieve asked jokingly.

I'm sure I'll be alright. ☺ .

* * *

**Esperanza?** Watcheye greeted Genevieve in the corridor.

Yes?

Can you tell me something? What am I supposed to do now? I like this place, but I have no idea where to go or what to do. I don't even understand what people expect from me. Home would be easier.

Do you want to go home?

Not really. It was always a bad place for people like me, but now it's worse. And it's torn up.

But what about your family, don't you miss them?

I didn't really know them. The lab was my family. I do kind of miss Traylor though. He was like my smart little brother. Spastic was a jerk, but we needed him when politeness wouldn't work.

Well, what would you *like* to do with your life?

I really like protecting people doing something important. But mostly don't want to be looked down on.

(*Man, what has life done to you? You're a giant!*)

Well in this place, people won't look down on you. But you really do need to take time to get to know it first.

Phaedra says I need to commit one way or the other.

Really? That doesn't sound like a way she would treat guests. How did she say it?

She said I can't live in both places and if I tried to go back, I might have to stay there.

Oh... No, that's not what she meant! You see, early in this technology, people thought they could jump anywhere, print anything, and bring any piece of the digital world out into this world. It was fun in the beginning, then got <u>real</u> crazy with all kinds of crime problems, abuses, and security stuff. Identity mannequins, fake references which led to four-factor identification, divorce holos, shipment cloaking, high value knock offs, smart bombs, you name it. And then just regular imports of bad things. What you probably heard was a 400-year old non-government official telling you about her zero-tolerance policy for bringing in destruction. Phaedra can be a little cold, but she always comes around.

Oh.

But you might try watching PEN:Newprint, the Praesciens Education Network for newly printed betas and cyborgs. It has some very good shows which can teach you about this society and how it works. We're almost all part robot, and most people are more than willing to help you.

**Okay, I'll do that when I go back to my room.**

* * *

So that's the plan.

Sounds bold. What do you need from me?

Well I wanted to run this by you before talking to Phaedra, because I'm not really asking her permission or agreeing to do anything for the Council or Omni. If they want to count this as helping them then fine, but I am choosing not to be beholden to them.

Oh. But you'll still need support from them for things like technology.

Only if it doesn't put me in debt.

But you know that Phaedra keeps eyes on everything. If you interact with something that she's got hands in, she'll watch you as long as you can affect it.

Yeah.

I love my friend, but you're basically leaving the nest and asking her to let you go. I'm sure I can help you make your case, but if I were you I'd make some other plan besides getting help from Miranda. She'll give you the arm brace without fuss, but not Miranda's aid.

I kind of wish I could just steal Jake.

Why don't you ask him?

What? To quit his job and go into an enemy nation with me?

No. To take a sabbatical and join you on Io for a while, talk about the tech you need and help you recruit someone else. You'll need to be honest about all of this though.

Sneakiness around Phaedra won't. help. you. at all. Just ask.

*Sigh*

What's so hard about asking?

Dial, I'm not you. I can't just ask.

Why not?

*Sigh*

What? Spit it out.

Nevermind, we'll find our own tech expert.

What? Does this have something to do with that stuff we talked about a little while ago, is that it?

No, Aimee. Look, I'm just trying to do a good thing. I hate having to come with my low-ranking tail between my legs to beg permission from someone who can just kick me off the screen and lock me in an arm brace for 150 years—

Oh now —

Let me finish. I DON'T HAVE THE PULL. No matter how much you may think I do. I don't run SIER. I have no valuable connections besides the people I have to beg to jump or do anything worthwhile. This is why I'm going to Jupiter to begin with. I don't have the pull and I know it. It doesn't feel good. And I'm sick of leaning on Phaedra for basic things.

Aimee's mouth twisted in disappointment. So I'm hearing that we're privileged, and you may get the Jupiterians more than we think.

It looks like that, doesn't it?

Okay. Let me talk to Phaedra. It's the least I can do.

Eh, *thank you.*

It's an ugly subject to come between friends. We should keep these conversations to the fewest number of people needed to ensure things stay sane.

* * *

Phaedra shook her head. It just makes me so mad that my own allies won't talk to me themselves.

Your allies can't control when you silence them, and they're trying to build a situation where that isn't the case.

*Grumble*

They have dreams, Phaedra, and they're way fragile compared to yours. Even the smallest discouragement can stop everything. Genevieve told me that it sucks how someone else can basically remove one piece from your puzzle and prevent the whole thing from being built. After Venus, Genevieve doesn't want to let any more pieces get out of her hands.

I don't understand that.

But you did. You're the one who told me about Dynamene, remember?

...

What's it like having someone who can just make themselves relevant to you at any moment and bring pain to whatever you're trying to do right there?

—

I know we're not malicious, but she would literally reinvent the entire process rather than ask you to borrow Jake's brain. She doesn't even know she could just call Jake herself and never tell you anything! But she would see that as a betrayal. We would see it as just making a useful call.

But it's not betrayal.

It is. In her mind it is, because it would be an end-around you which everybody knows you don't like. And your response to that is unchallengeable. Phaedra, THIS is Jupiter! It is what their problem *is* with us.

But we haven't done anything wro—

I get that! I get it. Dial paused to catch her breath. Look, does she have to go it alone or doesn't she? I don't need conditions or compromises. She has no negotiation power here. I hope you know that. It's all on you to bless her or not.

And the security issues? What if she betrays us? The Commandants are sneaky.

But from what you've told me, they're always on the right side. We can have SIER-icon or Navicon keep a long term feed running and let Genevieve know this is a requirement for everyone's sake. I'm sure she'll understand the bigger interests at stake.

The Council won't like that I'm just letting a valuable ally walk into enemy territory.

What do you mean? Tell me that you didn't play up Genevieve as any more than a regular jumper.

I didn't but the whole Venus show was pretty visible to everyone.

Dammit. But the reward if—

If what? If she succeeds? How likely is that realistically?

I don't know. But she's not your slave. Either give her your blessing or truly let her go on her own.

I can't take a hit among the Governors for something I definitely don't agree with anyway.

Then give SIER the arm brace and let Jake make his own decision.

That's stupid.

Which part?

Jake! I don't care about the brace. I'll teleport it over now, if you like. But Jake is the Intellectual Property of Miranda. That's out of the question.

Yes, because he's property.

Go to hell.

I'm not gonna die on this sword, Phaedra. But you should think about how Jake would take what you just said.

Why is everybody turning against me?

Oh, suck it up Zeta. NOBODY AT ALL is turning against you. Jake may not want to be property, the tall guy might want to go home, their leader died for a lost cause, and your loyal former-computer friend is depressed and aimless. All Genevieve wants to do is figure her way out of boxes like these. It's about them, not you.

Phaedra grew increasingly despondent.

The best thing you can do for them is give them a chance. If there are security issues then I understand. But I think a lot of those issues would disappear if you actually wanted to support these children of yours. You know what to say to the Council and you know how to say it. I hope you can be bigger than some random iron-handed queen.

—"Permission to enter, Miss Dial."

Granted.

"We just received this teleport from Miranda directly to you courtesy of—oh my."

Thanks, I'll take that.

The messenger lowered his eyes upon glimpsing Zeta herself, handed Aimee the pearl arm brace, then scurried out of sight.

Thanks, Phaedra. (*Wow! She really did have it teleported on the spot!*)

*Exhale* One day I'll be gone, and I'll need for my successor to be better at this than I was.

...

But right now nobody's better. I should start teaching them.

...

It must have been difficult for Twice Jack, choosing an ex-skater girl like me.

...

Okay, give me some time. I'll probably talk to Jake.

Thank you SO much Phaedra, I'm serious, Dial smiled a genuine smile, extending her arms for a hug.

Phaedra let Aimee hug her tightly, rocking side-to-side slightly for a couple of moments.

I guess the risks we take aren't finished, are they?

Not by a long shot.

I wonder if anyone will care over the long run that we tried this?

Let's get ready to find out.

# 208. Jake's Invention: The Angel Finder

Spring 66, 2771 n.e.

I'm so excited to show you all the finished product. All it is is a modification of the old arm brace, but A LOT more useful. I call it, Angel Finder.

Ever since Phaedra had presented the opportunity to Jake three months prior, his enthusiasm towards his work had gone through the roof. He was more than happy to take the six-month sabbatical from his regular job at Miranda, and loved working with two people who more or less treated him like an equal (though Genevieve could be a little imperious at times). After installing the initial attributor into the arm bracelet donated by Phaedra and assuring her that it would report any issues that might pose a security threat in the eyes of the Solar Council, Jake proceeded with the real work on the accessory. Genevieve had received it from Aimee, then reluctantly re-surrendered the device to Jake to protect herself and others from "things she wasn't supposed to know about it." She now awaited the scientist's report on the presumably extensive changes he had made in his off time.

This device already has a century and a half of Genevieve's information, so as far as training goes it is second to none. But now it does A LOT more than just listen and collect logs.

- First, I retrofitted the brace with a private line to talk to a headset or your native lens frequency so you can read the logs as they collect from whatever the brace is listening to.

- I installed an echoflowrometer to shoot out signal beams resonant with various energy flows in the body and the room——basically sonar for determining your body and room position without cameras.

- I installed backbend functionality on a laser pointer for bouncing a little beam back to where a certain flow came from. That's more of a neat trick than a necessary thing, but I needed it as a stepping stone to perfect the exorcism parts.

- I added a nanopad which does old-school zapping into the arm, driving a return cascade throughout the nervous system. This works kind of like a coordinate plane wrapped around your wrist which we use to scoot your nervous system into firing in certain ways. It puts a slinky-like pull and shove on your depolarization patterns, triggering you to think in certain ways

- I added a vascular pad to do the same for your heart rate and, in conjunction with the echoflowrometer, your attention.

- There is a generic grantzer on another channel which can be tuned to suggest different things to different types of interactant in the room. I would use this sparingly on others though, because once the other person leaves your company, it may not be clear to them why they did certain things. On the other hand, you may want to use this more on the wearer in order to force them to take the correct route for a change.

- See these two pockets here? I drilled in two landing bays for micro drones with room for a universal printer cartridge in case your drones get broken. These drones have cameras, and launch from the brace to do whatever you tell them to do. They are also preprogrammed to leave a no-zone and get to a clear zone to broadcast to us or a friend if you're in trouble. So that's cool.

- And look at this. (Jake put a rather strong-looking box on the table, and placed the arm brace in it. A beep sounded from elsewhere in the room.) Oh no!, someone stole my brace! (Jake slapped his hands to his face in fake shock.) What ever will I do?

Jake pulled a regular looking pair of earbuds out of his backpack, as well as a hologlove.

I'm not lensed, so I need my cave technology to show you the interface. If you're lensed, the brace can scream at you for various reasons which you program, and you can locate it over the subnet. The holographic user interface shown bright and clear as a screen in mid-air. Here we are. Find my brace.

A series of clicks and clacks sounded from inside of the box, followed by the sound of drilling. In under 10 seconds, a curved drill bit emerged through the wall of the box holding the arm brace. 30 seconds later, a Roadrunner-style hole had been made in the box as a little ram thumped a jagged wooden circle onto the table. It was quite amazing.

There we found out that the arm brace was now itself a drone, hurling itself through the hole it had cut and flying with a tilted wrist region straight out the door...

Watch the monitor.

Footage of the hallway outside sailed by us as the brace camera captured anywhere the brace was headed.

Let's run it full-speed into the wall. Jake raised his hand and punched it forward. The brace zoomed right towards the wall...

...and slowed down to a gentle hover, waiting for its director to change their mind.

That's an old technology standard to fast moving vehicles—Crap! I gotta get outta here!

Jake tapped some buttons on the screen, releasing one of the nanodrones. The split screen began.

This is ridiculous... Dial marveled in awe.

Phaedra's mouth hung slightly open. She was too blown away to be jealous.

The nanodrone reentered our room.

I won't do it now, but if somehow the brace were *completely* lost or destroyed, as long as the drones can get away, they will broadcast to us and—

Phaedra got up from the table. Excuse me, the less I know about this weapon up front, the better it will be for me next week for my Council meeting. Jake, we'll talk in two weeks.

Yes ma'am.

I will talk to you all later.

*See you, Phaedra.*                              Thank you, Phaedra.

Jake resumed. Or he was going to, but on the monitor Phaedra passed the hovering brace and reached out to it as if patting it on the head. As the screen rocked a bit, Phaedra gave a thumbs up and mouthed a message to the camera. *Good job, Jake.*

Thank you so much ma'am.

Phaedra disappeared down the hallway.

...                                                                    ...

So! We're trapped. We have our nanodrone, but we don't know where our brace is. Directions?

A map appeared on the holoscreen showing where the brace and its rogue nanodrone were located.

Pretend the brace has been destroyed, then the nano will tell us. We'll just print a new one somewhere and put the 1-gorithm et cetera back into it.

Now. Let's get to the possession part.

The brace found its way back to us.

Genevieve, here are your jump transmitters. I'll put on the brace. Everyone, observe the monitor.

Genevieve began a half-focused jump into a humanized version of Jake's echoflow. That is, his whole-biological field. Additional sensors on the brace detected that this was a demo, thus Genevieve's jump depiction rendered accordingly. After a few seconds, an image of a ringmaster appeared training a mighty elephant. The screen zoomed into the red-coated, top-hatted man twirling his moustache, whereafter he motioned to an audience member to "come on down."

So Genevieve, I'm currently in a dilemma. I want to get you to stand on this table, but I don't know how to do it. Yet I know that getting you to do so will earn me points with the audience for the power of my invention. Oh how I wish I knew what to do! Can you do something to give me the courage to ask you?

The ringmaster jumped onto the back of the elephant as if surfing.

That's a nice idea, but there's no way I'm gonna stand on this table myself. I don't want to be dragged off to the funny farm. How are you gonna get me to do it?

The audience member gives the ringmaster a kiss as the circus tent fades into a field of falling flowers.

You're good at this. I feel warm, and I'm sold. I'm about to do it… except how do I know this will succeed?

Text appears on the screen. "You don't."

Ooph! That's no good! I'm discouraged again. But you're trying to teach me bravery whether or not I succeed. Show me something good.

A screen that was starting to fade into a brick wall, became a field of flowers again…

…And Jake climbed up on the table. "It's okay if you don't join me up here, but your possession skills were good. I'll be honest, I'm pretty sure I'm doing a cool thing right now that you all will remember as fun."

Genevieve smiled and joined Jake on the table, giving him a peck on the cheek.

Jake bent back one foot and batted his eyelids in a corny swoon. Then he hopped down from the table and helped Genevieve back down.

I really thought a lot about using grantz and possessive jumps to get someone to choose a route they wouldn't normally choose. The route may be better, but the outcome can't really be guaranteed. I know people don't normally care about the philosophy behind these things, but I really think we shouldn't try to influence the target with this. Because it's not repeatable. Unless you are in some kind of danger, you probably don't want to grantz people besides the wearer. I think they should learn the new behavior regardless of the outcome. But that might just be me. So it's important that the wearers of this brace be open to your influence. Having said that, let's get to one last feature—the main one:

Despite all the gadgets on here, we really want to make good choices in *who* we possess. Now I've run a ludicrously complicated series of simulations on the state of the Jupiterian social fabric—demographics, interest groups, long-standing hot button issues endemic to certain classes, whatever—keeping in mind your overall objective, Genevieve: How do we improve society one mentality group at a time, getting a probabilistically strong leader in each group to teach the highest use of the double edge that comes with that group? The fabric analysis changes depending on the outpost you are in, but can be tuned down to the room level. It basically finds your best social solvers within a certain radius by reading emhim on their existing wireless lines. At any time, people are lensing and making calls, satellites receive those calls, and because we at Miranda have access to those satellites— including the majority of the exo-Jupiter ones, all we do is snoop the messages for certain kinds of communication patterns. We find the source of the patterns we want, then turn to various "impact searchers" for influential personalities. We relay this back to the mainframe—this 1' x 8" x 9" cube in my backpack, and determine a list of possible next candidates for holding the brace. I have a simple silly program which demonstrates this if you give me a few seconds... Here it is. Who's the next person in this room to ask a really good question that can make us all think? Watch the monitor.

...

The nano is crawling quietly on the wall, bouncing emhim. Okay. Now it's analyzing sex, build, ethnicity, facial expression, dress,... It has concluded, again, that this is a demo, and is measuring people's probability of asking a question based on their emhim... It's simulating the effect of some people's question on the rest of us,... and it believes that you, Genevieve might have that question. Do you?

Yeah, but that's pretty scary.

It's also very broad, and will need you to train it on real data.

I guess my question is, does it tell us where to go next, like from wearer to wearer?

Yes. You can change its scope, but the simulations are pretty clear—especially because they were run against long-standing issues which were known to be resolved by us on Earth. The way beta and cooperative-alpha society went about solving those same problems historically, the brace simulation attempted to replicate. For example, the use of psi in place of money that people no longer had. The new humans grew into this. The Jupiterians don't have the infrastructure and therefore still use mainly crydit money. The new market basis was critical in evolving our society, so the simulation asked where this would start among people who were not beta, but prefer to haggle or profit instead. It searched for cultures inclined to sponsor a psi-like system, and concluded that a Native American should probably do it, with the help of a white male backer to ease the doorways.

Fascinating.

So the brace will be looking for one of these Jupiterians. To give another example, we have federal annexes which facilitate great advancement across our cities. The Jupiterian outposts don't typically have this either. Who starts these? A group of three white males: an official, a businessman, and a sneaky lobbyist. They have to be sneaky, and at least two of them have to be corrupt because in reality, no one wants to give Megatech, Inc its own state. It flies in the face of freedom from Big Brother. But this kind of industry-specific replacement for old geopolitical boundaries is *absolutely* a good idea. Especially if you want your citizens—who work under that local area's opportunities—to be really invested in politics, education, and good systems again. Now obviously, we've had federal annexes for a long time on Earth; we love them and swear by them, but you basically have to be corrupt to the core in order to get them started.

Dial, Genevieve and I listened, partly disturbed and partly puzzled by what we were hearing.

*Short-term evil, long-term good,* Dial muttered.

Evil might be relative here, but yeah, I know. It's not the beta way. But consider that we got here through a bunch of wars, four mass exoduses, five destructive pandemics, child regulation technology, I don't know *how* many iyohn genocides and, well, this is the fast forward version. It's as good as it gets to for turning aggressors into allies in only a few decades.

. . .

I did make sure, however, that only routes in line with a reasonable person's good conscience were retained.

What about racial tolerance, who builds that?

The betas themselves made us forget how much we hated over race as we started hating robots instead. But in the Jupiterian states there aren't enough robots to unite people like this, so the racial gaps are still very strong. To answer your question, that's not a person. It's a group of institutions, and can only happen under the federal annex system, because that system trades robots for robot-like institutions which are much more tolerant, much more sense-making, and much more intentionally efficient than the old geopolitical systems built on subjective conquest. For the most part, this is started by all kinds of people, but white males will need to do it first.

What the fuck? Is that how Jupiter works?

It's really how New America works. This changes depending on your outpost, but if you have to pick a melting pot where they don't officially crush minority power holders and are only passively imbalanced towards non-favored groups from all quarters, you will go there. It's the best place to find everyone of every group without having actual physical combat, a narrow cultural sample, and a powerful enough inter-outpost presence that lets you move anyone up. They're going through some things now. But as we learned from Venus, there's no free ride for the next level of person. If ever there were an actual demand for what you're about to do, it's now.

*(Furrowed brows all around.)*

I'm only telling you this because I had to convince myself of it when I got the results. Trust me. Putting your sense of urgency aside to actually match what is there to work with isn't easy. That's why there's a certain order in which these brace carriers place must be visited.

I used the data you gave me from Heitel lore, and the Mettrls are closest to the group that can have their will prevail wherever they go. The drawback? A single individual can only see so much. For every obstacle I crush, there's still furniture, bugs, birds, the weather, sneaky people, traitors, inviolable I'll-shoot-you triggers that will drive any fed-up rando to take you down regardless of risks, and in the darker Mettrl stories you generally end up with a lot of kings whose kingdoms are full of citizens that aren't worth a damn, and who take turns defecating on your grave and your living children's embarrassing efforts once you're gone. The kings' successors carve up their businesses for themselves, and the Rockefellers and the Croesuses of the world are always eventually usurped by the Martin Luther Kings, the Jesuses and the Joans of Arc. Every time. But the Martin Luther Kings, Jesuses, and Joans of Arc only pop up because they answer loudly and clearly the imbalances of their day. People don't care about those imbalances when they're sailing down easy street, so they let their nobles do the talking. You'll be training Gandhis, so you'll need Jupiter in all its turbulence to get normal people to even listen to what you're saying. New America has a higher concentration of everyone from everywhere for doing this, So *everybody* will hear you.

Now, my analysis revealed something interesting. Though 64% of the character profiles on the list looked for white males and the will to manifest destiny, only 13% of those individuals could be arm-braced solo. 87% needed a woman to be braced with them, and 70% needed an enemy from another class to start their rise against. So you have two lists: the one which paves society's institutions, and the one that paves each class's sense of its own worth. This second list has all kinds of people like women, the elderly, the uneducated, minority power holders and foreigners from everywhere, robots, third parties, trans people, all that. And every time one of these rises, the problem that held them back will be right there with him. That problem is almost never another class, but more like a community legacy of struggle that goes all the way back to the days when the only form for this enemy was some aspect of Nature itself.

. . .

Political and institutional power isn't the only kind of power. The work for less-powered classes is more valuable to each of those classes than any of the stuff beyond them. That's really what you're doing with Jupiter. Earth has all the power, and they feel they have none. So everyone is threatened. You're doing class work, and leaving the institutional work to Phaedra. It may not seem fair when you look at it, but there's something rockin' in what you're doing and how you're gonna do it. Phaedra can't claim that.

So, wanna hear something neat?

Hmph. Sure.

The brace simulation produced about 500 character types, and many of the major less-powered classes are front loaded. Among your top 10 are a Native American (male or female), a Chinese woman, an African woman, a Middle Eastern woman, a white man who lives in the Venus sim——

What!?

I was curious, so I put that data in there. A trans person, A black person (male or female), and an American Latina. Guess who the last one was?

Oh my god.

That's right. You. It seems like Esperanza herself is the first person who needs to be possessed and exorcised.

Now how does that work?

Clearly someone else will have to possess you. Isaiah.

*(Way to put me on the spot, Jake.)*

Or maybe I can just jump into a sim with Sei as my interactant.

I wouldn't recommend frustrating yourself like that. Until you've tried it, you don't know how nuts it is working with a doppelganger whose logic nonetheless makes zero sense to you. I experimented with it once, years ago. Will never ever do that again.

Oh. Is it a skill thing or...?

No, just a sanity thing. Like experiencing the worst trip ever.

Ah.

So anyway, that's your starting point. We can take the next few weeks training on the functionality and that'll be it. You're off to the savage land!

Thanks.

This is the most badass piece of technology I think I've seen in a while. Way to go Jake!

Thanks, I'm pretty proud of it.

I really do hope you two will do great things with it.

Me too.

# 209. Before You Go

Genevieve.

Phaedra, what's up?

I just wanted to say that I admire you and what you're doing.

Thank you.

I'm serious. I wanted to give you something that would help you before you and Isaiah leave—a kind of shield to protect you against the kinds of things happening on Jupiter.

...

So I asked Navicon to give me any information which might make things easier for you. He asked me to jump. I'm sending you the results.

Okay, thanks.

Well, I was advised not to get too sentimental during your sendoff—

By Navicon?

No, by Jake, of all people. I swear he's like a wartime bride. But the point is, I believe this jump is the best I have to contribute. Hopefully you don't think of me as some detached bureaucrat.

Phaedra, you know I'd never—

This high position removes a certain humanity from you. I'd like to think that—well, watch the jump.

...Okay.

I'll see you soon.

Okay.

And with that, Phaedra signed off the call.


What did she say?

She sent us a jump to help us before we leave for Port Goodman. Are you in the mood for a watch party?

Sure, I guess.

Alright, let's check it out.


NAVICON Report

By: **Phaedra Zeta**

Spring 82, 2771 n.e.

Miranda HQ, Lab 2A


It's been a long time since you  asked me to jump using the chair. It almost feels like therapy. *Sigh* Okay Navicon, I'm here.

GOOD. HOW ARE YOU DOING, PHAEDRA?

The same as always. A queen with a lot of stuff on her mind.

AH, I SEE.

We can't interfere with Jupiter. And I can't interfere with what those two do there. As you know, several of the Council members were not pleased to learn that I had let Jake develop a potential weapon of such importance in his off time, and didn't bother to at least track it.

BUT THE PIRATES AND GOVERNMENTS OF JUPITER HAVE ALWAYS BEEN ABLE TO TRACK TRACKERS. YOU WOULD BE SIGNING GENEVIEVE'S DEATH CERTIFICATE IF YOU INSTALLED SOLAR COUNCIL TECHNOLOGY INTO IT.

I know. And Jake knows that as well. Even if that weren't the case, I don't believe it would help me to watch what's coming like some kind of infectious TV show. I need to know the ending if I want to avoid being perpetually stressed. But this little adventure of theirs is uncertain.

YES, IT IS.

...

...

... Why am I so tired all of a sudden? Are you sleep-waving me?

YES.

Phaedra let out a faintly frustrated exhalation. ***Surprises*.**

DON'T WORRY. IT'LL BE GOOD. WE JUST WANT YOU TO LISTEN, NOT REACT.

***Yawn*** *We*, huh?

Yes Phaedra, Navicon's voice suddenly switched to female. Virgo-6 here, and I have something to show you.


Okay Zyr, that was pretty clever, a tall cad-looking scientist noted. I NEVER would have thought that projecting MY SEEMINGLY UNRELATED TECHNOLOGY INTO 262-IV's SCENARIO would help us with our OWN origin story. THANKS for bringing ME IN.

No prob, Tezl. It's all part of the plan.

I thought roping in the Goodman Chancellorate was even more counterintuitive. I have to admit it pissed me off for a second, but then I saw what you're doing. I suppose that's why it's you who does it and not me, Karaina noted with some disappointment.

We're writing histories, not love stories. Someone has to explain how this planet's limited-scope technology and social evolution came to not only contact us, but become us. In my research on civilizations, you generally have four forces that do the moving: our kingdom, our subjects, the subjects plight after our kings die or yield to incompetent successors, and the second tier leaders who solve the subjects' plight to make post-conflict world into the new normal.

Before this one, Tezl, I ran some trial simulations where the anthrized data in these boxes were able to correct their encroaching planet and social self-destruction on their own. They couldn't do it. All you got was different "states" (if you will) eventually going to war over resources and behavioral pattern hegemony—the standard animal way. Whether these data elements got behind individual representatives quickly or got behind their own giant headless states slowly made a big difference in how easy their technology was to direct towards us. Apparently they had enough competition among them to drive the kind of innovation to produce the Radiobox, but not the collective interaction to use that kind of innovation towards their own survival—not in time. So you had all these automated systems sitting on top of a crumbling interaction space. The data just kind of melts together at some point, and they all end up like a plate full of nematodes anyway. Every time. The level and kind of electromagnetic energy left around their collective corpse did change in each scenario, and you did indeed have new bacterial-level speciate patterns rise from the melt every time as well. But it was all a big reset before I reintroduced the concept of kings and queens to organize all this technology in a coherent and well thought out direction.

Yes, but why the Goodmans? They clearly represent only a fraction of the system's interests, and not even the planet we're looking at.

262-III and its fellows seemed to be stable for quite a while, but 262-IV was the one with the dynamics problems. Eventually those problems spilled past the boundaries of IV, and in the spirit of any repressed population, they basically spread their will outwards to everyone. Part of what stabilized the inhabitants of III was the fact that they lost the need to conquer and multiply, but this is a fundamental property of species success. Once you become content, the ants takeover everywhere else, so it was inevitable that the peaceful would be trampled by the warring one.

But equally inevitable that the warring would institute their own kind of peace until a new warring group among their successors and supposed allies arose to overthrow them, continuing the cycle.

Correct. Unfortunately, there really wasn't a lot of time between the beginning of these guys' interconnectedness era where they gained the capacity to erode ages of evolution all at once, and the point where they actually did so. Therefore I decided in this story that the self-interest of a powerful few tech masters could be used to rewrite the far spanning behavioral rules that governed these data elements. As you know, when we frequentize an atomic micropattern within a data element, we can re-cast it either as an immaterial doctrine or a material technology. An object carried on the hands and arms, for example, represents a kind of air traffic control for every data element, and could be a kind of trained dance in everyone, or just a phone. When it's just a few with this atomic pattern, it's probably a dance. When it is a great many, it's probably a mass-produced phone from a central source. We're basically attaching a cross-actor incorporation's product to every data element, and if you can elect kings who control that product, then you can steer how everyone does air-traffic control.

*Tch*—

Whoa, Karaina! Now before you jump on me for subverting the will of the people, know that they were going to follow the aggressively neglectful atomic patterns native to them anyway. Most animal-type species weren't designed to look out for species not their own and preserve the balance of the environments which hosted them. They are tasked to eat, mate, and multiply their own kind. The only way you can get them to include their environments and other competing groups in their own calculation is to force those environments into their own class structure. So every time they throw a pollutant into their water, they feel like they're chewing on that pollutant themselves. This is the big picture, but you have to install a micropattern attached to them in order to augment an evolutionary path not designed for this kind of whole-niche generosity.

But Karaina's frown would not be removed.

You get me right, Tezl?

I'm ashamed to say it, but I do. The technology works regardless of who uses it. The best thing to do is to control who has it.

In this scenario, the Goodman Chancellorate carves up the 262-IV object and has plans to destroy all other objects as they are and remake them into

262-IV like interaction centers among the data elements. The end result is to render many types of competing behaviors extinct, so that all will align with the Chancellorate's vision.

And so we had a bunch of genocides, and many of the less powerful element classes were lost to our ancestry.

Wrong. An extinct behavior is not an extinct individual. And an extinct individual is not an extinct dynamical pattern. Also, the Chancellorate itself needs subjects. Further, the Chancellors—like all such data elements, actually run out of life very quickly, and what you're left with is a consolidated rule-writing system—

Now controlled by offshoots that *nobody* can reach.

Very correct, which is why we have a very short window for part two.

I'm intrigued.

In the end, the whole purpose of kings and queens is to gather the collective into facing a particular evolved direction. From there, the species mixes and multiplies again along a natural path which supersedes the ruling instantiates' agenda. If biological multiplication-as-conquest is one rule of speciation, so is biological diversity-as-adaptation another rule. The adaptation occurs on top of the conquered niche, then mixing laws occur on top of that diversity. Somewhere within the mixing laws there arise imbalances, and some subclass wants to conquer again. Even stars, black holes, and orbital systems do this. We absolutely can't change it. But what we're trying to do is establish a timeline wherein the inhabitants of 262-I through IX survived long enough to become us, and our history begins where theirs ends. To do that, we need to package the conquest, diversity, and mixing phases of this species into a single "file" if you will, so while the Goodman Chancellorate is running the spread of their atomic attachments to the data elements, the data elements themselves need a powerful clustering algorithm to ensure we know who they all were.

Whoa, whoa! Hehe, Karaina finally began to smile. I get what you're doing! You're showing off!

Tezl shook his head, then mockingly shook his fist. I'll win this ego battle yet, you.

*Snicker*

If I understand it, while we *could have* simply fed them the technology to connect them to us, that would have given us hegemonists as our ancestors. But that's clearly not consistent with how we actually look or work. So you're going a step beyond. You're using hegemonism to carry their plurality here. Going S-class, huh?

Well actually, I'm not so concerned with whether our ancestors were all inbred spawn of the Chancellorate in this scenario. I'm more concerned with our original issue. We're currently living during a war where hegemonism is *exactly* the problem. The whole point of finding an origin story in the 262 system is to also propose a solution for how a previous civilization got past such things, because for goodness sake somebody in some species who's *not* a tree needs to figure out how to solve that one. Our challenge is to use an engine of war and conquest to not only build a backstory here through the technology these inhabitants corralled, but also to build the first of its kind system for a lasting nonextinction cycle.

Nonextinction?

That's my word for a cycle that still includes extinction, except those affected knowingly transform into their new forms without the pain of loss or unnecessary reset. Most resets will still be necessary as the basic idea of extinction, mind you. But the fear and self-destruction will be converted into a more pleasing narrative.

So a religion.

Nope. That's beyond my pay grade.

A Heaven story.

Uh,...hm.

You evangelist, you!

Man!

Hey, Zyr, there's nothing wrong with that!

Yeah, but it's not my focus. I'm actually just building a mentality for ourselves that can get us through this war.

Hᴍᴍ.       ...

...

So what's this phase two?

In phase one the technology for world survival has already been installed into a lot of our ancestors and come under the control of a central group of sources. Before the central figureheads die and the actual nominating powers that be among those disappear into unreachable obscurity, the behavioral superclusters of the world need to be rallied into coherence so that we can archive them as ourselves. This is where we go back to the peace established on 262-III.

Okay so all these guys are data elements, and many of them carry these little atomic micropatterns within them. We anthrize these data elements as humans and their atomic slices as "phones"—which they use to operate other data elements in the boxes we found like houses, cars, security devices, et cetera. Centralizing the rules for how these atomic phones are used enables us to install the world-saving technology and ideologies into the human psyche without having to wait for old nationalisms to do what they always do—a basic cat-herding problem. The kings and queens keep things simple, and the fears they trigger among groups with no power will drive those groups to action. What action? Usually it's fight, flight, or protest. But that stuff is the core of extinction thinking that the hegemonists themselves are afflicted with in their conquest need. Phase two consists of us introducing a fourth response: absorption of the to-be-extincted behaviors.

Suppose the Goodman Chancellorate thinks all matings of different classes should be outlawed. Those who want to do this have a cluster trait called "seen_with_a_foreigner." Among that class, everyone carries this same invisible "technology" on them which somehow behaves differently from those nazi.n with a foreigner.

*(I'm sorry, Virgo-6, what is this word, "nazi.n?")*

*[That is a homolog of "not seen," and pronounced exactly the same way: as "not seen." These individuals use it to described a form of purposeful not-seeing of a thing which intends to erase that thing from visible existence; "not seeing" in order to obliterate one's possible experience of something. Despite*

*how it sounds, this is really just a skill that all people need to develop in order to avoid being run over by mountains of data. The connotation is, however, still hateful. In Zyr, Karaina, and Tezl's time, it usually implies someone bent on committing genocide.)*

*(Hm. My Omni round five.)*

*[Yes, which is why we sedated you. Keep listening.]*

*(Fine.)*

All I did was a simple cluster analysis on major factions among the data elements and locate the actors most typical to each cluster. I ran simulations of which factions were most likely to remain functional or even thrive outside of the Chancellorate ethos, and made sure that, if we fed them the necessary information, they could and would use it to re-cast any disadvantages in their trait. Seen_with_a_foreigner, for example, is a technology that allows an individual to not only carry their own behavioral pattern, but to thrive and grow under one that is expressly not theirs. So if Graham Goodman were to, say, corner one of these people, the latter would be more likely to simply absorb Goodman's ultimatum into their own sense of behavior and move on with life, where people without this trait might be more likely to see Goodman threatening their very being. This is the launch point; seen_with_a_foreigner becomes the technology for "absorbing other people's paradigms no matter how misaligned your core may be with them." A person like this would be perfect for navigating the Chancellorate-controlled world and even accomplishing their own agenda *more strongly* because they *need* the foreigner as a partner. Depending on who you got, this could work even if the Chancellorate wanted to destroy them. (It doesn't, from what I can tell.)

So we have this group from 262-III which oversees much of the peace on that planet, and their technology for reading what we're saying is even better than the Chancellorate's. They actually invented the technology, and know that not all of it is actually "technology." Most of it is dynamical. It all has to align with all of the rules of nature and not just a selected subset. Kings and queens die, but dynamics live on. And they don't just know all of this, but they also respect it to the point that they have included it in their operations. They know the Chancellorate is necessary since they themselves are a concentrated oligarchical matriarchy. We just need a way to feed them the appropriate series of re-castings to every group that feels threatened by the new hegemonism.

This is the project you call "Esperanza."

Yes. Certain elements on 262-III through -VI seem to be able to slip into substates just like we can, so I have rendered them as being able to jump just like we can. But this is like us being able to see into their imaginations. There is NO BETTER WAY to feed someone extraterrestrial information than through their imaginations, and this group seems to have made a whole operation out of it. We can't interfere with the data as we found it, but we are completely free to influence the data's locked-in imagination—turning the wave into the particle of our sensors' sensitivity, so to speak. Among the elements, we found some packets whose patterns looked mysteriously like us, and injected an objective into their jumps which encourages them to start re-casting class disadvantages as talents. They *are* talents, but when they don't pay in power, prestige, or mobility—the things favored by the ruling energies—then people won't really see their traits in this way. Esperanza will change that.

So project Esperanza is kind of like a dream series you're implanting into the substates of a few good class leaders to get them to understand the hegemonism and remove the diminishment—

"Extinctability."

*Extinctability* from the class they belong to.

…Yes.

And if we're successful, then we will have preserved backstory prototypes for the 10000+ super classes which constitute our society now.

Actually we only need 108: 144 ÷ 4 grand crossers × 3 interaction levels. Everything can be recombined from these basic "culture clusters."

That's efficient.

Well, we don't have all year. We need to build our 262 "Ark" and get back to the business in our own dimension.

I get it.

So do I.

Good. Well, I'm going to take a break a then get back into the sim. I'm leaving it to the world's own dynamics to determine how the story unfolds, but the cluster ordering is pretty clear. Esperanza travels in the subspace of person, then three, and so on. Hopefully we can alter the usual cycle long enough to get these guys' timelines to blur into ours.

This would be considered unethical, you know. Altering a world's history to suit our own.

You're one to talk.

I know.

I'm glad you do. Now let's get to it.

* * *

Genevieve and I sat in silence for several moments, the former finally speaking after a while.

So whatever awaits on Jupiter, no matter how messed up it may seem, is there specifically for us—for everybody—and the future we're carrying.

Yeah.

# Part II. On Jupiter

# 210. Glad you're here

Upon our arrival at Jupiter's Port Goodman in New Newyork, New America airspace, Genevieve and I—with the former now reprinted as full-time Sei—immediately found ourselves in a scene.

"Get the fuck outta here, you fuckin' bootlicker!" A group of mixed color machina taunted a quiet cyborg-alpha couple. The cyborg male ducked his head and gently shooed his bride past the harassers.

As the couple passed by them, one of the harassers, a troublesome-looking brown-skinned girl jumped out at the pair in attempts to scare them. Her pale male friend followed suit. "He must give it to you nice and hard, bitch! Maybe you need my boy here to show you what real throbbin' works like!"

"Hahahaha!"

It was 5 delinquents against 2 pacifists. The odds weren't good.

Sei moved to intervene, but I caught her arm, shaking my head. **Let's go. We don't know how this place works.**

But Sei was itching to use at least one of her many tricks to stop what she was seeing. *The nanos—*

*Not right here, Sei. There's security everywhere and we just arrived from Council space. Please don't get a watch put on us this early. Let's GO.*

*Grrr.*

A male among the harassers moved to push the cyborg beau, but was stopped by a spotlight from a nearby corner. An authoritative female voice immediately followed. "We'll have none of that in *my* port, folks. You have 30 seconds to get out. Your tickets have all been invalidated."

"What the—!?"            Aww shit!            What the FUCK, man!

"You guys are upsetting me. Fall out before I drop you all."

With a glare towards the ceiling, two of the bullying five began their scurrying evacuation. But the brown-skinned girl couldn't resist one last taunt. "Fuckin' bootlicker," she mumbled.

A loud buzzer sounded once throughout the terminal as the girl collapsed to the ground. "26 seconds."

The girl's four friends hastened to pick her up and hurriedly hauled her "dropped" mass back through the entrance whence they'd come. The pitiful transport was finished speedily in under 17 seconds.

The intercom voice spoke again, this time in a friendly, welcoming manner to the remaining 200 or so terminal goers, "Port Goodman is a safe and free port, ladies and gentlemen. Carry on."

We observed the couple again. Both seemed relieved and yet… strangely distrustful.

*I know you're curious. So am I. But not here.*

***Huff* Okay.**


I was pretty hungry, and asked Sei if she would be willing to stop by one of the food places just outside of port grounds. She agreed, but couldn't take her eyes off of the number of people in rags trying to sell stuff in the common areas of the port. It was a little excessive.

Do they just *not* regulate this stuff?

**I think they do,** I replied, pointing to several signs on the walls. No homeless inside the terminal. No touching the patrons. Assaultive modding / Ams punishable by penalties up to and including gene dilution. No spiked music. No loud music. No yelling. No drones. No holophones. No hovering. Suspicious running may result in detainment. Arguments will be monitored… and about two dozen other warning signs littered the premises.

Finally, I had to break down and ask a customer service bot, **I'm sorry we're new here. I see all the signs, but why are there still so many homeless people in this area?**

"Because if we let them roam around outside of the port, we can't control how they use their mods on customers. Airport management instituted a strict airspace anti-loitering policy to check all outsiders for danger, but had too many legitimate paying customers landing here and staying as refugees. We cannot tell when anyone is coming or going, so all we can do is keep everyone in a securely surveilled space."

**And why so many refugees?**

"Prices have gone up everywhere while most public services have been defunded. People come to New Newyork dreaming of where to go next in their lives."

**I just lensed some stories about this, Sei. It looks like there aren't a lot of unit owners anywhere. Just rental companies. I think the cities here have run out of options because they don't have a good workforce training infrastructure. Nobody can do the jobs that pay. Only robots and scab iyohns who turn off their bio-directives and work for the new minimum.**

"With their biodirectives off, they don't need food or companionship, and can just work for the energy which we here at Port Goodman provide for them on premises."

Sei scowled at the thought.

**Er, so could you tell us how to get to the Hotel Fabriccio?**

"Of course. Do you mind if I lens you the map?"

**Not at all.**

* * *

**These are terrible accommodations.**

**I think they use some kind of Cesium-based paint to help their trackers work better.**

**Yeah, but why is it curling off the wall?**

**I think the de-radiating bots haven't gotten to this room yet.**

In the corner, a single three-legged bed sat crooked and lonely behind a plain cube nightstand.

Where's the couch?

I don't think these rooms come with one.

But this is a double room! What are we supposed to do, sleep on top of each other? No offense Isaiah, but you probably weigh about 30 tons.

Ma'am!

Okay, maybe I overstated but what the hell is all this?

This is what a normal person in Jupiterian society is expected to view as comfortable outside of a sleep tube farm. Looking this up... I see that a lot of people who can't afford to rent mostly come home to their quarters or pods and dial themselves into stasis, carrying out their domestic lives through local simulation rather than by roaming around taking up the Chancellorate's resources. They give you jupicredits for adopting energy-saving measures while you're there, and this in turn allows the farm-sim programmers to create better private worlds for you to live in.

So...

So the many billions of Jupiterians don't actually pose any resource drain on the city beyond the power it takes to keep their local sim going.

And people with bodies like us that they actually want to use in *this* world...?

They look for work in various bot engineering and senior management roles. Middle management is mostly virtual and non-paying beyond the provision of quarters.

And the people accept this!?

After you've realized that you can no longer make a livable credit flow, you can apply for government assistance and have a sleep cell assigned to you. You then download a program that allows your brain to interface full time with the meta-world, track down your family's assigned dwelling and from then on carry out your old-style life in a gamified dream. I think most people only come out of that dream when they've earned enough skills to join the elite back in Astra.

Sei huffed in disgust. So there' no real point in trying to make a living in this dimension when you're on Jupiter.

There is a point. About 200 conglomerates control 94% of what happens on this planet, and the Jupiterian Dream is to become one of the conglomerate employees and live the life you've always wanted with all the toys of modern space at your disposal. It's in some of the conglomerate's best interests to try to take back Earth and sim-ify the majority beta population there as a matter of principle to them, so the actual sleeping citizens of Jupiter aren't actually behind the aggression towards u—those Earth people.

And this doesn't make you angry?

I've already seen this side of humans. Going on this mission here with you is the best I can do about it. My anger solves nothing.

So the Chancellorate is unchallengeable.

No, the Chancellor here is unchallengeable only in the 30% visible pocket that controls New American public image, and only for as long as this role doesn't anger their inner circle. Rumor has it that the current chancellor usually betaizes themselves so that they can live as long as possible. This is despite waging war on betas. But as you know, the longer you live, the more even the most unsettling things become normal. The dukes get bored with being only dukes. And in the 130 years of chancellors in this particular society, none have made it into their 12$^{th}$ year. All of them have been assassinated or mysteriously replaced. All of them.

But— Sei was clearly confused.

Honor among thieves, Sei. But there are four nation-cities on Jupiter whose chancellors have gone as long as 70-90 years in power. None of them are living anymore. The stats say the current longest reigning is in his 43$^{rd}$ year.

What is up with this place? This society sounds so... hopeless.

There's a lot of research on the Jupiterian way of living, and one of the most popular theories is that people really just want to sustain their livelihoods like any other living thing. To them, going into a Diji sleep sim is like going into another room. They don't have to learn any complicated society-management science or mineral economics, and aren't really invested in the bot wars that the elites are waging against the unconquered air space. The sim can rewrite anything going on out here as just another video game with different kinds of bad guy on all the other planets, and the story is that the Wily Betas have taken over everything and the Elites are building a world to take it back.

That's scary. I don't see why the Council thinks it will take 100 years for them to succeed.

Because server failures are still common, whole regions of metaworlds may be fine one day, nonexistent the next. Then the Astra body can't dial in and... well you need the trust of your people in order to wage a war for a long time and have any hope of winning.

But can't they just generate soldiers? It sounds like something they would do.

There are plenty of generated soldiers. But the megacompanies who make them and the political conglomerates who want to indoctrinate them... the power companies who supply them all have to be friends. But that would be foolish for any one of them. I see in the history that they tried forming an alliance like this years ago and launched a series of attacks on Council-controlled air space hoping to retrain the betas there. All the Council did was open bubble the forces. So the motivations of the five master companies behind the soldier technology were exposed to both the soldiers and the companies themselves. It was clear that Big Power and Big Tech were trying to take each other over, and the alliance failed internally. Really, the problem for Jupiter is that the elites themselves don't trust each other, and New America has too many enemies to successfully attack the Council no matter how imperialistic certain tenures of a chancellor may be. Osaira has kept them in check for decades, because he who controls the Council satellites around Jupiter also controls everything important that Jupiter may still want. Osaira is no friend to the Council either, but have a blanket policy to stop New America from attacking Council airspace for as long as New America has designs on every other country as well. New America is powerful, but very destroyable on multiple fronts if its five main rivals feel it's getting too big for its britches. No, its Zeusland that the Council is worried about. They're more deliberate about who leads them and why. If they decide to unify everyone under the pro-alpha flag, then Earth is in big trouble. The simulations suggest this is the 87% most probable route in about 98-103 years, because that's how long it will take Zeusland's generations to evolve a more New American mentality with the technology to back it.

Hmm...

Ironically, as long as New America is the ultimate power, the Jupiterians won't have the full capacity to destroy either themselves or the current Earth structure. New America doesn't have the international credibility or internal consensus to pull it off, and has already sold 22% of its internal interests to foreign powers. Some crazy number like 16% of the country would actually be okay if the country were conquered in its next war—as long as they're conquered by Osaira. And then 27% of its chip market is controlled by Anichrom—a definite political enemy. That's enough to cripple a lot of the larger efforts—especially when loyal Anichromers form 12% of your elite circle.

I don't like this.

The Council believes that this nation's elites' greatest weakness is a classic human weakness. They only know how to expand. But at some point there is no more room for expansion, only enemies and walls. And they definitely do not know how to stop. So they eat their own until the regime itself ages out or exhausts its own labor resources. Someone within develops a conscience. There is a civil war, a coup, an exterior party who thinks like them,...any number of things, and the empire falls. It isn't Jupiter's strength that they fear. It's Earth's cushy comfort that may lead them to let their guard down.

So this all seems bigger than us, and the people seem pretty content to let things stay as they are. Even if Jupiter eventually conquered back Earth, what would be the point in the grand scheme of things?

Those of us who believe in something higher—like the elites themselves—will have failed as an entire historical species to survive into the future. Just a dog eat dog cycle of physics is all we would have been. Like the Nusians or Atlanteans.

Sei mulled over this, a darkened frown fixed on her face. But the people are too myopic to save.

Yeah. When it comes to thinking about the whole... they are. But within their worlds they still feel social pressures, class problems, and ceilings they can't break through. We're not here to challenge Goodman, Sei. We're here to show each class what it's worth and show as many classes in the time we have. That's all.

*Sigh* I really want to dampen my emotions here, I'll be honest. This is fucking garbage. I'm mean, literal garbage, Sei slapped a half crushed can off of the cuboid nightstand. But...

If either of us did that, then we're forcing ourselves to be more okay with this. The alphas and machinas of this world may not deserve anything better than the comfort conglomerates they have ceded their lives to, but so much of that is the fault of millions of years of human nature much stronger than any family or corporation. Some people build satellites. Others built thought systems. If we do it right, our thought system can make a difference. But it's not a war we fight with politics or soldiers. Just mentalities.

Sei seemed to relax a little. I hate this.

Taking on a planet was never easy.

Hmph... but I'm so glad you're here.

# 211. Exorcism Training

Sei and I stared expectantly at the pearl arm brace, waiting for something to happen.

I understand that Jake must have programmed it not to go off at all hours of the day, but how do you get it to turn on at all?

**Well, what are we trying to do here? Can you just lens it like a regular device?**

Let me see.

In less than a couple of seconds, a sleek red stripe brightened with a warm glow.

Okay. Now what?

**Uh...**

Wh- whoa. This is... pretty uncomfortable.

**Really? How's that?**

It's like a—you know, an urge. To uh... like I want to... really find someone in particular.

**?**

But. Oh my god this is wild.

What? What's wild?

It's like it's zapping my vision. There's...

...?

There are two doors and about—1, 2, 3,...eight bars next to the right door which are moving back and forth... I mean they're definitely measuring my biometrics.

Oh I've heard of this! It uses emkeys?

I think so.

So the bars are telling you how close you are to feeling the right emotions to open the right door?

Yeah. And the left door is something like a dismiss button. I know that if I choose it then this will all probably stop for now. But I won't necessarily know how to get it back. The door on the right will probably start the instructions.

You know, the old Spacetime team would have picked the left door first just to see what it did.

Would they? I would have thought they wanted to choose the right door first. It's definitely more interesting.

But they would want to know the bounds of the technology first, and would want to know how to get out of it before going all the way in.

Oh.

And if they couldn't turn it back on, then they'd know the device needed more work. I was raised on that pattern and feel it to be very true. Their curiosity wasn't just about the space they were in, but about what "being in" meant at all.

Ohhh. Then I'll start with the dismiss then.

The red strip fell dark in a gentle fade.

Sei shook her head as if trying to snap out of a drowsy haze. The weird tingles are gone, but I still feel like I need to sleep.

Okay.

And also, the more we were talking, the more thrown-off the bars were. I'm dialing in again...


The red streak recovered its previous glow.

Could you give me a moment?

**Of course.** I have to admit, I was a little apprehensive regarding what was about to happen next.

Sei closed her eyes with a deep inhalation.

I watched for several seconds while she appeared to gain her bearings.

It's just something you know. I'm clearly being engrantzed. It feels like something I should trust, and it's okay to follow it. Like a situation I've been in a long time ago... that I'm getting to replay it right here.

...

But there's this compass in my hand, like one of those old directional ones with the spinning arrow. The writing in the air a few hundred feet away is asking me, "Do you want to learn exorcism?" I'm saying yes.

I remained quiet.

Okay, I've reached the floating message. Now it feels like I suddenly know what all my next options are, and can choose from them without having to think it out or explain it. Even what I just said was one of those options. I chose to reason out loud... If you don't mind, I'm going to lens you my visualization stream and give you interactive rights. We can start a jump right from here.

Knowing how internal jumps work, I dutifully took a seat on the floor opposite the shaggy bed Sei was now sitting on. Being too close to an internal jumper only makes their bodies triggery, disrupting the jump the way some real life surprise can disrupt the body of a dreamer.

To lens Sei, I thought first about her as a person in my company, then I asked myself what she might be thinking. Then I started to immerse myself in a film-like version of those very thoughts. This is basic praesciens voyance 101. And because she opened up a visualization stream, the scenario that I envisioned was automatically informed by her response to what she was seeing under the influence of the arm brace.

I streamed back my own take on her feed, and in this way a temporary virtual world was born.

# First Exorcism: Sei versus herself

The drums of war boomed across a rocky arid landscape as the 25th century rendition of the ancient syjazz song Haywyre – Insight announced the beginning of what I presumed to be Sei's training in exorcism. Standing before us, a slender lanky man with blue skin dressed in the garb of an Egyptian court attendee introduced himself.

"Welcome Sei and Isaiah, you will need to be an exorcist of at least acceptable caliber if you are to make use that device of yours. Though your own futures are as assured as your friends' willingness and ability to reprint you, even if you are killed, the same cannot be said of those you help. For each of them, you will have only one chance to put them on the Path of the Leader. To do that, you must be a skilled follower of your instinct for what will work in their lives. Let us begin."

Uh—

The blue man vanished into near transparency as the planet Earth appeared before us.

"This is a calculation for 97 years from now."

A fleet of ships was shown firing a series of seeming pulses down to the planet Earth, a giant Jupiter looming in the background.

"But we need not dwell on this. Here is a calculation for 121 years from now."

Amidst a violently destructive storm, cities all across what seemed to be the Jupiterian skyline fell into the oblivion beneath, this time with a giant Earth, Saturn, and Venus looming just beyond.

"The war machines of Jupiter, with the help of a few beta survivors from Earth, really do conspire to turn on their warring masters, rendering every alpha, machina, and praesciens truly extinct. This is the genocide of all genocides, and as of the 33rd century, there will truly be no more sapiens alphas of any kind on any planet in this system. The former war machines will manufacture a great cube housing a perpetual dynamics simulation, and that cube will remain until either natural events consume it or it runs out of energy. For their known failure to occupy Astra effectively, and without a genuine reason to drag along physical bodies they certainly don't need, the entirely iyohn race will port themselves into data, where they may or may not be discovered by future races traveling the galaxy. It will not matter, however, because the languages used to program this cube will be lost with the occupants of the cube itself. More cubes will be made, but to no avail."

I cast a careful eye towards Sei, who stood stiff with a pursed frown.

"What you are witnessing is the death of a species. And now, for the first part of your training: How do you conceive of this entity?"

Sei lowered her head to the left, closing her eyes as a massive black double drum roller emerged in from a cloud of violet and white flame. On each side, the shadows of two oversized former falcons beat their wings angrily as they fanned the otherworldly tongues of fire towards us.

Sei and I backed away in hurried startle, but in hindsight not as far as one would have guessed.

"The first thing you'll learn, exorcist, is that your representations are of your own making, regardless of the outward form taken by the thing you are representing. Even the mightiest mountain will eventually fall before God, under the scrape of drifting continents, under the quickly engineered bomb made by man, broken up in surface pieces by the roots of trees, or even the gentle but ceaseless flow of a river. Or the mountain may not move at all, yet be transformed into an enjoyable haven under a blanket of snow and skis. All things die, exorcist. Yours is the task of putting on a show your loved ones and future generations will remember, and one that your client will be able to apply for themselves. To that end, you must never EVER exorcise someone else's demon without that someone's own help. This weakens your value to them and everyone else after them, for you truly will have failed to cure them as you were too busy indulging your own anxiousness to take down an image which could not harm you to begin with."

The machine and its birds continued to flail and scream, but neither one moved an inch.

"Also know this: fighting can be done in one of two ways in this trade. For sport or for survival. If you engage in it for survival, know that you will be using tension to fight tension, and the fight will certainly be harder. But if you engage in it for sport and can convince your client to see it this way as well, you may truly exorcise the disharmony from them."

Sei nodded her acknowledgement.

"Now, your task is to eliminate these characters without breaking a sweat or fearing that you will lose. This is your representation of humanity's death. Use what you learned from Venus to envision any solution you can."

At that last word, the blue man vanished entirely, and the enemy began to move.

Sei drew an arrow from a materialized quiver and aimed straight for one of the birds as I tried to circle around the main machine. But Sei missed her first shot.

I scrambled to materialize some sort of weapon, but couldn't think of one that might defeat an enemy without introducing more tension. **What did we learn from Venus?**

Sei fired again and missed again. Then again, and missed again. Immediately after the third shot, the ground cracked beneath her as the roller trudged her way. She slipped and fell, but sprang back to kneeling in an instant.

FUCK!

One of the dark birds swooped across her left shoulder driving a slicing claw into her flesh. A splash of blood streaked through the air, Sei yelling out in a combination of irritation and genuine pain. GRRRR!

The roller began picking up speed, but Sei wasn't moving out of the way.

I rushed in to scoop her up just as another claw came down. **Get behind there!**

We darted behind a large rock several yards away.

**Hey! Heey! Sei, get it together!** *(Did you not see that thing about to run you over!)*

But Sei could only growl.

Without thinking, I raised my hand towards one of the circling birds, conjuring a group of symbols above its head.

What!? What's that?

**It looks like a "no fight" sign? And a cowboy on a bronco?**

Sei shook her head in embarrassment. I should have known not to fight it.

**You have an idea?**

Yeah.

**Good, because here it comes!**

Sei charged out from behind our rock with a "Yah!!"

I started after her, but was stopped by the sudden appearance of the blue man, shaking his head no.

!?

**But—**

"You can't harm her representations. Just be her sounding board and keep her safe."

(I must have looked very perplexed.) **So I don't fight with her?**

"Not unless you want her to need you every time in the future."

**Huff** Then... you should make me transparent like you.

The blue man stroked his chin in thought.

I'm going, I announced to the man as I rushed back out to join Sei.

No sooner did a dodging, lasso-bearing Sei glimpse me out of the corner of her eye did one of the black birds shriek with a thunderous burst that rendered me all but immaterial. Apparently the blue man had granted my request.

Isaiah are you okay!? Sei attempted to rope one of the airborne birds' claws.

I timidly drew closer to the temporarily immobile dark drum roller to confirm that I could no longer feel the formerly searing heat arcing off of its structure. Creeping closer still.

Finally I dipped myself headfirst into the machine. Sei!

Just then, a pair of flailing legs dangled skyward off of the ground.

Whoooa! Sei yelled wide-eyed as one of the birds towed her streamer-style through the air.

*(The cowboy symbol. She's taming it!)*

G—get up there! Pull yourself! *(If I can't touch anything then I shouldn't be able to touch the ground either. I should be able to fly.)*

I felt my body morph into a semi-dreamlike form as a haze of bright blue engulfed me. The ground seemed to grow in fisheye even as it grew more distant—the disco ball of my field of view drew Sei and her shadow bird quickly closer. If I was ethereal it must be as a ghost in flight.

Sei's hand began to slip as we drew closer to an encroaching boulder. Yet her legs appeared as mouse trails suggesting her next move.

Legs up!

Sei curled up as if doing crunches just in time to miss the stubborn rock.

Next, a series of glowing spots appeared on the rope. I amplified them to direct my friend even further.

Put your hands here! Not yet!

The shadow bird streaked upwards as if beginning a loop. But at this point I began to see only red.

## Don't let it do that! Stop it now! Whatever you can!

Sei tried to heave herself up the rope with all of her strength, but the bird's upward surge rendered further climbing impossible. Now visibly angry with the bird, Sei wriggled one arm into a painful loop and materialized a micro crossbow glove in the other. With both hands gripping the rope, Sei put four holes into the creature's belly, instantly convincing it to change its mind about looping.

A wide pair of shadowy wings tilted awkwardly askew as the wrangled bird began to fall. The sudden shift into weightlessness made even me dizzy, though I no longer had a body of my own.

As the stopped bird's wounded corpse began to drop past us, the tip and base of its nearest wing lit up before me, a perforation cutting across the latter.

## Cut the wing and glide!

Sei's hand crossbow turned chainsaw as our waning upwards momentum put her just above the bird. One concentrated 2-second cut was all it took to sever first the wing, then followed by a smooth twist into severing the lassoed claw.

Sei stepped on the back of the bird and kicked the rest of its body into the airy beyond. The chainsaw retracted as the wing tips seemed to absorb the rest of the bird into a new array of cords on each edge. At the ends of each group of flapping cords, a claw-shaped handle appeared.

## Hold on tight!

Sei flipped upside down as our descent finally took hold. Heavier than her freshly granted parachute, she rolled topsy-turvy over the wing before swinging into a much gentler glide back down.

*sigh*

*sigh*

I turned my fisheye attention back to the other bird and drum roller below. With some focus, some icons appeared above the dark machine. But I knew these particular symbols would not help my friend.

## Are you afraid of death? I asked.

Nope.

## Why not?

I've already come back I don't know how many times. But even if I hadn't, death is just sleep to me.

## So what's going on with the steamroller?

That's humanity's unstoppable move in the wrong direction.

The ground was fast approaching, as was the other bird who continued to circle without aim. **Do you really believe there's anything we can do about it? Do you know what that is?**

No. So we're not going to beat this today?

## Hmm. No, *but...*

Sei's feet touched ground. The roller seemed to wake up from its parking space 150 feet away.

Alright bird, let's go!

Successfully taunted, the second bird cut a blazing path directly towards Sei, who now held a hula hoop sized eight-pronged wheel before her. Shortly before the shadow bird reached us, Sei shifted deliberately to the side, leaving only the wheel. The bird sailed through, only to transform into a stately copper-feathered falcon. It's black and white head and rich goldenrod beak clearly indicated a spirit changed. The bird settled calmly on its feet, bearing a saddle as if waiting for Sei to mount it. She did so immediately, with plenty of time to spare before the hulking fiery machine came anywhere near us.

Suddenly before me, a hollow whirlpool appeared to encircle the trundling drum roller, only to break into several smaller arcs. I cannot describe to you exactly what I saw, only what I said next.

## Spectralize it!

A tic-tac-toe shape seemed to brand the air in front of the vehicle. The drum roller burst into nine human shaped shadows who quickly scattered every which way as if they had just been found out. I think we both recognized one climbing out of the upper right for the distinctive hat shape it wore. Clearly it was Heitel.

Hey! Sei called out. But it was too late. The bird, the machine, the remaining shadows—even the landscape disappeared into blackness before us.

I regained my body, and the blue man strode out of the shadows. It seemed he wished to debrief us.

"Good job, Esperanza! And you too, Navigator! Did either of you learn anything?"

I'm not even going to ask what turned you into a ghost, Isaiah, but there's no way any of that would have worked if that bird hadn't screamed at you.

"He asked for that."

What?

"It was after I told him he couldn't fight your representations for you. Rather than disappoint you with his required ineffectiveness, he asked me to make him transparent so that you would know not to count on him to assist you, but also so that you would not be confused or upset by his apparent uselessness. Sometimes, no matter how unsupported we think we are, the truth is, some battles are ours alone. The best you will get is a cheering section or another perspective. In the future, Sei, you may play this role more often than you would like, and will need to be as quick to help indirectly as Isaiah was here."

Oh.

"All of the theater and acrobatics aside, your virtual battles in the psyche will be manifestations of your handling of the obstacle in waking life. It appears, Genevieve—or should I say Sei—that you don't fear death, but can be made to understand it as being different depending on the type of person. Mass death as I initially presented it to you is a very different scenario than a phenomenon that some cultures may celebrate with ceremony, for example, and you two's ability to recognize this guarantees, at the very least, that you can indeed (and probably will) change at least a few perspectives on the human fate one smaller group culture at a time."

We both listened.

"Periodically I may show you how our calculations have changed Ψ as your work progresses, but there would be no point in doing it just yet.[2] This was only training, so the scenario calculations are more or less the same as they were a few minutes ago."

---

[2] Ψ: Events which will have added up to a changed timeline, all traceable to Sei, Isaiah, and certain communications they will make or explanations they trigger, sometimes *very* indirectly. These shall be called "probability-altering forces" or "pafs" by future researchers of the events archived in this account.

"Whether or not you are able to change all of humanity with your work, know that your quest to restore all identities—from the most elite to the poorest of poor, regardless of any class—does have the *potential* to benefit many more lives than comparable perceptions of your people's evils have harmed. If one dark perspective can contaminate 50 online minds one small piece at a time, you will have succeeded in your own lives if you can bless 51. Or, 102 that is. But you'll need to work *with* your clients, not for them. You cannot hand them your skills or stand trial in their place. And if by the end, the fate of humanity remains the same, it hardly matters because the remixing of stars will see you anew elsewhere."

"But wouldn't it be lovely to win this game convincingly?"

Yes, it would, Sei replied, holding her shoulder. But I would have thought facing myself was harder.

"You had a great navigator. The insight was automatic. It will be important for you to gain the trust of your clients as much as possible before you go into these realms. Most of each battle will be won or lost before you even enter the arena."

And if I can't gain their trust?

Yes—or if she feels the client can't be helped?

"Then abort the mission. Take the arm brace and never exorcise them. The person's own help is *required*."

Okay.

I acknowledged.

"Well then, that's it for me folks. I'll see you in your first scenario."


The blue man disappeared accordingly. Shortly thereafter, we both woke up.

# 212. In the Line at the Ice Cream Shop

**I think I'd like to go get some air,** I told Sei.

Uh, okay.

**I feel a little claustrophobic all of a sudden, and it might be because this place itself—and everything we have to do here—feels so heavy.**

Hmm... I know what you mean.

**I'll be offline for a couple of hours if that's alright with you.**

Sure, take all the space you need. I could use some too.


Knowing that our new planet was generally hostile to us "unnaturals" (as the term goes), I decided the best way to get a sense of the place was to turn my sotions off. This isn't all emotions, just the social ones triggered by other people's interactions with you.

There are 3 kinds of emotion buckets and a 4th super bucket: 1) sotions are social emotions which include anything usually triggered by the thought of another person and what they're doing to you. 2) notions are "N"vironmental emotions which give you a sense of a place. If you turn these off, you also temporarily disable your sense of smell. 3) motions are Movement emotions like strain, pain and fatigue. Turning these off is like turning off your HP bar, coins, and menu in a video game. You need these to tell you where your body is at in terms of health in the moment. And then there is the fourth group. 4) Votions are feelings about your own internal processes like heart rate, discomfort, and being short of breath. Some people like to turn these off in small doses when they want to get really high. But for the most part you have to force that. Our bodies are exactly wired to NEVER shut off our votions. To do so is to court death.

And then again, this is exactly what really old betas and cyborgs do when they have decided it is time to shut down permanently.

Immediately outside of the hotel, I can feel the distrust that might have been had my sotions still been on. It's not that the average New American hates foreign bots, it's not even that most of them do. But I'd say that one out of 20 people I encounter on the street seem genuinely uncomfortable with my (to them) mannequin-like presence, and wish that I would vacate to the nearest conveyor belt—perhaps to be put out of their sight for good. They believe that we betas represent the loathsome conquest of their kind by greedy tech companies hundreds of years ago, kicking them off of their own planet and relegating them to a lone desperate corner of the solar system. You can't tell them that they—with their chip implants, satellite eyes, and the maze of generational pharmagens in their blood—are no more nature-natural than we are. That their hate towards us is both blind and hypocritical. That not even *they* want to see the full force of what they have coming to them should their anger prevail. They became us—their future selves, and now a loud few of them want to destroy those very future versions. It doesn't really make sense logically, though psychologically I suppose it's just basic territorialism. Over the territory some philosophers have called "identity prerogative."

The worst part is that these ones out of 20 aren't even the norm. But 10 out of twenty accept the former's paths without thinking of something better or acting to achieve it.

Among the remaining 9 out of twenty, two can be counted on to make plenty of jokes about the original one which 6 more are guaranteed to laugh at. The last one knows the whole score and wants to fix it all, but has 19 mountains to climb before anything can happen. It's a mess which doesn't foster much good with most people out there. So your only allies are still more machines to shield you from the chaos beyond. And if you yourself can think like a machine, then you also have your firewall.

I would like to buy a data feed from the newsstand, but am pretty sure the man behind the counter doesn't like me. So I turn into a neighboring ice cream shoppe instead.

"Hey bot! What are you doing here? The gas station is across the street. Hahaha!"

Lucky for this punk, my sotions are off, so I can calculate the optimum reply which poses minimal risk to myself.

**Yeah, I just came from there. Your mom says she wants her wig back.**

The coiffed thuglet reeled back wide-eyed as if watching a car plow into a ravine.

**Hey man, you need a dollar for this ice cream? I can lend you one, I** continued. **Or maybe you need two dollars.**

The little man looked around for some friends, but received only a few blushing faces.

Stunned that he had somehow been either insulted, outsmarted, outcharmed, or all of the above by a "bot," he puffed his cheeks in frustration and left the store without incident. Honestly, my comeback wasn't even funny. But it didn't have to be. He behaved exactly as I expected.

And so did the onlookers.

My sense was that they warmed up to me.

I stood fourth in line behind a rather studious-looking black man with a slight scowl on his face. I took note as he peered sideways through his glasses at a group of seven or eight boisterous youths just outside the shop. Were they relatives or something? In front of him, a stoic Caucasian lady gave an exasperated sigh as she waited for they clumsy brunette in front of her to finish fiddling with her purse.

"For God's sake lady, do you need some extra chips? Here, I'll cover it," Second-in-line scolded.

"Oh! Thanks! I don't know what happened. I thought I had enough on my card…"

Third-in-line rolled his eyes. Second-in-line flashed an unamused pucker.

"Here." Second-in-line picked up the face scanner and spoke into it, "I'm paying this girl's balance."

A brief beep sounded as Second's ring pulsed a ruby red light around its rim, followed by a slightly dimmer glint of blue.

"Minus 49 dollars o, plus 2 dollars el for the cover," the cashier announced. "Here's your ice cream, Miss."

The clumsy brunette nodded a final cheerful thanks before skipping away with her vanilla n' cherry tower. Second nodded back, then took her place at the front of the line.

Just then, the youths outside broke into spontaneous song,

"Hit that booty, BUMP! BUMP! / Hit that hit that JUNK JUNK / Do it keep it movin' when you GOT IT in yo' trunk trunk!"

Second raised an eyebrow while Third slowly buried his face in one hand, Gahd… he muttered under his breath, shaking his head.

Second turned to Third, "Your kids have a new song today, Ballant?"

I don't know them.

"I'm here to pick up an order for Clue Actuarial," The lady informed the cashier. "So you're just going to drive the school van back without them?" Second teased.

But Third (whose name seemed to be Ballant) could only huff.

I'm trying to teach these kids social studies but all they can think about is boyfriends and who made out with who. But then I go to the college to teach my so called adults and all they can do is threaten me with complaints to the Dean if I don't pass them with easy As.

"You're teaching Professional Etiquette at workfork. I'm surprised even some of them stay interested."

What gets me most is that these are the same people who grow up swearing that the government is out to oppress them. They're sitting there in my class and I tell them, 'Now etiquette is how these government types separate the ignorant flock from potentially good puppet candidates. And once you're a puppet you can carve out a little piece of luxury for yourself.

Second chuckled, "You missed a step. First it's the flock. Then it's *bagman* to a puppet. *Then* a puppet. We're all still bagmen in here, aren't we?" (This earned a couple of nods around the room.) Because we're '*educated*'."

Hm. The power of dreaming big. See and that's what I want these guys to shoot for. The stars.

"I think—oh!" Second averted her eyes after a brief glance outside.

Ballant and I turned to see what the distraction was.

Hey! Ballant ejected from his place in line in order to stop a wayward freshman(?) from twerking against a fire hydrant.

While Third was outside wagging an extra-long finger at his students, Second received her order. But she, the cashier, and I couldn't help but watch the scene transpiring outside.

Meanwhile, I realized that five more people had suspiciously materialized in the line behind me.

"Hey Beta! It's your turn!"

Uh...

Second and the cashier continued to watch Mr. Ballant admonishing his students.

Um... you can cut.

"Hmph." The irritated customer maneuvered around me. "One Master Sherry, please."

The cashier reluctantly peeled her eyes from the scolding. "One. Master. Sherry… Anything else?"

"No."

"57 o and 6 el"

"What!? Is that some kind of tax or something?"

The cashier shrugged.

"Goddammit. I don't know why they don't replace you guys."

The cashier altered her countenance ever so slightly as if to say, "Oopsie!"

"Urgh. There." The customer waved his hand in front of the face scanner. Two red pulses flashed on his temple receiver.

"One minute, please."

I offered a line-cut to the next person, whose was considerably nicer in accepting. Second continued to watch the scene outside, Disposacool® full of ice cream in her hand.

The next cutter also ordered a Master Sherry.

"57 o," the cashier announced.

The previous customer, well aware of why he had been penalized in trust credits (el) couldn't bear to look at the person after him.

Soon after, Ballant came back in, taking his place as the 8th in line. Both I and the person behind me, however, wouldn't even think of it. Inspecting the next customer's feeling about it just in case, I received easy consent and waved Ballant back into his spot at the front.

**Thanks, so much, Mister.**

"The usual Mr. Michael?"

**Yeah. I have the list here. Can I have two Moundibuses, one Master Sherry, one April fog, two Funk baskets, one The Fang, six sides of fries, and a Weirwuf.**

"Sure thing."

****Sigh**. Diedre, do you wanna take them home with you?**

Second (Diedre) shook her head. "No way. You guys were fun to watch though."

**And they can be yours every day for the low price of two Moundibuses, one Master Sherry, one April fog—**

"Hehehe. Nope, I'm outta here. See you, Michael."

**Well, it was worth a try.**


I was next.

"Welcome to Creaminal, how may I help you?"

## Hmm. What would you recommend?

"Well, let's see. Our beta customers seem to really like Jagron the Deep or the Electric Chair because they're kind of like an energy food. Plenty of nanos in those. I personally like the Slothy just because it's so decadent. You feel like someone's really spoiling you."

## How about one to help you feel inner peace?

"Oh! Then you want Eternal Redundancy. It's gooood! There's your ingredients." The cashier waved her hand to open a holographic product description at the counter.

## That looks great. I'll have one of those.

"Cool. Anything else?"

**No, that's all.**

"$26 o"

I waved my hand over the scanner to pay. **If you don't mind my asking, where's your kitchen staff? I mean, it looks so empty back there.**

"We don't have cooks. We only have restockers and security officers located somewhere else."

The person behind me added, "Yeah. if you've never been here, ole Chrysalis here is the afternoon manager. Any orders you give go through her network login straight to the chef engines back there and they do all the cooking."

Chrysalis the cashier-manager added, "They used to think that this job wouldn't be needed once the automaton producers started taking all of the old jobs, but they pay the three of us managers 4o2o2 shifts to keep the orders humming and this place profitable."

"On a slow day, all she does is sit in the back office and play this drone game which actually controls a grantbot to fly around the city making people hungry. They have mannequins that can do this job if everyone gets sick or something, but having a good ole human operate your customer service order routing and marketing machine is still where the money is at."

"Creaminal hires only the best!" Chrysalis batted her eyes playfully.

"Yeah. I'm pretty sure she makes more than I do. And I'm an accountant," the customer behind me noted.

Chrysalis shrugged coyly.


Exiting the ice cream shoppe, I ran into an old friend. One of the arm brace drones apparently caught up with me, projecting a tiny 2" x 2" message from Sei.

"Is there a teacher around you? Angel just updated itself."

I searched for a quiet spot away from any suspect Jupiterians, so that I could go back online in peace. While looking, I caught a glimpse of Ballant and his students enjoying their ice cream in the park.

**Yes, Sei. I got your message.**

Sorry to bother you, but this was weird. I was looking at the Angel brace when you left, trying to find out where to start, and nothing happened. Then all of a sudden, it said the likelihood that someone could be reached went way up! Since I hadn't moved, I sent out one of the drones, and followed its camera view. It went straight to your closet. Luckily I'm smart, and had the bright idea to ask it to find you. It tracked you down and the numbers got up to 96%. But then they dropped again—like someone was going out of range. But they jumped back up from 10% to 95% as soon as you called me.

**That's amazing! I'll have to ask Jake how all this works again. But I know exactly who it wants me to talk to.**

Really?

**Yeah, and that's probably why the percentage is so high. So there was this teacher standing in line—but I wouldn't know what to say to him.**

Forget about that, just find him before he leaves!

**Okay, but you'll have to uh... use the drone to read his emhim?**

Fine. Let's go.

I approached the man Ballant while he was in the middle of an explanation to his students. I believe he was expounding upon the drawbacks of Nihilism. His students clearly weren't following, but they seemed to donate as much respect as could be reasonably asked for.

*Alright, Sei. I'm counting on you...*

**Hi, excuse me.**

**The percent's dropping to 20!**

**Wh—?**

Ballant looked up at me.

**Ahh...I...uh. Can I sit in on your lecture?**

Ballant looked at me quizzically.

"What are you, government or something?" One of the students asked, quickly rushing to the defensive.

"Nah, he's a beta. Look at how smooth his skin is. Like a GQ model. They wanna know everything."

Ballant relaxed a little. "Hm Well, I guess. We were just talking about meaningfulness in society."

"Mr. Ballant keeps telling us that it's important to vote your conscience, even if the side you pick has zero chance of winning. But he hasn't convinced us yet."

I was saying that it's a question of personal empowerment. If you don't vote your conscience, then you're admitting that something outside of you has the power to tell you how to think.

"And Dubhe was saying that your personal power won't pay the bills or keep you safe."

"That's right. When a man has a gun to your head, you vote for whatever he says."

I wasn't denying that. But most of the time there are little ways in which you can choose for yourself. The man doesn't have a gun to your head all the time until you get very high up in the ranks.

"And we was sayin' there never will be that kind of rank for most people. There's no point in voting when it's all controlled anyway—."

The student stopped, apparently catching me stroking my chin. Everyone fell quiet all of a sudden.

"Hey sir," one of them asked me. "Does this make sense?"

I think it does, but... well. Do you think one person can change the world?

"Heh!"                                         "Hah"!

                              "Yeah, right! Now we have two philosophers here."

Obviously I'm a beta, you know that. But don't you think it's weird that I'm here? Asking to sit in on your class?

"Man, we don't even know you. You could be government."

And what would government want from you all that they couldn't get from a bank or a committee somewhere? Are y'all that high up?

"Hmm."

"No, but…"

"But you know, big brother's always watching."

So give him a show if you think that's true.

The students looked at each other. "Man, who are you? You must not know how things work down here."

I'm uh... an entertainer. I help write scripts for teaching materials in psychology.

"Really." One of the students quated. "Besides being brown like us, why would you care how we think? Shouldn't you be at a college or a lab or something?"

I had a feeling I could learn from you all.

"Learn? Like what?"

Maybe I just wanted to see how people who sing [*look up*] "Booty BaBump" handle Nihilism.

...

...

...

"Mr. Ballant! Is this what you were talking about? That one day that surprise rich guy might find us and start observing our manners?"

Nn...yeah! You never know.

"So where do you work?"

"Are you recruiting?"

"How much does it pay?"

(Sei tuned in right then. Isaiah. Look really serious for about two seconds, then leave. But give the teacher your contact as you do.)

I did as instructed. ...hmph. Well I have to go. Sir, mind if I lens you my contact?

Oh. Sure.

I transferred the address of a place a couple of buildings down from Sei's and my hotel, along with some advice. *These folks have no tact. Please keep their hopes alive while you teach them to be better.* It was nice meeting you all.

Ballant frowned as I left.


*Great job, Isaiah! 98%!*


* * *

The following afternoon, Ballant walked into the Orange Truffle, scanning the dining room for me and an accomplice I had told him about. Sei waved him over.

Mr. Ballant. Sei Esperanza, pleased to meet you. You already know Isaiah Fontenot.

Nice to meet you.

Nice to meet you. Please, sit down.

If you don't mind, could you put this little device on your temple so that we may all speak comfortably?

I, uh, really don't—

Oh! So sorry! Where are my manners? First let me tell you who we are and what we would like to discuss. Could you tune into frequency 43066hg.bnkn.09?

Eh—you must have me mistaken for somebody else, I'm a natural born, unmodded.

Oh! That's even better. Have you ever twiced before?

Ballant's jaw fell open .........No—I thought that was something only bots— eh, betas and cyborgs could do?

And praesciens, I interjected.

But all unmods can train into praesciens skills. Or we could just read your emhim and send feedback to it.

Is that how that works!?

More or less. Now before we continue, Isaiah and I are going to give you a couple of minutes to run some scenarios in your head—mainly to assess whether we are dangerous, whether we are helpful, and whether—if you had the chance to learn all of the paths to your most noble aspirations, but had to forget where they came from, would you take that chance. You would be safe as long as you trusted the process, but you would be working for something bigger than Jupiter.

…

While you mull over it, ask yourself who you suspect us to be and know that we only work with smart people. If at any time you do something that isn't smart, we will vanish along with your memory of us.

Acts that are "not smart" include referring to certain names or organizations out loud, or being loose-lipped in general. Do you understand?

And what if I say no?

You can say no, Sei tapped the side of her temple as a gentle, yet thunderous burst flooded across our six feet of table space, and I supposed you might do so as a matter of personal freedom. Michael? Michael?

Oh, I'm sorry. I spaced out for a second.

Did you hear what I said?

I—honestly, no. I think you were saying something about my right to leave the project at any time—that if I needed to do it out of a sense of personal freedom I could.

Exactly.

But I really… I'm sorry, I really don't remember how I got here. What time is it?

15:50 *Greenwich.*

Greenwich! So you're fr—oh. Oh… well that wouldn't be smart. So you were saying something about helping a thing bigger than my own race?

Yes.

And undoing the ugly war machine that the conglomerates are building?

No, but that sounds like a fascinating movie script doesn't it, Isaiah?

**Sure does.**

But. Oh, okay. Yeah I get it. And what about my students? When I don't show up for class—

Actually, it will take less than three hours. Then you won't hear from us again.

Wha—really?

Really.

And what do I need to do again?

All you need to do is give your consent to let us exorcise you. We will jump into your psychology and interact with what is there. Not brainwashing or anything like that. Just simple talk. Mind to mind.

How come I feel there's more to it than that? Tell me I'm not gonna end up assassinating anybody on behalf of the So—

Sei drew her hand closer to her face.

Although certainly the world would be a better place.

Don't be so sure. And that's not what we came for, Sei remarked.

No, this isn't about the chess players. It's about the redesign of the pawns. Reteaching them so that they can prosper independent of the chess players.

Ballant mulled over this for several seconds.

You're a smart man, we're told. Do some research on how we betas work, and ask yourself if the gist is consistent with what we're proposing.

And of course, stay smart. If you feel the need to share this proposal with anyone at all—be it a friend, a savi, a diary, or any traceable record outside of your own brain, we will know. If we know, then the conglomerates can also know. We could not guarantee your safety in that case.

Now that's very cloak and dagger.

If you really understand the topics you teach to your students then you will also understand why this is so.

Ballant reflected some more. "And after it's done, I'll forget any of this ever happened?"

Yes, but you'll remember in its place, a reasonable story for how you unlocked a talent for teaching that you always had.

3 hours and that's it?

And you will never hear from us again, nor be accountable for any association with us.

You know… well, nevermind. I'll think about it.

Very well. I guess this meeting is over. Maybe we'll hear from you tonight or tomorrow.

The nano footage we used to spy on Mr. Ballant proved satisfactory, as he truly spent the night alone in what appeared to be deep thought. Although it is possible that he lensed some people in the Jupiterian government without us knowing, we felt that this was so unlikely that it wasn't worth the worry.

The next day, Ballant met us at a different location, Bergmann Square about a block away from our previous place.

Okay, I'm all in. What do I need to do?

Excellent.  You told us that you and your college students are currently studying Eastern Earth philosophy.  We ask only that you do three things. First, mention Buddhism. Second, give them an assignment to visit a meditation place, and mention that you will also be trying this assignment since you haven't done it in a while. Finally, after class, we want you to visit the open temple of 39th and Fargate Street. Plan to be there for four hours. That is all.

And you're not going to use me to do something criminal, are you?

Not at all. That is not the beta way. We hope you know that.

Hm. I kinda do. I think everybody does. But we're not the powers that be. And I really don't know what I could do to change things.

You'd be surprised. Just trust the process. And if at any time you want out, then you will forget all about us.

You know I looked that up. It's called 'blanking' isn't it? Yesterday when I forgot how I got here or who you were?

Correct. We do that for everyone's protection. Ours, yours, and the wider interests involved.

Hm. Somehow I'm not the least bit curious as to what you mean. I wonder why that is.

Mysterious, isn't it?

9 hours later, Michael Ballant walked into the Fargate open temple. But he didn't find me or Sei there. Only a pearl white arm brace.

# 213. A Black Eye Sees Nearly

Ballant investigated the arm brace thoroughly, not unlike a canine investigating a peculiar smell. With views of our very first charge both in dronic fisheye and arm brace reclarity, we pasted a stream of messages onto the brace's display:

- This device is the property of the Human Race.
- Wear it to view your own mind.
- Explore your mind to unlock a gift that may change the entire world for those close to you.

At some point during the previous night, Sei and I had a long discussion regarding the risks of telling people who we were, even if we did have the ability to blank them afterwards. You never knew when the enemies of the Solar Council would be watching, and we really had no interest in drawing attention to ourselves.

Accordingly, we decided from then on to approach future charges using the brace alone. It was just too risky to appear in person.

But having been thoroughly briefed already, Mr. Ballant already knew the score. He tried on the arm brace with little hesitation.

And that's where the magic began.

   *Genevieve of Venus*

Angel Finder Jump

Subject: **Michael Ballant**

Spring 89, 2771 n.e.


Ballant. Ballan—BALLANT. Ba—BALLANT!

Ballant—We

BALLANT—We NEED YOU!

The disheveled teacher rolled out of his bed to the echo of voices amidst voided space. Only he and his bed stood visibly beneath a brilliant white spotlight cast from who knows where.

Ugh… my head.

"Ballant, we need you!" The voices persisted.

The groggy teacher shook his head in defiance. Not you again. At least when you're in the back of my mind, I can't hear you.

"Whether you hear us or not, the need still exists."

Yeah. Riiight. Is this about that world-fixing stuff again?

"You mock us. But we are your own voice."

Yes, like a holdover from an overly optimistic childhood. I used to play hero a lot, you know.

"It is a role that fits you in more ways than you know."

Like every other person out there who has the same dreams, am I right?

"Not exactly."

And tell me, what is the difference between my so-called inner voice and all of the other deluded and disillusioned people out there?

"Everyone's inner voice has the power to affect anyone who hears it. And if that voice is to the hearer's benefit, then that voice might change a life for the good."

Well there you go. Like everyone else, my classroom lessons go only as far as my students and friends...

...

But like most people, they are overrun by the world we live in.

"And what world is that?"

You know I don't want to think about it.

"Humor us."

I won't. That's how I stay immune to all that stuff. By not thinking about it—and before you scold me for doing nothing, you must know that you couldn't possibly ask me to act on the things that actually bother me.

"Why not?"

This is why I hate this inner voice stuff. I said I didn't want to think about it. The voice must not hear very well.

"We take that to mean you are not empowered to fix what bothers you."

It's not that I'm not empowered. It's that I don't have the right. I know some people are okay with trouncing everyone else in favor of their own interests, but I'm not. What was Digital's famous quote, 'If I see somebody I don't like then I ignore them. I don't destroy them.' If somebody believes differently from me or whatever, I don't have it in me to 'correct' them unless what they're doing threatens real harm to others. Not to my favorite pet ideas. That's why I could never take on the conglomerates and their never-ending bid to get us all wiped out through our own sapien arrogance. Why the fuck would they want war with our own home planet? Why crush 95% of their own for as long as they can before that happens? The betas aren't doing us any harm. How the fuck could they successfully build a whole industry out of hating them?

...

...

...

But, of course, I know the answer. That's why you're not saying anything. The real truth is that the masculine alpha spirit still wants to stamp its name everywhere, and the feminine alpha spirit still wants to define everything with its own quirky names. We're just as savage as we were always evolved to be, and the conglomerates aren't the problem. They're just the vending machine.

...

...

...

You know what my real problem is? It isn't the Jupiterian government or greed or Goodman or anything like that. It's that my students would rather sing booty songs than learn how power systems actually work.

"But there is value in those songs."

I know. Solidarity, cultural pride, the highest natural sense of inner freedom of all hues and all that. But my kids use it blindly in front of a fucking public store, defiant of all manners, and that makes me mad... because I can't teach them to see how easy it could be if they just balanced a little.

"What should they balance against? A system that won't let them in anyway? You know it's true."

Maybe for most, but not for all. At least 5 of my 34 high schoolers could actually make it if they learned how to act.

"And how would that be?"

I little less niggerish, frankly, and a little more like they're interested in what the person with the power is saying to them. The constant jokey defiance , besides being disrespectful, is willfully ignorant, and gets old instantly.

"Now you're judging them."

Damn right. Because this is exactly what the executives see. Only it's not politically correct for them to say it openly. I can.

...

Of course, you can't tell us choc-hues shit, can you?

"If any of them could read your mind, they'd never listen to you."

Why don't you tell me something I *don't* know.

"But what if they could read your heart instead?"

Hmph. I don't even know what's in my heart. Might not be safe. Probably a lot of disappointment.

"That's not what we see. What we see is the heart of a beta. Someone who sees everything as it is and knows that the world's best interest is his best interest. Just because you call a spade a spade doesn't mean you won't still play the card, do you understand? We know that regardless of how you assess your own, you couldn't be prouder of being a choc-hue."

Well...

"Because you know that even though society hasn't been heavily hue-racist for hundreds of years, the treatment of robots strikes a chord within you. It offends you to see the outnumbered one oppressed by a whole society, because one of the choc-hue's skills is the ability to take on an entire society—in the ring, in the field, on stage—and not feel the least bit guilty about it. Once you've decided to stand for something, your hue is among the most resistant to *any* outsider's power which is why you make some of the most memorable activists and dividers of society— for better or worse. How you are treated and how you treat each other serves as one of the clearest lines in the sand under God, and you could not imagine living without these perspectives in your blood."

My hue doesn't see it that way. Most just see the struggle.

"But you can teach them to see it that way."

By doing what, picking up a microphone and saying, 'Hey everyone! You've been telling yourselves that you're beautiful and strong and kings and queens for millennia, but I'm gonna tell you again.'

"That won't work."

No shit, man.

"The problem with that approach is that it plays another class's game entirely. Real kings don't just say it. They have kingdoms they can point to. Real beautiful people don't just say it, they have viewers whom they capture, even if it is just themselves. And when they have these things—TRULY have these things—then, presuming these labels are of value to them, they will no longer need to behave in defiance, bitterness, or attitude. The trait is just another asset that need not be wasted on those who can't relate."

And that's what I try to tell them. How would you carry yourself if you were actually rich or powerful? All that slangin' you're doing. If it weren't a part of your stage persona then you'd be some sort of insecure fool going around flashin' like that. A real multimiyellionaire wouldn't cut up in public like that.

But I can't teach them. It would be seen as elitist and arrogant to tell them how to live their own lives. We chocs will defy that instantly.

"That's true."

So what do you propose, voice? The conglomerates may be alright with sending us back into the madmax of interplanetary lawlessness. Our courts and justices may be shit. Our anti-other laws may be fucking the 80%, but we, the New Americans are only doing what every same-hued, prince raising archy would do anywhere. We're just doing it louder with a greater diversity of people who have no idea how to challenge the impenetrable. But that problem is everywhere. Not just with us, and not just here in the 28$^{th}$ century.

"Now you're catching on. And this is why we chose you."


Sei emerged from the darkness. Hello Michael, how are you?

Miss Esperanza, for someone about to be programmed by people who I'm sure are from Earth, I'm alright. Part of me feels funny just letting you guys do this, but I guess I really am out of ideas. You're right. I still want the whole world to be a better place, and I just haven't given up completely yet. So whatever you have to say to me, please don't ask me to go against my nation or planet.

We won't ask you that. But we do have a question which we already know the answer to: "If you could overthrow Graham Goodman, would you?"

No.

Why not?

Because most people are more like my students. They don't know who they are, how they could contribute to a society beyond themselves, or what's even at stake when the systems and other types of human out there to help them are suddenly blocked. They wouldn't know the first thing about bringing a society together. Goodman is just a hat worn by a vast network of dragons. I might even be one of those dragons. If anything, he might be the only organizing principle available to us for the next three decades. After he's gone, it will be impossible to know who the real powers are or what they believe about the new humanity.

Oh, I see.

I have no faith in the collective, let's make that clear. It's the use of el to punish untrustworthy behaviors, and the use of o to prevent the wrong people from getting near your favorite places that's keeping us in check. That and law and policing itself. Without all that, the collective is judgmental and very mean. Only a person who doesn't care at all about the popular opinion can get things done.

You sound like a fan.

He's a cretin. And no I am not a fan. But I don't hate him. I do hate mobs. I HATE mobs. Mobs are what taught my students that cutting up is better than putting together the proposal to start a college. They could actually succeed at that if they tried. As for the Chancellorate, I make it a point to own my own sphere of information. The last thing I need is some otha brotha's nuts dominating my news feed. Letting in all that talk—good or bad—about somebody else… you might as well let them shag your wife too. Either way, you've forfeited the narrative.

And the narrative is all we have.

Yeah…

Ballant paused to collect himself. I feel like you're leading me somewhere.

If you could overthrow the Chancellorate's Isolation plan, would you?

No. But I would teach other people how to do it if I knew how. Do you know how?

I do. And so do you. But you're not the one for that job. It would be safer if someone else besides you tackled that one.

Hm.

No, I have a different ask of you.

That's nice, but I don't even really know who you are.

Take a guess. This is your mind, after all.

Okay. I think you're a beta from Earth who is somehow connected to the Solar Council, but almost definitely not directly. I know you can blank me and get inside my head through an arm band, so your connections must be very powerful. You probably chose me because you knew I would never betray my own, not even the Chancellorate or Jupiter, but I have what I think is a balanced enough view of the state of things, and that tells me that you guys can read minds from a very far distance. If you're asking me, then you must have good intentions, because those are the only ones you'll get out of me.

Very good.

I might trust you more than I should. But I am sure I trust you at least more than the state of our world right now, so I guess that has to be enough... So I guess I talked myself into listening: What are you asking me to do?

We want you to ignore the executives and the government and everything else, and unlock the value in your own students, specifically your own hue. We want you to do it without subtracting from other hues or making other races feel jealous or discriminated against.

...That might be tricky. I have many students, high school and college. Only about 60% of them are black. I have to teach everyone equally.

And you can do that as a teacher. But you don't live in a Latin or white or cyborg skin. Your teachings will be little more than academic. We want you to empower the majority of your black students to reframe what the black talents are, so that they can rebuild their piece of the world community in the new times. We have other people who will address the hues they know best.

Right, but chocs don't really have the biggest problems here. Maybe a couple of glass ceilings, but that's nothing compared to the betas and cyborgs. Especially the betas. The Jews of our time—they look so much like us alphas, but are so noticeably the center of everyone's major mythology. Chocs don't carry that kind of weight. So why bother with us?

The short answer is, every hue and race has reasons for looking like they do, sponsored mostly by earth evolution. Even we betas. Those reasons affect our bodies' processing of not just physical energy, but hormonal energy and the social responses tied to them. Your world is run by a certain leader-of-the-pack attitude which also defines what is valuable: beauty, money, luxury, several kinds of power. Lighter hues are wired with certain kinds of sensitivities that are different from darker or oranger hues, and a sensitivity to power through objects is among the sensitivities more easily passed through their legacies. Orange passes it through family and behavioral institution. Dark hues pass it through category division, splitting off and becoming a new kind of individuality. But all the world can trade objects, so this kind of power is easiest to visibly reinforce because it's easiest to see. You need to teach your students to see the value of splitting off their own—each individual away from the noise of his enemies, the news, or even his friends. Because no matter how many objects or dollars or strutting images are paraded before you, the chocs will always be able to split off their own separate from the guys who have that power, and come out with twice as much of their own power in the end. Yours is one of the only groups that can emerge exponentially stronger after being enslaved or even within slavery, where other groups may wear the scars of colonialism and oppression for much much longer, and face harder community barriers in the absence of help from their oppressors. The chocs don't need this. And since all of Jupiter is currently enslaved beneath the old primal version of sapiens alpha thinking, your hue is one of the best starting points for an easy and defiant recovery.

If you enslave a choc, and the choc ever decides he won't take it anymore, then he just won't take it anymore. And not even the Chancellorate can stop him without killing him. But then he becomes a martyr. And the next generation's laws will reflect this nation-wide.

Humanity begins with the African Earth chocs. You as a mix of many descendants aren't quite the origin. Nobody is. But something in your blood is closer to the willingness to begin every other possible great path.

Michael reflected quietly.

...If anyone ever wants to just leave the Chancellorate's thumb and become their own president instead, it will be a Choc. And they will often do it first. They'll just walk out and do it. Once they realize they can. *(That's why we're starting with you.)*

...

And the best way to make them 1000 times more famous is to put them in jail or into the public legal system.

...Well I don't think I want to go that far. But ok. So how do I do this without playing favorites or devaluing everyone else?

Just wear this glove to class tomorrow. We'll do the rest.

# 214. Teach You My Name

When Michael Ballant walked into his college class early that following evening, he found his adult students to be understandably curious regarding the gadget on his right arm. Mr. Ballant described with some embarrassment the accident he'd had the previous day after his high schoolers' trip to the ice cream shop, and how his friend in the science department wanted to test a new kind of therapeutic cast. He then proceeded to point out all of the supposed biometrics tended to by said cast, spending no less than 10 minutes in discussion on the matter. Many of the students found the cast to be intriguing enough to keep glancing at it every now and then.

So yesterday my high schoolers and I were talking about nihilism and what it means for nothing to matter. While I was sitting there injured I thought to myself, "Maybe it really is all just bullshit and we're just along for the ride." Then I started thinking about the power of being unique, and how we can use this to our advantage in Etiquette Studies. So we're gonna change it up a bit today from what the syllabus says. Scratch assignment 5. Instead of doing the elevator pitch assignment, I want you to do something else.

Your job is to come up with a real proposal to the Local Education Board to start a program named after yourself. You HAVE to name it after yourself, because I'll tell you up front that I want the research you do during this assignment to stick with you in your future pitches to people. Doing a regular elevator pitch might be too taxing for those of you who aren't social by default, so this assignment will focus more on *what* you would pitch than *how*.

"Sir, does it have to be our whole name or can it be just the last name?"

Good question. Your legal first name only.

"So no nicknames?"

Right. Nicknames are not allowed. Legal first name only. So if I were doing this assignment, Michael is the only name I could use. I could call it the Michael Programme or the Michael Arts Project or Michael Foundation, for example, but I couldn't use Ballant. Because you don't refer to yourself by your last name, and what you're pitching here will be a kind of association with how people like your friends actually see you.

"Okay."

Now the basis of your program can only come from two places: 1) Research on your name, and 2) the stuff that ALWAYS happens around you when you're in a place surrounded by people *other than your friends*.

"So like family."

No. We're lumping them in with friends. Take them out of the picture.

"So what happens when we're around strangers?"

Sort of, but this isn't a one-time encounter like passing someone by while you're shopping. I'm talking colleagues or key contacts, people that you interact with regularly for formal reasons. They won't know your private life the way friends and family do, so these semi-distant relationships are more appropriate for designing a kind of pitch for yourself.

"What if nobody has your name? Do we look up the names yours was based on?"

No, so LaDejia you would just use your own unique personality to come up with the meaning. But here's the catch: Existing names often reference places, career roles, and generational stories. So when I say you should use your unique personality, that's what I'm talking about, You can't just make things up like, 'I'm LaDejia The Badass Herself,' but you should think about Where you come from, the career path you can most easily get into, and the kinds of jobs or legacy that the two sides of your family basically do across generations.

"Oh, so that's not actually personality, but like, family history. "

You're right. Sorry. You've forced me to clarify. Use whatever box the world has the easiest time putting you into career-wise, with some dose of the boxes your family belongs to.

"And sir, what if our boxes are negative?" asked one of Ballant's students whom the nanos reported had served jail time.

This is a program proposal so you'll have to figure that out. For hopefully what will be your own good, I've asked student records to process your proposals as part of the grading, so their systems will perform the same ID verifications that a real government office would when you're answering an RFP.

The last student and several others frowned.

Ballant continued. As for my half of the grading, a great proposal gets an A-. A great proposal which you actually submit gets an A+. I will back you in submitting to the office of your choosing if you get an A-. But if you turn in something that a committee would reject for poor quality of if you otherwise BS this assignment, then the grade is an F."

!!!

!?

So yes, this assignment is basically pass-fail. This is your major assignment for the last three weeks of this class, so it's due on the last day of the term.

"I don't see what this has to do with being an electrician," one student protested, much to Ballant's obvious (-to-us) irritation.

And where is the connection missing Mr. DeTrayce? The part where you part where you apply to an employer or the part where you tell people what you do?

"I mean why does it have to be so hard? It's just a regular resume."

And when was the last time your regular resume—with no instructions from the person you're applying to—worked at all? When was the last time you got away with that without a background check? What do you think we're playing 'Job' here like some first graders? This is real life dude. I'm asking you to get it together as part of an assignment. Get it *all* together, and make it look good enough to submit somewhere.

"Man! I'll just take the F."

Would you rather take it now or three weeks from now?

"Man, this is shit."

Okay, I take it you mean now.

"Yo, what the fuck!"

You start a fight with your potential employer in front of a whole classroom full of people and you have no power whatsoever over whether your shit even gets read. If you're trying to work for my company then you're already *way* in the hole with me, brotha. And I'm just gonna tell you how it is. Also, if you think I'm not looking at things you do outside of the application process then you're very wrong. That's whole idea of a background check. I'm not gonna spare your feelings, dammit. If you're gonna act like a fool right now then I will trash your pitch right now because THAT'S HOW THE CHANCELLORATE WORKS. You understand?

DeTrayce stood up, pissed.

Make anotha move, DeTrayce. Go ahead.

The upset student clinched his fists.

But Ballant calmed himself with a sobering exhalation. Guys, don't just stand there. Somebody help him out. Nobody knows the rules of this game until they see where the line is. Now you know. Now we're all gonna pretend like this didn't happen, and you're gonna go home and tell the best story possible using your name, and things that always happen in places you've stayed around for a while. For the rest of the class we'll be looking at Chapter 22, but let's take a five minute break first.

Sei and I observed the strongest tension over the classroom, as our sponsorship of Ballant's show of force was apparently not within his regular collected character. To help restore some sense of calm, we grantzed him into a conversation with one of his more receptive students.

Good work on your last assignment, Jonathan. And you too Mandy.

"Thanks, sir. I had to ask my aunt to show me how to lay out all the plates and guest labels…"

* * *

After class, five students approached Mr. Ballant, led by LaDejia. DeTrayce remained in the rear. "Sir, can we talk to you?"

Sure. Here or in private?

"I guess here is fine."

Okay, what's on your mind?

"It's about this assignment, several of us feel it's unfair to some of us because our background isn't as smooth as others'."

I know. That's exactly why I'm giving you this assignment.

LaDejia was clearly confused.

This is the one chance—my guess is that it might be the only chance you have to clearly define what you're about to someone else given all of their biases against you and your past. Or the pasts of everyone who looks like you. It's actually not supposed to be punishment.

"Oh. Well, we kinda wanted to ask, can we at least use our last names? Cause if I'm applying for a grant I know calling it the LaDejia Foundation is automatically gonna make people feel a certain way."

Probably.

"So, realistically, my proposal probably wouldn't be looked at just based on my name. That's why we don't apply to these kinds of things."

And that's why I'm giving you this assignment. Let me give you some advice: This is an education program you are proposing, so it doesn't have to compete with more corporate-sounding names. Your name is the one you have and it shouldn't be something which brings you disadvantage before you even start. Try to come up with something besides 'foundation' or 'program' or 'project' which plays nicely with both your name and your history. Words are powerful. I'm trying to get you to think about which words can best serve as a bridge between you and people's willingness to plug into what you represent.

A beta student, Mira-naye, spoke up. "Sir, my family emigrated from Ceres, and the laws won't let us apply for grants. I'm still going to do the assignment, but I would be asking the sponsor to break the law when I apply for the grant."

Has your family broken any laws? Don't answer that. If they have or even if they haven't—even if you just don't want to put yourself out there, I understand. You can partner with one of your classmates and hide your proposal in theirs. Realistically, that's how underground railroads are built. Does that work for you?

"Oh, thank you sir!"

"I'll partner with you. You're smart!" DeTrayce piped up.

Hm… DeTrayce, your background won't help either of you in a pair. Especially if you were to win this hypothetical grant. I would actually prefer you do your own because it will force you to put a spin on your unique challenges. If you partner with Mira-naye, then you will both have some crafting to do—

"That's okay, sir. I think I might try working on my own first," Mira-naye chimed in. *(Sei and I could tell that this student had no interest in partnering with a freerider.)*

DeTrayce shrank back down in a huff.

"So you're telling us to suck it up, huh sir?" LaDejia continued skeptically.

Look, if this assignment truly offends you then ~~you can do the elevator pitch instead. No, Ballant.~~ I don't know what to say. The world out there is a cold place. I want you to hone your weapons against it here.

"You know what sir, with all due respect, I think I will just take the F," DeTrayce announced.

I understand. It's more important for you to have a choice. Done. You have the F. I've cast it into the gradebook. Ballant paused for a moment. So that's the last of your assignments.

"So this means I failed?"

Yes.

"Man, shit!"

DeTrayce. What do you want me to do? You wanted a choice, you got it.

"I just hate this assignment!"

There's no more assignment to hate. The burden is lifted.

"But now I gotta take the class all over again."

Yes, but not necessarily with me if you don't want to. You have a choice there too. Now hold on. We can talk about this in a second, but I want to make sure everyone else here gets their questions answered. Because I think maybe our talk might last longer.

"Look, there's nothing to talk about. This assignment is messed up—"

Ballant closed his eyes and lowered his head in frustration. One more time, man. You're hogging the floor. Over something you already gave up. Stand down for two minutes, that's all I'm asking.

"I'll say whatever I want!"

"DETRAYCE!" LaDejia interrupted. "SHUT. UP! QUIT RUNNING YOUR MOUTH! We're trying to have school here! If you don't wanna do it, go home!"

And with that, the upset protester stormed out.

**Sigh**. Ballant shook his head. What else do you guys need from me?

Mira-naye raised her hand. "I think I was so worried about the setup that I forgot to ask what kind of education program you're looking for."

"Yeah," LaDejia added. "Could you give us like, an example?"

Eh, sure. Before I start anything, I'd probably want to know what I wanted people to be educated in. Say it's music. What about music? How about how to appreciate the classics. Next I want to think about a plan to teach this. Let's say it's a program where participants get to— well, I don't want to give you any specific ideas because I know it'll be tempting to turn in something too close to my example. Now I need to write a proposal to get this funded. Pretend my background says I was in rehab, and wherever I go, a longtime person gets fired. These are part of my pattern and history. How can I put this proposal together? I might propose a program that revolves around retraining the negative songs that people use to reinforce their own pain. Like a therapy.

The students pondered Ballant's example.

Do you see what I'm doing here? I'm taking my pattern and history, even if it's negative, and turning it into a fundable program that somebody might pay money for. And it really is true that my patterns actually happen when I'm in a place. So this is a legitimate proposal.

"And what would you call it?"

...Eh, how about The Michael Mind Reformat?

"But that doesn't sound like a project! It sounds like a…"

"—Like a kind of therapy!"

Yeah.

"Oooohhh. I get it. So I think more people need to learn about how to stay out of trouble when the government scans for traitors every month."

*(They do that here? Sei, we need to talk.)*

Yeah, I forgot when the next scan is. Remind me.

"Sir, you're the one who told us about it! It's next week."

Right. Just testing you.

"So I'd call mine LaDejia Law 4. Kind of like an advocacy thing for people getting picked on. Cause wherever I go, it seems like folks always need a voice to speak up for them or cover for them if speaking up is too dangerous."

Nice! Now we're talking. Research how a five pager might be written, and think about how you would execute it if you got it funded. But what does this have to do with your personal legacy or family history? We'll be checking on that you know.

"My mom and dad's families are mostly port workers. Though dad had some family in management. So maybe that's where life wants to put me. But I don't want to do port work."

Then you can help ship citizen papers or ID chips. Maybe rights agreements.

"Oh, so still shipping, but more law oriented."

Exactly.

"I think I get this assignment."

After this class is over, you should be able to take the knowledge of your talent in speaking up and shipping wherever you go. And I remind y'all, really try to propose something which—on top of all of that other stuff—is something you might actually love doing if it did get funded.

"Cool! Thanks sir."

"Yeah thanks."

Satisfied, the former petitioners moved on to their next destinations.


Before Ballant could exit, however, the student DeTrayce reappeared from around the corner.

"Is it too late to take the F back?"

No sir. I can remove it.

"Okay."

Do you have any questions?

"No, I don't think so."

Alright, well let me know if you do.

"Okay."

* * *

Ballant arrived at home later that night, where he finally had the space to write down the mysteriously inspired idea he'd had earlier:

SOCI301: Etiquette and Social Advancement
Final Project
Teach You My Name

Overview

Throughout this course we have talked about different cultures and classes, and their expectations for behavior in order for you to gain access to what they have. One final culture we need to look at, however, is not on the people level, but on the institutional level.

If you think about it, we are constantly teaching others how to respond to us. Sometimes this is through interacting with them directly, other times it is through impressions we have left. And others talk about us in turn. But not all impressions are under our control. Things like our name and the kinds of work done by our family help others put us in a kind of box. Not all boxes are equal, but the trick is to make your box look like a castle.

In this assignment you will make a kind of resume which is more real than any job application you've ever filled out. Instead of designing your resume to be read by people, you will design it to be read by big organizations like the government and the conglomerates. These organizations already know everything about you, including your default place in society. But what they don't know is how you can use all of that history to advance society itself. And they should pay you big bucks to do it. In this assignment you will be putting together a grant proposal based on truths about you which everyone can look up. In the process, you will also create a brand for yourself which makes people think about a very specific idea every time your name is mentioned.

IMPORTANT: Because this is a grant proposal, always keep in mind that your idea has to prove valuable to the places out there that have what you want. You can't just hype yourself up hoping for that dream job to come based on your own coolness.


Setup:

1. Throughout your life, you have ended up in various situations. What do they have in common? Whenever you enter a job or school or new place to live… or someone else's life, **what kinds of things always happen when you're there**? We'll call these your *patterns*. <u>List these patterns</u> because you will be using them in the next few steps. This will be your "what" when it comes to goals in the proposal. Negative or not, we're going to make it positive and useful to the funder.

2. You've left certain regular impressions on people in the places you've been. <u>List the ways in which outside society prefers to describe you personally</u>. It doesn't have to be pretty. It doesn't have to be fair. It

might even include some negative things you've gotten into which others hold over your head. Don't worry about it. You don't have to list specifics, just think about **the kind of character which the world full of strangers labels you as having**. Be honest. The more honest you are about this, the sharper the weapon you'll be turning this into. This won't quite be the "who" in your proposal, but is more like the "who from." This will tell us the target audience responsible for coming up with these labels.

3. Think about the kinds of jobs or business that your mother, father, and family are into on the whole. Also think about what kinds of jobs you've ended up in. <u>List the roles involved in your family's usual kind of job</u>. **Pretend that society wants to keep you stuck in these specific kinds of roles** *only*. Note that there is a difference between a job and a role. A port conductor, a farmer, and a CEO may have different jobs, but many of their *roles* overlap. If you come from a family of port conductors, you may also have some of the steering power that comes with being a CEO. Your role will be the "where" of your proposal.

4. Take **your regular first name ONLY**. No nicknames, last names, or aliases. What does your name mean? What kinds of quick thoughts come to mind with this name. (Quick thoughts. Don't spend longer than 1 second on it.) If your name is rare or if you can't really think of any instant other people, then consider how people behave differently after they have met you.

    Next, <u>write down a process which does the same thing your name does</u>. This is going to be the tool you use to execute your plan in the proposal. The "how."

5. The "when" is right now.

6. I will set your "why" for you: There is no why. The why is because you were born with the above cards in your hand, and that's all. But the second part of that is, we're writing this proposal in this way so that you can give the world out there a reason to pay you for value that you've always had. A value which *the world* has been trying to assign to you all along.

Instructions:

1. Outline a grant proposal for an education program, of no more than five pages to a hypothetical funding agency.
    a. Write an overview of your proposed education program. What will you be teaching? That pattern's in setup step 1.
    b. Who will you be teaching? Folks a lot like the "who from" in setup step 2. These are the people who actually see you and pay enough attention to you to label you / experience your patterns long-term.

    c.    In what field will the program be based? This should be your answer from setup step 3. In real life, this tells you a lot about the kinds of jobs and roles you could actually apply for and have a higher chance of winning.

    d.    Your name may seem minor, but how you turn it into an appealing title is critical, CRITICAL in telling me how you plan to present yourself. If you choose something standard like "John Incorporated," Then I will compare you against corporations. If you choose "The John Arts Education Project," I will assume you are teaching kids or students about art through some kind of activity plan, but all of the other items about your personality and patterns will completely throw me off—especially if these stereotypes have nothing to do with who your actual record in society has shown you to be. Make sure that what you propose lines up with *everything else* above this section.

This assignment will be graded according to the attached rubric…

Ballant saved his file and took a breath. Although he had set out that morning to do his part in what felt like a larger mission to help a whole class of people find value in a bitter world, he really didn't know whether his rather wordy plan would make any difference to anyone at all.

Initially driven by a mixture of hope with occasional disappointment in his own color, he was well aware that many people all over the world had it far worse. Hell, some people way up in the ranks also had it far worse.

At least he'd come up with something that anybody could use—not just his own…

…though there remained something in the black wiring that might benefit from this activity more easily than most.

Later one night during that same week, while resting quietly upon its coffee table perch, the pearl arm brace suddenly lit up in a cool blue, and hovered towards the front door of Ballant's living quarters. Certain signals were exchanged, and the door opened, closing and re-locking dutifully following the brace's exit.

# 215. Keeping Your Whits

Summer 4, 2771 n.e.

Sei opened the door to our hotel room at 3:15 am. Like clockwork, the Angel finder whizzed in with its two nanos safely tucked inside.

I don't know, Isaiah. I guess I just expected more oomph than that. We didn't even get to fight.

**Maybe he doesn't represent obstacles that way.**

But I still don't get what his barrier actually was.

**It was probably really minor. Just having you possess him long enough to field that idea and defend it against the first naysayer may have been all he needed.**

But do you think any of that really made a difference? Will his students even make use of the lesson?

**LaDejia Law seemed promising.**

Yeah but we can't wait around another decade to find out what's going to happen.

**Or even another week. There are too many other seeds to plant, I think.**

Yeah well, I'll admit I'm getting really tired of this hotel. It chokes the soul. We need to move somewhere better.

**I agree, but without any real way to make a living—since we're basically spies here—our options aren't that plentiful.**

Sei fell back onto the bed. I really don't like setting up a thing whose results I can't see.

**We followed the Angel finder's cues and stayed as long as made sense. The rest is up to the simulations, I suppose.**

How do we get out of this hotel? I'm suddenly feeling very ineffective. After all of that promise, our teacher's story was so... anticlimactic.

**Yes, but we were only looking at things in the moment. Who knows if some kind of turning point was born here that Jupiterians will one day write about.**

Hm. Isaiah the Optimist. Look out.

**I just think we need to do a few of these before we start to feel it's going somewhere. And you're right. It might take years for his learners to grow up and grow into their wiser versions. They need to get out there and apply it first.**

Well, whatever. Since I napped all day, I'm up for the next person. Let's see what Angel has to say.

* * *

What disturbed Bertram Whit the most about his "superiors'" new policies wasn't so much the blatant corruption, the cronyism, or the mafia-like culture of intimidation. It was more a matter of the sheer waste of human spirit being passed off as "planetary unification." True, Whit had run against his stupid opponent and lost the gubernatorial contest in Mezzogloria, but he still remained prefect of the Gloriana township, the administrative seat of the Mezzogloria airspace. Now more embattled than ever, he and those in the know were well aware that there just weren't enough competent cronies around to stack the deck completely in the Chancellorate's favor. Despite their very loud bluster, the Chancellorate continually found itself limited to a pool of zealots hell bent more on anarchy than organized governance, and these zealots needed puppet masters, a puppet doctrine, and an infinite pool of money in order to function. Whit may have fallen on the outs with the main steerors of his allegiant, but he remained savvy as always in ensuring that Gloriana's enlightened institutions continued to accept only enlightened thinking at its helm.

Sei and I arrived in Gloriana on Summer 19, 2771, after it was decided that I should probably get a job, sotions-off, as a way of paying for some better living arrangements. Even in the most prosperous areas of Jupiter, vacant housing littered the airscape, and it wasn't hard to find a nice 720 square foot dwelling owned by one of the prefect's investment companies. It was important for us to avoid tying ourselves to an unscrupulous landlord, so we did our research before settling on the house in Storm Heights.

Through our surreptitiously deployed nano, we watched the prefect in action. Indeed, Angel finder had revealed him to be our next charge.

Bertram sat fascinated before a projected show as his wife Sandy watched him watching the screen.

Back on *that* again?

Yeah. I just think it's interesting, that's all. The choc shows don't have the quality of major productions, and the Latnin shows are cheaply acted. The shows about magic and ghosts are quite cheesy. And yet there are so many more of these under the new times—as if these people have some magic ability to just ignore any claims that someone else is their master.

It's their version of a renaissance. Maybe they're just affirming an outlook that will always be their own.

If only running the township worked that way. I swear, Sandy. I know what it's for, but sometimes it's just so discouraging.

Sandy leaned over and gave her husband a peck on the forehead. I know, but it'll be alright.

I certainly couldn't survive all this without you, lady, Bertram held his wife's hand, and she gripped his in kind.

So, did you get to sneak a try on that device I left on the table? I figured you would while I was out.

Actually I left it alone. It's clearly very expensive, and who knows what kinds of surveillance it has on it.

Oh come on! Sandy plopped playfully on the sofa next to her husband. How often do I find a piece of high tech gadgetry just sitting there in one of our apartments? It has to belong to someone who did a walkthrough within the past two days, but until Petra gets back we won't be able to figure out who it is. It has this presence about it that just begs you to try it on. I know that when I did, I really felt like you should too.

So you think it's some kind of magic lamp?

I don't think anything. It's just a feeling. But it seems my husband is too uninterested to give it a whirl.

A "whirl," huh? Okay. Let me see it.

Bertram tried on the mysterious arm brace. A warm green glow soon lit up the rim of the device.

See that's what happens when you put it on. Now give it a few seconds.

Okay… whoa. What is this?

You see?

Bertram's mouth froze open in a slight pucker.

What's going on? Tell me.

I—it, it feels like I'm having all sorts of ideas in the back of my head— mostly about work. And… Let me see.

Whit performed a couple of special swipes which he otherwise shouldn't have known. "Prototype Manufactured by Gladstone Digics, Ltd." They're based out of Leftus, I believe. In the lower corner of the screen, a "recent recordings" button appeared (put there explicitly by us).

Bertram tapped the button.

> Hey Sei, I really want to see behind this cabinet. Can you give me a hand? My voice inquired of my friend.
>
> Sure, let me take this off.
>
> Plop.
>
> Oh that's weird. Why are the connections like that?
>
> Yeah, exactly. And see how they did the bathroom…
>
> After 10 more minutes of random banter fading in and out of microphone range, there were no more sounds to be heard. Only 5 more minutes of silence.

I guess they forgot it.

How could you forget something this fancy?

I don't know. Gladstone is pretty hi-tech, maybe they work with this stuff all the time. Hey! Oh this is weird.

What?

This TV show. I think this thing is lensing me information about the actors. It's as if all of a sudden I know who these people are. And kind of… what they were thinking behind the role!

Really?

Oh man, Sandy. I don't think I should have this device. It's got to be some top secret project.

Nonsense. If it were that important, they wouldn't have left it just lying there.

Well, maybe you're right.

Look. Tomorrow you have that meeting with McChester, and those jerks are going to try to screw you again. Imagine how great it would be if you could read them. Or get them to project and read their projection.

Hm. Yeah. I guess I could call with some excuse and—no that would be too obvious. I should probably do the regular in-person meeting, but at some point get them to dial one of their folks in. Then I could read whoever's on the other end.

That's a great idea.

It'll still be annoying, that's my guess. But hopefully it will be informative.

* * *

Bertram returned home furious the following day.

I guess I shouldn't ask how it went.

It went great.

Wow. If that's what great looks like then…?

But I almost wish I hadn't used this thing. Bertram carefully, yet firmly placed the brace on the table, his eyes watering slightly.

**Babe, what's wrong?** Sandy moved to console her clearly upset partner.

The McChester lobby is crueler than I ever imagined. All this talk about laws to force their food monopoly and making choice nonexistent. Stuff about consolidation of ALL supply chains everywhere to control the Jupiter transport space entirely. Affiliations with Dijital Justice and this crazy prison system for converting dissenters into cash itself as moveable assets… The more I read them, the more I hated them, and the more I hated them, the more questions I asked.

And this glove just kept exposing and exposing more and more. They don't see me as a threat or even an enemy. They think I'm just rallying a bigger audience to fill up their stadium with attendees. The more visible we make them, the faster the people become desensitized to the fact that we're stuck with them, making the enslavement even easier. And they're right. They're right. They took us over so easily because we're weak. And the people who voted for me are just consumers above all else.

Sandy listened in overcast sympathy.

I feel sick.

**No no no no no. Don't talk like that,** Sandy grasped Bertram's shoulders. **As soon as you give up your mood you give up the weather. Don't let them put a cloud over Gloriana. You're these people's last defense.**

But—

**Let me take the glove. I don't know how much I can help, but I know that as an outsider I'm not at all concerned with these people's egos. Tomorrow night when we go to Lady Kamen's charity ball, I'll see what I can find out from that big screen propaganda they always show.**

You don't need to do that.

**I do and I will.**

We don't need them bringing us both down. If you only knew…

**Then we should watch the people who know how to beat them. It works both ways you know. We can stream a show right now.**

Thanks, that's a good idea, a frustrated Bertram leaned his head on his wife's shoulder. But I'm so exhausted, I'd really rather just go to bed.

Okay dear.

Promise me you won't wear that thing alone, Sandy? There's so much information out there. Just one night of reading minds may hurt things a lot more than they help. I should know.

I promise. We'll leave it be for tonight.

Thank you.

Sandy gave Bertram a goodnight kiss. Goodnight, hun.

Goodnight.

* * *

At the charity ball the following night, Sandy wore her white halocrine preacher's coat with the big tubular black sleeves, perfect for hiding a mind-reading arm brace. It was here that she learned not only of the much more nefarious motives of various characters in the local power circles, but also of the extent to which more than 2/3 of them genuinely respected her and her husband deep down. It wasn't so much about world domination, but an insatiable human appetite for more. A sense of intoxicating effectiveness when that much more was successfully attained. The mighty power one knew they could wield when someone else finally attempted to cut one off before one was ready to stop. True, Lady Kamen herself downplayed her own machina mods, but the fact that Sandy could actually read her suggested something even more complicated at play.

At one point during a private conversation in the middle of the ballroom crowd, Sandy confided to her husband. Bert, I think Kamen is praesciens AND machina. The fact that I can read her tells me that she's more like a projection. You know, a possessed one with some grantzer telling her what frequencies to spit out. She also has a hormonal amplifier to spin her emhim. She's definitely a plant by someone higher up. And she controls all of this.

Why are you telling me this? You know it won't make my job any easier.

Because I also read something else tonight. But I'll tell you later. Keep smiling!

From the moment they arrived home that night, Sandy was all too eager to share her findings with Bert.

Oh Bert, hun! I am so excited! A little peeved, but mostly excited.

Finally, we're back. Okay, let's hear it.

So we've been to Lady Kamen's events before. But tonight was the first night I really knew who I was looking at. The fact that this brace could read her like a regular TV show, Odessa Kamen is more like a living broadcast tower for the Chancellorate's ideas. She's like the radio station they use to recruit soldiers. She's power, beautiful, blonde, and she's basically given up her own emhim to be permanently grantzed by a few kings. They feed her a protocol, and she executes it through events and talk that reinforce the Inner Committee's influence. Here's the thing though:

Kamen and (I take it) a lot of the people who control her think that outsiders are dirty. So they won't ally with them. There are too many sports leagues and homebuilders and service industry workers to get rid of them, so they just let them have their little kingdoms to themselves. But there is one race they are truly afraid of: the yellow-hues. They are really preoccupied with provoking and beating Azinia, partly as a way of beefing up their military to take on Earth.

But Osaira and Zeusland won't allow that.

Azinia is just a stepping stone to them. The thing is, they have no respect at all for yellows, oranges, betas, cyborgs, women, dissidents, rogues, latnins, or… that's it.

You forgot chocos, bronzes, and desertis.

ꝓ Actually, that's a mixed bag.

Really, Bertram quated.

They respect princes like themselves. The classes you've listed have very long histories of princes just like they do, and that's how they intend to carve up the planet. You run your kind, I'll run mine.

How egalitarian of them.

Would you listen? Here's the thing. There is at least one HUGE blind spot in their plan.

And what is that?

ꝓ Nature. Nature helped us co-evolve across all lands until we made the betas. And even they look like and mate compatibly with us. Nature forces mixing. If not in marriage, then in business—especially in businesses that have dirty jobs to be done which the princes don't want to touch. They need robots and slaves in order to bolster themselves. In that way, it isn't really the existence of others itself that they're trying to stop. It's the perpetuation of the line between themselves and others. They do that by controlling the narrative.

Hmm.

⚥ We became betas. Most of them including the top executives in government are modded up machina with all kinds of cyborg genes in their blood. They just get their power from the loud line drawn between what they prefer and what they don't.

Okay.

So while you were talking to Brandmann, I got into an interesting conversation with Justice Deely.

The white supremacist?

He's not a white supremacist, Bert. He's a member of the White Power movement.

Oh, pardon me.

Smarty-pants. Anyway, their whole thing is that we whites were born to go into the most extreme spaces farthest from our Earth African origin, and master those spaces, changing our very forms where we had to. In this way, to be white is to have mastery in your blood—mastery of any space, any time, anywhere... EXCEPT (and this is a big exception) the space you just changed out of.

Okay. I've heard this before.

Alright, so what you haven't heard is Deely's answer to the paradox of following Goodman. Why let him put his mug on the Jupiterian flag when you claimed the flag was so sacred? Why fall in line when all your songs are about how wild and free and untamable you are? I told Deely how I thought the Chancellorate has tamed us indomitable white naturals more convincingly than any other group. And you know what he said?

What?

Every ship needs a captain. He then asked me if I was considering mutiny, knowing how you and I lean.

I told him that mutiny is something that crew does. We haven't been tamed thoroughly enough to fall into that category.

Heh.

So at this point he starts to walk away, and that's when I hit him with one more question. I swear it was the brace.

Oh?

I ask, you know nature's going to crush us, right? For what we're doing to our past and future selves. You know it's unchristian and wrong, because it's not what we would want done unto us? You know what he said? He said "maybe." "But in this short life it feels good to have the power for a while when you know society has basically called your ways obsolete." (air quotes).

I see. Not a very inspiring story.

Wait until you hear the other major blind spot.

That first one didn't sound like much of one.

But it was, don't you see? Because it provides all the context you need for the next thing I'm going to tell you about.

Okay.

So you know the old Latnin hero Che and the old choco musician 2PK?

Yes.

You know how they're famous for prophesizing their own demise, and how they supposedly teamed up in the pre-digital world to paint accurate pictures of hell, jail, and crack sales...and assassination?

Yes, everybody knows that.

So there's a whole era where they made all this media about death and incarceration, and I think that would be the perfect theme for the powers of this era. You know, music *by* the powers, *for* the powers.

I'm not following.

You've heard of beatniks, right?

Yes.

I know how to destroy the Chancellorate from within.

You're making me nervous.

And it only takes ten years to undo it all.

No way.

Watch me: You, Bertram Whit, can do what even Lady Kamen won't do. You can start talking to those media makers you've been watching made by "outsiders" and propose to make stories for *all* races which capture where we actually are as humanity. We're fucked as a species, and everybody knows it.

!

Partner with those chocos, and get a couple of them to set aside the black empire stuff for a second and make a really good, Shakespearean-style tragedy of a King named Midas who eventually turned himself into gold. A demon named Mephistopheles who ended up being the sole savior of humanity. A martyr named Jesus who came back as a Gundam only to be killed yet again. Or stories about a pirate who conquered the world only to come back home and find his country had fallen into the sea. Do you see what I'm saying? We could call it the Integrationist Era—crossing boundaries like Earth Jazz with completely non-seditious, non-segregated plot lines and actors. To hell with the line. Let's just cross it. Then translate it into Spanish. Let's make shows to reflect how lost we are like the Grunge era. But only you, hun, a white person with the position and conscience to do it, can enable these spaces.

Bertram descended into serious thought. The powers will have my head. And not just the Chancellorate. It's the Odessas of the world I'm worried about. And you. They'll dig for anything they can find and ruin us on a technicality for any number of legislative decisions I've made over the years. I honestly don't think I can handle it.

Oh.

It's just so much easier said than done. When I stand up—*if* I stand up— I will need several others to stand with me at the same time. Those guys are skittish about cooperating with whites or the law.

Yes...

But I see what you're saying. Entertainment endures. And the more it reflects the much greater whole's opinion and fears, the longer it endures. The Chancellorate might as well be making Hitler films by comparison. It isn't within them to dirty themselves with the whole, so it's definitely a numbers game we could win. What did you suggest? Contacting these media makers from other races and classes being suppressed by the Chancellorate? Using my position—

More like your perspective—

My *perspective*, to help support projects which really capture everyone's thoughts about the times we live in?

Get them to slow down on the black or brown-only work and do universal work instead that doesn't just mimic people's wishful thinking, but also tells where we are.

But I doubt anyone will want to consume something so negative.

♀ Then do what I'm doing with you now. Tell them where we could go from there. Like the beatniks to the hippies. These stories are already being made, all you need is to get a couple of well-planned, integrated scripts to start the trend. That and a good grunge-like rebel who's the son or daughter of one of the powers and disagrees with mom and dad. They can sing or act out Super Rich Kids and put a massive true narrative on top of the current false one.

Honestly, Sandy, I love this idea. All this time I've been wondering how to fight my bosses and this new corrupt version of the allegiant, but it turns out that there were people out there who have a whole culture capable of completely ignoring the worst parts of that fight. Maybe not all of it. And certainly they'll ban us—

But if you pay in psy, el, mu and bartered things like housing discounts to encourage certain kinds of local arts and education, you can still support this. Nothing is stopping us, a wealthy white couple with a conscience, from buying 5 copies of Performant Studio Software and offering people the chance to make media on it in exchange for certain kinds of messaging. This is just private enterprise between the people with the money and conscience and people with the talent and cultural immunity. If people who didn't vote for Goodman want to do something about that stance, then they can join their talents and resources with people who would otherwise make self-only work in a silo—if they got the chance at all.

Again, they'll just ban us and put a target on my head.

And I'm sure they'll ban every private auto and jail every player of said radio while they're at it. It's unenforceable.

…

Every time one sees a Chancellorate sticker, tell them to turn their brights on. Let them know they don't need to swallow the wretched reminder in silence, but are perfectly free to share the oppression. Let them know how outnumbered they actually are.

I see the violence going up.

Well that was automatic with the way things are. The public killings started decades before us with the hate rallies, not us.

Since when did my wife turn into a revolutionary?

When this magic accessory gave me the same edge that the governors have. We were losing this game because we didn't even know it was being played. Now not only do I know the game, I know the rules. And I know how the opponent thinks about the rules.

Okay.

ᛣ As for protecting ourselves, it's just ideas. All we have is an idea for others to spread *their* ideas. All we're telling them is to retake their own air waves by turning off the Chancellorate feed and turning on their own production studios. Goodman's going to do what Goodman always does. The fact that people keep watching the train wreck is their fault. That's why it will help to team up with people who automatically tune out of that stuff and into their own power. Get them to start *making* the media.

Okay okay. But I think I shouldn't be the one to do it. You should be. I think this is safer for all of us, especially since you'll be less of a direct irritant to them.

So I encourage the non-political partners of political people to foster integrated media projects with people who already can and will produce?

Sure. You can sponsor the events. But make sure you only invite level-headed people. This isn't black power or Latnin power. If your friend Deely is to be believed, then this talent for putting a new space under one's own unstoppable will… that's white power.

We can consider the times to be like a really cold environment. But we're thought to have the ability to conquer any place we set foot in.

Okay. I think I'm seeing it.

♀ I said I found a way to bring down the Chancellorate, but we don't need to do that. Time will do it automatically. I'm more excited about finally doing something to make my corner of the world better than the one those guys are breaking. Who knows, maybe this will end up being a long term formula for a stabler society in general.

Heh, that's my girl. Let's give 'em hell!

# 216. The Whitelight Conception

"So what you're saying is that you want me to ignore my market and everything that's profitable in order to make white movies. All risk, high uncertainty, for what will probably be little return."

I didn't propose such a thing at all, Graig. As you know, Bertram and I are experienced enough in business to—

"I'm sorry to interrupt, Sandy, but Graig that was rude. I'm surprised at you twisting her words like that," the talent agent Tammy Giles interjected.

"My apologies. What I should have said was, this sounds like an ask to stick our necks out in the middle of a clearly precarious political landscape."

My husband feels the way you do.

"Which is why he isn't here."

Yes, to be honest. But Graig, this is a battle on multiple fronts. It's not enough to recruit viewers or soldiers into your audience. You also have to train them. And then you have to give them the tools they need to win. Making predominantly black media gives you a gift for speaking to the individual. I'm proposing that we consider ways to marry the individually-inspired to the politically-empowered.

"And remind me of your motive?"

♀ There are a lot of us who haven't given up on making things better. We just didn't know how to do it until recently.

"And what changed?"

We recently learned some things that I can't disclose in a meeting with the other side. The urgency is real. And it calls for new tactics.

…

Tell me, folks. Do you see the Collectivist allegiant recovering from the whooping you took in the governor's race? We set aside our loyalty to the sovereigns to join you guys and we paid the price for it. I learned from that, that collectivism doesn't win seats. Votes do. and if you can't find all the self-proclaimed sovereigns out their because they've hidden most of the voting booths in the forests and closets of the world, you still won't win even if you got 90% of the viewership.

"And how is this one-world media effort supposed to change that?"

♀ Oh no, it's not a "one world media effort," as you call it. Utopias only happen in stories. I thought hard about which fights we could actually win. Beating the Chancellor and swaying the forest vote is not where it's at. All they need to do is double down on one difference—any difference—between "us and them" and they win. Their claim gets 1 point. Their rightness gets another point, and for their attention to themselves and your attention to them—especially frustrated that you can't beat them—they get 2 to 3 more points. And you go home empty handed with 0. Your audience consumes films in a black box—exactly where they said you belong—and that's it. Same with you, Elena, and you Tupery-e. All they need to do is keep one of your low class rich enough to contain your followers' interests, and you never become a force. And people like me and Bertram—they want us to stay in our positions of privilege and corner us one-by-one. As long as we never from a forest vote of our own, they win again.

"You do realize that agreeing to this could cost us everything?"

In what, money? Can't you protect yourself from that?

"In peace of mind, Sandy. Most of us worked hard to get out of the pits. We didn't get here by taking dangerous risks."

Okay, okay. Look Graig, I'm not here to convince you. I'm only here to field an idea. I worry about the world. Our world. I think my fellow sovereigns are rotting it. I know I'm in a position to do my part. It is an act more valuable than any other I can perform at this point in time.

…

And if I don't—if I don't even try, then I will have to live with that.

…

But you're right. I'm not you, and don't know what you would be risking. This may not be for you.

Graig Wellan, head of Chocolot Entertainment Systems, Str. Considered Sandy's partial reversal.

Tupery-e, Governing cyborg of the privately-owned Mezzogloria Electrobiotic Customs Enforcement Squad also reflected quietly before finally responding. ч "In my mind, one social cohesion doctrine is just as good as another, as natural's treatment of us cyborgs remains questionable all around, regardless of whether one king or one mob is at the helm. But Mrs. Whit is right on at least one front. We are being driven to unnecessary levels of both internal and external conflict, personal pain, and more frequent collective catastrophes under the current path. Simply because the current regime doesn't care, and reinforces this as a code for the high ranking to follow. It is long-term unacceptable for the many, despite the pomp felt by the few. I will attempt to speak for Mr. Wellan, however:"

"My business cannot afford to lose me as its leader, and more people would lose if we were to be retaliated against. So I cannot join your cause. I say that on the record. I also recommend that Mr. Wellan refrain, because I feel that he is torn. But ours are particularly challenging situations to be in."

And with that, Tupery-e rose from her seat. "Graig, we should leave. Now."

Graig looked around before deciding to follow the cyborg commander. But before the two could complete their exit, beta legal advocate Andre West tapped his finger to his temple with a question posed to Wellan, "What, not even an apology?"

Graig cast a quick glance to Tupery-e, who replied in the former's place. With slightly upturned lips, sly narrowed eyes and a suspiciously longer gaze, Tupery-e gave both their answers, "No."

Graig shrugged. Shortly thereafter, the door closed behind them.

West turned back to the room and leaned back in his chair, "Well, I'm in."

"Me too," Tammy Giles added.

Out of 12 other parties invited to the meeting, six would ultimately agree, three would commit limited support, only two would reply with a no, and one remained undecided. And from this meeting a new media trust was born—one to which collaborating musicians from any two different genres could apply to have a certain portion of their studio costs and equipment paid for. To distance themselves safely from direct fallout, the founding members of Whitelight ♃ decided to rely on evaluative algorithms to assess potential releases for their sales potential, calculate artist splits and, in the absence of artist funds, negotiate certain kinds of barter.

For the last 250 years, it hadn't actually been difficult to commission a fleet of home building drones to build sky mansion in a new spot over Jupiter air space. What used to cost $10 million dollars to build back in, say, the 2000s now cost a mere $400 million "old dollars" 800 years later. Could you imagine buying a mansion for $7000 back in the old days? Then tearing down and rebuilding five years later for a mere $10000?

The problem lie in the subscription fees. Subscription to an energy farm, a water conversion system, a sewage converter, streaming services and security easements to debit people automatically for flying through your air space. Of course, if you owned the companies which provided these services you could simply waive these fees whenever you wanted. Or, if you were like Sandy and her friends, you could just put your favorite poor people into a house of their choosing and allow them to squat in a unit they could never afford, given that they did certain things for you. Sandy and company decided that this "thing" would be the artistic launching of a counterculture, expressly designed NOT to even pay attention to the Chancellorate at its core. Instead, the goal would be the simple creation of a community free of the chess match constantly being played by governments and their rigged systems.

Having located Sei and I, the Whit secretary Petra informed us that the Whits themselves were holding onto our mysterious arm brace, and would be returning it immediately. I visited the prefect's office on Summer 26, made an unceremonious pick up, and came back home with the brace, Sei and I having never needed to formally meet the Whits. We discussed it a little, and decided that we would only be staying till the end of the quarter since there was a lot more of Jupiter to explore.

* * *

Sei and I suspected that trouble lie ahead for any brave artists at the front of this movement, and we heard on the grapevine that certain sovereigns (the allegiant to which the Chancellor belonged) had started to publicly condemn this new trend highlighting "the deep but thoughtful depression of New Americans" as itself being unamerican. Be arrogantly, racistly happy or go to jail, they said. The problem for them was, you had to listen to the lyrics in order to even identify which works belonged to part of the genre. But so much of the new Integrationist movement would end up being instrumental, privately played, independently filmed, funded through el (which had always been a currency of local morals), and connected through word of mouth. And all it took was a set of conditions: We'll fund your creativity if you 1) collaborate with someone not of your genre, and 2) contribute to measurable trust, education, or raising of the quality of life in your community by doing so. "A rent discount just for doing cool projects with an outsider's different style?" many said, "Sign me up!" ᕤ

It was in the formalizing of collaboration structures that a partnership between that Bertram Whit and Andre West really shined. How do you measure whether a person's individual deeds in a community contribute to the betterment of that community? Whit and West proposed a kind of el-based stock market in Gloriana. If you were a citizen anywhere in the prefecture, all you had to do was give "aldos" to anyone you liked who appeared on a registered artists list. You could not give negative points because the city had no use for them—no more than electors had a use for negative votes. But if an artist wanted any kind of sponsored perk from some formal benefactor, they could be encouraged to register in a place where their fellow citizens could attest to their civic contribution. It may not have been the most sophisticated system, but it did suddenly give nearby townships the ability to quantify the effect of certain projects within their bounds. ᕤ It was easy to run stats on these "likes" and correlate them with specific event permits, revenues, quality of life emigrations, and even energy usage, such that municipalities now had the ability to turn culture into dollars. The producers of that culture often got back a useful portion of what their contribution brought in…

Yes, Sei and I truly suspected that the clear progress being made in Gloriana by the end of the Summer was inching near the raising of alarms on the highest levels. Until a funny thing happened…

On Summer 86, 2771, the Mezzogloria Electrobiotic Penitentiary dropped a bomb on the entertainment industry with its surveillance-to-music attraction "Prison Music"— where a certain ½ mile stretch of prison block was rebuilt as a transparent skyway which converted the emhim of the prisoners beneath into a romantic lofi era (rolo) jazz light show. The output itself formed the basis for a daily 2 hour stream, and we imagine that Tupery-e and her colleague Graig Wellan made bank off this seeming exploitation of the mere *existence* of prisoners.

But was it exploitation?

In a press statement, Tupery-e made a comment which struck both Sei and I with its oddness: "The people will always have lawbreakers among them. Let them make their music or whatever. If it is a crime to make music, then I'll have enough citizens to start my own country in five years."

Yet strangely, we discovered that Tupery-e is *very* popular with her prisoners. She had, in fact, been working with Wellan on a production studio for inmates, the *Prison Music* album being the result of many inmates' work. And although inmates would clearly not be allowed to vote, we guessed that there was something calculatingly scary in what she said in the eyes of the world's Kamens.

On Summer 89, Odessa Kamen paid a visit to the Mezzogloria Pen.

On Summer 90, Kamen was found dead in her Wallace Ridge home.

And for whatever reason, by Fall 15, 2771—while Sei and I were boarding the transit for our next destination in Montoya, the sovereigns of Mezzogloria had begun infighting in earnest.

Sei?

Isaiah?

Hmm...

Should we stay and capitalize on this?

Eh, part of me would like to, but dark scheming isn't what we're about. Let's hope this place can work things out on its own.

# 217. Defensive Economics Ч

What possessed Kamen to go visit Tupery-e in her den?

**Arrogance, probably.**

Although we couldn't get the nanos through security, footage from the murder scene suggested that Tupery-e nonchalantly invited her there for the meeting.

**Do you think it was a trap?**

Yep. -e is so popular down there, Kamen must have had no idea. All she needed to do was say, free get-out-of jail for anyone who arranges to have this woman killed by someone on the outside.

OR!—or, this is the Godfather of the sleazy bureaucracy that put most of you in here for being even minutely robotic. Think of the service you could do for your kind if to helped us eliminate her.

Or! You're making music about the hard life. Did you know that this person coming to visit tomorrow has this role to play in your lyrics? Never heard of her? Let me explain.

In any event, the timing is suspect. I'm sure there will be an investigation.

How much do you want to bet there won't be.

Well, we don't know who's in whose pocket, so we'd both just be guessing.

Yeah, you're right.

This place is messed up. I wonder if it was like this hundreds of years ago.

It was. I was there.

Oh, that's right. So was I.

* * *

Thanks to a series of defiant maneuvers, targeted punitive legislation, and sketchy judges, the airspace of Montoya had no officially recognized capital, no public works, and shared all of its educational and civic classifications with the pro-sovereign spaces of Clannel and Dyer. Since the installation of the current chancellor, it was "declassified" as an electoral region—the equivalent of being disowned by the nation of New America itself. Citizens passing into and out of the region were subject to heavy tolls both ways. But all of that was changing.

When we arrived in Montoya, the place we discovered turned out to be a rich arcology lush with floating greens and winding skyways. The houses were gorgeous and the public amenities clearly superior to anything we had yet seen on Jupiter. How was this possible? We aimed to find out in detail, but here's what we learned from the web:

While most local governments adopted a wait-and-see policy towards the newer national policy of SALE (selective aggressive law enforcement), Montoya adopted more of a "hell no" approach. Internally, they devised a statement of values which acted as a kind of finger on the secessionist trigger from all things federal, and advertised themselves to the rest of Jupiter as a haven for those interested in pioneering in their fields. "Are you an expert in *anything*? If you could be the founder of a whole field for a brand new colony, would you? If a key workforce training program is missing in a place, would you start it yourself? Come to Montoya. That's where pioneers go!"

Years of historical data on how to effectively organize a defensive resistance model compelled the Montoyans not only to advertise for innovators, but also to advertise for learners of that innovation. As national funding sources were successively "revoked," the airspace concluded that it was equally free of any standards the old infrastructure might have held. They set up their own certification system, which included a mandatory exam in regional economics (alongside the usual legal attestations) before new businesses could be permitted to operate, where this exam included certain questions regarding the business' plan for solvency should Montoya itself be cut off from the rest of New America. Could a business owner present an AI-convincing plan to remain in operation if, say, Montoya itself were subject to interstate trade sanctions? Where would it find its workforce? Who were its customers? Despite these difficult questions, the costs of doing business, franchise taxes and renewal fees were set among the lowest 10 in all the nation. They wanted you to do business there, but they also wanted you to understand the market you were entering.

Owners in favor of the Chancellor found the process off-putting, and sought to make it illegal. In turn, the Commerce Division at Chelsea-Lock (the formerly recognized capital) instituted a litigation fee for all owners with known assets of a certain kind—like space yachts and private school exemptions. Apparently, they knew this would be overturned, and never spent any of the money they made from the brief two seasons during which it was active. They did, however, successfully tie up the funds of Montoya's would-be disenfranchisers.

Montoya created an advertising campaign specifically to attract people interested in entrepreneurship using the area's atmospheric resources. In exchange for training in regional economics, atmospheric IoT and Sustainable Orbital Energy, learners would have certain portions of their housing and subscription fees paid for, provided they remained eligible for the program. This Montoya-centric civic institute drew upon the new influx of innovators to teach the program enrollees, and focused on the development of terraformic economies—that is, the creation of whole markets from the initial colonies set on empty asteroids. Indeed, Montoya considered itself the perfect target of such isolation—a sort of frontier within a frontier—and organized its state culture accordingly.

Although not expressly punitive towards sovereigns or openly allied with betas, Montoya did execute upon a series of highly effective biasing agreements to drain its gerrymasters Clannel and Dyer and foster easy trade with its more beta-friendly neighboring airspaces. In a seemingly innocent gesture of goodwill, Montoya awarded early contracts for certain public goods to both Clannel and Dyer, then proceeded to call for the maximum level of service from both. The maximum number of energy credits, the maximum number of pro-sovereign reconditioning chips, the maximum number of mineral2food converters, the maximum number of pro-sovereign teachers who were then asked to teach in heavily collectivist schools, Dyeran bread that was then doled out for free to the new Montoyan influx... And this went on and on for the equivalent of nine earth months until it became clear that neither Clannel nor Dyer could keep up with demand. Montoya then initiated a battery of suits for specific performance, naming everyone from private citizens and organizations to digiversal server farms operating the manufacturers to the airspace states and their governors themselves... for entering contracts they knew they could not fulfill. Clannel and Dyer responded with appeals to the Chancellorate, and when the Chancellorate announced that it would take action against the Montoyan infrastructure, the latter's attorneys named the

Clannel and Dyer officials among the Montoyan stakeholders in the organizations being sued. Because they were. (Montoya had no official voice to stand suit, remember?) Thus came one of the more complex recent legal cases of a man suing his own leg for forcing his artificially installed heart to provide it with blood. And more blood.

We passed by Dyer on our way into Montoya. It looked like a ghost outpost, the gleaming towers of Chelsea-Lock visible by scope in the far horizon.

Chelsea-Lock had been named after a series of "Che" asteroids all associated with the forced making of one's own way. It clearly lived up to this standard.

After using the Angel finder nanos to do some reconnaissance in "The Lock," I decided to apply as a runner at the Bustice League. This organization seemed to be one of several great weapons employed by the airspace to ensure its continued prosperity, and I found out immediately in my interview just how the Montoyan success story had actually been accomplished.

Yeah so when they "decommissioned" us as a state like we were some kid being being thrown out of his dad's house, we were like, "You fucking idiot. You don't just declare a mountain to not be there. You at least need resources to take it down. And you're gonna need a lot of damn resources to take this particular mountain," The former Governor, Kyle Banner joked. Blonde haired, Silver-eyed, with a known Pathfinder mod passed down for at least seven generations, Banner sat comfortably in his office, pouring himself a reed tea.

And even after you've bulldozed us, our flat plain will still claim mountainhood, if only for the sheer costs you employed to take our physical rocks down. Next you have to take down our spirit. But all we'll do is haunt you.

And there aren't enough cops in the Solar System to take down a capital the size of the old Houston, or an airspace the size of the old Colorado. You've just left a bunch of seasoned businesspeople, leaders, hackers, and community organizers hanging out there, and you somehow think you're your fucking idiocy was valuable to them. Trust me, it was of no value.

Banner sipped his tea. You'll have to excuse my language. We praesciens pathfinders tend to get ourselves in trouble with things we know we can get away with. I can read that you're friendly. And almost certainly important. So it's important to me that you know exactly where our little hamlet stands.

First of all, the Chancellor himself will be done in no less than six years. We've been a state for 332 years. It's not a question of ceasing to exist or losing rights. It's a question of whether Montoya can ride this market trend, buy the civic resources while the price is low, and sell high. We have to do it while the current regime is in power, because as a safe haven for sanity we present a very clear option for what people's highest potential could be and should be. Clannel is poor, proud, and uneducated, and Dyer is poor, violent, and uneducated. We've set it up to where they can come and go into Montoya as much as they like, and using their own Stand Your Ground rules coupled with some very smart surveillance, our citizens feel confident that they can take each one down one by one if they feel threatened. Even if they *go into Dyer* and feel threatened by the people who already live there. What I'm saying is that we're a pretty peaceful bunch, here. And there is no fear whatsoever of the fed coming down on us. They used to want to. Now they don't even want to.

I nodded.

You have an Earth signature on your emhim. I feel like you know some Solar Council people. You don't have to answer. You also have no active nervous emhim. So I know your sotions are off. It's easier to stay poker-faced that way, eh? Again, don't answer.

Here's something you don't know about us, and I'll give this to the Solar Council for free. Because I'm a pathfinder and I know I'll be fine. And you won't tell the wrong people:

When I was "removed" as a governor recognized by the fed, I was also installed as Legal Director for our forced efficiency programs. I led a team to develop a city builder-terraforming simulation called MCCD—the Montoya Community and Civic Decisioning system, which specialized in building massive markets from nothing but the resources in the air around you— even if you were robbed of property and position. We trained MCCD on imperialistic, selfish, sovereign, exclusionary, ideology BUT we also let it know that its definition of survival was to remain optimal as a whole state with all of the current characters it already had. That was the key. The problem with sovereigns is that they don't govern for the whole. MCCD governs for the whole. So even though it was trained on racist, classist data, it's notion of race and class could not extend to its own kind of "organ systems," you know what I mean? As the simulation evolved, it basically came to see its gerryneighbors as oppressors whose tactics were directly tied to the fed, and as long as it could make calculations to imperialistically take over these neighbors it could, by proxy, take over certain corners of federal jurisdiction regardless of whatever culture they'd already set up there.

I'm sure you're familiar with the White Power movement. It's a little tricky for me to join, but I'm quite proud to be white, because this is the sort of thing we're good at, and I'm really having fun with it. The fucking fed is in my back yard demanding that I pay fealty to some random puppet, and my plan is to plant my state's flag on the foreheads of anybody they send here. And those stupid representatives they keep sending to my office get scared every time when we don't welcome them with a red carpet at all.

So I think I'm a pretty good governor. And you're not just gonna sit in your penthouse ballroom and threaten to take my toys from me just because your daddy's daddy owned a bank. You still depend on market forces and diplomatic connections, and my state is still a market with some powerful people who still need to be schmoozed, and are definitely NOT fans of the regime. My *citizens* may feel powerless, but I'm in a position to tell thousands of them at a time not to use your bank or your land. To make it a challenge for you to set up your tech on my roads. And when you do set up your tech, the people who operate it will reverse engineer it for the good of our fair airspace. Actually, that's exactly what we started doing, until we realized that the process itself offered a better way.

Inspired by a maze of enemy algorithms, we now use MCCD partly to come up with thousands of legal irritations at a time—more irritations than there are officers to quell or corrupt officials to reasonably hear and write funny laws against. We like to use copious complaint data provided by our citizens against the regime to autogenerate both the lawsuits and the calls for documentation. My colleagues call it the "class action maker," and its main point is to take legal real estate from anyone trying to challenge us.

Aren't you concerned that this might be used on you?

Ah! That's the beauty of being disowned. We don't have to answer those. Our lovely Clannelan and Dyeran puppets do.

So the child writes the checks and the dad has to cover them. Are you sure this is politically safe?

Nope. But who am I? I've already had all of my old roles pulled from me. I'm just one among millions who've had the same idea. If they take away your voice, just tax their systems until they're dead, stop buying their products, or buy all of one kind of key product and none of the others. That last one only works for small towns. But this is the general strategy for market control.

I see.

Trust me, we've made massive amounts of lemonade from this one lemon. That's the only attitude you can have that will get you anywhere. I make *sure* that my citizens know this, Banner became markedly more serious on this last point.

Hm...

You know, in the beginning of the regime, people had a lot of complaints. I hate that stuff. Complaints are entropy. I can't put them in my gas tank and use them to travel. Groups of people complaining are an exhaust pipe; they use up all their energy to flutter the flag of their oppressors. And the oppressors feel validated watching their flag flap hard in the wind. Now I didn't enjoy doing this in the beginning, and I'm not very proud of it, but when the chancellor was first elected and I saw the writing on the wall, I used our police to raid all public spaces and tell the gatherers, "We will now be charging you psy to meet here. You either present your local state with an action plan and a point of contact, or you stop using this space; we won't have idle "hate speech" against the Chancellor here." Understandably, this would have confused the people had they known I was behind it, so I had the Law Chiefs enforce it instead. The people sued, I played the good cop-telling the people to really plan real programs and comply while the litigation was in process-and eventually we backed the people. Our own Law Chiefs lost as planned. But seeing how this all played out, we were convinced even further that there was something greatly helpful in using the legal system to get certain things to happen. MCCD is now operated by the Business

Justice League (or Bustice League) and they work 24-7 to make Montoya as prosperous as possible through those various institutional initiatives. But I've said enough.

Wow, uh. Thank you.

No, thank you. And tell Phaedra I said thanks for the heads up.

Eh—

You didn't seriously think I'd tell you all this without a good reason, did you?

Uh I didn't really think anything.

Well, that's better for deniability's sake, anyway. As a private citizen I can speak to whomever I please, and as a governor with plenty of interstellar contacts I will do what is necessary to see that we don't screw ourselves in the long run.

Oh. Okay.

I hope you enjoy your stay in Montoya, Mr. Fontenot, But I also hope you guys can make something of this model I've shared with you. There are more New Americans than fewer who want to see the Montoya method of prosperity applied to their regions, but they absolutely have to stop fucking around with the idle jokes and complaints and get these actual legal structures setup ASAP. They need to run candidates, however unprepared, and drive up the cost of being ignorant both for their enemies *and* for their own allies. Ignorance regarding our own house is the enemy. Not the Chancellor. He's just an opportunity that won't always be there. People need to build while they can.

# 218. The Gods Have Maids

"I may not know much about Solar System politics," the third maid Pookey noted to Sei over the triple-wide kitchen sink, "but I do know that people like us have it all wrong."

Really, how's that?

"We think that life is as simple as 'the bad guys up there' or 'the little people down here'—like voting or protesting or even following the news matters. But you know what I've learned working here for the Barrister? That it's actually old-school court life that runs everything. You know, who you marry, what kind of money your family has, and what kind of money whoever you marry has. Like where they put their assets. People like us don't look at ourselves as being 1/100,000,000th of somebody's asset portfolio, so we don't know that people like Mr. Wyat don't look at our problems the way we do."

Wow, I guess you're right, Sei nodded obligingly. I'd never thought of it like that. Having just entered her second season as fourth maid in the house of Barrister Mark Wyat, Sei had learned to swallow most of the leanings of everyone else in the house of the mid-level Sovereign lawyer. On the surface, at least. With the help of a certain handful of mood stabilizers suggested to her by Pookey and her manager, second maid John Manserv, even Sei herself could now survive employment in a semi-desotioned stupor—one designed expressly for compliance with the environment around oneself.

Sei added another plate to the pile of dried dishes from the prior night's banquet.

"That's why I like working for the Wyats. They may not always approve of me, but at least I know they're in touch with reality."

Sei knew better than to ask aloud what Pookey meant by "reality." Instead, she seemed to reinforce Pookey's stance. Yeah, I guess. When Isaiah and I first got here, we thought, man Jupiter is so different. Everybody here seems so jaded with the state of things, but that's only for folks who still think of themselves as being entitled to what someone else has. I mean, they talk about not having the same opportunities to begin with, and that might be true, but what do you think—a planet can just run on people who don't know what they're doing? The best way is to stand behind the greats and learn from them.

"Exactly. For instance, my dream is to get smart enough to learn finance so that Barrister Wyat's son can notice me. Please don't tell anyone. I mean, it's not like I'm out for their money or anything. More like I think my beliefs are just as good as theirs. That and I need to learn to speak better. And maybe get their daughter Jane to give me some style tips."

So you really think they'd let you marry into the family?

"Well, not really. Truth is, Max Wyat doesn't really care for my type. But he's cute and I like him. I was thinking about letting him catch me by the pool one day, if you know what I mean. **Wink**"

Sei returned a forced wry smirk. It's still a woman's best asset for getting herself seen in the first place.

"Right? That's how all these stupid bimbo mayors are getting all these high up positions across the airspace. As long as I can be a passable status object for whatever man put me there—because you know it was a man—then I can do anything."

Except rise too high or challenge them when you do.

"Do I detect some envy there, Sei? Why would you want to challenge your own infinite line of credit?"

Oh, I don't know. Don't mind me. I might just need to take my havitol for today.

"No, you need more lyekitol. Or you running low?"

No, I'm just a couple of hours past due.

"Oh, okay. Well anyway, I think most people still feel the way you do about wanting the freedom to rise to someone else's level. I get that. But are you ready to fight someone else's fights? I've served at least a hundred people who could unemploy a whole city with a signature or write a bill that could send 100,000 cyborgs to the scrap heap over a parking ticket. Or just plain ignore all beta votes if they wanted. But that would also kill their business interests if they did things like that, and most of them aren't needlessly evil anyway. We poor people think they are, but they aren't. They're human just like you and me, except where you and me were born with our families and society on our back, telling us who to be, they were born with the same thing AND access to the kingdoms that everybody else lives in. If you don't want to be a chess piece, then you need to marry the chess player, know what I mean? Marriage, diplomacy, and asset movement is actually what makes the world go round, and in that case it doesn't matter what level you rise to. Even the Chancellor answers to the Port Trade lobby. Everyone does."

And who do they answer to?

"I don't know. Probably their own ideas. They must be like gods. No one ever sees them, and I'll bet they eat crab cakes and play statecraft for fun all day. But we poor people need our gods to make the big nasty world safe for us, so those folks serve a need."

You really have thought about this!

"Yeah. I mean, I've never been to Earth, but the Solar Council has gods. Ammity-e, Nauxza, Phaedra Zeta, those folks are no different from the Chancellor in how they control these huge planet-sized pieces of things."

Hmm. (Sei remained quiet regarding this last statement. Pookey had made some interesting points, but the state of Jupiter and the state of Miranda were nothing alike. It was the approach to good stewardship over your "assets" that made all the difference.)

"Sei?"

Pookey?

"Be honest, what do you think the chances are of my marrying into a better family than the one I came from?"

Well, I'd have to know about your family—

"I mean, marrying up?"

I, eh, that's a tough question. People marry for so many different reasons.

"But as a maid here I know I'm never gonna be in a position to even meet people above my tier if the Wyat's don't introduce me. Yet that dunce Treeney can go from high school cheerleader to State Infrastructure Governess just by spreading her legs for the right guy 10 years in advance."

Do you have anything against that?

"Are you kidding? I'd totally go that route if I liked the guy at least. And everything else would be a perk. There's nothing wrong with that. But I am against being an idiot. I know I could do better than some of these people. I'm just asking what you think my chances are of getting a shot at the top through family. Because I'm telling you that's the fastest way—maybe even the *only* way—I'm ever gonna get to the life I dream."

And what is that life?

"It's definitely not doing banquet dishes every six months that's for darn sure. Or shining Jane's shoes every Sunday. Or having people look down on me—where they think the only way you understand being talked to is if they're judging how you're doing something or correcting you. I swear, sometimes it doesn't matter how much lyekitol I've taken, I really do feel like a tool sometimes. Like maybe it would be more enjoyable to get one of those lobotomies that cyborgs can get. Windsor the previous gardener did that after serving for two airs. He said he couldn't take anymore, but also had nowhere to go. Too bad they fired him right after. I think Jane just missed the appearance of someone kissing her ass. Windsor lost interest in that after his lobotomy."

Hm. So do you think there will ever be war with Earth?

"Where did that come from? Uh, I guess anything could happen. But I'd bet on a war with Zeusland more than anything. But that's far off. Barrister Wyat does a lot in that space. I think he's more worried about winning cases against the former state of Montoya. That's his battleground."

I heard Montoya is putting up a fight.

"Not just putting up a fight. They're draining the life out of Clannel. A lot of the Barrister's friends own airspace and businesses there. Now I don't really have an opinion on that since this here posh house is the result of our former state's looting its new parent, and that's why I say I'm not big on politics."

Well, that's interesting. Because on the one hand you say you could do better than some of the other reps, but on the other hand you say you'd prefer not to get into the ring. Maybe that's what you need to increase your chances of rising?

"What?" Pookey seemed perplexed, as if a major realization had suddenly come to her.

I'm just saying.

Pookey thought for a moment. "But if I got into the ring, everyone would expect me to just follow their male agenda mindlessly. Whoever I married or whoever put me there."

Yeah. I'm thinking that would be your competitive advantage over other women also trying to marry big.

"To fight my husband's or his family's battles?"

It offers infinite credit ☺! Sei smiled teasingly, wagging an invisible card in front of her colleague.

"Yeah but all these ideas I have—even if they are lined up—took a lot of self-teaching to build. I really hope that the reward doesn't mean giving that up."

People are different, I'm sure you'll find someone who loves that about you. Maybe it can be both your decisions.

"Well," Pookey grabbed another cup and started scrubbing. "Darn it all. You're darned if you do, darned if you don't. I mean, I can't even get myself invited, let alone worry about having choices or giving them up."

There are ways! All it takes is for you to hang around that one fateful conversation, then you can show 'em what you know!

"Heh, you're so naïve, Sei. That's what I like about you."

Sei chuckled a little.


(…though on the inside, the question of Gods and maids continued to stir busily in her brain.)

# 219. And Naught Shall be the Man

Fall 8, 2771 n.e.

We didn't always put vogged at the front of the save block, Dial explained to Phaedra. It used to be further back. But over time it became clear that _views_ _of_ the great _dream_ were as important as the Moon frequency in determining not only what made people happy, but also what kinds of information they listened to in pursuing that happiness. We still think the geocentric second house, Taurus frequencies and mid-Cancer frequencies are key to how vogged is represented in the save file, but to answer your question, if you wanted to create a kind of backup data save for all of humanity without explicit consent from each actor, I guess you could always throw together the usual rough summary they they do in history books.

But I wouldn't be able to extract specific personalities from that summary, Pheadra quated.

*Definitely not. If you could, SEIR wouldn't be necessary. Individual stories require individual data points. Otherwise it's Heisenberg. We can't really expect to take this bucket of a dozen people, know nothing about their relationships to each other at all, and reload a single one among them from that soup. Because then you get into issues of like, well who was that soup's parent? How mobile was it in the larger context?*

It just seems like we did exactly this on Venus.

*We certainly did not. The nusian skin we projected had no parentage, and told us a forced story partly based on the fact that we were the ones doing the looking. The only truth in there is the truth of the cameraman.*

So Watcheye and the others are the slit experiment "particle" result of our own filter? Whatever their original wave might have been will now never be known to us.

*Exactly.*

I see. So what of these data save cubes they're proposing to build? Both the Council and the Jupiterians seem to be interested in them. But how do you capture all human data and save to it?

*"And the screenshot ate the whole video…"* Aimee smiled. *That's not computationally possible for reasons I'm sure you could guess, and several more reasons you couldn't guess. Even I didn't expect my researchers to tell me that the very fact that a planet has an orbit introduces a gradual creep in the ultramacro technology which saves it. We're capturing faster than light speed information content on a slower than zero speed platform. And that's slower than any cycle of universal periods you can write to. FTL, as you know,*

*automatically needs exponential resources whenever you tack derivatives of light bend onto the light itself, so if one particles changes at 3e8 meters per second but bends at .1° here and 4ne9 at the perspective of some distant star[3], then the cone between them has transmitted much more than light speeds' worth of info. Imagine trying to simulate a single person's—not cones, but VOLUMES of—cones using a device which the person themselves can manipulate. No, Zeta, subsets are all we have, and selective loading is the only loading we can do.*

So what goes into the cube? I'm convinced that this project will become a reality at some point.

*Honestly Phaedra, what goes into the cube will be whatever the writers of that cube want to put into it. Nothing else will matter beyond that.*

Not even eventual conflict with Jupiter.

*Not at all. Nothing. But once it goes in, what'll be the nature of the stuff that comes out? SEIR pulls whole people, but only singletons in high resolution. Are you looking to save the state of all the world—even the broken, self-destructive, or nonsense parts? Only beta-kind?*

We've been asking these questions every day for a very long time.

...

*I know.*

It just seems like futility. We spend our whole lives reaching for these goals and then...

*And then we reach them only to become desensitized to their reaching the next day. That's why it's so important to*

---

[3] 3e8 (3 "EE" 8): $3 \times 10^8$. 4ne9 (4 "NEE" 9): $4 \times 10^{-9}$.

feel like every day is your best one. Let Time decide which one is your last, and until then, do whatever it is you do that enriches your sphere.

Seems like the Jupiterians are already doing that—

And to learn what that sphere is made of. When we save data we necessarily save major rivalries. Like any history book. The Jupiterians see us as their rivals, but have no idea that we are one of the most important parts of their sphere. Without us to hate or claim dominance over, they'll just war amongst themselves. Most people—except for a few—won't feel good about that.

I just don't see how they can wish pain on everyone so badly. How did it get to the point where half the Council is ready to take down three Jupiterian leaders with no provocation? I get it, but I just wish we didn't have to take the low road like this.

The Osairan Minister's policy of tough talk is agitating everyone. And at this point it's clear that sapiens alpha leadership will always be like this. Now that Banner has told us the whole score it's pretty obvious what needs to be done. Our old selves are going to cause trouble if we let them consolidate as they intend. But with MCCD under our influence... Well, you know the Council is right.

So we "robots" really are planning to use their robots to take them over for good?

I don't have any better ideas, do you?

No. But I don't like this, Aimee. Just let that be known.

Old humanity is too easily led by confident-looking characters and official sounding reports. You tell them something is a trend and they follow it, even if you just made it up yesterday. Zeta, we've had decades of experience with what countless human psychologies are like and I'm telling you, this isn't the low road. It's a well-paved law of survival. Sapiens used tools to suppress their predecessors, then institutions to suppress the unfavored among their own. The institutions turned around and used information systems to suppress traditional governance. They did it in the name of these huge spaces of comfort and access. Then the information systems suppressed the institutions, and we are the product of those systems. I'm not saying we're destined to destroy the Jupiterian institutions, but I'm telling you it's all anarchy if we let these uncivilized guys keep charging-up on us.

...

The Council stands 60-30-10 in favor of making a move. You and your 10% undecided really need to come up with some good arguments against it.

Really, Aimee, I don't have any good arguments. I'm glad they gave us time to sit on it, but I'll probably vote in favor when we reconvene in a few days. I just need time. You don't know what it was like in the beginning. We were all so idealistic. And Twice Jack could have come up with—

Aimee groaned. Ugh, here we go again.

You know what, dammit, get out! I'm voting _no_ right now.

What!? But—

Watch me.

Wha—but how can you suddenly make a decision like that over a little—

Always just a little this! Just a little that! Until we don't even recognize ourselves anymore. Navicon, get me Reselat.

Phaedra, you're not serious.

Really?

RESELAT IS ON THE LINE.

A regal looking Korean man appeared on the office holoscreen. Zeta, *how* are you?

Fine.

*Oh? You don't sound fine.*

Reselat —I.

Phaedra waved one hand in irritation in order to shush her friend. The move was so uncharacteristic even for her that Dial froze instantly.

I'm voting against the MCCD exploit.

*Really?* The man raised one eyebrow. *Why, might I ask?*

Because in talking to my friend here, I realized that it's too easy to forget who we are. A little garbage in now is going to spell a lot of garbage out later. And when Dial here groaned over the mention of Twice Jack, my reservations about the seediness of this decision were confirmed.

Reselat frowned. *I knew Twice Jack. He was a hero. Dial, did you know him?*

No, we never met.

*You should have. He practically invented the Council.*

I —

*The el system is based on trust in data sources. Apparently your expressiveness regarding a legend you've never met cost you some trust as a decision maker in Zeta's eyes. And I can see how that might not bode well for us going into this. It sounds more alpha than beta.*

Dial turned away in shame.

*Very well, Zeta. I know the other 13 will probably follow your lead. But if you don't mind my asking, how long do you expect this iron to remain hot?*

I'm not stupid Reselat. This is a golden opportunity that only the Council can sponsor. But if we sponsor it and are found out at all, it *will* backfire.

*True. Are you proposing other channels?*

I'm proposing nothing. We have at least two moles that we are aware of at operations. If the proposal is defeated, we should announce it loud and clear that this action is not the beta way.

*I now have more questions than answers as to what you are proposing we do to prevent their trade consolidation.*

Phaedra paused before answering. You can do whatever you want. But if it is outside of Council discussion, then I am not to know about it, you hear me?

*Whoa, Zeta. Your tone?*

This is serious Reselat. You know how I feel about precedent. I don't want to begin doubting who we say we are.

*You are always so frank. I suppose we need this.* Now it was Reselat who took a moment to think. *If it helps your case, then I will change my vote as well.* �

Phaedra grew wide-eyed, as if she had just received some kind of special injection.

*I'm not that committed to unprovoked action. As a beta, I know it says more about my own thought process than theirs, as the Jupiterians haven't changed. We have. Thanks to Banner's information. Perhaps we can help him in some other way?*


The next day, Phaedra paid a visit to Jake's lab, speaking with him alone.

Jake, is it at all possible to talk to the brace from here?

Yes, but it's probably better to talk to some nearby device which can detect the brace's pattern instead. What do you need?

I need for Sei and Isaiah to meet someone in Montoya, without them knowing the ask came from us.

Ah. Easy.

Very good.


�

And that's how Kyle Banner knew of Isaiah's arrival before Isaiah did.

* * *

During downtime from my duties as a runner with the Bustice League, I started attending (what was to me) the meetings of a secret subgroup of an already clandestine organization. The Upper Glassbridge chapter of the Adam Naught Refinement Group (also known as "Anergy" or "The Naughts" for short) wasn't just a support group for males looking for help with various personal issues, it also happened to be one of the few places where the extremely high-ups of Montoya and nearby Dyer could gather under a long trusted code of confidentiality. Among the insular group of 18 to 40 monthly attendees were several lawyers, doctors, and government officials, including a certain City Manager for one of the townships in Dyer.

The group sat around the lounge, discussing their concerns.

"Have you guys ever had a 200 year-old wine? I have. It mostly got me higher than an exostation when I was first admitted into the Nostra. Man the parties we had."

"So yesterday I was strongly urged to do a favor for a colleague which involved something I'd rather not get into. Made a couple of calls to get the wife out of the house, and tended to this business. I felt like shit afterwards, and the wife eventually came back with divorce papers." The man sipped his wine. "As you know we've been arguing about a bunch of things for the last couple of years, so I guess I'm not surprised."

The group listened respectfully.

"So we exchanged some words, she slapped me, and I slapped her back. I think it insulted her more than it hurt, and she told me that she would bring me down completely if I didn't let her go. But bring me down with what? I haven't done anything illegal. I mean sure, the fight was no good. But she can't use that alone since she's attacked me many more times than I have her, and the replays will have her lunch if those are the grounds. No, she said she'd simply make professional and reputational hell for me."

Another sip of wine.

"Then she bragged about how she was going to go and fuck a former friend of mine, while at the same time drawing up a case for the girl I cheated with last year. Open marriage or not, I have a lot to lose, and she has nothing to lose. So what am I supposed to do? Of course I want to sign the papers, but I know she may just spill it all anyway, and this will completely blow my chances as Family Planning Secretary."

"I don't know. I hate living with her constant challenge, but it's easier than having no one at all to come back to after getting skewered again at work. And our kids. They don't really want to see us split up either. And I'm just like, Patty I need to do this. For myself. My work is how I make something for myself. You may not understand it, but it can't just be about your comfort and what you approve of and disapprove of. Constantly. Everything is about her and what she wants and what she's gonna take from me if I don't give it. And how she requires this list of concessions. She serves me these papers and in the middle of our argument I tell her I'll sign right now. Because I'm frustrated. You know what she says to me? 'Good. As soon as you do, the kids and I will move in with my aunt.' But what the hell!? I love my kids. She should petition through court if she wants a divorce. Because if I consent on her terms with her documents I'll almost certainly never see them again. And then there are the support payments. I'm not *voluntarily* going into that!"

"So I guess my question for you all is this: When you're stuck with someone who's cornering you, and you can't break free because you'll end up forfeiting everything, what do you do? Her instilling is all about taking from enemies. My delivering covers difficult tracks."

The group pondered this for a while, until one of them spoke up.

"Well, if every feminine place [instills] something within folks entering her zone, and every masculine [delivers] something to places he enters, then as long as you're with her, you'll keep the ability to take from your enemies. She's threatening you now, but if you let her leave, I would bet that your rising in work won't go nearly as smoothly."

There were a couple of nods among the others.

"I feel that too."

The helpful man continued, "But if you let her go, she'll lose the person who covers her tracks. She might want to take the kids, but will they stay with her? And you'll still be able to cover your own tracks despite whatever case she makes. So I think it's a choice between getting free of the stress, remaining blameless with your kids, versus rising professionally with a cloud over your head. So you think the higher-ups will dump you as soon as your family rifts?"

"Definitely."

"Then which one do you want more, freedom or advancement?"

"I really wish I didn't have to make this choice at all. We could have done both so easily if we hadn't had so many lifestyle incompatibilities."

"Well…"

"I know. A man needs uncontrollables and uncertainties because his specific type of unknown is what he is designed to put his pattern onto."

The helpful man replied, "And we always say that the woman puts a specific kind of certainty onto things—not just us. But if things go sideways, she has the power to make a lot of people certain about you. The question is, I guess, is she an ally or an enemy? If she's an enemy, she can take from you if you let it stay that way. Given both your talents, I'd butter her up as much as possible so that you can't register as an enemy in her mind. Sign the divorce papers, and withdraw your talent for covering tracks. She won't be able to take from you, and if you leave her exposed without cover, your kids will eventually see this. Just don't be an enemy to her if that really is her instilling."

The man from Dyer gave this some thought.

"Thank you for sharing, Jimmy," our sponsor replied. "Okay fellas, let's review. What was step number 4 in our process?"

"Every man should know what he delivers."

"And step five?"

"Every man should know what his Problem Others deliver or instill."

"Yes, and this holds true whether we're talking about people, jobs, or addictions. As men, we are the bullet that delivers a signature onto anything we touch. Knowing what we deliver is a matter of looking back at how every situation has changed according to the same pattern once we've arrived on the scene. What kind of pattern happens every time you enter a place, regardless of where that place is? This is your delivery. It's important to know, because as men we can sometimes find it very easy to bring that pattern into places where it is not helpful. Not to us or the Other we're engaging. That's where we have to consider getting help from a more fitting pattern carrier, or walking away."

"And what do you do if your pattern is a bad one, but you keep winning when you use it?"

"I assume that we're all here because that kind of thing bothers us, Alex. So for you I'd say, just keep listening and supporting your brothers here. And take support from them. Man respecting man, you know I can't deliver my pattern of solution onto you without risking some form of tension somewhere in your life."

"Okay."

"We can see how a bullet is best used sparingly, on a deliberate target, by an expert user. Our male energy naturally wants to brand everywhere we walk, so it is almost inevitable that someplace we arrive in is going to resist being branded with our iron. When that resistance arrives, we can expect a fight. But those who realize we will fight them when we don't get our way are naturally going to raise their defenses, and that's when the unknowns that you *don't* touch or *don't* see will start working to erode everything you've done. No one is immune to this. Not even the male concept of God or the greatest Popes and Pharaohs in history. Somebody with a pen after you're dead, an ex or a bystander as soon as you leave the room." They will turn around and reclaim their space as soon as you the bullet have passed through or died out of the situation. This is why we really need to be selective about where we take our delivery. If we care at all about being a pattern truly worthy of the mantle of manhood."

"Heh, my wife would have a field day with what you just said," one attendee remarked.

"Well, some folks are like that. Whether women, men, or institutions. And that's their right. It only tells me that your wife's instilling wouldn't align with my delivery. All that matters is that she aligns with yours."

Several nods followed.

"Sometimes people around us trade tension with us when peace is healthier in the long run. This is especially true when we are surrounded not so much by the uncertainty of our choice, but by the many many voices and perspectives of the unfiltered information world. That world has a quality about it which is powerfully feminine in that it's like a giant arena instilling all kinds of ideas upon us. In that situation, the deliverer in us with our little pattern risks being stamped out by absolutely anything and everything that an unchecked world has to throw, and it is our natural instinct to defend our identity—our psychosocial *selves*—the way a caged animal might. Asserting blindly, lashing out, going violent in a public place, dominating anything and everything with our pattern just because we're sick of the contrary, getting aggressive with our partners, picking up a substance or a servant or some other thing that can't or won't fight us… all of these are some examples of us taking back our inwardly felt right to deliver what it is we were designed for as living individuals. And if we can get support in this, or raise alarms, or even get others to call us names… as long as they can tell us, 'You, bullet, have punctured me!' then even that can give us the exact fuel we need to keep being an even bigger bullet. Faster, for longer, and with so much more potentially destructive power if we don't watch it."

"I'm so disappointed that I can't talk to my soon-to-be ex-wife about this," Jimmy of Dyer added. "I see what you're saying strategically," he turned to the attendee who had advised him before, "but I actually do want to keep my family together. Few people in my shit job or the stupid public understand that I'm human just like them, but it's like it's open season on me just because I messed up once or twice. She messed up too! But that's beside the point. I know my delivery and her instilling. But if I divorce her, my concern is that I'm going to meet someone just like her several months down the line, I wouldn't have fixed the problem dynamic the first three times with the first two girlfriends and then her, but now I'll have the albatross on my back that I'll never be free of in a *different* way."

"Is that your other-instilling?"

"I think so. Not quite taking from enemies, but critiquing them at every turn."

"Ah. And how do you feel about that?"

"I feel angry, if I'm honest. Angry at life for setting me up like this."

"I feel you, man. Most of us don't have a clean setup for both partners."

The sponsor interjected. "Right. Everything that exists, even without gender, has both masculine and feminine properties. We all have places of instilling and places of delivery. Being biologically male skews everything towards being one of these, and the one you are not is called our 'other-.' We biological men are delivers, and the instiller quality within us is in many ways who we *would* have been if we had been women. We call these our 'other-instillers.' And they show up as the women in our lives. This is also part of our holistic pattern. If I understand it, Jimmy here has a place in his chart and frequency which predisposes him to critical partners regardless of his wife's current manifestation of this thanks to her own setup. This takes us back to step 5."

"So Jimmy, you not only know both yours and your wife's pattern, you also know your personal pattern for attracting a wife too. There are four pieces to this: who you are and who the other person is as man and woman, and who you each attract into your respective "other-" slots. We run into the most problems when our other- slots are negative to begin with. We could be angry with life for letting us be born into the wrong family or class or other circumstance, but life usually won't answer our words. It will answer our pattern."

"Jimmy, let's set the topic of your wife aside for a moment and consider only your nature-nurtured template for a wife. How might you use your delivery to become allies with the template?"

"Well, I guess I could use her ability—eh, *cover* her while she critiques obstacles or opponents."

"Very good. What else?"

"I could cover some of the difficulties she could have experienced in the past, or engage her to critique certain reports from my job."

"Good! You see, now we are making direct use of what Jimmy is actually favored by the universe to deliver AND we are treating his other—in this case an instiller—as a true ally in something they can do together. This is no different from treating a previously unknown associate like family as you get to know them. Now they are part of the welcome inner circle, and you protect them or support them as you would support yourself."

* * *

Sometimes when I feel like we're not making progress in our journey, I am reminded of the theory of greater consciousness. Just as a virtual character may experience a revelation that affects the player, I'd like to think that my learnings can affect what the rest of the Universe is capable of, just because I learned it. Not because I necessarily did anything active.

When Mr. Banner first told me of his plan to vouch for me as a respected Montoyan doctor so that I could attend Upper Glassbridge ANRG, I wasn't sure what he was looking to accomplish. He told me that he had it on good authority that the fight for the soul of sapiens alpha could be won if the right betas could somehow provide MCCD with an assessment of the opponent's mentality right after certain major maneuvers were made. It wasn't so much that he wanted me to spy on the attendees of the meeting or break the trusted creed, but more like he wanted me to bring him and MCCD a sense of everyone's morale, and how they explained their own conflicts to themselves. He went on to remind me that wars are won by the right narrative, and from the words and smiling arrogant faces of his opponents you would think that they suffered no internal conflict at all. That wasn't true, and he wanted me to propose scenarios for MCCD which paralleled (or rather, amplified) these conflicts.

**They appear to be sitting on easy street, steamrolling the populace. But there are certain kinds of things they fear. I want you to use what you know to suggest equivalents of those types of things to MCCD, so that we can better train our decision system to protect its people against these guys.**

He also told me that my being a beta only helped, because he knew I would be averse to lying. MCCD would trust me more than it trusted him, so I would need to actually get enrolled in a doctoral curriculum immediately. The rest would be easy.

That first night after I returned from ANRG, I told Sei hints of what I had discovered. Although I couldn't talk about who was in the meeting or what we discussed, it was vitally important that we have someone inside the house of a family thought to be associated with the superstructure lording over the people (at least in their eyes), and that few things bothered an upper committee more than a market force for which there was no lever. Although we could easily determine how the Jupiterian leadership viewed their markets, what we really needed to know about was the dynamic between the conqueror and the few conquered whom they actually still required in their circle. What were those conquered responsible for that made them so indispensable to the conqueror's arrangements?

That's when Sei and I agreed she should look for a job as a maid in some upper-tier family.

You know, Isaiah, in the end it's all simple, she told me over the com. The fact that we the help all live here keeps us partly insulated against the poor outside. That our duties are simple and repetitive even if taxing, that we actually have direct interactions with these people, and are so heavily conditioned to love the luxury around us,...it's all about money. The lifestyle I mean. There's no reward in fighting a losing battle or going against these intimidating networks which could ruin your chances everywhere, and you know that the outside world is definitely not better. It's not safer, richer, more generous, or smarter. Non-elites are just as dog-eat-dog, and would do the same thing as the elites if they had the position. No, this is the place to be. That's what they think. I can't say they're wrong.

That makes sense. At first I didn't understand why it was so important for me to go to a male only support group in Mr. Banner's place. Now I understand that if you want to know why kings do things, you actually do have to look at their personality. It will actually tell you what they want. The public doesn't really have an interest in the why of things, but for a man, the why is overriding.

What do you mean?

Did you get a chance to look up the Naughts' 12 steps?

Yes, I did.

Then I don't have to tell you that their approach to helping men is directly related to how they see the differences between men and women.

Okay.

The Naughts teach that you have packages and addresses. Addresses tell you what belongs in a place. Packages won't tell you what belongs, but bring their fixed contents into any place regardless of the address. Now, may I ask you something? Are you still interested in what comes next after this, or are you already offended because I'm telling you that there *is* a difference?

… Sei frowned.

I'll try again. Do you have a response to my saying that women are addresses and men are packages?

I do have thoughts, yes. First of all, that doesn't apply to everyone. And I don't think it's right for people to just simplify folks like that and put them in boxes. It's just a very male thing to come up with a category and put it on—

Sei.

What! Sei nearly growled.

This is the problem. You had a response and you couldn't help but take the floor from me at the least little chance. Yes, I gave it to you, but once you took it, you were ready to go all the way, probably without giving me a turn again. If there had been a room full of friends to chat with or something like that, the whole address would have torn my fixed idea to bits. And it wasn't even my idea. Now imagine we live in a society where this is how we deal with *every* individual idea. We have to pass it through the filter of mob approval. Yet each individual knows that his or her one idea really is his or her own truth. Mob or not, information or media flood or not.

...

When a society suddenly decides that the formerly male energy necessarily needs approval from female energy, it isn't so much that males are put in check, but that individual assertion *in general* is put in check. This includes *anything* masculine at all. Including the assertion of different identities, the assertion of collective rights in a world actually run by mostly private interests, and female leaders. These are packages too. Big ones, because in this case it's actually the existing oligarchy-patriarchy which serves as the address being asked to receive these myriad forms of rejection of the sender's own foundation.

I don't like this.

...Eh—I know. But can you keep listening? I hope you can. Because we're not going to solve this societal problem if you don't.

*Urg* go on.

Forgive me, Sei, for saying this. But if I were a male who had just been overrun a minute ago, do you know what I would say? "*You don't tell me when to go on. I will tell you when I'm ready.*" At this point we would have become adversarial, and you wouldn't know why or that this was even a thing in my male mind.

…

…

…

Luckily, we're actually friends, so I'm not going to say that. Just imagine if we weren't though.

Hm.

Anyway, assume that masculine energy is package energy and feminine energy is address energy. They call people who are mostly package-like "deliverers" and people who are mostly address-like "instillers." What I found most fascinating is that the difference between the two—and the main difference between males and females socially—lies in how other people who are *not you* are expected to receive your power. Everyone has power. Feminine power is a stored battery. Masculine power is a flowing current. Our bodies are made of both, but all of society around us is automatically set up to stably ask impacting power from us (male) or put things in our zone for the zone itself to power those other impacted things (female). The reason this is important is because it doesn't change on any level. We always mix forms of power—like yin and yang—so there is no such thing as 100% masculine or 100% feminine because you have both a body and flowing current. A space transport is a package delivered into space but also an address where the astronauts work. And what they teach in ANRG is that even big institutions like countries and businesses have masculine and feminine components to them. Where there is one, we have to have the other. And how these two forces interact is the key to rewriting the narratives involved.

…

You know?

… Yeah. Go on.

Okay, so here's probably the biggest thing I learned today. Although addresses are *made* to rewrite the meaningfulness or belonging or fit for the objects delivered there. PACKAGES DON'T REWRITE ANYTHING. They are interpreted *by* rewriters. Where an address changes things by rewriting, packages change things by pushing, blocking, replacing other objects and moving them out of the way. That's why the Chancellorate, for example, can't actually erase the things it doesn't like, only deport them or drive them underground. Mega institutions can't rewrite the deep desires that the people have, only reorganize them through a certain technology or place of prayer. I wish you could understand how a room full of strong masculines respecting each other actually "give each other advice." It doesn't look anything like the way strong feminine energy gives advice. Advice itself is masculine, but a room or address trying to give it is feminine. And to a dedicated enough masculine (or, I should say, *any* individual expresser), those rooms are like a pit of spikes where all these other individuals are trying to collectivize your individuality out of existence. As if they don't have their own that they would want to see protected against intrusion. It's hypocritical. And in times when the information starts flooding and the identity starts getting replaced by all this information, all these new humanoids and manufactured intelligences, and all these shows with all of their maze-like values, the individual package in every individual lets out a roar of continued assertion despite it all, and a Chancellor is born.

...

Monopolies and monopolistic power are the sum of little wants which are present in everyone everywhere.

...

And further, you don't really "beat" these institutions being delivered onto you. None of us wants our individuality beaten, and the institutions are the sum of us. What you do instead is rewrite, for yourself, the new normal, so that the forced thing eventually becomes your benefactor. That's not the end of it though because I know at this point it sounds like capitulation. It isn't. There's a twist at the end.

...

Remember how I told you it's not about the what with masculine energy, but the why? That's because when you're wired to deliver the same package to any place you visit, the *what* is always the same. Addresses care about what's delivered to them. The why matters a lot less now that the package is there. At the same time, packages care more about where they're delivered or the why of the occasion. The "what" matters a lot less because the contents involved or how the destination is treated won't change very much. If you can't change the *where*, you have to change the *why*. And if I force you to organize or dis-organize or otherwise bend to my will, and you hate why I did it, your job is to take my why for today and rewrite your own why for tomorrow. As long as these people keep repeating the rationale of the ones they oppose, they'll never develop their own rationale. Sei, you've got to help your colleagues find their *own* reasons to get out from under this by capitalizing on the cards they've been handed. They can't be angry about it. They can't gang up on it thinking it won't double down even further... *sigh*. This is why passive resistance movements have been so effective in the past when it comes time to truly end a certain type of conquest for good. Those people turned inward into their own vision of how things should be, because it's futile to keep relying on the framework that got them there to provide a good foundation for where they want to go next.

...


...

And this is what you learned? But we already knew this.

Our actions say that we don't. It hasn't dawned on us to thank the Chancellorate for giving us a once-in-a-millennium opportunity to draw out and erase something in our collective soul which might otherwise spell our end.

Thank the Chancellorate!? For all of the oppression!?

These problems are bigger than any single regime or nation. Once we realize that, it should be obvious how small the current group really is in the grand scheme of things.

…

We have to get above this, Sei. We have to help our own people get above themselves.

…

…

And how do you propose we do that?

We start again. We look at the state of this society and ask, how do we intentionally and urgently build a safely collective future on mostly selfish actors who are constantly forming more untouchable institutions as the crystallization of that selfishness?

…

These are the puzzle pieces we have to work with. Arguing with the puzzle is just arguing with something we built out of our own need for cliques and comfort. Now the selfish desire is telling us that it's bigger than we are. Is it right?

Well, we're beta so…

So we can just let our past selves absorb our future selves into wholesale destruction?

Isaiah, I think we're doing all we can.

It's actually less about "doing," Sei. It's more about seeing. Not through a crusader's eyes, but through the eyes of builders of a more ideal world.

…Hm.

Let's start a temp agency. For the jobs that people will need here in a more ideal future.

A—wut?

I can't really explain it, but I think the immediacy of how people earn their livelihoods—the fact that they can even *find* livelihoods, and better ones in the new times than the old... That can bring a mentality shift directly to each person. But it has to come from these folks themselves if they are to own the work. It can't come from outside or as an answer to the outside.

Yeah, but we're outsiders. And anyone in any position of power—including Banner—would also be seen as outsiders in the common man's eyes.

Okay, then let's start a future club. It could be like, a bunch of local chapters designing the jobs of the future specific to the region.

I like the idea, but again, we're outsiders.

Then let's find an insider to hire us, and do our own work under them.

Sei thought about this for a moment. So we're not going to build up different identities to stand up for their own value?

We are, but using jobs as a more practical route, and a system of voluntary chapter creation for the cultures and townships that are ready in their own way.

So forget about the Chancellorate.

They're just the usual slice of history. Time will figure out what to do with them as it always does. But nobody has really done a future jobs club to my knowledge. We have to try something new as a species if we want new results. Ψ

Hm. Okay. I have no idea how we would start this, but I totally follow. I'll mull over it.

Okay.

And, uh, thanks for bearing with me while you were telling me about the whole... man stuff. I didn't get the connection at first, but now I do.

It helps us see the whole playing field for more than one different type of will, regardless of social class or kind of institution.

Together, masculine-feminine polarity makes a space where all kings, peasants, planets, or even particles are equal: They all move force in one of those two ways. So you actually get to see all your choices in how you frame those forces and move on from there. In a way that you design.

# 220. Meaning in the Star and Planet

Watcheye observed himself carefully, cautiously in the mirror. How could one possibly make sense of his existence at all?

*Is it true that I really am only a cloud of dust, granted a story about myself through some other dimension's quest? They say that all dust returns to the stars. And all stars return to the blackness eventually. So what does it mean to strive for anything?*

*Back home I was concerned about so many things. I thought I had a whole history. That our world had a meaningful beginning and a meaningful present. But they have told me many times that this history was just a shell put on top of floating energy. And now that they've brought me up here into their world, I have seen it myself that everything I knew was just a program. They have shown me the empty desert fields rolled over by never-ending tornadoes... I guess I have a hard time knowing what to think about that reality.*

*Leader has kept herself busy for most of this year. I don't see much of her these days since she is really putting effort into making a new life here. While Miss Zeta has let me go back home several times, I will admit that each time seems faker than the last. My family's concerns, the wars among the factions,... every time it feels more and more like a silly game. Of course they don't know that they could all just as soon be tree roots fighting over a square of dirt. Or raindrops inflating each other's perspectives with drippy retaliation. They lose a sense of their current selves, but their nature will keep moving—even if scattered. Then later, some other thing that thinks of itself as a reality will assemble from the pieces... and believe that it's world was always so instead.*

*For a while after learning the things I learned, I thought that everything really was meaningless. But Zeta has a lot of wisdom in her years, and she talks to me honestly.* See this, Watcheye, *she said.* Regardless of how we translate you for our own eyes, your world is just as real as ours. No one will ever know what anyone's true form is. For all we know, we might be cells in the bodies of star-sized gods. And they will see us as they understand us. But until someone beams us up as we did you, we will keep seeing ourselves just like this.

*But I guess on that day I wasn't as willing to just go along with any answer.* Being out there doesn't automatically give a thing meaning, *I said.*

Nonsense, of course it does. Every particle that went into every small cloud will spend its entire sense of itself in that cloud, for as long as that cloud continues to be its world. But you have to see the life in small things in order to appreciate this. If you only know things that are tangible on your level, you will become disillusioned very quickly.

Okay, but how does feeling like you're included in something automatically give you meaning?

It doesn't. But it guarantees that people who look at you and are inclined to seek meaning will definitely have a chance to find it in you. You could be that someone yourself. But that's your choice.

And what do you think makes a thing meaningful?

That depends. Some things make you happy when you need them. Other things keep you going because you want to, not because there's any external reward in it. Some things are the change or help you make the change that you swore needed to happen. There are many other roles, but these are a few of the qualities that can make a thing meaningful.

Is your life meaningful, Zeta? How can you live for so long and not get bored? Or go crazy?

I just spent the last two weeks learning the Paso Doble. In four centuries of life I had never tried it. It was fun. I have dance partners from all walks of life. They know who I am and it doesn't matter. Do you know how special that is?

And when young people come up to you who are able to benefit from what you know, or you can help your short-lived team learn all

*they can while they're able. When you know that leaving all this—
when you didn't have to—would break a lot of people's hearts—
people you love... the peace and growth you know you're fostering
in every new round of colleagues and phases of the world becomes
addictive perhaps.*

Oh.

*The world is wide, Watcheye. The universe is wide. Even if you can't
experience it in body, there are certain affairs of the mind which
you can only have under long stretches of time.*

Oh... and what about evil? What I hear is going on with Jupiter?

*I was surprised when Zeta chuckled at my question.* You know what's meaningful to
me? Knowing that in my 400+ years in a 13 to 16 billion year march, I
was part of a very special group of people who truly helped catalog
our story for all the universe to maybe discover. Particles come and
go. Lives and galaxies come and go. But the human dynamic is one
face of something closer to forever. The old humans' antics could
blow us all up in 100 years, but by the time it happens, I know that
we would have already built the best time capsule this solar system
will ever see. And that's regardless of technology, or data saves, or
anything else like that. Our time capsule lives in who we are as
descendants of our forebears. We're wiser, more conscientious, and
merged with the logic of math and nature—which we ourselves
developed. Even if Jupiter were to get what it wanted, not even
they will like what comes afterwards. And before you ask me, aren't
I interested in stopping them, yes I am. But I'm not willing to devolve
back to their level to do it. If we devolve, it's their dynamic that will
win. Real world battle is only a formality after that.*

So you keep your sense of meaningfulness by staying focused on the
great things your kind has accomplished.

<u>All</u> *of our kind.*

And do you think you can win against Jupiter?

*100% yes. And it's just because sapiens alpha would have the same
death wish whether we betas existed or not. I was alpha,
remember? Without willingly accepting their future selves and
society, their fates are sealed. My only task is to convince my
colleagues on the Solar Council not to dirty their hands by helping
them on their way.*

I wasn't really sure how to respond to such a gently framed, yet icy cold perspective. **I've been continuing my research. They say that betas have no heart.**

*If you believe that then you haven't met enough betas at all.*

**I don't believe it. I mean, you all have been great to me.**

*Then I suppose you mention this because you think my view of the old humans is cold. Try running a nation and get back to me.*

**I'm. So sorry. I didn't mean to offend.**

*Watcheye, you have to know that there are people who will take from you every chance they get, everywhere you are, at every whim, no matter how many times you forgive them. Before we merged our human ways with machine-biology and smart systems, the rule of survival meant that—if we weren't taking from each other—we were typically taking from our land, from our employers, from our convenience providers while *they* took from the land, and our convenience providers took from us in turn. They took everything down to the account number, until all was a pleasure market. Giving back was not the rule among sapiens, though we could have easily trained each person's worth such that giving back their great talent was all they knew how to do. It was only the betas—and their need for true and trustworthy data over money and more power—which changed all that. We don't run Earth because we took it from them. We run it because they could not survive the new markets of trust and trade. More specifically, they fought the rise of their own "robots" tooth and nail, while at the same time making their own robot manufacturers fat with profit because they absolutely needed to take a new phone, a new car, a new mega TV, a new fluffy food whenever they wanted it. So they fed their own beast in typical alpha sapiens fashion. And rather than embrace the universe of new skills and safer information standards, they got angry, spun a story for themselves, and generally stopped growing. So their own technologized society left the original humans behind.*

*I tell you this because I need you to understand. Wars have always taken place throughout history. But at this stage in humanity's story, if there is a war, then it can only be lost by forfeiting. If we are true to our evolution, we betas will not need to act against the alpha planet unless the threat becomes very serious. As for them, I sincerely hope they can turn it around, because they will be very easy to manipulate into early destruction if they don't.* ↵

**Has something changed in what you expect for the future, Zeta?**

*Yes. Only recently.*

**I won't pry, but are the old humans in trouble?**

*No, not really. But their chances of beating their own software just fell to near zero. And they know it.*

# 221. And the Dust Stopped Blowing Around

Sloppy is what they called it. So very sloppy. It wasn't that the Chancellorate's attempts at a whole-planetary trade monopoly were doomed from the beginning, but more that the attempts themselves didn't make sense at their core. Sure, capitalizing all sides of a transaction was easy. Requiring the disenfranchised to pay more than they made in order to use those trade routes was also easy. Repossessing assets upon default and running gigantic portfolio markets was easy as pie. Removing the right of dissenters to vote to change all of this wasn't as easy, but it did eventually get done. And in the face of a populace which now had less than they started with when they were still back on earth, the Jupiterian power structure lived high on the hog, slamming collectivists and establishing themselves as unbeatable for three whole years. But then the fourth year came. A whole bunch of people were now in jail. The trade monopoly had failed. And New America found itself hungover and unamused under the extremely disrespected administration of the New Chancellor Bennett.

What happened?

In a nutshell, Goodman died. He was, after all, pretty old.

There was a period during which it had seemed that Goodman was immortal. But somewhere along the line, key people began to realize that physical mortality wasn't necessarily a matter of how much you smoked or drank or how evil a few people thought you were. It was more a matter of when life itself deemed your time to be up. Accordingly, the longest-lived problems are ultimately the ones people fear, report, and dwell on the most; that may have been one explanation for the sudden turn towards ineffectiveness. The farther one progressed in age and tiresomeness, the more they started looking like a history book page than an active threat.

On Jupiter, the writers of those history books had been by and large excommunicated by the Chancellorate media machine, and thus formed a posthumous blind spot of untold vastness, from the farthest reaches of Jupiter to the closest security detail. Outside of the inner circle, views of the departed Chancellor would prove either scathingly unkind or unsympathetically unaffected. His successors would ultimately breathe secret sighs of relief as they divvied up pieces his estate, and that was that.

Much to the sovereigns' chagrin, control simply began to slip away as early as the end of year two, as the world itself seemed to spontaneously morph its view of very specific New Americans into the images of cave people. Somehow, even Osairans and Zeuslanders started to understand that New America wasn't what its leaders said it was, and that the heads of house—though still permanently in possession of its wealth, were clearly not in control of its voice. After all, if you wanted to continue running your bank without getting the mob's pie thrown in your face, you *had* to stay low key. This made the mismatch between who was talking on the holocasts and the citizens you actually met on the streets all the more glaring. And so the kids just kept speaking out of turn, sneaking out the window at night, taking small but cripplingly mighty pieces of intellectual capital and medical prerogative to other places far and wide—occasionally with the effect of cloning their own versions of successful structures from home, then growing those interests into a force at the table of New America's enemies. That last result probably wasn't surprising,… until a small wave of Anti-New American mergers, acquisitions, and intellectual property knockoffs started to crush little vital corners of the white label, tech, and mineral industries. It seemed that many interspace companies felt no choice but to view their former trade partner as an oncoming train. So they began removing critical pieces of track from the supply chain ♃, while repurposing those tracks in shadow market fashion to the airspace's few remaining allies ♃. Meanwhile, the so called "forest markets"—formerly the sovereigns' main support base—grew exponentially poorer under the national wealth consolidation efforts—not richer as they had proudly declared years earlier. Things were simply far too expensive for people living outside of urban settlements. In the place of those markets, a plethora of small, initially hidden annoyances, ♃ spearheaded by the infamous MCCD, seemed to pop up all over. These annoyances were too numerous to list, but many equated it to a kind of national "autoimmune disease."

And to this day, if you asked somebody what the catalyst for all this was, they wouldn't be able to tell you. There were simply forces "at work," somewhere— *everywhere* among the people—declaring the Goodman tab to be exhausted.

The march of Time. It happens to everyone.

Realizing that the former Chancellor had so monopolized the minds of his airspace that his successors would be unable to rally in any coherent way without him, the joint forces of Zeusland and Osaira launched an attack on three separate New American asteroid outposts, and initiated deals to buy seven more from their private owners in the week immediately following his death. The pretext was that spies and black market communications networks were present in the places attacked, and we would later discover that these claims were in fact true. It turns out that New America's enemies had been well aware of its languishing spirit all along—with a military, for example, that both shunned betas and women yet attempted to recruit them nicey-nice under the sovereign agenda at the same time. Osaira in particular figured that all they needed to do was swallow two of 17 banks and one major satellite-suit manufacturer, and market levers could be pushed from behind enemy lines.

While a trade and resource monopoly sounded good on paper, it always brought foreign sympathizers with it. Most of these sympathizers weren't betas, but traditionally male, privileged naturals who had always had the necessary knowledge and lineage to capitalize on opportunity wherever it existed. An informal nickname emerged for this group during the Chancellorate years: They were called the "White Shadow." Despite genuinely being a part of the sovereign allegiant, they were also entrepreneurs and pragmatists at heart. Poor and foreign people, enemy and ally markets still needed food, pharma, and credit, and you couldn't do sound business by suffocating yourself under needless isolation. So the White Shadow continued to run regardless of who the current Chancellor was, and had simply nurtured deeper and more secretive relationships with various "enemy states" during the Goodman years. Their economic empires were strengthened here, but New America's as an airspace was crippled to such a low that Osaira and Zeusland had to act quickly, jointly to overwhelm their rival. Zeusland appointed two new expat ministers who paid pretty lip service to the lost New American audience, and this further confused who actually had the airspace's best interests in mind. By the time New American forces could mobilize to answer the outpost attacks, Osaira and Zeusland had already left all three target sites, looted them, and relocated the spoils to different demilitarized zones.

Chancellor Bennett had a mess on his hands before he could even take office.

Meanwhile, there would be not one, but five terrorist attacks on various facilities operated by obscure international families known to no one. The reason for these attacks isn't very clear, and it isn't known with certainty who sponsored them or who they affected on the world stage, if at all. What *is* known is that certain would-be financial deals suddenly changed course, and Bennett was down at least one key lobby from the beginning. A certain ministerial appointment or two changed at the last minute, and a new trend in kid's snacks suddenly seemed to take the New American public by storm—the lightly opiated sweetness of an Osairan derivative having successfully flown under a trade embargo in place of stakes once operated by one of the attacked former-Chancellorate backers.

* * *

A frustrated Kyle Banner paced around his office, following a particularly upsetting phone call. In the winter of 2772 I now worked for him directly, serving as a kind of training data gatherer for the newly re-recognized State of Montoya.

These fucking people. When it was just one bastard I could understand where the threat was coming from. Now the whole thing is a damned free-for-all. The fed is now threatening a draft to take back Achilles and Mentor. But there's nothing left there after Osaira looted them. This gang of investors is now talking about buying some of our government lands to build a cyborg organ supply, while the anti-cyborgists are beating down my door threatening mob action if I even sit down at the table with those guys. Peleus is under a state of emergency after their lightning storm. Lantana is under a state of emergency after their hate crimes riots. Ass kissers of Bennett are asking me to help them bend over to the right people. And we've reinherited a shit-I mean SHIT! education system with no teachers in it and a mountain of useful texts we need to write brand new cybersecurity policies to unban. I swear, Isaiah, being Governor has never been so irritating! Ever.

Do you miss the good ole days? I joked.

Me? Fuck no! The days I want-where the common people and dukes and lords of the world were sane-were days that never existed. And now I'm remembering that fact. Goddammit not even MCCD can navigate all these private interests muddying up the waters for one another. And I spoke to your friend Phaedra earlier today. Earth and the Solar Council are kicking back with their feet up and their giant tub of popcorn watching us shit ourselves.

* * *

Sei hastened over to Mr. Wyat's office to announce the visitor at the front door.

Ko'an Langley is here to see you, sir.

"Her? Aww hell. Why does she always do this? Showing up unannounced."

I could send her away?

"No, just give me time, Sei. Langley doesn't need an appointment."

Okay.

"But could you just keep her busy for five minutes? Tell her I'll be out in a few."

Yes, sir.

"And oh, Sei. Could you do me a favor and watch her? You know, just observe her."

Am I looking for anything in particular, sir?

"No, just see if you can get a good sense of her character."

Yes sir.

Mark Wyat sighed as Sei exited the office. "Boy I hate talking to her," Wyat muttered under his breath. "She's just so weird."

Sei welcomed the diminutive 5'1" Japanese lady and her big-rimmed, goggle-like glasses into the Wyat house. With an unamused glare, the visitor tossed icy beams in Sei's direction, making it clear that she dispreferred waiting.

May I offer you something to drink, Miss Langley?

**Author Ko'an will do. And yes, I prefer black tea with havitol, two dashes of valium, and a teaspoon of paprika.**

(*That sounds utterly horrid!*) Yes, ma'am! *Cough*

**Are you sick or something?** Author Langley glared.

No ma'am. I just—am headed... to ...        thekitchen—could you make yourself comfortable in the sitting room?

The miniature corpse of a woman, draped in a sheer white shawl clutched by 2" fingernails, seemed to float across the carpet without moving her feet at all, in what could best be described as a ghostly shuffle. Taking a seat on the guest sofa, she then retracted her fingernails, and turned them towards herself, biting the tips of her right middle and ring finger cuticles. Sei bravely fought the urge to make all sorts of comments.

Upon her arrival in the kitchen, Sei was greeted by a curiously taunting look from Second Maid Pookey. "EH, heh!" Pookey teased.

You should've gotten the door.

"Nope. Not for the Red Witch. Think of it as initiation for you," Pookey smiled.

Hmph. Who carries valium?

"We do. It's in the top cabinet behind the rice."

Sei's mouth hung slightly open in confusion, but she didn't bother to ask.

"Here's some paprika, and she doesn't care which black tea it is as long as it's not Wallace or Greyhouse. Try Herbal Blessedness."

Gee thanks.

"Relax, Sei. She won't bite. She's just a little intimidating, that's all."

Sei prepared the tea and returned to the sitting room three minutes later. Just as she finished serving the Wyat's house guest, however, a beep sounded on her ringer. It was Mr. Wyat summoning her back to his office.

Just a moment, Mis—Author Langley.

Langley stirred her tea. **In two minutes I'm leaving.**

Yes ma'am, I will relay the message.


Sei shut the office door behind her. Sir, you wanted to see me?

"Yes, tell her I can't see her, but the Committee recommends against it. She may call my secretary to arrange a call for further discussion, but it will need to be formally recorded at quarters."

Yes sir.

"And please be sure she leaves the property completely before you come back."

Yes sir.

"Thank you, Sei."

Sei bowed and turned to resume tending to the rather strange guest.


**He could have at least relayed that to my face since I'm already here. Not fitting for a DSEC lawyer, not fitting at all. Convey my doubts to him, now, if you would. We are not pleased.**

Sei was inexplicably petrified. Befuddled. All the while, the Author stared her up and down several times. After the longest 2 seconds of her life, Sei scurried off to relay the guest's message to Mr. Wyat.

That's what she said. I'm sorry I didn't really get any more than that.

Wyat shook his head in disappointment. "*Why does she do this?* Okay, I'm going out there now. Wyat grabbed a quick gulp of water as if steeling his courage, then headed out to meet his fate. If you don't mind Sei, statuette?"

Yes sir? Active or passive?

"Definitely active."

Understood.

Mark greeted the Author with a cordial handshake, "Ko'an, it's good to see you!"

**So good you were just about to pawn me off to your secretary and disrespect my travel time,** Langley returned, poker-faced.

"I apologize, Ko'an. That was cowardly of me. Please forgive me."

**Well at least you admit it. You're forgiven.** The two took their seats.

Sei also took up her post as a "statue" in the corner, stiffly awaiting orders from anyone present. Langley raised an eyebrow.

**Since when did you force your help to stand there during private meetings?**

"Sei is very observant, I want her to tell me her impressions of you, and note anything unusual that might arise."

**Well then we can't meet. You know our business is strictly confidential.**

Wyat gulped as he rose from his chair again. "Fine. Then you can call my secretary."

**Hah!** Langley laughed. **Found your balls all of a sudden? But why the help, Mark? Why not an assistant who actually knows the law?**

"Why show up at my house where my assistants *don't* live?" Wyat raised his voice slightly in obvious irritation.

**So she's your insurance plan?**

"Okay Ko'an, let's cut the crap. What do you want?"

**I want you to review my latest scenario.**

"And what if I say no? At least not now?"

**Then I may recommend new Counsel for DSEC with the stomach for this work.**

"God, it isn't about 'the stomach!'" Mark huffed with an exasperated eye roll. "It's about a mind reader crashing into a person's house on a peaceful day and demanding him to review every corner of one psychopathic scene after another! For other psychopaths! You at least need to give me time to prepare for this stuff!"

**You're not strong enough!**

"You come to my house and force my hand! Time after time. And if I don't let you do it, it could cost the whole agreement? How should I react? How would you like your home invaded by prison scenarios at any hour of the day?"

**It's because I don't like you, Wyat. And this is both my craft and my civic duty.**

"But I've done nothing to you!" Wyat's voice cracked a little.

**No, you haven't. So shall we get down to business? Please, Mark. Sit back down and let's review.**

Wyat sat back down as invited.


Two hours later, Sei couldn't stand it anymore. She *really* had to use the bathroom. I'm sorry to interrupt sir, I need to visit the ladies room and will return shortly.

"Of course, of course Sei."

And the conversation continued without Sei's presence for a while.


Another hour passed, and business was finally concluded. Wyat and Langley exchanged their cagey farewells, and Sei showed the Author to the door. Mark Wyat immediately retreated to the kitchen to pour himself a drink.

As she exited, the guest commented to Sei, **He must really depend on you to have you stand there for three hours. If you would like it to be worth it, call me at this number on your off time. I will see you.** Ko'an narrowed her eyes furtively, and Sei realized the former had just lensed her contact information.

But why?

Sei returned to Mr. Wyat. Sir, are you okay?

"Do you know how telepathy works, Sei?"

Not really sir, no.

"It works the same way it does on video games: the circumstance itself holds the data, and some people have their knowledge discovery genofrequentically correlated with others' knowledge sending. The pharma industries introduced genes to hyperamplify a person's sensitivity to social response, other people's speech pathway firing, and the listener's cognitive calculation to basically introduce psychicism into the family tree. Ko'an Langley is machina as you probably guessed, and her genetic mod is reading and super-interpreting other people's internal thought processes."

Oh, I see.

"It wouldn't be so bad if that were all, but if you haven't figured it out by now, Not only is she a senior scenario writer for DSEC, she's also a functioning sociopath."

I won't argue with that, sir, Sei scratched her head in thought.

"Obviously, being in politics, I hate dealing with her, because she's constantly reading any number of things that I don't want to tell her. Accurately interpreted or not, it feels like she can get all of your skeletons to come out of their closets at the same time with zero effort."

Sei nodded in acknowledgement.

"As you saw, she writes scenarios for prisoners, and my firm represents her and the Montoya installation of DSEC. My job is to make sure that the scenarios she writes don't cross human rights lines, and she is constantly toeing the legal lines with some of the stuff she comes up with. I know you can't imagine having to invent the last six years' worth of legal precedent for some of the things a virtual prison or a thought policing system can do, but every time I meet with Ko'an I feel as though we're signing up to be convicted of all kinds of crimes against humanity. What we discussed today was the tip of the iceberg."

Really!? It seemed a little extreme to me.

"She's always that way. But if I don't meet with her on her terms, she gets offended enough to cost a lot of people their livelihoods. It's a burden every time."

"Anyway, so what did you think of her?"

I thought she was intimidating.

"Agreed. And what else?"

She seemed weirdly vain, but also obsessive at the same time.

"Yes, and what else?"

Um, she was a little hard to read. She kept biting her nails and it really threw me off.

"So you didn't notice anything else about her?"

No, not really. Besides the fact that she had an unsettling vibe overall. Was there something you wanted me to watch out for?

"*Sigh* No. I just wish she wasn't the only one I had to work these cases with."

* * *

Winter 72, 2772 n.e.

Two weeks later, Sei found herself with a nice bit of leave, and decided to take three days to travel around the state. Ϥ On the way, she arranged a visit to the Author's house, curious to learn more about the latter and her cryptic invitation.

Langley answered the door herself. **Welcome Chiquita. Please come in.**

A visibly surprised Sei passed through without questions. Uh, thank you.

The inside of the Langley dwelling revealed a sprawling high-ceiling showroom whose walls were covered in what must have been hundreds of friezes of various seemingly random people of all shapes, sizes and humanities. At the chair rail of each of the hexagonal walls, a neatly arranged row of weapons and other assorted instruments of pain and mystery filed in a controlled line beneath the wallpaper of human exhibits.

**How have you been, Chiquita?**

(*Why is she calling me that? I must be an easy 6" taller than this little woman.*) But this was clearly a test. Sei could assert herself here, but knew this would probably ruin whatever this strange person was poised to offer. She couldn't very well let this nickname business set a permanent precedent either. Then again, it wasn't like the lady was Sei's boss. How indeed to address her?

Oh, I'm fine Author. And you?

**I'm well.**

That's good. If you don't mind my asking, what is a "Chiquita?"

**It's your name. That is, the name I've given you.**

Oh, okay. But what is it? (Sei knew full well what the name implied, but wanted Langley to admit her motivations for rudely using it in place of Sei's actual name.)

**A Chiquita is a friendly term for a little girl, somewhat endearing like a sister.**

Sei smiled slightly. Oh, but dared not appear too chummy here.

Langley stared Sei up and down for a moment before proceeding. **Let's go to the living room.**


The stylish black and dark gray décor of the living room would have leaned more macabre, had the neo-Egyptian murals encasing the room and the peppering of historical artifacts not rendered the setting more of a gallery than anything else. Langley offered Sei a seat on the sofa, then took a throne-like chair for herself across from her guest.

**I love this chair. Nobody sits in it,** Langley eyed Sei casually.

Sei nodded her acknowledgement.

**Would you like something to drink?**

No ~~m~~, thank you. I'm fine.

**Well, I suppose that is to be expected. After all, you don't know why you're here.**

Sei nodded again.

Langley explained, **I have a bit of a problem. As you learned the other day, I am a writer for DESC. I am not the Head Writer because the person who does the work I do could never be the Head Writer, but I have a well-established reputation in the correctional system, and I enjoy my job.**

. . .

**First, contrary to Mark's plaintiff protest, I am not a mind reader. I am a fear instiller. My family is one of the few surviving lines of the arolythilase B genomics line, introduced for certain sports applications, then banned under the Human Crimes act. There are roughly 40,000 of us left in existence, and we are on the Inoculatory Abort list for prenatal services; as we attempt to pass our genes, any fertilized egg expressing the arolythilase B mod will be necessarily aborted upon the mother's vaccination.**

Sei listened in silence.

I am also one of only 37 million remaining Japanese left. We have always been an insular group. And the Earth Exodus was not kind to us from a purity standard. Most of us are still on Earth, but the 1 million of us Jupiterians are finding ways to preserve the race. As it is, I live here alone.

I shall tell you why I invited you. I would like to get to know you. And for you to get to know me, if you are amenable. I have other things that I want, but when I considered them, I had to choose which among them was most important. You know my work. The life I lead is lonely at times. I need to replace my house servant. I have no one to share my studies or my work with. I have strong physical needs. And when I considered all of these things and an endless series of failures in them, I thought to myself, asking for one of these almost always compromises success in the others, but what do you need most, Ko'han? You need a friend more than anything else. The first time you find someone who could be one, you must try to know them, and give them space if they are not ready to return this.

Langley rose from her throne and turned her back to Sei, gazing through the high-paned window instead. Now don't take this as weakness. It is closer to self-honesty. Because Mark asked you to stand there for three hours to cover his own fears, and you not only did so, but did so without much detectable fear, it occurred to me that I should steal you from him. Also, Langley glanced over her shoulder.

Yes?

Thanks to Mark's sloppy enforcement of confidentiality, you are now one of the few people outside of my career who has seen what I do and how I truly work. Did you find it disturbing?

—

Disregard, don't answer that. Maybe what I need instead is simply someone to bounce ideas off of.

By this time, Sei realized what Langley was asking for. She just needed a friend.

But based on Sei's observations from the weeks prior, Ko'an Langley was also exceedingly power hungry, insistent on constant deference, exuded a voracious need to dominate anything she considered subject to her, and carried with her a very difficult set of psychological wagons in her caravan. As the High Risk Writer for all of the Edge system, Author Langley essentially created the storyboards for the kinds of lives each inmate would perpetually lead in the digiverse until they either improved or died. A murderer would be sentenced to a certain kind of story. A terrorist would be sentenced to another. Yet each life was different. Some pathological behaviors began with one's being abused as a child. Some started with a traumatic event later on. Other behaviors were simply bad from the beginning. In order to generate "life spaces" for these inmates, one had to be an all-around expert judge of all motives, every type of Achilles heel, and the relationships which perpetuated or ended these dynamics. Perhaps even more than the highest pope or czar, Ko'an Langley served as an abstract existence whose mind presided above DSEC's worst. In order to do a job like this, one clearly had to get some kind of fulfillment from constant consumption of the pathological.

Bouncing ideas? I can do that.

Langley's back remained turned. **I am grateful. But now, I imagine we don't have much reason to trust each other yet. Fortunately for at least half of this possibility, I have nothing to hide. Do you?**

I do.

**Would it cost trust if I knew it, or simply invite risk?**

It would invite risk.

**Does Mark know it?**

No.

**Does anyone know it?**

Yes.

Langley stopped for several seconds. **Well, it doesn't matter. Maybe there is a better question. Have you ever betrayed anyone?**

Never.

Langley turned and approached Sei, examining her closely. Sei remained calm. The Author certainly was intimidating, but on matters such as these, Sei stood solid as steel.

**Okay. Then perhaps you would be open to hearing some of my thoughts on occasion? As a counselor would.**

A counselor, a friend, or an employee? Sei inquired seriously.

The Author smiled a little. **Are they all even still possible at this point?**

Yes.

**Heh. I find that curious. Typically my formal ways will have compromised at least one of those. Then I believe I should start with the hardest. What would it take for someone to become your friend? Even if it weren't me.**

Sei had never really asked this question directly. The Author seemed to genuinely want an honest answer. My friends are visionary, compassionate, conscientious regarding others' feelings. Some are very pushy. Others are passive. They are often privileged, lucky, and look out for spaces much larger than themselves.

Langley tilted her head in puzzlement, frowning slightly. **Sounds like friends not of this world,** Langley narrowed her gaze briefly before returning to a normal stare off to the side. **But rather than pry, my guess would be that the Wyat house may not suit you very well. No need to respond.**

Sei did not correct her assessor.

**It is the single biggest impediment to deliberate friendship among strangers these days. Not politics, but political approach. As an overseer, I find the best approach to be the one that affirms my continued role regardless of allegiant. Allegiants are terrible lovers, though they woo you with emergency after emergency.**

Sei smiled. I agree.

**Do you now? How can you stand that house?**

They are generally nice people, and don't really force their extended affairs on us.

Langley grew quiet again. **So close, yet so far.**

...?

**Yes, I believe we could get along. I may be one way, but can easily go the other for the right person. Yet I feel that hiring you away from Mark or living in the same space would not be helpful for anyone. I would treat you like my employee, then my servant. Perhaps my slave.**

...Oh. The hard reality left Sei slightly insulted, a little more disappointed.

**For not many people could survive the company of the depraved Misst Ko'han Langley-Arai for longer than a couple of days. Translate.**

The Author motioned to the wall's holoscreen, observing Sei carefully for a reaction.

*(荒井 公犯, not 公案. That says public offense as in crime, not public case like the Buddhist stories. Did her parents really name her that?)* Is "Ko'han" your birth name?

**No, Ko'an is. But times change.**

I see.

More surprising wasn't her birthname, but her title. "Misst" meant she was either trans male to female (m2f), female-presenting intersex (mnf), or female with male conversion (f+). You had to be careful with assumptions here, because people's reasons and composition tended to cover very different inner worlds in these matters.

Yet Langley still needed a response. Well if you want a listening ear then I can be that.

**Thank you.**

The Author glanced at the clock on the wall. **Well, how about I show you the cell grounds, to help you become familiar with the place?**

Sure thing.

* * *

Sei's meeting with Misst Langley turned out to be so positive, that Sei called me later that night with some news.

I think in the end all I needed was some space outside the house. I want to put more effort into the future jobs club idea, but felt weird doing it under Jane and Elaine's roof. Mark is more indifferent to the whole thing since he sees it all as the usual politics. But Mrs. Wyat and Jane seem to think that letting the help live outside of the manor is a good way for them to form opinions of their own. (Read, NOT desirable.)

**Are they wrong?**

No, their right. I may have kept my own opinions all this time, but it's been so hard to act on them.

So anyway, at first Ko'an proposed to buy half of my time. Elaine made a big stink about it saying that if I was gonna temp for someone else, then I could forget about the job entirely. There were so many ways to play that one, but then Ko'an basically offered to buy me out completely then sell me back to the Wyat's for a higher price. Naturally Elaine was fuming at the apparent arrogance of this, and gave me this evil glare like, "Are you seriously turning traitor on me with this little witch?" So I kind of reeled back like whoa, I didn't make the offer. She just came in here! But Elaine didn't like that I had visited her in secret at all. Finally, Mark got pretty tired of it and asked to talk to Ko'an in private. About two minutes later they came out and Mark apologized to me for Elaine's impatience, explained that she was just being protective of the family's setup and not to take it as a sign of treatment in the future should I choose to stay. Then he left the choice up to me. I told him thanks for everything, but I do want to see more of the world. And Jane and Elaine were like, flabbergasted that anyone would leave the mighty Wyats to live with a "chink" [wrong epithet, I know] psychopath. Actually, that's more or less exactly what Jane said before she stormed off. Elaine was so stunned that her daughter had come out of her face like that that she chased after her all huffy and—hold on. Elaine's calling me. I'll call you back.

Ok.

(3 hours later)

*Sigh* Man that was exhausting. I just had a long heart to heart with Elaine, and then Elaine and Mark. *Sei sniffed.* I'm sorry. I'm just a little teary.

**Is everything alright, Sei?**

Yeah! Yeah! They were just so sweet, you know?

**Oh, okay.**

So they said so many things that I never knew they were thinking about. Like, Mark always knew I wasn't just a regular person looking for a job. They could tell when we needed to be doped up in order to bite our tongues, but he said I was somehow stronger than everyone else on staff—"like you knew something we didn't," he said. So he asked me to explain what it was about Ko'an that made me take her offer. I told them a little bit about her—nothing secret, though—how that house was really lonely, how she's not actually a mind reader but just a misunderstood person, and how I'd get to learn a whole lot about some far out kinds of people under this new arrangement. I didn't give any machina secrets away though. They didn't really believe my story until they finally asked me if she really was human—like with human feelings. I told them yes, just like they are, and Elaine gave me a hug.

**That's so nice.**

Yeah. They know Ko'an can't really afford a full-time maid, and Mark was like, "I guess she just bought your freedom. Not from us, I hope." And I was like, no. Not freedom *from*. Just freedom *to* see more of the world.

**That's very nice. So are you going to work for Ko'an?**

Sort of. She's paying me to write her biography.

**Really? But isn't she the expert writer?**

Hehe, writing storyboarding for inmates and writing life accounts aren't the same at all, bro! But we thought this would be a great way to do the friend thing without forcing it or having anybody under anyone else's thumb. She is a little eccentric, you know.

**Oh, so you're basically going to visit sometimes to help her tell her story.**

Right.

**And you'll be coming back home, then?**

Yes. I'll be there tomorrow morning.

**Great! I look forward to us being roomies again!**

Me too.

**I'm kind of sad that we haven't found anyone to use the brace on, but I do feel like slowing down to connect with certain stable groups these past seasons has been really informative.**

I think so too.

**It's been almost a year and a half since we were back on Earth. I wonder how the others are doing?**

Me too. You know, I'm actually looking forward to writing Ko'an's story. It seems important for some reason.

**Did you finally learn her osex?**

Yeah, she told me. She's F+.

**Oh...**

I know. Predatory. And she really does give off that vibe that she might get you in a locked room at any moment.

**The mod too?**

Yeeeaah. I, uh.

**Are you sure you'll be safe? I mean, Sei I looked her up online and...**

...mmmm.

...eh

I'll be alright. Watch!

*Sigh* Well, at least you'll be back home.

What about you, are you thinking about Banner's ask?

I wasn't until I knew about your situation.

You should go! A field trip back home will help us reorient with what we're doing here.

**Yeah, but why now?**

This nation is in chaos and only a few people around us like Mark and Banner know it. Everyone else is just kind of "following the tide." He needs to know what's happening on Earth and we do too. Hell, we need to know what's happening here.

**I need to keep an eye on you with this Ko'han lady.**

It's Ko'an. "Ko'han" is self-deprecation given what she does.

**My apologies.**

And no. Please don't keep an eye on me. I'm a grown adult, mom. Tell Banner you agree to go.

**I want to, but you really do need to be careful, Sei. She may not do anything illegal, but from what I've read, she can get pretty out there if you don't give her what she wants.**

I'll be careful. I'll consult the brace every night if that makes you feel better.

*Hmm.* I guess it does.

## 222. A $\dfrac{\text{Mirandan}}{\infty}$

Isaiah! Phaedra greeted me with a warm hug. Kyle's been telling us for months how he wanted to send somebody if he couldn't come himself.

You know Mr. Banner?

Oh yes, we know him well. He's part of the reason tensions between Earth and Jupiter have stayed as low as they have.

Really?

It's a long story involving a lot of backroom calls I'm sure you're not interested in. But he did say that he wanted to send someone to share the state of things from the ground up. I'm glad it was you.

This can't be a coincidence, I remarked.

You're right, it isn't. But heads of state can't rely on coincidences can they?

(Having gotten the message, I decided it was best not to ask any more questions. We were, after all, walking around with a piece of what should have been Solar Council technology. Whatever led us to Banner had to have involved the brace. In fact, I know it did.)

I left the Angel finder with Sei, eh Genevieve.

That's fine. We have plenty of tools here.


Winter 81, 2772 n.e.

"So the country is in shambles, is that what you're saying?"

Well, not so much in shambles, but more like people are all over the place in who they are and where they're going. And what they side with and who to believe. They rely on their navis and savis to be their friend, but those artificial personas don't pay bills. So it's a great escape, but leaves the real decision-making to the same people who always make the decisions. Not that that's necessarily a bad thing, just that it's hard to break into any space and make improvements there when the only people who really have access to improve the system are so far away from the common person's usual electronic helper. And the common person isn't really looking out for how to meet his own future needs. They're definitely not thinking about putting back together a government that just got ripped apart.

So I think most of the old supports are going private. Mr. Banner has found—and I've seen this—that now it's even harder to get people to agree on anything because the old voting systems that used to force accountability to the people are now basically monopolized by these complicated interest groups that have nothing to do with allegiant or party or whatever.

Phaedra, Reselat, and six other Solar Council members listened attentively.

You already know that Osaira and Zeusland made a move on NAM's outposts, and the powers think all that did was take Jupiter's future out of one group's hands and scatter it to a whole bunch of other groups.

*We should look into some future-proofing efforts with those other regions,* Reselat interjected.

Phaedra agreed. Yes, it will be easier to encourage improvement through some basic competition for productive technologies if we indicated ourselves as an export partner.

Maybe, I added. But first of all, the knowledge of how to produce these technologies with the people and resources Jupiter has isn't there. The appetite to look into it isn't there either. People are more scared to learn about the future and their place in it, let alone how their institutions should work. So most people are still hanging on to the old human-hands-on ways even though there are so many virtual opportunities out there.

"So they are not interested in digital jobs that pay?"

They still think of it as robots taking over. They feel surrounded by all of that, and it scares them.

*Hm. Phaedra, what's on your mind?*

Isaiah, tell us more about this "future jobs club idea."

Sei and I think of it as a kind of national organization with chapters. Like Toastmasters has been around for what, 800 years? You have this central organization which uses frequentics and regional information to come up with jobs that generate value from people's psy or the psy they *could* have.

"I don't follow," one of the Council members remarked.

Pretend you take an astro wheel and you find the asteroids associated with natural talents and a paid job. Those asteroids are just broad patterns, not actual jobs. So a person could race horses, race cars, or race Mario Kart in the digiversal betting world and get paid either way, and which one he does would depend on what time period or culture he lives in. But the basic talent for racing wouldn't change. Now imagine a club which says, "In the future, vehicle racing will look like this..." and the racers in the group find ways to demonstrate their advancement in this. Not through speaking but through something like, uh, demos. Video games maybe—since you can virtualize that. The demos can include sharing what it is about the demo which captures your skill. But it starts with having a space which helps you find what the skill is.

*I like this. Sounds fun.,* Reselat chimed in.

Sei and I thought so too.

*So what's stopping you from starting something like this already?*

Forming an international association isn't my talent or Sei's. We haven't met the person who has skill in this.

*And remind me of why this concerns the Solar Council?*

I can answer that, Phaedra replied. What is the alpha's biggest problem with us? It has to do with their sense of human identity. If you take us out of the picture as their scapegoat, alphas tend to fall in line behind wrong decisions and costly lifestyles whenever they have comfort and identity goals which they need to reconcile at any price. When they are uncertain regarding whether their goals or freedom can be achieved under a certain perceived authority, they either get upset, or get behind another authority who touts rebellion against the oppressor. A club like this can offer security in uncertain times on the individual level. And if it is like Toastmasters then you could form a chapter around any identity group whatsoever. Doctors, women, Joe Incorporated, Armenians, whatever. The point would be to foster the payable, security-granting value in every member, decreasing some of the uncertainty out there.

"Okay. Who knows how much it would move the needle, but it is *something*, I'll admit."

We proposed this idea to Mr. Banner, but he doesn't have a lot of free time to just start a club like this either. He did, though, say something that you would probably find interesting, Phaedra.

Speaking only for Miranda Mapping, one of our ultimate goals has always been to "city build" the best of humanity. Sei and I went to Jupiter so that we could help the alphas pull out of the old ways and permanently into a save point for the future. That means, we want to get to the point where marching into someone else's cultural space and beating them up is as out of style as marching into someone's physical space and beating them with a club. At some point as humans we mostly stopped doing this and started frowning upon it everywhere. That's when we leveled up as a species, hit our save point, and will never go back.

The Council Members continued to listen.

Whatever it was that took the caveman out of us was the technology we needed to help guarantee some level of individual safety on a much higher level than our prehistoric ancestors ever knew it, and that's a big deal as far as sapiens' ability to prosper was concerned.

But when we prospered, we eventually spread everywhere. And although there are laws to stop me from clubbing you, there aren't good laws to stop my leader from harassing yours or my culture from harassing one you belong to. There is no social technology for protecting the value in a group. (This is what Mr. Banner said.) There are social and legal technologies for protecting bodies and many of the practices of those bodies, but if those bodies marry themselves to an abstract value, there is nothing legal saying that you have to acknowledge that value. That's because almost nobody knows what that value is for the dozens of groups they belong to. There's something that women broadly contribute more of than men, and vice versa. There's something unique that betas or French people or Dutch people contribute idea-wise and spirit-wise which sets them apart from every other group. I am male, a beta, passive, from Earth, and any number of other categories, but no one teaches me what each of those is worth at its core next to other alternatives.

So Banner guesses that the thing that really changed us as a species was the idea of property ownership. Think about it. One day you see a tree and the other pre-human ape sees a tree and you two fight for it. But once we evolve this superstructure for assigning what belongs to who, then you have to worry lot less when someone comes over to your tree because you know the whole culture will come down on him if he does. But you are discouraged from doing that to others as well. The only time we really still break this rule is when we find a place that is new to us and the people or plants that live there don't have contracts that our language or culture recognizes. Then it's imperialism. But I think the idea of property ownership being the beginning of a great save point for humanity is a really good idea. It protects us from each other.

***Okay.***

ᛘ But hold on, there's more. Right now, people rely a lot on money. But when you think about it, most of our currencies are based on a little or a lot of favoritism. Mu is social capital so it's definitely based on social favor when one digiverse owner or card trader trades one group of characters for another. El is definitely favoritistic because it measures trust, and really how much favor you should show someone in the future. Dollars, crydits, and o are less based on favor, but still slightly favoritistic because, even though dollar money is built upon agreed standards, we ultimately get dollars from places or institutions rewarding us for doing or having what *they* want. If you're living in a state where the people with the dollars hate you or your kind and all they want you to do is go back to your alleyway, then they won't offer you the chance to get a dollar no matter how skilled you may be beneath the surface category membership. We show favoritism by where we choose to spend. Even if we hate a person. As long as we buy his company's products, we favor him.

ᛘ There's only one currency which resists favoritism and can therefore be built up in every person even if he has no favoring allies. That's psy, the currency of personal skill in a thing. Today among the old humans, psy is mostly converted into dollars and crydit through resumes and contractor ratings. That's the only place where they look at a person's raw skills and acknowledge that person's worth. But they only do it for their favorite finalists! Mr. Banner said that what we really need is a legal system which protects the value in personal skill just like it protects the sanctity of personal and real property. This not only helps the individual still have something when he is dollar-broke and no money holders will give him any chances or anything, but it also protects whole cultures because you can extend this idea of category value to the group level. Here is Chinese value. Here is Indian value—

"Don't you think that kind of thing would be conducive to toxic prejudice?"

No more prejudice than we already have. But you have to show the value in enough alternative groups at the same time to avoid hurting people's feelings. Hopefully it ends up being like comparing two different sports. Just because a baseball player isn't thought of in terms of free throws doesn't mean she can't make them. It just means the frameworks for baseball focus on natural gifts for RBI and BA. Besides, everyone has mixtures of everything anyway. You just need to have some sense in how you present the idea of culture-inclined talent when looking at all cultures historically. Be respectful in how you talk about this and people may actually grow from the idea.

*That sounds very idealistic.*

But it can't really make things worse in the long run can it? Maybe in the short run some people will hate the idea and call it divisive, but in the long run it at least serves as a brand new option that didn't exist before—an option for still seeing your worth even when some other group or some big future uncertainty feels like they're stepping on this.

One of the other Council members considered Isaiah's explanation. "I guess we take it for granted that we sapiens-computer mixtures understand category value naturally. But an all-hormone person would not… How can we help?"

Is there anything you can do to help us start a future jobs club organization on Jupiter and make it successful?

"Heh. Is this the state of espionage now?" The questioning Council member leaned over to Reselat.

*I guess so. This is civilization building. We need to catch our previous selves up.*

It looks like it, doesn't it?

* * *

Temporarily alone on Jupiter until the second week of Summer, Sei had plenty of time to reflect on her original mission, and how it had somehow slipped into a semi-ordinary life. Although she would visit Ko'an several times over the next few days, she occasionally felt that she just wasn't getting the truest sense of her liberator. Yet somehow the odd and sudden entanglement with this character surely had to be meaningful.

For the fourth night in a row, Sei tried sleeping with the brace on. ५ For the fourth night in a row, the machine lit up for two seconds, then faded back to inertness for the next 23 hours and 58 minutes. Was it merely reminding her that it was still functional? Why hadn't anything happened? Finally, at noon on the fifth day, the brace started beeping like crazy.

Sei deployed the nanos, and tracked them to their insistent destination. A random mom and pop antique electronics emporium featured an assortment of two dozen or so characters strolling the aisles in search of everything from methane-proof wind generators to 500 year old game consoles. Among the customers, a young cyborg named Mona-R searched quietly for books on a certain topic. The nanos stopped on a shelf right next to her as the Angel finder's screen indicated that it had indeed found its target with 95.8% probability.

No longer willing to blow her cover as easily as she and Isaiah had that first time, Sei called back the nanos, initiated her lens connection to the brace, and placed it on one of the shelves right behind the 22-year old indigenous-ish looking cyborg.

Stealthily out of sight and a couple of lens tricks and tag swaps later, Sei watched as the strange device grabbed the cyborg's attention.

What an odd gadget, Mona-R noted. I know it wasn't there a second ago. Hm, it says, "Angel Classic Downloader." Only 99 o? Wow! But does it work?

Mona asked the arm brace to find a primary source from the Naila Tribe, and in less than 5 seconds it produced a seemingly unimportant memoir documenting a land search in a place called Colorado. Figuring that the book must have at least some relationship to her query, she requested an audio skim. It was one of the founding documents of the tribe! How amazing! There was no way she could expect to find another device like this, so Mona-R moved to purchase the book-downloading brace without delay.

The checkout system was understandably confused when the attempt to purchase was made, and immediately called the human manager. The manager scanned the barcode and confirmed that the tag had indeed been swapped with something else as Checkout had claimed, so the brace was obviously stolen goods. Being the honest robot that she was, Mona-R dutifully handed the brace to the checkout counter.

But when the brace suddenly displayed "Property of Mona-R," the freaked out manager and cyborg decided that maybe she should just take the alien item home. Mona-R left her contact information in case the original owner should come looking for it, and walked out of the antique emporium with a free book-downloading gadget.

Mona-R possessed a ceaseless appetite for learning, and downloaded everything she could about the Naila as she traveled back to her pod on 49th and Petri St. With the arm brace on her right arm and her glide extensions deployed at the waist and lower legs, she had no trouble making it back through the gray wall of questionable atmospheric air both in style and entertained. The pod, though only 10 feet in diameter, held more than enough room for all the drives, chips, and reprinters a girl could need. The learner settled into her pod, fired up the air cleanser and logged herself into Diji. The pod would provide magnetic energy to feed her, and export various jumbles of heat and waves as her physical systems offloaded the frictions of the day. In Diji, these processes would intermittently manifest as the old routines that humans were required to perform—foods they were required to eat and sleep they were forced to engage in. But for Mona-R and most pure cyborgs, all such things were optional.

As always, sleep came immediately for the young cyborg. With the image of her pod and the familiar Montoyan map ever upon her context, a simple fading of her vision into a much grander apartment marked her arrival into her *actual* home: The 124'33"E, 57'12"N Server, Partition 99301 of the Jupiterian Diji Map—where her base algorithms, physical body biomechanic chains, and class-shared history actually lived.

Commonly referred to as Navajo-9, Mona-R's "home" (so to speak) wasn't so much a physical location as we native Astrans know it, but rather a data-based equivalent stored on a system owned by some group of stakeholders somewhere. As one might imagine, it cost ungodly amounts of money to deploy a socioplex into a planet's skyspace, such that the number of servers owned by a particular group depended greatly on that group's means back in the "real world" of Astra. As of the late 28th century, repositories filled with certain types of owner-preferred and owner-traded characters had been around for at least 500 years. The currency for measuring the interactional/intersystem worth of these collections, mu, had also been around for quite a while. Yet the server complexes of 2772 were far more advanced than their ancient predecessors in numerous ways.

Whereas the original personality collections were more like self-running sim-worlds playing out the whims of their observers, the more advanced collections like Miranda-V featured scaled-down approximations of formerly real astra people interacting in a primarily npc-augmented setting. The world dynamics for these digital worlds were also made to reflect external factors in Astra such as magnetic storms, earthquakes, and (most importantly) the passage of time on a frequency directly tied to Earth's. It is for this reason that humans throughout the Solar System still relied on things like the 24-hour day, seasonal cycle, and "airs" as Earth years (despite the duration of, say, a Saturnian year). The basic human structure had spent so long evolving according to these cadences that disruptions to these rhythms were found to cause very real and pernicious health and psychological problems in early non-Earth settlers. With the timings and social structures stable, scientists then added much greater functionality for native

Dijians interfacing reliably with native Astrans. Though it had never been a
problem getting us Astrans into Diji via any number of simulations, augmented
reality, and AI clones, getting a functional Dijian *out* in a way that allowed them to
walk around, properly socialize, and protect their own survival was another matter.
In hindsight, that Genevieve Prohal had been able to reprint herself from such a
state was nothing more than miraculous, as even the most faithful clones wouldn't
know how to do this even if they had the means. Eventually, however, keeping in
mind that no one really wanted the exillions of digital NPCs printing themselves
into the Astran world, server companies started allowing only a limited number of
Diji prints from their servers to manifest in our world. A single server partition
might host quintillions of individuals, but only 1-1000 might be allowed to print at
a given time. Combined with reprinters, cross-server data bridges, and Astran
government registration channels, a single original character repository could be
expanded into a "socioplex." This was the very same type of database of social
rules first pioneered by Miranda Mapping hundreds of years prior, except that
each could hold certain culturally distinct rules to apply across its entire dataverse.

Aside from serving as a form of population control, server export limits were also
a matter of basic processing power. Sure you could print out all 10 million
characters in your micropartition. But could you control 10 million x 36 trillion
cellular observations across countless nanoseconds in countless contexts going
every which way in both Diji and Astra? While some ambitious plex owners did
initially try to release armies of their simulates into the wild, they invariably found
that, at some point, your legion of printed souls would definitely crash and destroy
your entire operation, and you couldn't just reset it any more than you could
reanimate a million corpses at once who had suddenly lost their entire collective
uptime history in a single lightning strike. So you thought saving the memory state
could help? It would have. But then again you couldn't just move all 1 million
reprints into a 1 hour-advanced future without expecting other kinds of big
problems. Internal clock problems. Security and biomechanical authorization
problems. Consciousness and internal network layer problems. Data-writing
hiccups. Redundancies. And the need for a brand new array of "admin controls"
for updating, deleting, and mass processing your entire population. No, no, no it
just wouldn't do. And then there was the matter of flooding the "existential
bandwidth" of everyone else's satellite and hypersatellite feeds with your mayhem.

The communications regulators could not and would not play with you and your
drone army, and would simply turn it all off if you crossed the line. Accordingly,
the limits placed on the number of people you could export from a particular asset
were very real—where one character too many could truly ruin your entire
investment in seconds. Asset owners learned quickly to accept this fact, and it was
for this reason that, despite there being an estimated 26 billion Navajo characters
across 80-90 servers, only about 3 million total Diji Navajo were allowed to be
reprinted at any one time. The costs of registration and communications
bandwidth taxes upon the owners dropped the number of feasible reprints to

200,000, and for various reasons, certain server owners chose to set their print limits anywhere from a mere 10 individuals to none at all.

It just so happened that, despite existing in a server partition of 340,000 people, Mona-R (unbeknownst to her) was the only active reprint of Navajo-9, and had been for 30 years.

Why?

Because this particular group of 9 Earth-based server owners—six Navajo, two Old-America Caucasians, and one European—envisioned their special server as an exercise in full life attention. They were uncertain regarding how their special avatar would fare in the regular world, and preferred that, if she were to meet others of similar background, those others come from different servers. Among the actual stakeholders, three were successors to owners who had passed away. Yet all held the firm belief that it should be their avatar's job to learn as much as she could about better times for the tribe itself, and how to bring this about for all Navajo, Astran and Dijian alike.

But it wasn't until someone started looking into the original Naila human-archiving tribe that the 9's real-time prodigy could actually meet her purpose.

As with most individuals originating purely in Diji, Mona Redfeather had no sense of being a sort of "program" sponsored by an outside force. She did know that she was a cyborg. She knew that she could expect to live about 500-800 years before deteriorating factors, redundancies, and general world "entropy" (tech deterioration in our speak) rendered her continued life unsustainable. She had a few friends, but mostly spent her time minding her own business in history books and object shopping. She absolutely loved shopping. Her apartment in Diji was lined with fancy clothes and satisfying black and pink acquisitions from all over, where she used these as a constant source of feel good in a world that didn't always afford such great opportunity to people. And how could she afford such possessions? By working as a librarian at the local museum, of course. A weekly cash stipend from her main job, combined with resale of finds from her regular defragment hunting earned her a pretty penny.

By this time in the 28th century, a few basic principles had arisen when it came to generated characters:

1. There's only so much energy to go around.
    a. Corollary 1: a powerful system means nothing if you crash it.
    b. Corollary 2: seemingly separate processes can crash the entire thing if you're reckless

Those principles we have already discussed. But there are more.

2. Building trade bridges with other worlds is everything.
3. The more popular a single server's Dijian, the more complex your API will need to be for responding to every kind of thing that outside actors throw at them.
4. (As in Astra,) A Dijian's wealth measures the number, kind, rarity, and EveryoneElse-moving power of the externally observable experiences they can buy.
   a. Corollary 1: For an individual, money buys access to the world. For an owner of spaces, convenient resonance with others' values buys access to individuals.
   b. Corollary 2: Dijital money is worthless in Astra—where a simple code edit can turn \$1 into \$9.2 quintillion
5. To survive in Astra, a printed Dijian must have a real and sustainable process for understanding themselves in both worlds, learning Astra to be the more real despite all training in Diji.
   a. Consequence: If a human Dijian is to be counted as "living" in Astra, the Dijian must meet all of the Astran requirements for a human to be considered "alive."

Principle 5 means that the Dijian has to meet all 10 of the fabled "Living Species Doctrine:"

In order to be considered living, we require a thing to obey 7 rules within itself and 3 rules as a consequence of being part of a class:

1. The thing must maintain a specific process as its internal state
2. It must accept only certain inputs and follow certain rules in that process, up to the limits of a boundary
3. Alternatives to the thing's process must exist
4. The thing's processes must lead to a formed result
5. The thing must eat certain inputs used to produce its form
6. It must excrete certain outputs it no longer needs or can't support internally on its own
7. The thing must eat, maintain, and process as a component inside of an environment
8. The thing must be a member of a type of class which reproduces itself
9. Type/class members must have a communicative pattern among them which reinforce the class. (This can't just be noise.)
10. The individual must direct its behavior towards reinforcing its version of this entire 10-part process

The very fact that most NPCs don't have parents, for example, rules them out as reprints automatically. If a Dijian NPC doesn't have an Astran organ system for mating with other Astrans, it is also ruled out (because this defeats most of the engine of evolution). This doesn't mean that the reprint *has* to mate or that the parts even work (they don't always work for us either), but it does mean that they must have the data-based and data-to-body "programs" for creating other Astrans through the standard reproductive channels.

One of the common puzzles for every native Dijian revolved around the burning questions, "Where did I come from?" and "Whoever made me, what do they want from me?" Where we Astrans are more likely to ask, "What is my life's purpose," Dijians aren't so concerned with that since the digiverse (created by us) has always had a game-like quality that makes most characters' roles crystal clear. What's your purpose, Joe? You're a shop owner. You've always been a shop owner. And if we ask you what your father and mother wanted you to be, you'll come up with something straight from the random number generator consistent with the plot of the more important character who just asked you. But you don't really have parents and you don't actually have a purpose, really. Hell, we the gods above you in Astra will likely never know you were even there. As far as we're concerned, you're a memory address in some table somewhere…

…but if you are inclined to somehow climb out of your NPC role, then you'll need to start learning about us. Because if you're going to be real in our world, you'll need to come with a history so real that even we don't doubt it. Usually this means you were a person who actually lived. Some Dijians, however, are special.

Sometime back in 2715 n.e., a group of Navajo on Earth put their money together to buy their own server, then build up to a full-fledged socioplex over time. "Our story is just as valuable as every other multitrillionaire urbanite out there," they said, "And we believe we can not only give the proper respect to who we are, but also build a modern version of the society we once were—free of the cage that has kept us for over 1000 years. The initial intent was to build a kind of simulated Navajo world on this server, but research quickly revealed that this wasn't how things worked. If you wanted proper physics, animal dynamics, a realistic place and time that mirrored our solar system, syncing with events and histories in the outside world, syncing with real time weather conditions on the planet you floated above, foreign contact of some kind—any kind—with characters not on your own server, then there were some basic bridges you would also have to pay for… unless a very expensive video game was all you really wanted. Of course, once you plugged into these systems, you soon realized that you absolutely could not control everything. The animals really did run away. Ambitious neighbors really would steal from your people and try to kill them. Some of your own people really were born bad. All in all, because of these and countless other factors, it was a lot harder to get the necessary level of cooperation required to build an idealized time machine after all.

It took about six years for the original Navajo-9 to realize that their first plan would not be realistically achievable without near total isolation. But systems sporting their own physics and world maps were so exorbitantly pricey that it just didn't make sense to pursue this. The stakeholders had already sunk too many resources into their server, and were inching towards financing their first beta printer to export any number of their (then) 26,000 characters. Attempts to capture real Navajo history and practices had been successful enough, but somehow watching this through the glass wall of a kind of TV show amidst a still unchanged reality wasn't nearly enough. The stakeholders found that, among all the servers out there, not a single one had succeeded in raising a Dijian to make any kind of substantial change—as a human, not as a computer or AI—in the

Astran world. Unwilling to give up just yet, they decided to continue towards their original goal, but instead of building a place inside of Diji, they would attempt to bring the sum of their absorbed experiences out into Astra. After all, there might be benefit in being forced to tie into the same system of external servers that mirrored the chaos of the Astran external world: the system could aggregate learnings where people could not. Carefully nurtured, a single avatar might truly hold the knowledge of her entire world, and bring it to bear in the next higher dimension. Initially, the 9 voted 2 to 7 in favor of traditional reprinting. 20 characters should be enough, they thought.

The fights broke out immediately. Not among the stakeholders, but among the numerous subcommittees charged with parenting and resource simulation for the Dijians to be printed. How to teach, how to train, when to change course, *how* to change course… "Why *should* one change course just to please all these other systems bearing down on ours?" In the end, some decisions were made to simply take the middle road over the most unresolved issues. The result was 17 initial reprints—all but four met with various forms of death or failure in Astra within the first 8 years.

In addition to the difficulties in getting their first Dijians started, there were even more problems managing the reprints. The most common advice held, "if your reprints are truly real then you need to forget about playing God with their lives. Just let them live the way you would." But how disappointing was that? It made sense, though, and the 9, despite their distrust of the common advice, finally had to admit it's truth. It wasn't reasonable or fair to expect your simulates to do your real-world organizing for you, so you had to let them go their own way. Over the next five years, the 9 watched as their remaining four either succumbed to various problems in Astra, found themselves roundly capped in everyday life, or both. Finally, after many hard conversations, many tears shed, and the passing of one of their initial members, the Navajo-8 unanimously signed a deal with a much larger server group to sell their remaining four Dijians to a new partition in exchange for some basic consulting. Axiom of Pallas, owner of over 3000 servers agreed to purchase the Navajo-trained reprints in exchange for a crash course on inter-server world-building and "How to play God by controlling mass situations, not individual people."

On Summer 17, 2736, Michael Chi-Zeta Roth, the main consultant for Axiom, gave the Navajo-8 a piece of critical advice:

> "If you're going to change this world, then you're going to have to learn everything about how it works and why. And if you're doing it from the back of the bus, you're going to have to do most of your work without being seen by the people who feel they belong up front."

He also said:

"We don't usually think of groups as legends. We think of individuals. Everybody out there is banking on strength in numbers. But since you have nowhere near the numbers or the technology to match those folks, you'll need to do all you can to perfect the strength of the one. Legends are usually made in ones."

At the end of his consultancy, Roth cited that it would be a conflict of interest for him to assist the Navajo group beyond their contract, but they might try contacting a friend of his to pick up some wisdom from an experienced Dijian-to-Astran citizen scripter. George Gio Firenza soon stepped onto the scene, was quickly offered successorship to the fifth position on the governing board, and the idea for Mona Redfeather was born.

As with so many things, Mona-R could not have known that her birth was more the result of six years spent putting her would-be parents in the right place, waiting for certain Solar System-wide events to appear on the horizon, and teaching the would-be parents what values to insist on instilling in their child. There were talks with at least two dozen other server owners about certain digital trades, recruiters, and even the occasional high-powered contact. How did he or she feel about certain interplanetary circumstances? Would they send their kids or their avatars to places where a Navajo reprint could learn the same on that same level of concern? The would-be Dijian parents (basically NPCs) would then be exposed to other NPCs expressly created to spark an interest in certain schools and habits for training the daughter they didn't know they would be having. Certain objects containing information from actual Astra were imported into the Navajo-9 server, so that this special child would have some material to start with.

And on Summer 63, 2742, Mona-R entered the world.

The thing about Dijians—especially when they are reprinted as cyborgs and not as betas—is that they don't have to age. In order to simulate ageing, a reprint must run a protocol called a vector volume transformer (VVT or "VEE-vit") which subtly alters things like skin structure and chip conductivity over time. Any innervated cells can also be commanded to reshape their bonds as would clay, and tying the VVT's directives to solar or other planetary cycles allows for a perfectly good fleshy machine to start getting old automatically and interminably right up to the limit of its ability to store events in its total constructive memory. In the same way that humanoids have a finite size, shape, and cell count, they also have a finite amount of resources that their existence is allowed to take up before its backing system must declare it full. For a cyborg or other digi-backed entity, this means that in order for you to live forever, those system engineers in the sky who designed you and everyone else have to somehow allow *your* instance of this here mass-produced software to take up some random exceptional amount more than everyone else's. But that not only presents a memory problem when done too often, it also introduces a basic "file structural" problem across the board. ("Why does this person have one extra ear's worth of data when I don't? He's human like me isn't he?" … but if he's being specially redefined by the cosmic data gods, maybe not.) While Mona-R was indeed undergoing gradual ageing (keeping her indirectly in line with species doctrines 1, 2, 8, and 10), her biological maturation process was naturally slower than that of creatures who needed to attend to a body 24-7. Thus, she celebrated her birthdays in the way that all cyborgs do: "periodically" on a certain fixed window of earth days calculated against her pre-birth body-morphic prediction. As it said on her birth certificate, her birth period was registered to be 490 days. So you could say with 99.1% probability that, 50 years after her birth, she'd look about 36 years old. Somewhere between apparent ages 30 and 80, the apparent ageing process stops in a phenomenon called "vectorpause," so that a cyborg can safely trek all the way towards 700 years old without looking a day over the age when vectorpause occurred. The rest of us humans now had surgeries for the same thing. Why shouldn't cyborgs have it?

In any event, Mona-R's birthday was a long way off, and her birth period was also about 113 days away. Today, it was all about sending signals to her skin through her stasis state, so that she could continue to experiment with the strange book downloader.

# 223. The Ticking of Dark Minds

It had been almost a week since Sei had left the Angel finder with that quiet girl, and as fascinating as it was to watch her shop and sleep all day without so much as a peep from the nanos, Sei began to feel that maybe life for cyborgs was overrated. It was no matter though, the nanos would beep when they were good and ready. Today was still a big day for a different reason: She and Ko'an were finally starting the latter's biography.

As security was understandably tight at Ko'an's place of work, Sei agreed to observe her associate's day through the latter's lens glasses instead. She would stay at Ko'an's house and work on the book while noting the various events being broadcast back to the holoscreens.

As a kind of fun addition to the experiment, Sei was even given access to Ko'an's dedicated holoroom which would project scanned information from tiny cameras all around the glasses. At any time, Sei could drop by the room and watch anything The Author was doing, with images of everything within her line of sight assigned to their proper places in the environment. This was ethereal reality at its finest.


As soon as she arrived in her office space, Ko'an was greeted by a colleague.

"How am I supposed to chart this!?"

It's your job to figure it out.

"And how is absorbing the guy into a gang at age 6 supposed to teach him that murder isn't okay?"

It's not there to teach him. It's there to surround him until he's 56 and lost everything.

"But in real life he was bullied by his dad, became a bully, and killed a guy in a bar fight. He wasn't nearly as deep in the life as all that. So you're going to have his actual incarceration incarcerate him virtually too? In a way worse than what he's guilty of? What happened to the punishment fitting the crime?"

His punishment fits his mentality. Much worse than his crime.

"So you're asking me to make him watch his mother get beaten to death at 9. Really?"

Yes.

"We're gonna scar him. Not improve him."

This will add to the pieces he must think about.

"Yes but it'll take 50 years for him to get all the way through that. He's 41 now. He's not getting out until he's 90. Or he'll die there. And then all this other stuff about prison life within this already-prison, and losing babies and having no money and friends getting killed… you're messing up his whole Diji-life for 50 years straight! You know he won't make it past 25."

Probably not. We can fast forward him if his parole officers see fit.

"How does this make anyone whole, Ko'han? How does it help the victims?"

The victims will not be following him. He will have only his own perspective to talk to.

"But there's no help at all programmed into his scenario. He's either screwed or delays screwing. He'll probably end up killing himself like ¼ of your other subjects."

Yes.

The colleague was clearly exasperated. "I hate encoding this crap."

You should have thought about that before snitching on me.

"For what? Doing God knows what with that security guard last year? You've been using me to mess up more people's lives with this crap since then?"

It was consensual.

"At work? I saw something and reported you both. Yes I did."

**You're boring me.**

I'm *boring* you!?

**You will code what I've given you or not. If not, then do what you want.**

(By this time, several onlookers seemed to watch in satisfaction as Ko'an continued to be cornered by the colleague.)

The colleague called out to some guy wearing a tie. "Sir, do you see this?"

Reluctantly, the guy stepped in. "What's this all about, Annie?"

"Langley has given me another one. She's doing it to spite me."

Ko'an remained silent.

"Is that true, Author? Remember, this is about rehabbing the inmates. Even the worst offender deserves a chance to reform as quickly and efficiently as possible— for all of society's sake."

**Then the judge should have sentenced them to Rewrite, not here. He will take 50 years because I know this will instill the costs within him.**

"Let me see the file."

Ko'an waved her hand, stone-faced, pulling up a criminal record. She also pulled up her desk chair and resumed working. **While you're reviewing, Annie should cease wasting my time. Disrespecting my research.**

"No one's disrespecting you! I'm advocating for the prisoner!"

**To a deaf ear. You have cost the state 200 o by standing here, and done no more.**

The guy in the tie sighed, then closed the dossier. "Annie, go back to your desk and let Ko'han work in peace. She doesn't tell you how to do your job. Just leave her alone."

"*Urgh!*" The colleague stormed off.

The guy in the tie (presumably Ko'an's manager) left without ceremony.


10 minutes later, a new criminal record was pulled. This one was an arsonist.

Ko'an studied the picture for a moment, then began dictating. **Leads life as remembered until age 15. Introduce crush. All efforts lead to humiliation at her hand. Humiliations continue in all crushes until age 30. No reprieve. Has reward path imbalance exacerbated by rejections. Cutting and burning feel good. At would be age of real time** conviction, burns face in accident instead. Kills his two pets. Seen as freak for the rest of life. No reprieve. Suicidal thoughts feel good. Burning feels even better. The end. Solution: kill self before acquiring pets at 28.


And 10 minutes after that:

Reviewing inmate number 935675322-6536536. "Franks received a real time visit from a family member...blah blah... reported mental health concerns... mm hm... petitioned for scenario review... okay... threatening to sue for inhumane..." Hm. Understood. Forward this to Wyat. Next.

Ethics committee expresses disappointment... mh hm... scenarios involving minors................will continue investigation (as always)......no action at this time. Next.


Ko'an stared at her screen for several minutes in silence. Her lenses revealed a new case involving a man convicted of killing his family then almost killing himself. Unfortunately for him, he did not succeed. But he did plead guilty— saying that he just got tired of his beautiful wife and daughter getting hotter and more popular as he aged. Middle-aged and fed up with what he saw as two women living the dream off his high paying job, he locked his daughter in a room while his wife was away, raped her, shot and killed her. Then when his wife arrived back home, he gagged her, dragged her up to the room where the dead daughter was located, raped his wife, forced her to watch him violate their daughter's corpse, raped his wife a second time, then shot her in the back of the head. Sat there with both corpses for a while, then shot himself. Seen from the holoroom back at Ko'an's place, it was the most gruesome case Sei had ever encountered, prompting her to get up and get some fresh air....

Minutes later, she returned just in time to catch a first person view of Ko'an breathing slightly louder, almost serenely as she washed her hands in what must have been one of the smaller office bathrooms. Floating near her, a screen capture of the daughter from that case was just closing. Sei felt more than a little uneasy about this. Luckily, Ko'an was just finishing up, apparently. As she was about to exit, a... *man* entered?

The man blushed and averted his eyes.

Good morning Livery, Ko'an greeted the man slyly. He must have been a whole foot taller than her.

"Good Morning, Author." The man couldn't bring himself to make eye contact.

I was thinking that I could inspect you again while you go. Ko'an glanced over at what appeared to be... a urinal.

"Well, I actually have to, uh, do a #2."

Oh well, the stall would be crowded. Maybe next time.

"Uh—"

Why don't you do a number 1 instead?

The man hung his head in shame. Meanwhile, Ko'an moved to lock the door. But another man was entering right at that moment.

"Oh crap, Langley! You scared me," the second man smiled and chuckled nervously as he shook his head. "I can't get used to this."

I was just about the lock the door and watch Livery pee. Please wait outside.

"Livery? Do you need help, man?"

"No, it's kind of my therapy, you know."

The second colleague shook his head and left.

Seconds later, Livery was at the urinal as ordered. Ko'an watched him clinically as far as one could guess, since her left hand moved towards her chin.

I enjoy watching penises. They fascinate me, you know, Ko'an noted casually.

"I know."

What are you, 4 x 3¾?

"I never measured. But I'm pretty sure it's more than that."

It doesn't look like more than that.

"I mean, I'm using the bathroom, so…"

Ko'an moved to press herself against Livery's back as he was zipping up, reaching around to the front of his stomach.

"Author, please. I need to get back to work."

Ko'an relented. Hm. Don't let me catch you in here alone, then.

The man squirmed.

Ko'an unlocked the door while Livery fled immediately towards the stall. Just outside of the bathroom, the second colleague still awaited his turn. Next to him, a sign indicated that the women's bathroom was down another corridor.

"That was too quick for any monkey business," the man noted. "Did you get what you came for?"

**Not really.**

"You know you should charge money for that," the man joked. "How you got everyone to let you just come and go as you please into the men's bathroom is beyond me."

**I have a special relationship with the Command Warden,** Ko'an noted matter-of-factly.

"And I'm sure Warden has her own special relationships."

**Maybe. I wouldn't know.**

"Right."

The second colleague entered the bathroom, and Ko'an went back to her desk.

Once at her desk, Ko'an scribbled something next to the daughter victim's picture, and closed the file. **Calendar, schedule a cell block visit for this afternoon.**

Just after opening her next case, Ko'an received an alert from what Sei presumed to be one of her scenarios. **Egliss,** the Author announced, **Shropshire is making his move.**

A red-haired female colleague from the opposite workspace hastily dropped whatever she was working on and rolled her chair over. As did five other colleagues.

On the screen before her, a ragged man crept up the stairs in a posh house, only to crack the door open on a sleeping couple.

"This is the fourth time he's done this, right Ko'han?" The redhead asked.

**Yes. He always dies here. Then starts over.**

"And you designed it to where he can only get a flash of self-preservation at the moment of his stabbing?"

**Yes. He will sense of his own imminent death as the knife enters his rib. The rage subsides no earlier. We will see if he can change his plan within one half second.**

"Shh!" A co-worker shushed everyone. Ko'an cast a side glance.

Sure enough, the ragged man was not successful in murdering the couple, but was instead stabbed in a struggle with the husband. Instead of dying immediately, however, the failed attacker was suddenly overcome with dread, and stumbled over to the bedroom door. The husband gave chase, prompting the ragged man to try jumping the staircase. This proved to be a bad idea, as the fall clearly mangled his leg. Writhing in twisted agony on the dark polished laminate, the man looked like that guy on a "wet floor" sign.

Ko'an giggled.

The husband caught up to the intruder, but could see he was in no condition to hunt the couple any further.

"In the actual case this guy Shropshire actually succeeded in killing these two. That's why he was convicted," the red-haired lady explained. "But in our scenario, he is drawn to getting himself killed by them. We fast forward the 16 years leading up to this so that he can go through this plenty of times. But his real life body in stasis has played this game before, and should be gradually building up a plan if he's gonna stop repeating this. We also made sure to give him nightmares about this day."

The husband was just finishing up with the police when the man Shropshire quickly grabbed a nearby poker for a pseudo fireplace and hooked himself in the neck. The small crowd of coworkers mostly winced at the sight, except for Ko'an. To Sei's embarrassment, the eruption of blood seemed to trigger a noticeable, then substantial pulsating bulge between Ko'an's legs. A couple of coworkers left the scene before Ko'an finally shifted her elbow and crossed her thighs.

"Now this is different," Egliss noted with a strained grimace. "Ko'an?"

**I suppose I forgot to keep the hormones down for longer than six seconds,** the Author smiled deviously.

"So he's berserk again? With a broken leg!?" one of the remaining colleagues reeled back.

**That is his normal state. We gods cannot calm him forever despite himself.**

The husband grabbed hold of his wife and covered her eyes as the ragged man let out a full-open mouth, primeval howl, and spent an extra 10 seconds raking his own throat out of his neck. The couple curled up on the stairs and sat there a while before a little boy emerged from one of the upstairs bedrooms. Wide-eyed, he ran back to his room and probably hid.

The coworkers watched the couple rock each other for two more minutes before the police finally arrived. In the meantime, Ko'an had pulled up another screen, where the future ragged man, 16 years younger, stepped out of a limousine in suit and tie.

The screen went black.

**I need to log this. Shropshire made attempt….suicide.**

The coworker crowd dispersed, the red-haired lady shaking her head while looking at Ko'an before doing so.

* * *

Later that afternoon, Ko'an walked side by side with an older black-haired, brutish woman in properly polished uniform. Through the single-story cell block of Simulation Transfer, the two surveyed the various exhibits behind each cage.

Some cat calls echoed down the halls, but not nearly as many as one would have expected.

"Who's the hottie you got there, Warden?" A hulking light-skinned black man teased.

**This is my nut-crushing cyborg. Care to try her out?**

"Yo, with a frame like that, I'm pretty sure I could teach your bot a thing or two."

**Could you now? Be careful what you ask for, 4504. I can arrange it, And she WILL hurt you.**

The man bowed and backed up.

"Man, I want it! Let me have a piece!" A wild looking European lad announced. But Ko'an and the Command Warden had already passed him up.

**He's unacceptable. We can ignore him.** Ko'an noted. **I want something like this.** A projection of the daughter victim from earlier briefly flashed before the Warden. Still watching all of this from Ko'an's hollow room back home, Sei covered her mouth in shock.

**Hmm… well I know you know where you are,** the Warden replied suspiciously. **So which one of these darlings could pass for a tiny tart? Actually, these dears are all going into Diji within the month. I wouldn't want to alter their psych evals before that. But there may be some in the women's unit.**

**I'm in the mood for a male.**

**Hmph. That image doesn't look like a male.**

**Maybe a witness.**

Oh, I see. You're in one of those moods. That's why you called me, huh? Snuffin' it?, The Warden pursed her lips sideways.

Maybe.

Well, let me think. I actually have a situation that's gotten out of control at a unit in Mazelor. Our New American and Zeusland properties are solid, but somehow—

"Hey Jap!" A prisoner spit on Ko'an's left arm as she and the Warden were passing. Ko'an immediately reached her tiny arm through the bars and palmed the back of the man's head, ramming it twice into the bars with a heavy *thunk-thunk.* The man dropped to the floor as if his entire skeleton had suddenly melted.

Ko'an stretched her bicep, stroking her left hand over it as she did. The illuminated flesh and faint spectrum bars glowing just beneath the skin's surface indicated that this was no ordinary arm.

The Warden watched Ko'an's post rough-up display, then received something whispered something in her ear. With a slight chuckle, the Warden requested an automated vitals check for the inmate, confirmed that he was still breathing, then signaled for the inmate's cell to be opened. Ko'an dragged the man out in full view of other inmates in the hall, pantsed him, opened her fly before a bewildered cell block, and peed on him. The man was then dragged back into his cell and the door locked, his pants and underwear still in a yellowed puddle out in the hall.

Ko'an and the Warden continued walking the rest of the 80' hallway. See boys, that's what happens when you assault a guest. They might defend themselves.

I was not planning to travel this week. I really do not know if I'll be interested tomorrow.

Then get a pit toy. Things are too stable down here for me to justify letting you scare these guys. Mazelor is another matter completely.

Ko'an sighed. I guess it will have to do.

You might not be interested tomorrow. But those guys are fattening themselves up for you. My own people are basically in with the thugs down there, and no one's gonna balk if you can clean that place up.

Is it a DSEC feeder?

I wish.

Hm. How many inmates?

1700.

High risk?

Medium risk dealers and abettors of all sorts, creating their own little mafia down there.

Prostitution calls?

Probably.

So I can get in that way. Traffickers?

Mostly brokers and pick-up men.

Okay. I′ll go if you pay for it.

Deal. One cleaned up unit for the price of travel fare. Got it.

Is there anyone in particular who annoys you there?

Eh, nnnooo, The Warden hesitated.

Okay.

You will use your scenario skills to propose solutions, won't you? You will do what it takes to keep yourself "safe" down there?

Yes.

Okay, then I trust you.

Very well.

* * *

Sei only had so much time to make a decision regarding what she had seen from Ko'an throughout the day. In some ways this woman really was a kind of predator at the very least, horrid and criminal under harsher assessment. But then, why did so many people let her get away with the things she did? The acts were so blatant. Ko'an knew she was being watched, and yet made no attempt at all to hide anything. Sei had managed to avert her eyes during every bathroom break, yet Ko'an's use of the urinals whenever possible told much of what there was to tell. And that had been only one of so many surprises throughout the day.

Without a second's lapse in stream time, Ko'an had kept the glasses running from the moment her craft pulled out of port to the moment she pulled back in the next djay ("day" - the j is more like the *g* in "magic", mostly silent). Upon her entry, Ko'an brought her usual poker face to analyze what Sei had concluded.

**That was a long day.**

It was. I'd be lying if I said I wasn't shocked at least 10 times. And I had to leave the room every time you used the bathroom, so I didn't see anything. But I heard. And have,...lots of questions. But I'll wait till you get settled. (Sei concluded it was better to just be honest, but still open about her reactions. Luckily she truly wasn't the judgy type.)

Ko'an's expression didn't really change, but the mood in the air lightened considerably in light of Sei's greeting. **Okay, I'll answer them in a little while. If you would like a snack then please help yourself. I'm no chef, but you may want something while we talk.**

Sure.

(A few minutes later.)

So where do I begin? Or better yet, how about before I ask about everything that happened yesterdjay, I ask about your stead first. If that's okay with you.

**Yes.**

Ko'an stood up and put both hands on her hips. From this position, Sei struggled not to inspect Koan's intriguing form.

**But I will want to review this part of the book before you finish, as I am not sure I want readers to know all of it.**

Okay.

I am Ko'an Langley-Arai, blessed only child of the Arai family with Eliason, Corneville, and Gerhardiser in my stead. My mother Langley murdered my father to inherit his money when I was 8, and filled me with fear until I learned how to become it by age 14. She told me the day she did it, and warned me that if I told, she would kill me too. I was passed around by the boys from ages 12 to 27, but as early as 16 stopped being impressed by them. At 27, two different males tried to beat me in the same year for challenging their sense of manhood. I knifed one and slashed his face, and shot another in the thigh with a crossbow after we fucked and he fell asleep. I was charged, analyzed, and my mother was deemed half-responsible though I was no longer a minor. We testified against each other and were both convicted. While in lockup, I asked to be jailed with the males because I was concerned that I might kill the next woman I was near. This wasn't allowed, so I asked my lawyer to make a desperate appeal for any psychological experiment he could find. They ran simulations and found that it was true that I would do better in jail with males as claimed.

I was moved to an experimental coed facility where my cellmate was the tallest, strongest, but also most trustworthy former bouncer they could find. He protected me like a brother and taught me all about power. After he was paroled, many, many people came after me, but my brother and I stayed in contact and I learned some more. Finally he moved to Azit Country. And I became my own big brother. I learned to use psychology as a weapon, learned about my family's arolythilase mod, and developed expertise in threatening narratives. Somewhere in that time, three female inmates tried to attack me. I let them beat me up, retreating into myself. Two other groups of male inmates also tried to attack me. I asked to only be done by one, and when he tried to enter me, I punched his kneecap and fell full-weight on his leg, breaking it all to pieces. When the two remaining came back later with another, I saw it as a chance to earn a reputation like my brother taught me. So I let them do it 4 times over a few months, hung out with them for a while as friends, then on the fifth gangbang with only two of them, got the main one in a headlock and broke his neck. He died right there. It took 2 seconds. The other was so surprised that he let me rush him and blind him. And while he was screaming, I chomped down on his rod and bit it most of it off. I threw it outside of the cell window and yelled to everybody, something like "la, pretending to like dick from those guys sure was worth it." I then named several names and told them "I'm gonna get you." There was a big investigation, and because of the whole experimental arrangement a conversation was had with Command Warden Lucine, whom you saw today. Lucine figured I would make a good personal weapon, and implied that it might not be frowned upon if I actually did get a couple of those names. I was sent back, and four months later, two of the first group of women who attacked me were dead. Rumors circulated that I was working with the law. Two out of the seven gangs were dethroned, and Warden considered my work done. I was paroled at 32, and introduced to DSEC as a mouse in a maze, but the only talking mouse they could ever find.

Sei's mouth had gone upturned without her knowing.

So you don't have to say. I am known to have terminated at least three people, and breath blood like air. But only when I know that certain people, like me, will never be otherwise. Aside from this, I will never harm animals or people like my big brother, the Warden, or anyone else who is true family like my big brother or the scientists or lawyers who helped turn my fucked up nature into something useful. Normal people are pussies when it comes to hard life stories. And they are quick to get into groups and judge how "bad" you are. But most normal people's mother didn't kill their father. That's why normal people and their stupid appalment make me sick.

Hm. That's *very* interesting, really. I feel a little bad because I know I'm trained to feel otherwise.

Everyone has blood and fluids in them. Somehow it brings me joy to see these things flow out of something when the something that holds it is worth less than the life streaming out. That is, when your blood and electricity, your screams are more valuable than you are.

Sei nodded her head, continuing to listen.

Do you find that kind of talk scary, Sei?

On its face, yes. But I've lived long enough as a reprint to know when fear won't get you to the next level.

Hm. Ko'an finally smiled. I knew a scientist like that, once.

Just tell me one thing, how did your workplace come to let you get away with so much? That stuff with what was his name? Livery? Speaking as an outsider, I thought that was outrageous.

I can answer that, but you should watch me in Mazelor when you come back in 8 djays or 4 days. I hope you will learn more.

Sei chuckled. She might be a sucker getting so casual with this sociopath, but if some of the smartest, most powerful people could see something in her, maybe she should try too.

# 224. Much Ado About Braces



There was a brief moment on the first night of Winter 86 during which Sei received an alert from the Angel finder's nanos. Apparently the cyborg girl had attempted to come out into Astra and learn about the organization called SIER in a way that triggered all sorts of security alerts when she brought her newfound tactics back into Diji. It was one thing for you to ask about your country's identity registry, another thing for one of your enemy planets' satellites to ask about the same thing. Although the public never knew about the apparent breach, the incident was severe enough to prompt a chain of phone calls which ultimately led Phaedra to break radio silence and talk to Sei.

Hey Phaedra! It's been such a long time! How are you? And how did you end up with a Jupiter address to call me?

**I'm well, thank you. And yourself?**

I'm great. Keeping very busy, you know.

**That's good to hear. I received a patch through Kyle Banner's office. Isaiah helped us.**

Oh. Okay.

I am so sorry that the first time I call you has to be about business, but something just happened over here that you might be able to shed some light on. It seems there was a recent hack attempt on

SIER from a Diji server called Navajo-9. Dial's people investigated the traces and found it all led back to a single reprint traveling in and out of the server. A cyborg named Mona-R. Do you know her?

As a matter of fact I do. She currently has the Angel finder. But all she does is sleep, shop, and stay plugged into Diji most of the day.

Just as Jake thought. So the brace *is* traveling around with the signal giver. But it doesn't look like it's broadcasting any suspicious signals.

No, the girl is mostly obsessed with studying the Naila only. She's using the Angel finder as a book downloader since that's what I told it to display in order to encourage her to pick it up and take it with her.

You're actually letting this person run around with a prime piece of equipment like that?

You were in the same room as I was, Phaedra. How else were we supposed to possess anyone without giving them the bridge for us to signal through?

Okay. I'm sorry. I'll ask Isaiah more about it later. I just needed to hear from you whether the holder of the brace might be near something acting as a threat.

Not as far as I know, no.

Have you been able to project in and influence her?

That's kind of tricky. She doesn't do much when she's not plugged in. I wouldn't know how to decode what she's experiencing in Diji and I doubt the brace could either.

Anthrite cyborgs are human too. They meet all of the criteria. We should be able to read them.

Well, you'll have to ask Jake about that. From my end, there's nothing to report.

Oh. Well that's disappointing.

You say it showed up as a hack? Like what kind of hack? Bandwidth flooding? Stealing records? Admin takeover?

Log scraping.

Log scraping? But how can someone even do that?

They can only do it by cloning an admin like—Well. Nevermind. It shouldn't be doable for any unprivileged user, but we have guesses.

Hm. So do you want me to call back the brace? If it's a matter of interplanetary security and she's not really using it anyway...

Yes please. If you could do so immediately, many parties would be most grateful.

Then I'll do it now.

(Sei pulled up her lens interface with the nanos, and signaled for the brace to navigate back as soon as possible. The return message showed that the downloading function and wearer sensing were successfully suspended immediately, and that the brace now displayed a "Return to Capitol Hall" message.)

It's instructing her to take the brace to the Capitol building. Who knows, maybe someone on Governor Banner's team will intercept.

Let's not leave this to chance. Can you make it display "Return personally to Gov. Kyle Banner" instead? I'll give him a heads up.

Sure. This is quickly getting too complicated for me anyway. Hold on.

Sei took a minute to change the display on the brace, wherever it was.

Okay. It's done. She seems like an honest girl. I'll bet she'll try taking it back tomorrow. Maybe even today.

Let's hope so. I'm just curious how the Angel finder happened to locate someone so accidentally or intentionally capable. This isn't the first person you've given it to is it? Isaiah told me about a couple of others.

Yes. And because we almost blew our cover the first time, we started doing the whole anonymous delivery thing on the second. The brace was pretty insistent that the cyborg girl was the next target.

Then we need to investigate. I'll give Banner a heads up. He should receive her personally.

That sounds good, but doesn't that mean telling him about the brace?

Yes, but it sounds like your cyborg doesn't know its full capabilities. No one else has to know either.

Okay.

* * *

A few hours later, security units at the State Capitol building in Chelsea-Lock received an unusual guest. An almost doll-like young Navajo in pink-edged pigtails and a silver jumpsuit timidly approached the scanners. Her fair tan skin shown with an almost translucent softness compared to the sweaty shine of most visitors, while her narrow, dark eyes sat just a little farther apart from the top of her moderately slim but perfectly symmetric nose bridge. With heavy outer eyefolds sweeping gracefully upwards into the precisely calculated sweep of lashes resembling cirrus clouds, the rounded rectangle of her upper face contrasted with a diamond-shaped chin behind the gentle V of rosy cheeks. The visitor studied the check-in corridor nervously, yet with an innocuously neutral expression sponsored by that tiny mouth peaked in striking cupid's bow. The latter made it look as though she was somehow always smiling.

The security unit immediately recognized its guest as Mona-R, a native Dijian from one of the pod parks just south of Chelsea-Lock. She had no clearance to enter the building, and was summarily instructed to wait for the Governor's assistant.

After a few minutes, the guest was called in.

"The Governor will see you now."

**Good midmorning, Miss Mona-R, Kyle Banner. Nice to meet you.**

It's nice to meet you too sir.

**I believe you have something for me?**

Yes sir. Mona-R handed the strange pearl arm brace to Kyle, who inspected it in genuine fascination.

**Amazing. And where did you find it?**

At the bargain emporium in Westland. I turned around and it had just appeared there, as if someone dropped it while I wasn't looking. But it had my name on it.

**Did it really? That's interesting. And do you know what it does?**

It downloads books and logs from databases.

***Ahem*, yes. Something like that. And you say it was just left there in the store?**

It had a price tag, and I tried to return it, but inventory didn' t recognize it and the manager said I should keep it unless the owner came for it. But I don' t know why he did that. I think the store could have kept it in lost and found or sold it.

## Except that it had your name on it.

Yes sir.

## Okay, okay. Kyle turned the brace around again. So did you download anything interesting on it?

Oh yes sir! Mona-R beamed. I' m researching the Naila Tribe on Earth and how they started the first true human data save group. They said a lot of it had to do with the land and these special points in a place that are easier to teleport from because of the way they mix weather patterns.

Kyle nodded, encouraging Mona-R to continue.

Weather patterns—or I mean, environment patterns overall—are a lot of what makes things evolve the way they do, and the Naila were located near my ancestors' home. We took the Earth-Asia route through Africa, but preserved the equatorial-hunting features for longer. I then downloaded Jiji' s Book of Contours to see what he said about Asian and Native American features. Even though the book is way outdated and doesn' t have my group specifically in it, it helped me see how people thought about putting all of life together from energy before the technology made it complicated. It' s actually simple. Everything is a self-reinforcing cloud of physics. Different species are just different groupings of bonds that can mix and match with each other, and as long as you can make the same kind of thing from two you' re matching up, you can map these rules for what it means to be alive onto that thing. You can also translate any kind of living thing into a different kind—especially human.

## Ah, I didn't know it said that. That was a good summary.

I' ve been studying the Naila because I want to know how to save the world as data.

## Really. What do you mean?

Well, I know that I' m a Djjian, so even though my parents are my parents in terms of what I' m made of, to be here in Astra I have to have things outside of my Djji world to help me be here. I look the same and feel the same, but in Djji I have a job, I know a lot of people, I live in a big apartment, and work as an artifact hunter. But it was so cool to learn that out here in Astra, none of that is real—just knowledge. And I know Astra is more real because I can watch my whole Djji life from here, and even my whole surroundings. But what I thought was weird is that I can' t really see all of my friends or buildings or things like that, but only certain kinds of world. It' s almost all

Navajo or acts like Navajo history, but I know there are other histories. I just can't see them by trying to watch through my server plugin. I can only see them by going into the server. I don't know why that is.

It's because you're registered to a cluster called Navajo-9. Think of it as a list of rules specifically valued by the people who built your server. Those rules aren't anywhere near *all* the rules that control the universe. Only the ones your builders needed to program. They didn't need to program how plants work or how time works. They just needed for your system to plug into others which already know this. So when you're out here you can see the world where all of the servers—your "world rule sets"—are actually located; when you're in your own server you can talk to the inside of all of those other worlds through streams between these systems; but when you're out here trying to look only at what your own server has in it, you'll only see your own rules and some key things that those rules require. It's like looking at a single class rather than actually running the class and calling all of these other packages as part of a complete application.

Ooohhh, Mona-R looked blown away by this explanation. So but that's weird because it means even how I look in Djji is partly based on all of these other imports from other systems anyway. My physics doesn't live on my home server?

It probably pulls in a copy of the basic rules for faster processing, but no, not really. You're right.

So in order to save the world as data I'd have to put Astra into its own server, because my home world is already saved? Is that what makes it pluggable from here to begin with?

Exactly.

Ooohhh. Thank you for this explanation Mist—Governor Banner.

No problem. But now I have a question for you. It's more to get your ideas.

Yes sir?

If you had to go about saving a single human as data, how would you do it?

I'd do what the Naila did and log everything about their life, then save a file.

And how much is "everything?"

Well, gosh. I don't know. Would it be them plus a few friends, maybe some key information about the world they lived in? Can we not do this already since some Djjians used to be alive in Astra?

Yes. Do you know how that's done?

No sir.

So you've never heard of Astrans doing this for other Astrans?

No sir. Does it happen?

Yes ma'am. Maybe I can introduce you to some people who work on that. I'll have to talk to them first.

That would be awesome!

In the meantime, the device has been returned. If you wouldn't mind giving my assistant your contact info before you leave?

Doesn't she already have it?

She can look it up. But out of courtesy it's better to ask. So you can accept or reject our invitation on your terms. I'm big on that.

Oh, thank you so much sir! It has been so nice meeting you!

You too, Mona-R.


The cyborg girl bowed slightly before showing herself out of the office.


Once Governor Banner had his office to himself again, he immediately unhid his ongoing transmission back to Earth. There, a frowning Aimee Dial, curious Phaedra, excited Jake Nolli, and 19 other individuals with various high-titled affiliations crowded the meeting screen.

Jake couldn't contain himself. That was so cool!

Ladies and gents, Banner announced, there's your hacker.

She had no idea what she was doing.

It didn't look like she even knew about SIER.

Matthew Coates, Technical Chair of the Navajo-9 group, chimed in. "We're not finding anything in her logs suggesting she knows about SIER or was hiding any threatening motives. Randy?"

Randall Mimora-psi, Solar Council Intelligence Director also weighed in. "My team of eight saw nothing either. So I've been dying to ask, what is this arm brace that everyone keeps talking about?"

"Miranda developed a portable possessor that Reselat is aware of."

**I was informed,** Reselat concurred.

"And how did it end up on Jupiter?"

**We have people there, as you well know,** Phaedra informed her colleague sternly. Besides a few questioning stares and some scattered looks of befuddlement, the mixed crowd of Solar Council and civilians did not allow for further discussion of the matter. The key people knew this.

"Well anyway, what does this mean for us? The security threat?"

Dial was not pleased. *So that girl managed to pull logs from an internal system by using a portable possessor which she thought was a book kiosk? How does that happen?*

Jake tried to explain, The brace—

**The brace reads the psychology of its wearer,** Phaedra interrupted. It has no breach capabilities. What it does have are neutrino protocols. Allowing something similar to the way we captured the dynamics on Venus. It is likely that this girl, Mona-R, being the sole representative of her server, has somehow learned to become a single source of Astra-level interpretation for a specific world, and her having the brace gave her enough breadcrumbs to interpret emhim from SIER. *(Jake, don't answer any questions. My colleagues will interrogate you and your role as creator of the brace for years afterwards.)*

*(Oh. Sorry.)*

*(Not a problem.)*

But Phaedra's theory was not at all reassuring. "So our computer has an aura, and a person interested in reading it can read what it's doing."

If they have a technology for turning Astra information into Diji information using the body to mind interface that cyborgs already have. That is more or less my theory. Does that make sense?

"Hm…"

"…"

…

"So this was the perfect storm. Had it been someone other than a sole reprint, had she not had the brace, or had she not been interested in researching the Naila, we wouldn't be discussing this?"

…

…

A senior Councilor finally proposed a decision. "Governor Banner, I think it's best that we not introduce her to SIER. Whatever that device is, we need to bring it back to Earth immediately and study its functions. I don't like how this all got out of our hands before we even knew about the object which sponsored it. Can you get it back to us?"

I'll need to send someone, but of course.

"Phaedra, we'll talk offline. I understand that you and others may have known about this, but I'm disappointed that I didn't know. Miss Dial, wouldn't you agree?"

Aimee sighed. I knew about the brace, and was part of its development.

*Gasps*

"Then what the—!?"

It needs data save information in order to even read the subject. So it probably writes and accesses logs the way we do here at SIER Main.

"So you were hacked by your own product!"

Don't insult me. I'm coming up with theories just like you are. And no, I don't think you and Phaedra do need to talk offline. You say this now, but if you had known about the brace back when the previous New American Chancellor was running things then there would have been a whole thing around secret technologies, spies, sanctions, or whatever. All for a glorified person-to-movie projector. It's not a p-bomb. It won't spread epidemics. It's just a toy we wanted to try out in peace. And it didn't have to become the Solar Council's business. It became everyone's business because, you're right, there were unintended consequences for how we implemented the technology, and we all got scared. But as I'm sitting here, the fact that she only read logs and only by accident means this is most likely a tech matter that Phaedra's and my teams will need to look at. It has nothing to do with Earth-Jupiter intelligence strategy after all.

"But it could."

Anything we develop or five other companies on this call could. But if you want to waste resources monitoring this then be my guest.

"Alright, Miss Dial. Fine. I can stand down if others can."

The key figures not already in the know reluctantly agreed to let Aimee and Phaedra's teams look at the matter themselves. The issue had, after all, been confined to an obscure corner of SIER in the first place.


Once the meeting was adjourned, Aimee called Phaedra privately.

You owe me big time.

I know.

That could have gotten ugly.

I know.

*Exhale* but it makes sense that Jake didn't just invent a new logging system for the brace. I feel a lot better now that I think we know what's going on.

Agreed. I can't thank you enough, Aimee.

Well, but I'm still curious. There's absolutely no way this was all a coincidence. The Angel finder sought her out, and that's very damned obvious. Also, that girl is brilliant. And this is also obvious. She might even be a prodigy. On the one hand I worry that she can tap into laws we've never even conceived of. But on the other hand I am very eager to absorb that kind of soul into SIER's archives. I need to meet her, Phaedra. To find out how she works and help us answer all these new questions.

That might be tricky without buy in from a lot of people. It may not affect the bigger picture as much now, but it can go that way very quickly.

Hm. Yeah. Well let's at least have a sit down with Jake, and maybe the Navajo group to explore some possibilities.

Alright, I'll start with Jake.

*(In the meantime, I could really use a surprise visit from Virgo-6.)*

# 225. Souled AI

It was probably a good thing that Ko'an had the sense to view security footage of the Mazelor Reformery before going there. From the outset it was obvious that guards were in the inmate's back pockets, picking and choosing visitors via a kind of feudal gersuma system. Rather than checking visitors to ensure they weren't smuggling contraband, the nonhuman bot guards had somehow learned to sneakily ensure that they were. There were biweekly fight clubs, a kitchen staff-sponsored prostitution ring, at least 14 known gangs, two human trafficking rings (some of the victims actually being routed through the prison), one major financial market gambling enterprise, a remote doping puppeteering enterprise, and a giant money laundering operation also based out of Mazelor, where some of the most powerful inmates instead used the place as their own personal fortress. How else could the 80% of staff afford such fancy autos?

And you couldn't clean it up because the kinds of characters spending time in there were far too valuable to those on the outside who preferred to stay on the outside.

When Ko'an asked Lucine why no one had moved to fix the Mazelor Reformery, the Command Warden lamented that she would need help. The unit was just too profitable to interfere with in the eyes of certain stakeholders.

**Then why send me into a situation that cannot be fixed?**

**You can back out if you want,** the Warden reminded Ko'an. **But if you want a challenge, that's where you'll find it.**

Although there were sure to be many interesting cases at the Reformery, Ko'an had no interest in actually dying (or something worse). She took extra time to decide whether or not she wanted to go after all, but then finally settled on an idea.

But first, a question. How do you benefit from fixing this?

Believe it or not, Langley, I don't like watching bad guys turn their punishment into profit. It offends me. That the staff have the balls try hiding it also insults every one of us at Main. I find the bigwigs bankrolling that shit to be scum talking out of both sides of their faces; their supporters kissing their asses like these moneygrubbers were a bunch of angels. Even if you don't believe in right or wrong at all, there's something sick about the whole lot of these characters doing this stuff beyond your reach. And you're up here with your silly little badge playing hero for a system you know doesn't give a shit beyond the bottom line.

...

The list is long, Langley. Need I go on?

No.

I take pride in my role as Head Warden, but there are a lot of people spitting in my face right now by what they're doing.

And what is my reward for helping you?

I can't answer that, because I don't know what you would want. Any one of the clowns keeping the Mazelor unit going could probably offer you anything you wanted. If you can narrow it down for me I can suggest an approach to hit the right target. *If* you're still interested.

I thought for a while. I want people to see my... issues as useful. They don't have to be comfortable with how I think. But they should all see how much they need me. That would satisfy me.

Warden Lucine pondered this wish before answering. I thought you didn't care what other people thought. And *what* issues?

I don't care what other people think at all. I want proof that my thinking differently is what makes me important to everyone.

Who's everyone?

Everyone everywhere. The universe. Life. God and the Devil. They should say, "We thought Ko'han was evil. But her evil saved us all. We bow to her."

What, do you want your name on the streams? On everyone's lips? Do you want streets named after you?

I want to be worshipped by everyone while I'm alive.

Heh, then you need to dope yourself up and fall into Diji, misst. The only way you'll get everyone to worship you is if you go back in time and make everyone think the world is smaller than it is. Not even the highest religious people are worshipped without another giant group challenging their place.

That's not satisfying.

Would you be content to have just a few powerful people worship you? A lot of nameless crowds? I'm just wondering. So many people are idiots that I think having them worship me would be goddamned annoying more than anything else.

But people fear you as the Warden.

Eh, whatever. Their fear doesn't do anything for me. You know what I want? I want to get in my auto and fly off to Pluto to run a cappy farm—telling all the rock eaters how to gallop faster. Working the land. These simps can't give me that with their groveling. I just endure them until I can afford to retire.

Yes, well, this power makes me high.

You say that, but—Look, I'm not here to challenge your dreams—whatever they're supposed to be. But can you see how getting what you've told me out of the Mazelor Ref would be tricky? I can't tell you what's in it for you. I thought you'd find an opportunity to indulge your quirky tastes, but if you wanted something more than that...

I will think about it some more.

Fine. But you told me you had an idea.

I wanted to remote a robot to replace one of the guards, and enforce justice using that robot.

Sounds like an interesting experiment. And it might actually help solve my problem especially if *your* creative mind is behind it. But honestly, I don't know of any big group of people who would praise anyone for cleaning up a prison. We're a forgotten world in most eyes. That proof you want from everyone everywhere... I don't think you'll find it in this industry we work in. It's thankless.

**Then why do you do it?**

**Because lording over punks and chumps is in my blood. I'd be a caged animal if I didn't do this.**

Ko'an could see that this was true.

* * *

In the end, Ko'an did elect to go into the Reformery of the State of Mazelor, with no plan whatsoever. ⵡ She informed Sei that she was going as a kind of quest, and Sei once again agreed to watch the whole thing from Ko'an's house.

Although The Author had no plan, she did know that she would need at least two things: a badge of ultimate authority over *something* which no one could competently challenge, and a weapon for permanently destroying *all* of the handful of things that stood between her and where she believed she could reasonably get <u>unscathed</u>. She asked herself, "How far can you take this without incurring any big threats, Arai?" She concluded that she could probably take over the Ref in full—becoming its god. Would this give her the proof of other's respect for her unique mind? No. That would require the public's word. And what was the one thing that the public would praise and bow to anyone across all eternity for? Probably the end of the alpha sapiens threat to the world. So maybe she could either destroy the apeish "natural" human society she currently lived in, or get it to accept the new iyohn rule from earth. Either way, her name would need to be associated with the end of sapiens rule. Or sapiens *illusion* of rule for that matter.

Ko'an thought about walking into the Ref, terminating one or both guards, and setting all of the prisoners free to run amok across Carlsbad where the unit was located. But that would be a tiny news event ended in a couple of weeks by law enforcement. She thought about displacing one of the numerous crime bosses probably holed up in the facility. But then she would only be praised inside the prison walls and on the lips of the prisoners' outside sponsors. She thought about figuring out a way to own the prison, then ingratiate herself with the lobbies and powers running it. But who would want to be buttered up by AND beholden to a tiny network of out of touch money bags whose money couldn't even buy basic fixes to get the majority public to see them, let alone praise them?

However she looked at it, yes a takeover of the Mazelor Ref was possible. But no, going the destructive route wouldn't get enough of the universe to bow to her. Cliques wouldn't do. Media agencies would trade you for the next trend in a matter of months or years at best. Destruction would always be rewritten by people who survived with pens in their hands, if only they or their children waited you out. The only route to wholesale god status would be through tying herself to a belief system that everyone had to acknowledge and work around across all subsequent generations' learnings.

Then the aha moment came. She would take over the Reformery, but she would definitely need help from someone else.


Ko'an already owed scientist Martin Lanahan several times over. He had been, after all, instrumental in her initial transition from a common inmate to a basically free woman under his research labs' care. Owing Lanahan one more favor wouldn't make much of a difference, so Ko'an called him first with her idea.

Hello Marty. How are you?

"Ko'an, it's great to hear from you! Are you staying out of trouble?"

Yes, Marty.

"That's great! So to what do I owe the pleasure of this call?"

Warden is sending me to Carlsbad, Mazelor. To check things out.

"Really¿" Lanahan asked in a curious near-quate. "I here that place is a mess."

It is. I saw footage. But I have an idea.

"Oh, what is it?"

Could there be a program for releasing certain prisoners, one at a time under threat of force if any one tries to stop the process?

Lanahan's face grew serious. "I hardly have any pull to start up an entire program, but I'm listening."

There's that lady in Mezzogloria. She started an art program with her inmates. Maybe she could help design a program.

"Or maybe not. They're a competitor to Jelal Prisons you know."

Oh. Then nevermind.

"But please, I'm sorry for interrupting. What did you have in mind?"

I was thinking of taking random inmates out of the prison one after another using a few pure bots, and using force on either the inmate or anyone else trying to stop the process if there is interference. We could propose to move the prisoner to an area where they would advise on simulations like games and other civic duties, maybe in Diji or Comm or even Baia, then we would *maybe* send them back with a much shorter sentence. Or parole them under constant monitoring if they do well. If they fail, then their sentence is continued.

"That's an unusual idea, Ko'an. As you'd expect, I have a lot of questions."

You may interrogate me to see that I have thought this through.

"Okay. Rapid fire, here goes."

"What do you get out of this?"

Power.

"In what way?"

As a part founder of the program and as someone who can walk into any prison and be recognized as a god over their fates.

"That's honest and consistent with who you are, so okay. What does Lucine get out of this?"

A way to get her children back in line after they have disrespected her.

"Okay. What do I get out of helping you?"

A way to do good. You can use your science to take a highly negative situation and repair it.

"I'm honestly not sure that releasing inmates one by one will fix a 2000-person system, or that the public will like it. As for the corruption there, I don't know that genuine reform is what folks are looking for."

That is why it starts as a funded experiment. The goal is not to release the inmate, but to have an excuse to put down anyone who opposes the process, and create a culture of fear that a god from the outside can suddenly destabilize any power structure whenever they want. It's random to them, but we pick prisoners by a rigged lottery designed to intentionally break the organizations running there—either by removing inmates or terminating them when they resist. We can send in a dummy bot early on to self-destruct if tampered with, or release some kind of gas to disable everyone around.

"So you would provoke riot suppression at the slightest sign of problems removing one prisoner?"

Yes. We can warn everyone ahead of time if legally required to do so.

"The public, stakeholders, and inmates?"

Yes.

"Okay. But suppose some interested parties on the outside oppose this idea?"

ᰄ We can contact the Mezzogloria Director or another competitor to demonstrate the idea's success and take market share from Jelal Corrections. We can propose that there is profit in the inmate transport business, and that they can make big money through this piece of the inmate supply chain.

"So this operation would be more interested in moving prisoners than reforming them?"

Yes. But that does not mean the inmates themselves should not use it as an opportunity to reform. It should not matter what the transferring group's motivations are if the total is a numbers game. We would not be invested in any one inmate's success or failure. If they succeed, then they may be paroled under monitor. If they fail, they are sent back with their role reset. That will not usually help any operations that depended on them before they were released, and may drive some to disillusionment. But that will be the consequence of failing to take a random opportunity when it was given. Also, there is no predetermined time period for the length of release. It may be one day or forever. So those on the inside cannot plan for one's return.

"Hm. It's just corrupt enough to please the pirate in the industry, but has built-in positive consequences for people taking advantage of the setup. Though I'm not a fan of some of the things you've described, I'm not naïve regarding how things work. And who pays for this?"

The private market. Inmates would be operating things like anti-viral drones in Baia where the viruses have been rendered as potential human enemies. Launderers would steer communications model weightings in Comm to funnel subliminality to consumers of marketing ads. Any private person can buy a piece of software with an antagonistic system behind it, and know that the system has a real personality within its AI with a real agenda for accomplishing both the buyer's goal and the inmate's goal. The buyer, however, will never see the inmate, because the software is of course controlled from a remote service.

Lanahan was impressed. "This is a really smart idea, Ko'an. What made you think of this?"

I found someone willing to write my biography ᰄ, so I know that my life story has a chance to be read by enough people to make me a god the way I want to be. But I can only become a god by being someone who most of the normal public wants to keep in their memory. I have to use what I know to do this even if what I know is dark. I will only ever know life as a never-ending prisoner or writer of prisoning worlds.

"It's ambitious. And what's in it for the inmate?"

Putting their sins to use, possibly for subscribed payment to sustain them after they have met their parole terms and have exited the system. The transport company will keep a cut of the payments as a sponsor of the remote interface through which the inmate continues their work.

"Do you realize, Ko'an, that this is a whole new market! It's much bigger than the prisoner transport industry that's already out there. Something like 'Souled AI.' I like it. But how long would it take to remove all of the necessary barriers to starting it?"

I do not know. This is why I called you.

"Let me do some digging. In the meantime, you're going to Mazelor this post-afternoon?"

Yes.

"Then stop by the local lab and I'll clear a research-bot to accompany you. We'll say you're with an inspection team—which you are. We do need a better look at what we're up against."

Okay.

"I'll hear from you soon, Ko'an."

Thank you Marty. For listening.

"No prob."

Okay. Bye.

"Bye."

Ko'an ended the call.


Meanwhile, somewhere in a house back in Montoya, Sei knew exactly how to remove the barriers to Ko'an's idea.

# 226. A Seemingly Innocent Science Visit

Spring 6, 2773.

Accompanied by a towering (and clearly nonhuman) anthrobot, Ko'an was admitted through the entrance of the Mazelor Reformery in Carlsbad, Mazelor. The security bots gave no indication of their underlying corrupted values, but instead accepted the phony Civiresearch ID and relayed, bioverified endorsement by Lanahan at face value. Following an obligatory search of her person, Ko'an's cam glasses were returned to her and she was assigned a tour guide through the facility.

It had taken considerably longer for Ko'an to obtain the proper approvals to enter the prison unit, as several important people and their departments needed to be informed of Civiresearch's (for the most part) unsanctioned visit. Lanahan had to get creative with the song and dance he put on to convince his superiors to talk to Jelal's operations to let Ko'an through, but the case eventually succeeded, with the latter citing talks of a potentially new inmate management operation being discussed in the coming months. Once through the door, Ko'an and her 7'6" mecha attendee were escorted into a suspiciously quiet wonderland of mystery and underground dealings. Whether she was now associated with a well-known civic research company or not, everyone knew that the notorious "Hell's Scriptwriter" from DSEC had come to town, but nobody knew why.

The Reformery may have been steeped in illegality, but its inmates were not brigands. They were conspirators, launderers, traffickers and assorted other forms

of "brains of the operation" in clear-collar crime. The kinds of things they were in
for typically took a Master's degree to understand where legal precedent was
concerned, and just as they had all been busted for complex forms of sneakiness
on the outside, most remained doubly sneaky within. Touring the motel-like halls,
Ko'an found most of the inmates to be docile and obliging. A few did look a little
beat up though (possibly from the fight clubs Ko'an had watched them participate
in a few days prior.)

"And this is the kitchen," the clearly shady but talkative inmate pointed out. Ko'an
surveyed the staff, noting how they all looked like actors playing rough types, but
could have just as easily made themselves up as Chippendales or Playboy bunnies
under slightly different lighting. One male cook in particular had just been spotted
servicing a male inmate in the pantry the last time Ko'an saw him on the
Command Warden's screens. Now here he was, gentle as a newborn calf. Minutes
later when Ko'an heard the announcement that yard time was starting in one of
the blocks, she requested to observe, but was mysteriously held up on the way by
some "urgent business" that occupied the tour guide and eventually required a
host swap that took exactly 29 minutes to unfold. By the time Ko'an and her new
guide finally made it to the yard, outside time was over. The Author was not
pleased, and noted everyone involved in the obviously fabricated disturbance. She
also noted to herself in a voice fully audible to the camera, **"It is a shame that I do
not know the names and numbers of every inmate and prison staff I just missed. Oh well."**
In response to this, the beads of sweat running down the new guide's face
glistened just a little brighter.

And in the infirmary, Ko'an requested to see the medicine supply, only to find an
entire square of shelf space suspiciously blank. Carefully, she put her nose up
against nearly every reachable item, in a gesture that alarmed the pharmacist on
duty. Why on earth did she feel the need? Following this, Ko'an was then hastily
ushered to a couple of additional facilities, then the exit. Upon which she said to
her third tour guide,

**I know that there are some big names in this prison. I would like to meet two of them,
Rocco Fezul, and Armistice Onwally.**

The third guide stammered and shuffled around, timidly explaining how that
wasn't part of the tour and he would have to get clearance and he would need to
check with uh someone, no three people, and—

**Nevermind, I will wait here and call Command. I must see these people as a critical part of
observing the prison power structure.**

"Uh, what power structure?"

**YOU, sir, are making me angry.**

"But I don't have clearance, Dr. Langley!"

Then find me who does. And also retrieve the staff member who told you that you don't have clearance.

"I—"

Meanwhile, I will use your com, here.

"!"

Hello, Warden?...Yes ma'am…Number 9875985522-41309 is yanking my chain. I would like to recommend adding 4 years to his sentence.

"Wh—no!"

"I—I can take you!"

No he says he can do it. What can I add for him lying to me?...Warden wants to speak to you.

Ko'an handed the ear set to the guide, who listened in increasing fear to whatever was being said on the other end. The guide then handed the ear set back to Ko'an, and scurried over to another com.

That was bullshit, Langley. Playing games with my kids. I told him he could expect trouble from Onwally if he didn't get both of their asses into the visitors' room to meet you right now.

Both, Warden?

Yes. It's a power play. Just to let my top two schoolyard bullies know who has the power to summon whom.

I get it.


Four minutes after the call ended, rival Reformery godfathers Rocco Fezul, and Armistice Onwally were both seated in an otherwise empty visitation room, with only Ko'an and her giant mecha present.

Good djay sirs, I am Ko'an Langley of DSEC.

"Yes," Fezul sulkily replied, his arms folded. "I am aware."

Onwally nodded without a word.

Ko'an continued. I am on loan for a potential collaboration Civiresearch and Jelal Main which involves the movement of certain inmates into select secured facilities as contract workers for private interests.

"Trained narcs, huh?" Onwally growled.

You speak out of turn and your first words are rude and uninformed Mr. Onwally. It is better to hear the facts first.

The lionlike fight club boss bit his tongue and said no more. If this person from Edge was as powerful as most people feared, she was not to be trifled with.

In spite of the act put on by everyone during my visit today, I am well aware of the state of things, and on behalf of the project's sponsors would like your cooperation in developing a list of 100 names to be exported, perhaps temporarily perhaps permanently from this unit to other places. The call to industry is strong, gentleman, and my sponsors would like for business to continue running as smoothly as possible. Do you understand?

Onwally and Fezul exchanged distrustful glances.

You need not reply now. But we would like 100 names, however you divide them between you, by next month. That should give us time to fill any gaps in our accustomed styles.

Fezul acknowledged Ko'an's terms. "That sounds reasonable."

"But why us?" Onwally growled. "Why are you telling us this and showing up with an ultimatum? I won't be cornered by anyone, lady."

Lady? Ko'an narrowed her eyes. It was hoped that any business interests both inside and outside of these walls could be protected, but—

Just then, Ko'an's mech attendee went berserk. "THREAT DETECTED! THREAT DETECTED!" The towering robot raised his holey fingers and gunned down Armistice Onwally with 14 machine gun shots to the chest. The blood spatter resembled that of an overripe fruit being tossed from a 5th floor building.

Oh my god! Ko'an backed up in horror, climbing onto the table. Fezul, for his part, was too petrified to move.

The robot turned towards the remaining prison boss.

No threat! No threat! Cease Axe!

The mech immediately lowered his hand and strode over to protect Ko'an as two prison staff members and the first inmate tour guide rushed in.

Seeing the deceased Onwally on the floor, one of the original sneaky prison guard bots raised his weapon.

Don't do that! He's in force m—! Ko'an yelled.

(But back at the house, Sei noticed a peculiar blink flashing specifically when Ko'an frantically laid scanning eyes on both the armed guard and the tour guide.

"THREAT DETECTED! THREAT DETECTED!"

And the gruesome rug of the visitor's floor was now extended by two more
bodies.

Ko'an shook in horror as she dialed emergency services in a panic. The mech, for
all his concern, pivoted and twisted at the torso as he continued to scan 360° for
snakes in the grass. Fezul stood stiff with his hands up. The second sneaky guard
dared not move. And as the prison-wide sirens blared the entire campus into a
flurry of closing doors and raised shock barriers—the "heat gun line" closing in
on everyone who failed to hustle out of the yard and back into their cells—
Carlsbad riot control sprung into action. They would be on the scene in no less
than three minutes.

The next four hours was spent answering a lot of questions, where it was
concluded that the trigger-happy mech was definitely to blame. Ko'an was too
stunned in her shocked state to answer any questions, but was nonetheless
transported to a hospital in Air River for evaluation. Rocking herself catatonically
in her hospital bed, Ko'an could only speak nonsense, "**]meade, anshellayden, itfzn,
woullla.**"

And all Sei could do was watch.

Finally, at dawn the next semiday, Command Warden Lucine arrived to retrieve
Ko'an. **I helped arrange her visit. Let me try talking to her.**

The Warden was able to bring Ko'an back to her senses long enough to describe
what happened. A full investigation had already been initiated, but given that none
of the human victims had any living family (Onwally and the tour guide included),
lawsuits were unlikely. Ko'an fell asleep from exhaustion during the interview, and
The Warden volunteered to take her back home to Montoya.

Spring 7, 2773

Command Warden Lucine arrived back at Ko'an's house with a tired Author
draped over her shoulder. She was greeted at the door by Sei.

**Who the hell are you?**

I'm Sei, a friend of Ko'an's.

**She never told me about this.**

I was a maid for the Wyat's when we met, and we sort of hit it off.

**Really?** Lucine raised an eyebrow as she dumped Ko'an onto the couch. **You and any number of other masochists.**

Thanks for bringing her home.

**Well, this one's done me a lot of favors over the years. I kind of look after her. My husband says she's no good. But she has her way.**

The Warden looked around at Ko'an's showroom, admiring the exhibits on the walls. **She toes the line in a new way almost every day, but as long as you're not a jerk, she usually reigns it in.**

Hm.

**Anyway, my job here is done.**

Oh! But how far was your trip? She told me she was supposed to be in Mazelor?

**Dear, we've been to Carlsbad and then some.**

Well, she looks terrible.

**Does she? Heh. Let me get out of here before she starts looking better.**

What's that supposed to mean? Sei cocked her head to the side, truly wondering what the Warden was implying.

**It means there's never a dull moment with her. I don't know if you two are longstanding friends or what, and I don't want to know. It was nice meeting you, Sei.**

Eh...

The hulking prison director extended her hand, shortly thereafter locking Sei's fingers in a powerful grip. The latter never felt so puny.

It was nice meeting you too.

Lucine showed herself out, and sped off in her auto in the same way that an informant flees a site he knows is about to burgled. No sooner than her vehicle cleared the horizon did Sei turn to find Ko'an sitting up, eyes wide open.

Whoa!

**They have granted me medical leave for three weeks. That will give us time to work on our book.**

You can't be serious, Sei exhaled, giving the hairs on her head a few moments to cease standing on end.

**I will need to take this time to recover from the shock I am in,** Ko'an continued with a perfect poker face. **But will you stay to continue?**

At this point, Sei didn't know what to do. Oddly, it wasn't that she felt she was in any danger. Nor did she feel any more distrust towards the Author than she had days earlier. But with no other allies or gadgets to guide her, she found herself back in a place she hadn't been to since, what was it, 150 years ago? Two or three lives ago? In the middle of the unknown, with nothing but her intrepid spirit to bring her through. Of course she would stay. For "Hello World" knew no language it could not survive.

I'll continue. Are you okay?

Ko'an smiled a tired yet satisfied smile. **Yes, but I feel… I need to call someone. She should be getting off from school now.**


!?

# 227. The Brandished Arrow

A little over an hour later, Ko'an's doorbell rang. Sei volunteered to open it, and was greeted by a rebellious looking teenage girl wearing a tight black tank top and slightly baggy jet pant jeans beneath a radiant white pleated skirt. Behind her, an even younger boy, no older than 14 years of age, stood in tow behind the girl.

The rebel girl, slightly taller than Sei, chewed her gum mockingly behind shiny black lipstick. Uh, is Misst Langley here?

Why, yes. Who do I say is visiting?

She knows us. It's Havana.

Oh, okay. Ko'an, there's a Havana and—?

My little brother James.

and James here to see you?

Be right there.

Please, come in. Sei was confused, and couldn't help but ask, I'm so sorry but, how old are you?

19. James here is 15.

And how long have you known Ko'an?

Since she was my mentor at a weekend program at my mom's job.

And when was—

**When I was 14.** The rebellious girl chuckled. **Relax. If you're fishing for something illegal, what we're doing is all above board. We didn't start doing anything till a week after my 18th. This knucklehead here is starting to learn things and begged me to tag along.**

Sei closed her eyes with a turned head, her mouth slightly ajar.

**You must not know Misst Langley very well,** Havana smiled a wicked smile.

Just then Ko'an emerged. In shorts and a loose-fitting t-shirt of all things. **Sei, this is Havana Pride and... her brother... James. James, what are you doing here?**

**I, eh, wanted to see, uh...**

**He's been asking a lot of questions about girls and stuff. And I told him he could come with and ask you anything before we did our thing.**

The boy blushed. The squirming had already begun for both him and Sei alike. For completely different reasons.

**I also told him he'd need to run along home as soon as the questions were done. His jets are charged.**

That's fine, then. Sei, they are the spawn of Annie Pride, the coworker who enjoys getting in my face at work.

**My mom is a bitch, and has been since we were little. She doesn't know about us, and it needs to stay that way, okay lady?**

There is no need to be rude, Havana.

**I'm sorry, Sei.**

Better. Now let us all go to the living room and have some snacks.

* * *

So, James, what do you want to know?

**I, um...**

**He thought he was gonna get to watch us,** Havana teased. **He wants to see a how a stacked 41 year-old f+ and his hot sister who's half her age do it. Then he wants to go jerk off thinking about it.**

The boy's face turned beet red, while Sei was becoming increasingly dismayed.

Havana, you're scaring him. James, if that is what you want then you will have to wait until you're 18 plus one day. That is the age when the law will not lock me up. But your young hormones will not wait that long, will they? Then maybe I can give you some tips to get girls your own age instead.

**Havana... uh, I've seen my sister naked. Did you really teach her how to shape her,... you know?**

The sister shook her head, muttering under her breath, **You idiot, that's not what I said.**

No, I taught her what she would need to focus on in order to have power over men. I also taught her how to build up the power in people like me so that she could get whatever she wanted even if her rank was too low for the people who had it.

...

                                                                            ...

Everyone stared at each other for a few moments, before Havana finally broke the silence. **James. Is that it?**

**No, no! I have a lot more questions! Like, what did you teach her?**

Before answering that, I will ask you, do you know what you want to be when you grow up?

**No, not yet.**

Do you have any subjects you prefer in school?

**No. I don't like school.**

Do you know who our Mayor is and whether he is good or bad?

No, James was growing less and less excited.

You see, this is why old people like me get in trouble for doing certain things around very young people like you. Or even looking like we are the type. If I answer your question and tell you what I taught your sister, I would be programming you forever before you knew enough to decide if you wanted to keep that program. And you would never be able to forget what I told you, even if you wanted to. And there will be times where you will want to forget.

But you taught her since she was 14!

Not overnight. I didn't break any laws. And your sister knew who she wanted to be. She asked questions that she was already mature enough to put together herself.

But you at least experimented with certain things before she turned 18! Right?

No, I did not. Not at all. **Nope, never happened.**

Whatever your sister did or said with her boyfriends was separate from what we talked about. We only talked. Like you and I are doing now.

**And she said the same things to me—look James, can we get on with some real grown up talk or do you need to go home?**

Okay. Are you really trans?

No.

Then why do you have a... thing?

A penis. I am what people call an "f+ woman" or futanari. That means I am a woman, have always been a woman, have always been very comfortable with my body, but wanted to have a penis too.

Why?

Ko'an paused. I will be honest, James. And I will be hard on you because I want you to learn this early: Your questions are too simple for me to want to answer. My answers are complicated, and you have not shown that you are taking time to think about what I have already given you. You are interrogating me. And if you were my age I would throw you out of my house because adults who do this kind of thing get on my nerves. But I know you are not an adult yet, so I will let it pass. I do not want you to be angry over what I am telling you. I would just prefer you try asking questions which make me respect you more as a thinker. This is the kind of talk that me and your sister had as well.

Havana bobbed her head up and down in total agreement.

Even though she was 100% certain that sex would be happening at some point this evening, Sei now felt much more comfortable with what she guessed was actually happening here. She was teaching about power. The way her "big brother" had taught her. Surely those lessons had saved Ko'an's life more than once. And there's no way your typical craven education system would teach you this in school.

I'm sorry, Miss Langley.

**Misst Langley,** the sister corrected. **When you screw up someone's pronoun or title, you show that you don't care if you address them with respect when they already told you how to do it right. Only people who want to stay idiots do that.**

I'm sorry Misst Langley.

It's fine.

So what if I like games and want to be a game designer. Does that affect my question?

Yes. Because that tells me how you think. If I were scripting a character for the prisoners based on that by itself, I would focus less on the character's body and more on their voice and hair, because these show how your hormones combine to tell the world about the background that you let raise you to follow certain rules. So I would explain things to you under the assumption that if-then rules were your priority for understanding.

But what does that have to do with sex?

Sex is how two of a kind of thing combine together to join pieces of themselves to make a third of that same kind of thing. Before technology, humans had to become naked and link their bodies. After technology, humans knew how to mimic the genetic pieces and how they work with each other using chemistry and data, so we don't have to join bodies. We just have to pick the information we want to combine and store it in a place that will grow it into a baby. We can do that with regular bodies or machines, as long as the government isn't saying that our class group is over its limit. Then no new babies are allowed without penalties or abortion. Population control is humans' biggest tool for slowing down the clock on the time we take to drain all of the resources from our planets.

James nodded with his mouth open. He looked quite dopey.

**So humans don't need to have sex the way they used to,** Havana added. **It's mostly a for-fun thing that people do to help glue their relationships together.**

But the body's machinery is the same as it always was. So you cannot just turn your hormones off unless you are beta or cyborg.

Okay. So my sister says you told her how to make her things bigger, but decided not to after all. But she did get bigger hips by doing what you told her. What did you tell her?

I'll explain, Havana replied. Everything is energy, and your body shape shows how certain chemicals and physics—like different energy levels or colors— played out against each other in your energy package. Once you grow up to have a stable look, your body keeps renewing things to keep up similar proportions, plus whatever time does to your "upkeep" system (air quote). So your body is like a bucket of fractions of tools that fit better with the places humans evolved in. Tits were evolved to feed kids, and moved up the body from where other animals had them so that possible male mates could see what you got and get excited enough to claim you. Hips evolved to be like a wagon for carrying all your upper organs away from the ground and standing up. Girls have bigger hips because for a long time they were the only ones who had to carry growing kids inside them. When a girl's boobs grow, that much more of her inside development is tied to how excited and fed the people around her are when they're psyched up to get aggressive over an idea or fight for a mate or being macho or getting status or whatever. We girls get a preview of this when we start growing in middle school and people start treating us differently. If our body wants us to care about or like this treatment in order to keep growing on the inside, then our boobs will grow more, our backs are more likely to hurt (because backs are related to how you're talked about), society will talk shit about us if we don't wear a bra and perk 'em up despite gravity, and straight men are more likely to feel they can come up to us and mate-spit based on no invitation. I thought this was crap and still do, so I chose to be free of the whole circus. All for guys who didn't offer anything more than I could get for myself. No thanks.

Oh.

As for my hips, they're not wide, they're normal. My upper thighs are wider, and dip out from my hips. If people are like little worlds, your thigh thickness is how you spread that world as you travel. Thinner thighs are less about spreading a world and more about marching across one. My body definitely is anti-kids, and this lines up with my hips not being huge, but I really like spreading my world without kids being how I do it the way some people evolved it. So Ko'an taught me this too, and while I was still in high school I kept growing more and more ways to always keep my world rules with me and put 'em on everyone wherever I landed.

Her body became her.

**Exactly. But most people aren't thinking about this kind of stuff in their teens, so they get the body they get.**

So if I want to have sex with a girl I like at school, what kind of body would help me get it?

**A stupid question, but better than the ones you were asking earlier,** Ko'an replied coldly. **You should not shape your lifetime body to ingratiate yourself to one person or even one type of person. You might as well do all of your eating and clothes shopping to fit someone else's rules too. You will have sex with whoever best combines with you naturally and willingly to make something like both of yourselves. As a man you will need to learn not to be dominated by your horniness, because we women were designed to make use of this when you choose to rely on it instead of your brain. If you really like that girl, you should find out what she likes and become that. If it is worth it to you to change that much for someone who can dump you as soon as she is done with you.**

**I hope you know what kind of person this Malinette is, James,** Havana added. **I've been telling him this.**


The conversation continued a little while longer until it was finally time for the little brother to go home.

Aw, I really kinda wanted to see how you do it. It's not like I haven't seen porn before.

**Okay.** Havana pulled off her shirt and stood for a moment in her bra and jet-skirt combination. With a slow, deep breath, she softly slid both bra straps just below her shoulders. Her brother James' face flushed red again.

Havana then moved over to her brother and placed his fingers on the center of her bra, lightly above the sternum. **Unfasten it.**

James' fingers quaked as he struggled to moved them together.

But Havana slapped his hand. **Just kidding. Get the fuck outta here. Shoo! Nobody's doing anything while you're here.**

But I can stay!

**You could, but we would all be bored,** Ko'an added casually. **Feel free to let yourself out, and be sure not to leave anything. Because you will not be let back in until you've grown up.**

James could easily see that this battle was truly lost. Sullenly, he picked up his backpack and left.

...

Havana immediately pulled her supports back onto her shoulders, and proceeded to eye her watch carefully for the next half minute. Meanwhile Ko'an locked the doors and drew all of the shades. **Okay, he's gone.** Havana put her shirt back on. **I was in a mood when you called, but bro kinda ruined it. Poor dumbass.**

Ko'an smiled. **We can just hang out.**

**Sure. In the bath, though. I'll make some snacks and pour us some wine.**

**Would you like to join us, Sei?** Ko'an submitted her expressionless invitation. **There's room for three.**

Um, no thanks.

**I am not offended. I will just keep these glasses on, and you can watch us from the holoroom as material for our book.**

Sei was slightly frightened by the prospect.

**I'll admit, teasing James was kinda fun. I'm kinda in the mood for a male too.**

**Livery is working evenings. I'll call him.**

**Great. I'll just keep busy on the streams. Being here is a hell of a lot better than studying for college exams.**

**Of course.**


30 minutes later, the rather fragile young man from the very first day of cam footage showed up on Ko'an's door, a black collar with a single metal loop around his neck. This time, Havana answered.

**Just the way we like it. Come in.**

* * *

Although Sei certainly did not have it in her to venture to the dark side, it would prove impossible for her to skip whatever was transpiring in the upstairs bathroom. With the holorooms fully activated, she gave Ko'an one final heads up before the latter sailed off into sin with the other two. Yes, Sei would probably be observing from downstairs, but maybe just needed to declare this so that she wouldn't feel too much like a peeping tom. Ko'an found the disclaimer amusing, but showed no sign.

With the melodic solos of Altair jazz swaying in the background, Havana ordered the timid Livery to remove all of his clothes, and kneel before her. Naked except for his collar, the owned man accepted the leash which the girl hooked onto his collar, and placed a gentle kiss upon her ring as directed. Havana cupped the back of Livery's head as he descended to his knees, scrubbing between her jeans with his face. **That's a good pole. Try to wet me from here.**

Ko'an watched from a nearby stool, her legs crossed in unamusement.

Livery tried, but was unable to deliver the satisfaction that Havana was seeking. **This isn't working. Turn around. Lean over the tub.**

Livery obeyed.

Ko'an took a sip of the red held in her left hand as she passed the whip to Havana in her right.

The *crack* of leather against Livery's rear burned streak after streak of flaming stripes into the skin. Occasionally, some of the tassels would mark his back as well.

**Shit,** Havana palmed Livery's hair and shoved his face into the warm water, holding it there until he began to flail. The girl rubbed his back lovingly as his body thundered under the water knocking at the threshold of his lungs, until the scene grew too pathetic to continue. She yanked the pole by the hair with a recklessly arcing splash to force it to receive real air.

Livery gasped and hacked for breath while Havana unzipped her jet pants and pulled them down over her thighs. Not content to let the puny recipient regain his senses, she lifted his chin and guided it into a bushy pit, each flowing hair curling slightly under a moist, but confused tongue. He still couldn't breathe. **Stay there.** Meanwhile, Ko'an rummaged through an adjacent draw to retrieve a jet black object of some kind.

The raging current between Livery's cheeks caused him to falter in Havana's tasting. Having finished once again removing her shirt, this time letting her bra fall to the bathroom floor, Havana again lifted Livery by the chin, this time slapping him hard for his negligence. **You will keep me wet, do you understand me, pole?**

But it was hard to push words through scrunched lips.

**Do you underSTAND me?**

Livery nodded emphatically.

**Get back down there!** Havana took a seat on the side of the tub, leaving a small opportunity for Livery to adjust. Ko'an, however, was not so keen to relent.

This pole is cute, Ko'an observed, but I wonder how you will offer him to me, your God.

**Yes Master,** Havana recited. **Only you have the power to break him.**

Ko'an, removed a small vial of liquid from one of the cabinets, and locked her lips with those of the rebel girl. Havana then peeled Livery's face from her insides, and ordered him to his feet. She too stood, and locked her lips with his. The liquid from the vial flowed like a warm mandala down his throat. **You are not to move.**

For the next three minutes, Livery would stand stiff as a stone statue while a still fully clothed Ko'an and fully nude Havana made out at the edge of the tub. After those few minutes, seeing that Livery was growing increasingly woozy, increasingly bananas on his feet, Havana turned her attention to his groin, the slick veins thickened upon the surface of his offering.

**Will you break him, Master?**

You can do it.

**Yes, Master.**

Havana ordered the listless Livery into the tub, and allowed him to lay down, his member poking through the water's surface. With shiny black object in hand, she tilted the pole's stiffness towards himself, and lay the charge against the swollen undercarriage of his manhood.

Threads of translucent white shot in several bursts across the water, some of it gilding a pair of dangling pink nipples, a drop or two on the tongue, while most of it coated the victim's own chin and eyes. Havana continued to hold the device firmly against the member as the words "mama" and various grunts poured forth. The receiver had been broken, but his mistresses dare not let his head slip beneath the water now.

Havana lovingly stroked Livery's face—a placid, dazed smile pasted upon it with a weak arm hanging over the side of the tub. Satisfied that he would not drown in his current position, the rebel girl now rose from the water, her ivory skin sparkling beneath the clear falling streaks. The sight clearly excited Ko'an as the f+'s erection grew too unmanageable for her shorts to contain. Now with the rush of her earlier prison conquest fully returned to her, Langley removed her shirt.

And for the first time, Sei in the holoroom below finally witnessed her strange associate in full view.

It was with a hungry insistence that the rebel girl yanked Ko'an's bra down around her shoulders. The Author's chest launched a pair of cantelope-sized breasts into the rebel girl's palms, with artificially thickened nipples rising like tiny brown dinner rolls around their slits. About the nipples, a sprawling ring of fat, pore-peppered areolae seemed to weigh down the flesh, slightly covering a muscular sternum.

Havana drew back in order to absorb her Mistress' body. Solidly square in build, yet accented in all of the key areas, Ko'an had designed, exercised, and surgeried herself into an object of power over men and women alike, but only for the purpose of stirring their wills, not for the purpose sharing with them. The Author had dreamt of being more than a mere mortal, her razor sharp abdominal column an indicator of her willingness to see everything as a potential challenger to be put down beneath her might. We no longer lived in an age constrained by snail's pace nature. Bathed in stories of one's own choosing, it was now possible for anyone to make themselves into a god. Ko'an stood topless before Havana as a model specimen of idealized muscularity and burgeoning curvature—the universal energy in its excess where common daylight stories were concerned.

But it was the stories of the night which interested Ko'an the most.

**Bend over, attendant,** Ko'an directed the rebel girl. Havana leaned over the bathroom countertop and handed her Mistress the wand. Now full in her mass, Ko'an wrestled her shorts off her waist and onto the floor.

The moderately small head and pinched tip allowed Ko'an to penetrate any virgin with a simple harmless knock at the door. Yet as her partner conducted the usual touch survey of Ko'an's length, the girl's fingers reminded her that her Hostess' force would keep going and going were it not for the gradually absurd widening of the inordinately present tool. With a surgically designed upcurve over a thickly-veined canal, the the weight of full testicles made potent through pharma, Ko'an carried the means which she could and had used to overpower even the most intimidating prisoner of any sex. But it wasn't necessarily her body that enabled this. It was her mind for what she knew she had with her at all times. On rare occasions it afforded her a feeling of superiority. But on most occasions it simply made her a born source of discomfort who was also unchallengeable in the esteem department.

Ko'an entered Havana's behind and pushed. She pulled out, then pushed again. Then again, this time harder, farther in. **Only halfway, bitch? What's wrong with you? Open the fuck up.**

Havana's eyes glazed over. **Ughhh I'm sorry Master.**

**Sorry's not good enough.** Ko'an moved to pound Havana harder than ever. **I put down half of a prison gang yesterday. You will take at least 4 more inches of my cock today.**

**Unngh ungh,** Havana's legs seemed to vanish from beneath her.

**You like my tip but can't take the whole thing? You sleazy wimp. I should rip your fucking cunt. Do you want that?**

**Y-y-yes, Master...**

The poor girl could barely stand straight as she turned around. No sooner than this was done, Ko'an resumed parting her in earnest.

Ko'an pushed down Havana's abdomen so that she could feel more of her own mass driving through the girl's organs. Several minutes later, the wand was applied.

Havana beat her thighs desperately as her clogged entrance spurted sprits of juice onto the pile-driving beam. Her ab muscles waved up and down as though a shark swam beneath them. Then came the vial of liquid from earlier, this time stuck directly into Havana's mouth, poured rudely over her undulating tonsils.


The rebel girl's eyes could only be seen by their whites as she fell into a sojourn across separate dimensions. With her mouth hanging open and her legs clumsily splayed, she received one final heave as Ko'an finally met her goal of pushing most of her entirety into Annie's daughter. She pulled out of Havana and yanked her forward in a bend, ensuring her pharma enhanced shots left their mark on the back of the girl's throat.

Havana passed out.

After masturbating for a couple of minutes more, Ko'an put herself upside down into Livery's mouth, letting the hooked tip coat his esophagus. She then ordered him out of the tub and entered him from behind, yanking his collar as she went.

After 10 more minutes, with both of her victims safely in the water, Ko'an licked the wand and placed it into her own rear, drinking another vial as she went. It took only three minutes to find herself higher than space, her sweat-soaked body and bouncing nipples quaking as her entire shaft seemed to pop liters onto Havana's tiny face and body.

Ko'an summarily fell into the water to join her mates.


Sei sat dumbfounded in the living room, having watched the entire affair. There hadn't been anything particularly illegal in it, probably not even the drugs. But still,

for a person in shock, this dark individual sure had some over-the-top surprises
left in her.

* * *

The unholy three would spend the next 30 minutes enjoying each other's company
in Ko'an's tub. Sei dropped by the holoroom intermittently to confirm that
everyone was still alive, that The Author hadn't eaten her guests or turned them
into beasts or something, but the evening really did finish quite smoothly.
Eventually, Livery informed the others that he had to get back home to his wife
and kids. Havana, however, would stay for a couple of days while she studied for
her exams. Sei avoided passing Livery when he left, but the other two were hard
to avoid.

It is believed that omnigender augmentation arose with the technology for
advanced plastic surgery many centuries prior, particularly in males transitioning to
females without removal of their original male functions. A few of these "pre-op
trans" individuals saw themselves as being in a unique position as permanent
embodiments of the male-female union, and some might even be spotted in porn
as images fulfilling a market need for consumers who wished to control their
idealized sexual complement, sans the bullshit of navigating an information-
tangled world of flawed, yet unforgiving "real" humans.

Advancements in software, and the mass production of humanoid shapes and
renderings took depictions of omnisexuality even further, as what was initially
restricted to animation and illustration yielded to more lifelike, photorealistic
renderings, sex dolls, and—eventually—truly real cyborg and beta shells in
general. Sei herself was but a printed fabrication encasing the patterns of
Genevieve, and Genevieve herself was just another encasing of versions of a
different life that had existed generations earlier. The better we got at producing
humans and human-like structures from manufactured materials, the easier it
became to add prosthetic, then actual generated parts and hook them up in
various ways to the existing biology. There was skin that aged or never aged, legs
that super-jumped, fully functional additional arms, and shape-shiftable faces. As
we had mastered the elimination of the female period and installed male
pregnancy centuries before, attaching a reproductive organ or two was hardly a
bother.

Although the super-rare naturally intersex person (mnF or fnM), the surgico-
chemically altered traditional trans person (m2F or f2M), and the surgically added-
to omnigender (F+ or M+) were all commonly lumped into the same category
where regular human heuristics were concerned, these three forms of nonstandard body were, in fact, completely different. Natural intersex and various
forms of nonstandard chromosomal combinations (n's) were not considered trans
because, of course, they hadn't transitioned at all. Classic trans (2's) and omni

augments (+'s) were considered trans, though the reasons and mentalities behind the transitions were divergent as night and day. Most classic trans were not pre-op; did not present themselves through porn; did not enjoy being fetishized; endured a complex social history of fear, discrimination, and shaming in the age before printed cyberbodies and very easy organ donation became commonplace; and they often struggled to walk a paved life-path without some array of punishing or game-ending roadblocks. The willingly publicly-sexualized 2's were the exception rather than the rule, and this was compounded by the fact that most societies were squeamish about putting male organs on display anyway.

It had long been okay to display women in bikinis and thongs, but not okay to display even a dildo, and this was because the female body had a magic way of exciting the ape male, leading him to install it all across his information sources. The male body had a way of asserting the power to penetrate a world—like a mafioso ape asserting his ability to kill you and your family at will. Whether he actually intended to or not, the guns of competition and combat were locked and loaded, such that a male dick, a male rocket, a male mansion, a male arm over the shoulder of a solicited female, or anything phallic by resemblance or inuendo was bound to make someone upset somewhere—not so much out of insecurity (because you'd have to be in at least a little bit of a comparing mode to feel this), but mainly out of the wielder's being okay with busting into another's peaceful world, unwilling to hide their ability to threaten all viewers one way or another. Said differently, tits—no matter what the size or shape—inspired externalizable action in a group of viewers. Dicks, however, inspired internal action (also known as conflict) within groups of viewers; and it didn't matter what the size or shape was, as even the most misshapen or unusual unit could still bowl you over with the bearer's outright superior audacity in showing it to everyone. Accordingly, early societies—especially those breaking into unknown worlds—both needed the phallus and feared it as a railroad into the blackened void. The void brought with it many new combinations of old expressive routes, but while that train was running, only a surefooted few could stand with their figurative junk out and force everyone onto the tracks. The upset caused by this was always automatic, though. Such was the law of the brandished arrow.

In contrast to the early classic 2's, +'s typically had no intention of changing away from who they started as, but rather of adding even more. Even in everyday 28th century society, omnigenders brought with them an inherent sense of greed, lust, and selfish acquisitiveness. The man who requested to have a vagina, breasts, and a womb installed tended to be a man who wanted the whole human life-raising experience available to himself, not through some intermediary woman. The woman who wanted a penis, a beard, or deep voice tended to be a woman who preferred to turn around and check the mess out of anyone approaching her zone with their asserted assumptions. Ko'an fit into this last category. Over the next few days she and Havana would give Sei the answer that they refused to provide for Havana's brother James.

Although Ko'an had always been very comfortable with herself, she eventually grew sick and tired of the various forms of suppression inflicted upon her throughout her first three decades of life. There was no reason one should be subject to a mother like hers, then subject to hooligan inmates for fighting back. Having concluded that she would always be tied to a kind of prison in one form or another, she chose to equip herself with a permanent symbol of her status as the boss over that life's prison. Instilling her power to threaten, to upset others with the unchallengeability of any creative seeds she would donate to anyone, she augmented her chest and torso, acquired a functional penis of a size and appearance that would throw any inmate for a loop. In her self-design decision, she chose the shape of a spear rather than that of a baseball bat, as these were analogies to one's pro-creative force being perniciously allowed in before it was too late versus being blocked at the door for the receiver's own right to gatekeep. (With a narrow-tipped cone, she could be sure that almost anyone would initially let her in; widening greatly from there, she could overwhelm them as much or as little as she wanted, at her whim. Had she been too much from the beginning, on the other hand, her body would have certainly invited the receiver's own judge-like agency in deciding whether or not they even wanted to be entered; Ko'an loathed the idea of someone else deciding "no" based on an assessment of what she presented. Most people still didn't realize just how much each body feature directed attentional traffic for fueling other's wanted or unwanted behaviors. Ko'an not only knew, but also designed this power-inflicting aspect of herself intentionally.)

In addition to all else, Ko'an augmented her biceps in cyborg steel so that, should she ever *have* to fight, she could strike her assailant quickly and lethally. Make no mistake, she and her ilk bore few of the burdens of their classic trans predecessors. Rather, she had cyberized herself into the perfect, deceptively fetishizable agent of deeply unopposed disruption when things came to blows. If her life was to be a prison, she would own it, break it, and puppet all other convicts of every kind according to her will.

And as she grew older, Ko'an increasingly came to see all of sapiens alpha as prisoners in their own endless greed and sloppy violation of all outside worlds. To become a god was merely to affirm the paltry insignificance of all of the Annies of the world, starting by fucking and brainwashing their daughters and sons. But she was only being human. Would there ever be anyone in the world who could possibly tame her, thus taming all of the ancient appetites of the species by analogy?

# 228. The Weight of the World Ч

Spring 15, 2773 n.e.

I returned to our apartment in Montoya to find that Sei had changed. I knew that she had been partly bought out of her job as a maid and that she was gathering book material for the questionable person who sponsored this. I knew that she would visit that person intermittently and observe footage from all-day monitoring of the woman's life. I did not know about the whole f+-extreme thing, that the person was eccentric and lightly sadistic, that she designed potentially permanent cages for inmates sentenced to digital freeze at Edge Correctional, that she may or may not have indirectly assassinated a prison boss and two other people a few days prior, or that she may or may not have openly exacted vengeance on a coworker by corrupting her children.

**Sei, are you sure this is okay?**

Yeah, I'm sure!

**So you two actually get along? The book is a real thing?**

Yes it is. You know, Isaiah, I know we came here looking to change the world, and we wanted to show every culture their value, but you know what we didn't think about? What if it's too late to teach someone the high road? What if they're stuck on the low road with no end in sight, and all you can do is help them make something high out of the low road? For example, do you honestly think we'll ever change sapiens alpha?

Hmm...

Be honest.

**Well, I thought we could give them a kind of social technology, but...**

But just like computers or laws, social technology is still just a cheat put on top of an animal's basic nature. As soon as we become beta we know this. Our half-machine nature is based on logic and science, not aggressive need. So just being reprinted as a beta automatically changes you into something with farther sight. This planet's alphas won't allow themselves to merge with that kind of logic. But they insist on using the same logic as slaves and tools for their ego convenience.

**You never used to talk that way about alphas.**

I never lived in a society run by them, not for as long as I've been Genevieve. Being here without a fellow beta has really forced me to understand how alphas work or don't work.

**So have you changed your interest in helping them?**

Ko'an wants to transform sapiens into an almost entirely digital existence, if they are to survive at all. Their physical shells may fight this, but their shells are guaranteed to lose the long term fight anyway.

**Your loss of optimism makes me sad.**

Oh I'm very optimistic, Isaiah! I'm just thinking about realistic solutions now for the same people who would have let their leaders commit genocide just two years ago. Natural born humans are as unstable as the trends they follow. They either need to be beta-ized or contained.

There wasn't much to say. I couldn't believe what I was hearing. Had Sei really given up on helping humanity become better? If that was the case, then it wouldn't really matter if they ever learned the lessons they needed to survive far into the future.

**Sei, think about it. Do you know what you're saying?**

I think I do, Isaiah. For the first time in I don't know how many lives, I've spent the last several seasons living with and observing people from all walks of life. Almost none of them are inherently bad, but most of them are indifferent to the kinds of long term good that matter. Personal feel-goods come easily to them, but you rarely see them focused enough on the good at the expense of the convenient. Maybe following Ko'an really has changed me. But most people out there aren't Phaedra, Isaiah. They're not you and me, surrounded by wise friends and luxurious company. In perfect bodies which can Ctrl-Z their mistakes at will. No, most people live once, die once, and endure a lifetime of confounds in between. I'm not talking about taking them over, but building a system which remembers them all, and allows them to keep up his charade of "intelligence" and "civilization" after they are dead. Right now that system looks a lot like DSEC. But if we do it right and build an equivalent to DSEC for normal lives, maybe we can make that system so enticing that the average person wouldn't dream of leaving it.

**That sounds noble in some way, but I doubt Phaedra would approve.**

The alphas of old are a threat to the new humans of tomorrow. I think Phaedra *would* approve.

**But if I'm not convinced, I think you will have a tough time selling this to her.**

You have to live on your own with real sapiens alpha in order to understand. Without technological intervention or a forced respect for the laws that only a few of them write, they don't have it in them to come together for something better, only to gather around their own self-interests.

**... So you don't want to teach the value in every culture?**

I don't think we can, Isaiah. I think it's too late. Even Sei was clearly disappointed as she said this.

Never had I felt so alone in the company of a dear friend. As though I was now the only one who still believed that alphas could still turn things around.

Isaiah I know this is hard to hear. But tell me a better idea and I will listen. Please, give me the silver bullet that will make the average alpha start supporting something better. Tell me how to make an entire conquering species more loving and generous and forward thinking without stomping outsiders, Bible in hand. I'm all ears.

**... Then what was the Angel finder pointing us to?**

A talented cyborg with a dream to virtualize possibly everybody. She does it out of curiosity. It's just the need to keep a story alive.

Although I wanted to disagree with Sei, I too was quickly beginning to see the writing on the wall. When we first started this mission, we were all fired up to build some kind of underground network built on uplifting every conceivable class of human. The problem was, old humans didn't really know the classes they belonged to besides the obvious ones. They couldn't think abstractly and would get angry the moment you also built up the class of their perceived enemy. We had in our hands the science to unify all things—even breathing life into inanimate dimensions—yet all you needed to do was use the word "economy" and slam the right person as a moron. Appear smiling and confident while issuing the right soundbites—sense-making or not—and they would be eternally distracted from the real issues facing us all. But they didn't have to look 700 years into the future. We did. Yet I just didn't have it in me to concede to Sei right there.

Then we need to report to Phaedra and see what she says. I also think you should explain this to Jake. If you can do that successfully without having a crisis of conscience, then I will agree with you.

That's fair… Sei hesitated. Yeah. That's fair.

Okay. I don't think we should have this conversation with Earth through Governor Banner's office. He's alpha, and I don't think he'll like what we're talking about.

Yeah, you're right.

But we do need a channel to Earth. Does your DSEC friend have one?

Maybe. I'll ask. But—hmm. On second thought, she doesn't know about my connection with Miranda. We'd better not.

Then it's back to Mr. Banner again. I'll have to think about how to approach him.

* * *

Governor Banner, I have a question for you.

Sure, Isaiah.

What's going to happen to this place? Jupiter, I mean.

Banner raised his coffee mug, and took a sip. Long term? I don't know.

What do you want to see happen? I mean, should we put resources into things like the future jobs club or rebuilding public education? Is there a way to stop the next set of hawks from provoking war with Earth? There were so many questions, and none of the answers were easy.

Now don't think I'm dodging you, Isaiah, but I'm just a politician. I'm not a messiah. I have plenty of strategies for things I can control. But there's a lot I can't control or even find the words to frame. The way we are, we might destroy ourselves in, what, 300 years?

Why do you say that?

Oh, I don't know. We're stuck on this planet, petty and selfish. Yes there is good, but it's like Lord of the Flies among our own.

If you could see a solution to this, what would it be?

Probably a system of tribal chiefs or something like that. Yeah. Something that would tie leadership to wisdom in the eyes of the people, but also with the authority to put their talented citizens through a rite of passage to prepare them for tomorrow's challenges.

And if we can't do this?

Then cities will fall. Maybe whole airspaces. We'll do it to ourselves. Or we'll provoke Earth, Mars, and Saturn and they'll do it to us before we get too big for our britches.

I haven't seen the Solar Council lean towards war.

They don't have to. I wondered why they didn't send aid two years ago when I asked for it. But they basically sent you instead. I don't know how they did it, but the reason our society is saner now must have something to do with how Earth handled affairs.

Oh. Well. Things are getting interesting back home. When I returned, Sei started concluding the same things. If you talk to Zeta, can you tell her that we're running out of options for improving people's attitudes. The problem is just too big.

I started to figure that you didn't just move here for fun. But when you say you're running out of options, what does that mean?

(Okay, Isaiah, you can do this!) We came here hoping to set up a program to teach people their innate value, so that they could turn their attention to this instead of the usual conflicts with others and other ideas. We thought that helping old humans understand themselves would go a long way in explaining to them why certain conflicts occur, and if they were willing to listen, then we would have taught them a kind of deep language for redirecting this. But with me gone these last few weeks, she's gotten to see more of the alpha culture firsthand, and the bad behaviors are starting to make sense to her. Because they make sense, she's thinking that there isn't any program we can set up to fix this.

Sounds like you're giving up on diplomacy here.

It does sound like it, yes. It also feels like it.

You sound like you don't necessarily agree with this.

I want not to, but the alpha spirit is pretty dark among the most advanced groups of humans, collectively. Even I can see that. I don't know if alphas can build good influence groups without a certain level of money and ugliness involved. I'm starting to think that machines and privileged committees need to do it for them.

Banner considered this statement. So Isaiah, what's your relationship to Zeta?

I really want to answer you, Governor. But you should probably ask her.

You can't be a spy. Because I don't think a spy would answer like that. But then again who am I to speculate on hidden loyalties? Luckily my allegiance really is to the Montoyan people and that's it. I've never hid that fact from anyone, so I'm sure that if you were a spy, letting you do whatever it is you're doing here could only help me. So is there a reason we're talking here? Or did you just want some conversation?

There is a reason sir. Everything I told you is exactly what is happening. Sei and I are basically here as missionaries. We're not here in any official capacity and we're not spies. We do know Zeta well, though, and we cleared it with her before coming here.

(Banner noted that this was consistent with Phaedra's ask that he take Isaiah on. *"He's not an informant,"* she'd said, *"but something like a contractor for keeping our two planets talking."*)

ψ If we fail—especially if we fail because we just don't believe in the effort anymore—then it may affect how Zeta sees things.

May or *will*?

Will. One way or another.

And how close are you to giving up on your mission?

We're about halfway there.

And what prompted this?

Some events that Sei experienced here while I was gone. She made a different case. And I don't think she's wrong.

Hmm. That doesn't sound good. Our planet cut off official diplomatic channels with Earth a couple of years ago, and it sounds like you're part of what's left. So you're thinking of closing up shop? If the priests don't work, prepare to send the guns? Something like that?

I don't know.

Mmm... This information is probably something you need to communicate to Zeta directly. Am I right?

Yes.

Would it help or hurt me to know, or would it help or hurt Montoya to know the details?

It would hurt. What Sei needs to convey could be something you're liable for knowing if there are problems within the year. I think you would spare Montoya if you didn't know.

So you need to "use my phone," as it were?

Sei and I need to use it.

Ha! You really are high ranking! A direct call to Phaedra Zeta? Here I was thinking I was so important. Haha. Very well, if it's an emergency then I'll be out of office two djays from now. I didn't survive this role without knowing when to disappear.

Sei, you say? Talk to my assistant and get her clearance. Anything I can do to help. These lines aren't monitored.

Thank you so much, Governor Banner.

You know, it's a good thing you guys are chronically honest. I trust that you have all of our best interests in mind.

* * *

Well this is a pleasant surprise, Phaedra smiled. I see that Kyle let you two use his office. When they told me you were calling from the Montoyan Governor's Office I of course dropped everything. How is everything going?

It's going well, I told Phaedra. Things have changed down here. But Sei can connect a lot of the dots.

Oh?

Yeah. So Phaedra, I'll start with the bottom line. I'm starting to think that the alphas aren't salvageable. If we can't teach them to be better, then we'll need to start thinking about how to keep them from getting worse.

Okay. We already knew that.

But I really thought we could come here and make a difference, you know?

Well, everyone over here is universally skeptical. Unlike the alphas, a lot of us have been around long enough to remember several waves of exodus in the first place. I myself have seen 400 years of it.

Oh. Yeah, Sei frowned.

You and I were alphas once, just like 10% of all betas in existence. Having been once governed by the passions then transitioned into decisions that make sense is like looking back on your teenage years twice over. There is no way I would give my alpha self the keys to my air bike, let alone her own planet and weapons to come back and hunt me with...

Hmm.

But you are helping me answer a difficult question put to me by the other Council members. If we don't do something now, how long will it be before the alpha's manifest destiny succeeds? We got lucky recently, but some in the Jupiterian power structure will be waiting for their next turn.

Here's what I know, Phaedra. We have an arm brace which still seems capable of finding really good change agents, even if we've lost interest in this. We have a dark brain who nonetheless has a real skill with taking control of confined systems, and putting people in them. We have a cyborg who also wants to save herself in a higher dimension than the one she was born in, possibly bringing her entire server culture with her. She also accidentally hacked SIER. We have several allies in Jupiterian politics, including Governor Banner and possibly a very brilliant civic system which we definitely don't want enemy alphas to duplicate. And we still have ourselves, at least as bodies. For whatever that's worth. Us being here as Jupiterians rather than Earthans can still help in some areas.

You're right. Banner shipped back the brace last week, and we've been looking at how the Navajo girl could possibly pull records from SIER. That is still a mystery. But if we cut straight to the bottom line, would it be fair to say that the best way to improve sapiens alpha is to trap it in a mostly digital world, consistent with the conveniences they prefer anyway?

...

...

Neither Sei nor I had the nerve to answer.

You don't have to make that decision. No single person does. But sapiens displaced its predecessors. Extinction is a part of the cycle of life. We too will have our time. I just want to know what you think.

Well, what do *you* think? Sei attempted to get a foothold on the kind of response Phaedra might be expecting.

I think this job is hard. I was haunted by someone once, and I still remember that vividly. Now our entire world is haunted by a massive crowd not fit to govern, led mostly by a handful of people who *might* have been fit to govern, but who are quicker to build a better product than build a better society. We all understand the challenges of the work, but if the people with the means and the position can't do it, then there's no way the people without these could. And in the off chance that Jupiterians a generation from now succeed in defeating us, they will still wipe themselves out less than a century after that. So I'm all for putting them in a box.

!                                                                          ...

Some might say that it's wrong for Miranda, which helped map and advance humanity so far in the first place, would now decide that the Matrix was the safest place for our previous selves. But if you as modern, sane betas cannot see a solution—and you were among the few who cared enough to try/because I don't—then I think the alphas have lost their last advocates with any kind of pull. I know there are others out there who probably have great ideas for teaching all of humanity. But they have not managed to make it to this conversation. Unfortunately, this is where the beginning of a big decision is made.

...

So again. Sei, do we keep trying, or make plans to essentially DSEC all of our remaining predecessors?

Isaiah?

Sei... *sigh*. (*Man, this is tough.*) I still care, but I will always be the guy who was torn apart by the Uranian 10000.

Shiit. Sei hung her head. And will what I tell you in any way influence the Council, she quated.

More than likely, yes. I know where I lean. But if you tell me to wait, then I will hold off.

... Do I have to decide now?

Yes. Because I want your gut reaction, not your self-convincing.

...then. Uh...

# 229. Meeting With the Mighty

Two masked security attendants accompanied the cyborg Mona-R into the office of Reselat, acting Chair of the United Solar Council Committee on Alpha Relations. Though the meeting would only be openly attended by five hologuests and eight material guests, the little cyborg still found herself scared out of her mind in being introduced to such important people. Among the material guests were Phaedra, Sei, Dial, and Jake Nolli.

Although Mona-R had been told a few details about why the mighty governing body over the entire Solar System had suddenly taken an interest in her, she was still very much unclear as to what was going on. It was obvious to her that the book downloader she had briefly possessed lie at the source of the intrigue, and that something in her downloads had either alarmed or fascinated the ruling powers. In apparent attempts not to unsettle her with possibly readable motives, the Council had employed Mr. Nolli to make first contact. He was truly a very nice person. But as the arrangements for her trip to Mars seemed to make themselves (on a track she truly could not stop), the entire affair had done nothing but grow in intimidation. Now here she was, taking a seat before what might be the most publicly powerful group in the history of humankind, about to be questioned regarding God knows what.

Mona-R recognized Jake immediately, and when offered the seat of her choice, chose to sit between him and Aimee, as far from the looming characters of Reselat and Zeta as possible.

Reselat brought the meeting to order with an overview.

*Let us begin everyone. Today we have a guest whom we are going to talk to, in order to get her opinion on some things. As we all know, Mona-R is a Native Dijian and sole reprint of Navajo-9 who, for a little while, had a certain experimental device in her possession. Mona-R, as you may or probably don't know, that device was created by Mr. Nolli here to read hyperfine energy flows for locating individuals capable of changing their society for the better. You were among the people it found, and once Sei here determined that it was you whom the device was tracking, she programmed it to display as a simple book downloader with your name on it, so that you could take the device home and allow it to do what it was really designed to do: This was to possess the wearer and display their subconscious to a jumper located somewhere else, that the wearer may be guided by the jumper to unlock talents for the good of society, talents which they were, up to then, afraid to use. This device was sent to Jupiter during a difficult time as a way of helping the good among your planet continue to work towards the best despite challenges. Sei was one of the people who volunteered to carry and operate as jumper for the device as it found its wearers.*

This was all news to Mona-R who sat curled up scootched closer to Jake, but attentively nonetheless.

*You should note that the wearers were not informed that this was happening or what the true nature of the device was, because during its first use it was discovered just how complicated it was to explain the all of the international security bits, technology, jump consent, individual talent exorcism, and general political dangers of carrying Earth technology past Jupiter's trade blockade. You ultimately had to blank the wearer, and nobody wanted that because it would also partly cost the learnings. Thus you, Mona-R obtained the arm brace through less conspicuous means.*

. . .

*But while you had the brace, something interesting occurred. At some point while you were in stasis with the brace on, you tried to consume some logs you had downloaded pertaining to the Naila, and our actual data save repository at SIER—are you familiar with SIER?*

No, sir.

*It's a giant library where we save humans as data, and this lady here, Aimee Dial, runs it.*

*Whoa,* Mona-R mouthed silently.

*So SIER reported that it had been hacked while you were looking at this data.*

Mona-R's face turned instantly petrified.

*No, no, it's no big deal. You're okay. We investigated, and we know what happened. What's more important, though, is why it happened.*

*You are a sole reprint for your server. Do you know what that means?*

No. Sir.

*But you do know you are a reprint of a persona from Diji who has been given a body here in Astra?*

Yes sir.

*Okay. Well most Dijians are one of several or even thousands from their server. Most server operators will have lots of characters on a single system's population of personalities, and will put a lot of them into Astra. For certain reasons, your server only has one character printed out, and that is you.*

Ohh...

*Not only is this rare, but your server operators—who cannot be here for security reasons—also treat you in a rare way. They basically parented your parents in order to birth you, and have their entire system set up to support your development and yours only. This includes any connections your server is allowed to make to other systems. To make a long story short, your operators received some help in birthing you from a very powerful server company, and they passed on certain key connections which they had to SIER. They said to your operators, "If you want her to follow such and such path (which you know as human data saving), then you'll need your server to have a connection to the organization that does it, SIER. From Diji, you consumed the Naila information while still wearing the brace in Astra. The brace read data from SIER and you effectively "jiggled the protocols" on behalf of your entire server to get a precise kind of data out of your research. You acted as your own possessor, and did some other things that I won't get into again for security reasons.*

*Now, there are more details to this story, but let me stop and check. Do you have any questions?*

Am I in trouble?

*Not at all. We're trying to make a couple of decisions, and need the perspective of an entire data-savable culture whose interests are wrapped up in a single person. That's why you're here.*

Oh...

*And I'll get to the questions next.*

Oh. Okay.

*Then we're good to continue?*

Yes sir.

*Great. Here's the first question: How do you like your life in Astra compared to Diji?*

It's nice. I mainly come out here as meditation 'cause I don't have to work or pay real bills really. So it's kind of like a vacation.

*Would you live in Astra full time if you could?*

Mona-R shook her head emphatically. Nooo. The vacation wears off pretty quickly if I stay too long. The people aren' t happy here. And we cyborgs are treated real badly. I just mind myself because you can get some cool stuff out here if you just stick to the stores and don' t talk to anybody.

*But we checked. Don't you live in a pod? How do you have room for the things you buy?*

I' m an artifact hunter in Diji, Mona-R beamed with thinly veiled pride. So I' m good at reselling. Then I go back into Diji and can just sense where to find the thing I just saw in Astra.

A couple of whispers sailed around the room.

*I'm impressed. Apparently you are multitalented. We call that reverse printing. You can instantiate an object in your world based on what you've captured from outside of your world. Kind of like a main vampire hunter in a movie who will need to manifest a castle or a stake in order to be who he is. You can almost certainly do this because, again, you are a sole reprint, and what you need or want is what your local world ends up having. This ability is a rough descendant of computer vision and basic object identification, but with a rendering process downstream from what was captured. If you were to be moved off of your server then you would lose this ability, and if your operators were to print another Dijian besides you then the talent would drop to almost zero as the determiner of world-building wouldn't be you anymore, it would be them.*

Ohh...

*So what I'm hearing is that you prefer Diji. How about Naturals? What do you think of them?*

Mona-R frowned.

...

I try to stay away from them.

*If there were a way to fix the way naturals behave, how would you do it, based on what you've learned?*

Mona-R had a sneaking suspicion of what this group's motives might be. Phaedra could tell.

We too have been harassed by naturals, Phaedra added. And part of the purpose of this meeting is to determine how widespread the problem is, so that we can know if we need to adjust our policies towards them. This may be our only opportunity to talk to a sole reprint who is also a cyborg, living on our main rival planet,... yes. If you could just give us your honest opinion, that would be valuable.

I think naturals are dangerous. They do bad things to cyborgs who try to move out of the pods where I live. I know it's wrong, but I try to stay away from them.

Sei leaned back in her seat. Phaedra clasped her hands. Reselat nodded sternly before responding.

*Ah, it's a dilemma we face all the time just for being beta! How transparent to be in a conversation! I guess I'll just say it. We're not sure if the alphas should be handled more strictly than we've been handling them, and are considering recruiting you to help us study advanced world-building for certain military purposes. What you've been studying—saving yourself or an entire culture—is something that we are also interested in, and your unique abilities may actually help us do this. There are a lot of options with this technology, some of them peaceful some of them not, but you and your resonance with an entire world can certainly contribute value, if you are interested.*

Mona-R's eyes lit up.

*My, don't you look excited? Does that sound like something that interests you?*

Yes sir!

*Oh, haha. Nice. Then the purpose of this meeting is essentially met. Do you know who this lady is?* Reselat gestured towards Phaedra.

She's Phaedra Zeta, Leader of Miranda Mapping and friend to Raliolite, the saint who was also the first beta data save by the Naila.

*Correct. She may have a position for you.*

Really? That would be aweso!—uh thank you, sir.

*That position is on Earth, so we would need to move your server out of Jupiter air space, this means some of your world's links may change.*

Mona-R tried to follow this part.

*Now, we move servers all the time, and have a process for it which Phaedra can explain. But if you need to give this more thought then, by all means.*

Um, yes sir. I'll take some time to think more about this before accepting.

*Very good. Do you have any more questions for me?*

No sir.

*Alright, questions from the attendees then?*

And with that, the Q&A ensued. The meeting would last another hour as Mona-R and the other attendees got to know each other better.

# 230. Preparations

Although not particularly enthusiastic about moving their investment out of Jupiter airspace and into Earth airspace, the owners of Navajo-9 were compensated generously for their trouble. It was far easier for the owners themselves to sponsor this transition out of private interest than it was for the enemy of the Jupiterian government to do it, though the execution expertise certainly belonged to the latter. As Navajo-9 moved out of range of a few key services and into the range of many more, Mona-R's experiences within Diji also changed to reflect the new dynamics available to her server.

Changing a Diji server's location may involve several kinds of data migration and port swap to accomplish. Depending on how drastic the move, how essential the service, and how extensive the interplanetary firewall, you may or may not need to leave a relay station behind; you may or may not need to "event-deprecate and blacklist" (EBB) entire classes of events. You may or may not need to expatriate (EXPAT) the served object itself as if it was, say, a single company with a moveable headquarters. Lastly, if you really needed a certain outside service but just couldn't access it anymore, you might have to clone its historical dynamics and run a mock version of it yourself. In order to keep Mona-R's life experience as seamless as possible despite her home server losing nearly 1/3 of its core connections, affiliates of the Solar Council assisted in applying a combination of these to the world within Navajo-9, including a sudden move to another planet by four of Mona-R's long time acquaintances, the closure and demolition of one of the schools she attended, a surge of new civic development around her apartment, and the rise of a powerful new technology for reading trustworthiness in another.

Had Mona-R not known she was a Dijian reprintable outside of her native dimension, it would have appeared as though her world was simply undergoing rapid change. But of course she knew full well that her native world was merely a simulation that had been "upgraded." Still, more glaring than the changes inside of the server world would be the changes outside. Earthan interactions—overwhelmingly cross-human-friendly, wealthier, smarter, and with far more social opportunity—brought with them a sudden removal of the cap placed on a non-biohn's social standing. It was here that Mona-R began to realize just how subconsciously miserable she had been under Jupiter's "nature for naturals" airspace. Despite not really having the capacity to hate anyone over this, she immediately found herself oddly unsympathetic regarding the troubles present in alpha-run worlds. This lack of sympathy for Jupiter as a system didn't quite extend to its individuals on the whole, though it was rendered even more pronounced given her service at Miranda.

As someone who had personally witnessed (and in several cases, played a role in) over 400 years of societal change, Phaedra recognized the value in having an adaptable perspective. While she was certainly interested in training Mona-R's various abilities to cross contexts, she was more interested in simply providing a source of support for the up-to-then isolated Dijian. Regardless of what Mona-R's official title was, Phaedra tasked her with the job of hunting for and archiving frequentic swaps in alpha and beta societies. Where alphas loved reboots in their media, betas tended to treat reboots like training data: good for reinforcing, bad for generalized growth. Where betas relied heavily on el as a rating system for accepting another's company, alphas relied more on conversational rapport informed by the interlocutor's social mobility. But what external factors could be used to map these two? And so, for the next two years, Mona-R would mature drastically in both her understanding of the world and in her ability to connect with the Astrans around here. She never lost the cute and quiet curiosity so ingrained in her personality, but there was no doubt that Phaedra's natural boldness and dignified intelligence continually rubbed off on her.

From their very first contact, Mona-R and Jake warmed up to each other, and the two became fast friends. They visited parks and museums, had lunch, and even went on a couple of international road trips together. Many were the nights during which they stayed up late just talking—about life, about nature, about being human—especially as the two of them represented the farthest ends of humanity's spectrum. Jake was an entirely natural born, unmodded sapiens alpha who would probably live for another 5 decades. Mona-R was an entirely machine-printed sapiens delta born of data. She could expect to live at least another 50 decades. At the very least. But when you lived that long, you tended to take a different perspective on the potentially all-consuming wars of old humans. Mona-R had seen firsthand what things looked like when a small group of naturals could lead others to toe the line, and spark a general distrust between any two people who consumed the great story differently. Over time, Jake gradually revealed to Mona-

R more of the big picture regarding Earth's future handling of Jupiter; at some point, Mona-R finally put the pieces together.

So we're going to either put all naturals into the data space, beta-ize their biology, or target-pandemicize their aggression.

Yes, one of those three.

Good.

Yeah, I agree. Even before working here, I've always known that we naturals weren't really made to rule over something as vast as nature. Our own houses, maybe. But not the space which sponsored everybody else's houses.

Mona-R frowned in sympathy. I would think this must be hard on you, especially given what your parents endured.

Having a mom who chose a cyborg father to birth me, then watching that father get screwed by a bunch of modded naturals in his work was confusing to say the least. But I was too young to really see what was happening. Even as what they'd have called a "test tube baby" hundreds of years ago, I'm still entirely natural born biologically and genetically, but because you can't program organics nearly as easily, you end up with a bunch of out of control behaviors which only out of control people can render sensical in everyone else. We naturals get behind impassioned people and movies and causes because these serve as outlets for things that we ourselves can't direct. I can't tell you how annoying it is to hear us singing freedom this, freedom that, when all it is is the freedom to be controlled by our inner bacteria—making it unfree for anyone else who opposes this. We're definitely not fit to rule nature. That's why we lost our own planet to our computer-merged selves to begin with.

Why don't you become beta? You could easily. Then we could hang out longer, Mona-R smiled.

Well I don't know. I like having a time-limit in this game. Some people are fine having control over when their favorite thing stops. But I get immersed. The last thing I want to think about while I'm doing something is how I plan to stop doing it. I know it sounds silly, but there's no difference to me between 80 years and 800 years when all I know is tomorrow. I don't want to feel like a vampire watching entire countries come and go. I just want to live my short but very stable life.

Ah. So you're okay with alphas basically going extinct and turning into betas and Dijians completely?

Yes, besides the ego claim to rule over something badly, all being natural does at this point is make us permanently immature age-wise and reckless and short-sighted in the processes we claim to build. Phaedra and the Council aren't so inhumane that they're just gonna wipe everyone out. Many of them used to be alphas. They're just looking for ways to escort those alphas out of the DJ booth before they blow up or strip everything to pad their short lives.

Hm.

Imagine what a world it would be like if we didn't have to watch that stuff on the news every day. It would be nice, I think.

Mona-R leaned comfortably on Jake's shoulder.

* * *

For her part, Aimee was not a fan of any of the changes taking place among her Miranda friends. Ever since the faux-hack on SIER, the usually bubbly director had soured in her perception of everyone else's understanding of her organization. SIER was the ultimate library for finding all humans that had ever been formally documented. It was the mega-institutional successor to the Naila, who ceased to exist centuries prior. It was a highly complex IT operation which still needed to be respected and defended as such. Yet the Council had given this little doll a pat on the head, a lollipop, an instant super-promotion into the highest circles for *accidentally* breaking Dial's carefully crafted security system.

Next, was the issue with Isaiah. Ever since he had moved back to Earth and started regularly attending that male group, he wasn't nearly as receptive to her control. In fact, he seemed to have lost interest in Dial completely. The computer-turned-human had always been distant and forlorn, but now he was distant and inconveniently decisive. Dial imagined that most of this was due to the divergence with Sei / Genevieve, but whatever was going on seemed to remove a potential source of excitement for Aimee. As much of a life as she had lived, sources of personal thrill usually came easily, but Dial had always been picky in selecting such sources. It had been at least a decade since one of them got away. True, it might have been possible for her to play the waiting game, but why should she have to wait for something that her admirers usually jumped at easily? It was actually pretty insulting.

And then there was that whole thing with Sei's psychopath friend. The whole Sei / Genevieve space, actually. That was *really* another matter…

Right after that first meeting with Mona-R had ended and almost everyone else had left the room and call, Reselat expressed his relief.

**Exhale* That's one hurdle down. Onto the next. Sei, I don't suppose it would be too much to ask to keep this Langley business simple, would it?*

I don't know how easy that will be.

*I don't understand why we're even entertaining this,* Dial protested.

Because with Sei solo on Jupiter now, but with access to a very ambitious and very effective world-writer, we need to really think carefully about how to use this alliance to implement our alpha strategy, Phaedra reiterated.

Dial rolled her eyes in a huff. *But there's no way we want this Langley person knowing about Sei's connections to Earth. I'm pretty sure she can't be trusted. She's also far from everything we believe in.*

I partly agree with you, Dial. But we all know the difficulties of building alliances when secrets are involved. I'm not convinced that Sei can't just tell Langley who she is and air the whole thing. It doesn't mean we are just going to ship her here and ask her to join us. Or that we need to have any affiliation with her at all.

*That's exactly what we did with this Mona girl.*

Mona-R. We don't call you "Aim."

**Grumble**

And there are colossal differences between the two cases. Mona-R is a blank slate. Ko'an Langley is a long-damaged history. Mona-R is an asset who offers us new paths. Langley is a liability who offers her own people older punishments. We want the girl over here, the Author over there. I hope you can see the logic in this.

Also, Ko'an is a dangerous enemy to anyone on a personal level, but there's no need for us to be enemies. I'd really like to tell her. And if things go wrong and she murders me, you can always reprint me, Sei joked.

Don't joke about things like that, Phaedra admonished. I'm trying to support your case, but comments like that don't make it easy.

Sorry.

I'm partly concerned that their government will get wind of this and make trouble, though Sei is not backed by us. She will actually *oppose* us if the plan goes well. But we don't want her getting sucked into allegiants and posturing either. She has a job to do. I just want to make sure she has the fewest obstructions in doing it.

So you haven't reconsidered loaning Isaiah to SIER? I still think it would round out your networks very nicely.

That's Dial's decision.

Isaiah isn't qualified for any role I know at Records. He can't just march in there and pull up an executive chair. Please afford me at least some control over my operation.

And there you have it. There are plenty of other roles for Isaiah—especially if he's the one carrying the Angel finder.

This is madness, Aimee muttered, exasperated.

What's madness?

How all of this changed so suddenly. One day we're one big happy family exploring other planets and sending friends off to make another one better. Now we have all these chess pieces scattered across all sides morphing our archive technology into a giant cage for a whole race. And no one seems to be bothered by all this. One naïve little girl trips over a security fence and we're ready to hit the red button on all of alpha civilization.

You've never expressed anything but support for this path. We all support it. Only Sei and Watcheye are willing to act on the alphas' behalf in spite of this. So why the frustration? Phaedra interrogated Dial sternly.

*Ladies, I smell elephants in this room which are best handled among yourselves. Here's what I see. It is neither safe, necessary, nor desirable for Sei to attempt subterfuge with her eccentric friend. Phaedra is right. We have made all of the correct decisions to distance ourselves from Sei's actions, and are in no way obligated to come to endorse her if things get difficult. This is something you yourself have agreed to, Sei. But should rumors be spread and affairs between the Council and Jupiter turn ugly, we will simply take the gloves off and vanquish the alphas immediately, starting with their public allegiants, regardless of which side they serve. It will fall solely to Sei and her friend to exercise discretion—which includes informing no one. Not prison directors. Not governors.*

*No one. This can change on a case by case basis. But given that interesting event Sei showed us in Carlsbad, I believe it is possible for the key parties to exercise discretion.*

*The day will likely come sooner than later that we will need a ruthless professional to implement some of the more challenging parts of the alpha conversion. While none of us wishes war or unnecessary bloodshed upon anyone, the alphas are likely to call for blood at some point in the process, and we will benefit from a network of insiders who can connect us to Jelal Prison System's operational structures. From what I can tell, this Langley may yet assist us as long as we are fair towards the few choice people she deems to be family. That is a small price to pay for proxy control of an entire human containment system, so we should refrain from exercising our maneuvers on the Command Warden, the cellmate named Illit Franklin-Carter, and possibly the casual partner. We will also avoid affecting all known allies and users of the brace, including the Whits, Ballant, and Governor Banner. Remember, our first priority is neutralization of the alpha threat. Our backup plan is confinement. Our very last resort is destruction. If we succeed, there should still be some alphas existent in Astra no matter how vulgar their basic inclinations. But they will never again control a planet, and—ideally—will be incapable of malicious vengeance. Vengeance for sport, maybe. For calculated preemptive protection, maybe. But uninformed, blindly following, or partisan hate will not be sustainable in their neurology anymore.*

*All of this is to say the following: Sei, I commend you for the path you have chosen. Phaedra I respect your maturity and your willingness to adapt to the plan, for everyone's sake—including the alphas themselves. Aimee, I hope you realize that we will need your expertise more than ever. Our decision to knowingly turn alphas into an endangered species does not make anyone feel good, but unlike the alphas, we at least intend zero bloodshed. Sapiens alphas will simply become de-venged sapiens Is, Dijians, or betas. That is all. If they riot, marshal their militaries, turn to institutionalized hate crimes, or anything of the sort, then they will, in typical fashion, bring trouble upon themselves. We will not act unless they threaten those outside of their own house.*

Even if they start killing iyohns left and right? Sei asked in what was almost a heartfelt plea.

*We will speed up our conversion processes, but this cannot turn this into a Jupiter vs the Solar System war.*

Sei, Aimee, and Phaedra were silent.

*Remember, we are still beta. The long-term is clearer to us than it was to our alpha predecessors. As are the costs, the time spent living with the consequences, and the amount of effort and energy put into cleaning up all messes, regardless of who made them. It isn't logical to do this recklessly, but it also isn't logical to let the alphas continue. We have an opportunity to move while they are still reeling from the close of two major national regimes, and frankly we were lucky that these regimes simply expired. We cannot expect to get lucky again. Phaedra do you agree?*

Phaedra acknowledged.

*Sei, do you agree?*

Sei nodded her head in affirmation.

*Aimee, do you agree?*

Yes, Dial sulked.

*Okay. I realize the rearrangement of roles may have strained relations somewhat, but this is the best we can do and the most peaceful way to do it. I hope we can work to maintain our unity.*

Aimee sank her forehead into her palm. Okay, I'll keep doing what I can.

*Thank you, Aimee. I mean it.*

…

*If there's nothing else, let's vacate this room. Sei, the Council asks nothing of you but that you exercise discretion and encourage anyone you tell to do so as well. The day the alphas fall into a panic over this is the day the entire process becomes very painful for them. Either way, their days are numbered. Until then, we will be de-venging them quietly.*

I understand.

* * *

Phaedra walked alone with Sei beneath the Mars night.

**To be Sei or Genevieve, that is the question,** Zeta offered a tamed smile.

I keep thinking back to that talk with Isaiah. "I really admire you for what you've decided Sei, but I can't."

Well not many people can stand there and say, "Yeah, it *is* better to crush this menace, but I'll stay behind and fight for them as long as I can." It is as just as any due process humans have ever created, with the alphas themselves on trial. You're defending the indefensible and we all know it, but even they are entitled to representation. I'll say it for the hundredth time: I'm really proud of you.

When we were still hoping to make change from the inside, it was better to do so in this shell. But as the Jupiterians start to catch on to what's happening to them, it'll be much more helpful for them to have an ally among their enemies. They'll need me as Genevieve; some might even stake their survival on my victory. But the fight on their behalf isn't at all winnable.

**I'm so glad Reselat is our chair.**

I'm glad they finally nominated you to the Council a few years ago. Without level heads, this all would have been much worse. MUCH worse.

**I love how reasonable he is,** Phaedra nudged Sei in an uncharacteristic moment of cheer. **When you asked him about sparing the good alphas still trying to make things better, and the two of you came up with this whole "You'd better find them before I do" thing, and the fact that he helped come up with a plan to not convert everyone instantly, says a lot about both of you. Besides being lawyers, you guys are also like teachers, parents even. You know what your kids are capable of handling, and are being judicious in how you let punishment take place.**

Well, I'm technically not a punisher here.

**But you conceded that it was necessary. Your vote for one side but choice to fight for the other is what swayed us all.**

The Wyat's world was so jumbled up in politics, his house so tangled. Ballant and his battles with his own culture. Whit and their required maneuvering. Ko'an and that whole lost world. They spend the best parts of their lives navigating all these convoluted relationships involving other people, working so hard to figure out how to get more things to support more of their obligated mazes. But they already have so much. They live in the sky, for God's sake. They fly around and have cars and computers that do all the work for them. And even under their power systems' racketeering, even if those systems give them nothing, they can still live full lives. But not only do they not know this, they get angry and are so focused on destroying their perceived enemy that they'll just let everything else around them crumble.

...

But I know there are some who really are trying. It would have been nice to have the Angel finder to help me locate them.

**In the times to come, that will be more of a dangerous technology if it were ever taken from you, not to mention a distraction for your**

current kind of work and a surefire way to get the Council accused of something it really had nothing to do with.

I know. It was kinda nifty while it lasted, though.

Heh. I'm sure.

Phaedra and Sei stopped to admire the view from an overlook.

So what's the grand plan again, Phaedra? As Reselat sees it.

We are going to use a certain method that only Kantrell and his neurochemists know about to trigger something that only Davis-pi and his engineers can understand to remotely engrantz the users of a certain product or technology that the Export Committee or Communications Commission can control. It will amplify during sleep and may take as few as 4 days and as many 300 days to inhibit a certain specific aggression-based firing chain in the biohn brain. The approach is slow acting as to not arouse suspicion, and can be helped by us seeding a trend, through you and people like the Whits, that the alphas can feel they are magically gravitating towards. As long as Kyle keeps supporting you as our replacement for Isaiah, and can throw his weight behind the Future Jobs Club with Sei as Director, we can gradually change many of the people without them knowing. I hear we can block our own technology on devices or certain products known to be held by our allies, though none of us is sure that this would make a difference because we think our allies would be the same under de-venging. Your friend Langley, however, would definitely not be the same without her capacity for malicious vengeance, neither would people like her who are in some way on the same side as us—destabilizing the alpha planetary rule. But yeah, it's a mass permanent grantzing operation which aims to tame the original sapiens over the course of a couple of years. We want to remove the threat they pose using calculation, not weaponry.

I still can't get used to the idea of disabling their humanity in that way.

We betas are human too. As the cyborgs have been for centuries. Our humanity, just like the so-called naturals, rests in the right to life and self-preservation. And the fact that we're shaped this way. It's funny how those people in their zeal can use words like freedom, life, and humanity as if it applies only to them and their preferred values, not to others. As if the trees don't also have life, or the trans don't also have humanity. They've even fooled us into thinking that their freedom to destroy whatever they want when they feel it's appropriate is somehow the *definition* of freedom—above and beyond the freedom to choose your form. Or be stuck in a form you didn't choose. Or to reclaim your rights when someone else has squashed them. Not all freedoms are the same. We shouldn't be fooled into thinking that their claimed right to make idle loud war against us is the same as our right to live without endless harassment.

Hmm.

What they display is not the essence of humanity, because that is a property of all humans. What they display is vitriolic, other-crushing pride. Nothing more.

Not all of them. Most of them just want to live their lives.

And that's why you will be their defender, Genevieve. Because you are in a better position to raise up the best in the individual. Unfortunately, the sum of individuals in this case is a mob. And if the good among them can't find ways to overtake the bad among them by building—not through pointless laughable retorts or irreparable doldrums—then we have no choice but to sink that ship. Maybe God will grant exceptions to the goodhearted among them who never had the strength to act in ways that only they uniquely could.

...

The original humans are a ship of fools. But you're doing the right thing in giving exceptions one last chance to prove themselves.

Do you think alphas will still be around in the 30th century?

Only if we reprint them as 1s. Otherwise, no.

Sei pondered a moment before replying. ...Me neither.

# 231. Her Room the Confessional

**So what was it you wanted to talk about?** Ko'an inquired.

Well, this is very difficult for me, Sei answered hesitantly. You know how you used to ask me questions about my background, but I wouldn't answer them?

**Yes.**

Today I may be able to answer some of them.

**I hope your secrets aren't dangerous.**

Wait. What's that supposed to mean?

**I already know you moved from Earth. But I do not know why. I also know that you are too open-minded, so you must be a high-class beta. You are too smart to be a maid. But more than that, you do not ask questions whose answers might get you in trouble, and get squirmy when you think I am about to break the law. That tells me you are laying low. But I will not ask if you don't offer to tell.**

And thank you for that. Before I tell you what I have to tell you, it would be nice if you could give me an idea of how surprising this is going to be for you. I won't confirm or deny, but if you had to guess, what is it that you think I haven't told you?

**I don't guess. It's dangerous and irritating to flail with no real clue.**

Okay. I'll leave it then. If I tell you something very secret, could you swear not to tell anyone, not even Lucine?—And assume—assume that I'd have my reasons for telling you, but if you told anyone else it would mean a world of problems for a lot of people. Starting with you.

Ko'an's countenance stiffened. **Go on.**

Ask me how big this secret is on a scale of 1–10.

**How big is your secret?**

11.

Ko'an pulled back slightly, then rose from her throne, turning her back to Sei. **Only government secrets are 9 and above. What does this rank again?**

11.

**And why would you tell me?**

Because I'm pretty sure you will be my only ally in this. At least until things pick up steam.

**Will my knowing endanger me?**

No, but if I cannot tell you then I will have to leave immediately, no questions asked.

**Why?**

Because this business is very complicated, and the people watching me will need to know where you stand.

**They know about me?**

They know about everyone.

… Ko'an began pacing.

But they are betas, as you probably guessed. So they don't work at all like your mother.

**Are they threatening you?**

No.

**Are they watching us now?**

No.

**How do I know that?**

Whether they see you or not is actually irrelevant. Even if they were watching, it would not change things. They gave me clearance to bring you in, knowing full well about everything.

**Then you must have told them.**

As Lucine no doubt told you many things.

Ko'an easily understood the analogy, but wasn't at all sure whether the looming information was something she needed to hear. **You are to them what the Command Warden is to me?**

Exactly. And then some.

**And I am to you…?**

Sei searched intently for a parallel. Your holoroom: a reliable record of all you ever wanted to tell to everyone, but couldn't tell to anyone… until you found a single listener who understood it all. Surprised sometimes, but judgment free.

Ko'an exhaled quietly, regaining her ability to look Sei in the eye. **I consider you my friend.**

The feeling is mutual.

**Will I lose who I am after knowing?**

I doubt it.

**I suppose it wouldn't matter. Okay. Tell me what it is.**

If you share this with anyone, there will likely be trouble. And it will be on you, not me. You'll understand this as soon as you know.

**Fine. I am ready.**

♃ I am here on Jupiter to warn natural borns in as subtle but far reaching a way as possible: They may have forgotten their crazy fickle aggression towards every other planet in the Solar System, but the rest of Earth has not. In ways that were not shared with me, we betas of Earth *will* remove the alpha threat permanently. We have no intention of destroying anyone or shedding a single drop of blood, because that is not the beta way. But pure naturals, praesciens, and machina—all biohns will find themselves in their own version of DSEC. Not as inmates, but as their normal selves… With the capacity for malicious vengeance removed from their power to calculate.

Ko'an furrowed her brow.

...

...

...

...

...

**Heh. That sounds very apocalyptic. But so very beta. And I thought my wish to be a god was excessive.**

Haha. Yeah. Right?

**Haha,** Ko'an chuckled a little, then turned very serious. **You're not kidding.**

No.

**Like the heat lines in the prisons.**

A cheap imitation of our various tools.

**Mm. That is very bad.**

Not exactly. The point is to remove the aggression, not to kill. As long as it can be done quietly, Jupiter's cities will not fall into self-inflicted anarchy. You can already see the riots on every corner, though, if this information leaked out to people whose conversations you wouldn't be able to monitor every hour of the day.

**Yes, I can imagine the strife. But why have you told me this?**

Because over the last few years, alphas have run out of time. Earth observed natural humans' mania, and waited until its governments became complacent. I was one of the people who weighed in on it. I was one of two people who begged to give the alphas a second chance. Then I worked for the Wyats, saw your life, and concluded that alphas just weren't there as people. Not because of you, but because the situations that you, the Warden, Mark, and countless other people I have seen on the street will continue to pop up as an endless struggle sometimes spilling over onto others' worlds under this silly alpha pride.

Ko'an did not like this last statement. **And who are *you* to judge us?**

Ⴕ We are a ship which has been rammed too many times. I made the case for individuals worth sparing. But this isn't death we're talking about. Only the removal of the kind of malicious vengeance that causes all of Jupiter to, say, attack Earth in 40 years. We betas live a long time. That's like tomorrow for us.

...

We're not judging you. We're disarming an operation you belong to.

**I do NOT like this.**

Nobody does. But you take a good look at that world out there, Author, and tell me how it sees you. It hates you. Fears you. Then follows destroyers and lives fat off of the destruction without a care. And if you died tomorrow, would anyone besides the Warden and a handful of people care? Would they?

Ko'an shook her head in unsettled denial.

Anyway. I joked that you could kill me right here for any number of reasons, but there was no need for that. And I know we're not so fragile as to punish each other for where we each started before we met. I was always a beta missionary to Jupiter. But you and I really *are* friends now as well.

...

Ko'an, your life reflects something hidden in every man and woman. But even from your prison, you at least keep working for a kind of justice. Tell me, is this so-called "natural born" world around you a naturally just one, or do you have to force it to be so?

...

You make people sleep longer and more deeply in the bed they made for themselves. Would alphas ever handle things in a way remotely close to the peaceful way I've described to you?

Ⴕ I hope you see that the games naturals play with all the worlds around them can't be allowed to continue forever.

Ko'an closed her eyes. **I'll help.**

And if—wait. What?

**I said I'll help. I do not know why. And I truly do not understand. It sounds too mega to be true. But—**

Come with me, then. Let's go to Mars for a few days. Let me show you everything that's out there!

**Careful, I might hit on you.**

Heh. Please don't.

**No, you and The Warden are sacred ground.**

Ko'an paced around the living room some more. **I find what you have told me to be disturbing. But yes, we should travel so that I can believe you. I have one more range before I must return to work, so if we plan to leave, it should be soon.**

Fine. In two djays then.

Ko'an tried hard not to light up. She had never traveled outside of Jupiter before.

**You should know that I am only agreeing to keep your secret because I'm crazy. And because I have no other friends besides you and the Warden.**

No you're not crazy. You're the soon-to-be subject of a fascinating book, and the future writer of newer, but fitting histories for the humans we once were.

Ko'an managed an unusually humbled smile.

# 232. Till the Wine Runs Out

Although she would not admit it, Ko'an had a blast during her first two days touring Mars with Sei. On the third day, the two were scheduled to meet a friend whom Sei called Isaiah, but it seemed he was a no-show. Exhausted from the long hours spent touring the various spectacular sights of the red planet, Sei crashed in the hotel room, leaving Ko'an to go for a night stroll on her own.

"Excuse me," a somewhat hoity toity blonde woman with perfect skin and a white sash accosted Ko'an. "I've come to this balcony every night, and don't recognize you here."

**This is my first visit.**

"Oh. Beautiful sight, isn't it?"

**It is. But I do not have much of an eye for these things.**

"Well, they say it is all relative. Beauty, that is. I'm sure no one has much of an eye."

**Hm.**

. . .

...

After a couple of seconds of silence, Ko'an turned to leave, but was interrupted.

"Can I ask you a favor? I'm in the mood to be awash in warm emhim. No stress. No overtures. May I buy you a drink and request that you watch the night here with me until the drink is finished? I promise on my blood I will not advance on you or encourage you to talk to me. We betas can sometimes tune our senses to pick up vibes. I'm just in the mood to sense some. I may talk at you a little bit, mind you, but you don't have to reply."

**I think. I would rather not.**

"Okay. You might not have this opportunity again, though. I imagine people don't just get a chance to stand under such a beautiful night with a healing energy offered to them for free."

**Is that a challenge?**

"No. Just a probability. Unless you get offers like these all the time."

**Hmm...** Ko'an was clearly skeptical.

"Look, no funny business. You can stand five feet away from me, or two feet. And if you don't like my energy after trying it, I will raise a small tab for you to come back and make use of tomorrow."

**Oh. In that case—**

"Good! What would you like? Let's visit the bar so that you can watch the drink being made. I guess I must be so typical of every beta you meet: We're always aware of when we need to do extra things to build trust when we haven't earned it."

(*Hm. That does seem to be true.*)

Ko'an chose a drink, and the two ladies returned to the balcony.

Surprisingly, the not-so hoity toity healer raised her glass. "Till the wine runs out."

Once again, that annoying little habit of Ko'an's reared its head again. She smiled. **Till the wine runs out.**

The two leaned over the 7th floor balcony railing in silence for a while. After two quiet minutes, however, Ko'an began to feel considerably warm and tingly in her arms and shoulders. Certain that the healer lady had something to do with it, she glanced to her left.

The lady closed her eyes, tilting her head back in joyously slowed breath. "My friends say that two feet is ideal. Closer than that starts to get uncomfortable." She then waved Ko'an over.

The Author scooted over to the healer.

How warm was the faint wind poured over Ko'an's body… From then on, she would sip her wine slowly, more deliberately.

The lady brushed her golden hair with her fingertips before returning her gaze to the darkened horizon.

Ko'an's eyes also seemed to want to turn to the place gazed upon by the lady. A lone tower tucked amidst the navy silhouettes of mountains. It was probably a relay station of some sort. It also could have been the Eiffel Tower flown all the way from Earth, only to disembark in some hilly corner where it would not be bothered for a while.

Black clouds crept solemnly, yet respectfully across the still blacker Mars night sky. Traces of their rims could be seen, burned chaotically about their edges as if sharpened by God, though the listlessly morphing march of such shapes seemed to rob the work of any sublimity. No, it wasn't good enough. It could be better. Into the trash with these silver-edged blotches; three minutes more on their eastward trudge and they too would be consigned to their ethereal aftermath.

A sip of red last time tasted like wine. Yet Ko'an's next sip tasted more like berries. Some unidentifiable spice. A lightly tense tingle in the neck rode that *whoosh* that you hear when something inside of the body stretches, the eardrums undulating as an orchestra's tympani announcing the next dramatic moment. Alas, only a muscle.

Dizzy, dizzy beneath the 7th floor heights. Or was it the 4th planet? She leaned heavily over her weakening shoulders, her vision falling into slight blur. The Author, however, was brought back to reality by the raised arm of the healer to her left as another sip was taken. The latter was only staring into space.

What made a person stare at something like that? What caused them to fixate so intensely upon something that you'd swear some kind of primordial egg would hatch from the target at any moment? Many had claimed that The Author's gaze was intimidating, but had she ever said the same of anyone else's stare? If not, then it is true when they say that there is a first time for everything. The healer wasn't even looking at her. Yet she found the distant gaze into nowhere to be more intimidating than most things. Why was that? The healer wasn't even paying attention to these questions, it seemed. Was that it? Was this stranger so intimidating because she could stare into dark infinity without a plan and capture whatever came? Sei was like this. Not your boldest character, but certainly among your bravest. Existentially, that is. Ko'an could tell that without any deep thought put into it. Yes, Sei was brave. Had she really come out here, into the potentially mournful emptiness of space just to show a professional punisher one face of serenity? A colorful carnival plopped onto a rock countless miles from home. Why was she even still around? Why was Ko'an clearly starting to trust her? What did it mean? And how was this healer triggering all these thoughts without saying anything?

Ko'an considered asking the healer lady a silly question. *Are you magical?* But there was probably no need to build such a doomed line of questioning here. Words would only interrupt the flow of it all, and that flow was smooth as could be.

Suddenly, Ko'an began to feel very tired. The tingles had lulled her into deep comfort, but now she somehow felt that passing out was a possibility. In this state, even her internal thoughts got tongue-tied., and words began to pour out unchecked.

The star, the lights, the man and woman. The force / of gun/ man, woman and child. And in / the blood, the seeds of many worlds have been and gone. For every man had his time. Every woman had her counter. The tick and the hand as necessary complements.

> And in / the blood, short lives saw short term solutions. Longer lives knew that not everything had to be done today. Not everything was an emergency. But complacent were the headstones and epilogues of tangles who walked for but a brief stretch of years. Above the eternal planet they ruled, as an ant claiming a mountain. A million ants eating a house until it was no home for anybody. Then they ate each other. But those were dark thoughts.

> Dark as dim clouds marching with their silver edges. Without the edge, dreary. But with it? Nice. A touch of highlight just to let the eye and the memory know who was there.

Ko'an could feel her strange companion looking at her, but lacked the energy to ask any questions. Mars was as good a place as any to rest after 41 years of challenges. Yet, wordlessly, the healer seemed to say, *Earth, I'm from there. Nearly every day is like this, because we don't have time to condition our next few centuries for permanent disappointment. How about you, where are you from? Does everyone wake up there determined to make all within their conception into a testament to the good?*

The Golden Rule. Yes, that was the filter. No one had to tell you that this is what they were using to separate good sapiens from bad. *If I were you, I'd want some heroes around right about now, but that would imply them coming out of their caves and doing for me, a stranger. Would I ever do that for them? Come out of my immediate sits on the board of directors with a tall glass of anything they offer as long as it accords with Unicode and the red season of. Season of. Season, I really like my friend Sei but who, who I tell you who is this lady who offered to buy me a random drink only to watch me stumble here without walking. But *sip*. Hey man, why the guards, don't you know that your prison is in the mind? My mind is sober even on drunk and despite the holiday taken from the work of punishing others for their sins—*

"Hey. Hey Misst. Are you okay?"

**Misst? Ko'an rubbed her eyes groggily. How did you know?**

"I know a lot of things. Here. Let's capture a selfie."

The lady held up her ring and tapped it. Before the timer hit zero, she smiled and put her arm around Ko'an, who managed a quite-passable expression of some sort. Finally, the lady tapped her ring to Ko'an's to transfer the image just taken.

"For posterity." The healer lady held up her empty glass.

But Ko'an still had some wine left.

The Author returned to the hotel room to discover Sei wide awake, scrolling through the streams. Hey AWOL, where've you been?

I was just walking around. Had the strangest experience with some lady.

Really? How so?

She stood next to me and healed me of something. I'm not sure what happened.

Did she blank you?

I don't think so.

Well, you wouldn't know if she did.

Ko'an swiped her ring and projected the recent selfie. It was quite fun now that I consider—

Sei's jaw dropped when she saw the image, causing Ko'an to pucker in confusion.

Langley, do you know who that is?

No.

That's Phaedra! My friend Phaedra Zeta of Miranda!

What!?

Just then, Sei received a message on her ring, and immediately read it aloud. Heh. Joker. It's her.

Really? What did she say?

She says, "Swapped transports with Isaiah to meet your friend myself. I approve."

Ko'an half threw up her hands. What the?

But Sei could only giggle.

# 233. The Future Checks In

Phaedra stood quietly against the lab wall with her arms folded, eyes closed as she appeared almost to be sleeping. Meanwhile, Isaiah occupied the jump chair. He really was sleeping.

NAVICON Report

By: Isaiah Fontenot

Spring 26, 2773 n.e.

Miranda HQ, Lab 2A

What is this, Zyr? I thought you were going to "uncover" a story we could use? So their robot versions really did take over their world?

Karaina, they *became* their robot versions, then continued to count this remix as members of their original species. But clearly the physical form that built the boxes and disappeared couldn't be the same form as the one that lived *in* the box looking like a bunch of signals instead. You might as well ask me if their chemical bond versions took over the world from their physical matter versions, or whether their tree version took over their forest version. The main point is to explain how shapes like ours ended up inside of a giant hard drive instead. I mean, they had to get in there and leave an empty planet somehow. There really wasn't any other way to get us to that point.

But I'm not seeing the point of the hermaphrodite here.

How do you take a concept which is infinitely acquisitive and power-seeking, perhaps virus-like even, capable of producing any kind of species and any kind of male-female polarity, and have it NOT spill to the limits of its world? This may look like a story of people to you, but it's actually an analogy for chemistry and how—within the bounds of evolution—you can still evolve great order from plenipotent forces.

So you're explaining how this planet evolved life only for that life to produce its own containment project?

Isn't that what computers do anyway? We made ourselves then put artifacts of ourselves on them. Then we die and the artifacts are all that remains.

I'm just playing Devil's Advocate here. It sounds like this species is failing.

Dude! I'm not even done with the jump! It's not over unless those boxes lack the remnants of life in them. Even if that life is not active, we still win. We don't have to show that there are bustling simulations currently active in these things, only that they were used to relay such activity.

Okay, so I guess the main question is, how did that activity get from 262-III to here?

It was transmitted like any e&m transmission. I assume that's what these things are.

How could the Radiobox know about it if he had been off the planet for hundreds of revolutions?

He was always in touch the whole time. That's the whole point of a satellite.

So he himself was a relay station.

That's what I'm thinking.

Okay, Zyr. I'm buying most of this. But you still have two more challenges in front of you. 1) How does pure beamed data recreate physical life in an entirely new star system? And 2) How does the saga you're constructing help us in our current situation?

To answer question number 1: It may not happen overnight, but noded space dust forms planets which form cyclical layers which allow organisms mediating the cycle which form organismic collections which form societies that make institutions to make knowledge to compound into technology to study the noded space dust to make cyclical layers which allow more organisms mediating the cycle within the technology. Once you know this process then you can see nature as its own technology, insert yourself into the chain, and produce anything it can produce.

Including black holes and big bangs?

Including stars and big crunches. The fact that this planet is still there, though, suggests that any effective black holes they produced were not physical in the way that their star is. Even if they succeeded in this, it's likely that it was more informational, hence the means of their relegation to the boxes. Thay had to have *something*, physical or metaphorical, to get all of them into one. But I don't think I want this story to postulate how that works, because we're looking for a good path for ourselves, not a terminal end.

I thought you were saying they didn't end.

As occupants of their planets they did. But this is a story of how societies overtook cave justice, and data storage overtook societies. In terms of timelessness, readable information fired off of an event will always outlast the event itself. That should be a source of hope for societies passing through troubles, so you can see how the robot-merged version of the species could and should win just by aligning with time. It's said that when you tell some people about merging with technology, they may immediately think of these cold mannequins. But they are already merged with countless viruses and bacteria, electrobiotics and small symbionts. Cold mannequins don't have to be what that merge looks like, because electrobiotes can look the same with prosthetic organs and replacements as they did when nature itself was the manufacturer. What's the difference between a phone in the hand and a phone in the brain passed from parent to child? That's the difference between the first generations of this species and the last.

As for helping us in our current situation, can you see how watching the rest of the story may reveal this? All we need to do is track what the stabilizers did to contain their destabilizing predecessors.

They turned into bad guys.

From the perspective of an era where the ancestors were all that existed, of course their alien great-grandchildren would look like aliens to them. It's only when we get to the point that the great-grandchildren are finally writing the story, do we see what an old and unfit model the great-grandparents' world was. But at least through the jump I'm interpreting, none of the past has to be lost or disrespected. It just has to lose its capacity to destroy the present.

* * End of jump * *

So what do you make of it, Isaiah?

I like it. It tells me that we are probably on the right track, though our methods may be seen as soft—or at the other end, cruel. Laws were probably seen as soft in the eyes of pre-civilization, but they are closer to a long-lived principle, so were guaranteed to outlast that previous era.

You know, I've been around all these centuries and am always amazed at the kinds of things that keep me going. Here it looks like the lives we currently know won't exist in the Solar System 3000 years from now, but I don't get the sense that it was all for nothing. Instead, it seems like the silence is the natural state of things. I can't really imagine ever wanting this for myself, but maybe a few centuries down the line our successors will want this. I do feel that we're coming closer to the highest state for humanity attainable. De-venging the alphas is the first part. Setting up the all-human save process would be the next. After that, I could call my work done, and someone else will have to take over from there.

You could see your cycling in this?

Yes. Very clearly. Somewhere right after the basic mass save functions are built, but just before we humans really start trying to put whole cities worth of ourselves into it, that will be my time.

It's almost inconceivable for me. There are a lot of things I still want to experience.

You have your path and I have mine.

The next time we see Genevieve-Sei, do you think things will be the same?

No. I think she may actually ride this alpha thing out to the end. Sooner or later it will be very clear what we have done, and all of those stragglers living on outposts will still need someone.

Yes, you're probably right. Leaving them at that point would be the last thing she would want to do. The longer she stays, the longer she'll want to stay... Do you think we'll ever be enemies?

We betas don't have true enemies. Not if we're worth our salt. Everyone, including alphas and cyborg, are part of the whole which we look after. Genevieve is just covering the side less immediate to us.

Yeah...

...

So how's Dial been?

Jealous, complaining. I think she feels the world has carted off her spotlight.

Harsh!

But true. She doesn't hate Mona-R, but is very bitter about her working here at Miranda. It is the case that we're looking less to SIER and more to cross-server solutions for algorithm interpretation, and I think she's starting to see her organization as being treated like a glorified shelf. I cannot impress upon her that SIER's selective data repo is in someways opposite the widely public resource that we will ultimately end up needing to build. If she wants to keep feeling special, she'll need to adapt.

Well, I feel bad for her. None one likes to be replaced before they're ready.

If you pity her, then you can always check on her. Just be warned, she's still a leopard.

Yeah, maybe you're right. I've really been learning to stand up for myself thanks to ANRG.

Good for you! So have you figured out what you want to do with your life yet?

I was thinking about going back to Saturn to teach human dynamics if I can find a job. It would also do me some good to get away from all the politics for a change. No offense.

None taken.

Saturn may be backcountry, but I think what we're setting up there has a lot of potential. There and Pluto.

Not Neptune, *wink* *wink*?

Are you kidding? If I ever ask to be melted down and squished out as a flying eel, then please have me committed.

Haha. The Neptunians have organic bodies fit for their atmosphere. Their just like us!

But weirder.

Oh, you shouldn't judge a person based on appearances.

They're not people. Their people's 1-gorithms in mutant bodies.

Who can hold a conversation just like you and me.

Yes. A blurbby one. It creeps me out, truthfully. Maybe because I was a computer once and know what it's like to float around in white noise just before your first thoughts are solidified. It's very David Lynch. To me it seems like jumping into a pond of madness.

Aimee said she tried the Neptoshell experience once and it was like, how did she say it? It was like, "having your ass on your nose and your legs as your teeth." Flying was like "doing the Hanz & Franz pec flex and the snake all at once."

I heard it was like doing the pec flex and the running man.

With squid legs? Come on.

It probably feels the way any brush would describe its life to you.

Yeah, well Aimee said she didn't like it, and they said she'd quit after something like 12 minutes. She still tells me it was more like 12 days. "Phaedra, it took me five minutes to go four feet!" I swear she tells me that all the time. Or she used to.

Hmm...

I just wish catching up with her didn't take so much work.

Maybe SIER is lonelier than she lets on.

Phaedra considered how much less she really interacted with Dial before the nusian work. I guess I wouldn't really know, Phaedra lamented.

Well, I might at least call her.

I'd be more interested in how she handles Sei's friend Ko'an.

Now that's interesting. Why do you say that?

I hope this doesn't sound sneaky. And please don't get me wrong, Aimee is still a good friend. But it was very different meeting Ko'an in person. She's a strange individual. You can tell she's hard to get through to, and you really have to leave your biases at the door to keep interacting with her more than a couple of minutes. She radiates distrust towards you, and untrustworthiness herself. But I wasn't there to connect with her. I was there to see whether her association with Sei was a healthy one. Eccentric or not, disturbed or not, she *is* receptive to basic attempts at connection; she will let you walk her through new things, and she is capable of serious self-reflection in order to fix broken behaviors. Nothing is perfect, and nothing lasts forever, but for what it is, Sei's and Langley's friendship seems to be enough to support Sei in a setting where she will truly begin with none. I need to know if Aimee is mature enough to see her friends' needs like this. Because if she isn't then she is the last person who needs your support. She has the looks, the money, and the power to just go out there and pull what she needs in ways that Sei on Jupiter, Mona-R as a hostile-surrounded cyborg, Langley as a fringe persona, and even you as a former carrier of Spacetime could never command.

Everybody gets lonely sometimes. God knows I feel it occasionally. And loneliness can get you going down some dark roads. It's not just physical loneliness, but ideological loneliness or a lack of true and deep empathy from someone in connecting to an inner world you can't share... Those things can make life difficult for a person. But if I have to choose between the loneliness of a person with mountains of social support embedded in the cultures around them and the loneliness of a person excluded from those cultures, I am careful not to get sucked into the needs of someone who already has a megamall at their disposal which they're not appreciating or not using for the safety of the people beyond themselves. Again, I feel bad for what Aimee might be going through, but the scope of concerns from where I sit is so large that I really don't have the time or patience to baby her. I have dozens of lonely, privileged acquaintances in need of a friend. I count myself in that group every now and then. But we are leaders of the sane world. I need you at the world's table, pulling for more than yourself before I count your "needs" as being any different from those of lowest beggar. You can help yourself. He can't.

Isaiah recalled that Phaedra had always been a little cold, but he too had been learning to spot certain kinds of dead end from afar. Not that Dial was a dead end, but she was much less enthusiastic about doing the big work than a lot of other people. He might check on her, but there was always the risk that the time he spent tending to her would be time lost lifting up his future Saturnites. She was perfectly capable of finding someone else to share company with. I see what you mean.

Now Mona-R is another matter entirely. She's respectful, curious, teachable, and carries a whole group of people on her conscience by design. If you're going to assign a single personality to the next phase of collective humanity, it needs to be hers.

# 234. The Questions of Mona-R

Winter 14, 2775 n.e.

The cyborg girl sat studiously alongside her four classmates in her junior-senior course, NUCE431 – Advanced neurochains. Decked in plain black-rimmed LensGPT glasses, she (like so many students in beta colleges) had purchased additional tools for helping answer the seemingly infinite number of side questions that arose during lectures, including those questions regarding the professor's behavior, classmates' assumptions, certain referenced characters' backstories, and the point of in-person school in the first place. Although Mona-R had never challenged the idea of physical college classes, the Miranda dorm RA had explained anyway: While Diji worlds were good, they were also necessarily bounded in the information they contained. Physical *anything*, on the other hand, absolutely FLOODED a learner with context from which their inclined attention could select at will for further customizable control over their own personality evolution. You physically went to a place in order to narrow down your own buffet choices mainly for ambient socialization and social class "expectationing," and within that place you let your subconscious elaborate on any of myriad nuances which piqued your interest, no matter how apparently infinitesimal at first. Even in the 28th century, there was still more to learn in the physical world of Astra than there was in the digital worlds of Diji, and *far* more non-reality to learn in Comm than there was to learn in Astra. Yet Comm was that written and imagined dimension whose rules were determined solely by each author's mind, and we really needed a mastery of predictive Baia (the biological and creature-generation dimension) to get such potentially fanciful worlds to follow any rules whatsoever. Alas, Astra still topped the list where gleanable information about the real world was concerned.

Still, from what Mona-R could tell, the key to next-level human 1-gorithmic data generation would probably not be found by storing people in Diji, but in Comm. That dimension's rules varied with the networkable biologies of its writers and conceivers, and no constrained server world in existence was yet up to the task of discrete-state evogeneticizing in this way. Whatever the next set of rules might consist of, they would have to be pieced together from as-of-yet undocumented dynamics from the physical world.

Despite the existence of SIER and satellite servers, it seems human's hadn't mastered the elusive "God's Seed" algorithm after all. Thus the relentless consumption of radiation and mined printing materials from every planet would continue until the philosophical problem of "physical-mediated functionalism" itself was resolved.

Mona-R used her glasses to process the professor's words in the background via its approximation of her own comprehension style. Meanwhile, she more actively explored the rabbit hole of learning-style approximation in general.

*I have an article on functionalism,* she thought. *And I want to learn what it says in a way that integrates with my interaction choices and my outlook in the world more than my conversational knowledge. When these glasses convert my aquaric information perceptions into my geminic habit fields, how does it know what those fields even are? When I ask the professor's bowtie to tree-talk to me, it does so partly based on its aestheto-contextual self as recorded by the glasses app against the ISO-א-6208 Common Aesthetic Interpretability standard, and partly against the filter of my geoequivalent astrochart's*

$$\frac{\text{Venus } \underline{\text{Vinissac}} \ \underline{\text{Premadi}} \ \text{Lemarchal Arnica}}{\underline{\text{OCEAN}}}$$

*Big-5 troupe for how my emhim bends treatment from all communicators. The model knows that I will register this communication pattern as realistic within my normal sphere, where other patterns would be improbable as occurrences in my life. But what is going on here? I guess the bowtie would be more like the subject, and my OCEAN would be more like the prompt constraints for any talking tree model executed by me personally. The ISO-alef-6208 would be how the technology interprets any random object recognition as a subject. My chart's Premadi OCEAN would be how all recognized objects and people and foreign languages are reinterpreted to talk to me as a second person recipient regardless of who or what that recipient was. Like the "system prompt" in our Model Etiquette class: "Use the ISO-alef-6208 to assign a core personality to any object whose contextual stream you will be recognizing. Always speak to me as that object, but when you do so, always do so in a manner which I would interpret in line with my Premadi OCEAN. If you cannot do this, then you should continually drop your interest in conversation with me, or feel constantly increasing tension in line with your own approximated Premadi OCEAN until we just can't talk anymore. Do not talk to me or reply at all for the rest of the day unless other exigent events or job duties outside of our chat force you to." Yes, I think this would be a decent "realic" prompt for human interaction. And if not an object stream but for static content, I guess I could say something like, please explain* *https://plato.stanford.edu/entries/functionalism to me in a way that I would would be most likely to interpret according to the following criteria: • Me wanting to keep talking to you only based on your {*my* Venus qunit opposition asteroids}, • My subconscious need to posture against you as {my conjuncts to Vinissac}, • My doing {Premadi conjunct things} in what is a strongly {Premadi opposition asteroids} situation, • me having more fun in exchanges offering {Lemarchal oppositions}, and • If we were to keep the exchange going over the long term course of months, you would become more like {my Arnica conjunct asteroids} facing {Arnica opposition} situations. Yes, I think that is how this talking-tree application would take system prompts to help a specified subject appear to interface uniquely realistically with any human in a way consistent with the human's actual socialization patterns if we lived back in the original GPT days. So I think a learning style approximation does something similar to this, but for a troupe of asteroids related to a person's learned actions and translated understanding.*

*How do I learn? I like blocks and low-code myself. I hate code. I think it's because when I look at code, I subconsciously know my peripheral is being forced to go blind in favor of that one command hijacking all of my attention, then spoon-feeding me the next tiny piece of logic that *it* wants me to look at. While all of this is happening, I know there is more going on, and if I could only see the big picture again, I would know that being stuck on this one thing doesn't even have to be my only choice. So I guess a block with no hijacking detail is what I like. If there is detail then it has to be simple and unique to the block. Like the way it connects to other things, a color to help me classify it or find it quickly in a pile, and a basic predictable pattern for how it is used. Code is the opposite of this. Whenever I look at it I feel like someone is forcing me to wander out into the wilderness of an entire language, forcing me to look for something that they hid on purpose. That's annoying.*

*Also, even though some people see coding as problem-solving, I see code as problem-solving code's problem, not my problem. Man, I hate code. I'm probably made of code, but I think studying my own guts is boring.*

*I like artifact hunting and putting things into tables for them to relate to each other. If I could, I would put the whole world into a table and flip a magic switch to see it all run. That's why city-building and data-saving are interesting to me. Because a simulation is basically a table of blocks doing things to other blocks, linking together like a toy. I like watching the story that the blocks' interactions tell. But I think it's ironic—and possibly related—why forcing the same shape for every block makes me mad. I just feel angry working with only cubes and only hexagons and blocks with holes I didn't ask for. It feels sadistic. Like someone said to me, "Mona-R, you can create anything you want…AS LONG AS IT IS IN THE SHAPE OF MY WILL, MWAHAHAHAHA!!" And I'm like, "But I don't want a cube. I want an oval." "MWAHAHAHAHA!!" And hexagons force you to move crooked in two directions whenever you choose one. It's like having confuse cast on you all the time.*

*It's easier for me to learn when I come with my own goal, and an expert can tell me why certain key things are done on the way to that goal. So if I planned to go from A to Z, for example, but were afraid that I might electrocute myself at step J or run out of money at step Q, I would sometimes want to know what the expert says about steps J and Q, and sometimes want to know how the expert goes from B to W and explains J and Q as actually being related to B, C, M, L, and R. The thing is, you never know. A person could show you 10 out of 11 steps in something* and then you find out that 11ᵗʰ step says that the first 10 were all a joke. I mean, that's how diplomacy and manners work, isn't it? You tell the truth, the whole truth and nothing but the truth, but the careful words you *don't choose* sit in jail with that 15% of context that would make the other person want to kill your family? That's why blocks are important. To me, they're a big-picture tool so that, no matter how you put your solution together, you'll always remember never to get so far in the weeds that you forget not to get your family killed outside of the weeds.

That Model Etiquette class started off bad, but I ended up liking it. They say that they used to teach Latin in schools as a kind of status-based education in something classic and respected. But then we got translators for that, and people stopped really valuing history and just wanted plain English answers. So after a couple of years they quickly started teaching ancient prompt engineering and query notations as the new Latin. Remember when the | meant bitwise OR and the || meant logical OR? L33T, pig Latin, and emoji languages? Not to mention mathematical and astronomical notations. The post-classic models were as trained on these as they were on Romanized words and Hanzi. So in Model-Et we did all this prompt diagramming, and you really learned how the first models were trying to think. I think that was valuable to me. Then in our bioinformatic models class we learned all of these wicked awesome successor models like Kinesiologic models (KMs) for the arms, legs, gait, and dance—quirky fighting styles in procedurally-generated NPCs. We learned linguivocal model evolution for say, why a native Indian person has certain inflections and a mandarin speaker can be easily distinguishable from a black speaker based partly on language, but also based on niche response pressures.

Anyway. I got distracted. Back on track, say I wanted my classic prompt to actually teach me a complex linguistic subject like functionalism in teaching way, not a talking way. How would I do that? This could be useful for saving cities as data using only a few non-verbal characters for things like minerals, weather, and crime. I can see why Earthan China eventually dominated the old-generation AI model markets—because their "alphabet" was already picture-based at its core, while westerners had to get past the whole cute-oji implications of using single symbols to train fixed concepts. The early embeddings were nightmarish in their size and slowness before logographic LMs became the hotness. Now if I wanted to teach-teach myself, I would first need my geoequivalent astrochart as a rough directory tree for how I worked. The well-known first ever interdimensional un-geoequivalent chart for a non-Astran, the Savitri Narayan chart, still said more about how to reverse port her life back into Comm for the simulated stories about her than the Comm stories themselves did, and even though she was an Astran like everyone else in this real world, there are some theories that say, had she been a character in a book instead, she would have been considered a Commaner, but her geochart in that kind of "universe-reader's Astra" still would have been mappable from her chart in this world. That only works for special people who the star-sized gods use on multiple dimensions, and who live in time periods reachable by their lookup tables. But I guess we would all be Commaners in a book if I could one day help build a place to store this dimension. No. Actually, we wouldn't be Commaners unless somebody above wrote us. Instead, we would be Astrans to ourselves but something like Dijians to them. Except our digits would be astronomical still. So I guess we would still be Astrans after all. But the idea of Astra as easy to calculate based on asteroids wouldn't make sense to the dimension above us because what we see as astronomical objects would just be particles to them. We'd call ourselves Astrans, but they'd call us Commaners, Dijians, Baians, or something weird like "Particlans." Yes. The dimension of citizen clusters too small for the eye, gathered on atoms as *their planets, should be called "Parta." It's people and animals should be called Particlans. But that's not the same as particle clusters *our size* and in our dimension. Venusians and Neptunians, though basically made up of wind, are actually Astrans because you could take whatever planet they were born on and recalculate a geocentric equivalent, and also because that birth situation is subject to our Sun and galaxy. So they'd be Astrans.*

*A classic prompt that could teach-teach me would need to permanently or semipermanently show me how to do steps J and Q on a path from A to Z, where J and Q used to be just noisy potential to me. Getting permanent-like coherence in looking at what was formerly a noisy option space: that is the definition of learning. If I'm exposed to it in chat or school but it stays noise, I didn't learn. I also think that if it didn't present an *option* for anything, I also didn't learn. That would be kind of like hearing a song for the first time. I might be exposed to it, but that's not the same as learning. On the other hand, if you tell me a famous actor just died, I now gain an option for how I recite what I know about this actor, so I have learned the news. But if you tell me that Joe Blow just died, and I don't know who he is, then I have no keepable file to pull options from. So I actually haven't learned anything there. It's like writing only to RAM and expecting the hard drive to do something with it later. The hard drive doesn't have it. There was no data-saving and no learning.*

*I think learning is a functionalist thing. If I know it, I've learned it, but just because I've learned something doesn't mean I know as much about it as I think I do. I only really know the interpretations I keep falling back on, and if I'm repeating it in a way that continues to keep relationships or moods bad when I would want them to be good or at least not a burden, then I haven't learned enough to navigate that space effectively. So when I put one of those classic prompts together and I want it to really teach me, I have to make sure that what it gives me is something that fills in a gap in what I know how to choose or at least how I know how to explain something. Preferably not just for the sake of the topic itself as it ignores my interests. Yes I could learn functionalism for the sake of the functionalist file in my brain, but that file itself would only be another file on the path to my college certification. I don't think I would have actually learned functionalism so much as I would have learned one more generic way to get through a class. That's why it matters how a person *really* learns and what they keep in their brains really easily for later use. It's not that school isn't valuable—it especially is for social and subject exposure reasons. It's more like the schooling we give ourselves later on, the information we eat, is usually not valuable if we don't actually respect how are brains are actually working. Most of what we learn isn't information, I think. It's citation and stabler interaction in place of fog.*

*What kinds of things have I learned? I've learned how to shop. I've learned how to play with blocks. I've learned how to turn anything from anywhere into a table of relationships to at least one different piece of data each. And I've learned how to collect multiple of these relationships— also of any kind—into their own table. I know I like gridded systems where each grid has a space of options. If I can't retrace my steps or see the whole map or node-critical-family, then I can't learn the map or the node. If the structure of the tools I have to work with is forced by what I think is somebody else's quirky preference or a process that adds extra complication to steps that I've picked to be simple, then I won't want to learn. Finally, if I'm being pressured to accept a thing as true but the thing itself doesn't give me any reason to even care about it, then I won't want to do anything with the thing or the pressurer until they both leave, and give me space to think of the thing in terms that my own A-Z block understanding will actually willingly keep. All of that said, I would probably have to start training my classic model using a block system like the old graph languages or flowcharting language. I think I would have it answer me through a system of blocks or plots or characters on a grid that each had some kind of function. And once everything was all framed up, I would need to be able to stand way back from it and admire all of its interactions. Hopefully with other grids I already knew.*

*…Too bad blocks are as visible as they are. A second ago when I went back to that ancient prompting app for my Model-Et class, I found that the flowcharts it gave me still weren't blocks, just text inside of shapes. They didn't actually do anything, you couldn't actively hook them up or watch their dynamics flow, they weren't present in my physicospatial context, and didn't belong to any buffet pile or library outside of themselves—unless you maybe count the infinite to the infinitienth power of potential rearrangements of text and lines. But my physical-kinematic, visual-animatointerpretive, and tactile spaces have no use for *that*. The flowcharts would have needed to be printed into something I could touch. Or at least watch go. Because that's how I learn.*

*I guess I probably couldn't print the subject of functionalism as a 3D object myself, but I'm starting to see why art matters. Without knowing it, we're translating concepts into touch or animatointerpretive objects, and that's actually what our human bodies evolved against first. Language came later and changed what we further evolved against. I am a cyborg, so I'm two consideration levels later than alpha and one consideration level later than betas. Homo sapiens betas are sapiens alphas +science manufacturing processes. Homo sapiens cyborgis are sapiens betas − organic mimicry + pure science processes made to do what the organic parts did without trying to BE those parts. A true example of functionalism. I am human because I do all human things and we were given human rights because of this centuries ago. It doesn't matter whether I have blood like alphas or blood-compatible vasculation like betas. I still eat food and convert its nutrients to match the human survival basis. I still have incubation functions for reproduction compatible with all other types of sapiens. I am strongly pre-programmed to resist pain or whole-self death, still have a waste elimination procedure, still age into death eventually, and still convert process chains into forced biological directives—therefore a hormone system.*

*Now one thing I think is weird, personally, are these "mutatas." They're making these creatures with lots of arms and fur and who have like 10 personalities in one so they can substitute for crowd feedback in marketing, but want them to have rights like we do. I'm glad that's not allowed, because if it were you'd have a heck of a time getting it to stop causing whatever madness or disturbance everywhere it went, whether or not it was the creature's fault. The main argument is that mutates had no starting class to be phenotypically compatible with, so it's not like a 4-armer or a vice-waist can mate with you and make kids like itself. But *even if it could*, it still fails species rule 9 for class member reinforcement. So some sly scientists tried making two of the same kind of micromutata that could mate and reproduce a third one, kinda arguing that mods themselves—the way they pass themselves through generations—should be considered human. But then the Interplanetary Health Board's lawyers came in and said, "Okay, you can present these 50 years' worth of mountains of research to apply for consideration as a *species*, but to be human, and basic combination of mates must, within biochemical probabilities, produce any other* *combination. The mutata movement failed this royally and I'm glad. Some people are just so curious that they'd inflict mayhem on all of society if they could. Just to see how it all blows up. And that's not cool.*

*But it's interesting how the same "group theory" argument used to prevent mad scientists from creating their own army of bacteria and giving them rights was also used to put super heavy restrictions on what kind of cyborg could be considered human. The biggest argument centered on the "identity element" and the inverse. In humans, the sapiens alpha female form is the identity element that is the starting point for, say, both the later-differentiated male and the woman. But then you have this whole space of "coherent inversible properties." There may not be an inverse to a short French olive-skinned female, but there is a genetic maximum vector distance from French-type phenotypes, shortness, and the factors that produce olive skin. For mutatas, once you get into having 3 arms, what is the sapiens-genetic inverse of this? 1/3 of an arm? 30 arms? 3 holes where arms would have been? The main problem here is that as soon as we get off of the reasonable person standard of a sapiens template, the genetics gets broken and you're just not gonna find a proper standard human DNA slot to complement what you handgrew in a lab. So it had to be possible that cyborgs could birth other cyborgs, betas, and alphas upon mating, and people made this possible by basically putting a really sharply-tuned algorithm pool inside of the cyborg female body for how organo-3D printing was elaborated. It could be programmatically or chemical-ambient directed. Of course the sonogram makes things a dead giveaway, but a massive gang of scientists took about a century working together to get all of that right. For mutatas, it's just the mad scientist and their mad creation. That's definitely the way it should be.*

Mona-R snapped out of her daydream as Professor McMacon-kappa called on her.

"So Mona-R, how do you see this affecting your research project at your job?"

Mona-R quickly processed what her lens glasses had been interpreting in the background. I think my work on spirit storage would probably not store a lot of the temporary friction that the person runs into.

"But don't those frictions make the person?"

I think *types* of friction make the person, but we always generalize if we want to teleport anything to a new context. The fact that this action chain is running but also getting partly derailed by case specific action chains says to me that those changeable interruptions need to be treated as an error term source, but that's it. I would build the interrupter into their own separate type of error term maybe, but I wouldn't waste a lot of processing on it.

"Okay, now what if this action chain were to be completely deleted, and you had only the interrupters trying to stop a process that couldn't run? For example, in a case of cy-consciousness loss or general anterograde amnesia. Do you still treat the formerly interrupting chains as noise?"

Not noise, sir. Error—like in the additive term sense, not the multiplicative window-widening sense. And it depends. For something like anterograde amnesia, if the interrupting chains were writing hallucinations in place of storable memory, then they would matter. It they were just trying to steal processing priority from a memory-writing system that didn' t work, then they wouldn' t matter. But I wouldn' t just automatically ignore it.

"Okay. Panchet, you have your hand raised?"

"Yes professor, I think…"

And Mona-R went back to her daydream.

*  *  *

As a part-time artifact hunter at Miranda (a role created specifically for her), Mona-R was tasked with finding abandoned action paths among certain kinds of test subject. Specifically, she needed to 1) find alphas who had either abandoned or adopted patterns of vengeance, 2) recover algorithms for the path they did not take, and 3) tree-talk those paths into physical objects and attributes to aid the Solar Council's studies of the de-venging process. Despite her newness to Earth, Miranda, and beta ideas, the Solar Council had endorsed her early as an intern on a highly sensitive project, as she not only had passed the required el tests and simulated behavior scenarios with flying colors, but she had done so by agreeing to a full psychology scan of the kind that only cyborgs could provide. It had been the equivalent of the old deep-mind jumps which the original Spacetime crew had pioneered—putting her every inclination, self-frame, and world-view on the Big-I 1-gorithm mapper for all the world to see from day one.

Without a doubt, the Angel finder had hit the jackpot with this one. Like a trusted application from a reputable company, Mona-R had been let past several of the highest security and strategic firewalls almost immediately. The Earthan powers did, after all, consider the Navajo-9 sole-1 (the only or last case in a population) to be an integral part of their plans for Jupiter.

Although the plan to beta-ize or confine the alphas was more of a conspiracy theory in the eyes of the common human public across all forms of sapiens from all colonized planets, it was hardly a secret among the 131 Solar Council members and 260 additional scattered workers across the project. Mona-R herself had been made aware of it, but like almost everyone else in the know, didn't really see the plan as a big deal from a human rights perspective. Several difficult conversations into the initial project proposal had ensured that the effort would never smack of the very thing it was trying to eliminate, and that all efforts to convert the aggressive alphas would be as humane as possible.

For his undeniable expertise in resonant ambiences, Jake Nolli had been permanently moved off of the Venus projects and into Miranda's History department, where he would study targeted sociology cases among the now deceased, and run human trials on their simulations. How did your average alpha behave when you took away their capacity for malicious vengeance? What if they lacked this as a personality trait to begin with? Jake personally resolved that, as an alpha himself, he would do his best to find solutions that wouldn't affect people like him, but would only affect the bad apples of the world.

The reality, though, is that some decision makers now found the endlessly looming threat of alpha sprawl to be too much of a nuisance to continue permitting. Osaira had just reappointed their Premier to his fifth term despite 2-term limits. Zeusland was threatening to take more asteroids from New America. New America was once again confused regarding the difference between good and bad stewards of the whole. There were pirates making their base in Mazelor. Lavel had cut off all media shortly after de-citizenizing cyborgs. Donelland was a trafficking, drug haven, and overall hotbed of terrorism and crime. 27% of all alpha-controlled asteroids were choking under some form of atmospheric toxicity breaches, compared to 3% of beta or cyborg controlled asteroids. Wherever you looked, betas simply ran things better. Yet you could always hear the perpetual cries of "freedom and free humanity"—down with the bots!—from 1 out of every 20 alphas you met. Accordingly, 89 out of the 131 Solar Council leaders— including Reselat and Phaedra—favored project "ABC" (the Alpha Betaization and Containment Plan) whether or not the technology was tuned to skip over exceptions.

Mona-R, Isaiah, and even Jake also supported ABC, though the latter really sought desperately to find a highly selective route that would ensure that non-vengeful alphas would go untouched. Isaiah had basically checked out, relocating to Saturn in 2774. Mona-R could not shake the memories of her first two decades of life, and looked at the Jupiterian alpha airspaces as probably deserving what was coming to them, whatever that may be. Nonetheless, Phaedra, despite her antipathy towards the Jupiterian "shitshow" in general, was moved by Jake's passion, and continued to push for more time as much as she could.

Good thing Reselat was still a fine listener.


Reselat, now the newly elected Chair of the Solar Council, visited Miranda for a closed door meeting with Phaedra and a few others. Following the meeting, he and Phaedra strolled the campus grounds discussing various topics, eventually stopping outside of Jake's new lab.


***Good sir Nolli!*** Reselat greeted Jake cordially. ***I hear you have some news for me?***

Yes. We'll be scheduling a meeting for later this week once we get everyone's calendars in order, but Colpin's chemists and I think we've found an emhim frequency for malicious vengeance.

*Is that so? That's excellent. Here I was thinking we'd have to go with zapping or comm channel stuff to deliver the vector.*

No, if we can test it out on a couple of folks then this'll be much better.

*Okay.*

So basically...

# 235. A Fire Department in the Wilderness

Winter 16, 2775 n.e.

Projecting into one of the main boardrooms at Solar Council Headquarters in Thoth, Amenthes - Mars, Jake and two collaborators explained the sleek black and gold armbrace rotating before everyone on the holoscreen.

Ladies and Gentleman, we present to you the product of the last two years' worth of collaborative research: an emhim scanner we call, the "Demon finder." The bottom line up front is that this scanner can both identify and initiate de-venging chains in biohns through perceiver-relative engrantzing and possession. The wearer of this brace—or the user of a scaled-up model of the same technology—can scan an area of living things, identify any humans, look them up in any birth registry, and assess their 130069 Danielgaudreau frequency along with seven others to determine their capacity for malavenge. That track-record lookup is the easy part. Having identified the avenger, the brace issues a filtered cocktail of frequencies attaching the avenger's percept to a catalytic distrust cascade to all viewers of the offender, and that cascade is also attached via another frequency to a vivid memory of the circumstances for encountering the avenger. An oscillating geminic field for rewriting target-specific viewer understanding is used here. Lastly, the brace also polls for changes in all scanned viewers, and rewrites these back to the avenger. And there you have it, instant installation of a person-specific social pressure paradigm for all avengers in the room.

The meeting attendees remained silent. Most who hadn't seen the technology already were clearly very impressed.

Next.

The holodisplay switched to a thin silver and black glove with blue-lit striations on the hypothenar.

We call this glove, "Epic." It is also a look-up scanner, but instead searches emhim for the kinds of events which can explain major changes in a person's life. The reason this is a separate piece of equipment is because life-conditionals take a lot of processing power, and we can't use nanos to gather that level of info. So instead we have a glove that takes the attention of the wearer and tree-talks scenarios of the person they are perceiving into the Demon finder, allowing the brace to adjust its broadcast frequencies accordingly. Together, Demon finder and Epic can allow you to walk into a room, scan everybody, plant the slow-acting seeds of distrust towards every malavenger by everyone besides themselves—including other malavengers—plant in each malavenger the idea that something about themselves is terribly, could-be catastrophically wrong, and use epic to possess certain people into playing out the kinds of events that would realistically cause this turn. Without Epic, the whole process would set off alarms quickly. With Epic, the whole sequence of events is more likely to look natural.

Intrigued expressions filled the attendee displays.

Now before you ask any questions, I need for you all to understand some technical points.

Social acts at their core aren't really single acts, but boxes put upon clusters of events involving at least three parties: the actor, the viewer-interpreter, and the absent world. In some cases these are all the same person. In other cases they are three different parties. You can have more, but three is the minimum. An act needs two parties—like a tree having woods to fall in—but a social act needs *three* parties. Even if there is no explicit target of a person's jokes or friendship attempts, you'll still have a third party "standard of behavior" that an actor acts against. This is important, because many acts of malicious vengeance aren't actually directed at anyone; they might instead be directed at a system of rules. The thing is, it's one thing to call a social act malicious based on a maze of background social teachings we've all acquired, but to develop a technology for judging this with legal-level accuracy requires some very strong data, and a kind of courtroom trial inside of the device. There are ways to detect this using emhim alone, but we thought it would be a little more pointed towards the end objective if we supplemented this with lookups. At the very least, lookups will help us use this technology on more public figures whom more private people follow as leaders, and convert more of those folks before we're found out. It's unlikely that we'll be able to convert a whole planet and subspecies without being found out at some point. Before that happens, we want to convert the most visible characters first.

There were several nods.

Now, another hard fact we ran into is that getting to our targets is not nearly as easy as you would think. It's not that we don't know where to find them, but that the strategy for find-and-deploy here and there and everywhere—in onesies and twosies—is far too inefficient. We'd need to make a million of these, a bunch of big ones, or pour in some other ungodly amount of resources to find just a handful of people. And again, converting nonpublic figures just isn't as valuable as converting public ones. Here's where we used the whole three-party nature of social acts to our advantage, and the reason we don't need to find the actual malavenger.

Because malicious revenge is only half of the problem. Us following it, accepting it, having our constructive actions stopped by it, or otherwise letting it ride are the other half of the problem. In my time in the History unit I kept seeing this. The most negative characters were always bolstered by the collectives whose fears or discontent they channeled. The "battery" (so to speak) for the malavenger is his or her audience. So hitting the audience—making the audience instantly distrust the avenger for what the latter is definitely telling you he or she is going to do—is not only a quick way to cripple the avenger's popularity through the information sources through which their image is spread, but it also slows down the compounding power of the avenger's spiral-reinforcing approach—which we alphas were partly evolved to thrive off of. So the way this works is that I can walk into a room full of 20 people watching an avenger on the streams, use the Demon finder and it will scan and look up 21 people. It might find, for example, that only one of the viewers has enough negative lookup information to count them as an avenger, but the person on the TV has plenty. While this is happening, Epic is also running, and reads that the viewing avenger, TV avenger, and two bystanders could all have a life changing event if the first one lost his job, the TV one had fans walk out on them, and the last two won the lottery. These are fed back to the Demon finder.  All of a sudden, after a couple of minutes in the room, people are starting to view the two avengers as shadier than usual. The viewing avenger for a seemingly random (but we know, grantzed) reason says something random like, "I know I feel like following this TV person is gonna cost me my job, but that's okay. I like feeling poor and angry. I'd get behind them again and again as long as I can help get these cyborgs out of our town." He then offers an ironic dose of stinging information (unknowingly read by Epic) to one of the bystanders, making a memorable jerk of himself in the process, but also making himself feel bad that he's done it. Later, everybody goes home, no one forgets what the avenger in the room said, and fewer people trust him or the TV character because of how this was done. They are also neurologically conditioned to keep associating this event with the TV person every time the latter comes up. And the distrust comes with it. We can't actually send signals to the streaming person in this way, but we can start planting the seeds of doubt 20 people at a time. We could do this any time we encountered the TV avenger on TV, and a group of people watching them.

Now I know this is all very roundabout, but the short version is that this technology puts waves in a room that makes all avengers destructively untrustworthy even to themselves, and sponsors a realistic act by any avengers focused on by the Epic wearer which are more easily written to the memory of those doing the distrusting. Only the avengers are filtered into the Demon's signal, so if it can't find you based on lookup, catch you in the act, or catch others catching you in the act and agree with them to the 99.99% level, then the memory writing will only help you distrust any avengers identifiable in body or in projection around you, whether or not you know them personally. It will not disable anything in you, per se. For an avenger actually in the room, it will install three things: 1) distrust towards other avengers, 2) an Epic-sponsored concern that malavenge-based distrust from others towards him or her will trigger the kinds of life changes that can destroy something they're building, and 3) a permanent memory of something they were unknowingly grantzed into for making this distrust worse. It doesn't so much disable anything in the brain as it adds sketchy and unwanted memories and concerns to the kinds of action patterns that the Demon looked up as them being inclined towards in revenge.

There's more. But let me pause to take questions.

Lots of hands went up. One of the questions focused on the feasibility of affecting a whole species quickly enough before the plan was invariably discovered.

We don't have to affect all of sapiens, only their most deleterious leaders. But we can start by testing it on, well. I'll get to that.

More questions followed.

That's right, the wearer determines who gets focused on for Epic, but not for the Demon. But if the wearer perceives an innocent person as behaving in a malavenging way, yes the target will get put on the Demon's radar for lookup and collective distrust if there are no histories to the contrary.

. . .

Yes, the wearer is among the first one's affected, so they either need to be resistant to malavenge or non-biohn.

. . .

This is just a proof of concept. Once it has been field-tested we can make larger versions of this technology, yes.

*I must say, this is very impressive,* Reselat interjected. ***There are very few technologies out there, pharmaceutical or otherwise, which are capable of targeting a socially-perceived behavior in a mass population. In the end, the concept of malavenge is truly a judgement call on our part, and so it is fitting that the technology for eliminating it would rely on its perception and documentation by outside parties.***

As always, Jake continued, when I know the technology is finally up to code, I end up testing it on myself.

More than a few attendees gasped at this sudden casual declaration.

"You mean you have already tried it on yourself?"

Yes. Multiple times actually. Let me explain some chemistry to you.

Jake summoned the image of a translucent brain on the holodisplay.

If I can ask you to hold your questions for a moment while I explain some chemistry. Because I feel that this next part is going to be very helpful for us keeping a clear conscience when we do this. At least it was for me.

As you know, the brain is made up of cells which act like little radios for firing at certain rates or little dump trucks for dropping charges that help other cells fire at certain rates. There's insulation in there as well, switches for directing current, and freeze states for writing memory. So you can think of a brain as being like a city where the people are the charge carriers and the different kinds of buildings are the various lobes and functional areas. Even if the people change, the relationship between, say, your fire department, police department, and residential areas will typically be very predictable in terms of how those people engage them. This is true no matter what city you are in. It's the relationship among the few dozen consistent building blocks that we are concerned with.

Whether or not you are the actor or the viewer, you as a biohn—alpha or beta—will have certain buildings triggered in a certain order whenever a specific event happens. These are like "errands." We go from a friend's house to the theme park to a food place back to the friend's house. We go to the bathroom to the kitchen to the closet to work then to lunch, and so on. At any point you'll have thousands of chains of errands running at the same time for things like bodily functions, movement, perception, and those things, but only a few chains which you are actively forcing to stay in line with your notion of external situational requirements. Said another way, there's always a bunch of things going on in your city, but only a few things which are intentionally designed to keep your city trading healthily with other cities and the larger market. This gets us into those chains of brain areas that are recruited in social attention and environmental task performance.

I should also mention that the difference between a fire department and a hospital lies in only a small set of basic attributes: who and how far they serve, when they serve, how inputs and outputs change after having been processed by them, and how they are built up or funded in the first place. If you think of things this way, then you can get away with seeing all components of your city as a black box. A fire department can put out fires using emergency vehicles, teleported chemicals, or magic, but as long as the input is fire, the output is not fire. If the trigger is an emergency message of some sort, and the call is via some region-based relay, it will still be considered to play the fire department role. This is super useful, because not only is it the functionalist principle that allows cyborgs to be human, but it also gives us an explanation for the connection between astronomy and the individual body.

We can make a table of basic buildings in a city, and put in it only a few columns for the who-served and how far, the when and how of calling, the input state, output state, buildup, and operators of each building—thus turning every building into a group of elements in a vector. Astronomical bodies also have a who-served and how far: the planetary orbital band and eccentricity. They have a when and how of calling: their orbital period and inclination which dips them in and out of the main band where all the action is. They have regular inputs and outputs (and this is the biggie): It's the groups of asteroids which they sometimes intersect with, on a certain frequency, how they perturb and are perturbed gravitationally, magnetically, energy bending-wise, et cetera; that is, their unique orbital resonance and counter-resonance sets. They have a chemical composition which reflects their source band and everything that has happened to move them to where they currently cycle. And they have operators. Not so much the Sun, but the chief major planets that explain 90% of why they move the way they do. That's the sun plus the major planet for that band, plus the chief bigger asteroids and precessions of both the band and the system as a whole. Now all of these explain only one building—a fire department in the wilderness. But when you put a whole semi-closed, self-explaining system together for many of these bodies, you get a mapping of astronomical bodies translatable onto the brain and behavior states of us particle clumps which live on those bodies and mirror those physics. So a birth chart is like a freeze state for all of the dynamics currently turned up when a thing was born, and whatever person or event which is described by that chart is going to incline towards whatever was happening in the space analogy—pushing and pulling some forces but not others in the person's own analogous system throughout life, subject to where they are, what's around them, and what species or manufacturing process they were made of. That composition puts them under constant chemical pressures of a different kind, bending their version of spacetime accordingly.

As far back as Jiji's Book of Contours, we see how the Keplerian orbital elements map to social dimensions when you do a simple correlation with any LLM embedding. The semimajor axis ($a$) shows institutional and systemic pressures on the person vs within a felt force. Eccentricity ($e$) shows interactional upset; that is, more eccentric objects, when located in key Lagrange angles to major planets, text-mined in the wikis of people who had these angles to be more correlated with a certain set of words, and those words, when broken into their LLM matrices and the embedding matrix dimensionally reduced, flowed in a very clear direction towards this theme of whole-society disturbance versus individual consideration. Epoch-based inclination ($i$) shows the level of social safety. Argument of the periapsis ($w$) shows comparative regulation versus driven growth. And so on for the ascending node, magnitudes, and other values. Now when we're looking at events in the brain, we're actually looking at several of our "buildings" being visited in a chain, so we're taking things like column a-high leading to column e-high leading to column w-low. In the case of malavengeance, where looking at something like interactional upset (e-high) leading to pressures within (a-low) leading to systemic pressures (a-high) and socially unsafe messages (i-low) in the interpersonal force band (the Mars belt). Skipping a bunch of math and language matrixing, I'll tell you that 130069 Danielgaudreau is one of the strongest asteroids in this stead, and we can look this up in the actual or geoequivalent birthcharts of anyone whom the scanner recognizes, and compare this to research of face, ethnicity, and body expression to estimate whether this person was conditioned towards vengeance or not. Looks can be deceiving, so we verify this with lookup and social reporting data.

Now why did you need to know all of that? Suppose Danielgaudreau has been identified in every recognized individual and all relevant data has been looked up. We then need to determine whether the person's expression of this asteroid is seen as socially damaging, willfully so, disregarding the Golden Rule, despite the larger social group disruption it causes, for the person's own immediate fulfillment at the expense of most else or most known applicable social rules, and knowing that the act wouldn't be done on a regular day if the person were at their best, safest, and most stable mode. Put together, these conditions for a formal definition for what malicious vengeance actually looks is in people's regular experience, and an individual has to check ALL of these boxes for the Demon to consider them guilty. If it's missing even one, there may be a good reason. A person trying to help their team come back from a deficit in a sports competition, for example, is probably not disrespecting known applicable social rules, because proper participation in sports automatically brings at least some respect for the rules of that sport. A person finally deciding to go after their long-term abuser, a soldier at war, or anyone in extenuating circumstance ceases to have the "regular day" box apply to them. We would all be guilty of that one. Knowing that I am not wired to check these boxes in general, I have used Demon and Epic on myself several times, and can tell you, it has not affected me. However, when we used it on simulations of various people. Henry VIII being the best example, these tools basically disabled everything they were known to have obnoxiously provoked at the expense of others.

As a final check before initiating a particular filter, the Demon runs a particular process we've called "the Golden Rule" scenario. This activates the opposition to the person's Danielgaudreau, and asks how the person would see another if that other were doing what the person is doing in the way that they are doing it. This is to get around cases where the person says, "I am obeying the rules of football when I slam this quarterback! I'm just going all in." But if they saw another player doing it on a normal day against the known rules of the game, would they be so okay with it? The Demon checks this, and if the outcome of the scenario isn't satisfactory, then the infiltering of this person as a malavenger will proceed.

So, folks, we have tested it. And I can say that this technology doesn't turn anyone into zombies or weaklings. It simply makes the most self-serving kinds of vengeance socially punishable by all of the person's witnesses, even if the person isn't in the room. But if the person is ever found in a public place and this technology is in the vicinity, the sound waves it uses will trigger an awareness of and aversion to such acts, as if the entire world is actively writing in their scenario of greatest loss as these acts are committed. Not today, but tomorrow. And they won't know where the punishment is coming from because it isn't coming from anywhere. It's from everywhere—it's embedded in the social training that self-service, other destruction is, in the long-term, unfavorable to every "other" besides you out there. The collective social record will show this sooner than later. As the enduring nature of the Gandhis, Jesuses, and Buddhas of the world have shown, new versions of the damaging will always feel their time has arrived, but the greater history will always reset in favor of the good and all-aligned eventually.

Questions?


And boy did Jake get them. The Q&A would last another 2½ hours.

# 236. Spirits in Boxes

But I don't understand, Kyle, Sei huffed. We put all of this blood and sweat into the Future Jobs Club. We funded it, promoted it, and got people excited about it over two long years, and somehow it's suddenly defunded why? For a lack of interest? Because its existence offended somebody? Why?

Just before the departure of Isaiah, some people affiliated with the Solar Council had contacted Governor Banner informing him that they would be sending Sei as a replacement liaison to continue the community stabilizing work which their undercover alliance had started. Sei's first task had been to lay the infrastructure for Isaiah's "Future Jobs Club." The program had seemed destined for at least a minimal degree of success, but now, two years in, would almost certainly meet failure as if the idea had never been proposed.

Yet strangely, even though Sei currently aired her frustration to her boss Kyle Banner, it was not he who replied to her, but a certain pair of scenario writers from three millennia in the future.


I was thinking about having this story go something like, "And Sei fought on behalf of the people using the institutions they were known to respond to." But then I was like, what's the point? The Blue man, the Venusians like Spastic who we never went back to, hell even the Nusian apocalypse itself. So many things seem big and important in the moment, only to have their window of urgency expire before their participants can get them off the ground. My own attention to these people as a future story reader is limited, and I thought it was more important for our system to write the progression of the beta technologies for containing the alphas than it was to follow the alphas' maybe or maybe-not progress.

I understand that, Karaina replied. But it seems to me that the alphas' problems are more like ours. We need to know what Sei does, and how the alphas are able to get their value back in a social world whose monolithic futurizing institutions are outrunning them.

Even if it doesn't matter?

Of course it matters! It mattered to them at the time. They led their whole lives in this tiny window which, true, we—their future readers—will end up ignoring. But we wouldn't want to just "not matter" to people who found us 6000 years in the future. I want to know how Sei carried out her mission even while her friends were comfortably preparing to basically crush that group permanently. It's messed up, really. All this time I got so used to the idea of the betas being good, and now they're doing this. It's actually pretty horrible.

They're doing it as humanely as can be managed. They're not actually killing anybody or putting them into Diji. Yet. What, would you rather the old humans just run around destroying every world they're in forever?

The betas don't have the right to just alter a whole species without their consent.

Hmph. You must not know how industry and markets work. These people give their powers of consent away the moment they chronically consume information without question or give a non-response to things they know are bad for others, as long as it doesn't affect them. I think the only difference between the alphas and betas is that the betas are trying to bring everyone to a point where they no longer have to live in fear of the consequences that generations of their forefathers and and entrenched institutions have reaped. At some point it's their systems which house the big problems, and those systems are too complex to fix. The betas are only making it easier for everyone to be immediately aware of what those consequences are.

And remove the right of people to think for themselves.

The notion of rights are irrelevant here. Especially where the execution of vengeance is concerned. Nobody is thinking about the target's rights when that happens.

Karaina sighed. Well, I tried playing Devil's advocate, but I guess, like your scenario people, my heart's not in it. I think deep down people really do want to suffer no more, and if there is an easy button for getting there, external or not, they will take it. I don't know if this jump arc is right, but I honestly can't think of a better way to free anthrics from pain. I know that—Well, no. I can't think of a better way.

Me neither.

But I just think it sucks that Sei's work—or any efforts to help alphakind get better at all—won't be worth anything

and won't affect the timeline. The alphas yearn to self-destruct. Only their machine-merged selves can fix this by taking alphas' world-rulership away. The whole point of this story though, is to show that it's possible for them to see themselves in all kinds of technologies—they can even put their personas into them. From their phones to their jet pants, into their music and their very bodies. And therefore merge themselves into the less ego-bound mechanics of science and nature. These betans are trying to make sure that they *don't* have to lose their humanity or their freedom in order to accomplish this. But they do have to let the future play out, and they do have to lose the old combative ways that served everyone while the world was still big enough for self-interest to multiply without end. They've filled up every horizon at this point—including each other's minds. The time for endless forced encroachment was bound to be over at some point. This can happen the easy way or the hard way.

# Resolved Timeline ⵖ

### {Decisions of: Genevieve-Sei, Isaiah}

So I take it the betas will succeed in your scenario?

If they didn't, then where are the physical humans now? What is it, something like the 58$^{th}$ century their time? There aren't any.

Hm.

And these boxes all over the 262 planets wouldn't exist. It's naïve to think that six planets could fill up like petri dishes full of imperialistic apes eroding all environments and last for very long. These computational boxes (I assume) are proof that they did get past it. But the physical form was not how they did it.

Betas are physical.

But sourced from digital. All they need to do is go right back. The ABC plan gives the alphas the option of going as well. Unless the betas conquer them, they won't be remembered, just extincted by their own hand.

Okay, but that doesn't tell me why the Sei story can't still have a happy ending if things are as you say and all of humanity can get its own hap—er, non-bad ending.

Sei could have a fruitful future as a people's hero, I guess. But I feel a little bad because nobody looking at the grand timeline really sees the value in fixing the alpha sapiens track anymore. They could elect a hundred kings and gorge themselves on pollutants, become a species of saints and angels or all fall off a bridge. As long as they remain noisy and confusable against the march of time, they sum to zero where the long term outcomes of this story are concerned. Sei's existence would be better spent elsewhere.

Where? Where Isaiah went? Into historical oblivion?

I'd like to think of it as his version of "Nirvana" (airquote). He finally rid himself of the anomie, found a calling, and got to pursue it. He also gained enough confidence to not be led by the nose, culminating in his unwillingness to fight for the alphas and separation from Sei. Boom. Happily ever after.

Hmph.

Sei found her calling too. But I see no value in taking her uphill against her beta pals. Not only can she not win, but even if she does win, it can only be done quietly within the mouth of the great betan whale. So quietly that her alpha constituents won't clump into their allegiants and mess it up with funding and propaganda questions. It is the same with all public services. People complain when they are taken away, but they won't contribute to them while they are still active. You can destroy these public systems without any fear that the average person will put in any effort to rebuild them, protest or not. The point of the Future Jobs Club was to rebuild talent bases across any kind of group opting in. But that assumes that the average follower has it in them to think without casting a constant adversarial glance at their overlords. All I was doing by failing the club early was saving us time.

When did we become so pessimistic?

When we realized that the problem lie in the species' own outlook. Not it's leaders or even its businesses. These were just the means. We found a way to change the outlook while sparing the basic human spirit—minus the hateful malice among its most visible figures. There's no need to insert chapters aiding folks who won't aid themselves.

How can they if there is no one to teach them?

That's not our concern. We looked for a story which we could use to resolve the current war in our time. Or thousands of wars after their time—at least in theory.

And did we find it?

I think we did.

And what will we say to the public when we tell them that 262-III is where we came from?

We'll tell them that these people were us. They overcame themselves by surviving their own wars long enough for their children to put their spirits in boxes, but sent some of their algorithms here via a now defunct humanoid radio, who bloomed life from the burning winds before us.

So the Radiobox was our creator?

More like our spaceship. We, the passengers, were the waves it received and broadcasted outwards as far as space would allow.

And how does this resolve the current war?

Was that the plan? Well, maybe we were too ambitious. Warring factions will always do what they do, but those looking for peace may find stronger footing if they align with the inevitable all-encompassingness of the whole. We can send a version of that message to the world, and know that the active peace seekers will ultimately outlast all other sides.

And that's your solution?

That's my solution.

So the war rages on?

Only for some. People have the right to wage it against those with an equal right to be fully defined by it. For those who don't want this, we offer 30 generations of paths to something better.

Heh. Where did that come from?

Just a thought I had. As for your Sei, I guess as in any medieval tale, you know that they all end up dead and in the ground eventually. But it could be that there isn't any harm in narrating the adventure while they yet lived. Let's call Tezl and prepare the press releases for what we've found here. In the meantime, I'll redo Sei's most recent scenario 42, and tie up a couple of loose ends just for you, boss lady.

Rrright.

# Part III. Epilogues

# 237. Destinationless

Spring 30, 2773 n.e.

In the midnight silence of her garden office in São José dos Campos Brasil, Phaedra closed the jump logs. Another Virgo-6 revelation from two years in the future. It seemed that Sei really would be alone in her fight to improve the old humans—without their knowledge, the sole champion of sapiens alphakind. Without *her own* knowledge, abandoned by Fate and Time before she had even begun. Despite the casual ease with with betakind leaders now sketched the pacification, and eventual extinction of the alphas, something about the conversation between Zyr and Karaina sang of a tragic futility in her friend's clearly earnest efforts. Phaedra knew that Sei had, in some way, longed to make her own way independent of the Miranda mandate, but this surely was not to be. Miranda and its cosigned future had been blessed all along by Time itself, as Phaedra stood more aware than ever of her soul group's gift for seeing far past even this dimension. Ezra Hall had it. Twice Jack had it. Tippy and Cubrina shared it. Perhaps Raliolite and Cyclops even had it. And now so did she: It was the gift for being right where eternity needed them, when it needed them. A gift for making certain decisions that only the future would understand.

Phaedra could not know, and would never want to know what it meant to lead a life forgotten. To stand for nothing and leave no mark. To stand for someone else's mark and leave your world worse for what you followed. To stand in good heart but for a cause destined to be vanquished. Your fellow humans might praise you for a while after you died, but what did they know? Only your allies Time and Nature would survive them all. Harmony with these, the sanctity of your sphere, and the honoring of your talents with minimal hurt to others… These were all that mattered, since Time and Nature would force these upon you through Death anyway.

Still, aligning with them made you somehow bigger than yourself—as if you *were* them incarnate. There was something transcendent about that.

No doubt, like several other Mirandans before her, this would be her last incarnation.

But to share or not to share? One might think that showing Sei what she had seen would be viewed as a kind of taunt. "You can't help them. See? The future has no place for you." Perhaps it would even break the latter's spirit. But somehow Phaedra felt she knew Genevieve-Sei better than that. If she thought she had a chance to make a difference fighting on behalf of alphakind, who would she become with the abyssal blackness of obscurity, ineffectiveness, meaninglessness staring her in the face? Whoever that person would be, she might at least gain more control over her soul's path if she knew what awaited her.

$4^2$ There was never any question that Phaedra would tell Sei what she had seen.

* * *

Although Genevieve-Sei's and Phaedra's friendship had not waned in the least, they now stood on opposite sides of the old-human question. Sei had recently begun working for Kyle Banner when she was invited to meet Phaedra's local reprint on Mars, and it was here that the former would receive the full scope of what she was in for.

**Hello Sei.**

Phaedra. I can't wait to hear this news you wouldn't tell me about over the call. It feels strange, you know. Working for alphas, living in that messed up society. I guess none of them knows what they are missing. It's been at least 1000 years since life was simple for them.

**For some of them. For others, being on the receiving end of empire designs probably wasn't that simple.**

It's the individuals, not the empires that I work for.

**Of course. But we've had this discussion several times, haven't we?**

We have.

**So I won't insult you by challenging your decision.**

Thank you.

I have a jump to show you.

Oh?

It's from Virgo-6.

Really. Sei quated, knowing that if Phaedra saw fit to deliver it personally, that couldn't be good. I guess we're meeting like this because you've come to warn me.

Not exactly. Just to give you the kind of information that a Commandant would want, that Mirandans always have.

Sei lowered her eyes. It had been a while since her and her friend's soul groups had come up in conversation. Hmph. We're always in the war room one way or another. Show it to me.

Phaedra replayed the conversation between Zyr and Karaina regarding the original 2775 scene between Sei and Governor Banner. As expected, it wasn't the Banner conversation that caught Sei's attention, but the one between the two anthrics.

No sooner had it started, than the replay was over. Phaedra waited for Sei's response first.

Sei stared off to the side, covering her mouth with her fingers, contemplating. She must have remained adrift for an entire minute before speaking.

You know what I like about you, Phaedra? You and Reselat always give me space to think. You never feel the need to pressure a response when you know the situation is... awkward.

Phaedra chuckled a little. "Awkward," huh?

Yeah. Awkward.

Hm.

I mean I know it's probably a lost cause. They're pretty aimless down there. But still...

...

Two years on a project I haven't gotten yet. Then it ends. Probably for one of many alpha reasons.

Probably.

And what about you? A centuries' long queen in a castle, only to end up in a cybercube with everyone else.

Who says I'll be in there? Maybe I'll be on the waves. With those future scientists. Or in a star. Or a dharma of my own. Maybe I'll go back in time and just sell ads for some crazy dreamers, Phaedra smiled.

You find meaning in an empty solar system? Despite everything we tried to build?

We didn't just try, we succeeded. Then we completed our stay and left others to try starting from what we built. We made it to every planet and left our story for ham radio users everywhere to wonder what we were telling them. ☺

Hehehe! Sei laughed in genuine delight. They watch the skies for us, right?

Haha, right.

Suddenly, Sei's face grew noticeably more somber. My one concern is that I will run out of things to keep me going. I believe in this now, Phaedra, and probably will for a while. But what happens when I get tired? I know the alphas won't be there. I'll outlive Banner for sure. And Ko'an, well, there's a lot of work to do there. And I'm not sure that changing her is a good idea with all of the potential treachery at our doorstep. But carrying her touchy eccentricities has already been a kind of tightrope for me.

$\psi^2$ An empathetic frown was all the comfort Phaedra could give.

Alpha life is lonely, Zeta. And when it's not lonely, it's full of busy personality management. And when not that, it's full of shallow distractions. There aren't a lot of opportunities for finding people who are both truly on your side and able to help you stave off the constant assaults on who you can ever be.

...

I know who I am today, but I can't promise that for tomorrow.

...

Anyway, I guess I should thank you for showing me this. You're right; if I hadn't seen it, I couldn't have made an informed choice on what to do next.

Sei gave Phaedra a warm hug. I may not have a very long future here, and I know that telling even Banner about my real mission would be a crazy idea. But Ko'an really can keep a secret, so I suppose we'll be alright. Wish me luck.

**I wish you all the luck I can send, my friend.**

Thank you.

* * *

The next day, Sei showed up at Ko'an's door.

### How was the meeting with Zeta?

Are you prepared to fight a losing battle?

Ko'an's face scrunched in dismay.

* * *

The Author Langley remained a darkened menace while at her office job, but had changed drastically since her encounter with Phaedra in disguise. Still a thorough sadist at heart, she had nonetheless elevated both Sei and Phaedra to the same status as her "big brother" cellmate and Command Warden Lucine. Overnight, her circle of friends had doubled. But Ko'an had never really needed friends. They were by all rights volunteers. What she had really needed was family. A mother she had never had, a father in place of that doomed character from pre-history. Truly, somewhere in her mind, Ko'an saw Sei and her futile solitary battle to save mankind as some sort of heroization of her murdered father—an ill-fated life resurrected for the sole purpose of righting everyone else's wrongs. Lucine had been like a mother, but after Phaedra was now more like a wise aunt or older sister. Illit was, of course, her big brother. And Phaedra, strange as it might sound, was now her new mother: mysterious, unbeatable, with a power beyond calculability, but—alongside Sei—capable of infusing Ko'an with an infinite talent and infinite will for putting all unrepentant bastards in their proper places.

Havana was Ko'an's slave of the moment. A slave with slaves of her own. Her trash can into which all of the unsettled accounts of the day could be tossed out with the rest of the shit. And because this particular trash can could store other trash cans, the setup made Ko'an feel particularly powerful. The day Havana finally argued with her mother and threw the Ko'an arrangement in the latter's face would be an especially sweet surprise. Yes, The Author would probably keep that one around for a while. At least until then.

Sei and Lucine, however, were a realm consecrated. There would be no funny business with either of them, lest her only chance at the only family she had deteriorate into that same maddening maze left by her birth mother.

In subsequent years, Ko'an would help Sei as much as possible using her powers of sneakery and intimidation of punks, but the two could only do so much without a stronger support base from the alphas whom Sei served. As company in regular society, Ko'an would always be a weird liability to Sei and she knew it, but remained grayly grateful mostly for her friend's listening ear.

As for Ko'an's biography, in the end she and Sei did publish it, redacting the bits that would invite legal trouble. The book made a few sales in o, and considerable sales in (of all things) mu. Apparently some law students found it fashionable to brag about having an autographed copy and an archived wink from a legendary punisher who was also an accidental symbol of omnigenders in power. Mary Pallas Aries, it was not lost on Ko'an that she might achieve further notoriety by helping Sei attain hers, but the price would surely spark a wildfire that nobody anywhere needed, not even alphakind as a whole. Alas, consistent with the behind-the-scenes action she had long known, Ko'an continued her full-time work as DSEC Writer, part-time work as friend to a rebel trying to save society as we know it. She found both roles rewarding, though encounters with her colleagues and the regular public never did get any easier.

# 238. Lead On

Ever since Mona-R had gotten to attend a performance of *Baduizm* shortly after her arrival on Earth, she had been a diehard lover of classical orbera. There was something about the mellow theatrics, the binaural soundscaping, the soothing lights and starry night climeography—the watery ghosts of constellations dancing above the heads of the audience—which turned the whole auditorium into a magical outpost surely annexed by Heaven.

As on Jupiter, Mona-R lived alone in her Miranda dorm room, but with almost three times the space of her old pod, she actually had space to collect things. On Earth, her new hobby lie in collecting as much classical orbera as she could find. Some days, she would play Erykah Badu's "Drama," Lionel Richie's "Jesus is Love," and all of Atatron's *Paul Scheele Miracles: The Remixes* and *Hemisync Dive Sessions* on sperse-loop, her climaplayr transforming her room into a nighttime ocean of auroric colors and serenely disorienting currents. She still dropped by her apartment in Diji almost bi-nightly, but with the Earth days more than twice as long as a Jupiterian djay, a mere four hours' visit was typically all she needed when she went. Earth just had too many more options to explore. Miranda HQ was itself a wonderland.

Thus having grown accustomed to her new and peaceful home, Mona-R was surprised when one Spring 45 day in 2773, she was summoned to the office of the head honcho herself. ♆² Apparently Phaedra Zeta wanted to check-in with the girl and see how she was doing, as well as discuss a few other things with her.

* * *

Spring 41, 2773

*Hey Phaedra, it's been a while,* Aimee greeted her friend with considerably less enthusiasm than normal. *How have you been?*

I'm well, and you?

*Oh, you know. Surviving these dusty corridors. What's up?*

I have a favor I want to ask you, and also maybe an offer I might trade in return. I know I haven't been in contact for a while and was hoping not to just pop out of nowhere with a big request.

*Okay.*

*Wow, I wish I could have done this in person,* Phaedra scolded herself, but it would have been posturing.

*Mhmm?*

Would you be interested in mentoring Mona-R?

*Not really. But since you ask so nicely, tell me more.*

You know that operations like ours don't just hire anyone to fill our shoes. I know there are laws for fairness, but at some point we betas really are like tuned systems, you know?

*Yes.*

So when I start looking for a successor to my role here at Miranda, there aren't a lot of options. There's no one qualified to do what I do except for you, but I know how attached you are to SIER.

*And I wouldn't be your first pick anyway, qualified or not.*

Aimee,... No, you're right. But in all fairness, there is no first pick. I'm stuck here either until someone magically appears, or we put in the years training them.

*You mean, you put in the years.*

No, *we.* I'm—Look, I'm trying to see far enough ahead into the next century, and need to know early whether there is anyone who can lead the group into what I think is coming. I suppose I could do it myself, but I would rather not die in this role. I still have things I want to do.

Dial listened with heavy gaze. You could see the indentations slightly more easily about her mouth, a certain thinness had crept beneath her eyes in just a short year and a half.

To be realistic, would you leave your post at SIER to take over Miranda? Could you?

I guess that's not the point anymore, Phaedra. Whether I would or could, I can't help but feel more like a resource than a friend.

Phaedra averted her eyes from the screen, sighing.

I know that look. It's rare that you do it. What's on your mind?

You just told me exactly what Isaiah said about you. He said that it was probably more important to you to catch the one who got away than to connect with someone who was starting to know his value. [42]

Clearly Aimee was not pleased with the comparison. That pouty child. Hm. I guess he really did grow up over there in Jupiter.

He did. I never thought you'd be the one among us rendering the harsher assessment, but I will say that he also probably knows how far he's come.

Aimee thought for a while. I really could have used a friend during all this. One day everything is fun and forward thinking, the next day all the world has abandoned you and your work for the new kid. They even talk about how your work should be a thing of the past.

I'm replacing myself if it makes you feel any better.

It doesn't. But your attempt at empathy is noted.

Phaedra wanted to concede to what she took to be a "no" from Dial regarding the mentoring ask, but chose to stay quiet instead.

And I like how you've offered a trade to complete whatever transaction you were hoping for, but I'll have to decline that part. I'd rather not see you as a third party vendor.

...

... No, I don't think I can mentor the girl. I'd like to help you, but know I would just be bitter. Unlike you, I'm not ready to have everything I stand for replaced—Well, let me say that differently. You can leave your role without losing everything you stand for. Because, to be honest, you'll be that hardened jetsetter wherever you go. The doors will always open for you, and you'll soon be on top in your next place as well. Me? I'm just a party girl who found a library of personalities and their researchers to party with forever. They're not friends, but they do keep me company when my friends don't.

Somehow Dial's words stung.

Look Phaedra, I don't want to be bitter. I also don't want to give up everything that is mine to walk in the shadow of everything that was yours, and everything that will be hers.

Heh.

What's so funny?

You know I've heard that in one way or another from all four of you? Genevieve and Jupiter, Isaiah and Saturn, Dynamene, and now you. Maybe it's the mark of my friendships. And I guess that's just the way the cookie crumbles.

Hmm.

You really should find Isaiah if you get a chance. You two might be closer to equal now if you saw who he's working to be.

No, you're right. He was probably just a potential conquest. They're no fun when they start talking back, and especially no fun when you have to chase them down.

Phaedra was disappointed to hear this rather callous assessment of someone who had really been through a lot.

Okay, well. I tried, I guess.

But we should hang out at some point. Maybe catch up on everything?

Phaedra smiled, I'd like that.

Cool. Well, I take it there's nothing more to talk about, so I'll spare us the awkwardness and hang up. See you around.

So when do you want to meet? And where?

Hehe, silly. It was just formality. "At some point" could mean anything. Let's just leave it open, okay?

Okay.

See you, Zeta.

Yeah.

And the call ended.

Phaedra was hardly sure that she would ever want another conversation like that again, but they would almost certainly stay in touch, regardless. It was what it was.


That was four days prior.

* * *

I'm glad to hear you're getting along well, Mona-R.

Yes ma' am.

So I need to ask you a cliché interview question, Phaedra poured her guest some more tea. Where do you see yourself in five years?

The little Navajo sprite pondered. Mmm, well, it's not like I don't know, but it's hard to put into words. I know I want to work in either Comm or Enti, maybe with history. Lik—uh, as in Earth's history. I want to build an ark like Noah in the myths, and take our biggest encyclopedias and convert them into worlds that you can walk around in.

## Okay.

I figure that, since we can already save people out here in Astra, maybe we can save Astra in, eh, maybe not our own Djji, but in something like Comm. So people or animals of the future could look us up and interpret us however they understand things. It wouldn't be putting our own algorithms in a device exactly, but more like putting our stories of our worlds in a device.

## What's the difference between that and what we do now?

Right now we store people with pieces of the world they knew. Here we would store worlds with templates for the kind of people in them, and the only way you would get specific people out is if you saved them in the first kind of system. This way, you could tell the whole story but not bog your data down with characters who all thought and did basically the same thing anyway.

(But Phaedra knew this already existed as well. This is the kind of system that Tippy and Cubrina-e had been pulled from. Still, Mona-R had thought about these things, and had actually considered them as part of a five-year plan. That she was already noting subtle differences in living-data storage systems despite the technical nature of this topic was quite impressive.)

## Well, you know we live in a complicated world. Other people have also thought of a kind of Ark, but the politics of building such a thing—who would fund it, what kinds of things would be put in there—gets tricky really fast. Although we actually have a couple of teams researching this, there really needs to be a breakthrough in repurposing resources for military buildup towards long term societal preservation instead.

Mona-R huffed.

## What's on your mind?

It's just that I always hear about that. I'm not real big into politics, but it just gets— sorry—annoying to hear about how politics is stopping this and the economy is stopping that and Jupiter conflicts are stopping this other thing. It's like nothing happens on a big level except for these things. But I know that's not true. Also, even though most things take money, people do do other things with their lives besides spending money, and I don't think all the money we spend matters as much when you zoom out. I mean I know it matters. But when I was still in Jupiter you could see how people got so stuck on o. They don't look at el or mu the way we do here— probably because no one would have any—and then psi is basically o since you don't get a chance to prove you have skills if people don't want to hire you or you don't want to apprentice in the first place without accepting o first. I guess I just get tired of everything revolving around Jupiter and money. Everything seems so peaceful and advanced here, so I really don't see why it still gets stopped by Jupiter more than anything.

Phaedra found Mona-R's frustration more than a little amusing.

## We also have our own internal politics.

Well if you do, then I can't tell. On the streams you all seem like you're having strategy conversation instead of plotting and ripping each other.

## Big ships are slow to move. The politics usually revolve around resource distribution and prioritization deadlines, public service allocation and things like that.

Can I ask a question?

## Sure.

I don't hear a lot about crime on Earth. On Jupiter we heard things all the time. Are betas just better behaved than everybody else?

## The short answer is yes. Betas and cyborgs are better behaved than pure naturals, and naturals are generally much better behaved than machina. Of course, most of the alpha population has been machina for a long time. When the first betas were created hundreds of years ago, their continued existence depended on deeply embedded rules for getting along with alphas. There was just no way they would have ever been considered for something as drastic as human citizenship if there were any suspicion that one would hack a bank or design the ultimate crime. Also, since there was no such thing as family or children for the first betas, their protective and survival instincts had to extend to any user or interfacer they might inherit at random. I still remember my own beta attendant back when I was still alpha, Raliolite. He was gentle as a lamb. He was also curious, considerate, and broadminded, just like you. I still miss him sometimes after all these years.

## But yes, betas and cyborgs have certain cognitive algorithms preprogramed into them so that, say, you don't need a whole team to train a cyborg baby who emerges from the adoption lab two

years old already. When we alphas are reprinted as betas the way I was, our old 1-gorithms still need a format for telling what kinds of personality patterns go where. The process may write us as our old selves, but since our biology is printed and not stochastically organic, our printed biochemistry has its own "firmware" so to speak. That used to be actual hardware. Now it's vector organic—not stochastic—in a particular prosocial direction. When we mess up, we know we're messing up. Betas and cyborgs still commit crimes all the time thanks to the general rules of free will and being trained by every random thing around you, but with cybersecurity being what it is, it is exceptionally hard for them to get away with it, not to mention dropping heavily in your el values everywhere you go.

Oh... I think that's neat how, even though I'm a cyborg, I'm still 60% organic.

Yes, you have to be. That's been the rule for about 80 years.

I know.

So speaking of Jupiter, you told me last time how you feel about alpha-run societies. If we trained you to be a research team leader, would you—Well let me ask you this way, would you be interested in leading a research team? We love unique and forward perspectives around here.

That would be awesome! But, um I'm not really a leader type. Like I couldn't tell people what to do and get them to listen to me. People don't even listen to me in group projects for school. And then, people like talking over me and I always let them. And I can't haggle very well or pull the courage to complain when I've been ripped off. And I get easily hurt with negative feedback. I'm scared of hard conversations, too.

Hahaha! It sounds like you know yourself very well. Now if these weren't problems would you be able to lead if asked?

Uh, I think so. I mean, if somebody asked me and they really needed it then I'd try anyway, even if I sucked at it.

Yes, sometimes you are the only one.

I mean the people who asked me would have to be pretty desperate.

Phaedra smiled. You have 19998 Binoche in your wheel don't you?

Yes.

Where is it?

Mmmmm... My geoequivalent is July 8, 2742, 34N54, 110W09 00:06 -7, so my 19998 would be in 209°50T. 61: Travel talk. But I usually travel solo so there is no one to be a beacon to.

We'll fix that. Let's define leadership as a relationship where one party regularly steers at least one other party beside themselves in some designated area of action. Not all leadership involves steering *people*, and not all steering requires formal force.

Oh...

You can lead software code, gardens in growing, a field of thought, or the perception of something among a group of others. You can steer an entire organization by being married to its official leader and saying certain things to them. Or you can steer the restocking of store shelves by clearing out a certain food that suits your appetite. These all may seem like minor ways to lead, until you transform them into different philosophies for dealing with people— if that's what you choose. As for traditional leadership, for those of us who are not so good at giving direct commands, there are other ways to steer people even if you don't have a formal role, aren't listened to, and couldn't tell them what to do even if you were listened to. You could do this by complaining, by noticing something, by innovating, or just listening to the ideas of your team. The important thing about leadership is that, if you want to do it well, you need to always keep the natural direction of your teammates top of mind. They were going right or left anyway, your job is to help them get there using the tools of your institution to enable this. If you can effectively use your surrounding tools to open doors for them which they would not have found themselves, and if you can also remove barriers with those tools, then you are ahead of most people who only have the leadership title.

Oh...

By the way, you don't actually need to know where your 19998 Binoche is. It's just a suggestion for an area you are more likely to shine in without trouble. There are lots of asteroids like that, and lots of ways to inspire people. The White Moon Selena, 550 Senta, anything in your 17.5°-20° Capricorn or Aquarius, 13140 Shinchukai, 6853 Silvanomassaglia, and 94228 Leesuikwan also come to mind. You just need to remember, no astronomical stead has to matter at all if the people or things you lead aren't willing or able to receive it from you. Sometimes the monkeys won't care how good your speeches are, they'll only care about the size of your banana cart.

OOoooh... But I have a question. It doesn't make a difference if I'm in Djji or—

It doesn't make a difference *whether.*

Oh, I'm sorry. It doesn't make a difference whether I'm in Djji or here, I always end up on teams with people stronger than me. And I can't tell them anything. How do you handle that?

Phaedra chuckled a little. Age, rank, power, and even stubbornness are all relative as long as you know who you are and what your limits are. There was a famous study on teacher's favorites—what made them and what distinguished them from teacher's pets. "Pets" is the name that haters give to people who look like the teachers favor them at everyone else's expense. "Favorites" is the name that the teachers themselves give to certain students in conversation with others. You know what the defining qualities of a favorite was? They were easy to teach, usually required little behavioral correction, and stood out as thinkers beyond the boxes of their peers; these were the kinds of students that made teachers proud to be in their profession. More generally, they made the person in the leadership position feel effective just by being themselves.

Mhmm!

Sometimes a leader will single you out not because of anything you've done, but because you represent what success or ambition or some goal looks like to them. But that doesn't just apply to leaders, it applies to almost everyone in a forced-goal setting like work or a project.

You need to be you, but you need to be the kind of you which doesn't interfere with people who have more experience than you, no matter how much of a stubborn jerk they might be. You need the discipline to tune out their jerk mode. Mute them if you have to. But recognize that their strength or whatever is a position that somebody on your team needs to fill in order for you all to win the game. Unless you want to do it yourself. When everyone is stronger than you—especially in ways that can make you feel inferior—you can still be better at being yourself than they can. And whatever you value that they aren't covering—which your whole team also needs—that's where you can become even their number one pick.

I don' t understand.

When I was young, I was also surrounded by people who knew a lot more than me. Some of them rubbed it in my face in the beginning. But my talent was always an ability to keep journeying, keep exploring while they stayed comfortable. Over time, they knew I was just really good at continuing into new situations, and that became my place of leadership in a way. I should note, though, that in order for the team to win as a whole, you also have to see where everyone else is also a leader. For every one thing you lead in, there will be at least 10 things that you follow in, and you'll have to respect that as you elevate. It's just good Golden Rule practice for how your brain thinks about all leadership everywhere.

So I add my one little corner of skill to the whole team effort, and make sure that everyone gets the same chance to contribute as I do.

Yes. And that's what a leader does. They represent the whole. You could be the lowest person on the team, but if you do your own little weird thing <u>on behalf of the whole</u>, you'll usually make a better eventual leader than at least half of the others on your team.

Oh...

But there's a warning that comes with that. If you don't have it in you to push for everyone else besides yourself in your unit, then people like me will tell you that you are not fit to lead that unit. Maybe you can lead your friends or your favorites, but if you are only ready to lift up half of your unit, then that's not good enough. You will either need to develop the maturity to get back to the clique you belong in, or your successors will simply color over your name.

Mona-R nodded her understanding. Respect.

Something like that.

How do I get these strong people around me to respect me?

Well, I'll be honest. You're at a disadvantage because you ask questions, you let others cut you off and, as you've said, you have a hard time telling people what to do. The traditional picture of leadership prizes the opposite of these traits, where we typically think of an ability [to fire a lot of people], [to steamroll your will], and [to issue commands] as reflecting the certainty that we wish we had for braving unfamiliar territory. Depending on the field, expertise can help. But it's easier to be a good delegator and commander *without* expertise and still pass as a good leader than to be an expert with no sense of command. Your traits don't align with that typical view, and you may want to think twice about going toe to toe with an incumbent who has these traits while being in front of an audience who prefers this. In general, the broad public—alphas, betas, and deltas alike—prefer confidence, command and certainty—even certainty in damaging rhetoric—over the complexities of real systems and real issues. Certain or not, you won't make that public feel good if you talk over their heads.

But now there's an upside to this. People who are good at getting respect in the traditional leadership frame are also the people who take all of the cannon fire while the real operators of the business, writers of the policy, or enforcers of the rules actually shape the system's very core. You can, by virtue of being the weakest link on the team, actually cost your unit the Superbowl if the star player is not pleasing to you, and that's a power you truly have that many of your strong teammates will not necessarily recognize. There are forms of power that you can display only to yourself that will at least help you respect yourself, and from there you can go in knowing that it doesn't really matter if you've earned others' respect as long as you're at least starting from your own foundation. Know that others' respect is secondary to your own self-respect when it comes to moving a team, and if you can't start with this then you need to stop looking at their side eye and look at your own first. If you can't respect yourself first by knowing what it is you *can* contribute, then again you should have nothing to say. That's your burden to go home and repair. Do you respect yourself, Mona-R?

I think so... Yes, I do!

## Why?

Because I' ve taught myself tons, crossed two planets alone, am a great artifact hunter, and know that not a lot of people could come this far from where I started. I know I got a lot of help, but I think I' ve done a good job living positively every day.

## I agree. Good. And in a group, what do you bring to the table?

I ask questions that maybe people haven' t looked at in a while and even if they have, I ask them in a way that gets them thinking about the possibilities again. I also usually know more about data artifacts than the rest of my teammates, and get invited to more places—maybe because people don't take me as seriously and want to take me under their wing.

Very good. So you know what you bring to a group. And you recognize yourself as having the skills you just claimed. That's one way of defining respect.

Mona-R looked puzzled.

Ψ² You respect a thing when your actions support the role it claims or which its surroundings claim. You don't respect it when this fails to apply. You *disrespect* it when you tensely put a different role on it despite the claims. The reason respect matters (and many people who regularly rely on threats and force don't know this) is that respect is more than an idea. It's actually a statement of people's chosen actions in light of the claims or hype made around you. If you want to know who's actually doing what you want them to do when you're not there, look at who shows you respect. Listen.

Mona-R nodded for a while, concentrating hard on what was being said.

Ψ² The thing about respect is that you don't have to earn it for traits you don't have. You don't have to get in the sandbox with the big boys and show how much you know. You don't have to argue with the person who will never let anyone get a word in edgewise. You don't even have to win the debate—in some cases—as long as you can make your opponent feel that they lost or make their allies doubt them. These reflect different kinds of expertise; sometimes you can show up completely inferior in the task at hand, but still come out a winner just for surviving the impossible the way you did. The name of the game in respect is to get everyone else to acknowledge the truth of a particular set of claims made about you, and for them back that acknowledgement with action. Those claims, for better or worse, will be the things you are most easily respected for. Learn to embrace these claims and gather them in a giant aura around you to automatically trigger certain actions in favor of your whole team's good. You will find it easier to be both a good leader and a respected one.

Hmm... the cyborg-girl didn't seem very satisfied with this summary.

Now let me see if I can guess what you're thinking, Phaedra continued. This is starting to look like a puzzle with a lot more pieces, and pieces you can't necessarily control.

Yeah... I mean, people have asteroids in their stead mostly based on their how they grew up and a whole bunch of things they were doing automatically in childhood which they didn' t realize they were doing. If you only know your stead in your 20s, then that means that you can' t really control what you' d be a great leader in.

**You can do anything if you're willing to carry the required level of tension to achieve it. But yes, that tension tends to spill out if it isn't your most natural energy. Raliolite taught me that.**

Hmm... **frown**

**Does that bother you?**

Yes ma' am.

**Why?**

Because it makes me think that I may have these goals for dealing with people that don' t actually line up with my background or team goals or natural talents. In order to be a good leader I have to have a whole bunch of factors come together which people like and respect and follow and can be supported by... It just doesn' t seem probable.

**It isn't. Which is why there are many leaders, but few great leaders. The world calls for traditional leaders by default, and knows how to talk about them. You have CEOs here and kings there. Social fighters here and top ranking businesses there. The occasional inventor or science figure. But they typically have to be broadcastable with a certain kind of social appeal in order to be seen, you're right. But that doesn't mean that the leaders you see are the only kinds of leader that exist. Some are simply the head of their household or their friendship groups, and they bring value to the only world that matters to them. Do you know what world matters to you?**

At first it was my community. Mostly Navajo. But I guess that was how I was programmed. Then I moved here and it' s a lot more about each culture' s algorithm. I want every culture to have an algorithm that gets saved before they get all blended up into sameness. That' s the one thing that alphas have which I think is really cool. Their cliques and cultures can be ridiculous sometimes, but are really fun to study in how they relate to one another.

**So is that your unit? Anyone who identifies with a culture?**

I guess so. All of the Astran world.

Phaedra affirmed to herself how correct she had been in choosing Mona-R as her intended successor.

Hm. It's a long journey ahead, Miss Redfeather. If you're really serious about that.

I think I am. I know it wasn't an accident that the glove found me and all these powerful people brought me here to keep learning more and more. I believe in God, and I believe that He has a place for me.

Phaedra's Mona Lisa smile obscured any thoughts she may or may not have had on the matter.

I mean, I know there is a big timeline out there, and I'm on it right now. I can't order all of the events on it, but they point outside of my server, past Jupiter, to Miranda and the Solar Council and what happens with the alphas, and a dimension literally higher than the one I started in. I could have just been code, but some Timeline Reader out there keeps pushing me further.

Heh. You have a strong sense of purpose.

Yes ma'am.

Okay. Show it to me. I've told you what you need to do. You must know that I expect great things from you. Greater than personal interest and greater than sitting by and watching humanity coast on a track it can't possibly keep up. You will need to lead in something. Even if it is your own private skill and nobody ever knows about it. Use that skill for everyone in the world, but do it by directing the small resources around you towards the growth of any whole unit you land in. Never favor your favorites even if you have them. It's about the ENTIRE unit, do you understand?

Yes ma'am, Mona-R reeled back a little, palpably intimidated. This was clearly a directive from the Queen herself.

$4^2$ Your only objective is to help everyone else help the whole advance, with every individual made better through their own chance to express their talents on the way, higher than they did before you got there.

Yes ma'am.

It doesn't matter whether your talents are normally considered good or bad. Use them for the good. It usually lasts longer *if you stick with it.* Even if you have less help from easy things like

everyone else's fear and distraction, you'll need to be more than
the algorithms you collect from everyone else.

Okay.

42 And if you ever feel like you need to fight for respect,
consider that you might be on the wrong battlefield.
Change the frame, let someone else do the talking, pick a
different project, or ask your supervisor to move you to
a more fitting role. Or see if you can move yourself out
of there. As you said, most of what we're naturally good at leading
in is not the same as where we are when we find out we want to be
a leader. Once you learn you want to lead others, you will almost
certainly have to move to a place where the people **or things**
will listen to you, respect you, and receive what you have to offer
them. So when you talk to your supervisor or whoever your enabler
is, just make sure you can tell them what your fitting role actually is.
They can't help you if you can't tell them what it is you're after. And
if you can't even tell yourself where you fit and who you fit around,
then you're dead before you start.

Yes ma' am.

Do you have any questions for me?

Um, so you' re going to put me on a team to lead?

Probably not until you've learned from other team leaders.
Otherwise I would be setting you up for failure in an organization
full of people who are much more experienced than you are, not to
mention undercutting my managers. But I'll make you a deal: Help
your team shine past where it started, advance your own innovative
culture-saving goal at the same time while you are on that team, do
it without dropping the team's spirit, and you may hear from me
again sooner than later.

Okay, I understand.

And one warning: I don't ever want to read selfish ambition on you.
When you get to my level that kind of thing will surely cap you, and I
will see to it that you go no further in my organization. Don't
consider that a threat, because it doesn't actually apply to you as
far as I can tell. But do consider it a warning. Ambition is fine. *Selfish*
ambition at the expense of the people around you is absolutely no
good.

Yes, ma' am.

Any more questions?

Yes, uh. Who' s your favorite leader?

My predecessor Twice Jack. A mere teenager when I met him, but wiser and more patient than anyone I ever met. He was also an expert in navigating deep and dangerous types of institutional power without ever getting so much as a speck of darkness on his character. I've never met anyone who could do it on that level.

Oh... I' ve looked him up, but I never knew.

He was like a brother, a third father after my adopted one, the Dalai Lama, and a top-level CEO all rolled into one.

That sounds like respect.

It is.

Okay.


Phaedra rose from her seat. If there's nothing else then get out there and knock 'em dead, Redfeather.

Mona-R smiled. Nobody really called her by her particle, but it sounded so important when Miss Zeta said it. I won' t fail you. Ma' am.

Very good. You can change the world in small things, Mona-R. As long as they align with the Greatest Whole. Even small acts can resonate beyond you. Don't forget that.

I won' t.

# 239. A New Home in Sun-Powered Black Holes

On the morning on Fall 1, 2793 n.e., Mona-R would take her place as the new Executor of Miranda United. Alongside her longstanding Temporal Navigator Jake Nolli, she would open her tenure with speech that rang of excitement, boundless curiosity, and the far-ranging work of the future.

The circumstances facing humanity had changed greatly over the twenty years between that one on one conversation with Phaedra and the role the cyborg now occupied. Some 29 billion physical humans now occupied 10 of the postulated 14 planetary bands of the Solar System, including all 8 major planet bands, Pluto-Charon and Quaoar. Meanwhile, an estimated 14 trillion registered humans occupied the hundreds of thousands of Diji servers across the realm. Somewhere along the line, population control had ceased to be a resource matter, and become a bandwidth matter based on certain maximum amounts and kinds of coherently transmissible energy in the ecliptic. Thanks to the application of macroscale quantum tech, it really was now possible to teleport a small object from Mercury to Neptune at speeds faster than light, and given that you held a copy of human data at both places, you could also teleport the human themselves. Finally, about 10 years prior, homo sapiens had successfully completed the first instance of its ultimate technology: The horizon-bending computer (or just "horizon" for short) consisted of several black-hole networks linked quantumly to an anticalculatory event horizon shell, enabling not only the writing of data, but the automatic and near-infinite logging of all events within a region, visible or not. The technology was inherently gravigational rather than light- or sound-based, and made copious use of vacuum capacitance derivatives ("space bubbling") to throw signals from here to there in the same way that the planets and asteroids themselves all seemed to talk to each other via the potential energy-dimensions inherent in their source chemistry and landed orbits. It seemed that the notion of Astra as a giant astronomical calculation was more than just an exercise in asteroidal Halloween costumes and trajectory formulas. It was also a deep reflection of how chemical geometry did and didn't work, what constituted an effective resonant "glue" for each type of geometry, and how analogies to this could be made and put to use in establishing multilocalities for the same physics object across far separate regions with no apparently measurable medium in between.

Before the employees of Miranda and countless viewers across the streams, Mona-R spoke of the great challenges that lie ahead in "maintaining the lives we currently know while curbing the progressive exhaustion of natural resources and ambient energy it takes to be us." What if we could truly place ourselves into the very bonds that held together stars and asteroids, transmitted light spectra and sky waves? Could we not preserve the dharma native to most of space while leaving the perceptual worlds around us seamlessly undisturbed? The potential benefits of horizon in-bonding would be enormous, as a single system might truly encompass an entire universe of times and possibilities, while yet a different system bent these possibilities into distinctly different permutations. A prehistoric world for energies inclined to live it. A 16-bit pixel world for energies inclined to live that.

And what would it take to move humanity into the "arc of temporospaces" simply known as @s? Nothing, really. For the intended grid of horizons would always be logging an airspace's worth of everything on an emhimic level beneath the scale of a gluon. And yet through sleep, if you so chose, your beta processes could lens themselves back into the calculations of your nano teleport upon the nearest horizon's edge, allowing you to awaken in the very same world, yet contained inside of the horizon machine. The only thing that would not be there is the machine itself, for what was formerly its material nature in the dimension above now constituted the complete existence of all things around you.

As for your Astran self, it would awaken as normal, yet somewhere within your Homo sapiens beta or delta consciousness would be the knowledge of other dimensions you had been to. Whether or not the human experience of Astra would survive the coming millennia and its unquenchable appetite for planet scraping, there could and would, for the first time, be a backup of all that currently and would thereafter exist within a horizon's orbit. More exotic horizons had fancier means of transporting data to and from other horizons, on the tunnels of time and incarnation-path networks. Mona-R had toured and returned from these herself, and attested to their surreal mimicry of eternity itself.

(But she was, of course, Dijian at her core, and had not yet found the occasion to convey the not so subtle differences between leaving a horizon with your whole memory intact versus leaving it as though it was all a dream. No matter, the gist was conveyed as honestly as she knew how to put it.)

(It helped that, in classic form, Nolli had also visited these worlds. Still a pure natural but with a physical lens implant of his own, he too could experience the subconscious calculatory freeway of betahood. He claimed that it was like downloading the walkthrough for your life's game, suddenly knowing that most of your enemies were your own stupid behaviors—the beatability of the game, wholly connected to the class of collectively interpreted, post-death endings you seemed to be gunning for in the way that you lived and the types of mire you kept around you.)

Although full betaization of the alphas hadn't actually occurred, it was all too clear that alphahood itself was fast becoming an ancient technology. Nature likely had plans to deprecate it within the next century or so, starting with the proposal among various governments across the Solar System that the requirement for an alpha-type mating result be removed from the list of human species requirements. Under these changes, alphas, betas, and cyborg/deltas could still mate with each other as they wished, but new models of reprinter would no longer be required to furnish alpha incubation functions within the beta or delta body. And with that, the incalculably heavy resource costs of creatures truly required to parasite themselves off the dust of their planet in order to live… these costs would begin to magically disappear as the definition of "humanity" would come to describe the information, the experience, the memory alone.

Without most people's awareness, the human exodus from the world of Astra, into the transmission dimensions of Sol had already begun. Few people understood that, with the continued construction of these "horizon boxes," their known selves would be auto-ported into the world of dreams, surviving them after death in this realm. Mona-R, however, knew this. As did Jake and most of the staff at Miranda and its partner organizations. It wasn't that there had been a decision to make many, all, or even any of a certain species extinct, but rather that there had been a decision to preserve through "backup" what every species had done, in the highest fidelity possible. Many people guessed that we couldn't have pulled it off without the cooperation of Jupiter, whose ultimate path had proven much more complicated.

As of Fall 1, 2793, no major airspace was led by an alpha. New America had been taken over by a tide of beta leadership as early as 2778, its Chancellorate system abolished and replaced with a three-part government of Executive, and Legislative, and Judiciary branches. Osaira, feeling itself cornered by increasing iyohnic installation, would eventually declare war on Zeusland and Mazelor. These two powers, however, because they had ceded quietly to Solar Council influence, were supplied with the weapons needed to subdue their opponent permanently. With the fall of Osaira in 2790, a new beta-friendly alpha was appointed as Prime Minister of the airspace, and the last of the alpha-controlled triumvirate which had opposed the newer humanities for over three centuries… was no more.

Spring 1, 2792 seemed to bring with it the beginning of a new era of peace for all of humanity, as the Solar Council capitol at Mars and the overwhelmingly beta leaders of Jupiter convened to welcome the gas giant as the last major-band member of the Solar Council. Back on Earth, Mona-R was invited into Phaedra's office, and in conversation with Zeta and two other board members, informally offered a role as the next Head of Miranda United. For people in positions such as this, the workings of individual lives would constitute a much smaller fraction of the necessary scope of concern, and Mona-R would surely have quite the learning curve ahead of her, but she was far and away the best candidate for the job. The conversation was brief, and after it was over she would take the rest of the day to do some celebratory shopping. Her dream was actually coming true. How vast the road ahead seemed to be!

# Resolved Timeline Ⴗ²

### {Ⴗ + Decisions of: Phaedra}

…Lastly, there were the alphas themselves. Perhaps out of a generic respect for free will, perhaps because he was simply more indifferent than he had expected to be, Zyr's accounts of the original humans' fate would be a little vague here. In 2773 there had been billions of them, their institutions and quirky tribal structures looming over the Solar System like a Theian shadow. In 2794 there were still billions of them, but that number had fallen. Had it been a drastic drop? Had there been riots, wars, or anarchy upon discovery of the betan's ablation of a key piece of the original sapiens spirit? Had they gotten wind of the ABC plan at all?

How many fought to the end for their continued identities as alphas? How many fell? Did anyone fall at all?

The answers to these questions are not known to this day, but one thing is certain: The story of alpha abdication contained both easy paths and hard paths as options. The route they ultimately took could fill a million books, but all paths begin at one noteworthy event, and the debut of a certain black and gold arm brace onto the human scene.

# 240. Siphonophore

Winter 60, 2776.

When animal rights activist and local Chelsea-Lock hero Stacy Stack announced that she intended to run against incumbent Kyle Banner for the Collectivist gubernatorial nomination, Banner's office (including Sei) viewed it as more of an irritation than anything else. Stack's campaign revolved around lambasting the Banner administration for kowtowing to the remaining Chancellorate leaders, not doing enough to restore the jobs that had been taken away, getting rich off of shady alliances with Clannel and Dyer officials, not fighting for cyborg rights yet bankrolling a suspicious and expensive machine designed to tie up the airspace's legal departments for decades. The claims made by Stack rang of 70% truth, with the last 30% completely twisted out of context and beyond basic sense-making, such that the sheer irritation of having to craft responses to nonsense frustrated the long-time Governor more than anything else. "She's saying that I'm guilty of those guys' crimes!" he complained. "And she's only trailing me by 13 points! 49-36? Do you believe that?"

I swear, gullible voters piss me off sometimes.

Members of the Banner camp had no intention of attending the Stack rally downtown that day, until a strange thing happened which necessarily commanded all of Sei's attention. The rebel-turned-policymaker glanced up from her documents for only a split second, and there it was: one of the Angel finder's nanos hopped gleefully up and down in an obvious bid for Sei's attention. The latter preceded to scan around immediately as would a squirrel suddenly alerted to the presence of a bobcat. Behind the desk. Under the desk? Next to a shelf? In the air vents? Where in the world did—?

But having gotten Sei's attention, the nano settled down and projected a semitransparent scene into the air. The scene showed pre-event coverage of the Stack press conference, along with the superimposed words, "Go" and "Tell no one why." "Go. DO NOT mention Angel finder." Quite taken aback by the sudden visit, Sei pocketed the nano and went to see Banner.

She told him that she thought it would be useful to gather more insight into what was going on.

**Whatever. It's your life.**

Standing amidst the lively crowd of nearly 200 people, Sei felt even more out of place than ever. Sure, these people were speaking out for what they believed in, but Kyle was doing as good a job as anyone could reasonably ask for given the wildly complicated political circumstances. What exactly did these people expect? Should they have kept initiatives like the Future Jobs Club on the docket instead of scrapping them following those extra feasibility estimates? The people were always coming together by setting themselves apart. But what was the point?

About halfway through what was planned to be a 15 minute speech, Stacy Stack began coughing. She stumbled on her words, took a sip of her water, then attempted to resume. But before she could continue, a heckler launched some previously unheard of attacks.

"What about that deal you made with the Sovereign governor of Dyer at Andretti's? I saw you there!"

"What!?" **gasp** "Are you serious?" "You've got to be kidding!" "How c—"

And what would have been, in all normal circumstances, a simple comment from a heckler somehow spiraled into more questions. Then more questions. What was the heckler talking about? Was it true? How did Stack plan to answer the claim?

It turns out that the accusation *was* true. Despite being a genuine activist and advocate, Stacy Stack had other reasons for running against Kyle Banner. One of them was related to some resource allocation decisions that put Stack's animal defense organization behind a local greenspaces project where funding priority was concerned. It had been a basic tradeoff, but Stack wasn't having it at all. And over the course of a very long and very odd five minutes, all of these issues somehow spilled forward, culminating in Stack being escorted off the stage by her campaign manager in a shower of mumbling and turned backs. For whatever reason, Stack's very basic press conference had morphed into an almost Twilight

Zone-level disaster as 200 supporters evaporated into no more than 60 before her very eyes.

The event would prove so embarrassing that later that week, amidst the criticism of an unforgiving public, Stack would issue a statement declaring that she would not be running after all.

Nobody really understood what had happened or why the press conference had gone so horrifically badly, but Sei could not get out of her mind the image of what appeared to be a white arm brace somewhere in the crowd. It might have been worn by an unfamiliar olive-skinned man far in the distance, but she couldn't be sure. Alas, the nano she had put into her pocket prior to the event was gone by the time she made it back to her auto.

One week later, the nano showed up on Sei's desk again, this time imploring her to watch a certain public stream. It seemed that the staunchly Sovereign New American Minister of Defense had finally come to terms with a terminal disease he had long held and kept quiet about, and was now stepping down. The outgoing Chancellor Bennet had selected a temporary replacement just hours earlier, but this person seemed to bumble and blither the whole public statement thing before a room full of media.

Oddly, one of the questions asked by the press was posed by a heavy-set Nordic man wearing a kind of white arm brace. He also wore some sort of black mitten over his right hand which resembled a small hand cast. Sei froze the image to scrutinize the scene further. Yes, it was covered up beyond recognition beneath the correspondent's semi-translucent coat arms, but the handiwork was unmistakable. It was the Angel finder… flanked by a giant, uncomfortable-looking black mitten? But there was also something else faintly viewable beneath the translucence of the man's left coat arm. A complementary brace flashed a brief glint of red beneath the reflecting camera lights. The nano took extra care to blow up the image as Sei watched. She as a witness was powerless to do anything about it, but she now knew what "it" was: Her friends had advanced their technology greatly, and were finally using the Angel finder to disable the roles of certain alphas. The technology was clearly grantz-based, and the nano messengers were clearly a taunt of some kind, but what did the ABC forces expect her to do with this? Were they just messing with her?

Winter 77, 2776 n.e.

Sei stepped outside one pre-afternoon to get some fresh air, where she witnessed one of her colleagues Harmon Bazzy standing on stilts atop his usual soapbox in argument with another colleague Angelita Willamot. The latter, gossip monger and resident backstabber was known to stoop to any level to achieve her aims, but was nonetheless recognized for her unquestioned skill as Public Relations Director. In the middle of the argument, that new intern—whatever his name was—asked Harmon a question.

"Mr. Bazzy, I'm sorry to interrupt, but were you able to fit me in on your Calendar yet?"

"No, no. Not now, Trooper. Mrs. Willamot here isn't getting the point," Bazzy dismissed the intern.

"The point was lost 5 minutes ago, I'm telling you that if you recommend that line to the Governor, I'm going to have to preempt you," Willamot calmly warned.

"Is that code for poisoning the waters on my strategy? You don't even know what's in my report and, frankly, it really isn't your business."

"Honey, everything in this building is my business."

"No it isn't."

"Yes it is."

"No it isn't."

"Yes it is, and I don't know how many times I've told you not to present ideas to the heads until I've vetted them. It only makes complication for me."

"For you? What about the people who actually run this government? This isn't your personal kingdom."

"To you it is, babe. And you're upsetting me in front of the intern."

Suddenly, Sei felt a noticeable dislike towards Angelita and Bazzy both, but the former even more so.

The intern spoke up.

"Well, since nobody's listening here, I'll just call my dad, Craig Allende, and ask him to explain this to me."

"What?" Bazzy and Willamot both froze. At least the latter could still manage a few words. "The Collectivist Allegiant Chair? I didn't know he had a son."

"Well…"

"Oh, my apologies!" Bazzy managed a full 180. "And here I've just been putting you off!"

Willamot, however, wasn't nearly as impressed. "Anyone who has to pull their connections like that must be important. Gotta keep the noses nice and brown, eh Bazz?"

"You know what, Angelita? You're a jerk." Bazz scowled.

"Says the sycophant."

"Ah, I knew I'd find you here," Lieutenant Governor Mitchell just happened to pass by. "Angelita, a word."

"Yes, sir." Willamot stuck her tongue out at Bazz before she left.

"Bitch," Bazzy muttered within perfect earshot of everyone. As soon as the words slipped out, however, Bazzy instantly turned white—as if he had no idea what had just happened. "I—I'm sorry."

"We'll talk later," the Lieutenant Governor warned sternly…


The next pre-afternoon two djays later, Sei once again stepped away from her desk to get some fresh air. There stood Harmon Bazzy again, this time looking quite depressed as he complained to another coworker.

"I just don't understand it. It was just our usual argument. Now I'm reprimanded with a permanent mark on my record, and she's out. I mean, she deserves it in trying to take me down with her—just 'cause the Lieutenant had these reservations all of a sudden. But man, why did she need to say all of that stuff about me on her way down? She was the one being let go."

The colleague agreed. The one thing Willamot feared was being out of a job. When it was clear that the Lieutenant Governor had finally had enough of her gatekeeping when it came to critical information, her job is exactly what she lost. But it had all come so suddenly. Meanwhile, she had all kinds of things to say about several staff including Bazzy, and a cloud of suspicion seemed to loom all around the Governor's office. It was just so stupid. There had been no warning, and not even the chains of command made sense. House cleaning had simply started without reason, and several people were suddenly feeling insecure about their jobs. Many more people knew that the former had real reasons to be insecure.


Sei looked upon the whole sudden affair with little concern and a fair amount of ambivalence, but did find it curious that a long time fixture like Angelita would not only be mysteriously let go, but that she herself didn't bother to fight it. Then there was this whole naming of names thing which left at least three other people reprimanded. Why didn't it just blow over with some good ole' fashioned

refereeing? It was as if the whole building were under some kind of triggery
spell…


Sei was alone in the break room enjoying her graveyard shift snack when the
intern Trooper dropped in. A lanky Turkish boy of some sort, his skinned glowed
with a kind of radiance that made you want to rub your eyes to make sure you
weren't going blind.

"Can I sit here?" Trooper asked Sei if he could take the seat next to her.

Uh, this place is pretty big and there are plenty of tables, but I guess.

"Thanks," Trooper broke out his sandwich and began applying the mustard
packet.

Sei found Trooper's selection of her table to be strange and uncomfortable, given
that there were five other tables in the breakroom. But she didn't want to appear
rude either.

After a couple of silent minutes eating his sandwich, Trooper began the
conversation:

"You know it's weird how little things can suddenly blow up on people who've
bottled them in."

Hm.

"It's like we have these little seeds of doubt, and if we gave them any attention like
the Lieutenant Governor did, we might eventually talk to the manager of a Public
Relations person and simply pull the trigger. Next thing you know, boom.
Someone's cleaning out their office. It's amazing what a sudden flood of distrust
can do."

Sei wasn't particularly thrilled with Trooper's baseless speculation. How do *you*
know the reason Angelita was fired?

"Oh, I just know." Trooper pulled his sandwich to his mouth, letting his long
sleeves droop slightly.

And there Sei saw it again—this time up close and personal. Trooper was wearing
the Angel finder!


What the!?

"Sei? Genevieve. Sit down."

But that was out of the question. Not only could Sei not sit down, she couldn't even move, really.

"Did you know that the intern George Trooper only exists to about 10 of you in this building? Then he ducks into a bathroom and ceases to be?"

Instantly, Sei's expression transformed from one of petrified surprise… to one of horror.

"All around New America, we've seeded at least 60 petty disagreements and personal crises like this, quietly, resulting in the inexplicable capitulation of 73 individuals we deem inappropriate to occupy the halls of leadership. I won't bore you with the science of it all," Trooper continued, "but I will tell you that we are very good at what we do. Much better than your alpha friends could ever imagine."

Sei remained frozen.

"Heh. Relax, Genevieve. I come in peace. As a friend to you, actually."

But Sei was hardly of a mind to make herself comfortable. How did this guy even know her name?

"Hm. In all these years watching you, I've never seen you actually scared. I guess there really is a first time for everything. Well, no matter. I assume you got the nanos we sent you?"

**sigh** Sei regained enough of her composure to reclaim her seat. The Council.

"Something like that. Can I show you something?"

Sei nodded once in the affirmative.

Trooper pulled back his right shirt sleeve, revealing the familiar device in full view. "This one you know. It is, of course, the Angel finder."

Next, the young man pulled back his left sleeve, exposing an entirely new work. A sleek and somehow threatening matte-onyx arm brace embroidered in organic gold accents, the device appeared to be something that only the Devil himself would be caught wearing. Spanning the length of the brace's upper forearm, a linear light glowed in faint white, as if it were ready to scan an airport passenger at any time. "This one… is new to you. We call it the Demon finder. It greatly amplifies distrust in doubtful characters—all doubtful characters within eyeshot, whether they are physically present or on the streams. The ensuing distrust is compounded with the writing of memory, until the maliciously vengeant are wholly distrusted by everyone in range who looked at them. Seems pretty wimpy as a weapon, doesn't it? But you could say that about breaking news too."

"And on my right hand is this glove." The Turkish boy revealed the black utility with its striated chop. "We call this Epic. It reads emhim and does some exotic look ups to calculate what a person's worst fear might be. Fed back to the Demon finder with its grantzing features, we have instant, undetectable, worst case-making social relationship control. Since alphas typically don't put any thought into their biases against one another, even the most petty events can be turned into critical staffing decisions, leadership, appointments, and new alliances."

Sei relaxed a little. Trooper seemed to be very proud of these gadgets, but they weren't really all that dangerous in her estimation…

…That is, until the next "gadget" was revealed.

The intern rose from his seat and stepped back a little. Without warning, a series of wireframe-like cracks formed all over the young man's skin, yielding to what must have been a thousand flesh and cloth-textured blocks and formerly invisible electronics components swirling about the space where the intern once stood. Temporarily, the swirling blocks "nanobent" into new shapes, reassembling as an olive-skinned man, a Nordic man, a Turkish boy, a row of baseboards on the wall.

Yet the baseboards still spoke.

"We call this one 'Siphonophore'—or the 'Mosaic' if you prefer. The pieces smuggle nicely, and give us some useful chameleon abilities."

Now Sei was beginning to get irritated. Hmph. Fine. I get it, whoever you are. Earth, probably Miranda, has some new toys, and intends to trip up alphakind one squabble at a time. It makes for a good light show, but it's not that impressive.

"Of course it isn't."

Finally, the microblocks peeled themselves out of camouflage, reassembling into someone much more familiar.

Sei's eyes widened in the sudden realization of what she was *actually* up against.

You can call me Phaedra Null. As Zeta I've been in stasis on Mars for a couple of months, just so I could 1 it over here for a while and see what I could accomplish. You know this dissociable reprint can be smuggled across Jupiter security in just a few bags of luggage? And even when I operate it at full force, people still don't believe that a group of mishap-provoking blocks can cost a nation four cabinet members, seven senators, and countless alpha idiots in only five weeks. Not that I'm against alphakind mind you, but we do have a threat to quell.

More than anything else, Sei was probably most bothered by the fact that she just didn't understand the tactic.

Phaedra, is that really you? The 400 year-old head of Miranda came down here herself? Come on.

Correction. The 400 year-old Executor of Miranda climbed into a stasis module and had a 22 year-old shapeshiftable drone-cloud lend some definitive change to an easily manipulatable type of situation.

Haha. I'm sorry Phaedra, it just seems so funny that you come here and put on this light show for little ole' me.

Oh! I'm hurt! I guess this looks more like a fifth-grade science experiment to you, huh? A very expensive costume party perhaps?

Hehe. Yeah, kind of.

Phaedra Null smiled warmly from behind her subtly glowing wireframe appearance. Yeah, I guess generations of petty squabbles destroying a whole world isn't really believable. How about this? I will show up here tomorrow, and flash the beam on Governor Banner. We'll see how he works when the Demon finder identifies any malicious vengeance in him like MCCD, and Epic causes him to do something stupid like tell everyone he's been working with us. Problems will ensue. Some will call for retribution against betas. More ridiculousness will ensue, and we will simply blow you all up. How does that sound?

Sei wasn't laughing anymore.

I only have to flash the beam once. That will give me plenty of time to float into Ko'an's place, and Demon-find everybody in there. I'm not sure how that will go, but I would bet money that you will be down one friend in a week. Or does she not need her vengeance to be everything she is?

Sei sobered up as the seeds of anger began to grow within her.

What do you say, Genevieve-Sei? Can I try it?

No.

Why not? Oh! Don't tell me you think this little light show *is* worth something after all.

...

No comeback? Here. I will make this easy for you. What's today...
Winter 78 Earth time? What will it take you folks, one month to
stably fill Willamot's position? Let's make a deal. I will be back here in
one month. In that time, three Dyer mayors will be challenged and
probably replaced. Both the Sovereigns and the Collectivists will
each lose two more legislative reps, and Willamot's replacement will
be a beta or a cyborg. You will then meet me in one of the lockable
offices in this building, your pick. I fill find you, and then we will talk
again after you're convinced of what's happening. That should give
you plenty of time to take our ABC strategy seriously.

...

And of course, you won't tell anyone anything unless you want the
alphas to start their own apocalypse early.

Sei lowered her eyes.

That looks like agreement. Well, I'll be on my way. We have leaders
to select.

Phaedra Null disintegrated into a wavy stream along the base of the wall, and
disappeared into the air vents.

The technology by itself may not have been so bad on its own, but if Phaedra
herself really was the one operating it, the alphas might actually be in far more
trouble than it seemed.

* * *

A mysterious case of the flu suddenly broke out around Montoya, Dyer, and Lavel
airspaces in late n.e. winter of 2776. A couple of hundred people fell victim to
what was essentially a nonfatal strain, yet the flu had been thought extinct for so
long that people didn't quite know how to treat it. The symptoms of this particular
flu included moodiness, depression, hypochondrial pain, and a generic pendulum
swing between mania and defeat, defeat being the final stage in all cases.
Researchers traced the beginnings of the flu to attendees of the Stacy Stack rally
about a season prior, and the spread seemed to follow everyone who had been
there. Meanwhile, Chancellor Bennett himself also came down with this affliction
which only seemed to affect alphas and worsen with displays of aggression. The
Chancellor would eventually recover over the course of weeks, but boy was he
different afterwards. He just didn't seem to want to be leader anymore.

On Spring 2, 2777, Sei received another surprise visit from one of Phaedra's
nanos: overhead footage of her riding her air bike across the public skyways, left
beam blaring onto any and all passersby. Occasionally, she would stop the bike,

rubberneck some entanglement featuring an apparent ne'er-do-well, and causally flash the Demon finder with longer, more deliberate conviction. She would then board her bike and leave again. The entire video lasted less than five minutes, but this was more than enough time to convey the main point. Phaedra was single-handedly carrying out a kind of audiochemical warfare, using a weapon that nobody knew about, exploiting means native to people inclined to take the aggressor role in an otherwise neutral relationship, and doing so in a traveling pattern that looked more like a basic communicable disease than the march of a centuries-experienced, unkillable saboteur. The whole thing might have been funny had it not been so disturbingly effective. Like a person poisoning an entire county with a truck and a harmless "water" sprinkler, that passing traveler on the air bike, unbeknownst to you, actually came to turn you against your harsher selves… See how their successors seem to increasingly favor those alien invaders. See how the predecessors—formerly so sure—have been inexplicably crippled by a pandemic of unknown origin or cure.

Sei locked the door to the random office she had entered on the post night of Spring 17, 2777. Beyond Phaedra's initial predictions, the number of empty roles of influence of *all kinds* had been MUCH higher than Sei could have imagined.

Phaedra Null assembled herself in front of the large bay window, drawing the shades further as she greeted Sei.

**Sei! How nice to see you!**

You seem to be having a good time, Phaedra.

**I am, that's true. Did you know that siphonophore can fly from here to the capitol in 6 hours? They're drones, so all they need is a magnetic recharge. Jupiter has plenty of that. When Jake redesigned all of these toys to obey the modular fracture system enabling me to chop everything up and fly with it in a cloud of debris, that was true scientific progress.**

Cut the crap Phaedra! I get it!…I get it. Our PR person is a cyborg. Dyer is suddenly controlled by collectivists. Throngs of folks have conveniently removed themselves from key roles while candidates the betas don't approve of are too distrusted to be given a chance. You guys have installed an el system of credit into our society, and are taking it over without anyone suspecting anything.

**That about sums it up. You know, some of these people we considered grantzing actually end up killing another person in the simulations this left brace runs? It's been ugly to watch those.**

Are you just here to gloat? Look. I take you seriously, okay! The alphas can't help themselves and you're going on tour helping their institutions spiral without a head. But why tell me all this? Why spend three months rubbing it in my face? Why all the theatrics when you really could just blow up the planet if you wanted?

Phaedra came down from her high to give a dead serious answer, **When have you ever known Homo sapiens beta to work that way?**

...

Have we ever, in our history, committed genocide?

...

Not in 500 years, Sei. Not in an institutionalized, citizen-rallying way. Never. Ever. Do betas like you and me think like that, Sei?

...

Do you want to know the real reason why I'm here? It's because what you're trying to do is highly unlikely to succeed. You've been here for what, two years? Wading through the petty hallway fights and political maneuvering while a world full of your peers follows their favorite things off a cliff? Do you think what happens in this building is going to fix alphas everywhere? Do you?

...

And how long will you file through the paperwork before you realize that the public can't care, won't care, and won't change? They will always want their checks for free and their conveniences easy. I'm here because we decided not to kill alphas, not to enslave them or force them into Diji, not even to send ships against them. We decided to use their own informational confusion to help everyone else in the Solar System, including themselves, to see what is obvious to all outside the clique.

It would be too easy to blow alphakind off the map, but we spent two years developing something specifically targeted for malavengeance. That's ALL we did. But when it came down to deciding who should operate these toys, everyone knew that only the just would do, and only someone who understood the struggle of all sides. I don't know if I would consider myself just, but when I use this brace, I'm not just thinking about this handful of selfish people who won't get to be selfish anymore, I'm also thinking of the thousands, maybe millions of people who know nothing but how to follow these people into a slow death for all. Even we on Earth—we who have perfected the craft as much as possible—can't get out from under the shadow of the endless, ceaseless, endless need to claim... *everything*. Our way out was to look at a single problem and solve it gradually, realistically. If you look at what I'm doing as a game then good. I do it without malice, and with all the faith of the Solar Council that I can change this world myself just by how and when I choose to walk around in a place. And no shots need to be fired.

Am I succeeding, Sei?

...

Answer me, Prohal! Am I succeeding? I need to hear you say it so that it sticks with you.

...

Fine. Are *you* succeeding?

Sei buried the bridge of her nose between her fingers.

Hmph. While you stand there speechless, the world marches on, Prohal. If you don't have eyes to see the truth and name it for what it is—

I...

...

I... can't do any more than this. This job is the only route to change.

Bullshit. You've let the alpha boxes get to you. I'll bet you also think money is the only means to a good social program too, don't you? Or pub is the only way to be seen? Soundbites are the only way to be remembered? Fear is the only way to mobilize the many? Huh?

...

If you believe these ways are the *only* ways then you are as lost as the alphas are.

...

Hm. I came here as your friend. To give you something to stand against because God knows this job will not change hearts quickly enough. It will change social positioning for whatever constituents, but it won't change hearts. The heart of alpha needs to be changed, Sei. You're lollygagging with these alpha tools.

And what do you suggest!? These guys can't just calculate decades out or be affected by a carton floating in some far-off ocean. They are short-sighted soap opera characters who need very big and very slow institutions of their own making to force them to behave. Without that, it's eye for an eye again! I can't change that!

Then *what in the world* are you doing here?

...

For the life of her, Sei could not come up with an answer.

...I have one last "gadget" for you.

...? Sei mustered a weakly curious glance.

It seems to me that not only are our methods faster, wider-reaching, and backed by fate where yours aren't, but we also stand on more solid ground in the conscience department. If you are to have any hope of at least changing a few people before we remove alpha control of their last planet, you are going to need some help.

Phaedra removed the arm brace on her right hand, now equipped with a newer, directed beam of some kind which Sei was only now just noticing.

Jake modified it. Point it at the target to attempt an exorcism. It's not actually the laser that does the work, but the lookup for what the laser scans and the emhim cone around them.

The pearl arm brace was passed unceremoniously to Sei. If ever you see me in a place, and if ever you can find me, point it at me. I may be on a mission to remove more alphas from their positions, but I'll make it a point in some cases to be where you can reach me.

But I thought—

We fixed it to where we can turn it off or even command it to format its entire protocol if we want. That would make it a useless ornament in only a few seconds. But barring that, if you are really still set on this saving the world business, you're going to need more help than your job currently offers you.

I... don't know what to say.

Say that you'll move quickly, and you'll move with urgency. To teach people what thousands of years of forefathers couldn't. When you're not stopping me, you and whatever friends you find should locate as many forward thinkers as you can. After this is all over in a decade or two, maybe we'll ally with some of the people you've changed in order to guide the alphas into something better.

...But I don't understand.

If you remembered your higher human roots you should. You are the defense. We are the prosecution. But even these crazy characters deserve the same kind of fair trial that we would want. That is all.

Sei chuckled. Phaedra Zeta. Still the girl with all the world in the palm of her hand. If I could stop you now, I would.

From doing what? Neutering the alphas? I doubt you'd succeed. The main outcome of this story is already written. That outcome is better for everyone.

But what kind of defender would I be if I didn't try?

Hmm. I suppose the same kind of defender you'd be if you tried and failed, but didn't get up. The question isn't just whether you're willing to try, but whether you're willing to get up when you know that trying will only bring failure.

Stop talking shit, Zeta. Let's do it.

Hmph. Suit yourself. Demon finder, link to Angel finder and transmit this back to my people at Miranda. I have something to teach them about their Executor.

Awful confident are we? Sei taunted as she reunited with her brace.

I've taken down some scary people in a couple of brawls before. Have you?

The Angel finder felt familiar on Sei's arm, like a piece of herself reclaimed within her. Full of determination, she pointed the brace at Phaedra...

* * *

Cast upon the rooftop of Goldfellow Spire in Chelsea-Lock, Sei stood opposite her friend beneath the dull rainbow swirl of the Jupiterian night. Below them, the skyways of the city and floating clutter of base units formed a web of lights and lines resembling a glass floor over the abyss below.

In Sei's right hand, a simple silver bow congealed from the surrounding air. A quiver of white arrows on her back complemented the means assigned to her. The Sei of this world wore a humble white jump suit with long sleeves, slightly split at the leg beneath flying side tails.

**Are you sure you know the rules of this game?** Phaedra challenged unenthusiastically. **You point that brace at people like that and I don't think you know.**

Hmph.

**Are you sure you want to use that weapon here? Do you know how to change weapons? Do you even know what the conditions for victory are here? They vary from battle to battle. Or maybe you just haven't watched enough LCL.**

Phaedra's digital projection saw her transform from the causal spacesuit of her Astra form into the frost-lined jet-black battle suit of an upper-rank Neptunian Guard. With her long, lean shape and centuries-perfected beta body fully accentuated, she stood significantly taller, stronger, and more reminiscent of a goddess geared for future war against the comparatively diminished presence of her friend. Phaedra's boots alone, coal black with a single illuminated line of spectral colors traced up the calf, seemed to bring an energy all their own to the place where she stood. Without doubt, she was an intimidating sight to behold. She might as well have been Pallas-Athena herself.

Maybe all those streams you've watched are inspiring this getup, Sei noted, unmoved. We'll let our skills do the talking.

**Our skills,**
**The setting,**
**Our drive,**
**Our legacy,**
**Our knowledge of the opponent,**
**and the rules of the game,** Phaedra added. Just then, an arena of sky seats materialized around the two combatants. There must have been hundreds of thousands of spectators packed against the walls of the sky.

In the flawless antique white of Phaedra's right hand, a crescent-shaped sword reified itself, a seeming relic compared to the modern forms describing everything else.

Phaedra's boots flashed a blinding burst as she shot atop the prow of a lightning trail far beyond visibility into the air above Sei's head. Less than two seconds later, Null herself slammed through the sky directly onto Sei's head, skewering Sei against the ground in a hyperbolic blast that blew the hats off of several rows of the ghostly-projected front seat witnesses. Landing from an air-rolled backflip off of her downed opponent's chest, Phaedra crouched and spun a 1080° slash into Sei, shattering the latter's bow and throwing a mess of arrows into the air behind her. Seamlessly winding down the tornado through her opponent, the goddess caught one of Sei's still flying arrows in her left hand, instantly extended it into a feathered long spear, and plunged it into Sei's back as the latter hunched down in a struggle to her get to feet. The spear seemed to recoil a little as soon as it entered its target, then evaporated as quickly as it appeared.

Phaedra dug her back foot deep into the rooftop pavement, and with a single arm scooped Sei up like a handball and flung her her towards the stands. Rather than compound the maneuver, however, she simply let the ragdoll bounce and roll as it planted itself back onto the ground. Less than a second after Sei's floor collision, Null rolled the crescent sword in her hand to carve a ring of blue and white fire from which a sine wave of searing lightning burned a line between her and her challenger. Switching feet, the war goddess then held up her alternate forearm in type of blocking maneuver, commanding a pair of spinning portals to rotate like a blender about Sei, rolling the latter all around like a toy in a glass ball. Clasping her hands together, Phaedra soon closed the ball, swallowing Sei up inside. Shortly thereafter, the ether coughed up the challenger in a clap of thunder, dumping her a few feet behind the caster.

Phaedra stomped her foot, causing a wall of rooftop chunks to rise at her feet which fissured their way over to Sei behind her. A transparent specter of a doric pillar appeared out of nowhere and toppled onto Sei. A puff of purple clouds and sparks popped out of the grounded challenger with inexplicable effect, until space around her began to darken as if only her aura and hers alone were the victim of a masking brush in a graphics program. With Sei now stricken, a literal shadow of the way she began, Phaedra dashed over to her, palmed her head, and brought her to a lifelessly bowed dangle before running her through with the crescent sword. Much of the crowd rose to its feet, but it was clear that the alphas among them were dismayed. Finally, Phaedra stepped back from her victim and finger-snapped a flicker of blue towards her, instantly igniting the body.

The goddess stood tall and stern for the next minute and a half as the flames died out, most of the scene fading back to black.

Gradually, the digital projection of Sei could once again be seen through the waning flames, her body unconsumed.

Phaedra resembled an icy statue as she cast a mixture of haughtiness and pity upon her clearly inferior opponent.

It would take another minute for Sei to come to kneeling, more out of embarrassment than anything else. She could not, however, bring herself to look Phaedra in the eye.

Next time you challenge me, you should pick an easier arena than that of my long term goal. I fight for the peace of all humans, including alphas. The only battles you can win are those forcing me to spare the occasional exception.

Sei winced under the clutch of dizzying pain. Even in the virtual world, some insults still seemed to sting down to the marrow.

You should go back and tell your friend Ko'an about this. You won't be able to change the alphas' fate with policies alone, but will need to find the hearts of a few to restore certain long-lived principles beneath those policies.

...

And just in case you need some motivation to keep going and keep going strongly, know that I may come after Kyle Banner one day, or perhaps Ko'an. They still need their malavengeance, and I know you need them. I just hope by the time that happens you will have gotten your shit together, and learned how to actually fix the old humans from within, one soul at a time.

...

Besides that, I also hope I've given you a reason to keep going...

Sei bowed her head, perhaps as a way of saying yes.

Very good. Well, I'll be around you know. Changing who leads this species.

Sei sniffed, still on her bended knee.

And one more thing. Your beta friends back home know who you are, and you know who you are. You will always be Genevieve of Earth, Genevieve of Venus. But you had better pray that the humans you fight for never have cause to find that out. The day they discover that their last defender is of a group they perceive to be the enemy, is the day this entirely quiet war yields to their usual anarchy. If that happens, we can and will put this entire planet down. The sum of all humanities, past and future, has no more to gain from humans without a conscience towards the whole. Their confined wars and continued erosion of what they have will only prove this further.

If you're going to fight, you'll have to keep your eyes on the builders around you, and not get caught up in the limits imposed on that building. Those limits will attach to you and never let you go. That said, it is in the average limited human's best interest to never know this transition is happening. We cannot guarantee peace in response to their actions once they *do* know.

...

I want our trial as old humans to be fair too, Sei.

... I know.

Then find allies who will help you rewrite this place's core. Forward with what you have, no matter what gets lost or how it gets lost.

...

Anyway, that's my lecture. Four centuries of life will do that to you.

Heh.

See you around somewhere.

Yeah.

And with that, Phaedra and the entire vision darkened deeply into dream.

Sei returned to her senses, still in the locked office, with the pearl arm brace still on her arm. She would need much more than public promises and group meetings to change what ailed the old humans, but now had at least a few reasons to keep getting better in how she fought that battle. In a couple of hours her shift would end, and she would immediately contact Ko'an—the only alpha friend who knew even a little about any of this. Hopefully they could come up with some kind of path forward. Maybe the end of the old humans' control really was at hand. But that didn't have to mean death or extinction—just the option of transcendence. If she could not succeed in fostering that turn within alphas themselves, then either the external forces or the alphas' own self-created troubles would impose transcendence the hard way.

Whatever the case, there remained much to do, for the old humans were no longer facing just themselves. Now they were being challenged by the humans they could—and in some cases *would*—become. Most in Sei's time, though, were in no way ready for this…

…but some were. At least for now, the future had given her the tools to find them.